The Ghastly Gothic Tomes

Vol. 1

The Ghastly Gothic Tomes

Vol. 1

Published by NRM Books.

ISBN: 978-1-965179-04-8

CREDITS
Cover Art by: Nathan Reese Maher

COPYRIGHT

Table of Contents

The Castle of Otranto

By Horace Walpole

INTRODUCTION

Horace Walpole was the youngest son of Sir Robert Walpole, the great statesman, who died Earl of Orford. He was born in 1717, the year in which his father resigned office, remaining in opposition for almost three years before his return to a long tenure of power. Horace Walpole was educated at Eton, where he formed a school friendship with Thomas Gray, who was but a few months older. In 1739 Gray was travelling-companion with Walpole in France and Italy until they differed and parted; but the friendship was afterwards renewed, and remained firm to the end. Horace Walpole went from Eton to King's College, Cambridge, and entered Parliament in 1741, the year before his father's final resignation and acceptance of an earldom. His way of life was made easy to him. As Usher of the Exchequer, Comptroller of the Pipe, and Clerk of the Estreats in the Exchequer, he received nearly two thousand a year for doing nothing, lived with his father, and amused himself.

Horace Walpole idled, and amused himself with the small life of the fashionable world to which he was proud of belonging, though he had a quick eye for its vanities. He had social wit, and liked to put it to small uses. But he was not an empty idler, and there were seasons when he could become a sharp judge of himself. "I am sensible," he wrote to his most intimate friend, "I am sensible of having more follies and weaknesses and fewer real good qualities than most men. I sometimes reflect on this, though, I own, too seldom. I always want to begin acting like a man, and a sensible one, which I think I might be if I would." He had deep home affections, and, under many polite affectations, plenty of good sense.

Horace Walpole's father died in 1745. The eldest son, who succeeded to the earldom, died in 1751, and left a son, George, who was for a time insane, and lived until 1791. As George left no child, the title and estates passed to Horace Walpole, then seventy-four years old, and the only uncle who survived. Horace Walpole thus became Earl of Orford, during the last six years of his life. As to the title, he said that he felt himself being called names in his old age. He died unmarried, in the year 1797, at the age of eighty.

He had turned his house at Strawberry Hill, by the Thames, near Twickenham, into a Gothic villa — eighteenth-century Gothic — and amused himself by spending freely upon its adornment with such things as were then fashionable as objects of taste. But he delighted also in his flowers and his trellises of roses, and the quiet Thames. When confined by gout to his London house in Arlington Street, flowers from Strawberry Hill and a bird were necessary consolations. He set up also at Strawberry Hill a private printing press, at which he printed his friend Gray's poems, also in 1758 his own "Catalogue of the Royal and Noble Authors of England," and five volumes of "Anecdotes of Painting in England," between 1762 and 1771.

Horace Walpole produced *The Castle of Otranto* in 1765, at the mature age of forty-eight. It was suggested by a dream from which he said he waked one morning, and of which "all I could recover was, that I had thought myself in an ancient castle (a very natural dream for a head like mine, filled with Gothic story), and that on the uppermost banister of a great staircase I saw a gigantic hand in armour. In the evening I sat down and began to write, without knowing in the least what I intended to say or relate." So began the tale which professed to be translated by "William Marshal, gentleman, from the Italian of Onuphro Muralto, canon of the Church of St. Nicholas, at Otranto." It was written in two months. Walpole's friend Gray reported to him that at Cambridge the book made "some of them cry a little, and all in general afraid to go to bed o' nights." *The Castle of Otranto* was, in its own way, an early sign of the reaction towards romance in the latter part of the last century. This gives it interest. But it has had many followers, and the hardy modern reader, when he reads Gray's note from Cambridge, needs to be reminded of its date.

H. M.

PREFACE TO THE FIRST EDITION.

The following work was found in the library of an ancient Catholic family in the north of England. It was printed at Naples, in the black letter, in the year 1529. How much sooner it was written does not appear. The principal incidents are such as were believed in the darkest ages of Christianity; but the language and conduct have nothing that savours of barbarism. The style is the purest Italian.

If the story was written near the time when it is supposed to have happened, it must have been between 1095, the era of the first Crusade, and 1243, the date of the last, or not long afterwards. There is no other circumstance in the work that can lead us to guess at the period in which the scene is laid: the names of the actors are evidently fictitious, and probably disguised on purpose: yet the Spanish names of the domestics seem to indicate that this work was not composed until the establishment of the Arragonian Kings in Naples had made Spanish appellations familiar in that country. The beauty of the diction, and the zeal of the author (moderated, however, by singular judgment) concur to make me think that the date of the composition was little antecedent to that of the impression. Letters were then in their most flourishing state in Italy, and contributed to dispel the empire of superstition, at that time so forcibly attacked by the reformers. It is not unlikely that an artful priest might endeavour to turn their own arms on the innovators, and might avail himself of his abilities as an author to confirm the populace in their ancient errors and superstitions. If this was his view, he has certainly acted with signal address. Such a work as the following would enslave a hundred vulgar minds beyond half the books of controversy that have been written from the days of Luther to the present hour.

This solution of the author's motives is, however, offered as a mere conjecture. Whatever his views were, or whatever effects the execution of them might have, his work can only be laid before the public at present as a matter of entertainment. Even as such, some apology for it is necessary. Miracles, visions, necromancy, dreams, and other preternatural events, are exploded now even from romances. That was not the case when our author wrote; much less when the story itself is supposed to have happened. Belief in every kind of prodigy was so established in those dark ages, that an author would not be faithful to the manners of the times, who should omit all mention of them. He is not bound to believe them himself, but he must represent his actors as believing them.

If this air of the miraculous is excused, the reader will find nothing else unworthy of his perusal. Allow the possibility of the facts, and all the actors comport themselves as persons would do in their situation. There is no bombast, no similes, flowers, digressions, or unnecessary descriptions. Everything tends directly to the catastrophe. Never is the reader's attention relaxed. The rules of the drama are almost observed throughout the conduct of the piece. The characters are well drawn, and still better maintained. Terror, the author's principal engine, prevents the story from ever languishing; and it is so often contrasted by pity, that the mind is kept up in a constant vicissitude of interesting passions.

Some persons may perhaps think the characters of the domestics too little serious for the general cast of the story; but besides their opposition to the principal personages, the art of the author is very observable in his conduct of the subalterns. They discover many passages essential to the story, which could not be well brought to light but by their naïveté and simplicity. In particular, the womanish terror and foibles of Bianca, in the last chapter, conduce essentially towards advancing the catastrophe.

It is natural for a translator to be prejudiced in favour of his adopted work. More impartial readers may not be so much struck with the beauties of this piece as I was. Yet I am not blind to my author's defects. I could wish he had grounded his plan on a more useful moral than this: that "the sins of fathers are visited on their children to the third and fourth generation." I doubt whether, in his time, any more than at present, ambition curbed its appetite of dominion from the dread of so remote a punishment. And yet this moral is weakened by that less direct insinuation, that even such anathema may be diverted by devotion to St. Nicholas. Here the interest of the Monk plainly gets the better of the judgment of the author. However, with all its faults, I have no doubt but the English reader will be pleased with a sight of this performance. The piety that reigns throughout, the lessons of virtue that are inculcated, and the rigid purity of the sentiments, exempt this work from the censure to which romances are but too liable. Should it meet with the success I hope for, I may be encouraged to reprint the original Italian, though it will tend to depreciate my own labour. Our language falls far short of the charms of the Italian, both for variety and harmony. The latter is peculiarly excellent for simple narrative. It is difficult in English to relate without falling too low or rising too high; a fault obviously occasioned by the little care taken to speak pure language in common conversation. Every Italian or Frenchman of any rank piques himself on speaking his own tongue correctly and with choice. I cannot flatter myself with having done justice to my author in this respect: his style is as elegant as his conduct of the passions is masterly. It is a pity that he did not apply his talents to what they were evidently proper for—the theatre.

I will detain the reader no longer, but to make one short remark. Though the machinery is invention, and the names of the actors imaginary, I cannot but believe that the groundwork of the story is founded on truth. The scene is undoubtedly laid in some real castle. The author seems frequently, without design, to describe particular parts. "The chamber," says he, "on the right hand;" "the door on the left hand;" "the distance from the chapel to Conrad's apartment:" these and other passages are strong presumptions that the author had some certain building in his eye. Curious persons, who have leisure to employ in such researches, may possibly discover in the Italian writers the foundation on which our author has built. If a catastrophe, at all resembling that which he describes, is believed to have given rise to this work, it will contribute to interest the reader, and will make the "Castle of Otranto" a still more moving story.

SONNET TO THE RIGHT HONOURABLE
LADY MARY COKE.

The gentle maid, whose hapless tale
    These melancholy pages speak;
Say, gracious lady, shall she fail
    To draw the tear adown thy cheek?

No; never was thy pitying breast
    Insensible to human woes;
Tender, tho' firm, it melts distrest
    For weaknesses it never knows.

Oh! guard the marvels I relate
Of fell ambition scourg'd by fate,
    From reason's peevish blame.
Blest with thy smile, my dauntless sail
I dare expand to Fancy's gale,
    For sure thy smiles are Fame.

H. W.

CHAPTER I.

Manfred, Prince of Otranto, had one son and one daughter: the latter, a most beautiful virgin, aged eighteen, was called Matilda. Conrad, the son, was three years younger, a homely youth, sickly, and of no promising disposition; yet he was the darling of his father, who never showed any symptoms of affection to Matilda. Manfred had contracted a marriage for his son with the Marquis of Vicenza's daughter, Isabella; and she had already been delivered by her guardians into the hands of Manfred, that he might celebrate the wedding as soon as Conrad's infirm state of health would permit.

Manfred's impatience for this ceremonial was remarked by his family and neighbours. The former, indeed, apprehending the severity of their Prince's disposition, did not dare to utter their surmises on this precipitation. Hippolita, his wife, an amiable lady, did sometimes venture to represent the danger of marrying their only son so early, considering his great youth, and greater infirmities; but she never received any other answer than reflections on her own sterility, who had given him but one heir. His tenants and subjects were less cautious in their discourses. They attributed this hasty wedding to the Prince's dread of seeing accomplished an ancient prophecy, which was said to have pronounced that the castle and lordship of Otranto "should pass from the present family, whenever the real owner should be grown too large to inhabit it." It was difficult to make any sense of this prophecy; and still less easy to conceive what it had to do with the marriage in question. Yet these mysteries, or contradictions, did not make the populace adhere the less to their opinion.

Young Conrad's birthday was fixed for his espousals. The company was assembled in the chapel of the Castle, and everything ready for beginning the divine office, when Conrad himself was missing. Manfred, impatient of the least delay, and who had not observed his son retire, despatched one of his attendants to summon the young Prince. The servant, who had not stayed long enough to have crossed the court to Conrad's apartment, came running back breathless, in a frantic manner, his eyes staring, and foaming at the mouth. He said nothing, but pointed to the court.

The company were struck with terror and amazement. The Princess Hippolita, without knowing what was the matter, but anxious for her son, swooned away. Manfred, less apprehensive than enraged at the procrastination of the nuptials, and at the folly of his domestic, asked imperiously what was the matter?

The fellow made no answer, but continued pointing towards the courtyard; and at last, after repeated questions put to him, cried out, "Oh! the helmet! the helmet!"

In the meantime, some of the company had run into the court, from whence was heard a confused noise of shrieks, horror, and surprise. Manfred, who began to be alarmed at not seeing his son, went himself to get information of what occasioned this strange confusion. Matilda remained endeavouring to assist her mother, and Isabella stayed for the same purpose, and to avoid showing any impatience for the bridegroom, for whom, in truth, she had conceived little affection.

The first thing that struck Manfred's eyes was a group of his servants endeavouring to raise something that appeared to him a mountain of sable plumes. He gazed without believing his sight.

"What are ye doing?" cried Manfred, wrathfully; "where is my son?"

A volley of voices replied, "Oh! my Lord! the Prince! the Prince! the helmet! the helmet!"

Shocked with these lamentable sounds, and dreading he knew not what, he advanced hastily,—but what a sight for a father's eyes!—he beheld his child dashed to pieces, and almost buried under an enormous helmet, an hundred times more large than any casque ever made for human being, and shaded with a proportionable quantity of black feathers.

The horror of the spectacle, the ignorance of all around how this misfortune had happened, and above all, the tremendous phenomenon before him, took away the Prince's speech. Yet his silence lasted longer than even grief could occasion. He fixed his eyes on what he wished in vain to believe a vision; and seemed less attentive to his loss, than buried in meditation on the stupendous object that had occasioned it. He touched, he examined the fatal casque; nor could even the bleeding mangled remains of the young Prince divert the eyes of Manfred from the portent before him.

All who had known his partial fondness for young Conrad, were as much surprised at their Prince's insensibility, as thunderstruck themselves at the miracle of the helmet. They conveyed the disfigured corpse into the hall, without receiving the least direction from Manfred. As little was he attentive to the ladies who remained in the chapel. On the contrary, without mentioning the unhappy princesses, his wife and daughter, the first sounds that dropped from Manfred's lips were, "Take care of the Lady Isabella."

The domestics, without observing the singularity of this direction, were guided by their affection to their mistress, to consider it as peculiarly addressed to her situation, and flew to her assistance. They conveyed her to her chamber more dead than alive, and indifferent to all the strange circumstances she heard, except the death of her son.

Matilda, who doted on her mother, smothered her own grief and amazement, and thought of nothing but assisting and comforting her afflicted parent. Isabella, who had been treated by Hippolita like a daughter, and who returned that tenderness with equal duty and affection, was scarce less assiduous about the Princess; at the same time endeavouring to partake and lessen the weight of sorrow which she saw Matilda strove to suppress, for whom she had conceived the warmest sympathy of friendship. Yet her own situation could not help finding its place in her thoughts. She felt no concern for the death of young Conrad, except commiseration; and she was not sorry to be delivered from a marriage which had promised her little felicity, either from her destined bridegroom, or from the severe temper of Manfred, who, though he had distinguished her by great indulgence, had imprinted her mind with terror, from his causeless rigour to such amiable princesses as Hippolita and Matilda.

While the ladies were conveying the wretched mother to her bed, Manfred remained in the court, gazing on the ominous casque, and regardless of the crowd which the strangeness of the event had now assembled around him. The few words he articulated, tended solely to inquiries, whether any man knew from whence it could have come? Nobody could give him the least information. However, as it seemed to be the sole object of his curiosity, it soon became so to the rest of the spectators, whose conjectures were as absurd and improbable, as the catastrophe itself was unprecedented. In the midst of their senseless guesses, a young peasant, whom rumour had drawn thither from a neighbouring village, observed that the miraculous helmet was exactly like that on the figure in black marble of Alfonso the Good, one of their former princes, in the church of St. Nicholas.

"Villain! What sayest thou?" cried Manfred, starting from his trance in a tempest of rage, and seizing the young man by the collar; "how darest thou utter such treason? Thy life shall pay for it."

The spectators, who as little comprehended the cause of the Prince's fury as all the rest they had seen, were at a loss to unravel this new circumstance. The young peasant himself was still more astonished, not conceiving how he had offended the Prince. Yet recollecting himself, with a mixture of grace and humility, he disengaged himself from Manfred's grip, and then with an obeisance, which discovered more jealousy of innocence than dismay, he asked, with respect, of what he was guilty? Manfred, more enraged at the vigour, however decently exerted, with which the young man had shaken off his hold, than appeased by his submission, ordered his attendants to seize him, and, if he had not been withheld by his friends whom he had invited to the nuptials, would have poignarded the peasant in their arms.

During this altercation, some of the vulgar spectators had run to the great church, which stood near the castle, and came back open-mouthed, declaring that the helmet was missing from Alfonso's statue. Manfred, at this news, grew perfectly frantic; and, as if he sought a subject on which to vent the tempest within him, he rushed again on the young peasant, crying—

"Villain! Monster! Sorcerer! 'tis thou hast done this! 'tis thou hast slain my son!"

The mob, who wanted some object within the scope of their capacities, on whom they might discharge their bewildered reasoning, caught the words from the mouth of their lord, and re-echoed—

"Ay, ay; 'tis he, 'tis he: he has stolen the helmet from good Alfonso's tomb, and dashed out the brains of our young Prince with it," never reflecting how enormous the disproportion was between the marble helmet that had been in the church, and that of steel before their eyes; nor how impossible it was for a youth seemingly not twenty, to wield a piece of armour of so prodigious a weight.

The folly of these ejaculations brought Manfred to himself: yet whether provoked at the peasant having observed the resemblance between the two helmets, and thereby led to the farther discovery of the absence of that in the church, or wishing to bury any such rumour under so impertinent a supposition, he gravely pronounced that the young man was certainly a necromancer, and that till the Church could take cognisance of the affair, he would have the Magician, whom they had thus detected, kept prisoner under the helmet itself, which he ordered his attendants to raise, and place the young man under it; declaring he should be kept there without food, with which his own infernal art might furnish him.

It was in vain for the youth to represent against this preposterous sentence: in vain did Manfred's friends endeavour to divert him from this savage and ill-grounded resolution. The generality were charmed with their lord's decision, which, to their apprehensions, carried great appearance of justice, as the Magician was to be punished by the very instrument with which he had offended: nor were they struck with the least compunction at the probability of the youth being starved, for they firmly believed that, by his diabolic skill, he could easily supply himself with nutriment.

Manfred thus saw his commands even cheerfully obeyed; and appointing a guard with strict orders to prevent any food being conveyed to the prisoner, he dismissed his friends and attendants, and retired to his own chamber, after locking the gates of the castle, in which he suffered none but his domestics to remain.

In the meantime, the care and zeal of the young Ladies had brought the Princess Hippolita to herself, who amidst the transports of her own sorrow frequently demanded news of her lord, would have dismissed her attendants to watch over him, and at last enjoined Matilda to leave her, and visit and comfort her father. Matilda, who wanted no affectionate duty to Manfred, though she trembled at his austerity, obeyed the orders of Hippolita, whom she tenderly recommended to Isabella; and inquiring of the domestics for her father, was informed that he was retired to his chamber, and had commanded that nobody should have admittance to him. Concluding that he was immersed in sorrow for the death of her brother, and fearing to renew his tears by the sight of his sole remaining child, she hesitated whether she should break in upon his affliction; yet solicitude for him, backed by the commands of her mother, encouraged her to venture disobeying the orders he had given; a fault she had never been guilty of before.

The gentle timidity of her nature made her pause for some minutes at his door. She heard him traverse his chamber backwards, and forwards with disordered steps; a mood which increased her apprehensions. She was, however, just going to beg admittance, when Manfred suddenly opened the door; and as it was now twilight, concurring with the disorder of his mind, he did not distinguish the person, but asked angrily, who it was? Matilda replied, trembling —

"My dearest father, it is I, your daughter."

Manfred, stepping back hastily, cried, "Begone! I do not want a daughter;" and flinging back abruptly, clapped the door against the terrified Matilda.

She was too well acquainted with her father's impetuosity to venture a second intrusion. When she had a little recovered the shock of so bitter a reception, she wiped away her tears to prevent the additional stab that the knowledge of it would give to Hippolita, who questioned her in the most anxious terms on the health of Manfred, and how he bore his loss. Matilda assured her he was well, and supported his misfortune with manly fortitude.

"But will he not let me see him?" said Hippolita mournfully; "will he not permit me to blend my tears with his, and shed a mother's sorrows in the bosom of her Lord? Or do you deceive me, Matilda? I know how Manfred doted on his son: is not the stroke too heavy for him? has he not sunk under it? You do not answer me — alas! I dread the worst! — Raise me, my maidens; I will, I will see my Lord. Bear me to him instantly: he is dearer to me even than my children."

Matilda made signs to Isabella to prevent Hippolita's rising; and both those lovely young women were using their gentle violence to stop and calm the Princess, when a servant, on the part of Manfred, arrived and told Isabella that his Lord demanded to speak with her.

"With me!" cried Isabella.

"Go," said Hippolita, relieved by a message from her Lord: "Manfred cannot support the sight of his own family. He thinks you less disordered than we are, and dreads the shock of my grief. Console him, dear Isabella, and tell him I will smother my own anguish rather than add to his."

As it was now evening the servant who conducted Isabella bore a torch before her. When they came to Manfred, who was walking impatiently about the gallery, he started, and said hastily —

"Take away that light, and begone."

Then shutting the door impetuously, he flung himself upon a bench against the wall, and bade Isabella sit by him. She obeyed trembling.

"I sent for you, Lady," said he — and then stopped under great appearance of confusion.

"My Lord!"

"Yes, I sent for you on a matter of great moment," resumed he. "Dry your tears, young Lady — you have lost your bridegroom. Yes, cruel fate! and I have lost the hopes of my race! But Conrad was not worthy of your beauty."

"How, my Lord!" said Isabella; "sure you do not suspect me of not feeling the concern I ought: my duty and affection would have always — "

"Think no more of him," interrupted Manfred; "he was a sickly, puny child, and Heaven has perhaps taken him away, that I might not trust the honours of my house on so frail a foundation. The line of Manfred calls for numerous supports. My foolish fondness for that boy blinded the eyes of my prudence — but it is better as it is. I hope, in a few years, to have reason to rejoice at the death of Conrad."

Words cannot paint the astonishment of Isabella. At first she apprehended that grief had disordered Manfred's understanding. Her next thought suggested that this strange discourse was designed to ensnare her: she feared that Manfred had perceived her indifference for his son: and in consequence of that idea she replied —

"Good my Lord, do not doubt my tenderness: my heart would have accompanied my hand. Conrad would have engrossed all my care; and wherever fate shall dispose of me, I shall always cherish his memory, and regard your Highness and the virtuous Hippolita as my parents."

"Curse on Hippolita!" cried Manfred. "Forget her from this moment, as I do. In short, Lady, you have missed a husband undeserving of your charms: they shall now be better disposed of. Instead of a sickly boy, you shall have a husband in the prime of his age, who will know how to value your beauties, and who may expect a numerous offspring."

"Alas, my Lord!" said Isabella, "my mind is too sadly engrossed by the recent catastrophe in your family to think of another marriage. If ever my father returns, and it shall be his pleasure, I shall obey, as I did when I consented to give my hand to your son: but until his return, permit me to remain under your hospitable roof, and employ the melancholy hours in assuaging yours, Hippolita's, and the fair Matilda's affliction."

"I desired you once before," said Manfred angrily, "not to name that woman: from this hour she must be a stranger to you, as she must be to me. In short, Isabella, since I cannot give you my son, I offer you myself."

"Heavens!" cried Isabella, waking from her delusion, "what do I hear? You! my Lord! You! My father-in-law! the father of Conrad! the husband of the virtuous and tender Hippolita!"

"I tell you," said Manfred imperiously, "Hippolita is no longer my wife; I divorce her from this hour. Too long has she cursed me by her unfruitfulness. My fate depends on having sons, and this night I trust will give a new date to my hopes."

At those words he seized the cold hand of Isabella, who was half dead with fright and horror. She shrieked, and started from him, Manfred rose to pursue her, when the moon, which was now up, and gleamed in at the opposite casement, presented to his sight the plumes of the fatal helmet, which rose to the height of the windows, waving backwards and forwards in a tempestuous manner, and accompanied with a hollow and rustling sound. Isabella, who gathered courage from her situation, and who dreaded nothing so much as Manfred's pursuit of his declaration, cried—

"Look, my Lord! see, Heaven itself declares against your impious intentions!"

"Heaven nor Hell shall impede my designs," said Manfred, advancing again to seize the Princess.

At that instant the portrait of his grandfather, which hung over the bench where they had been sitting, uttered a deep sigh, and heaved its breast.

Isabella, whose back was turned to the picture, saw not the motion, nor knew whence the sound came, but started, and said—

"Hark, my Lord! What sound was that?" and at the same time made towards the door.

Manfred, distracted between the flight of Isabella, who had now reached the stairs, and yet unable to keep his eyes from the picture, which began to move, had, however, advanced some steps after her, still looking backwards on the portrait, when he saw it quit its panel, and descend on the floor with a grave and melancholy air.

"Do I dream?" cried Manfred, returning; "or are the devils themselves in league against me? Speak, infernal spectre! Or, if thou art my grandsire, why dost thou too conspire against thy wretched descendant, who too dearly pays for—" Ere he could finish the sentence, the vision sighed again, and made a sign to Manfred to follow him.

"Lead on!" cried Manfred; "I will follow thee to the gulf of perdition."

The spectre marched sedately, but dejected, to the end of the gallery, and turned into a chamber on the right hand. Manfred accompanied him at a little distance, full of anxiety and horror, but resolved. As he would have entered the chamber, the door was clapped to with violence by an invisible hand. The Prince, collecting courage from this delay, would have forcibly burst open the door with his foot, but found that it resisted his utmost efforts.

"Since Hell will not satisfy my curiosity," said Manfred, "I will use the human means in my power for preserving my race; Isabella shall not escape me."

The lady, whose resolution had given way to terror the moment she had quitted Manfred, continued her flight to the bottom of the principal staircase. There she stopped, not knowing whither to direct her steps, nor how to escape from the impetuosity of the Prince. The gates of the castle, she knew, were locked, and guards placed in the court. Should she, as her heart prompted her, go and prepare Hippolita for the cruel destiny that awaited her, she did not doubt but Manfred would seek her there, and that his violence would incite him to double the injury he meditated, without leaving room for them to avoid the impetuosity of his passions. Delay might give him time to reflect on the horrid measures he had conceived, or produce some circumstance in her favour, if she could — for that night, at least — avoid his odious purpose. Yet where conceal herself? How avoid the pursuit he would infallibly make throughout the castle?

As these thoughts passed rapidly through her mind, she recollected a subterraneous passage which led from the vaults of the castle to the church of St. Nicholas. Could she reach the altar before she was overtaken, she knew even Manfred's violence would not dare to profane the sacredness of the place; and she determined, if no other means of deliverance offered, to shut herself up for ever among the holy virgins whose convent was contiguous to the cathedral. In this resolution, she seized a lamp that burned at the foot of the staircase, and hurried towards the secret passage.

The lower part of the castle was hollowed into several intricate cloisters; and it was not easy for one under so much anxiety to find the door that opened into the cavern. An awful silence reigned throughout those subterraneous regions, except now and then some blasts of wind that shook the doors she had passed, and which, grating on the rusty hinges, were re-echoed through that long labyrinth of darkness. Every murmur struck her with new terror; yet more she dreaded to hear the wrathful voice of Manfred urging his domestics to pursue her.

She trod as softly as impatience would give her leave, yet frequently stopped and listened to hear if she was followed. In one of those moments she thought she heard a sigh. She shuddered, and recoiled a few paces. In a moment she thought she heard the step of some person. Her blood curdled; she concluded it was Manfred. Every suggestion that horror could inspire rushed into her mind. She condemned her rash flight, which had thus exposed her to his rage in a place where her cries were not likely to draw anybody to her assistance. Yet the sound seemed not to come from behind. If Manfred knew where she was, he must have followed her. She was still in one of the cloisters, and the steps she had heard were too distinct to proceed from the way she had come. Cheered with this reflection, and hoping to find a friend in whoever was not the Prince, she was going to advance, when a door that stood ajar, at some distance to the left, was opened gently: but ere her lamp, which she held up, could discover who opened it, the person retreated precipitately on seeing the light.

Isabella, whom every incident was sufficient to dismay, hesitated whether she should proceed. Her dread of Manfred soon outweighed every other terror. The very circumstance of the person avoiding her gave her a sort of courage. It could only be, she thought, some domestic belonging to the castle. Her gentleness had never raised her an enemy, and conscious innocence made her hope that, unless sent by the Prince's order to seek her, his servants would rather assist than prevent her flight. Fortifying herself with these reflections, and believing by what she could observe that she was near the mouth of the subterraneous cavern, she approached the door that had been opened; but a sudden gust of wind that met her at the door extinguished her lamp, and left her in total darkness.

Words cannot paint the horror of the Princess's situation. Alone in so dismal a place, her mind imprinted with all the terrible events of the day, hopeless of escaping, expecting every moment the arrival of Manfred, and far from tranquil on knowing she was within reach of somebody, she knew not whom, who for some cause seemed concealed thereabouts; all these thoughts crowded on her distracted mind, and she was ready to sink under her apprehensions. She addressed herself to every saint in heaven, and inwardly implored their assistance. For a considerable time she remained in an agony of despair.

At last, as softly as was possible, she felt for the door, and having found it, entered trembling into the vault from whence she had heard the sigh and steps. It gave her a kind of momentary joy to perceive an imperfect ray of clouded moonshine gleam from the roof of the vault, which seemed to be fallen in, and from whence hung a fragment of earth or building, she could not distinguish which, that appeared to have been crushed inwards. She advanced eagerly towards this chasm, when she discerned a human form standing close against the wall.

She shrieked, believing it the ghost of her betrothed Conrad. The figure, advancing, said, in a submissive voice —

"Be not alarmed, Lady; I will not injure you."

Isabella, a little encouraged by the words and tone of voice of the stranger, and recollecting that this must be the person who had opened the door, recovered her spirits enough to reply —

"Sir, whoever you are, take pity on a wretched Princess, standing on the brink of destruction. Assist me to escape from this fatal castle, or in a few moments I may be made miserable for ever."

"Alas!" said the stranger, "what can I do to assist you? I will die in your defence; but I am unacquainted with the castle, and want—"

"Oh!" said Isabella, hastily interrupting him; "help me but to find a trap-door that must be hereabout, and it is the greatest service you can do me, for I have not a minute to lose."

Saying these words, she felt about on the pavement, and directed the stranger to search likewise, for a smooth piece of brass enclosed in one of the stones.

"That," said she, "is the lock, which opens with a spring, of which I know the secret. If we can find that, I may escape—if not, alas! courteous stranger, I fear I shall have involved you in my misfortunes: Manfred will suspect you for the accomplice of my flight, and you will fall a victim to his resentment."

"I value not my life," said the stranger, "and it will be some comfort to lose it in trying to deliver you from his tyranny."

"Generous youth," said Isabella, "how shall I ever requite—"

As she uttered those words, a ray of moonshine, streaming through a cranny of the ruin above, shone directly on the lock they sought.

"Oh! transport!" said Isabella; "here is the trap-door!" and, taking out the key, she touched the spring, which, starting aside, discovered an iron ring. "Lift up the door," said the Princess.

The stranger obeyed, and beneath appeared some stone steps descending into a vault totally dark.

"We must go down here," said Isabella. "Follow me; dark and dismal as it is, we cannot miss our way; it leads directly to the church of St. Nicholas. But, perhaps," added the Princess modestly, "you have no reason to leave the castle, nor have I farther occasion for your service; in a few minutes I shall be safe from Manfred's rage—only let me know to whom I am so much obliged."

"I will never quit you," said the stranger eagerly, "until I have placed you in safety—nor think me, Princess, more generous than I am; though you are my principal care—"

The stranger was interrupted by a sudden noise of voices that seemed approaching, and they soon distinguished these words—

"Talk not to me of necromancers; I tell you she must be in the castle; I will find her in spite of enchantment."

"Oh, heavens!" cried Isabella; "it is the voice of Manfred! Make haste, or we are ruined! and shut the trap-door after you."

Saying this, she descended the steps precipitately; and as the stranger hastened to follow her, he let the door slip out of his hands: it fell, and the spring closed over it. He tried in vain to open it, not having observed Isabella's method of touching the spring; nor had he many moments to make an essay. The noise of the falling door had been heard by Manfred, who, directed by the sound, hastened thither, attended by his servants with torches.

"It must be Isabella," cried Manfred, before he entered the vault. "She is escaping by the subterraneous passage, but she cannot have got far."

What was the astonishment of the Prince when, instead of Isabella, the light of the torches discovered to him the young peasant whom he thought confined under the fatal helmet!

"Traitor!" said Manfred; "how camest thou here? I thought thee in durance above in the court."

"I am no traitor," replied the young man boldly, "nor am I answerable for your thoughts."

"Presumptuous villain!" cried Manfred; "dost thou provoke my wrath? Tell me, how hast thou escaped from above? Thou hast corrupted thy guards, and their lives shall answer it."

"My poverty," said the peasant calmly, "will disculpate them: though the ministers of a tyrant's wrath, to thee they are faithful, and but too willing to execute the orders which you unjustly imposed upon them."

"Art thou so hardy as to dare my vengeance?" said the Prince; "but tortures shall force the truth from thee. Tell me; I will know thy accomplices."

"There was my accomplice!" said the youth, smiling, and pointing to the roof.

Manfred ordered the torches to be held up, and perceived that one of the cheeks of the enchanted casque had forced its way through the pavement of the court, as his servants had let it fall over the peasant, and had broken through into the vault, leaving a gap, through which the peasant had pressed himself some minutes before he was found by Isabella.

"Was that the way by which thou didst descend?" said Manfred.

"It was," said the youth.

"But what noise was that," said Manfred, "which I heard as I entered the cloister?"

"A door clapped," said the peasant; "I heard it as well as you."

"What door?" said Manfred hastily.

"I am not acquainted with your castle," said the peasant; "this is the first time I ever entered it, and this vault the only part of it within which I ever was."

"But I tell thee," said Manfred (wishing to find out if the youth had discovered the trap-door), "it was this way I heard the noise. My servants heard it too."

"My Lord," interrupted one of them officiously, "to be sure it was the trap-door, and he was going to make his escape."

"Peace, blockhead!" said the Prince angrily; "if he was going to escape, how should he come on this side? I will know from his own mouth what noise it was I heard. Tell me truly; thy life depends on thy veracity."

"My veracity is dearer to me than my life," said the peasant; "nor would I purchase the one by forfeiting the other."

"Indeed, young philosopher!" said Manfred contemptuously; "tell me, then, what was the noise I heard?"

"Ask me what I can answer," said he, "and put me to death instantly if I tell you a lie."

Manfred, growing impatient at the steady valour and indifference of the youth, cried —

"Well, then, thou man of truth, answer! Was it the fall of the trap-door that I heard?"

"It was," said the youth.

"It was!" said the Prince; "and how didst thou come to know there was a trap-door here?"

"I saw the plate of brass by a gleam of moonshine," replied he.

"But what told thee it was a lock?" said Manfred. "How didst thou discover the secret of opening it?"

"Providence, that delivered me from the helmet, was able to direct me to the spring of a lock," said he.

"Providence should have gone a little farther, and have placed thee out of the reach of my resentment," said Manfred. "When Providence had taught thee to open the lock, it abandoned thee for a fool, who did not know how to make use of its favours. Why didst thou not pursue the path pointed out for thy escape? Why didst thou shut the trap-door before thou hadst descended the steps?"

"I might ask you, my Lord," said the peasant, "how I, totally unacquainted with your castle, was to know that those steps led to any outlet? but I scorn to evade your questions. Wherever those steps lead to, perhaps I should have explored the way — I could not be in a worse situation than I was. But the truth is, I let the trap-door fall: your immediate arrival followed. I had given the alarm — what imported it to me whether I was seized a minute sooner or a minute later?"

"Thou art a resolute villain for thy years," said Manfred; "yet on reflection I suspect thou dost but trifle with me. Thou hast not yet told me how thou didst open the lock."

"That I will show you, my Lord," said the peasant; and, taking up a fragment of stone that had fallen from above, he laid himself on the trap-door, and began to beat on the piece of brass that covered it, meaning to gain time for the escape of the Princess. This presence of mind, joined to the frankness of the youth, staggered Manfred. He even felt a disposition towards pardoning one who had been guilty of no crime. Manfred was not one of those savage tyrants who wanton in cruelty unprovoked. The circumstances of his fortune had given an asperity to his temper, which was naturally humane; and his virtues were always ready to operate, when his passions did not obscure his reason.

While the Prince was in this suspense, a confused noise of voices echoed through the distant vaults. As the sound approached, he distinguished the clamours of some of his domestics, whom he had dispersed through the castle in search of Isabella, calling out —

"Where is my Lord? where is the Prince?"

"Here I am," said Manfred, as they came nearer; "have you found the Princess?"

The first that arrived, replied, "Oh, my Lord! I am glad we have found you."

"Found me!" said Manfred; "have you found the Princess?"

"We thought we had, my Lord," said the fellow, looking terrified, "but —"

"But, what?" cried the Prince; "has she escaped?"

"Jaquez and I, my Lord —"

"Yes, I and Diego," interrupted the second, who came up in still greater consternation.

"Speak one of you at a time," said Manfred; "I ask you, where is the Princess?"

"We do not know," said they both together; "but we are frightened out of our wits."

"So I think, blockheads," said Manfred; "what is it has scared you thus?"

"Oh! my Lord," said Jaquez, "Diego has seen such a sight! your Highness would not believe our eyes."

"What new absurdity is this?" cried Manfred; "give me a direct answer, or, by Heaven—"

"Why, my Lord, if it please your Highness to hear me," said the poor fellow, "Diego and I—"

"Yes, I and Jaquez—" cried his comrade.

"Did not I forbid you to speak both at a time?" said the Prince: "you, Jaquez, answer; for the other fool seems more distracted than thou art; what is the matter?"

"My gracious Lord," said Jaquez, "if it please your Highness to hear me; Diego and I, according to your Highness's orders, went to search for the young Lady; but being comprehensive that we might meet the ghost of my young Lord, your Highness's son, God rest his soul, as he has not received Christian burial—"

"Sot!" cried Manfred in a rage; "is it only a ghost, then, that thou hast seen?"

"Oh! worse! worse! my Lord," cried Diego: "I had rather have seen ten whole ghosts."

"Grant me patience!" said Manfred; "these blockheads distract me. Out of my sight, Diego! and thou, Jaquez, tell me in one word, art thou sober? art thou raving? thou wast wont to have some sense: has the other sot frightened himself and thee too? Speak; what is it he fancies he has seen?"

"Why, my Lord," replied Jaquez, trembling, "I was going to tell your Highness, that since the calamitous misfortune of my young Lord, God rest his precious soul! not one of us your Highness's faithful servants—indeed we are, my Lord, though poor men—I say, not one of us has dared to set a foot about the castle, but two together: so Diego and I, thinking that my young Lady might be in the great gallery, went up there to look for her, and tell her your Highness wanted something to impart to her."

"O blundering fools!" cried Manfred; "and in the meantime, she has made her escape, because you were afraid of goblins!— Why, thou knave! she left me in the gallery; I came from thence myself."

"For all that, she may be there still for aught I know," said Jaquez; "but the devil shall have me before I seek her there again — poor Diego! I do not believe he will ever recover it."

"Recover what?" said Manfred; "am I never to learn what it is has terrified these rascals? — but I lose my time; follow me, slave; I will see if she is in the gallery."

"For Heaven's sake, my dear, good Lord," cried Jaquez, "do not go to the gallery. Satan himself I believe is in the chamber next to the gallery."

Manfred, who hitherto had treated the terror of his servants as an idle panic, was struck at this new circumstance. He recollected the apparition of the portrait, and the sudden closing of the door at the end of the gallery. His voice faltered, and he asked with disorder —

"What is in the great chamber?"

"My Lord," said Jaquez, "when Diego and I came into the gallery, he went first, for he said he had more courage than I. So when we came into the gallery we found nobody. We looked under every bench and stool; and still we found nobody."

"Were all the pictures in their places?" said Manfred.

"Yes, my Lord," answered Jaquez; "but we did not think of looking behind them."

"Well, well!" said Manfred; "proceed."

"When we came to the door of the great chamber," continued Jaquez, "we found it shut."

"And could not you open it?" said Manfred.

"Oh! yes, my Lord; would to Heaven we had not!" replied he — "nay, it was not I neither; it was Diego: he was grown foolhardy, and would go on, though I advised him not — if ever I open a door that is shut again — "

"Trifle not," said Manfred, shuddering, "but tell me what you saw in the great chamber on opening the door."

"I, my Lord!" said Jaquez; "I was behind Diego; but I heard the noise."

"Jaquez," said Manfred, in a solemn tone of voice; "tell me, I adjure thee by the souls of my ancestors, what was it thou sawest? what was it thou heardest?"

"It was Diego saw it, my Lord, it was not I," replied Jaquez; "I only heard the noise. Diego had no sooner opened the door, than he cried out, and ran back. I ran back too, and said, 'Is it the ghost?' 'The ghost! no, no,' said Diego, and his hair stood on end—'it is a giant, I believe; he is all clad in armour, for I saw his foot and part of his leg, and they are as large as the helmet below in the court.' As he said these words, my Lord, we heard a violent motion and the rattling of armour, as if the giant was rising, for Diego has told me since that he believes the giant was lying down, for the foot and leg were stretched at length on the floor. Before we could get to the end of the gallery, we heard the door of the great chamber clap behind us, but we did not dare turn back to see if the giant was following us—yet, now I think on it, we must have heard him if he had pursued us—but for Heaven's sake, good my Lord, send for the chaplain, and have the castle exorcised, for, for certain, it is enchanted."

"Ay, pray do, my Lord," cried all the servants at once, "or we must leave your Highness's service."

"Peace, dotards!" said Manfred, "and follow me; I will know what all this means."

"We! my Lord!" cried they with one voice; "we would not go up to the gallery for your Highness's revenue." The young peasant, who had stood silent, now spoke.

"Will your Highness," said he, "permit me to try this adventure? My life is of consequence to nobody; I fear no bad angel, and have offended no good one."

"Your behaviour is above your seeming," said Manfred, viewing him with surprise and admiration—"hereafter I will reward your bravery—but now," continued he with a sigh, "I am so circumstanced, that I dare trust no eyes but my own. However, I give you leave to accompany me."

Manfred, when he first followed Isabella from the gallery, had gone directly to the apartment of his wife, concluding the Princess had retired thither. Hippolita, who knew his step, rose with anxious fondness to meet her Lord, whom she had not seen since the death of their son. She would have flown in a transport mixed of joy and grief to his bosom, but he pushed her rudely off, and said—

"Where is Isabella?"

"Isabella! my Lord!" said the astonished Hippolita.

"Yes, Isabella," cried Manfred imperiously; "I want Isabella."

"My Lord," replied Matilda, who perceived how much his behaviour had shocked her mother, "she has not been with us since your Highness summoned her to your apartment."

"Tell me where she is," said the Prince; "I do not want to know where she has been."

"My good Lord," says Hippolita, "your daughter tells you the truth: Isabella left us by your command, and has not returned since;—but, my good Lord, compose yourself: retire to your rest: this dismal day has disordered you. Isabella shall wait your orders in the morning."

"What, then, you know where she is!" cried Manfred. "Tell me directly, for I will not lose an instant—and you, woman," speaking to his wife, "order your chaplain to attend me forthwith."

"Isabella," said Hippolita calmly, "is retired, I suppose, to her chamber: she is not accustomed to watch at this late hour. Gracious my Lord," continued she, "let me know what has disturbed you. Has Isabella offended you?"

"Trouble me not with questions," said Manfred, "but tell me where she is."

"Matilda shall call her," said the Princess. "Sit down, my Lord, and resume your wonted fortitude."

"What, art thou jealous of Isabella?" replied he, "that you wish to be present at our interview!"

"Good heavens! my Lord," said Hippolita, "what is it your Highness means?"

"Thou wilt know ere many minutes are passed," said the cruel Prince. "Send your chaplain to me, and wait my pleasure here."

At these words he flung out of the room in search of Isabella, leaving the amazed ladies thunderstruck with his words and frantic deportment, and lost in vain conjectures on what he was meditating.

Manfred was now returning from the vault, attended by the peasant and a few of his servants whom he had obliged to accompany him. He ascended the staircase without stopping till he arrived at the gallery, at the door of which he met Hippolita and her chaplain. When Diego had been dismissed by Manfred, he had gone directly to the Princess's apartment with the alarm of what he had seen. That excellent Lady, who no more than Manfred doubted of the reality of the vision, yet affected to treat it as a delirium of the servant. Willing, however, to save her Lord from any additional shock, and prepared by a series of griefs not to tremble at any accession to it, she determined to make herself the first sacrifice, if fate had marked the present hour for their destruction. Dismissing the reluctant Matilda to her rest, who in vain sued for leave to accompany her mother, and attended only by her chaplain, Hippolita had visited the gallery and great chamber; and now with more serenity of soul than she had felt for many hours, she met her Lord, and assured him that the vision of the gigantic leg and foot was all a fable; and no doubt an impression made by fear, and the dark and dismal hour of the night, on the minds of his servants. She and the chaplain had examined the chamber, and found everything in the usual order.

Manfred, though persuaded, like his wife, that the vision had been no work of fancy, recovered a little from the tempest of mind into which so many strange events had thrown him. Ashamed, too, of his inhuman treatment of a Princess who returned every injury with new marks of tenderness and duty, he felt returning love forcing itself into his eyes; but not less ashamed of feeling remorse towards one against whom he was inwardly meditating a yet more bitter outrage, he curbed the yearnings of his heart, and did not dare to lean even towards pity. The next transition of his soul was to exquisite villainy.

Presuming on the unshaken submission of Hippolita, he flattered himself that she would not only acquiesce with patience to a divorce, but would obey, if it was his pleasure, in endeavouring to persuade Isabella to give him her hand—but ere he could indulge his horrid hope, he reflected that Isabella was not to be found. Coming to himself, he gave orders that every avenue to the castle should be strictly guarded, and charged his domestics on pain of their lives to suffer nobody to pass out. The young peasant, to whom he spoke favourably, he ordered to remain in a small chamber on the stairs, in which there was a pallet-bed, and the key of which he took away himself, telling the youth he would talk with him in the morning. Then dismissing his attendants, and bestowing a sullen kind of half-nod on Hippolita, he retired to his own chamber.

CHAPTER II.

Matilda, who by Hippolita's order had retired to her apartment, was ill-disposed to take any rest. The shocking fate of her brother had deeply affected her. She was surprised at not seeing Isabella; but the strange words which had fallen from her father, and his obscure menace to the Princess his wife, accompanied by the most furious behaviour, had filled her gentle mind with terror and alarm. She waited anxiously for the return of Bianca, a young damsel that attended her, whom she had sent to learn what was become of Isabella. Bianca soon appeared, and informed her mistress of what she had gathered from the servants, that Isabella was nowhere to be found. She related the adventure of the young peasant who had been discovered in the vault, though with many simple additions from the incoherent accounts of the domestics; and she dwelt principally on the gigantic leg and foot which had been seen in the gallery-chamber. This last circumstance had terrified Bianca so much, that she was rejoiced when Matilda told her that she would not go to rest, but would watch till the Princess should rise.

The young Princess wearied herself in conjectures on the flight of Isabella, and on the threats of Manfred to her mother. "But what business could he have so urgent with the chaplain?" said Matilda, "Does he intend to have my brother's body interred privately in the chapel?"

"Oh, Madam!" said Bianca, "now I guess. As you are become his heiress, he is impatient to have you married: he has always been raving for more sons; I warrant he is now impatient for grandsons. As sure as I live, Madam, I shall see you a bride at last. — Good madam, you won't cast off your faithful Bianca: you won't put Donna Rosara over me now you are a great Princess."

"My poor Bianca," said Matilda, "how fast your thoughts amble! I a great princess! What hast thou seen in Manfred's behaviour since my brother's death that bespeaks any increase of tenderness to me? No, Bianca; his heart was ever a stranger to me — but he is my father, and I must not complain. Nay, if Heaven shuts my father's heart against me, it overpays my little merit in the tenderness of my mother — O that dear mother! yes, Bianca, 'tis there I feel the rugged temper of Manfred. I can support his harshness to me with patience; but it wounds my soul when I am witness to his causeless severity towards her."

"Oh! Madam," said Bianca, "all men use their wives so, when they are weary of them."

"And yet you congratulated me but now," said Matilda, "when you fancied my father intended to dispose of me!"

"I would have you a great Lady," replied Bianca, "come what will. I do not wish to see you moped in a convent, as you would be if you had your will, and if my Lady, your mother, who knows that a bad husband is better than no husband at all, did not hinder you. — Bless me! what noise is that! St. Nicholas forgive me! I was but in jest."

"It is the wind," said Matilda, "whistling through the battlements in the tower above: you have heard it a thousand times."

"Nay," said Bianca, "there was no harm neither in what I said: it is no sin to talk of matrimony — and so, Madam, as I was saying, if my Lord Manfred should offer you a handsome young Prince for a bridegroom, you would drop him a curtsey, and tell him you would rather take the veil?"

"Thank Heaven! I am in no such danger," said Matilda: "you know how many proposals for me he has rejected — "

"And you thank him, like a dutiful daughter, do you, Madam? But come, Madam; suppose, to-morrow morning, he was to send for you to the great council chamber, and there you should find at his elbow a lovely young Prince, with large black eyes, a smooth white forehead, and manly curling locks like jet; in short, Madam, a young hero resembling the picture of the good Alfonso in the gallery, which you sit and gaze at for hours together — "

"Do not speak lightly of that picture," interrupted Matilda sighing; "I know the adoration with which I look at that picture is uncommon — but I am not in love with a coloured panel. The character of that virtuous Prince, the veneration with which my mother has inspired me for his memory, the orisons which, I know not why, she has enjoined me to pour forth at his tomb, all have concurred to persuade me that somehow or other my destiny is linked with something relating to him."

"Lord, Madam! how should that be?" said Bianca; "I have always heard that your family was in no way related to his: and I am sure I cannot conceive why my Lady, the Princess, sends you in a cold morning or a damp evening to pray at his tomb:

he is no saint by the almanack. If you must pray, why does she not bid you address yourself to our great St. Nicholas? I am sure he is the saint I pray to for a husband."

"Perhaps my mind would be less affected," said Matilda, "if my mother would explain her reasons to me: but it is the mystery she observes, that inspires me with this — I know not what to call it. As she never acts from caprice, I am sure there is some fatal secret at bottom — nay, I know there is: in her agony of grief for my brother's death she dropped some words that intimated as much."

"Oh! dear Madam," cried Bianca, "what were they?"

"No," said Matilda, "if a parent lets fall a word, and wishes it recalled, it is not for a child to utter it."

"What! was she sorry for what she had said?" asked Bianca; "I am sure, Madam, you may trust me — "

"With my own little secrets when I have any, I may," said Matilda; "but never with my mother's: a child ought to have no ears or eyes but as a parent directs."

"Well! to be sure, Madam, you were born to be a saint," said Bianca, "and there is no resisting one's vocation: you will end in a convent at last. But there is my Lady Isabella would not be so reserved to me: she will let me talk to her of young men: and when a handsome cavalier has come to the castle, she has owned to me that she wished your brother Conrad resembled him."

"Bianca," said the Princess, "I do not allow you to mention my friend disrespectfully. Isabella is of a cheerful disposition, but her soul is pure as virtue itself. She knows your idle babbling humour, and perhaps has now and then encouraged it, to divert melancholy, and enliven the solitude in which my father keeps us — "

"Blessed Mary!" said Bianca, starting, "there it is again! Dear Madam, do you hear nothing? this castle is certainly haunted!"

"Peace!" said Matilda, "and listen! I did think I heard a voice — but it must be fancy: your terrors, I suppose, have infected me."

"Indeed! indeed! Madam," said Bianca, half-weeping with agony, "I am sure I heard a voice."

"Does anybody lie in the chamber beneath?" said the Princess.

"Nobody has dared to lie there," answered Bianca, "since the great astrologer, that was your brother's tutor, drowned himself. For certain, Madam, his ghost and the young Prince's are now met in the chamber below — for Heaven's sake let us fly to your mother's apartment!"

"I charge you not to stir," said Matilda. "If they are spirits in pain, we may ease their sufferings by questioning them. They can mean no hurt to us, for we have not injured them — and if they should, shall we be more safe in one chamber than in another? Reach me my beads; we will say a prayer, and then speak to them."

"Oh! dear Lady, I would not speak to a ghost for the world!" cried Bianca. As she said those words they heard the casement of the little chamber below Matilda's open. They listened attentively, and in a few minutes thought they heard a person sing, but could not distinguish the words.

"This can be no evil spirit," said the Princess, in a low voice; "it is undoubtedly one of the family — open the window, and we shall know the voice."

"I dare not, indeed, Madam," said Bianca.

"Thou art a very fool," said Matilda, opening the window gently herself. The noise the Princess made was, however, heard by the person beneath, who stopped; and they concluded had heard the casement open.

"Is anybody below?" said the Princess; "if there is, speak."

"Yes," said an unknown voice.

"Who is it?" said Matilda.

"A stranger," replied the voice.

"What stranger?" said she; "and how didst thou come there at this unusual hour, when all the gates of the castle are locked?"

"I am not here willingly," answered the voice. "But pardon me, Lady, if I have disturbed your rest; I knew not that I was overheard. Sleep had forsaken me; I left a restless couch, and came to waste the irksome hours with gazing on the fair approach of morning, impatient to be dismissed from this castle."

"Thy words and accents," said Matilda, "are of melancholy cast; if thou art unhappy, I pity thee. If poverty afflicts thee, let me know it; I will mention thee to the Princess, whose beneficent soul ever melts for the distressed, and she will relieve thee."

"I am indeed unhappy," said the stranger; "and I know not what wealth is. But I do not complain of the lot which Heaven has cast for me; I am young and healthy, and am not ashamed of owing my support to myself—yet think me not proud, or that I disdain your generous offers. I will remember you in my orisons, and will pray for blessings on your gracious self and your noble mistress—if I sigh, Lady, it is for others, not for myself."

"Now I have it, Madam," said Bianca, whispering the Princess; "this is certainly the young peasant; and, by my conscience, he is in love—Well! this is a charming adventure!—do, Madam, let us sift him. He does not know you, but takes you for one of my Lady Hippolita's women."

"Art thou not ashamed, Bianca!" said the Princess. "What right have we to pry into the secrets of this young man's heart? He seems virtuous and frank, and tells us he is unhappy. Are those circumstances that authorise us to make a property of him? How are we entitled to his confidence?"

"Lord, Madam! how little you know of love!" replied Bianca; "why, lovers have no pleasure equal to talking of their mistress."

"And would you have me become a peasant's confidante?" said the Princess.

"Well, then, let me talk to him," said Bianca; "though I have the honour of being your Highness's maid of honour, I was not always so great. Besides, if love levels ranks, it raises them too; I have a respect for any young man in love."

"Peace, simpleton!" said the Princess. "Though he said he was unhappy, it does not follow that he must be in love. Think of all that has happened to-day, and tell me if there are no misfortunes but what love causes. — Stranger," resumed the Princess, "if thy misfortunes have not been occasioned by thy own fault, and are within the compass of the Princess Hippolita's power to redress, I will take upon me to answer that she will be thy protectress. When thou art dismissed from this castle, repair to holy father Jerome, at the convent adjoining to the church of St. Nicholas, and make thy story known to him, as far as thou thinkest meet. He will not fail to inform the Princess, who is the mother of all that want her assistance. Farewell; it is not seemly for me to hold farther converse with a man at this unwonted hour."

"May the saints guard thee, gracious Lady!" replied the peasant; "but oh! if a poor and worthless stranger might presume to beg a minute's audience farther; am I so happy? the casement is not shut; might I venture to ask — "

"Speak quickly," said Matilda; "the morning dawns apace: should the labourers come into the fields and perceive us — What wouldst thou ask?"

"I know not how, I know not if I dare," said the young stranger, faltering; "yet the humanity with which you have spoken to me emboldens — Lady! dare I trust you?"

"Heavens!" said Matilda, "what dost thou mean? With what wouldst thou trust me? Speak boldly, if thy secret is fit to be entrusted to a virtuous breast."

"I would ask," said the peasant, recollecting himself, "whether what I have heard from the domestics is true, that the Princess is missing from the castle?"

"What imports it to thee to know?" replied Matilda. "Thy first words bespoke a prudent and becoming gravity. Dost thou come hither to pry into the secrets of Manfred? Adieu. I have been mistaken in thee." Saying these words she shut the casement hastily, without giving the young man time to reply.

"I had acted more wisely," said the Princess to Bianca, with some sharpness, "if I had let thee converse with this peasant; his inquisitiveness seems of a piece with thy own."

"It is not fit for me to argue with your Highness," replied Bianca; "but perhaps the questions I should have put to him would have been more to the purpose than those you have been pleased to ask him."

"Oh! no doubt," said Matilda; "you are a very discreet personage! May I know what you would have asked him?"

"A bystander often sees more of the game than those that play," answered Bianca. "Does your Highness think, Madam, that this question about my Lady Isabella was the result of mere curiosity? No, no, Madam, there is more in it than you great folks are aware of. Lopez told me that all the servants believe this young fellow contrived my Lady Isabella's escape; now, pray, Madam, observe you and I both know that my Lady Isabella never much fancied the Prince your brother. Well! he is killed just in a critical minute—I accuse nobody. A helmet falls from the moon—so, my Lord, your father says; but Lopez and all the servants say that this young spark is a magician, and stole it from Alfonso's tomb—"

"Have done with this rhapsody of impertinence," said Matilda.

"Nay, Madam, as you please," cried Bianca; "yet it is very particular though, that my Lady Isabella should be missing the very same day, and that this young sorcerer should be found at the mouth of the trap-door. I accuse nobody; but if my young Lord came honestly by his death—"

"Dare not on thy duty," said Matilda, "to breathe a suspicion on the purity of my dear Isabella's fame."

"Purity, or not purity," said Bianca, "gone she is—a stranger is found that nobody knows; you question him yourself; he tells you he is in love, or unhappy, it is the same thing—nay, he owned he was unhappy about others; and is anybody unhappy about another, unless they are in love with them? and at the very next word, he asks innocently, pour soul! if my Lady Isabella is missing."

"To be sure," said Matilda, "thy observations are not totally without foundation—Isabella's flight amazes me. The curiosity of the stranger is very particular; yet Isabella never concealed a thought from me."

"So she told you," said Bianca, "to fish out your secrets; but who knows, Madam, but this stranger may be some Prince in disguise? Do, Madam, let me open the window, and ask him a few questions."

"No," replied Matilda, "I will ask him myself, if he knows aught of Isabella; he is not worthy I should converse farther with him." She was going to open the casement, when they heard the bell ring at the postern-gate of the castle, which is on the right hand of the tower, where Matilda lay. This prevented the Princess from renewing the conversation with the stranger.

After continuing silent for some time, "I am persuaded," said she to Bianca, "that whatever be the cause of Isabella's flight it had no unworthy motive. If this stranger was accessory to it, she must be satisfied with his fidelity and worth. I observed, did not you, Bianca? that his words were tinctured with an uncommon infusion of piety. It was no ruffian's speech; his phrases were becoming a man of gentle birth."

"I told you, Madam," said Bianca, "that I was sure he was some Prince in disguise."

"Yet," said Matilda, "if he was privy to her escape, how will you account for his not accompanying her in her flight? why expose himself unnecessarily and rashly to my father's resentment?"

"As for that, Madam," replied she, "if he could get from under the helmet, he will find ways of eluding your father's anger. I do not doubt but he has some talisman or other about him."

"You resolve everything into magic," said Matilda; "but a man who has any intercourse with infernal spirits, does not dare to make use of those tremendous and holy words which he uttered. Didst thou not observe with what fervour he vowed to remember me to heaven in his prayers? Yes; Isabella was undoubtedly convinced of his piety."

"Commend me to the piety of a young fellow and a damsel that consult to elope!" said Bianca. "No, no, Madam, my Lady Isabella is of another guess mould than you take her for. She used indeed to sigh and lift up her eyes in your company, because she knows you are a saint; but when your back was turned—"

"You wrong her," said Matilda; "Isabella is no hypocrite; she has a due sense of devotion, but never affected a call she has not. On the contrary, she always combated my inclination for the cloister; and though I own the mystery she has made to me of her flight confounds me; though it seems inconsistent with the friendship between us; I cannot forget the disinterested warmth with which she always opposed my taking the veil. She wished to see me married, though my dower would have been a loss to her and my brother's children. For her sake I will believe well of this young peasant."

"Then you do think there is some liking between them," said Bianca. While she was speaking, a servant came hastily into the chamber and told the Princess that the Lady Isabella was found.

"Where?" said Matilda.

"She has taken sanctuary in St. Nicholas's church," replied the servant; "Father Jerome has brought the news himself; he is below with his Highness."

"Where is my mother?" said Matilda.

"She is in her own chamber, Madam, and has asked for you."

Manfred had risen at the first dawn of light, and gone to Hippolita's apartment, to inquire if she knew aught of Isabella. While he was questioning her, word was brought that Jerome demanded to speak with him. Manfred, little suspecting the cause of the Friar's arrival, and knowing he was employed by Hippolita in her charities, ordered him to be admitted, intending to leave them together, while he pursued his search after Isabella.

"Is your business with me or the Princess?" said Manfred.

"With both," replied the holy man. "The Lady Isabella—"

"What of her?" interrupted Manfred, eagerly.

"Is at St. Nicholas's altar," replied Jerome.

"That is no business of Hippolita," said Manfred with confusion; "let us retire to my chamber, Father, and inform me how she came thither."

"No, my Lord," replied the good man, with an air of firmness and authority, that daunted even the resolute Manfred, who could not help revering the saint-like virtues of Jerome; "my commission is to both, and with your Highness's good-liking, in the presence of both I shall deliver it; but first, my Lord, I must interrogate the Princess, whether she is acquainted with the cause of the Lady Isabella's retirement from your castle."

"No, on my soul," said Hippolita; "does Isabella charge me with being privy to it?"

"Father," interrupted Manfred, "I pay due reverence to your holy profession; but I am sovereign here, and will allow no meddling priest to interfere in the affairs of my domestic. If you have aught to say attend me to my chamber; I do not use to let my wife be acquainted with the secret affairs of my state; they are not within a woman's province."

"My Lord," said the holy man, "I am no intruder into the secrets of families. My office is to promote peace, to heal divisions, to preach repentance, and teach mankind to curb their headstrong passions. I forgive your Highness's uncharitable apostrophe; I know my duty, and am the minister of a mightier prince than Manfred. Hearken to him who speaks through my organs."

Manfred trembled with rage and shame. Hippolita's countenance declared her astonishment and impatience to know where this would end. Her silence more strongly spoke her observance of Manfred.

"The Lady Isabella," resumed Jerome, "commends herself to both your Highnesses; she thanks both for the kindness with which she has been treated in your castle: she deplores the loss of your son, and her own misfortune in not becoming the daughter of such wise and noble Princes, whom she shall always respect as Parents; she prays for uninterrupted union and felicity between you" [Manfred's colour changed]: "but as it is no longer possible for her to be allied to you, she entreats your consent to remain in sanctuary, till she can learn news of her father, or, by the certainty of his death, be at liberty, with the approbation of her guardians, to dispose of herself in suitable marriage."

"I shall give no such consent," said the Prince, "but insist on her return to the castle without delay: I am answerable for her person to her guardians, and will not brook her being in any hands but my own."

"Your Highness will recollect whether that can any longer be proper," replied the Friar.

"I want no monitor," said Manfred, colouring; "Isabella's conduct leaves room for strange suspicions — and that young villain, who was at least the accomplice of her flight, if not the cause of it —"

"The cause!" interrupted Jerome; "was a young man the cause?"

"This is not to be borne!" cried Manfred. "Am I to be bearded in my own palace by an insolent Monk? Thou art privy, I guess, to their amours."

"I would pray to heaven to clear up your uncharitable surmises," said Jerome, "if your Highness were not satisfied in your conscience how unjustly you accuse me. I do pray to heaven to pardon that uncharitableness: and I implore your Highness to leave the Princess at peace in that holy place, where she is not liable to be disturbed by such vain and worldly fantasies as discourses of love from any man."

"Cant not to me," said Manfred, "but return and bring the Princess to her duty."

"It is my duty to prevent her return hither," said Jerome. "She is where orphans and virgins are safest from the snares and wiles of this world; and nothing but a parent's authority shall take her thence."

"I am her parent," cried Manfred, "and demand her."

"She wished to have you for her parent," said the Friar; "but Heaven that forbad that connection has for ever dissolved all ties betwixt you: and I announce to your Highness —"

"Stop! audacious man," said Manfred, "and dread my displeasure."

"Holy Father," said Hippolita, "it is your office to be no respecter of persons: you must speak as your duty prescribes: but it is my duty to hear nothing that it pleases not my Lord I should hear. Attend the Prince to his chamber. I will retire to my oratory, and pray to the blessed Virgin to inspire you with her holy counsels, and to restore the heart of my gracious Lord to its wonted peace and gentleness."

"Excellent woman!" said the Friar. "My Lord, I attend your pleasure."

Manfred, accompanied by the Friar, passed to his own apartment, where shutting the door, "I perceive, Father," said he, "that Isabella has acquainted you with my purpose. Now hear my resolve, and obey. Reasons of state, most urgent reasons, my own and the safety of my people, demand that I should have a son. It is in vain to expect an heir from Hippolita. I have made choice of Isabella. You must bring her back; and you must do more. I know the influence you have with Hippolita: her conscience is in your hands. She is, I allow, a faultless woman: her soul is set on heaven, and scorns the little grandeur of this world: you can withdraw her from it entirely. Persuade her to consent to the dissolution of our marriage, and to retire into a monastery — she shall endow one if she will; and she shall have the means of being as liberal to your order as she or you can wish. Thus you will divert the calamities that are hanging over our heads, and have the merit of saving the principality of Otranto from destruction. You are a prudent man, and though the warmth of my temper betrayed me into some unbecoming expressions, I honour your virtue, and wish to be indebted to you for the repose of my life and the preservation of my family."

"The will of heaven be done!" said the Friar. "I am but its worthless instrument. It makes use of my tongue to tell thee, Prince, of thy unwarrantable designs. The injuries of the virtuous Hippolita have mounted to the throne of pity. By me thou art reprimanded for thy adulterous intention of repudiating her: by me thou art warned not to pursue the incestuous design on thy contracted daughter. Heaven that delivered her from thy fury, when the judgments so recently fallen on thy house ought to have inspired thee with other thoughts, will continue to watch over her. Even I, a poor and despised Friar, am able to protect her from thy violence — I, sinner as I am, and uncharitably reviled by your Highness as an accomplice of I know not what amours, scorn the allurements with which it has pleased thee to tempt mine honesty. I love my order; I honour devout souls; I respect the piety of thy Princess — but I will not betray the confidence she reposes in me, nor serve even the cause of religion by foul and sinful compliances — but forsooth! the welfare of the state depends on your Highness having a son! Heaven mocks the short-sighted views of man. But yester-morn, whose house was so great, so flourishing as Manfred's? — where is young Conrad now? — My

Lord, I respect your tears—but I mean not to check them—let them flow, Prince! They will weigh more with heaven toward the welfare of thy subjects, than a marriage, which, founded on lust or policy, could never prosper. The sceptre, which passed from the race of Alfonso to thine, cannot be preserved by a match which the church will never allow. If it is the will of the Most High that Manfred's name must perish, resign yourself, my Lord, to its decrees; and thus deserve a crown that can never pass away. Come, my Lord; I like this sorrow—let us return to the Princess: she is not apprised of your cruel intentions; nor did I mean more than to alarm you. You saw with what gentle patience, with what efforts of love, she heard, she rejected hearing, the extent of your guilt. I know she longs to fold you in her arms, and assure you of her unalterable affection."

"Father," said the Prince, "you mistake my compunction: true, I honour Hippolita's virtues; I think her a Saint; and wish it were for my soul's health to tie faster the knot that has united us—but alas! Father, you know not the bitterest of my pangs! it is some time that I have had scruples on the legality of our union: Hippolita is related to me in the fourth degree—it is true, we had a dispensation: but I have been informed that she had also been contracted to another. This it is that sits heavy at my heart: to this state of unlawful wedlock I impute the visitation that has fallen on me in the death of Conrad!—ease my conscience of this burden: dissolve our marriage, and accomplish the work of godliness—which your divine exhortations have commenced in my soul."

How cutting was the anguish which the good man felt, when he perceived this turn in the wily Prince! He trembled for Hippolita, whose ruin he saw was determined; and he feared if Manfred had no hope of recovering Isabella, that his impatience for a son would direct him to some other object, who might not be equally proof against the temptation of Manfred's rank. For some time the holy man remained absorbed in thought. At length, conceiving some hopes from delay, he thought the wisest conduct would be to prevent the Prince from despairing of recovering Isabella. Her the Friar knew he could dispose, from her affection to Hippolita, and from the aversion she had expressed to him for Manfred's addresses, to second his views, till the censures of the church could be fulminated against a divorce. With this intention, as if struck with the Prince's scruples, he at length said:

"My Lord, I have been pondering on what your Highness has said; and if in truth it is delicacy of conscience that is the real motive of your repugnance to your virtuous Lady, far be it from me to endeavour to harden your heart. The church is an indulgent mother: unfold your griefs to her: she alone can administer comfort to your soul, either by satisfying your conscience, or upon examination of your scruples, by setting you at liberty, and indulging you in the lawful means of continuing your lineage. In the latter case, if the Lady Isabella can be brought to consent—"

Manfred, who concluded that he had either over-reached the good man, or that his first warmth had been but a tribute paid to appearance, was overjoyed at this sudden turn, and repeated the most magnificent promises, if he should succeed by the Friar's mediation. The well-meaning priest suffered him to deceive himself, fully determined to traverse his views, instead of seconding them.

"Since we now understand one another," resumed the Prince, "I expect, Father, that you satisfy me in one point. Who is the youth that I found in the vault? He must have been privy to Isabella's flight: tell me truly, is he her lover? or is he an agent for another's passion? I have often suspected Isabella's indifference to my son: a thousand circumstances crowd on my mind that confirm that suspicion. She herself was so conscious of it, that while I discoursed her in the gallery, she outran my suspicions, and endeavoured to justify herself from coolness to Conrad."

The Friar, who knew nothing of the youth, but what he had learnt occasionally from the Princess, ignorant what was become of him, and not sufficiently reflecting on the impetuosity of Manfred's temper, conceived that it might not be amiss to sow the seeds of jealousy in his mind: they might be turned to some use hereafter, either by prejudicing the Prince against Isabella, if he persisted in that union or by diverting his attention to a wrong scent, and employing his thoughts on a visionary intrigue, prevent his engaging in any new pursuit. With this unhappy policy, he answered in a manner to confirm Manfred in the belief of some connection between Isabella and the youth. The Prince, whose passions wanted little fuel to throw them into a blaze, fell into a rage at the idea of what the Friar suggested.

"I will fathom to the bottom of this intrigue," cried he; and quitting Jerome abruptly, with a command to remain there till his return, he hastened to the great hall of the castle, and ordered the peasant to be brought before him.

"Thou hardened young impostor!" said the Prince, as soon as he saw the youth; "what becomes of thy boasted veracity now? it was Providence, was it, and the light of the moon, that discovered the lock of the trap-door to thee? Tell me, audacious boy, who thou art, and how long thou hast been acquainted with the Princess—and take care to answer with less equivocation than thou didst last night, or tortures shall wring the truth from thee."

The young man, perceiving that his share in the flight of the Princess was discovered, and concluding that anything he should say could no longer be of any service or detriment to her, replied—

"I am no impostor, my Lord, nor have I deserved opprobrious language. I answered to every question your Highness put to me last night with the same veracity that I shall speak now: and that will not be from fear of your tortures, but because my soul abhors a falsehood. Please to repeat your questions, my Lord; I am ready to give you all the satisfaction in my power."

"You know my questions," replied the Prince, "and only want time to prepare an evasion. Speak directly; who art thou? and how long hast thou been known to the Princess?"

"I am a labourer at the next village," said the peasant; "my name is Theodore. The Princess found me in the vault last night: before that hour I never was in her presence."

"I may believe as much or as little as I please of this," said Manfred; "but I will hear thy own story before I examine into the truth of it. Tell me, what reason did the Princess give thee for making her escape? thy life depends on thy answer."

"She told me," replied Theodore, "that she was on the brink of destruction, and that if she could not escape from the castle, she was in danger in a few moments of being made miserable for ever."

"And on this slight foundation, on a silly girl's report," said Manfred, "thou didst hazard my displeasure?"

"I fear no man's displeasure," said Theodore, "when a woman in distress puts herself under my protection."

During this examination, Matilda was going to the apartment of Hippolita. At the upper end of the hall, where Manfred sat, was a boarded gallery with latticed windows, through which Matilda and Bianca were to pass. Hearing her father's voice, and seeing the servants assembled round him, she stopped to learn the occasion. The prisoner soon drew her attention: the steady and composed manner in which he answered, and the gallantry of his last reply, which were the first words she heard distinctly, interested her in his favour. His person was noble, handsome, and commanding, even in that situation: but his countenance soon engrossed her whole care.

"Heavens! Bianca," said the Princess softly, "do I dream? or is not that youth the exact resemblance of Alfonso's picture in the gallery?"

She could say no more, for her father's voice grew louder at every word.

"This bravado," said he, "surpasses all thy former insolence. Thou shalt experience the wrath with which thou darest to trifle. Seize him," continued Manfred, "and bind him—the first news the Princess hears of her champion shall be, that he has lost his head for her sake."

"The injustice of which thou art guilty towards me," said Theodore, "convinces me that I have done a good deed in delivering the Princess from thy tyranny. May she be happy, whatever becomes of me!"

"This is a lover!" cried Manfred in a rage: "a peasant within sight of death is not animated by such sentiments. Tell me, tell me, rash boy, who thou art, or the rack shall force thy secret from thee."

"Thou hast threatened me with death already," said the youth, "for the truth I have told thee: if that is all the encouragement I am to expect for sincerity, I am not tempted to indulge thy vain curiosity farther."

"Then thou wilt not speak?" said Manfred.

"I will not," replied he.

"Bear him away into the courtyard," said Manfred; "I will see his head this instant severed from his body."

45

Matilda fainted at hearing those words. Bianca shrieked, and cried—"Help! help! the Princess is dead!"

Manfred started at this ejaculation, and demanded what was the matter! The young peasant, who heard it too, was struck with horror, and asked eagerly the same question; but Manfred ordered him to be hurried into the court, and kept there for execution, till he had informed himself of the cause of Bianca's shrieks. When he learned the meaning, he treated it as a womanish panic, and ordering Matilda to be carried to her apartment, he rushed into the court, and calling for one of his guards, bade Theodore kneel down, and prepare to receive the fatal blow.

The undaunted youth received the bitter sentence with a resignation that touched every heart but Manfred's. He wished earnestly to know the meaning of the words he had heard relating to the Princess; but fearing to exasperate the tyrant more against her, he desisted. The only boon he deigned to ask was, that he might be permitted to have a confessor, and make his peace with heaven. Manfred, who hoped by the confessor's means to come at the youth's history, readily granted his request; and being convinced that Father Jerome was now in his interest, he ordered him to be called and shrive the prisoner. The holy man, who had little foreseen the catastrophe that his imprudence occasioned, fell on his knees to the Prince, and adjured him in the most solemn manner not to shed innocent blood. He accused himself in the bitterest terms for his indiscretion, endeavoured to disculpate the youth, and left no method untried to soften the tyrant's rage. Manfred, more incensed than appeased by Jerome's intercession, whose retraction now made him suspect he had been imposed upon by both, commanded the Friar to do his duty, telling him he would not allow the prisoner many minutes for confession.

"Nor do I ask many, my Lord," said the unhappy young man. "My sins, thank heaven, have not been numerous; nor exceed what might be expected at my years. Dry your tears, good Father, and let us despatch. This is a bad world; nor have I had cause to leave it with regret."

"Oh wretched youth!" said Jerome; "how canst thou bear the sight of me with patience? I am thy murderer! it is I have brought this dismal hour upon thee!"

"I forgive thee from my soul," said the youth, "as I hope heaven will pardon me. Hear my confession, Father; and give me thy blessing."

"How can I prepare thee for thy passage as I ought?" said Jerome. "Thou canst not be saved without pardoning thy foes — and canst thou forgive that impious man there?"

"I can," said Theodore; "I do."

"And does not this touch thee, cruel Prince?" said the Friar.

"I sent for thee to confess him," said Manfred, sternly; "not to plead for him. Thou didst first incense me against him — his blood be upon thy head!"

"It will! it will!" said the good man, in an agony of sorrow. "Thou and I must never hope to go where this blessed youth is going!"

"Despatch!" said Manfred; "I am no more to be moved by the whining of priests than by the shrieks of women."

"What!" said the youth; "is it possible that my fate could have occasioned what I heard! Is the Princess then again in thy power?"

"Thou dost but remember me of my wrath," said Manfred. "Prepare thee, for this moment is thy last."

The youth, who felt his indignation rise, and who was touched with the sorrow which he saw he had infused into all the spectators, as well as into the Friar, suppressed his emotions, and putting off his doublet, and unbuttoning his collar, knelt down to his prayers. As he stooped, his shirt slipped down below his shoulder, and discovered the mark of a bloody arrow.

"Gracious heaven!" cried the holy man, starting; "what do I see? It is my child! my Theodore!"

The passions that ensued must be conceived; they cannot be painted. The tears of the assistants were suspended by wonder, rather than stopped by joy. They seemed to inquire in the eyes of their Lord what they ought to feel. Surprise, doubt, tenderness, respect, succeeded each other in the countenance of the youth. He received with modest submission the effusion of the old man's tears and embraces. Yet afraid of giving a loose to hope, and suspecting from what had passed the inflexibility of Manfred's temper, he cast a glance towards the Prince, as if to say, canst thou be unmoved at such a scene as this?

Manfred's heart was capable of being touched. He forgot his anger in his astonishment; yet his pride forbad his owning himself affected. He even doubted whether this discovery was not a contrivance of the Friar to save the youth.

"What may this mean?" said he. "How can he be thy son? Is it consistent with thy profession or reputed sanctity to avow a peasant's offspring for the fruit of thy irregular amours!"

"Oh, God!" said the holy man, "dost thou question his being mine? Could I feel the anguish I do if I were not his father? Spare him! good Prince! spare him! and revile me as thou pleasest."

"Spare him! spare him!" cried the attendants; "for this good man's sake!"

"Peace!" said Manfred, sternly. "I must know more ere I am disposed to pardon. A Saint's bastard may be no saint himself."

"Injurious Lord!" said Theodore, "add not insult to cruelty. If I am this venerable man's son, though no Prince, as thou art, know the blood that flows in my veins—"

"Yes," said the Friar, interrupting him, "his blood is noble; nor is he that abject thing, my Lord, you speak him. He is my lawful son, and Sicily can boast of few houses more ancient than that of Falconara. But alas! my Lord, what is blood! what is nobility! We are all reptiles, miserable, sinful creatures. It is piety alone that can distinguish us from the dust whence we sprung, and whither we must return."

"Truce to your sermon," said Manfred; "you forget you are no longer Friar Jerome, but the Count of Falconara. Let me know your history; you will have time to moralise hereafter, if you should not happen to obtain the grace of that sturdy criminal there."

"Mother of God!" said the Friar, "is it possible my Lord can refuse a father the life of his only, his long-lost, child! Trample me, my Lord, scorn, afflict me, accept my life for his, but spare my son!"

"Thou canst feel, then," said Manfred, "what it is to lose an only son! A little hour ago thou didst preach up resignation to me: my house, if fate so pleased, must perish—but the Count of Falconara—"

"Alas! my Lord," said Jerome, "I confess I have offended; but aggravate not an old man's sufferings! I boast not of my family, nor think of such vanities—it is nature, that pleads for this boy; it is the memory of the dear woman that bore him. Is she, Theodore, is she dead?"

"Her soul has long been with the blessed," said Theodore.

"Oh! how?" cried Jerome, "tell me—no—she is happy! Thou art all my care now!—Most dread Lord! will you—will you grant me my poor boy's life?"

"Return to thy convent," answered Manfred; "conduct the Princess hither; obey me in what else thou knowest; and I promise thee the life of thy son."

"Oh! my Lord," said Jerome, "is my honesty the price I must pay for this dear youth's safety?"

"For me!" cried Theodore. "Let me die a thousand deaths, rather than stain thy conscience. What is it the tyrant would exact of thee? Is the Princess still safe from his power? Protect her, thou venerable old man; and let all the weight of his wrath fall on me."

Jerome endeavoured to check the impetuosity of the youth; and ere Manfred could reply, the trampling of horses was heard, and a brazen trumpet, which hung without the gate of the castle, was suddenly sounded. At the same instant the sable plumes on the enchanted helmet, which still remained at the other end of the court, were tempestuously agitated, and nodded thrice, as if bowed by some invisible wearer.

CHAPTER III.

Manfred's heart misgave him when he beheld the plumage on the miraculous casque shaken in concert with the sounding of the brazen trumpet.

"Father!" said he to Jerome, whom he now ceased to treat as Count of Falconara, "what mean these portents? If I have offended—" the plumes were shaken with greater violence than before.

"Unhappy Prince that I am," cried Manfred. "Holy Father! will you not assist me with your prayers?"

"My Lord," replied Jerome, "heaven is no doubt displeased with your mockery of its servants. Submit yourself to the church; and cease to persecute her ministers. Dismiss this innocent youth; and learn to respect the holy character I wear. Heaven will not be trifled with: you see—" the trumpet sounded again.

"I acknowledge I have been too hasty," said Manfred. "Father, do you go to the wicket, and demand who is at the gate."

"Do you grant me the life of Theodore?" replied the Friar.

"I do," said Manfred; "but inquire who is without!"

Jerome, falling on the neck of his son, discharged a flood of tears, that spoke the fulness of his soul.

"You promised to go to the gate," said Manfred.

"I thought," replied the Friar, "your Highness would excuse my thanking you first in this tribute of my heart."

"Go, dearest Sir," said Theodore; "obey the Prince. I do not deserve that you should delay his satisfaction for me."

Jerome, inquiring who was without, was answered, "A Herald."

"From whom?" said he.

"From the Knight of the Gigantic Sabre," said the Herald; "and I must speak with the usurper of Otranto."

Jerome returned to the Prince, and did not fail to repeat the message in the very words it had been uttered. The first sounds struck Manfred with terror; but when he heard himself styled usurper, his rage rekindled, and all his courage revived.

"Usurper! — insolent villain!" cried he; "who dares to question my title? Retire, Father; this is no business for Monks: I will meet this presumptuous man myself. Go to your convent and prepare the Princess's return. Your son shall be a hostage for your fidelity: his life depends on your obedience."

"Good heaven! my Lord," cried Jerome, "your Highness did but this instant freely pardon my child — have you so soon forgot the interposition of heaven?"

"Heaven," replied Manfred, "does not send Heralds to question the title of a lawful Prince. I doubt whether it even notifies its will through Friars — but that is your affair, not mine. At present you know my pleasure; and it is not a saucy Herald that shall save your son, if you do not return with the Princess."

It was in vain for the holy man to reply. Manfred commanded him to be conducted to the postern-gate, and shut out from the castle. And he ordered some of his attendants to carry Theodore to the top of the black tower, and guard him strictly; scarce permitting the father and son to exchange a hasty embrace at parting. He then withdrew to the hall, and seating himself in princely state, ordered the Herald to be admitted to his presence.

"Well! thou insolent!" said the Prince, "what wouldst thou with me?"

"I come," replied he, "to thee, Manfred, usurper of the principality of Otranto, from the renowned and invincible Knight, the Knight of the Gigantic Sabre: in the name of his Lord, Frederic, Marquis of Vicenza, he demands the Lady Isabella, daughter of that Prince, whom thou hast basely and traitorously got into thy power, by bribing her false guardians during his absence; and he requires thee to resign the principality of Otranto, which thou hast usurped from the said Lord Frederic, the nearest of blood to the last rightful Lord, Alfonso the Good. If thou dost not instantly comply with these just demands, he defies thee to single combat to the last extremity." And so saying the Herald cast down his warder.

"And where is this braggart who sends thee?" said Manfred.

"At the distance of a league," said the Herald: "he comes to make good his Lord's claim against thee, as he is a true knight, and thou an usurper and ravisher."

Injurious as this challenge was, Manfred reflected that it was not his interest to provoke the Marquis. He knew how well founded the claim of Frederic was; nor was this the first time he had heard of it. Frederic's ancestors had assumed the style of Princes of Otranto, from the death of Alfonso the Good without issue; but Manfred, his father, and grandfather, had been too powerful for the house of Vicenza to dispossess them. Frederic, a martial and amorous young Prince, had married a beautiful young lady, of whom he was enamoured, and who had died in childbed of Isabella. Her death affected him so much that he had taken the cross and gone to the Holy Land, where he was wounded in an engagement against the infidels, made prisoner, and reported to be dead. When the news reached Manfred's ears, he bribed the guardians of the Lady Isabella to deliver her up to him as a bride for his son Conrad, by which alliance he had proposed to unite the claims of the two houses. This motive, on Conrad's death, had co-operated to make him so suddenly resolve on espousing her himself; and the same reflection determined him now to endeavour at obtaining the consent of Frederic to this marriage. A like policy inspired him with the thought of inviting Frederic's champion into the castle, lest he should be informed of Isabella's flight, which he strictly enjoined his domestics not to disclose to any of the Knight's retinue.

"Herald," said Manfred, as soon as he had digested these reflections, "return to thy master, and tell him, ere we liquidate our differences by the sword, Manfred would hold some converse with him. Bid him welcome to my castle, where by my faith, as I am a true Knight, he shall have courteous reception, and full security for himself and followers. If we cannot adjust our quarrel by amicable means, I swear he shall depart in safety, and shall have full satisfaction according to the laws of arms: So help me God and His holy Trinity!"

The Herald made three obeisances and retired.

During this interview Jerome's mind was agitated by a thousand contrary passions. He trembled for the life of his son, and his first thought was to persuade Isabella to return to the castle. Yet he was scarce less alarmed at the thought of her union with Manfred. He dreaded Hippolita's unbounded submission to the will of her Lord; and though he did not doubt but he could alarm her piety not to consent to a divorce, if he could get access to her; yet should Manfred discover that the obstruction came from him, it might be equally fatal to Theodore. He was impatient to know whence came the Herald, who with so little management had questioned the title of Manfred: yet he did not dare absent himself from the convent, lest Isabella should leave it, and her flight be imputed to him. He returned disconsolately to the monastery, uncertain on what conduct to resolve. A Monk, who met him in the porch and observed his melancholy air, said—

"Alas! brother, is it then true that we have lost our excellent Princess Hippolita?"

The holy man started, and cried, "What meanest thou, brother? I come this instant from the castle, and left her in perfect health."

"Martelli," replied the other Friar, "passed by the convent but a quarter of an hour ago on his way from the castle, and reported that her Highness was dead. All our brethren are gone to the chapel to pray for her happy transit to a better life, and willed me to wait thy arrival. They know thy holy attachment to that good Lady, and are anxious for the affliction it will cause in thee—indeed we have all reason to weep; she was a mother to our house. But this life is but a pilgrimage; we must not murmur—we shall all follow her! May our end be like hers!"

"Good brother, thou dreamest," said Jerome. "I tell thee I come from the castle, and left the Princess well. Where is the Lady Isabella?"

"Poor Gentlewoman!" replied the Friar; "I told her the sad news, and offered her spiritual comfort. I reminded her of the transitory condition of mortality, and advised her to take the veil: I quoted the example of the holy Princess Sanchia of Arragon."

"Thy zeal was laudable," said Jerome, impatiently; "but at present it was unnecessary: Hippolita is well—at least I trust in the Lord she is; I heard nothing to the contrary—yet, methinks, the Prince's earnestness—Well, brother, but where is the Lady Isabella?"

"I know not," said the Friar; "she wept much, and said she would retire to her chamber."

Jerome left his comrade abruptly, and hastened to the Princess, but she was not in her chamber. He inquired of the domestics of the convent, but could learn no news of her. He searched in vain throughout the monastery and the church, and despatched messengers round the neighbourhood, to get intelligence if she had been seen; but to no purpose. Nothing could equal the good man's perplexity. He judged that Isabella, suspecting Manfred of having precipitated his wife's death, had taken the alarm, and withdrawn herself to some more secret place of concealment. This new flight would probably carry the Prince's fury to the height. The report of Hippolita's death, though it seemed almost incredible, increased his consternation; and though Isabella's escape bespoke her aversion of Manfred for a husband, Jerome could feel no comfort from it, while it endangered the life of his son. He determined to return to the castle, and made several of his brethren accompany him to attest his innocence to Manfred, and, if necessary, join their intercession with his for Theodore.

The Prince, in the meantime, had passed into the court, and ordered the gates of the castle to be flung open for the reception of the stranger Knight and his train. In a few minutes the cavalcade arrived. First came two harbingers with wands. Next a herald, followed by two pages and two trumpets. Then a hundred foot-guards. These were attended by as many horse. After them fifty footmen, clothed in scarlet and black, the colours of the Knight. Then a led horse. Two heralds on each side of a gentleman on horseback bearing a banner with the arms of Vicenza and Otranto quarterly—a circumstance that much offended Manfred—but he stifled his resentment. Two more pages. The Knight's confessor telling his beads. Fifty more footmen clad as before. Two Knights habited in complete armour, their beavers down, comrades to the principal Knight. The squires of the two Knights, carrying their shields and devices. The Knight's own squire. A hundred gentlemen bearing an enormous sword, and seeming to faint under the weight of it. The Knight himself on a chestnut steed, in complete armour, his lance in the rest, his face entirely concealed by his vizor, which was surmounted by a large plume of scarlet and black feathers. Fifty foot-guards with drums and trumpets closed the procession, which wheeled off to the right and left to make room for the principal Knight.

As soon as he approached the gate he stopped; and the herald advancing, read again the words of the challenge. Manfred's eyes were fixed on the gigantic sword, and he scarce seemed to attend to the cartel: but his attention was soon diverted by a tempest of wind that rose behind him. He turned and beheld the Plumes of the enchanted helmet agitated in the same extraordinary manner as before. It required intrepidity like Manfred's not to sink under a concurrence of circumstances that seemed to announce his fate. Yet scorning in the presence of strangers to betray the courage he had always manifested, he said boldly —

"Sir Knight, whoever thou art, I bid thee welcome. If thou art of mortal mould, thy valour shall meet its equal: and if thou art a true Knight, thou wilt scorn to employ sorcery to carry thy point. Be these omens from heaven or hell, Manfred trusts to the righteousness of his cause and to the aid of St. Nicholas, who has ever protected his house. Alight, Sir Knight, and repose thyself. To-morrow thou shalt have a fair field, and heaven befriend the juster side!"

The Knight made no reply, but dismounting, was conducted by Manfred to the great hall of the castle. As they traversed the court, the Knight stopped to gaze on the miraculous casque; and kneeling down, seemed to pray inwardly for some minutes. Rising, he made a sign to the Prince to lead on. As soon as they entered the hall, Manfred proposed to the stranger to disarm, but the Knight shook his head in token of refusal.

"Sir Knight," said Manfred, "this is not courteous, but by my good faith I will not cross thee, nor shalt thou have cause to complain of the Prince of Otranto. No treachery is designed on my part; I hope none is intended on thine; here take my gage" (giving him his ring): "your friends and you shall enjoy the laws of hospitality. Rest here until refreshments are brought. I will but give orders for the accommodation of your train, and return to you." The three Knights bowed as accepting his courtesy. Manfred directed the stranger's retinue to be conducted to an adjacent hospital, founded by the Princess Hippolita for the reception of pilgrims. As they made the circuit of the court to return towards the gate, the gigantic sword burst from the supporters, and falling to the ground opposite to the helmet, remained immovable. Manfred, almost hardened to preternatural appearances, surmounted the shock of this new prodigy; and returning to the hall, where by this time the feast was ready, he invited his silent guests to take their places. Manfred, however ill his heart was at ease, endeavoured to inspire the company with mirth. He put several questions to them, but was answered only by signs. They raised their vizors but sufficiently to feed themselves, and that sparingly.

"Sirs" said the Prince, "ye are the first guests I ever treated within these walls who scorned to hold any intercourse with me: nor has it oft been customary, I ween, for princes to hazard their state and dignity against strangers and mutes. You say you come in the name of Frederic of Vicenza; I have ever heard that he was a gallant and courteous Knight; nor would he, I am bold to say, think it beneath him to mix in social converse with a Prince that is his equal, and not unknown by deeds in arms. Still ye are silent—well! be it as it may—by the laws of hospitality and chivalry ye are masters under this roof: ye shall do your pleasure. But come, give me a goblet of wine; ye will not refuse to pledge me to the healths of your fair mistresses."

The principal Knight sighed and crossed himself, and was rising from the board.

"Sir Knight," said Manfred, "what I said was but in sport. I shall constrain you in nothing: use your good liking. Since mirth is not your mood, let us be sad. Business may hit your fancies better. Let us withdraw, and hear if what I have to unfold may be better relished than the vain efforts I have made for your pastime."

Manfred then conducting the three Knights into an inner chamber, shut the door, and inviting them to be seated, began thus, addressing himself to the chief personage:—

"You come, Sir Knight, as I understand, in the name of the Marquis of Vicenza, to re-demand the Lady Isabella, his daughter, who has been contracted in the face of Holy Church to my son, by the consent of her legal guardians; and to require me to resign my dominions to your Lord, who gives himself for the nearest of blood to Prince Alfonso, whose soul God rest! I shall speak to the latter article of your demands first. You must know, your Lord knows, that I enjoy the principality of Otranto from my father, Don Manuel, as he received it from his father, Don Ricardo. Alfonso, their predecessor, dying childless in the Holy Land, bequeathed his estates to my grandfather, Don Ricardo, in consideration of his faithful services." The stranger shook his head.

"Sir Knight," said Manfred, warmly, "Ricardo was a valiant and upright man; he was a pious man; witness his munificent foundation of the adjoining church and two convents. He was peculiarly patronised by St. Nicholas—my grandfather was incapable—I say, Sir, Don Ricardo was incapable—excuse me, your interruption has disordered me. I venerate the memory of my grandfather. Well, Sirs, he held this estate; he held it by his good sword and by the favour of St. Nicholas—so did my father; and so, Sirs, will I, come what come will. But Frederic, your Lord, is nearest in blood. I have consented to put my title to the issue of the sword. Does that imply a vicious title? I might have asked, where is Frederic your Lord? Report speaks him dead in captivity. You say, your actions say, he lives—I question it not—I might, Sirs, I might—but I do not. Other Princes would bid Frederic take his inheritance by force, if he can: they would not stake their dignity on a single combat: they would not submit it to the decision of unknown mutes!—pardon me, gentlemen, I am too warm: but suppose yourselves in my situation: as ye are stout Knights, would it not move your choler to have your own and the honour of your ancestors called in question?" "But to the point. Ye require me to deliver up the Lady Isabella. Sirs, I must ask if ye are authorised to receive her?"

The Knight nodded.

"Receive her," continued Manfred; "well, you are authorised to receive her, but, gentle Knight, may I ask if you have full powers?"

The Knight nodded.

"'Tis well," said Manfred; "then hear what I have to offer. Ye see, gentlemen, before you, the most unhappy of men!" (he began to weep); "afford me your compassion; I am entitled to it, indeed I am. Know, I have lost my only hope, my joy, the support of my house—Conrad died yester morning."

The Knights discovered signs of surprise.

"Yes, Sirs, fate has disposed of my son. Isabella is at liberty."

"Do you then restore her?" cried the chief Knight, breaking silence.

"Afford me your patience," said Manfred. "I rejoice to find, by this testimony of your goodwill, that this matter may be adjusted without blood. It is no interest of mine dictates what little I have farther to say. Ye behold in me a man disgusted with the world: the loss of my son has weaned me from earthly cares. Power and greatness have no longer any charms in my eyes. I wished to transmit the sceptre I had received from my ancestors with honour to my son—but that is over! Life itself is so indifferent to me, that I accepted your defiance with joy. A good Knight cannot go to the grave with more satisfaction than when falling in his vocation: whatever is the will of heaven, I submit; for alas! Sirs, I am a man of many sorrows. Manfred is no object of envy, but no doubt you are acquainted with my story."

The Knight made signs of ignorance, and seemed curious to have Manfred proceed.

"Is it possible, Sirs," continued the Prince, "that my story should be a secret to you? Have you heard nothing relating to me and the Princess Hippolita?"

They shook their heads.

"No! Thus, then, Sirs, it is. You think me ambitious: ambition, alas! is composed of more rugged materials. If I were ambitious, I should not for so many years have been a prey to all the hell of conscientious scruples. But I weary your patience: I will be brief. Know, then, that I have long been troubled in mind on my union with the Princess Hippolita. Oh! Sirs, if ye were acquainted with that excellent woman! if ye knew that I adore her like a mistress, and cherish her as a friend — but man was not born for perfect happiness! She shares my scruples, and with her consent I have brought this matter before the church, for we are related within the forbidden degrees. I expect every hour the definitive sentence that must separate us for ever — I am sure you feel for me — I see you do — pardon these tears!"

The Knights gazed on each other, wondering where this would end.

Manfred continued —

"The death of my son betiding while my soul was under this anxiety, I thought of nothing but resigning my dominions, and retiring for ever from the sight of mankind. My only difficulty was to fix on a successor, who would be tender of my people, and to dispose of the Lady Isabella, who is dear to me as my own blood. I was willing to restore the line of Alfonso, even in his most distant kindred. And though, pardon me, I am satisfied it was his will that Ricardo's lineage should take place of his own relations; yet where was I to search for those relations? I knew of none but Frederic, your Lord; he was a captive to the infidels, or dead; and were he living, and at home, would he quit the flourishing State of Vicenza for the inconsiderable principality of Otranto? If he would not, could I bear the thought of seeing a hard, unfeeling, Viceroy set over my poor faithful people? for, Sirs, I love my people, and thank heaven am beloved by them. But ye will ask whither tends this long discourse? Briefly, then, thus, Sirs. Heaven in your arrival seems to point out a remedy for these difficulties and my misfortunes. The Lady Isabella is at liberty; I shall soon be so. I would submit to anything for the good of my people. Were it not the best, the only way to extinguish the feuds between our families, if I was to take the Lady Isabella to wife? You start. But though Hippolita's virtues will ever be dear to me, a Prince must not consider himself; he is born for his people." A servant at that instant entering the chamber apprised Manfred that Jerome and several of his brethren demanded immediate access to him.

The Prince, provoked at this interruption, and fearing that the Friar would discover to the strangers that Isabella had taken sanctuary, was going to forbid Jerome's entrance. But recollecting that he was certainly arrived to notify the Princess's return, Manfred began to excuse himself to the Knights for leaving them for a few moments, but was prevented by the arrival of the Friars. Manfred angrily reprimanded them for their intrusion, and would have forced them back from the chamber; but Jerome was too much agitated to be repulsed. He declared aloud the flight of Isabella, with protestations of his own innocence.

Manfred, distracted at the news, and not less at its coming to the knowledge of the strangers, uttered nothing but incoherent sentences, now upbraiding the Friar, now apologising to the Knights, earnest to know what was become of Isabella, yet equally afraid of their knowing; impatient to pursue her, yet dreading to have them join in the pursuit. He offered to despatch messengers in quest of her, but the chief Knight, no longer keeping silence, reproached Manfred in bitter terms for his dark and ambiguous dealing, and demanded the cause of Isabella's first absence from the castle. Manfred, casting a stern look at Jerome, implying a command of silence, pretended that on Conrad's death he had placed her in sanctuary until he could determine how to dispose of her. Jerome, who trembled for his son's life, did not dare contradict this falsehood, but one of his brethren, not under the same anxiety, declared frankly that she had fled to their church in the preceding night. The Prince in vain endeavoured to stop this discovery, which overwhelmed him with shame and confusion. The principal stranger, amazed at the contradictions he heard, and more than half persuaded that Manfred had secreted the Princess, notwithstanding the concern he expressed at her flight, rushing to the door, said—

"Thou traitor Prince! Isabella shall be found."

Manfred endeavoured to hold him, but the other Knights assisting their comrade, he broke from the Prince, and hastened into the court, demanding his attendants. Manfred, finding it vain to divert him from the pursuit, offered to accompany him and summoning his attendants, and taking Jerome and some of the Friars to guide them, they issued from the castle; Manfred privately giving orders to have the Knight's company secured, while to the knight he affected to despatch a messenger to require their assistance.

The company had no sooner quitted the castle than Matilda, who felt herself deeply interested for the young peasant, since she had seen him condemned to death in the hall, and whose thoughts had been taken up with concerting measures to save him, was informed by some of the female attendants that Manfred had despatched all his men various ways in pursuit of Isabella. He had in his hurry given this order in general terms, not meaning to extend it to the guard he had set upon Theodore, but forgetting it. The domestics, officious to obey so peremptory a Prince, and urged by their own curiosity and love of novelty to join in any precipitate chase, had to a man left the castle. Matilda disengaged herself from her women, stole up to the black tower, and unbolting the door, presented herself to the astonished Theodore.

"Young man," said she, "though filial duty and womanly modesty condemn the step I am taking, yet holy charity, surmounting all other ties, justifies this act. Fly; the doors of thy prison are open: my father and his domestics are absent; but they may soon return. Be gone in safety; and may the angels of heaven direct thy course!"

"Thou art surely one of those angels!" said the enraptured Theodore: "none but a blessed saint could speak, could act — could look — like thee. May I not know the name of my divine protectress? Methought thou namedst thy father. Is it possible? Can Manfred's blood feel holy pity! Lovely Lady, thou answerest not. But how art thou here thyself? Why dost thou neglect thy own safety, and waste a thought on a wretch like Theodore? Let us fly together: the life thou bestowest shall be dedicated to thy defence."

"Alas! thou mistakest," said Matilda, sighing: "I am Manfred's daughter, but no dangers await me."

"Amazement!" said Theodore; "but last night I blessed myself for yielding thee the service thy gracious compassion so charitably returns me now."

"Still thou art in an error," said the Princess; "but this is no time for explanation. Fly, virtuous youth, while it is in my power to save thee: should my father return, thou and I both should indeed have cause to tremble."

"How!" said Theodore; "thinkest thou, charming maid, that I will accept of life at the hazard of aught calamitous to thee? Better I endured a thousand deaths."

"I run no risk," said Matilda, "but by thy delay. Depart; it cannot be known that I have assisted thy flight."

"Swear by the saints above," said Theodore, "that thou canst not be suspected; else here I vow to await whatever can befall me."

"Oh! thou art too generous," said Matilda; "but rest assured that no suspicion can alight on me."

"Give me thy beauteous hand in token that thou dost not deceive me," said Theodore; "and let me bathe it with the warm tears of gratitude."

"Forbear!" said the Princess; "this must not be."

"Alas!" said Theodore, "I have never known but calamity until this hour—perhaps shall never know other fortune again: suffer the chaste raptures of holy gratitude: 'tis my soul would print its effusions on thy hand."

"Forbear, and be gone," said Matilda. "How would Isabella approve of seeing thee at my feet?"

"Who is Isabella?" said the young man with surprise.

"Ah, me! I fear," said the Princess, "I am serving a deceitful one. Hast thou forgot thy curiosity this morning?"

"Thy looks, thy actions, all thy beauteous self seem an emanation of divinity," said Theodore; "but thy words are dark and mysterious. Speak, Lady; speak to thy servant's comprehension."

"Thou understandest but too well!" said Matilda; "but once more I command thee to be gone: thy blood, which I may preserve, will be on my head, if I waste the time in vain discourse."

"I go, Lady," said Theodore, "because it is thy will, and because I would not bring the grey hairs of my father with sorrow to the grave. Say but, adored Lady, that I have thy gentle pity."

"Stay," said Matilda; "I will conduct thee to the subterraneous vault by which Isabella escaped; it will lead thee to the church of St. Nicholas, where thou mayst take sanctuary."

"What!" said Theodore, "was it another, and not thy lovely self that I assisted to find the subterraneous passage?"

"It was," said Matilda; "but ask no more; I tremble to see thee still abide here; fly to the sanctuary."

"To sanctuary," said Theodore; "no, Princess; sanctuaries are for helpless damsels, or for criminals. Theodore's soul is free from guilt, nor will wear the appearance of it. Give me a sword, Lady, and thy father shall learn that Theodore scorns an ignominious flight."

"Rash youth!" said Matilda; "thou wouldst not dare to lift thy presumptuous arm against the Prince of Otranto?"

"Not against thy father; indeed, I dare not," said Theodore. "Excuse me, Lady; I had forgotten. But could I gaze on thee, and remember thou art sprung from the tyrant Manfred! But he is thy father, and from this moment my injuries are buried in oblivion."

A deep and hollow groan, which seemed to come from above, startled the Princess and Theodore.

"Good heaven! we are overheard!" said the Princess. They listened; but perceiving no further noise, they both concluded it the effect of pent-up vapours. And the Princess, preceding Theodore softly, carried him to her father's armoury, where, equipping him with a complete suit, he was conducted by Matilda to the postern-gate.

"Avoid the town," said the Princess, "and all the western side of the castle. 'Tis there the search must be making by Manfred and the strangers; but hie thee to the opposite quarter.

Yonder behind that forest to the east is a chain of rocks, hollowed into a labyrinth of caverns that reach to the sea coast. There thou mayst lie concealed, till thou canst make signs to some vessel to put on shore, and take thee off. Go! heaven be thy guide! — and sometimes in thy prayers remember — Matilda!"

Theodore flung himself at her feet, and seizing her lily hand, which with struggles she suffered him to kiss, he vowed on the earliest opportunity to get himself knighted, and fervently entreated her permission to swear himself eternally her knight. Ere the Princess could reply, a clap of thunder was suddenly heard that shook the battlements. Theodore, regardless of the tempest, would have urged his suit: but the Princess, dismayed, retreated hastily into the castle, and commanded the youth to be gone with an air that would not be disobeyed. He sighed, and retired, but with eyes fixed on the gate, until Matilda, closing it, put an end to an interview, in which the hearts of both had drunk so deeply of a passion, which both now tasted for the first time.

Theodore went pensively to the convent, to acquaint his father with his deliverance. There he learned the absence of Jerome, and the pursuit that was making after the Lady Isabella, with some particulars of whose story he now first became acquainted. The generous gallantry of his nature prompted him to wish to assist her; but the Monks could lend him no lights to guess at the route she had taken. He was not tempted to wander far in search of her, for the idea of Matilda had imprinted itself so strongly on his heart, that he could not bear to absent himself at much distance from her abode. The tenderness Jerome had expressed for him concurred to confirm this reluctance; and he even persuaded himself that filial affection was the chief cause of his hovering between the castle and monastery.

Until Jerome should return at night, Theodore at length determined to repair to the forest that Matilda had pointed out to him. Arriving there, he sought the gloomiest shades, as best suited to the pleasing melancholy that reigned in his mind. In this mood he roved insensibly to the caves which had formerly served as a retreat to hermits, and were now reported round the country to be haunted by evil spirits. He recollected to have heard this tradition; and being of a brave and adventurous disposition, he willingly indulged his curiosity in exploring the secret recesses of this labyrinth. He had not penetrated far before he thought he heard the steps of some person who seemed to retreat before him.

Theodore, though firmly grounded in all our holy faith enjoins to be believed, had no apprehension that good men were abandoned without cause to the malice of the powers of darkness. He thought the place more likely to be infested by robbers than by those infernal agents who are reported to molest and bewilder travellers. He had long burned with impatience to approve his valour. Drawing his sabre, he marched sedately onwards, still directing his steps as the imperfect rustling sound before him led the way. The armour he wore was a like indication to the person who avoided him. Theodore, now convinced that he was not mistaken, redoubled his pace, and evidently gained on the person that fled, whose haste increasing, Theodore came up just as a woman fell breathless before him. He hasted to raise her, but her terror was so great that he apprehended she would faint in his arms. He used every gentle word to dispel her alarms, and assured her that far from injuring, he would defend her at the peril of his life. The Lady recovering her spirits from his courteous demeanour, and gazing on her protector, said —

"Sure, I have heard that voice before!"

"Not to my knowledge," replied Theodore; "unless, as I conjecture, thou art the Lady Isabella."

"Merciful heaven!" cried she. "Thou art not sent in quest of me, art thou?" And saying those words, she threw herself at his feet, and besought him not to deliver her up to Manfred.

"To Manfred!" cried Theodore — "no, Lady; I have once already delivered thee from his tyranny, and it shall fare hard with me now, but I will place thee out of the reach of his daring."

"Is it possible," said she, "that thou shouldst be the generous unknown whom I met last night in the vault of the castle? Sure thou art not a mortal, but my guardian angel. On my knees, let me thank —"

"Hold! gentle Princess," said Theodore, "nor demean thyself before a poor and friendless young man. If heaven has selected me for thy deliverer, it will accomplish its work, and strengthen my arm in thy cause. But come, Lady, we are too near the mouth of the cavern; let us seek its inmost recesses. I can have no tranquillity till I have placed thee beyond the reach of danger."

"Alas! what mean you, sir?" said she. "Though all your actions are noble, though your sentiments speak the purity of your soul, is it fitting that I should accompany you alone into these perplexed retreats? Should we be found together, what would a censorious world think of my conduct?"

"I respect your virtuous delicacy," said Theodore; "nor do you harbour a suspicion that wounds my honour. I meant to conduct you into the most private cavity of these rocks, and then at the hazard of my life to guard their entrance against every living thing. Besides, Lady," continued he, drawing a deep sigh, "beauteous and all perfect as your form is, and though my wishes are not guiltless of aspiring, know, my soul is dedicated to another; and although—" A sudden noise prevented Theodore from proceeding. They soon distinguished these sounds—

"Isabella! what, ho! Isabella!" The trembling Princess relapsed into her former agony of fear. Theodore endeavoured to encourage her, but in vain. He assured her he would die rather than suffer her to return under Manfred's power; and begging her to remain concealed, he went forth to prevent the person in search of her from approaching.

At the mouth of the cavern he found an armed Knight, discoursing with a peasant, who assured him he had seen a lady enter the passes of the rock. The Knight was preparing to seek her, when Theodore, placing himself in his way, with his sword drawn, sternly forbad him at his peril to advance.

"And who art thou, who darest to cross my way?" said the Knight, haughtily.

"One who does not dare more than he will perform," said Theodore.

"I seek the Lady Isabella," said the Knight, "and understand she has taken refuge among these rocks. Impede me not, or thou wilt repent having provoked my resentment."

"Thy purpose is as odious as thy resentment is contemptible," said Theodore. "Return whence thou camest, or we shall soon know whose resentment is most terrible."

The stranger, who was the principal Knight that had arrived from the Marquis of Vicenza, had galloped from Manfred as he was busied in getting information of the Princess, and giving various orders to prevent her falling into the power of the three

Knights. Their chief had suspected Manfred of being privy to the Princess's absconding, and this insult from a man, who he concluded was stationed by that Prince to secrete her, confirming his suspicions, he made no reply, but discharging a blow with his sabre at Theodore, would soon have removed all obstruction, if Theodore, who took him for one of Manfred's captains, and who had no sooner given the provocation than prepared to support it, had not received the stroke on his shield. The valour that had so long been smothered in his breast broke forth at once; he rushed impetuously on the Knight, whose pride and wrath were not less powerful incentives to hardy deeds. The combat was furious, but not long. Theodore wounded the Knight in three several places, and at last disarmed him as he fainted by the loss of blood.

The peasant, who had fled on the first onset, had given the alarm to some of Manfred's domestics, who, by his orders, were dispersed through the forest in pursuit of Isabella. They came up as the Knight fell, whom they soon discovered to be the noble stranger. Theodore, notwithstanding his hatred to Manfred, could not behold the victory he had gained without emotions of pity and generosity. But he was more touched when he learned the quality of his adversary, and was informed that he was no retainer, but an enemy, of Manfred. He assisted the servants of the latter in disarming the Knight, and in endeavouring to stanch the blood that flowed from his wounds. The Knight recovering his speech, said, in a faint and faltering voice —

"Generous foe, we have both been in an error. I took thee for an instrument of the tyrant; I perceive thou hast made the like mistake. It is too late for excuses. I faint. If Isabella is at hand — call her — I have important secrets to —"

"He is dying!" said one of the attendants; "has nobody a crucifix about them? Andrea, do thou pray over him."

"Fetch some water," said Theodore, "and pour it down his throat, while I hasten to the Princess."

Saying this, he flew to Isabella, and in few words told her modestly that he had been so unfortunate by mistake as to wound a gentleman from her father's court, who wished, ere he died, to impart something of consequence to her.

The Princess, who had been transported at hearing the voice of Theodore, as he called to her to come forth, was astonished at what she heard. Suffering herself to be conducted by Theodore, the new proof of whose valour recalled her dispersed spirits, she came where the bleeding Knight lay speechless on the ground. But her fears returned when she beheld the domestics of Manfred. She would again have fled if Theodore had not made her observe that they were unarmed, and had not threatened them with instant death if they should dare to seize the Princess.

The stranger, opening his eyes, and beholding a woman, said, "Art thou — pray tell me truly — art thou Isabella of Vicenza?"

"I am," said she: "good heaven restore thee!"

"Then thou — then thou" — said the Knight, struggling for utterance — "seest — thy father. Give me one — "

"Oh! amazement! horror! what do I hear! what do I see!" cried Isabella. "My father! You my father! How came you here, Sir? For heaven's sake, speak! Oh! run for help, or he will expire!"

"'Tis most true," said the wounded Knight, exerting all his force; "I am Frederic thy father. Yes, I came to deliver thee. It will not be. Give me a parting kiss, and take — "

"Sir," said Theodore, "do not exhaust yourself; suffer us to convey you to the castle."

"To the castle!" said Isabella. "Is there no help nearer than the castle? Would you expose my father to the tyrant? If he goes thither, I dare not accompany him; and yet, can I leave him!"

"My child," said Frederic, "it matters not for me whither I am carried. A few minutes will place me beyond danger; but while I have eyes to dote on thee, forsake me not, dear Isabella! This brave Knight — I know not who he is — will protect thy innocence. Sir, you will not abandon my child, will you?"

Theodore, shedding tears over his victim, and vowing to guard the Princess at the expense of his life, persuaded Frederic to suffer himself to be conducted to the castle. They placed him on a horse belonging to one of the domestics, after binding up his wounds as well as they were able. Theodore marched by his side; and the afflicted Isabella, who could not bear to quit him, followed mournfully behind.

CHAPTER IV.

The sorrowful troop no sooner arrived at the castle, than they were met by Hippolita and Matilda, whom Isabella had sent one of the domestics before to advertise of their approach. The ladies causing Frederic to be conveyed into the nearest chamber, retired, while the surgeons examined his wounds. Matilda blushed at seeing Theodore and Isabella together; but endeavoured to conceal it by embracing the latter, and condoling with her on her father's mischance. The surgeons soon came to acquaint Hippolita that none of the Marquis's wounds were dangerous; and that he was desirous of seeing his daughter and the Princesses.

Theodore, under pretence of expressing his joy at being freed from his apprehensions of the combat being fatal to Frederic, could not resist the impulse of following Matilda. Her eyes were so often cast down on meeting his, that Isabella, who regarded Theodore as attentively as he gazed on Matilda, soon divined who the object was that he had told her in the cave engaged his affections. While this mute scene passed, Hippolita demanded of Frederic the cause of his having taken that mysterious course for reclaiming his daughter; and threw in various apologies to excuse her Lord for the match contracted between their children.

Frederic, however incensed against Manfred, was not insensible to the courtesy and benevolence of Hippolita: but he was still more struck with the lovely form of Matilda. Wishing to detain them by his bedside, he informed Hippolita of his story. He told her that, while prisoner to the infidels, he had dreamed that his daughter, of whom he had learned no news since his captivity, was detained in a castle, where she was in danger of the most dreadful misfortunes: and that if he obtained his liberty, and repaired to a wood near Joppa, he would learn more. Alarmed at this dream, and incapable of obeying the direction given by it, his chains became more grievous than ever. But while his thoughts were occupied on the means of obtaining his liberty, he received the agreeable news that the confederate Princes who were warring in Palestine had paid his ransom. He instantly set out for the wood that had been marked in his dream.

For three days he and his attendants had wandered in the forest without seeing a human form: but on the evening of the third they came to a cell, in which they found a venerable hermit in the agonies of death. Applying rich cordials, they brought the fainting man to his speech.

"My sons," said he, "I am bounden to your charity — but it is in vain — I am going to my eternal rest — yet I die with the satisfaction of performing the will of heaven. When first I repaired to this solitude, after seeing my country become a prey to unbelievers — it is alas! above fifty years since I was witness to that dreadful scene! St. Nicholas appeared to me, and revealed a secret, which he bade me never disclose to mortal man, but on my death-bed. This is that tremendous hour, and ye are no doubt the chosen warriors to whom I was ordered to reveal my trust. As soon as ye have done the last offices to this wretched corse, dig under the seventh tree on the left hand of this poor cave, and your pains will — Oh! good heaven receive my soul!" With those words the devout man breathed his last.

"By break of day," continued Frederic, "when we had committed the holy relics to earth, we dug according to direction. But what was our astonishment when about the depth of six feet we discovered an enormous sabre — the very weapon yonder in the court. On the blade, which was then partly out of the scabbard, though since closed by our efforts in removing it, were written the following lines — no; excuse me, Madam," added the Marquis, turning to Hippolita; "if I forbear to repeat them: I respect your sex and rank, and would not be guilty of offending your ear with sounds injurious to aught that is dear to you."

He paused. Hippolita trembled. She did not doubt but Frederic was destined by heaven to accomplish the fate that seemed to threaten her house. Looking with anxious fondness at Matilda, a silent tear stole down her cheek: but recollecting herself, she said —

"Proceed, my Lord; heaven does nothing in vain; mortals must receive its divine behests with lowliness and submission. It is our part to deprecate its wrath, or bow to its decrees. Repeat the sentence, my Lord; we listen resigned."

Frederic was grieved that he had proceeded so far. The dignity and patient firmness of Hippolita penetrated him with respect, and the tender silent affection with which the Princess and her daughter regarded each other, melted him almost to tears. Yet apprehensive that his forbearance to obey would be more alarming, he repeated in a faltering and low voice the following lines:

"Where'er a casque that suits this sword is found,

With perils is thy daughter compass'd round;

Alfonso's blood alone can save the maid,

And quiet a long restless Prince's shade."

"What is there in these lines," said Theodore impatiently, "that affects these Princesses? Why were they to be shocked by a mysterious delicacy, that has so little foundation?"

"Your words are rude, young man," said the Marquis; "and though fortune has favoured you once—"

"My honoured Lord," said Isabella, who resented Theodore's warmth, which she perceived was dictated by his sentiments for Matilda, "discompose not yourself for the glosing of a peasant's son: he forgets the reverence he owes you; but he is not accustomed—"

Hippolita, concerned at the heat that had arisen, checked Theodore for his boldness, but with an air acknowledging his zeal; and changing the conversation, demanded of Frederic where he had left her Lord? As the Marquis was going to reply, they heard a noise without, and rising to inquire the cause, Manfred, Jerome, and part of the troop, who had met an imperfect rumour of what had happened, entered the chamber. Manfred advanced hastily towards Frederic's bed to condole with him on his misfortune, and to learn the circumstances of the combat, when starting in an agony of terror and amazement, he cried—

"Ha! what art thou? thou dreadful spectre! is my hour come?"

"My dearest, gracious Lord," cried Hippolita, clasping him in her arms, "what is it you see! Why do you fix your eye-balls thus?"

"What!" cried Manfred breathless; "dost thou see nothing, Hippolita? Is this ghastly phantom sent to me alone—to me, who did not—"

"For mercy's sweetest self, my Lord," said Hippolita, "resume your soul, command your reason. There is none here, but us, your friends."

"What, is not that Alfonso?" cried Manfred. "Dost thou not see him? can it be my brain's delirium?"

"This! my Lord," said Hippolita; "this is Theodore, the youth who has been so unfortunate."

"Theodore!" said Manfred mournfully, and striking his forehead; "Theodore or a phantom, he has unhinged the soul of Manfred. But how comes he here? and how comes he in armour?"

"I believe he went in search of Isabella," said Hippolita.

"Of Isabella!" said Manfred, relapsing into rage; "yes, yes, that is not doubtful—. But how did he escape from durance in which I left him? Was it Isabella, or this hypocritical old Friar, that procured his enlargement?"

"And would a parent be criminal, my Lord," said Theodore, "if he meditated the deliverance of his child?"

Jerome, amazed to hear himself in a manner accused by his son, and without foundation, knew not what to think. He could not comprehend how Theodore had escaped, how he came to be armed, and to encounter Frederic. Still he would not venture to ask any questions that might tend to inflame Manfred's wrath against his son. Jerome's silence convinced Manfred that he had contrived Theodore's release.

"And is it thus, thou ungrateful old man," said the Prince, addressing himself to the Friar, "that thou repayest mine and Hippolita's bounties? And not content with traversing my heart's nearest wishes, thou armest thy bastard, and bringest him into my own castle to insult me!"

"My Lord," said Theodore, "you wrong my father: neither he nor I are capable of harbouring a thought against your peace. Is it insolence thus to surrender myself to your Highness's pleasure?" added he, laying his sword respectfully at Manfred's feet. "Behold my bosom; strike, my Lord, if you suspect that a disloyal thought is lodged there. There is not a sentiment engraven on my heart that does not venerate you and yours."

The grace and fervour with which Theodore uttered these words interested every person present in his favour. Even Manfred was touched—yet still possessed with his resemblance to Alfonso, his admiration was dashed with secret horror.

"Rise," said he; "thy life is not my present purpose. But tell me thy history, and how thou camest connected with this old traitor here."

"My Lord," said Jerome eagerly.

"Peace! impostor!" said Manfred; "I will not have him prompted."

"My Lord," said Theodore, "I want no assistance; my story is very brief. I was carried at five years of age to Algiers with my mother, who had been taken by corsairs from the coast of Sicily. She died of grief in less than a twelvemonth;" the tears gushed from Jerome's eyes, on whose countenance a thousand anxious passions stood expressed. "Before she died," continued Theodore, "she bound a writing about my arm under my garments, which told me I was the son of the Count Falconara."

"It is most true," said Jerome; "I am that wretched father."

"Again I enjoin thee silence," said Manfred: "proceed."

"I remained in slavery," said Theodore, "until within these two years, when attending on my master in his cruises, I was delivered by a Christian vessel, which overpowered the pirate; and discovering myself to the captain, he generously put me on shore in Sicily; but alas! instead of finding a father, I learned that his estate, which was situated on the coast, had, during his absence, been laid waste by the Rover who had carried my mother and me into captivity: that his castle had been burnt to the ground, and that my father on his return had sold what remained, and was retired into religion in the kingdom of Naples, but where no man could inform me. Destitute and friendless, hopeless almost of attaining the transport of a parent's embrace, I took the first opportunity of setting sail for Naples, from whence, within these six days, I wandered into this province, still supporting myself by the labour of my hands; nor until yester-morn did I believe that heaven had reserved any lot for me but peace of mind and contented poverty. This, my Lord, is Theodore's story. I am blessed beyond my hope in finding a father; I am unfortunate beyond my desert in having incurred your Highness's displeasure."

He ceased. A murmur of approbation gently arose from the audience.

"This is not all," said Frederic; "I am bound in honour to add what he suppresses. Though he is modest, I must be generous; he is one of the bravest youths on Christian ground. He is warm too; and from the short knowledge I have of him, I will pledge myself for his veracity: if what he reports of himself were not true, he would not utter it—and for me, youth, I honour a frankness which becomes thy birth; but now, and thou didst offend me: yet the noble blood which flows in thy veins, may well be allowed to boil out, when it has so recently traced itself to its source. Come, my Lord," (turning to Manfred), "if I can pardon him, surely you may; it is not the youth's fault, if you took him for a spectre."

This bitter taunt galled the soul of Manfred.

"If beings from another world," replied he haughtily, "have power to impress my mind with awe, it is more than living man can do; nor could a stripling's arm."

"My Lord," interrupted Hippolita, "your guest has occasion for repose: shall we not leave him to his rest?" Saying this, and taking Manfred by the hand, she took leave of Frederic, and led the company forth.

The Prince, not sorry to quit a conversation which recalled to mind the discovery he had made of his most secret sensations, suffered himself to be conducted to his own apartment, after permitting Theodore, though under engagement to return to the castle on the morrow (a condition the young man gladly accepted), to retire with his father to the convent. Matilda and Isabella were too much occupied with their own reflections, and too little content with each other, to wish for farther converse that night. They separated each to her chamber, with more expressions of ceremony and fewer of affection than had passed between them since their childhood.

If they parted with small cordiality, they did but meet with greater impatience, as soon as the sun was risen. Their minds were in a situation that excluded sleep, and each recollected a thousand questions which she wished she had put to the other overnight. Matilda reflected that Isabella had been twice delivered by Theodore in very critical situations, which she could not believe accidental. His eyes, it was true, had been fixed on her in Frederic's chamber; but that might have been to disguise his passion for Isabella from the fathers of both. It were better to clear this up. She wished to know the truth, lest she should wrong her friend by entertaining a passion for Isabella's lover. Thus jealousy prompted, and at the same time borrowed an excuse from friendship to justify its curiosity.

Isabella, not less restless, had better foundation for her suspicions. Both Theodore's tongue and eyes had told her his heart was engaged; it was true—yet, perhaps, Matilda might not correspond to his passion; she had ever appeared insensible to love: all her thoughts were set on heaven.

"Why did I dissuade her?" said Isabella to herself; "I am punished for my generosity; but when did they meet? where? It cannot be; I have deceived myself; perhaps last night was the first time they ever beheld each other; it must be some other object that has prepossessed his affections—if it is, I am not so unhappy as I thought; if it is not my friend Matilda—how! Can I stoop to wish for the affection of a man, who rudely and unnecessarily acquainted me with his indifference? and that at the very moment in which common courtesy demanded at least expressions of civility. I will go to my dear Matilda, who will confirm me in this becoming pride. Man is false—I will advise with her on taking the veil: she will rejoice to find me in this disposition; and I will acquaint her that I no longer oppose her inclination for the cloister."

In this frame of mind, and determined to open her heart entirely to Matilda, she went to that Princess's chamber, whom she found already dressed, and leaning pensively on her arm. This attitude, so correspondent to what she felt herself, revived Isabella's suspicions, and destroyed the confidence she had purposed to place in her friend. They blushed at meeting, and were too much novices to disguise their sensations with address. After some unmeaning questions and replies, Matilda demanded of Isabella the cause of her flight? The latter, who had almost forgotten Manfred's passion, so entirely was she occupied by her own, concluding that Matilda referred to her last escape from the convent, which had occasioned the events of the preceding evening, replied—

"Martelli brought word to the convent that your mother was dead."

"Oh!" said Matilda, interrupting her, "Bianca has explained that mistake to me: on seeing me faint, she cried out, 'The Princess is dead!' and Martelli, who had come for the usual dole to the castle—"

"And what made you faint?" said Isabella, indifferent to the rest. Matilda blushed and stammered—

"My father—he was sitting in judgment on a criminal—"

"What criminal?" said Isabella eagerly.

"A young man," said Matilda; "I believe—I think it was that young man that—"

"What, Theodore?" said Isabella.

"Yes," answered she; "I never saw him before; I do not know how he had offended my father, but as he has been of service to you, I am glad my Lord has pardoned him."

"Served me!" replied Isabella; "do you term it serving me, to wound my father, and almost occasion his death? Though it is but since yesterday that I am blessed with knowing a parent, I hope Matilda does not think I am such a stranger to filial tenderness as not to resent the boldness of that audacious youth, and that it is impossible for me ever to feel any affection for one who dared to lift his arm against the author of my being. No, Matilda, my heart abhors him; and if you still retain the friendship for me that you have vowed from your infancy, you will detest a man who has been on the point of making me miserable for ever."

Matilda held down her head and replied: "I hope my dearest Isabella does not doubt her Matilda's friendship: I never beheld that youth until yesterday; he is almost a stranger to me: but as the surgeons have pronounced your father out of danger, you ought not to harbour uncharitable resentment against one, who I am persuaded did not know the Marquis was related to you."

"You plead his cause very pathetically," said Isabella, "considering he is so much a stranger to you! I am mistaken, or he returns your charity."

"What mean you?" said Matilda.

"Nothing," said Isabella, repenting that she had given Matilda a hint of Theodore's inclination for her. Then changing the discourse, she asked Matilda what occasioned Manfred to take Theodore for a spectre?

"Bless me," said Matilda, "did not you observe his extreme resemblance to the portrait of Alfonso in the gallery? I took notice of it to Bianca even before I saw him in armour; but with the helmet on, he is the very image of that picture."

"I do not much observe pictures," said Isabella: "much less have I examined this young man so attentively as you seem to have done. Ah? Matilda, your heart is in danger, but let me warn you as a friend, he has owned to me that he is in love; it cannot be with you, for yesterday was the first time you ever met — was it not?"

"Certainly," replied Matilda; "but why does my dearest Isabella conclude from anything I have said, that"—she paused—then continuing: "he saw you first, and I am far from having the vanity to think that my little portion of charms could engage a heart devoted to you; may you be happy, Isabella, whatever is the fate of Matilda!"

"My lovely friend," said Isabella, whose heart was too honest to resist a kind expression, "it is you that Theodore admires; I saw it; I am persuaded of it; nor shall a thought of my own happiness suffer me to interfere with yours."

This frankness drew tears from the gentle Matilda; and jealousy that for a moment had raised a coolness between these amiable maidens soon gave way to the natural sincerity and candour of their souls. Each confessed to the other the impression that Theodore had made on her; and this confidence was followed by a struggle of generosity, each insisting on yielding her claim to her friend. At length the dignity of Isabella's virtue reminding her of the preference which Theodore had almost declared for her rival, made her determine to conquer her passion, and cede the beloved object to her friend.

During this contest of amity, Hippolita entered her daughter's chamber.

"Madam," said she to Isabella, "you have so much tenderness for Matilda, and interest yourself so kindly in whatever affects our wretched house, that I can have no secrets with my child which are not proper for you to hear."

The princesses were all attention and anxiety.

"Know then, Madam," continued Hippolita, "and you my dearest Matilda, that being convinced by all the events of these two last ominous days, that heaven purposes the sceptre of Otranto should pass from Manfred's hands into those of the Marquis Frederic, I have been perhaps inspired with the thought of averting our total destruction by the union of our rival houses. With this view I have been proposing to Manfred, my lord, to tender this dear, dear child to Frederic, your father."

"Me to Lord Frederic!" cried Matilda; "good heavens! my gracious mother—and have you named it to my father?"

"I have," said Hippolita; "he listened benignly to my proposal, and is gone to break it to the Marquis."

"Ah! wretched princess!" cried Isabella; "what hast thou done! what ruin has thy inadvertent goodness been preparing for thyself, for me, and for Matilda!"

"Ruin from me to you and to my child!" said Hippolita "what can this mean?"

"Alas!" said Isabella, "the purity of your own heart prevents your seeing the depravity of others. Manfred, your lord, that impious man—"

"Hold," said Hippolita; "you must not in my presence, young lady, mention Manfred with disrespect: he is my lord and husband, and—"

"Will not long be so," said Isabella, "if his wicked purposes can be carried into execution."

"This language amazes me," said Hippolita. "Your feeling, Isabella, is warm; but until this hour I never knew it betray you into intemperance. What deed of Manfred authorises you to treat him as a murderer, an assassin?"

"Thou virtuous, and too credulous Princess!" replied Isabella; "it is not thy life he aims at—it is to separate himself from thee! to divorce thee! to—"

"To divorce me!" "To divorce my mother!" cried Hippolita and Matilda at once.

"Yes," said Isabella; "and to complete his crime, he meditates—I cannot speak it!"

"What can surpass what thou hast already uttered?" said Matilda.

Hippolita was silent. Grief choked her speech; and the recollection of Manfred's late ambiguous discourses confirmed what she heard.

"Excellent, dear lady! madam! mother!" cried Isabella, flinging herself at Hippolita's feet in a transport of passion; "trust me, believe me, I will die a thousand deaths sooner than consent to injure you, than yield to so odious—oh!—"

"This is too much!" cried Hippolita: "What crimes does one crime suggest! Rise, dear Isabella; I do not doubt your virtue. Oh! Matilda, this stroke is too heavy for thee! weep not, my child; and not a murmur, I charge thee. Remember, he is thy father still!"

"But you are my mother too," said Matilda fervently; "and you are virtuous, you are guiltless!—Oh! must not I, must not I complain?"

"You must not," said Hippolita—"come, all will yet be well. Manfred, in the agony for the loss of thy brother, knew not what he said; perhaps Isabella misunderstood him; his heart is good—and, my child, thou knowest not all! There is a destiny hangs over us; the hand of Providence is stretched out; oh! could I but save thee from the wreck! Yes," continued she in a firmer tone, "perhaps the sacrifice of myself may atone for all; I will go and offer myself to this divorce—it boots not what becomes of me. I will withdraw into the neighbouring monastery, and waste the remainder of life in prayers and tears for my child and—the Prince!"

"Thou art as much too good for this world," said Isabella, "as Manfred is execrable; but think not, lady, that thy weakness shall determine for me. I swear, hear me all ye angels—"

"Stop, I adjure thee," cried Hippolita: "remember thou dost not depend on thyself; thou hast a father."

"My father is too pious, too noble," interrupted Isabella, "to command an impious deed. But should he command it; can a father enjoin a cursed act? I was contracted to the son, can I wed the father? No, madam, no; force should not drag me to Manfred's hated bed. I loathe him, I abhor him: divine and human laws forbid—and my friend, my dearest Matilda! would I wound her tender soul by injuring her adored mother? my own mother—I never have known another"—

"Oh! she is the mother of both!" cried Matilda: "can we, can we, Isabella, adore her too much?"

"My lovely children," said the touched Hippolita, "your tenderness overpowers me—but I must not give way to it. It is not ours to make election for ourselves: heaven, our fathers, and our husbands must decide for us. Have patience until you hear what Manfred and Frederic have determined. If the Marquis accepts Matilda's hand, I know she will readily obey. Heaven may interpose and prevent the rest. What means my child?" continued she, seeing Matilda fall at her feet with a flood of speechless tears—"But no; answer me not, my daughter: I must not hear a word against the pleasure of thy father."

"Oh! doubt not my obedience, my dreadful obedience to him and to you!" said Matilda. "But can I, most respected of women, can I experience all this tenderness, this world of goodness, and conceal a thought from the best of mothers?"

"What art thou going to utter?" said Isabella trembling. "Recollect thyself, Matilda."

"No, Isabella," said the Princess, "I should not deserve this incomparable parent, if the inmost recesses of my soul harboured a thought without her permission—nay, I have offended her; I have suffered a passion to enter my heart without her avowal—but here I disclaim it; here I vow to heaven and her—"

"My child! my child;" said Hippolita, "what words are these! what new calamities has fate in store for us! Thou, a passion? Thou, in this hour of destruction—"

"Oh! I see all my guilt!" said Matilda. "I abhor myself, if I cost my mother a pang. She is the dearest thing I have on earth—Oh! I will never, never behold him more!"

"Isabella," said Hippolita, "thou art conscious to this unhappy secret, whatever it is. Speak!"

"What!" cried Matilda, "have I so forfeited my mother's love, that she will not permit me even to speak my own guilt? oh! wretched, wretched Matilda!"

"Thou art too cruel," said Isabella to Hippolita: "canst thou behold this anguish of a virtuous mind, and not commiserate it?"

"Not pity my child!" said Hippolita, catching Matilda in her arms—"Oh! I know she is good, she is all virtue, all tenderness, and duty. I do forgive thee, my excellent, my only hope!"

The princesses then revealed to Hippolita their mutual inclination for Theodore, and the purpose of Isabella to resign him to Matilda. Hippolita blamed their imprudence, and showed them the improbability that either father would consent to bestow his heiress on so poor a man, though nobly born. Some comfort it gave her to find their passion of so recent a date, and that Theodore had had but little cause to suspect it in either. She strictly enjoined them to avoid all correspondence with him. This Matilda fervently promised: but Isabella, who flattered herself that she meant no more than to promote his union with her friend, could not determine to avoid him; and made no reply.

"I will go to the convent," said Hippolita, "and order new masses to be said for a deliverance from these calamities."

"Oh! my mother," said Matilda, "you mean to quit us: you mean to take sanctuary, and to give my father an opportunity of pursuing his fatal intention. Alas! on my knees I supplicate you to forbear; will you leave me a prey to Frederic? I will follow you to the convent."

"Be at peace, my child," said Hippolita: "I will return instantly. I will never abandon thee, until I know it is the will of heaven, and for thy benefit."

"Do not deceive me," said Matilda. "I will not marry Frederic until thou commandest it. Alas! what will become of me?"

"Why that exclamation?" said Hippolita. "I have promised thee to return—"

"Ah! my mother," replied Matilda, "stay and save me from myself. A frown from thee can do more than all my father's severity. I have given away my heart, and you alone can make me recall it."

"No more," said Hippolita; "thou must not relapse, Matilda."

"I can quit Theodore," said she, "but must I wed another? let me attend thee to the altar, and shut myself from the world for ever."

"Thy fate depends on thy father," said Hippolita; "I have ill-bestowed my tenderness, if it has taught thee to revere aught beyond him. Adieu! my child: I go to pray for thee."

Hippolita's real purpose was to demand of Jerome, whether in conscience she might not consent to the divorce. She had oft urged Manfred to resign the principality, which the delicacy of her conscience rendered an hourly burthen to her. These scruples concurred to make the separation from her husband appear less dreadful to her than it would have seemed in any other situation.

Jerome, at quitting the castle overnight, had questioned Theodore severely why he had accused him to Manfred of being privy to his escape. Theodore owned it had been with design to prevent Manfred's suspicion from alighting on Matilda; and added, the holiness of Jerome's life and character secured him from the tyrant's wrath. Jerome was heartily grieved to discover his son's inclination for that princess; and leaving him to his rest, promised in the morning to acquaint him with important reasons for conquering his passion.

Theodore, like Isabella, was too recently acquainted with parental authority to submit to its decisions against the impulse of his heart. He had little curiosity to learn the Friar's reasons, and less disposition to obey them. The lovely Matilda had made stronger impressions on him than filial affection. All night he pleased himself with visions of love; and it was not till late after the morning-office, that he recollected the Friar's commands to attend him at Alfonso's tomb.

"Young man," said Jerome, when he saw him, "this tardiness does not please me. Have a father's commands already so little weight?"

Theodore made awkward excuses, and attributed his delay to having overslept himself.

"And on whom were thy dreams employed?" said the Friar sternly. His son blushed. "Come, come," resumed the Friar, "inconsiderate youth, this must not be; eradicate this guilty passion from thy breast—"

"Guilty passion!" cried Theodore: "Can guilt dwell with innocent beauty and virtuous modesty?"

"It is sinful," replied the Friar, "to cherish those whom heaven has doomed to destruction. A tyrant's race must be swept from the earth to the third and fourth generation."

"Will heaven visit the innocent for the crimes of the guilty?" said Theodore. "The fair Matilda has virtues enough—"

"To undo thee:" interrupted Jerome. "Hast thou so soon forgotten that twice the savage Manfred has pronounced thy sentence?"

"Nor have I forgotten, sir," said Theodore, "that the charity of his daughter delivered me from his power. I can forget injuries, but never benefits."

"The injuries thou hast received from Manfred's race," said the Friar, "are beyond what thou canst conceive. Reply not, but view this holy image! Beneath this marble monument rest the ashes of the good Alfonso; a prince adorned with every virtue: the father of his people! the delight of mankind! Kneel, headstrong boy, and list, while a father unfolds a tale of horror that will expel every sentiment from thy soul, but sensations of sacred vengeance — Alfonso! much injured prince! let thy unsatisfied shade sit awful on the troubled air, while these trembling lips — Ha! who comes there? — "

"The most wretched of women!" said Hippolita, entering the choir. "Good Father, art thou at leisure? — but why this kneeling youth? what means the horror imprinted on each countenance? why at this venerable tomb — alas! hast thou seen aught?"

"We were pouring forth our orisons to heaven," replied the Friar, with some confusion, "to put an end to the woes of this deplorable province. Join with us, Lady! thy spotless soul may obtain an exemption from the judgments which the portents of these days but too speakingly denounce against thy house."

"I pray fervently to heaven to divert them," said the pious Princess. "Thou knowest it has been the occupation of my life to wrest a blessing for my Lord and my harmless children. — One alas! is taken from me! would heaven but hear me for my poor Matilda! Father! intercede for her!"

"Every heart will bless her," cried Theodore with rapture.

"Be dumb, rash youth!" said Jerome. "And thou, fond Princess, contend not with the Powers above! the Lord giveth, and the Lord taketh away: bless His holy name, and submit to his decrees."

"I do most devoutly," said Hippolita; "but will He not spare my only comfort? must Matilda perish too? — ah! Father, I came — but dismiss thy son. No ear but thine must hear what I have to utter."

"May heaven grant thy every wish, most excellent Princess!" said Theodore retiring. Jerome frowned.

Hippolita then acquainted the Friar with the proposal she had suggested to Manfred, his approbation of it, and the tender of Matilda that he was gone to make to Frederic. Jerome could not conceal his dislike of the notion, which he covered under pretence of the improbability that Frederic, the nearest of blood to Alfonso, and who was come to claim his succession, would yield to an alliance with the usurper of his right. But nothing could equal the perplexity of the Friar, when Hippolita confessed her readiness not to oppose the separation, and demanded his opinion on the legality of her acquiescence. The Friar caught eagerly at her request of his advice, and without explaining his aversion to the proposed marriage of Manfred and Isabella, he painted to Hippolita in the most alarming colours the sinfulness of her consent, denounced judgments against her if she complied, and enjoined her in the severest terms to treat any such proposition with every mark of indignation and refusal.

Manfred, in the meantime, had broken his purpose to Frederic, and proposed the double marriage. That weak Prince, who had been struck with the charms of Matilda, listened but too eagerly to the offer. He forgot his enmity to Manfred, whom he saw but little hope of dispossessing by force; and flattering himself that no issue might succeed from the union of his daughter with the tyrant, he looked upon his own succession to the principality as facilitated by wedding Matilda. He made faint opposition to the proposal; affecting, for form only, not to acquiesce unless Hippolita should consent to the divorce. Manfred took that upon himself.

Transported with his success, and impatient to see himself in a situation to expect sons, he hastened to his wife's apartment, determined to extort her compliance. He learned with indignation that she was absent at the convent. His guilt suggested to him that she had probably been informed by Isabella of his purpose. He doubted whether her retirement to the convent did not import an intention of remaining there, until she could raise obstacles to their divorce; and the suspicions he had already entertained of Jerome, made him apprehend that the Friar would not only traverse his views, but might have inspired Hippolita with the resolution of taking sanctuary. Impatient to unravel this clue, and to defeat its success, Manfred hastened to the convent, and arrived there as the Friar was earnestly exhorting the Princess never to yield to the divorce.

"Madam," said Manfred, "what business drew you hither? why did you not await my return from the Marquis?"

"I came to implore a blessing on your councils," replied Hippolita.

"My councils do not need a Friar's intervention," said Manfred; "and of all men living is that hoary traitor the only one whom you delight to confer with?"

"Profane Prince!" said Jerome; "is it at the altar that thou choosest to insult the servants of the altar?—but, Manfred, thy impious schemes are known. Heaven and this virtuous lady know them—nay, frown not, Prince. The Church despises thy menaces. Her thunders will be heard above thy wrath. Dare to proceed in thy cursed purpose of a divorce, until her sentence be known, and here I lance her anathema at thy head."

"Audacious rebel!" said Manfred, endeavouring to conceal the awe with which the Friar's words inspired him. "Dost thou presume to threaten thy lawful Prince?"

"Thou art no lawful Prince," said Jerome; "thou art no Prince—go, discuss thy claim with Frederic; and when that is done—"

"It is done," replied Manfred; "Frederic accepts Matilda's hand, and is content to waive his claim, unless I have no male issue"—as he spoke those words three drops of blood fell from the nose of Alfonso's statue. Manfred turned pale, and the Princess sank on her knees.

"Behold!" said the Friar; "mark this miraculous indication that the blood of Alfonso will never mix with that of Manfred!"

"My gracious Lord," said Hippolita, "let us submit ourselves to heaven. Think not thy ever obedient wife rebels against thy authority. I have no will but that of my Lord and the Church. To that revered tribunal let us appeal. It does not depend on us to burst the bonds that unite us. If the Church shall approve the dissolution of our marriage, be it so—I have but few years, and those of sorrow, to pass. Where can they be worn away so well as at the foot of this altar, in prayers for thine and Matilda's safety?"

"But thou shalt not remain here until then," said Manfred. "Repair with me to the castle, and there I will advise on the proper measures for a divorce;—but this meddling Friar comes not thither; my hospitable roof shall never more harbour a traitor—and for thy Reverence's offspring," continued he, "I banish him from my dominions. He, I ween, is no sacred personage, nor under the protection of the Church. Whoever weds Isabella, it shall not be Father Falconara's started-up son."

"They start up," said the Friar, "who are suddenly beheld in the seat of lawful Princes; but they wither away like the grass, and their place knows them no more."

Manfred, casting a look of scorn at the Friar, led Hippolita forth; but at the door of the church whispered one of his attendants to remain concealed about the convent, and bring him instant notice, if any one from the castle should repair thither.

CHAPTER V.

Every reflection which Manfred made on the Friar's behaviour, conspired to persuade him that Jerome was privy to an amour between Isabella and Theodore. But Jerome's new presumption, so dissonant from his former meekness, suggested still deeper apprehensions. The Prince even suspected that the Friar depended on some secret support from Frederic, whose arrival, coinciding with the novel appearance of Theodore, seemed to bespeak a correspondence. Still more was he troubled with the resemblance of Theodore to Alfonso's portrait. The latter he knew had unquestionably died without issue. Frederic had consented to bestow Isabella on him. These contradictions agitated his mind with numberless pangs.

He saw but two methods of extricating himself from his difficulties. The one was to resign his dominions to the Marquis—pride, ambition, and his reliance on ancient prophecies, which had pointed out a possibility of his preserving them to his posterity, combated that thought. The other was to press his marriage with Isabella. After long ruminating on these anxious thoughts, as he marched silently with Hippolita to the castle, he at last discoursed with that Princess on the subject of his disquiet, and used every insinuating and plausible argument to extract her consent to, even her promise of promoting the divorce. Hippolita needed little persuasions to bend her to his pleasure. She endeavoured to win him over to the measure of resigning his dominions; but finding her exhortations fruitless, she assured him, that as far as her conscience would allow, she would raise no opposition to a separation, though without better founded scruples than what he yet alleged, she would not engage to be active in demanding it.

This compliance, though inadequate, was sufficient to raise Manfred's hopes. He trusted that his power and wealth would easily advance his suit at the court of Rome, whither he resolved to engage Frederic to take a journey on purpose. That Prince had discovered so much passion for Matilda, that Manfred hoped to obtain all he wished by holding out or withdrawing his daughter's charms, according as the Marquis should appear more or less disposed to co-operate in his views. Even the absence of Frederic would be a material point gained, until he could take further measures for his security.

Dismissing Hippolita to her apartment, he repaired to that of the Marquis; but crossing the great hall through which he was to pass he met Bianca. The damsel he knew was in the confidence of both the young ladies. It immediately occurred to him to sift her on the subject of Isabella and Theodore. Calling her aside into the recess of the oriel window of the hall, and soothing her with many fair words and promises, he demanded of her whether she knew aught of the state of Isabella's affections.

"I! my Lord! no my Lord—yes my Lord—poor Lady! she is wonderfully alarmed about her father's wounds; but I tell her he will do well; don't your Highness think so?"

"I do not ask you," replied Manfred, "what she thinks about her father; but you are in her secrets. Come, be a good girl and tell me; is there any young man—ha!—you understand me."

"Lord bless me! understand your Highness? no, not I. I told her a few vulnerary herbs and repose—"

"I am not talking," replied the Prince, impatiently, "about her father; I know he will do well."

"Bless me, I rejoice to hear your Highness say so; for though I thought it not right to let my young Lady despond, methought his greatness had a wan look, and a something—I remember when young Ferdinand was wounded by the Venetian—"

"Thou answerest from the point," interrupted Manfred; "but here, take this jewel, perhaps that may fix thy attention—nay, no reverences; my favour shall not stop here—come, tell me truly; how stands Isabella's heart?"

"Well! your Highness has such a way!" said Bianca, "to be sure—but can your Highness keep a secret? if it should ever come out of your lips—"

"It shall not, it shall not," cried Manfred.

"Nay, but swear, your Highness."

"By my halidame, if it should ever be known that I said it—"

"Why, truth is truth, I do not think my Lady Isabella ever much affectioned my young Lord your son; yet he was a sweet youth as one should see; I am sure, if I had been a Princess—but bless me! I must attend my Lady Matilda; she will marvel what is become of me."

"Stay," cried Manfred; "thou hast not satisfied my question. Hast thou ever carried any message, any letter?"

"I! good gracious!" cried Bianca; "I carry a letter? I would not to be a Queen. I hope your Highness thinks, though I am poor, I am honest. Did your Highness never hear what Count Marsigli offered me, when he came a wooing to my Lady Matilda?"

"I have not leisure," said Manfred, "to listen to thy tale. I do not question thy honesty. But it is thy duty to conceal nothing from me. How long has Isabella been acquainted with Theodore?"

"Nay, there is nothing can escape your Highness!" said Bianca; "not that I know any thing of the matter. Theodore, to be sure, is a proper young man, and, as my Lady Matilda says, the very image of good Alfonso. Has not your Highness remarked it?"

"Yes, yes, — No — thou torturest me," said Manfred. "Where did they meet? when?"

"Who! my Lady Matilda?" said Bianca.

"No, no, not Matilda: Isabella; when did Isabella first become acquainted with this Theodore!"

"Virgin Mary!" said Bianca, "how should I know?"

"Thou dost know," said Manfred; "and I must know; I will —"

"Lord! your Highness is not jealous of young Theodore!" said Bianca.

"Jealous! no, no. Why should I be jealous? perhaps I mean to unite them — If I were sure Isabella would have no repugnance."

"Repugnance! no, I'll warrant her," said Bianca; "he is as comely a youth as ever trod on Christian ground. We are all in love with him; there is not a soul in the castle but would be rejoiced to have him for our Prince — I mean, when it shall please heaven to call your Highness to itself."

"Indeed!" said Manfred, "has it gone so far! oh! this cursed Friar! — but I must not lose time — go, Bianca, attend Isabella; but I charge thee, not a word of what has passed. Find out how she is affected towards Theodore; bring me good news, and that ring has a companion. Wait at the foot of the winding staircase: I am going to visit the Marquis, and will talk further with thee at my return."

Manfred, after some general conversation, desired Frederic to dismiss the two Knights, his companions, having to talk with him on urgent affairs.

As soon as they were alone, he began in artful guise to sound the Marquis on the subject of Matilda; and finding him disposed to his wish, he let drop hints on the difficulties that would attend the celebration of their marriage, unless—At that instant Bianca burst into the room with a wildness in her look and gestures that spoke the utmost terror.

"Oh! my Lord, my Lord!" cried she; "we are all undone! it is come again! it is come again!"

"What is come again?" cried Manfred amazed.

"Oh! the hand! the Giant! the hand!—support me! I am terrified out of my senses," cried Bianca. "I will not sleep in the castle to-night. Where shall I go? my things may come after me to-morrow—would I had been content to wed Francesco! this comes of ambition!"

"What has terrified thee thus, young woman?" said the Marquis. "Thou art safe here; be not alarmed."

"Oh! your Greatness is wonderfully good," said Bianca, "but I dare not—no, pray let me go—I had rather leave everything behind me, than stay another hour under this roof."

"Go to, thou hast lost thy senses," said Manfred. "Interrupt us not; we were communing on important matters—My Lord, this wench is subject to fits—Come with me, Bianca."

"Oh! the Saints! No," said Bianca, "for certain it comes to warn your Highness; why should it appear to me else? I say my prayers morning and evening—oh! if your Highness had believed Diego! 'Tis the same hand that he saw the foot to in the gallery-chamber—Father Jerome has often told us the prophecy would be out one of these days—'Bianca,' said he, 'mark my words—'"

"Thou ravest," said Manfred, in a rage; "be gone, and keep these fooleries to frighten thy companions."

"What! my Lord," cried Bianca, "do you think I have seen nothing? go to the foot of the great stairs yourself — as I live I saw it."

"Saw what? tell us, fair maid, what thou hast seen," said Frederic.

"Can your Highness listen," said Manfred, "to the delirium of a silly wench, who has heard stories of apparitions until she believes them?"

"This is more than fancy," said the Marquis; "her terror is too natural and too strongly impressed to be the work of imagination. Tell us, fair maiden, what it is has moved thee thus?"

"Yes, my Lord, thank your Greatness," said Bianca; "I believe I look very pale; I shall be better when I have recovered myself — I was going to my Lady Isabella's chamber, by his Highness's order —"

"We do not want the circumstances," interrupted Manfred. "Since his Highness will have it so, proceed; but be brief."

"Lord! your Highness thwarts one so!" replied Bianca; "I fear my hair — I am sure I never in my life — well! as I was telling your Greatness, I was going by his Highness's order to my Lady Isabella's chamber; she lies in the watchet-coloured chamber, on the right hand, one pair of stairs: so when I came to the great stairs — I was looking on his Highness's present here —"

"Grant me patience!" said Manfred, "will this wench never come to the point? what imports it to the Marquis, that I gave thee a bauble for thy faithful attendance on my daughter? we want to know what thou sawest."

"I was going to tell your Highness," said Bianca, "if you would permit me. So as I was rubbing the ring — I am sure I had not gone up three steps, but I heard the rattling of armour; for all the world such a clatter as Diego says he heard when the Giant turned him about in the gallery-chamber."

"What Giant is this, my Lord?" said the Marquis; "is your castle haunted by giants and goblins?"

"Lord! what, has not your Greatness heard the story of the Giant in the gallery-chamber?" cried Bianca. "I marvel his Highness has not told you; mayhap you do not know there is a prophecy —"

"This trifling is intolerable," interrupted Manfred. "Let us dismiss this silly wench, my Lord! we have more important affairs to discuss."

"By your favour," said Frederic, "these are no trifles. The enormous sabre I was directed to in the wood, yon casque, its fellow — are these visions of this poor maiden's brain?"

"So Jaquez thinks, may it please your Greatness," said Bianca. "He says this moon will not be out without our seeing some strange revolution. For my part, I should not be surprised if it was to happen to-morrow; for, as I was saying, when I heard the clattering of armour, I was all in a cold sweat. I looked up, and, if your Greatness will believe me, I saw upon the uppermost banister of the great stairs a hand in armour as big as big. I thought I should have swooned. I never stopped until I came hither — would I were well out of this castle. My Lady Matilda told me but yester-morning that her Highness Hippolita knows something."

"Thou art an insolent!" cried Manfred. "Lord Marquis, it much misgives me that this scene is concerted to affront me. Are my own domestics suborned to spread tales injurious to my honour? Pursue your claim by manly daring; or let us bury our feuds, as was proposed, by the intermarriage of our children. But trust me, it ill becomes a Prince of your bearing to practise on mercenary wenches."

"I scorn your imputation," said Frederic. "Until this hour I never set eyes on this damsel: I have given her no jewel. My Lord, my Lord, your conscience, your guilt accuses you, and would throw the suspicion on me; but keep your daughter, and think no more of Isabella. The judgments already fallen on your house forbid me matching into it."

Manfred, alarmed at the resolute tone in which Frederic delivered these words, endeavoured to pacify him. Dismissing Bianca, he made such submissions to the Marquis, and threw in such artful encomiums on Matilda, that Frederic was once more staggered. However, as his passion was of so recent a date, it could not at once surmount the scruples he had conceived. He had gathered enough from Bianca's discourse to persuade him that heaven declared itself against Manfred. The proposed marriages too removed his claim to a distance; and the principality of Otranto was a stronger temptation than the contingent reversion of it with Matilda. Still he would not absolutely recede from his engagements; but purposing to gain time, he demanded of Manfred if it was true in fact that Hippolita consented to the divorce. The Prince, transported to find no other obstacle, and depending on his influence over his wife, assured the Marquis it was so, and that he might satisfy himself of the truth from her own mouth.

As they were thus discoursing, word was brought that the banquet was prepared. Manfred conducted Frederic to the great hall, where they were received by Hippolita and the young Princesses. Manfred placed the Marquis next to Matilda, and seated himself between his wife and Isabella. Hippolita comported herself with an easy gravity; but the young ladies were silent and melancholy. Manfred, who was determined to pursue his point with the Marquis in the remainder of the evening, pushed on the feast until it waxed late; affecting unrestrained gaiety, and plying Frederic with repeated goblets of wine. The latter, more upon his guard than Manfred wished, declined his frequent challenges, on pretence of his late loss of blood; while the Prince, to raise his own disordered spirits, and to counterfeit unconcern, indulged himself in plentiful draughts, though not to the intoxication of his senses.

The evening being far advanced, the banquet concluded. Manfred would have withdrawn with Frederic; but the latter pleading weakness and want of repose, retired to his chamber, gallantly telling the Prince that his daughter should amuse his Highness until himself could attend him. Manfred accepted the party, and to the no small grief of Isabella, accompanied her to her apartment. Matilda waited on her mother to enjoy the freshness of the evening on the ramparts of the castle.

Soon as the company were dispersed their several ways, Frederic, quitting his chamber, inquired if Hippolita was alone, and was told by one of her attendants, who had not noticed her going forth, that at that hour she generally withdrew to her oratory, where he probably would find her. The Marquis, during the repast, had beheld Matilda with increase of passion. He now wished to find Hippolita in the disposition her Lord had promised. The portents that had alarmed him were forgotten in his desires. Stealing softly and unobserved to the apartment of Hippolita, he entered it with a resolution to encourage her acquiescence to the divorce, having perceived that Manfred was resolved to make the possession of Isabella an unalterable condition, before he would grant Matilda to his wishes.

The Marquis was not surprised at the silence that reigned in the Princess's apartment. Concluding her, as he had been advertised, in her oratory, he passed on. The door was ajar; the evening gloomy and overcast. Pushing open the door gently, he saw a person kneeling before the altar. As he approached nearer, it seemed not a woman, but one in a long woollen weed, whose back was towards him. The person seemed absorbed in prayer. The Marquis was about to return, when the figure, rising, stood some moments fixed in meditation, without regarding him. The Marquis, expecting the holy person to come forth, and meaning to excuse his uncivil interruption, said,

"Reverend Father, I sought the Lady Hippolita."

"Hippolita!" replied a hollow voice; "camest thou to this castle to seek Hippolita?" and then the figure, turning slowly round, discovered to Frederic the fleshless jaws and empty sockets of a skeleton, wrapt in a hermit's cowl.

"Angels of grace protect me!" cried Frederic, recoiling.

"Deserve their protection!" said the Spectre. Frederic, falling on his knees, adjured the phantom to take pity on him.

"Dost thou not remember me?" said the apparition. "Remember the wood of Joppa!"

"Art thou that holy hermit?" cried Frederic, trembling. "Can I do aught for thy eternal peace?"

"Wast thou delivered from bondage," said the spectre, "to pursue carnal delights? Hast thou forgotten the buried sabre, and the behest of Heaven engraven on it?"

"I have not, I have not," said Frederic; "but say, blest spirit, what is thy errand to me? What remains to be done?"

"To forget Matilda!" said the apparition; and vanished.

Frederic's blood froze in his veins. For some minutes he remained motionless. Then falling prostrate on his face before the altar, he besought the intercession of every saint for pardon. A flood of tears succeeded to this transport; and the image of the beauteous Matilda rushing in spite of him on his thoughts, he lay on the ground in a conflict of penitence and passion. Ere he could recover from this agony of his spirits, the Princess Hippolita with a taper in her hand entered the oratory alone. Seeing a man without motion on the floor, she gave a shriek, concluding him dead. Her fright brought Frederic to himself. Rising suddenly, his face bedewed with tears, he would have rushed from her presence; but Hippolita stopping him, conjured him in the most plaintive accents to explain the cause of his disorder, and by what strange chance she had found him there in that posture.

"Ah, virtuous Princess!" said the Marquis, penetrated with grief, and stopped.

"For the love of Heaven, my Lord," said Hippolita, "disclose the cause of this transport! What mean these doleful sounds, this alarming exclamation on my name? What woes has heaven still in store for the wretched Hippolita? Yet silent! By every pitying angel, I adjure thee, noble Prince," continued she, falling at his feet, "to disclose the purport of what lies at thy heart. I see thou feelest for me; thou feelest the sharp pangs that thou inflictest—speak, for pity! Does aught thou knowest concern my child?"

"I cannot speak," cried Frederic, bursting from her. "Oh, Matilda!"

Quitting the Princess thus abruptly, he hastened to his own apartment. At the door of it he was accosted by Manfred, who flushed by wine and love had come to seek him, and to propose to waste some hours of the night in music and revelling. Frederic, offended at an invitation so dissonant from the mood of his soul, pushed him rudely aside, and entering his chamber, flung the door intemperately against Manfred, and bolted it inwards. The haughty Prince, enraged at this unaccountable behaviour, withdrew in a frame of mind capable of the most fatal excesses. As he crossed the court, he was met by the domestic whom he had planted at the convent as a spy on Jerome and Theodore. This man, almost breathless with the haste he had made, informed his Lord that Theodore, and some lady from the castle were, at that instant, in private conference at the tomb of Alfonso in St. Nicholas's church. He had dogged Theodore thither, but the gloominess of the night had prevented his discovering who the woman was.

Manfred, whose spirits were inflamed, and whom Isabella had driven from her on his urging his passion with too little reserve, did not doubt but the inquietude she had expressed had been occasioned by her impatience to meet Theodore. Provoked by this conjecture, and enraged at her father, he hastened secretly to the great church. Gliding softly between the aisles, and guided by an imperfect gleam of moonshine that shone faintly through the illuminated windows, he stole towards the tomb of Alfonso, to which he was directed by indistinct whispers of the persons he sought. The first sounds he could distinguish were—

"Does it, alas! depend on me? Manfred will never permit our union."

"No, this shall prevent it!" cried the tyrant, drawing his dagger, and plunging it over her shoulder into the bosom of the person that spoke.

"Ah, me, I am slain!" cried Matilda, sinking. "Good heaven, receive my soul!"

"Savage, inhuman monster, what hast thou done!" cried Theodore, rushing on him, and wrenching his dagger from him.

"Stop, stop thy impious hand!" cried Matilda; "it is my father!"

Manfred, waking as from a trance, beat his breast, twisted his hands in his locks, and endeavoured to recover his dagger from Theodore to despatch himself. Theodore, scarce less distracted, and only mastering the transports of his grief to assist Matilda, had now by his cries drawn some of the monks to his aid. While part of them endeavoured, in concert with the afflicted Theodore, to stop the blood of the dying Princess, the rest prevented Manfred from laying violent hands on himself.

Matilda, resigning herself patiently to her fate, acknowledged with looks of grateful love the zeal of Theodore. Yet oft as her faintness would permit her speech its way, she begged the assistants to comfort her father. Jerome, by this time, had learnt the fatal news, and reached the church. His looks seemed to reproach Theodore, but turning to Manfred, he said,

"Now, tyrant! behold the completion of woe fulfilled on thy impious and devoted head! The blood of Alfonso cried to heaven for vengeance; and heaven has permitted its altar to be polluted by assassination, that thou mightest shed thy own blood at the foot of that Prince's sepulchre!"

"Cruel man!" cried Matilda, "to aggravate the woes of a parent; may heaven bless my father, and forgive him as I do! My Lord, my gracious Sire, dost thou forgive thy child? Indeed, I came not hither to meet Theodore. I found him praying at this tomb, whither my mother sent me to intercede for thee, for her—dearest father, bless your child, and say you forgive her."

"Forgive thee! Murderous monster!" cried Manfred, "can assassins forgive? I took thee for Isabella; but heaven directed my bloody hand to the heart of my child. Oh, Matilda!—I cannot utter it—canst thou forgive the blindness of my rage?"

"I can, I do; and may heaven confirm it!" said Matilda; "but while I have life to ask it—oh! my mother! what will she feel? Will you comfort her, my Lord? Will you not put her away? Indeed she loves you! Oh, I am faint! bear me to the castle. Can I live to have her close my eyes?"

Theodore and the monks besought her earnestly to suffer herself to be borne into the convent; but her instances were so pressing to be carried to the castle, that placing her on a litter, they conveyed her thither as she requested. Theodore, supporting her head with his arm, and hanging over her in an agony of despairing love, still endeavoured to inspire her with hopes of life. Jerome, on the other side, comforted her with discourses of heaven, and holding a crucifix before her, which she bathed with innocent tears, prepared her for her passage to immortality. Manfred, plunged in the deepest affliction, followed the litter in despair.

Ere they reached the castle, Hippolita, informed of the dreadful catastrophe, had flown to meet her murdered child; but when she saw the afflicted procession, the mightiness of her grief deprived her of her senses, and she fell lifeless to the earth in a swoon. Isabella and Frederic, who attended her, were overwhelmed in almost equal sorrow. Matilda alone seemed insensible to her own situation: every thought was lost in tenderness for her mother.

Ordering the litter to stop, as soon as Hippolita was brought to herself, she asked for her father. He approached, unable to speak. Matilda, seizing his hand and her mother's, locked them in her own, and then clasped them to her heart. Manfred could not support this act of pathetic piety. He dashed himself on the ground, and cursed the day he was born. Isabella, apprehensive that these struggles of passion were more than Matilda could support, took upon herself to order Manfred to be borne to his apartment, while she caused Matilda to be conveyed to the nearest chamber. Hippolita, scarce more alive than her daughter, was regardless of everything but her; but when the tender Isabella's care would have likewise removed her, while the surgeons examined Matilda's wound, she cried,

"Remove me! never, never! I lived but in her, and will expire with her."

Matilda raised her eyes at her mother's voice, but closed them again without speaking. Her sinking pulse and the damp coldness of her hand soon dispelled all hopes of recovery. Theodore followed the surgeons into the outer chamber, and heard them pronounce the fatal sentence with a transport equal to frenzy.

"Since she cannot live mine," cried he, "at least she shall be mine in death! Father! Jerome! will you not join our hands?" cried he to the Friar, who, with the Marquis, had accompanied the surgeons.

"What means thy distracted rashness?" said Jerome. "Is this an hour for marriage?"

"It is, it is," cried Theodore. "Alas! there is no other!"

"Young man, thou art too unadvised," said Frederic. "Dost thou think we are to listen to thy fond transports in this hour of fate? What pretensions hast thou to the Princess?"

"Those of a Prince," said Theodore; "of the sovereign of Otranto. This reverend man, my father, has informed me who I am."

"Thou ravest," said the Marquis. "There is no Prince of Otranto but myself, now Manfred, by murder, by sacrilegious murder, has forfeited all pretensions."

"My Lord," said Jerome, assuming an air of command, "he tells you true. It was not my purpose the secret should have been divulged so soon, but fate presses onward to its work. What his hot-headed passion has revealed, my tongue confirms. Know, Prince, that when Alfonso set sail for the Holy Land—"

"Is this a season for explanations?" cried Theodore. "Father, come and unite me to the Princess; she shall be mine! In every other thing I will dutifully obey you. My life! my adored Matilda!" continued Theodore, rushing back into the inner chamber, "will you not be mine? Will you not bless your—"

Isabella made signs to him to be silent, apprehending the Princess was near her end.

"What, is she dead?" cried Theodore; "is it possible!"

The violence of his exclamations brought Matilda to herself. Lifting up her eyes, she looked round for her mother.

"Life of my soul, I am here!" cried Hippolita; "think not I will quit thee!"

"Oh! you are too good," said Matilda. "But weep not for me, my mother! I am going where sorrow never dwells—Isabella, thou hast loved me; wouldst thou not supply my fondness to this dear, dear woman? Indeed I am faint!"

"Oh! my child! my child!" said Hippolita in a flood of tears, "can I not withhold thee a moment?"

"It will not be," said Matilda; "commend me to heaven— Where is my father? forgive him, dearest mother—forgive him my death; it was an error. Oh! I had forgotten—dearest mother, I vowed never to see Theodore more—perhaps that has drawn down this calamity—but it was not intentional—can you pardon me?"

"Oh! wound not my agonising soul!" said Hippolita; "thou never couldst offend me—Alas! she faints! help! help!"

"I would say something more," said Matilda, struggling, "but it cannot be—Isabella—Theodore—for my sake—Oh!—" she expired.

Isabella and her women tore Hippolita from the corse; but Theodore threatened destruction to all who attempted to remove him from it. He printed a thousand kisses on her clay-cold hands, and uttered every expression that despairing love could dictate.

Isabella, in the meantime, was accompanying the afflicted Hippolita to her apartment; but, in the middle of the court, they were met by Manfred, who, distracted with his own thoughts, and anxious once more to behold his daughter, was advancing to the chamber where she lay. As the moon was now at its height, he read in the countenances of this unhappy company the event he dreaded.

"What! is she dead?" cried he in wild confusion. A clap of thunder at that instant shook the castle to its foundations; the earth rocked, and the clank of more than mortal armour was heard behind. Frederic and Jerome thought the last day was at hand. The latter, forcing Theodore along with them, rushed into the court. The moment Theodore appeared, the walls of the castle behind Manfred were thrown down with a mighty force, and the form of Alfonso, dilated to an immense magnitude, appeared in the centre of the ruins.

"Behold in Theodore the true heir of Alfonso!" said the vision: And having pronounced those words, accompanied by a clap of thunder, it ascended solemnly towards heaven, where the clouds parting asunder, the form of St. Nicholas was seen, and receiving Alfonso's shade, they were soon wrapt from mortal eyes in a blaze of glory.

The beholders fell prostrate on their faces, acknowledging the divine will. The first that broke silence was Hippolita.

"My Lord," said she to the desponding Manfred, "behold the vanity of human greatness! Conrad is gone! Matilda is no more! In Theodore we view the true Prince of Otranto. By what miracle he is so I know not—suffice it to us, our doom is pronounced! shall we not, can we but dedicate the few deplorable hours we have to live, in deprecating the further wrath of heaven? heaven ejects us—whither can we fly, but to yon holy cells that yet offer us a retreat."

"Thou guiltless but unhappy woman! unhappy by my crimes!" replied Manfred, "my heart at last is open to thy devout admonitions. Oh! could—but it cannot be—ye are lost in wonder—let me at last do justice on myself! To heap shame on my own head is all the satisfaction I have left to offer to offended heaven. My story has drawn down these judgments: Let my confession atone—but, ah! what can atone for usurpation and a murdered child? a child murdered in a consecrated place? List, sirs, and may this bloody record be a warning to future tyrants!"

"Alfonso, ye all know, died in the Holy Land—ye would interrupt me; ye would say he came not fairly to his end—it is most true—why else this bitter cup which Manfred must drink to the dregs. Ricardo, my grandfather, was his chamberlain—I would draw a veil over my ancestor's crimes—but it is in vain! Alfonso died by poison. A fictitious will declared Ricardo his heir. His crimes pursued him—yet he lost no Conrad, no Matilda! I pay the price of usurpation for all! A storm overtook him. Haunted by his guilt he vowed to St. Nicholas to found a church and two convents, if he lived to reach Otranto. The sacrifice was accepted: the saint appeared to him in a dream, and promised that Ricardo's posterity should reign in Otranto until the rightful owner should be grown too large to inhabit the castle, and as long as issue male from Ricardo's loins should remain to enjoy it—alas! alas! nor male nor female, except myself, remains of all his wretched race! I have done—the woes of these three days speak the rest. How this young man can be Alfonso's heir I know not—yet I do not doubt it. His are these dominions; I resign them—yet I knew not Alfonso had an heir—I question not the will of heaven—poverty and prayer must fill up the woeful space, until Manfred shall be summoned to Ricardo."

"What remains is my part to declare," said Jerome. "When Alfonso set sail for the Holy Land he was driven by a storm to the coast of Sicily. The other vessel, which bore Ricardo and his train, as your Lordship must have heard, was separated from him."

"It is most true," said Manfred; "and the title you give me is more than an outcast can claim—well! be it so—proceed."

Jerome blushed, and continued. "For three months Lord Alfonso was wind-bound in Sicily. There he became enamoured of a fair virgin named Victoria. He was too pious to tempt her to forbidden pleasures. They were married. Yet deeming this amour incongruous with the holy vow of arms by which he was bound, he determined to conceal their nuptials until his return from the Crusade, when he purposed to seek and acknowledge her for his lawful wife. He left her pregnant. During his absence she was delivered of a daughter. But scarce had she felt a mother's pangs ere she heard the fatal rumour of her Lord's death, and the succession of Ricardo. What could a friendless, helpless woman do? Would her testimony avail?—yet, my lord, I have an authentic writing—"

"It needs not," said Manfred; "the horrors of these days, the vision we have but now seen, all corroborate thy evidence beyond a thousand parchments. Matilda's death and my expulsion—"

"Be composed, my Lord," said Hippolita; "this holy man did not mean to recall your griefs." Jerome proceeded.

"I shall not dwell on what is needless. The daughter of which Victoria was delivered, was at her maturity bestowed in marriage on me. Victoria died; and the secret remained locked in my breast. Theodore's narrative has told the rest."

The Friar ceased. The disconsolate company retired to the remaining part of the castle. In the morning Manfred signed his abdication of the principality, with the approbation of

Hippolita, and each took on them the habit of religion in the neighbouring convents. Frederic offered his daughter to the new Prince, which Hippolita's tenderness for Isabella concurred to promote. But Theodore's grief was too fresh to admit the thought of another love; and it was not until after frequent discourses with Isabella of his dear Matilda, that he was persuaded he could know no happiness but in the society of one with whom he could for ever indulge the melancholy that had taken possession of his soul.

Sir Bertrand, A Fragment

By John Aikin & Anna Laetitia Barbauld

. . . . After this adventure, Sir Bertrand turned his steed towards the wolds, hoping to cross these dreary moors before the curfew. But ere he had proceeded half his journey, he was bewildered by the different tracks, and not being able, as far as the eye could reach, to espy any object but the brown heath surrounding him, he was at length quite uncertain which way he should direct his course. Night overtook him in this situation. It was one of those nights when the moon gives a faint glimmering of light through the thick black clouds of a lowering sky. Now and then she suddenly emerged in full splendor from her veil; and then instantly retired behind it, having just served to give the forlorn Sir Bertrand a wide extended prospect over the desolate waste. Hope and native courage a while urged him to push forwards, but at length the increasing darkness and fatigue of body and mind overcame him; he dreaded moving from the ground he stood on, for fear of unknown pits and bogs, and alighting from his horse in despair, he threw himself on the ground. He had not long continued in that posture when the sullen toll of a distant bell struck his ears—he started up, and, turning towards the sound, discerned a dim twinkling light. Instantly he seized his horse's bridle, and with cautious steps advanced towards it. After a painful march, he was stopt by a moated ditch surrounding the place from whence the light proceeded; and by a momentary glimpse of moon-light he had a full view of a large antique mansion, with turrets at the corners, and an ample porch in the center. The injuries of time were strongly marked on every thing about it. The roof in various places was fallen in, the battlements were half demolished, and the windows broken and dismantled. A draw-bridge, with a ruinous gate-way at each end, led to the court before the building. He entered, and instantly the light, which proceeded from a window in one of the turrets, glided along and vanished; at the same moment the moon sunk beneath a black cloud, and the night was darker than ever. All was silent. Sir Bertrand fastened his steed under a shed, and approaching the house, traversed its whole front with light and slow footsteps. All was still as death. He looked in at the lower windows, but could not distinguish a single object through the impenetrable gloom. After a short parley with himself, he entered the porch, and seizing a massy iron knocker at the gate, lifted it up, and hesitating, at length struck a loud stroke. The noise resounded through the whole mansion with hollow echoes. All was still again. He repeated the strokes more boldly, and louder — another interval of silence ensued. A third time he knocked, and a third time all was still. He then fell back to some distance, that he might discern whether any light could be seen in the whole front. It again appeared in the same place, and quickly glided away as before. At the same instant, a deep sullen[Pg 131] toll sounded from the turret. Sir Bertrand's heart made a fearful stop — He was a while motionless; then terror impelled him to make some hasty steps towards his steed; but shame stopt his flight; and, urged by honour, and a resistless desire of finishing the adventure, he returned to the porch; and, working up his soul to a full steadiness of resolution, he drew forth his sword with one hand, and with the other lifted up the latch of the gate. The heavy door, creaking upon its hinges, reluctantly yielded to his hand — he applied his shoulder to it, and forced it open — he quitted it, and stept forward — the door instantly shut with a thundering clap. Sir Bertrand's blood was chilled — he turned back to find the door, and it was long ere his trembling hands could seize it — but his utmost strength could not open it again. After several ineffectual attempts, he looked behind him, and beheld, across a hall, upon a large staircase, a pale bluish flame, which cast a dismal gleam of light around. He again summoned forth his courage, and advanced towards it — It retired. He came to the foot of the stairs, and, after a moment's deliberation, ascended. He went slowly up, the flame retiring before him, till he came to a wide gallery — The flame proceeded along it, and he followed in silent horror, treading lightly, for the echoes of his footsteps startled him. It led him to the foot of another staircase, and then vanished. At the same instant, another toll sounded from the turret — Sir Bertrand felt it strike upon his heart. He was now in total darkness, and, with his arms extended, began to ascend the second staircase. A dead cold hand met his left hand, and firmly grasped it, drawing him forcibly forwards — he endeavoured to disengage himself, but could not — he made a furious blow with his sword, and instantly a loud shriek pierced his ears, and the dead hand was left powerless in his — He dropt it, and rushed forwards with a desperate valour. The stairs were narrow and winding, and interrupted by frequent breaches, and loose fragments of stone.

The staircase grew narrower and narrower, and at length terminated in a low iron grate. Sir Bertrand pushed it open—it led to an intricate winding passage, just large enough to admit a person upon his hands and knees. A faint glimmering of light served to shew the nature of the place. Sir Bertrand entered—A deep hollow groan resounded from a distance through the vault—He went forwards, and proceeding beyond the first turning, he discerned the same blue flame which had before conducted him. He followed it. The vault, at length, suddenly opened into a lofty gallery, in the midst of which a figure appeared, completely armed, thrusting forwards the bloody stump of an arm, with a terrible frown and menacing gesture, and brandishing a sword in his hand. Sir Bertrand undauntedly sprung forwards; and, aiming a fierce blow at the figure, it instantly vanished, letting fall a massy iron key. The flame now rested upon a pair of ample folding doors at the end of the gallery. Sir Bertrand went up to it, and applied the key to a brazen lock. With difficulty he turned the bolt. Instantly the doors flew open, and discovered a large apartment, at the end of which was a coffin rested upon a bier, with a taper burning on each side of it. Along the room, on both sides, were gigantic statues of black marble, attired in the Moorish habit, and holding enormous sabres in their right hands. Each of them reared his arm, and advanced one leg forwards as the knight entered; at the same moment, the lid of the coffin flew open, and the bell tolled. The flame still glided forwards, and Sir Bertrand resolutely followed, till he arrived within six paces of the coffin. Suddenly, a lady in a shroud and black veil rose up in it, and stretched out her arms towards him; at the same time, the statues clashed their sabres, and advanced. Sir Bertrand flew to the lady, and clasped her in his arms—she threw up her veil, and kissed his lips; and instantly the whole building shook as with an earthquake, and fell asunder with a horrible crash. Sir Bertrand was thrown into a sudden trance, and, on recovering, found himself seated on a velvet sofa, in the most magnificent room he had ever seen, lighted with innumerable tapers, in lustres of pure crystal. A sumptuous banquet was set in the middle. The doors opening to soft music, a lady of incomparable beauty, attired with amazing splendor, entered, surrounded by a troop of gay nymphs, more fair than the Graces. She advanced to the knight, and, falling on her knees, thanked him as her deliverer. The nymphs placed a garland of laurel upon his head, and the lady led him by the hand to the banquet, and sat beside him. The nymphs placed themselves at the table, and a numerous train of servants entering, served up the feast; delicious music playing all the time. Sir Bertrand could not speak for astonishment: he could only return their honours by courteous looks and gestures. After the banquet was finished, all retired but the lady, who, leading back the knight to the sofa, addressed him in these words: . . . .

The Old English Baron

By Clara Reeve

PREFACE

As this Story is of a species which, though not new, is out of the common track, it has been thought necessary to point out some circumstances to the reader, which will elucidate the design, and, it is hoped, will induce him to form a favourable, as well as a right judgment of the work before him.

This Story is the literary offspring of The Castle of Otranto, written upon the same plan, with a design to unite the most attractive and interesting circumstances of the ancient Romance and modern Novel, at the same time it assumes a character and manner of its own, that differs from both; it is distinguished by the appellation of a Gothic Story, being a picture of Gothic times and manners. Fictitious stories have been the delight of all times and all countries, by oral tradition in barbarous, by writing in more civilized ones; and although some persons of wit and learning have condemned them indiscriminately, I would venture to affirm, that even those who so much affect to despise them under one form, will receive and embrace them under another.

Thus, for instance, a man shall admire and almost adore the Epic poems of the Ancients, and yet despise and execrate the ancient Romances, which are only Epics in prose.

History represents human nature as it is in real life, alas, too often a melancholy retrospect! Romance displays only the amiable side of the picture; it shews the pleasing features, and throws a veil over the blemishes: Mankind are naturally pleased with what gratifies their vanity; and vanity, like all other passions of the human heart, may be rendered subservient to good and useful purposes.

I confess that it may be abused, and become an instrument to corrupt the manners and morals of mankind; so may poetry, so may plays, so may every kind of composition; but that will prove nothing more than the old saying lately revived by the philosophers the most in fashion, "that every earthly thing has two handles."

The business of Romance is, first, to excite the attention; and secondly, to direct it to some useful, or at least innocent, end: Happy the writer who attains both these points, like Richardson! and not unfortunate, or undeserving praise, he who gains only the latter, and furnishes out an entertainment for the reader!

Having, in some degree, opened my design, I beg leave to conduct my reader back again, till he comes within view of The Castle of Otranto; a work which, as already has been observed, is an attempt to unite the various merits and graces of the ancient Romance and modern Novel. To attain this end, there is required a sufficient degree of the marvellous, to excite the attention; enough of the manners of real life, to give an air of probability to the work; and enough of the pathetic, to engage the heart in its behalf.

The book we have mentioned is excellent in the two last points, but has a redundancy in the first; the opening excites the attention very strongly; the conduct of the story is artful and judicious; the characters are admirably drawn and supported; the diction polished and elegant; yet, with all these brilliant advantages, it palls upon the mind (though it does not upon the ear); and the reason is obvious, the machinery is so violent, that it destroys the effect it is intended to excite. Had the story been kept within the utmost verge of probability, the effect had been preserved, without losing the least circumstance that excites or detains the attention.

For instance; we can conceive, and allow of, the appearance of a ghost; we can even dispense with an enchanted sword and helmet; but then they must keep within certain limits of credibility: A sword so large as to require an hundred men to lift it; a helmet that by its own weight forces a passage through a court-yard into an arched vault, big enough for a man to go through; a picture that walks out of its frame; a skeleton ghost in a hermit's cowl: — When your expectation is wound up to the highest pitch, these circumstances take it down with a witness, destroy the work of imagination, and, instead of attention, excite laughter. I was both surprised and vexed to find the enchantment dissolved, which I wished might continue to the end of the book; and several of its readers have confessed the same disappointment to me: The beauties are so numerous, that we cannot bear the defects, but want it to be perfect in all respects.

In the course of my observations upon this singular book, it seemed to me that it was possible to compose a work upon the same plan, wherein these defects might be avoided; and the keeping, as in painting, might be preserved.

But then I began to fear it might happen to me as to certain translators, and imitators of Shakespeare; the unities may be preserved, while the spirit is evaporated. However, I ventured to attempt it; I read the beginning to a circle of friends of approved judgment, and by their approbation was encouraged to proceed, and to finish it.

THE OLD ENGLISH BARON:
A GOTHIC STORY.

In the minority of Henry the Sixth, King of England, when the renowned John, Duke of Bedford was Regent of France, and Humphrey, the good Duke of Gloucester, was Protector of England, a worthy knight, called Sir Philip Harclay, returned from his travels to England, his native country. He had served under the glorious King Henry the Fifth with distinguished valour, had acquired an honourable fame, and was no less esteemed for Christian virtues than for deeds of chivalry. After the death of his prince, he entered into the service of the Greek emperor, and distinguished his courage against the encroachments of the Saracens. In a battle there, he took prisoner a certain gentleman, by name M. Zadisky, of Greek extraction, but brought up by a Saracen officer; this man he converted to the Christian faith; after which he bound him to himself by the ties of friendship and gratitude, and he resolved to continue with his benefactor. After thirty years travel and warlike service, he determined to return to his native land, and to spend the remainder of his life in peace; and, by devoting himself to works of piety and charity, prepare for a better state hereafter.

This noble knight had, in his early youth, contracted a strict friendship with the only son of the Lord Lovel, a gentleman of eminent virtues and accomplishments. During Sir Philip's residence in foreign countries, he had frequently written to his friend, and had for a time received answers; the last informed him of the death of old Lord Lovel, and the marriage of the young one; but from that time he had heard no more from him. Sir Philip imputed it not to neglect or forgetfulness, but to the difficulties of intercourse, common at that time to all travellers and adventurers. When he was returning home, he resolved, after looking into his family affairs, to visit the Castle of Lovel, and enquire into the situation of his friend. He landed in Kent, attended by his Greek friend and two faithful servants, one of which was maimed by the wounds he had received in the defence of his master.

Sir Philip went to his family seat in Yorkshire. He found his mother and sister were dead, and his estates sequestered in the hands of commissioners appointed by the Protector. He was obliged to prove the reality of his claim, and the identity of his person (by the testimony of some of the old servants of his family), after which every thing was restored to him. He took possession of his own house, established his household, settled the old servants in their former stations, and placed those he brought home in the upper offices of his family. He then left his friend to superintend his domestic affairs; and, attended by only one of his old servants, he set out for the Castle of Lovel, in the west of England. They travelled by easy journeys; but, towards the evening of the second day, the servant was so ill and fatigued he could go no further; he stopped at an inn where he grew worse every hour, and the next day expired. Sir Philip was under great concern for the loss of his servant, and some for himself, being alone in a strange place; however he took courage, ordered his servant's funeral, attended it himself, and, having shed a tear of humanity over his grave, proceeded alone on his journey.

As he drew near the estate of his friend, he began to enquire of every one he met, whether the Lord Lovel resided at the seat of his ancestors? He was answered by one, he did not know; by another, he could not tell; by a third, that he never heard of such a person. Sir Philip thought it strange that a man of Lord Lovel's consequence should be unknown in his own neighbourhood, and where his ancestors had usually resided. He ruminated on the uncertainty of human happiness. "This world," said he, "has nothing for a wise man to depend upon. I have lost all my relations, and most of my friends; and am even uncertain whether any are remaining. I will, however, be thankful for the blessings that are spared to me; and I will endeavour to replace those that I have lost. If my friend lives, he shall share my fortune with me; his children shall have the reversion of it; and I will share his comforts in return. But perhaps my friend may have met with troubles that have made him disgusted with the world; perhaps he has buried his amiable wife, or his promising children; and, tired of public life, he is retired into a monastery. At least, I will know what all this silence means."

When he came within a mile of the Castle of Lovel, he stopped at a cottage and asked for a draught of water; a peasant, master of the house, brought it, and asked if his honour would alight and take a moment's refreshment. Sir Philip accepted his offer, being resolved to make farther enquiry before he approached the castle. He asked the same questions of him, that he had before of others.

"Which Lord Lovel," said the man, "does your honour enquire after?"

"The man whom I knew was called Arthur," said Sir Philip.

"Ay," said the Peasant, "he was the only surviving son of

Richard, Lord Lovel, as I think?"

"Very true, friend, he was so."

"Alas, sir," said the man, "he is dead! he survived his father but a short time."

"Dead! say you? how long since?"

"About fifteen years, to the best of my remembrance."

Sir Philip sighed deeply.

"Alas!" said he, "what do we, by living long, but survive all our friends! But pray tell me how he died?"

"I will, sir, to the best of my knowledge. An't please your honour, I heard say, that he attended the King when he went against the Welch rebels, and he left his lady big with child; and so there was a battle fought, and the king got the better of the rebels. There came first a report that none of the officers were killed; but a few days after there came a messenger with an account very different, that several were wounded, and that the Lord Lovel was slain; which sad news overset us all with sorrow, for he was a noble gentleman, a bountiful master, and the delight of all the neighbourhood."

"He was indeed," said Sir Philip, "all that is amiable and good; he was my dear and noble friend, and I am inconsolable for his loss. But the unfortunate lady, what became of her?"

"Why, a'nt please your honour, they said she died of grief for the loss of her husband; but her death was kept private for a time, and we did not know it for certain till some weeks afterwards."

"The will of Heaven be obeyed!" said Sir Philip; "but who succeeded to the title and estate?"

"The next heir," said the peasant, "a kinsman of the deceased, Sir Walter Lovel by name."

"I have seen him," said Sir Philip, "formerly; but where was he when these events happened?"

"At the Castle of Lovel, sir; he came there on a visit to the lady, and waited there to receive my Lord, at his return from Wales; when the news of his death arrived, Sir Walter did every thing in his power to comfort her, and some said he was to marry her; but she refused to be comforted, and took it so to heart that she died."

"And does the present Lord Lovel reside at the castle?"

"No, sir."

"Who then?"

"The Lord Baron Fitz-Owen."

"And how came Sir Walter to leave the seat of his ancestors?"

"Why, sir, he married his sister to this said Lord; and so he sold the Castle to him, and went away, and built himself a house in the north country, as far as Northumberland, I think they call it."

"That is very strange!" said Sir Philip.

"So it is, please your honour; but this is all I know about it."

"I thank you, friend, for your intelligence; I have taken a long journey to no purpose, and have met with nothing but cross accidents. This life is, indeed, a pilgrimage! Pray direct me the nearest way to the next monastery."

"Noble sir," said the peasant, "it is full five miles off, the night is coming on, and the ways are bad; I am but a poor man, and cannot entertain your honour as you are used to; but if you will enter my poor cottage, that, and every thing in it, are at your service."

"My honest friend, I thank you heartily," said Sir Philip; "your kindness and hospitality might shame many of higher birth and breeding; I will accept your kind offer; — but pray let me know the name of my host?"

"John Wyatt, sir; an honest man though a poor one, and a Christian man, though a sinful one."

"Whose cottage is this?"

"It belongs to the Lord Fitz-Owen."

"What family have you?"

"A wife, two sons and a daughter, who will all be proud to wait upon your honour; let me hold your honour's stirrup whilst you alight."

He seconded these words by the proper action, and having assisted his guest to dismount, he conducted him into his house, called his wife to attend him, and then led his horse under a poor shed, that served him as a stable. Sir Philip was fatigued in body and mind, and was glad to repose himself anywhere. The courtesy of his host engaged his attention, and satisfied his wishes. He soon after returned, followed by a youth of about eighteen years.

"Make haste, John," said the father, "and be sure you say neither more nor less than what I have told you."

"I will, father," said the lad; and immediately set off, ran like a buck across the fields, and was out of sight in an instant.

"I hope, friend," said Sir Philip, "you have not sent your son to provide for my entertainment; I am a soldier, used to lodge and fare hard; and, if it were otherwise, your courtesy and kindness would give a relish to the most ordinary food."

"I wish heartily," said Wyatt, "it was in my power to entertain your honour as you ought to be; but, as I cannot do so, I will, when my son returns, acquaint you with the errand I sent him on."

After this they conversed together on common subjects, like fellow-creatures of the same natural form and endowments, though different kinds of education had given a conscious superiority to the one, a conscious inferiority to the other; and the due respect was paid by the latter, without being exacted by the former. In about half an hour young John returned.

"Thou hast made haste," said the father.

"Not more than good speed," quoth the son.

"Tell us, then, how you speed?"

"Shall I tell all that passed?" said John.

"All," said the father; "I don't want to hide any thing."

John stood with his cap in his hand, and thus told his tale—

"I went straight to the castle as fast as I could run; it was my hap to light on young Master Edmund first, so I told him just as you had me, that a noble gentleman was come a long journey from foreign parts to see the Lord Lovel, his friend; and, having lived abroad many years, he did not know that he was dead, and that the castle was fallen into other hands; that upon hearing these tidings he was much grieved and disappointed, and wanting a night's lodging, to rest himself before he returned to his own home, he was fain to take up with one at our cottage; that my father thought my Lord would be angry with him, if he were not told of the stranger's journey and intentions, especially to let such a man lie at our cottage, where he could neither be lodged nor entertained according to his quality."

Here John stopped, and his father exclaimed —

"A good lad! you did your errand very well; and tell us the answer."

John proceeded —

"Master Edmund ordered me some beer, and went to acquaint my Lord of the message; he stayed a while, and then came back to me. — 'John,' said he, 'tell the noble stranger that the Baron Fitz-Owen greets him well, and desires him to rest assured, that though Lord Lovel is dead, and the castle fallen into other hands, his friends will always find a welcome there; and my lord desires that he will accept of a lodging there, while he remains in this country.' — So I came away directly, and made haste to deliver my errand."

Sir Philip expressed some dissatisfaction at this mark of old Wyatt's respect.

"I wish," said he, "that you had acquainted me with your intention before you sent to inform the Baron I was here. I choose rather to lodge with you; and I propose to make amends for the trouble I shall give you."

"Pray, sir, don't mention it," said the peasant, "you are as welcome as myself; I hope no offence; the only reason of my sending was, because I am both unable and unworthy to entertain your honour."

"I am sorry," said Sir Philip, "you should think me so dainty; I am a Christian soldier; and him I acknowledge for my Prince and Master, accepted the invitations of the poor, and washed the feet of his disciples. Let us say no more on this head; I am resolved to stay this night in your cottage, tomorrow I will wait on the Baron, and thank him for his hospitable invitation."

"That shall be as your honour pleases, since you will condescend to stay here. John, do you run back and acquaint my Lord of it."

"Not so," said Sir Philip; "it is now almost dark."

"'Tis no matter," said John, "I can go it blindfold."

Sir Philip then gave him a message to the Baron in his own name, acquainting him that he would pay his respects to him in the morning. John flew back the second time, and soon returned with new commendations from the Baron, and that he would expect him on the morrow. Sir Philip gave him an angel of gold, and praised his speed and abilities.

He supped with Wyatt and his family upon new-laid eggs and rashers of bacon, with the highest relish. They praised the Creator for His gifts, and acknowledged they were unworthy of the least of His blessings. They gave the best of their two lofts up to Sir Philip, the rest of the family slept in the other, the old woman and her daughter in the bed, the father and his two sons upon clean straw. Sir Philip's bed was of a better kind, and yet much inferior to his usual accommodations; nevertheless the good knight slept as well in Wyatt's cottage, as he could have done in a palace.

During his sleep, many strange and incoherent dreams arose to his imagination. He thought he received a message from his friend Lord Lovel, to come to him at the castle; that he stood at the gate and received him, that he strove to embrace him, but could not; but that he spoke to this effect:— "Though I have been dead these fifteen years, I still command here, and none can enter these gates without my permission; know that it is I that invite, and bid you welcome; the hopes of my house rest upon you." Upon this he bid Sir Philip follow him; he led him through many rooms, till at last he sunk down, and Sir Philip thought he still followed him, till he came into a dark and frightful cave, where he disappeared, and in his stead he beheld a complete suit of armour stained with blood, which belonged to his friend, and he thought he heard dismal groans from beneath. Presently after, he thought he was hurried away by an invisible hand, and led into a wild heath, where the people were inclosing the ground, and making preparations for two combatants; the trumpet sounded, and a voice called out still louder, "Forbear! It is not permitted to be revealed till the time is ripe for the event; wait with patience on the decrees of heaven." He was then transported to his own house, where, going into an unfrequented room, he was again met by his friend, who was living, and in all the bloom of youth, as when he first knew him: He started at the sight, and awoke. The sun shone upon his curtains, and, perceiving it was day, he sat up, and recollected where he was. The images that impressed his sleeping fancy remained strongly on his mind waking; but his reason strove to disperse them; it was natural that the story he had heard should create these ideas, that they should wait on him in his sleep, and that every dream should bear some relation to his deceased friend. The sun dazzled his eyes, the birds serenaded him and diverted his attention, and a woodbine forced its way through the window, and regaled his sense of smelling with its fragrance. He arose, paid his devotions to Heaven, and then carefully descended the narrow stairs, and went out at the door of the cottage. There he saw the industrious wife and daughter of old Wyatt at their morning work, the one milking her cow, the other feeding her poultry. He asked for a draught of milk, which, with a slice of rye bread, served to break his fast. He walked about the fields alone; for old Wyatt and his two sons were gone out to their daily labour. He was soon called back by the good woman, who told him that a servant from the Baron waited to conduct him to the Castle. He took leave of Wyatt's wife, telling her he would see her again before he left the country. The daughter fetched his horse, which he mounted, and set forward with the servant, of whom he asked many questions concerning his master's family.

"How long have you lived with the Baron?"

"Ten years."

"Is he a good master?"

"Yes, Sir, and also a good husband and father."

"What family has he?"

"Three sons and a daughter."

"What age are they of?"

"The eldest son is in his seventeenth year, the second in his sixteenth, the others several years younger; but beside these my Lord has several young gentlemen brought up with his own sons, two of which are his nephews; he keeps in his house a learned clerk to teach them languages; and as for all bodily exercises, none come near them; there is a fletcher to teach them the use of the cross-bow; a master to teach them to ride; another the use of the sword; another learns them to dance; and then they wrestle and run, and have such activity in all their motions, that it does one good to see them; and my Lord thinks nothing too much to bestow on their education."

"Truly," says Sir Philip, "he does the part of a good parent, and I honour him greatly for it; but are the young gentlemen of a promising disposition?"

"Yes indeed, Sir," answered the servant; "the young gentlemen, my Lord's sons, are hopeful youths; but yet there is one who is thought to exceed them all, though he is the son of a poor labourer."

"And who is he?" said the knight.

"One Edmund Twyford, the son of a cottager in our village; he is to be sure as fine a youth as ever the sun shone upon, and of so sweet a disposition that nobody envies his good fortune."

"What good fortune does he enjoy?"

"Why, Sir, about two years ago, my lord, at his sons request, took him into his own family, and gives him the same education as his own children; the young lords doat upon him, especially Master William, who is about his own age: It is supposed that he will attend the young Lords when they go to the wars, which my Lord intends they shall by and by."

"What you tell me," said Sir Philip, "increases every minute my respect for your Lord; he is an excellent father and master, he seeks out merit in obscurity; he distinguishes and rewards it,—I honour him with all my heart."

In this manner they conversed together till they came within view of the castle. In a field near the house they saw a company of youths, with crossbows in their hands, shooting at a mark.

"There," said the servant, "are our young gentlemen at their exercises."

Sir Philip stopped his horse to observe them; he heard two or three of them cry out, "Edmund is the victor! He wins the prize!"

"I must," said Sir Philip, "take a view of this Edmund."

He jumped off his horse, gave the bridle to the servant, and walked into the field. The young gentlemen came up, and paid their respects to him; he apologized for intruding upon their sports, and asked which was the victor? Upon which the youth he spoke to beckoned to another, who immediately advanced, and made his obeisance; As he drew near, Sir Philip fixed his eyes upon him, with so much attention, that he seemed not to observe his courtesy and address. At length he recollected himself, and said, "What is your name, young man?"

"Edmund Twyford," replied the youth; "and I have the honour to attend upon the Lord Fitz-Owen's sons."

"Pray, noble sir," said the youth who first addressed Sir Philip, "are not you the stranger who is expected by my father?"

"I am, sir," answered he, "and I go to pay my respects to him."

"Will you excuse our attendance, Sir? We have not yet finished our exercises."

"My dear youth," said Sir Philip, "no apology is necessary; but will you favour me with your proper name, that I may know to whose courtesy I am obliged?"

"My name is William Fitz-Owen; that gentleman is my eldest brother, Master Robert; that other my kinsman, Master Richard Wenlock."

"Very well; I thank you, gentle Sir; I beg you not to stir another step, your servant holds my horse."

"Farewell, Sir," said Master William; "I hope we shall have the pleasure of meeting you at dinner."

The youths returned to their sports, and Sir Philip mounted his horse and proceeded to the castle; he entered it with a deep sigh, and melancholy recollections. The Baron received him with the utmost respect and courtesy. He gave a brief account of the principal events that had happened in the family of Lovel during his absence; he spoke of the late Lord Lovel with respect, of the present with the affection of a brother. Sir Philip, in return, gave a brief recital of his own adventures abroad, and of the disagreeable circumstances he had met with since his return home; he pathetically lamented the loss of all his friends, not forgetting that of his faithful servant on the way; saying he could be contented to give up the world, and retire to a religious house, but that he was withheld by the consideration, that some who depended entirely upon him, would want his presence and assistance; and, beside that, he thought he might be of service to many others. The Baron agreed with him in opinion, that a man was of much more service to the world who continued in it, than one who retired from it, and gave his fortune to the Church, whose servants did not always make the best use of it. Sir Philip then turned the conversation, and congratulated the Baron on his hopeful family; he praised their persons and address, and warmly applauded the care he bestowed on their education. The Baron listened with pleasure to the honest approbation of a worthy heart, and enjoyed the true happiness of a parent.

Sir Philip then made further enquiry concerning Edmund, whose appearance had struck him with an impression in his favour.

"That boy," said the Baron, "is the son of a cottager in this neighbourhood; his uncommon merit, and gentleness of manners, distinguish him from those of his own class; from his childhood he attracted the notice and affection of all that knew him; he was beloved everywhere but at his father's house, and there it should seem that his merits were his crimes; for the peasant, his father, hated him, treated him severely, and at length threatened to turn him out of doors; he used to run here and there on errands for my people, and at length they obliged me to take notice of him; my sons earnestly desired I would take him into my family; I did so about two years ago, intending to make him their servant; but his extraordinary genius and disposition have obliged me to look upon him in a superior light; perhaps I may incur the censure of many people, by giving him so many advantages, and treating him as the companion of my children; his merit must justify or condemn my partiality for him; however, I trust that I have secured to my children a faithful servant of the upper kind, and a useful friend to my family."

Sir Philip warmly applauded his generous host, and wished to be a sharer in his bounty to that fine youth, whose appearance indicated all the qualities that had endeared him to his companions.

At the hour of dinner the young men presented themselves before their Lord, and his guest. Sir Philip addressed himself to Edmund; he asked him many questions, and received modest and intelligent answers, and he grew every minute more pleased with him. After dinner the youths withdrew with their tutor to pursue their studies. Sir Philip sat for some time wrapt up in meditation. After some minutes, the Baron asked him, "If he might not be favoured with the fruits of his contemplations?"

"You shall, my Lord," answered he, "for you have a right to them. I was thinking, that when many blessings are lost, we should cherish those that remain, and even endeavour to replace the others. My Lord, I have taken a strong liking to that youth whom you call Edmund Twyford; I have neither children nor relations to claim my fortune, nor share my affections; your Lordship has many demands upon your generosity: I can provide for this promising youth without doing injustice to any one; will you give him to me?"

"He is a fortunate boy," said the Baron, "to gain your favour so soon."

"My Lord," said the knight, "I will confess to you, that the first thing that touched my heart in his favour, is a strong resemblance he bears to a certain dear friend I once had, and his manner resembles him as much as his person; his qualities deserve that he should be placed in a higher rank; I will adopt him for my son, and introduce him into the world as my relation, if you will resign him to me; What say you?"

"Sir," said the Baron, "you have made a noble offer, and I am too much the young man's friend to be a hindrance to his preferment. It is true that I intended to provide for him in my own family; but I cannot do it so effectually as by giving him to you, whose generous affection being unlimited by other ties, may in time prefer him to a higher station as he shall deserve it. I have only one condition to make; that the lad shall have his option; for I would not oblige him to leave my service against his inclination."

"You say well," replied Sir Philip; "nor would I take him upon other terms."

"Agreed then," said the Baron; "let us send for Edmund hither."

A servant was sent to fetch him; he came immediately, and his Lord thus bespoke him.

"Edmund, you owe eternal obligations to this gentleman, who, perceiving in you a certain resemblance to a friend of his, and liking your behaviour, has taken a great affection for you, insomuch that he desires to receive you into his family: I cannot better provide for you than by disposing of you to him; and, if you have no objection, you shall return home with him when he goes from hence."

The countenance of Edmund underwent many alterations during this proposal of his Lord; it expressed tenderness, gratitude, and sorrow, but the last was predominant; he bowed respectfully to the Baron and Sir Philip, and, after some hesitation, spoke as follows: —

"I feel very strongly the obligations I owe to this gentleman, for his noble and generous offer; I cannot express the sense I have of his goodness to me, a peasant boy, only known to him by my Lord's kind and partial mention; this uncommon bounty claims my eternal gratitude. To you, my honoured Lord, I owe every thing, even this gentleman's good opinion; you distinguished me when nobody else did; and, next to you, your sons are my best and dearest benefactors; they introduced me to your notice. My heart is unalterably attached to this house and family, and my utmost ambition is to spend my life in your service; but if you have perceived any great and grievous faults in me, that make you wish to put me out of your family, and if you have recommended me to this gentleman in order to be rid of me, in that case I will submit to your pleasure, as I would if you should sentence me to death."

During this speech the tears made themselves channels down Edmund's cheeks; and his two noble auditors, catching the tender inflection, wiped their eyes at the conclusion.

"My dear child," said the Baron, "you overcome me by your tenderness and gratitude! I know of no faults you have committed, that I should wish to be rid of you. I thought to do you the best service by promoting you to that of Sir Philip Harclay, who is both able and willing to provide for you; but if you prefer my service to his, I will not part with you."

Upon this Edmund kneeled to the Baron; he embraced his knees. "My dear Lord! I am, and will be your servant, in preference to any man living; I only ask your permission to live and die in your service."

"You see, Sir Philip," said the Baron, "how this boy engages the heart; how can I part with him?"

"I cannot ask you any more," answered Sir Philip, "I see it is impossible; but I esteem you both still higher than ever; the youth for his gratitude, and your lordship for your noble mind and true generosity; blessings attend you both!"

"Oh, sir," said Edmund, pressing the hand of Sir Philip, "do not think me ungrateful to you; I will ever remember your goodness, and pray to Heaven to reward it: the name of Sir Philip Harclay shall be engraven upon my heart, next to my Lord and his family, for ever."

Sir Philip raised the youth and embraced him, saying, "If ever you want a friend, remember me; and depend upon my protection, so long as you continue to deserve it."

Edmund bowed low, and withdrew, with his eyes full of tears of sensibility and gratitude. When he was gone, Sir Philip said, "I am thinking, that though young Edmund wants not my assistance at present, he may hereafter stand in need of my friendship. I should not wonder if such rare qualities as he possesses, should one day create envy, and raise him enemies; in which case he might come to lose your favour, without any fault of yours or his own."

"I am obliged to you for the warning," said the Baron, "I hope it will be unnecessary; but if ever I part with Edmund, you shall have the refusal of him."

"I thank your Lordship for all your civilities to me," said the knight; "I leave my best wishes with you and your hopeful family, and I humbly take my leave."

"Will you not stay one night in the castle?" returned my Lord; "you shall be as welcome a guest as ever."

"I acknowledge your goodness and hospitality, but this house fills me with melancholy recollections; I came hither with a heavy heart, and it will not be lighter while I remain here. I shall always remember your lordship with the highest respect and esteem; and I pray God to preserve you, and increase your blessings!"

After some further ceremonies, Sir Philip departed, and returned to old Wyatt's, ruminating on the vicissitude of human affairs, and thinking on the changes he had seen.

At his return to Wyatt's cottage, he found the family assembled together. He told them he would take another night's lodging there, which they heard with great pleasure;—for he had familiarised himself to them in the last evening's conversation, insomuch that they began to enjoy his company. He told Wyatt of the misfortune he had sustained by losing his servant on the way, and wished he could get one to attend him home in his place. Young John looked earnestly at his father, who returned a look of approbation.

"I perceive one in this company," said he, "that would be proud to serve your honour; but I fear he is not brought up well enough."

John coloured with impatience; he could not forbear speaking.

"Sir, I can answer for an honest heart, a willing mind, and a light pair of heels; and though I am somewhat awkward, I shall be proud to learn, to please my noble master, if he will but try me."

"You say well," said Sir Philip, "I have observed your qualifications, and if you are desirous to serve me, I am equally pleased with you; if your father has no objection I will take you."

"Objection, sir!" said the old man; "it will be my pride to prefer him to such a noble gentleman; I will make no terms for him, but leave it to your honour to do for him as he shall deserve."

"Very well," said Sir Philip, "you shall be no loser by that; I will charge myself with the care of the young man."

The bargain was struck, and Sir Philip purchased a horse for John of the old man. The next morning they set out; the knight left marks of his bounty with the good couple, and departed, laden with their blessing and prayers. He stopped at the place where his faithful servant was buried, and caused masses to be said for the repose of his soul; then, pursuing his way by easy journeys, arrived in safety at home. His family rejoiced at his return; he settled his new servant in attendance upon his person; he then looked round his neighbourhood for objects of his charity; when he saw merit in distress, it was his delight to raise and support it; he spent his time in the service of his Creator, and glorified him in doing good to his creatures. He reflected frequently upon every thing that had befallen him in his late journey to the west; and, at his leisure, took down all the particulars in writing.

[Here follows an interval of four years, as by the manuscript; and this omission seems intended by the writer. What follows is in a different hand, and the character is more modern.]

ABOUT this time the prognostics of Sir Philip Harclay began to be verified, that Edmund's good qualities might one day excite envy and create him enemies. The sons and kinsmen of his patron began to seek occasion to find fault with him, and to depreciate him with others. The Baron's eldest son and heir, Master Robert, had several contests with Master William, the second son, upon his account: This youth had a warm affection for Edmund, and whenever his brother and kinsmen treated him slightly, he supported him against their malicious insinuations. Mr. Richard Wenlock, and Mr. John Markham, were the sisters sons of the Lord Fitz-Owen; and there were several other more distant relations, who, with them, secretly envied Edmund's fine qualities, and strove to lessen him in the esteem of the Baron and his family. By degrees they excited a dislike in Master Robert, that in time was fixed into habit, and fell little short of aversion.

Young Wenlock's hatred was confirmed by an additional circumstance: He had a growing passion for the Lady Emma, the Baron's only daughter; and, as love is eagle-eyed, he saw, or fancied he saw her cast an eye of preference on Edmund. An accidental service that she received from him, had excited her grateful regards and attentions towards him. The incessant view of his fine person and qualities, had perhaps improved her esteem into a still softer sensation, though she was yet ignorant of it, and thought it only the tribute due to gratitude and friendship.

One Christmas time, the Baron and all his family went to visit a family in Wales; crossing a ford, the horse that carried the Lady Emma, who rode behind her cousin Wenlock, stumbled and fell down, and threw her off into the water: Edmund dismounted in a moment, and flew to her assistance; he took her out so quick, that the accident was not known to some part of the company. From this time Wenlock strove to undermine Edmund in her esteem, and she conceived herself obliged in justice and gratitude to defend him against the malicious insinuations of his enemies. She one day asked Wenlock, why he in particular should endeavour to recommend himself to her favour, by speaking against Edmund, to whom she was under great obligations? He made but little reply; but the impression sunk deep into his rancorous heart; every word in Edmund's behalf was like a poisoned arrow that rankled in the wound, and grew every day more inflamed. Sometimes he would pretend to extenuate Edmund's supposed faults, in order to load him with the sin of ingratitude upon other occasions. Rancour works deepest in the heart that strives to conceal it; and, when covered by art, frequently puts on the appearance of candour. By these means did Wenlock and Markham impose upon the credulity of Master Robert and their other relations: Master William only stood proof against all their insinuations.

The same autumn that Edmund completed his eighteenth year, the Baron declared his intention of sending the young men of his house to France the following spring, to learn the art of war, and signalize their courage and abilities.

Their ill-will towards Edmund was so well concealed, that his patron had not discovered it; but it was whispered among the servants, who are generally close observers of the manners of their principals. Edmund was a favourite with them all, which was a strong presumption that he deserved to be so, for they seldom shew much regard to dependents, or to superiour domestics, who are generally objects of envy and dislike. Edmund was courteous, but not familiar with them; and, by this means, gained their affections without soliciting them. Among them was an old serving man, called Joseph Howel; this man had formerly served the old Lord Lovel, and his son; and when the young Lord died, and Sir Walter sold the castle to his brother-in-law, the Lord Fitz-Owen, he only of all the old servants was left in the house, to take care of it, and to deliver it into the possession of the new proprietor, who retained him in his service: He was a man of few words, but much reflection: and, without troubling himself about other people's affairs, went silently and properly about his own business; more solicitous to discharge his duty, than to recommend himself to notice, and not seeming to aspire to any higher office than that of a serving man. This old man would fix his eyes upon Edmund, whenever he could do it without observation; sometimes he would sigh deeply, and a tear would start from his eye, which he strove to conceal from observation. One day Edmund surprised him in this tender emotion, as he was wiping his eyes with the back of his hand: "Why," said he, "my good friend, do you look at me so earnestly and affectionately?"

"Because I love you, Master Edmund," said he; "because I wish you well."

"I thank you kindly," answered Edmund; "I am unable to repay your love, otherwise than by returning it, which I do sincerely."

"I thank you, sir," said the old man; "that is all I desire, and more than I deserve."

"Do not say so," said Edmund; "if I had any better way to thank you, I would not say so much about it; but words are all my inheritance."

Upon this he shook hands with Joseph, who withdrew hastily to conceal his emotion, saying, "God bless you, master, and make your fortune equal to your deserts! I cannot help thinking you were born to a higher station than what you now hold."

"You know to the contrary," said Edmund; but Joseph was gone out of sight and hearing.

The notice and observation of strangers, and the affection of individuals, together with that inward consciousness that always attends superiour qualities, would sometimes kindle the flames of ambition in Edmund's heart; but he checked them presently by reflecting upon his low birth and dependant station. He was modest, yet intrepid; gentle and courteous to all; frank and unreserved to those that loved him, discreet and complaisant to those who hated him; generous and compassionate to the distresses of his fellow-creatures in general; humble, but not servile, to his patron and superiors. Once, when he with a manly spirit justified himself against a malicious imputation, his young Lord, Robert, taxed him with pride and arrogance to his kinsmen. Edmund denied the charge against him with equal spirit and modesty. Master Robert answered him sharply, "How dare you contradict my cousins? do you mean to give them the lie?"

"Not in words, Sir," said Edmund; "but I will behave so as that you shall not believe them."

Master Robert haughtily bid him be silent and know himself, and not presume to contend with men so much his superiors in every respect. These heart-burnings in some degree subsided by their preparations for going to France. Master Robert was to be presented at court before his departure, and it was expected that he should be knighted. The Baron designed Edmund to be his esquire; but this was frustrated by his old enemies, who persuaded Robert to make choice of one of his own domestics, called Thomas Hewson; him did they set up as a rival to Edmund, and he took every occasion to affront him. All that Master Robert gained by this step was the contempt of those, who saw Edmund's merit, and thought it want of discernment in him not to distinguish and reward it. Edmund requested of his Lord that he might be Master William's attendant; "and when," said he, "my patron shall be knighted, as I make no doubt he will one day be, he has promised that I shall be his esquire." The Baron granted Edmund's request; and, being freed from servitude to the rest, he was devoted to that of his beloved Master William, who treated him in public as his principal domestic, but in private as his chosen friend and brother.

The whole cabal of his enemies consulted together in what manner they should vent their resentment against him; and it was agreed that they should treat him with indifference and neglect, till they should arrive in France; and when there, they should contrive to render his courage suspected, and by putting him upon some desperate enterprize, rid themselves of him for ever. About this time died the great Duke of Bedford, to the irreparable loss of the English nation. He was succeeded by Richard Plantagenet, Duke of York, as Regent of France, of which great part had revolted to Charles the Dauphin. Frequent actions ensued. Cities were lost and won; and continual occasions offered to exercise the courage, and abilities, of the youths of both nations.

The young men of Baron Fitz-Owen's house were recommended particularly to the Regent's notice. Master Robert was knighted, with several other young men of family, who distinguished themselves by their spirit and activity upon every occasion. The youth were daily employed in warlike exercises, and frequent actions; and made their first essay in arms in such a manner as to bring into notice all that deserved it. Various a but all their contrivances recoiled upon themselves, and brought increase of honour upon Edmund's head; he distinguished himself upon so many occasions, that Sir Robert himself began to pay him more than ordinary regard, to the infinite mortification of his kinsmen and relations. They laid many schemes against him, but none took effect.

[From this place the characters in the manuscript are effaced by time and damp. Here and there some sentences are legible, but not sufficient to pursue the thread of the story. Mention is made of several actions in which the young men were engaged — that Edmund distinguished himself by intrepidity in action; by gentleness, humanity and modesty in the cessations —

that he attracted the notice of every person of observation, and also that he received personal commendation from the Regent.]

[The following incidents are clear enough to be transcribed; but the beginning of the next succeeding pages is obliterated. However, we may guess at the beginning by what remains.]

As soon as the cabal met in Sir Robert's tent, Mr. Wenlock thus began:—"You see, my friends, that every attempt we make to humble this upstart, turns into applause, and serves only to raise his pride still higher. Something must be done, or his praise will go home before us, at our own expence; and we shall seem only soils to set off his glories. Any thing would I give to the man who should execute our vengeance upon him."

"Stop there, cousin Wenlock," said Sir Robert; "though I think Edmund proud and vain-glorious, and would join in any scheme to humble him, and make him know himself, I will not suffer any man to use such base methods to effect it. Edmund is brave; and it is beneath an Englishman to revenge himself by unworthy means; if any such are used, I will be the first man to bring the guilty to justice; and if I hear another word to this purpose, I will inform my brother William, who will acquaint Edmund with your mean intentions." Upon this the cabal drew back, and Mr. Wenlock protested that he meant no more than to mortify his pride, and make him know his proper station. Soon after Sir Robert withdrew, and they resumed their deliberations.

Then spoke Thomas Hewson: "There is a party to be sent out to-morrow night, to intercept a convoy of provisions for the relief of Rouen; I will provoke Mr. Edmund to make one of this party, and when he is engaged in the action, I and my companions will draw off, and leave him to the enemy, who I trust will so handle him, that you shall no more be troubled with him."

"This will do," said Mr. Wenlock; "but let it be kept from my two cousins, and only known to ourselves; if they offer to be of the party, I will persuade them off it. And you, Thomas, if you bring this scheme to a conclusion, may depend upon my eternal gratitude."

"And mine," said Markham; and so said all. The next day the affair was publicly mentioned; and Hewson, as he promised, provoked Edmund to the trial. Several young men of family offered themselves; among the rest, Sir Robert, and his brother William. Mr. Wenlock persuaded them not to go, and set the danger of the enterprize in the strongest colours. At last

Sir Robert complained of the tooth-ache, and was confined to his tent. Edmund waited on him; and judging by the ardour of his own courage of that of his patron, thus bespoke him:—"I am greatly concerned, dear Sir, that we cannot have your company at night; but as I know what you will suffer in being absent, I would beg the favour of you to let me use your arms and device, and I will promise not to disgrace them."

"No, Edmund, I cannot consent to that: I thank you for your noble offer, and will remember it to your advantage; but I cannot wear honours of another man's getting. You have awakened me to a sense of my duty: I will go with you, and contend with you for glory; and William shall do the same."

In a few hours they were ready to set out. Wenlock and Markham, and their dependants, found themselves engaged in honour to go upon an enterprize they never intended; and set out, with heavy hearts, to join the party. They marched in silence in the horrors of a dark night, and wet roads; they met the convoy where they expected, and a sharp engagement ensued. The victory was some time doubtful; but the moon rising on the backs of the English, gave them the advantage. They saw the disposition of their enemies, and availed themselves of it. Edmund advanced the foremost of the party; he drew out the leader on the French side; he slew him. Mr. William pressed forward to assist his friend; Sir Robert, to defend his brother; Wenlock, and Markham, from shame to stay behind.

Thomas Hewson and his associates drew back on their side; the French perceived it, and pursued the advantage. Edmund pushed them in front; the young nobles all followed him; they broke through the detachment, and stopped the waggons. The officer who commanded the party, encouraged them to go on; the defeat was soon complete, and the provisions carried in triumph to the English camp.

Edmund was presented to the Regent as the man to whom the victory was chiefly owing. Not a tongue presumed to move itself against him; even malice and envy were silenced.

"Approach, young man," said the Regent, "that I may confer upon you the honour of knighthood, which you have well deserved."

Mr. Wenlock could no longer forbear speaking—"Knighthood," said he, "is an order belonging to gentlemen, it cannot be conferred on a

129

peasant."

"What say you, sir!" returned the Regent; "is this youth a peasant?"

"He is," said Wenlock; "let him deny it if he can."

Edmund, with a modest bow, replied, "It is true indeed I am a peasant, and this honour is too great for me; I have only done my duty."

The Duke of York, whose pride of birth equalled that of any man living or dead, sheathed his sword immediately. "Though," said he, "I cannot reward you as I intended, I will take care that you shall have a large share in the spoils of this night; and, I declare publicly, that you stand first in the list of gallant men in this engagement."

Thomas Hewson and his associates made a poor figure in their return; they were publicly reproved for their backwardness. Hewson was wounded in body and more in mind, for the bad success of his ill-laid design. He could not hold up his head before Edmund; who, unconscious of their malice, administered every kind of comfort to them. He spoke in their behalf to the commanding officer, imputing their conduct to unavoidable accidents. He visited them privately; he gave them a part of the spoils allotted to himself; by every act of valour and courtesy he strove to engage those hearts that hated, envied, and maligned him: But where hatred arises from envy of superior qualities, every display of those qualities increases the cause from whence it arises.

[Another pause ensues here.]

The young nobles and gentlemen who distinguished Edmund were prevented from raising him to preferment by the insinuations of Wenlock and his associates, who never failed to set before them his low descent, and his pride and arrogance in presuming to rank with gentlemen.

[Here the manuscript is not legible for several pages. There is mention, about this time, of the death of the Lady Fitz-Owen, but not the cause.]

Wenlock rejoiced to find that his schemes took effect, and that they should be recalled at the approach of winter. The Baron was glad of a pretence to send for them home; for he could no longer endure the absence of his children, after the loss of their mother.

[The manuscript is again defaced for many leaves; at length the letters become more legible, and the remainder of it is quite perfect.]

From the time the young men returned from France, the enemies of Edmund employed their utmost abilities to ruin him in the Baron's opinion, and get him dismissed from the family. They insinuated a thousand things against him, that happened, as they said, during his residence in France, and therefore could not be known to his master; but when the Baron privately enquired of his two elder sons, he found there was no truth in their reports. Sir Robert, though he did not love him, scorned to join in untruths against him. Mr. William spoke of him with the warmth of fraternal affection. The Baron perceived that his kinsmen disliked Edmund; but his own good heart hindered him from seeing the baseness of theirs. It is said, that continual dropping will wear away a stone; so did their incessant reports, by insensible degrees, produce a coolness in his patron's behaviour towards him. If he behaved with manly spirit, it was misconstrued into pride and arrogance; his generosity was imprudence; his humility was hypocrisy, the better to cover his ambition. Edmund bore patiently all the indignities that were thrown upon him; and, though he felt them severely in his bosom, scorned to justify his conduct at the expence even of his enemies. Perhaps his gentle spirit might at length have sunk under this treatment, but providence interposed in his behalf; and, by seemingly accidental circumstances, conducted him imperceptibly towards the crisis of his fate.

Father Oswald, who had been preceptor to the young men, had a strong affection for Edmund, from a thorough knowledge of his heart; he saw through the mean artifices that were used to undermine him in his patron's favour; he watched their machinations, and strove to frustrate their designs.

This good man used frequently to walk out with Edmund; they conversed upon various subjects; and the youth would lament to him the unhappiness of his situation, and the peculiar circumstances that attended him. The father, by his wholesome advice, comforted his drooping heart, and confirmed him in his resolution of bearing unavoidable evils with patience and fortitude, from the consciousness of his own innocence, and the assurance of a future and eternal reward.

One day, as they were walking in a wood near the castle, Edmund asked the father, what meant those preparations for building, the cutting down trees, and burning of bricks?

"What," said Oswald, "have you not heard that my Lord is going to build a new apartment on the west side of the castle?"

"And why," said Edmund, "should my Lord be at that expence when there is one on the east side that is never occupied?"

"That apartment," said the friar, "you must have observed is always shut up."

"I have observed it often," said Edmund; "but I never presumed to ask any questions about it."

"You had then," said Oswald, "less curiosity, and more discretion, than is common at your age."

"You have raised my curiosity," said Edmund; "and, if it be not improper, I beg of you to gratify it."

"We are alone," said Oswald, "and I am so well assured of your prudence, that I will explain this mystery in some degree to you."

"You must know, that apartment was occupied by the last Lord Lovel when he was a batchelor. He married in his father's lifetime, who gave up his own apartment to him, and offered to retire to this himself; but the son would not permit him; he chose to sleep here, rather than in any other. He had been married about three months, when his father, the old lord, died of a fever. About twelve months after his marriage, he was called upon to attend the King, Henry the Fourth, on an expedition into Wales, whither he was attended by many of his dependants. He left his lady big with child, and full of care and anxiety for his safety and return.

"After the King had chastised the rebels, and obtained the victory, the Lord Lovel was expected home every day; various reports were sent home before him; one messenger brought an account of his health and safety; soon after another came with bad news, that he was slain in battle. His kinsman, Sir Walter Lovel, came here on a visit to comfort the Lady; and he waited to receive his kinsman at his return. It was he that brought the news of the sad event of the battle to the Lady Lovel.

"She fainted away at the relation; but, when she revived, exerted the utmost resolution; saying, it was her duty to bear this dreadful stroke with Christian fortitude and patience, especially in regard to the child she went with, the last remains of her beloved husband, and the undoubted heir of a noble house. For several days she seemed an example of patience and resignation; but then, all at once, she renounced them, and broke out into passionate and frantic exclamations; she said, that her dear lord was basely murdered; that his ghost had appeared to her, and revealed his fate. She called upon Heaven and earth to revenge her wrongs; saying, she would never cease complaining to God, and the King, for vengeance and justice.

"Upon this, Sir Walter told the servants that Lady Lovel was distracted, from grief for the death of her Lord; that his regard for her was as strong as ever; and that, if she recovered, he would himself be her comforter, and marry her. In the mean time she was confined in this very apartment, and in less than a month the poor Lady died. She lies buried in the family vault in St. Austin's church in the village. Sir Walter took possession of the castle, and all the other estates, and assumed the title of Lord Lovel.

"Soon after, it was reported that the castle was haunted, and that the ghosts of Lord and Lady Lovel had been seen by several of the servants. Whoever went into this apartment were terrified by uncommon noises, and strange appearances; at length this apartment was wholly shut up, and the servants were forbid to enter it, or to talk of any thing relating to it: However, the story did not stop here; it was whispered about, that the new Lord Lovel was so disturbed every night, that he could not sleep in quiet; and, being at last tired of the place, he sold the castle and estate of his ancestors, to his brother-in-law the Lord Fitz-Owen, who now enjoys it, and left this country."

"All this is news to me," said Edmund; "but, father, tell me what grounds there were for the lady's suspicion that her lord died unfairly?"

"Alas!" said Oswald, "that is only known to God. There were strange thoughts in the minds of many at that time; I had mine; but I will not disclose them, not even to you. I will not injure those who may be innocent; and I leave it to Providence, who will doubtless, in its own best time and manner, punish the guilty. But let what I have told you be as if you had never heard it."

"I thank you for these marks of your esteem and confidence," said Edmund; "be assured that I will not abuse them; nor do I desire to pry into secrets not proper to be revealed. I entirely approve your discretion, and acquiesce in your conclusion, that Providence will in its own time vindicate its ways to man; if it were not for that trust, my situation would be insupportable. I strive earnestly to deserve the esteem and favour of good men; I endeavour to regulate my conduct so as to avoid giving offence to any man; but I see, with infinite pain, that it is impossible for me to gain these points."

"I see it too, with great concern," said Oswald; "and every thing that I can say and do in your favour is misconstrued; and, by seeking to do you service, I lose my own influence. But I will never give my sanction to acts of injustice, nor join to oppress innocence. My dear child, put your trust in God: He who brought light out of darkness, can bring good out of evil."

"I hope and trust so," said Edmund; "but, father, if my enemies should prevail — if my lord should believe their stories against me, and I should be put out of the house with disgrace, what will become of me? I have nothing but my character to depend upon; if I lose that, I lose every thing; and I see they seek no less than my ruin."

"Trust in my lord's honour and justice," replied Oswald; "he knows your virtue, and he is not ignorant of their ill-will towards you."

"I know my lord's justice too well to doubt it," said Edmund; "but would it not be better to rid him of this trouble, and his family of an incumbrance? I would gladly do something for myself, but cannot without my lord's recommendation; and, such is my situation, that I fear the asking for a dismission would be accounted base ingratitude; beside, when I think of leaving this house, my heart saddens at the thought, and tells me I cannot be happy out of it; yet I think I could return to a peasant's life with cheerfulness, rather than live in a palace under disdain and contempt."

"Have patience a little longer, my son," said Oswald; "I will think of some way to serve you, and to represent your grievances to my lord, without offence to either — perhaps the causes may be removed. Continue to observe the same irreproachable conduct; and be assured that Heaven will defend your innocence, and defeat the unjust designs of your enemies. Let us now return home."

About a week after this conference, Edmund walked out in the fields ruminating on the disagreeable circumstances of his situation. Insensible of the time, he had been out several hours without perceiving how the day wore away, when he heard himself called by name several times; looking backward, he saw his friend Mr. William, and hallooed to him. He came running towards him; and, leaping over the style, stood still a while to recover his breath.

"What is the matter, sir?" said Edmund; "your looks bespeak some tidings of importance."

With a look of tender concern and affection, the youth pressed his hand and spoke—

"My dear Edmund, you must come home with me directly; your old enemies have united to ruin you with my father; my brother Robert has declared that he thinks there will be no peace in our family till you are dismissed from it, and told my father, he hoped he would not break with his kinsmen rather than give up Edmund."

"But what do they lay to my charge?" said Edmund.

"I cannot rightly understand," answered William, "for they make a great mystery of it; something of great consequence, they say; but they will not tell me what: However, my father has told them that they must bring their accusation before your face, and he will have you answer them publicly. I have been seeking you this hour, to inform you of this, that you might be prepared to defend yourself against your accusers."

"God reward you, sir," said Edmund, "for all your goodness to me! I see they are determined to ruin me if possible: I shall be compelled to leave the castle; but, whatever becomes of me, be assured you shall have no cause to blush for your kindness and partiality to your Edmund."

"I know it, I am sure of it," said William; "and here I swear to you, as Jonathan did to David, I beseech Heaven to bless me, as my friendship to you shall be steady and inviolable!"

"Only so long as I shall deserve so great a blessing," interrupted Edmund.

"I know your worth and honour," continued William; "and such is my confidence in your merit, that I firmly believe Heaven designs you for something extraordinary; and I expect that some great and unforeseen event will raise you to the rank and station to which you appear to belong: Promise me, therefore, that whatever may be your fate you will preserve the same friendship for me that I bear to you."

Edmund was so much affected that he could not answer but in broken sentences.

"Oh my friend, my master! I vow, I promise, my heart promises!"

He kneeled down with clasped hands, and uplifted eyes. William kneeled by him, and they invoked the Supreme to witness to their friendship, and implored His blessing upon it. They then rose up and embraced each other, while tears of cordial affection bedewed their cheeks.

As soon as they were able to speak, Edmund conjured his friend not to expose himself to the displeasure of his family out of kindness to him.

"I submit to the will of Heaven," said he; "I wait with patience its disposal of me; if I leave the castle, I will find means to inform you of my fate and fortunes."

"I hope," said William, "that things may yet be accommodated; but do not take any resolution, let us act as occasions arise."

In this manner these amiable youths conferred, till they arrived at the castle. The Baron was sitting in the great hall, on a high chair with a footstep before, with the state and dignity of a judge; before him stood Father Oswald, as pleading the cause for himself and Edmund. Round the Baron's chair stood his eldest son and his kinsmen, with their principal domestics. The old servant, Joseph, at some distance, with his head leaning forward, as listening with the utmost attention to what passed. Mr. William approached the chair. "My Lord, I have found Edmund, and brought him to answer for himself."

"You have done well," said the Baron. "Edmund, come hither; you are charged with some indiscretions, for I cannot properly call them crimes: I am resolved to do justice between you and your accusers; I shall therefore hear you as well as them; for no man ought to be condemned unheard."

"My lord," said Edmund, with equal modesty and intrepidity, "I demand my trial; if I shall be found guilty of any crimes against my Benefactor, let me be punished with the utmost rigour; But if, as I trust, no such charge can be proved against me, I know your goodness too well to doubt that you will do justice to me, as well as to others; and if it should so happen that by the misrepresentations of my enemies (who have long sought my ruin privately, and now avow it publicly), if by their artifices your lordship should be induced to think me guilty, I would submit to your sentence in silence, and appeal to another tribunal."

"See," said Mr. Wenlock, "the confidence of the fellow! he already supposes that my lord must be in the wrong if he condemns him; and then this meek creature will appeal to another tribunal. To whose will he appeal? I desire he may be made to explain himself."

"That I will immediately," said Edmund, "without being compelled. I only meant to appeal to Heaven that best knows my innocence."

"'Tis true," said the Baron, "and no offence to any one; man can only judge by appearances, but Heaven knows the heart; Let every one of you bear this in mind, that you may not bring a false accusation, nor justify yourselves by concealing the truth. Edmund, I am informed that Oswald and you have made very free with me and my family, in some of your conversations; you were heard to censure me for the absurdity of building a new apartment on the west side of the castle, when there was one on the east side uninhabited. Oswald said, that apartment was shut up because it was haunted; that some shocking murder had been committed there; adding many particulars concerning Lord Lovel's family, such as he could not know the truth of, and, if he had known, was imprudent to reveal. But, further, you complained of ill-treatment here; and mentioned an intention to leave the castle, and seek your fortune elsewhere. I shall examine into all these particulars in turn. At present I desire you, Edmund, to relate all that you can remember of the conversation that passed between you and Oswald in the wood last Monday."

"Good God!" said Edmund, "is it possible that any person could put such a construction upon so innocent a conversation?"

"Tell me then," said the Baron, "the particulars of it."

"I will, my lord, as nearly as my memory will allow me." Accordingly he related most of the conversation that passed in the wood; but, in the part that concerned the family of Lovel, he abbreviated as much as possible. Oswald's countenance cleared up, for he had done the same before Edmund came. The Baron called to his eldest son.

"You hear, Sir Robert, what both parties say; I have questioned them separately; neither of them knew what the other would answer, yet their accounts agree almost to a word."

"I confess they do so," answered Sir Robert; "but, sir, it is very bold and presuming for them to speak of our family affairs in such a manner; if my uncle, Lord Lovel, should come to know it, he would punish them severely; and, if his honour is reflected upon, it becomes us to resent and to punish it." Here Mr. Wenlock broke out into passion, and offered to swear to the truth of his accusation.

"Be silent, Dick," said the Baron; "I shall judge for myself. I protest," said he to Sir Robert, "I never heard so much as Oswald has now told me concerning the deaths of Lord and Lady Lovel; I think it is best to let such stories alone till they die away of themselves. I had, indeed, heard of an idle story of the east apartment's being haunted, when first I came hither, and my brother advised me to shut it up till it should be forgotten; but what has now been said, has suggested a thought that may make that apartment useful in future. I have thought of a punishment for Edmund that will stop the mouth of his accusers for the present; and, as I hope, will establish his credit with every body. Edmund, will you undertake this adventure for me?"

"What adventure, my Lord," said Edmund? "There is nothing I would not undertake to shew my gratitude and fidelity to you. As to my courage, I would shew that at the expence of my malicious accusers, if respect to my Lord's blood did not tie up my hands; as I am situated, I beg it may be put to the proof in whatever way is most for my master's service."

"That is well said," cried the Baron; "as to your enemies, I am thinking how to separate you from them effectually; of that I shall speak hereafter. I am going to try Edmund's courage; he shall sleep three nights in the east apartment, that he may testify to all whether it be haunted or not; afterwards I will have that apartment set in order, and my eldest son shall take it for his own; it will spare me some expence, and answer my purpose as well, or better; Will you consent, Edmund?"

"With all my heart, my Lord," said Edmund, "I have not wilfully offended God or man; I have, therefore, nothing to fear."

"Brave boy!" said my Lord; "I am not deceived in you, nor shall you be deceived in your reliance on me. You shall sleep in that apartment to-night, and to-morrow I will have some private talk with you. Do you, Oswald, go with me; I want to have some conversation with you. The rest of you, retire to your studies and business; I will meet you at dinner."

Edmund retired to his own chamber, and Oswald was shut up with the Baron; he defended Edmund's cause and his own, and laid open as much as he knew of the malice and designs of his enemies. The Baron expressed much concern at the untimely deaths of Lord and Lady Lovel, and desired Oswald to be circumspect in regard to what he had to say of the circumstances attending them; adding, that he was both innocent and ignorant of any treachery towards either of them. Oswald excused himself for his communications to Edmund, saying, they fell undesignedly into the subject, and that he mentioned it in confidence to him only.

The Baron sent orders to the young men to come to dinner; but they refused to meet Edmund at table; accordingly he ate in the steward's apartment. After dinner, the Baron tried to reconcile his kinsmen to Edmund; but found it impossible. They saw their designs were laid open; and, judging of him by themselves, thought it impossible to forgive or be forgiven. The Baron ordered them to keep in separate apartments; he took his eldest son for his own companion, as being the most reasonable of the malcontents; and ordered his kinsmen to keep their own apartment, with a servant to watch their motions. Mr. William had Oswald for his companion. Old Joseph was bid to attend on Edmund; to serve him at supper; and, at the hour of nine, to conduct him to the haunted apartment. Edmund desired that he might have a light and his sword, lest his enemies should endeavour to surprise him. The Baron thought his request reasonable, and complied with it.

There was a great search to find the key of the apartment; at last it was discovered by Edmund, himself, among a parcel of old rusty keys in a lumber room. The Baron sent the young men their suppers to their respective apartments. Edmund declined eating, and desired to be conducted to his apartment. He was accompanied by most of the servants to the door of it; they wished him success, and prayed for him as if he had been going to execution.

The door was with great difficulty unlocked, and Joseph gave Edmund a lighted lamp, and wished him a good night; he returned his good wishes to them all with the utmost cheerfulness, took the key on the inside of the door, and dismissed them.

He then took a survey of his chamber; the furniture, by long neglect, was decayed and dropping to pieces; the bed was devoured by the moths, and occupied by the rats, who had built their nests there with impunity for many generations. The bedding was very damp, for the rain had forced its way through the ceiling; he determined, therefore, to lie down in his clothes. There were two doors on the further side of the room, with keys in them; being not at all sleepy, he resolved to examine them; he attempted one lock, and opened it with ease; he went into a large dining-room, the furniture of which was in the same tattered condition; out of this was a large closet with some books in it, and hung round with coats of arms, with genealogies and alliances of the house of Lovel; he amused himself here some minutes, and then returned into the bed-chamber.

He recollected the other door, and resolved to see where it led to; the key was rusted into the lock, and resisted his attempts; he set the lamp on the ground, and, exerting all his strength, opened the door, and at the same instant the wind of it blew out the lamp, and left him in utter darkness. At the same moment he heard a hollow rustling noise, like that of a person coming through a narrow passage. Till this moment not one idea of fear had approached the mind of Edmund; but, just then, all the concurrent circumstances of his situation struck upon his heart, and gave him a new and disagreeable sensation. He paused a while; and, recollecting himself, cried out aloud. "What should I fear? I have not wilfully offended God or man; why then should I doubt protection? But I have not yet implored the divine assistance; how then can I expect it!" Upon this, he kneeled down and prayed earnestly, resigning himself wholly to the will of heaven; while he was yet speaking, his courage returned, and he resumed his usual confidence; again he approached the door from whence the noise proceeded; he thought he saw a glimmering light upon a staircase before him. "If," said he, "this apartment is haunted, I will use my endeavours to discover the cause of it; and if the spirit appears visibly, I will speak to it."

He was preparing to descend the staircase, when he heard several knocks at the door by which he first entered the room; and, stepping backward, the door was clapped to with great violence. Again fear attacked him, but he resisted it, and boldly cried out, "Who is there?"

A voice at the outer door answered, "It's I; Joseph, your friend!"

"What do you want?" said Edmund.

"I have brought you some wood to make a fire," said Joseph.

"I thank you kindly," said Edmund; "but my lamp is gone out; I will try to find the door, however."

After some trouble he found, and opened it; and was not sorry to see his friend Joseph, with a light in one hand, a flagon of beer in the other, and a fagot upon his shoulder. "I come," said the good old man, "to bring you something to keep up your spirits; the evening is cold; I know this room wants airing; and beside that, my master, I think your present undertaking requires a little assistance."

"My good friend," said Edmund, "I never shall be able to deserve or requite your kindness to me."

"My dear sir, you always deserved more than I could do for you; and I think I shall yet live to see you defeat the designs of your enemies, and acknowledge the services of your friends."

"Alas!" said Edmund, "I see little prospect of that!"

"I see," said Joseph, "something that persuades me you are designed for great things; and I perceive that things are working about to some great end: have courage, my Master, my heart beats strangely high upon your account!"

"You make me smile," said Edmund.

"I am glad to see it, sir; may you smile all the rest of your life!"

"I thank your honest affection," returned Edmund, "though it is too partial to me. You had better go to bed, however; if it is known that you visit me here, it will be bad for us both."

"So I will presently; but, please God, I will come here again to-morrow night, when all the family are a-bed; and I will tell you some things that you never yet heard."

"But pray tell me," said Edmund, "where does that door lead to?"

"Upon a passage that ends in a staircase that leads to the lower rooms; and there is likewise a door out of that passage into the dining-room."

"And what rooms are there below stairs," said Edmund?

"The same as above," replied he.

"Very well; then I wish you a good night, we will talk further to-morrow."

"Aye, to-morrow night; and in this place, my dear master."

"Why do you call me your master? I never was, nor ever can be, your master."

"God only knows that," said the good old man; "good-night, and heaven bless you!"

"Good-night, my worthy friend!"

Joseph withdrew, and Edmund returned to the other door, and attempted several times to open it in vain; his hands were benumbed and tired; at length he gave over. He made a fire in the chimney, placed the lamp on a table, and opened one of the window-shutters to admit the day-light; he then recommended himself to the Divine protection, and threw himself upon the bed; he presently fell asleep, and continued in that state, till the sun saluted him with his orient beams through the window he had opened.

As soon as he was perfectly awake, he strove to recollect his dreams. He thought that he heard people coming up the staircase that he had a glimpse of; that the door opened, and there entered a warrior, leading a lady by the hand, who was young and beautiful, but pale and wan; The man was dressed in complete armour, and his helmet down. They approached the bed; they undrew the curtains. He thought the man said, "Is this our child?" The woman replied, "It is; and the hour approaches that he shall be known for such." They then separated, and one stood on each side of the bed; their hands met over his head, and they gave him a solemn benediction. He strove to rise and pay them his respects, but they forbad him; and the lady said, "Sleep in peace, oh my Edmund! for those who are the true possessors of this apartment are employed in thy preservation; sleep on, sweet hope of a house that is thought past hope!"

Upon this, they withdrew, and went out at the same door by which they entered, and he heard them descend the stairs. After this, he followed a funeral as chief mourner; he saw the whole procession, and heard the ceremonies performed. He was snatched away from this mournful scene to one of a contrary kind, a stately feast, at which he presided; and he heard himself congratulated as a husband, and a father; his friend William sat by his side; and his happiness was complete. Every succeeding idea was happiness without allay; and his mind was not idle a moment till the morning sun awakened him. He perfectly remembered his dreams, and meditated on what all these things should portend. "Am I then," said he, "not Edmund Twyford, but somebody of consequence in whose fate so many people are interested? Vain thought, that must have arisen from the partial suggestion of my two friends, Mr. William and old Joseph."

He lay thus reflecting, when a servant knocked at his door, and told him it was past six o'clock, and that the Baron expected him to breakfast in an hour. He rose immediately; paid his tribute of thanks to heaven for its protection, and went from his chamber in high health and spirits. He walked in the garden till the hour of breakfast, and then attended the Baron.

"Good morrow, Edmund!" said he; "how have you rested in your new apartment?"

"Extremely well, my lord," answered he.

"I am glad to hear it," said the Baron; "but I did not know your accommodations were so bad, as Joseph tells me they are."

"'Tis of no consequence," said Edmund; "if they were much worse, I could dispense with them for three nights."

"Very well," said the Baron; "you are a brave lad; I am satisfied with you, and will excuse the other two nights."

"But, my lord, I will not be excused; no one shall have reason to suspect my courage; I am determined to go through the remaining nights upon many accounts."

"That shall be as you please," said my Lord. "I think of you as you deserve; so well, that I shall ask your advice by and by in some affairs of consequence."

"My life and services are yours, my lord; command them freely."

"Let Oswald be called in," said my Lord; "he shall be one of our consultation." He came; the servants were dismissed; and the Baron spoke as follows:

"Edmund, when first I took you into my family, it was at the request of my sons and kinsmen; I bear witness to your good behaviour, you have not deserved to lose their esteem; but, nevertheless, I have observed for some years past, that all but my son William have set their faces against you; I see their meanness, and I perceive their motives: but they are, and must be, my relations; and I would rather govern them by love, than fear. I love and esteem your virtues: I cannot give you up to gratify their humours. My son William has lost the affections of the rest, for that he bears to you; but he has increased my regard for him; I think myself bound in honour to him and you to provide for you; I cannot do it, as I wished, under my own roof. If you stay here, I see nothing but confusion in my family; yet I cannot put you out of it disgracefully. I want to think of some way to prefer you, that you may leave this house with honour; and I desire both of you to give me your advice in this matter. If Edmund will tell me in what way I can employ him to his own honour and my advantage, I am ready to do it; let him propose it, and Oswald shall moderate between us."

Here he stopped; and Edmund, whose sighs almost choked him, threw himself at the Baron's feet, and wet his hand with his tears: "Oh, my noble, generous benefactor! do you condescend to consult such a one as me upon the state of your family? does your most amiable and beloved son incur the ill-will of his brothers and kinsmen for my sake? What am I, that I should disturb the peace of this noble family? Oh, my lord, send me away directly! I should be unworthy to live, if I did not earnestly endeavour to restore your happiness. You have given me a noble education, and I trust I shall not disgrace it. If you will recommend me, and give me a character, I fear not to make my own fortune."

The Baron wiped his eyes; "I wish to do this, my child, but in what way?"

"My lord," said Edmund, "I will open my heart to you. I have served with credit in the army, and I should prefer a soldier's life."

"You please me well," said the Baron; "I will send you to France, and give you a recommendation to the Regent; he knows you personally, and will prefer you, for my sake, and for your own merit."

"My lord, you overwhelm me with your goodness! I am but your creature, and my life shall be devoted to your service."

"But," said the Baron, "how to dispose of you till the spring?"

"That," said Oswald, "may be thought of at leisure; I am glad that you have resolved, and I congratulate you both." The Baron put an end to the conversation by desiring Edmund to go with him into the menage to see his horses. He ordered Oswald to acquaint his son William with all that had passed, and to try to persuade the young men to meet Edmund and William at dinner.

The Baron took Edmund with him into his menage to see some horses he had lately purchased; while they were examining the beauties and defects of these noble and useful animals, Edmund declared that he preferred Caradoc, a horse he had broke himself, to any other in my lord's stables. "Then," said the Baron, "I will give him to you; and you shall go upon him to seek your fortune." He made new acknowledgments for this gift, and declared he would prize it highly for the giver's sake. "But I shall not part with you yet," said my lord; "I will first carry all my points with these saucy boys, and oblige them to do you justice."

"You have already done that," said Edmund; "and I will not suffer any of your Lordship's blood to undergo any farther humiliation upon my account. I think, with humble submission to your better judgment, the sooner I go hence the better."

While they were speaking, Oswald came to them, and said, that the young men had absolutely refused to dine at the table, if Edmund was present. "'Tis well," said the Baron; "I shall find a way to punish their contumacy hereafter; I will make them know that I am the master here. Edmund and you, Oswald, shall spend the day in my apartment above stairs. William shall dine with me alone; and I will acquaint him with our determination; my son Robert, and his cabal, shall be prisoners in the great parlour. Edmund shall, according to his own desire, spend this and the following night in the haunted apartment; and this for his sake, and my own; for if I should now contradict my former orders, it would subject us both to their impertinent reflections."

He then took Oswald aside, and charged him not to let Edmund go out of his sight; for if he should come in the way of those implacable enemies, he trembled for the consequences. He then walked back to the stables, and the two friends returned into the house.

They had a long conversation on various subjects; in the course of it, Edmund acquainted Oswald with all that had passed between him and Joseph the preceding night, the curiosity he had raised in him, and his promise to gratify it the night following.

"I wish," said Oswald, "you would permit me to be one of your party."

"How can that be?" said Edmund; "we shall be watched, perhaps; and, if discovered, what excuse can you make for coming there? Beside, if it were known, I shall be branded with the imputation of cowardice; and, though I have borne much, I will not promise to bear that patiently."

"Never fear," replied Oswald, "I will speak to Joseph about it; and, after prayers are over and the family gone to bed, I will steal away from my own chamber and come to you. I am strongly interested in your affairs; and I cannot be easy unless you will receive me into your company; I will bind myself to secrecy in any manner you shall enjoin."

"Your word is sufficient," said Edmund; "I have as much reason to trust you, father, as any man living; I should be ungrateful to refuse you any thing in my power to grant; But suppose the apartment should really be haunted, would you have resolution enough to pursue the adventure to a discovery?"

"I hope so," said Oswald; "but have you any reason to believe it is?"

"I have," said Edmund; "but I have not opened my lips upon this subject to any creature but yourself. This night I purpose, if Heaven permit, to go all over the rooms; and, though I had formed this design, I will confess that your company will strengthen my resolution. I will have no reserves to you in any respect; but I must put a seal upon your lips."

Oswald swore secrecy till he should be permitted to disclose the mysteries of that apartment; and both of them waited, in solemn expectation, the event of the approaching night.

In the afternoon Mr. William was allowed to visit his friend. An affecting interview passed between them. He lamented the necessity of Edmund's departure; and they took a solemn leave of each other, as if they foreboded it would be long ere they should meet again.

About the same hour as the preceding evening, Joseph came to conduct Edmund to his apartment.

"You will find better accommodations than you had last night," said he, "and all by my lord's own order."

"I every hour receive some new proof of his goodness," said Edmund.

When they arrived, he found a good fire in the chamber, and a table covered with cold meats, and a flagon of strong beer.

"Sit down and get your supper, my dear Master," said Joseph: "I must attend my Lord; but as soon as the family are gone to bed, I will visit you again."

"Do so," said Edmund; "but first, see Father Oswald; he has something to say to you. You may trust him, for I have no reserves to him."

"Well, Sir, I will see him if you desire it; and I will come to you as soon as possible." So saying, he went his way, and Edmund sat down to supper.

After a moderate refreshment, he kneeled down, and prayed with the greatest fervency. He resigned himself to the disposal of Heaven: "I am nothing," said he, "I desire to be nothing but what thou, O Lord, pleasest to make me. If it is thy will that I should return to my former obscurity, be it obeyed with cheerfulness; and, if thou art pleased to exalt me, I will look up to thee, as the only fountain of honour and dignity." While he prayed, he felt an enlargement of heart beyond what he had ever experienced before; all idle fears were dispersed, and his heart glowed with divine love and affiance; — he seemed raised above the world and all its pursuits. He continued wrapt up in mental devotion, till a knocking at the door obliged him to rise, and let in his two friends, who came without shoes, and on tiptoe, to visit him.

"Save you, my son!" said the friar; "you look cheerful and happy."

"I am so, father," said Edmund; "I have resigned myself to the disposal of Heaven, and I find my heart strengthened above what I can express."

"Heaven be praised!" said Oswald: "I believe you are designed for great things, my son."

"What! do you too encourage my ambition?" says Edmund; "strange concurrence of circumstances! — Sit down, my friends; and do you, my good Joseph, tell me the particulars you promised last night." They drew their chairs round the fire, and Joseph began as follows: —

"You have heard of the untimely death of the late Lord Lovel, my noble and worthy master; perhaps you may have also heard that, from that time, this apartment was haunted. What passed the other day, when my Lord questioned you both on this head, brought all the circumstances fresh into my mind. You then said, there were suspicions that he came not fairly to his end. I trust you both, and will speak what I know of it. There was a person suspected of this murder; and whom do you think it was?"

"You must speak out," said Oswald.

"Why then," said Joseph, "it was the present Lord Lovel."

"You speak my thoughts," said Oswald; "but proceed to the proofs."

"I will," said Joseph.

"From the time that my lord's death was reported, there were strange whisperings and consultations between the new lord and some of the servants; there was a deal of private business carried on in this apartment. Soon after, they gave out that my poor lady was distracted; but she threw out strong expressions that savoured nothing of madness. She said, that the ghost of her departed lord had appeared to her, and revealed the circumstances of this murder. None of the servants, but one, were permitted to see her. At this very time, Sir Walter, the new lord, had the cruelty to offer love to her; he urged her to marry him; and one of her women overheard her say, she would sooner die than give her hand to the man who caused the death of her Lord; Soon after this, we were told my Lady was dead. The Lord Lovel made a public and sumptuous funeral for her."

"That is true," said Oswald; "for I was a novice, and assisted at it."

"Well," says Joseph, "now comes my part of the story. As I was coming home from the burial, I overtook Roger our ploughman. Said he, What think you of this burying? — 'What should I think,' said I, 'but that we have lost the best Master and Lady that we shall ever know?' 'God, He knows,' quoth Roger, 'whether they be living or dead; but if ever I saw my Lady in my life, I saw her alive the night they say she died.' I tried to convince him that he was mistaken; but he offered to take his oath, that the very night they said she died, he saw her come out at the garden gate into the fields; that she often stopped, like a person in pain, and then went forward again until he lost sight of her. Now it is certain that her time was out, and she expected to lie down every day; and they did not pretend that she died in child-bed. I thought upon what I heard, but nothing I said. Roger told the same story to another servant; so he was called to an account, the story was hushed up, and the foolish fellow said, he was verily persuaded it was her ghost that he saw. Now you must take notice that, from this time, they began to talk about, that this apartment was troubled; and not only this, but at last the new Lord could not sleep in quiet in his own room; and this induced him to sell the castle to his brother-in-law, and get out of this country as fast as possible. He took most of the servants away with him, and Roger among the rest. As for me, they thought I knew nothing, and so they left me behind; but I was neither blind nor deaf, though I could hear, and see, and say nothing."

"This is a dark story," said Oswald.

"It is so," said Edmund; "but why should Joseph seem to think it concerns me in particular?"

"Ah, dear Sir," said Joseph, "I must tell you, though I never uttered it to mortal man before; the striking resemblance this young man bears to my dear Lord, the strange dislike his reputed father took to him, his gentle manners, his generous heart, his noble qualities so uncommon in those of his birth and breeding, the sound of his voice — you may smile at the strength of my fancy, but I cannot put it out of my mind but that he is my own master's son."

At these words Edmund changed colour and trembled; he clapped his hand upon his breast, and looked up to Heaven in silence; his dream recurred to his memory, and struck upon his heart. He related it to his attentive auditors.

"The ways of Providence are wonderful," said Oswald. "If this be so, Heaven in its own time will make it appear."

Here a silence of several minutes ensued; when, suddenly, they were awakened from their reverie by a violent noise in the rooms underneath them. It seemed like the clashing of arms, and something seemed to fall down with violence.

They started, and Edmund rose up with a look full of resolution and intrepidity.

"I am called!" said he; "I obey the call!"

He took up a lamp, and went to the door that he had opened the night before. Oswald followed with his rosary in his hand, and Joseph last with trembling steps. The door opened with ease, and they descended the stairs in profound silence.

The lower rooms answered exactly to those above; there were two parlours and a large closet. They saw nothing remarkable in these rooms, except two pictures, that were turned with their faces to the wall. Joseph took the courage to turn them. "These," said he, "are the portraits of my lord and lady. Father, look at this face; do you know who is like it?"

"I should think," said Oswald, "it was done for Edmund!"

"I am," said Edmund, "struck with the resemblance myself; but let us go on; I feel myself inspired with unusual courage. Let us open the closet door."

Oswald stopped him short.

"Take heed," said he, "lest the wind of the door put out the lamp. I will open this door."

He attempted it without success; Joseph did the same, but to no purpose; Edmund gave the lamp to Joseph; he approached the door, tried the key, and it gave way to his hand in a moment.

"This adventure belongs," said he, "to me only; that is plain—bring the lamp forward."

Oswald repeated the paternoster, in which they all joined, and then entered the closet.

The first thing that presented itself to their view, was a complete suit of armour, that seemed to have fallen down on an heap.

"Behold!" said Edmund; "this made the noise we heard above." They took it up, and examined it piece by piece; the inside of the breast plate was stained with blood.

"See here!" said Edmund; "what think you of this?"

"'Tis my Lord's armour," said Joseph; "I know it well—here has been bloody work in this closet!"

Going forward, he stumbled over something; it was a ring with the arms of Lovel engraved upon it.

"This is my Lord's ring," said Joseph; "I have seen him wear it; I give it to you, sir, as the right owner; and most religiously do I believe you his son."

"Heaven only knows that," said Edmund; "and, if it permits, I will know who was my father before I am a day older."

While he was speaking, he shifted his ground, and perceived that the boards rose up on the other side of the closet; upon farther examination they found that the whole floor was loose, and a table that stood over them concealed the circumstance from a casual observer.

"I perceive," said Oswald, "that some great discovery is at hand."

"God defend us!" said Edmund, "but I verily believe that the person that owned this armour lies buried under us."

Upon this, a dismal hollow groan was heard, as if from underneath. A solemn silence ensued, and marks of fear were visible upon all three; the groan was thrice heard; Oswald made signs for them to kneel, and he prayed audibly, that Heaven would direct them how to act; he also prayed for the soul of the departed, that it might rest in peace. After this, he arose; but Edmund continued kneeling—he vowed solemnly to devote himself to the discovery of this secret, and the avenging the death of the person there buried. He then rose up. "It would be to no purpose," said he, "for us to examine further now; when I am properly authorised, I will have this place opened; I trust that time is not far off."

"I believe it," said Oswald; "you are designed by Heaven to be its instrument in bringing this deed of darkness to light. We are your creatures; only tell us what you would have us do, and we are ready to obey your commands."

"I only demand your silence," said Edmund, "till I call for your evidence; and then, you must speak all you know, and all you suspect."

"Oh," said Joseph, "that I may but live to see that day, and I shall have lived long enough!"

"Come," said Edmund, "let us return up stairs, and we will consult further how I shall proceed."

So saying, he went out of the closet, and they followed him. He locked the door, and took the key out—"I will keep this," said he, "till I have power to use it to purpose, lest any one should presume to pry into the secret of this closet. I will always carry it about me, to remind me of what I have undertaken."

Upon this, they returned up stairs into the bed-chamber; all was still, and they heard nothing more to disturb them. "How," said Edmund, "is it possible that I should be the son of Lord Lovel? for, however circumstances have seemed to encourage such a notion, what reason have I to believe it?"

"I am strangely puzzled about it," said Oswald. "It seems unlikely that so good a man as Lord Lovel should corrupt the wife of a peasant, his vassal; and, especially, being so lately married to a lady with whom he was passionately in love."

"Hold there!" said Joseph; "my lord was incapable of such an action; If Master Edmund is the son of my lord, he is also the son of my lady."

"How can that be," said Edmund?

"I don't know how," said Joseph; "but there is a person who can tell if she will; I mean Margery Twyford, who calls herself your mother."

"You meet my thoughts," said Edmund; "I had resolved, before you spoke, to visit her, and to interrogate her on the subject; I will ask my Lord's permission to go this very day."

"That is right," said Oswald; "but be cautious and prudent in your enquiries."

"If you," said Edmund, "would bear me company, I should do better; she might think herself obliged to answer your questions; and, being less interested in the event, you would be more discreet in your interrogations."

"That I will most readily," said he; "and I will ask my lord's permission for us both."

"This point is well determined," said Joseph; "I am impatient for the result; and I believe my feet will carry me to meet you whether I consent or not."

"I am as impatient as you," said Oswald; "but let us be silent as the grave, and let not a word or look indicate any thing knowing or mysterious."

The daylight began to dawn upon their conference; and Edmund, observing it, begged his friends to withdraw in silence. They did so, and left Edmund to his own recollections. His thoughts were too much employed for sleep to approach him; he threw himself upon the bed, and lay meditating how he should proceed; a thousand schemes offered themselves and were rejected; But he resolved, at all events, to leave Baron Fitz-Owen's family the first opportunity that presented itself.

He was summoned, as before, to attend my lord at breakfast; during which, he was silent, absent, and reserved. My Lord observed it, and rallied him; enquiring how he had spent the night?

"In reflecting upon my situation, my Lord; and in laying plans for my future conduct." Oswald took the hint, and asked permission to visit Edmund's mother in his company, and acquaint her with his intentions of leaving the country soon. He consented freely; but seemed unresolved about Edmund's departure.

They set out directly, and Edmund went hastily to old Twyford's cottage, declaring that every field seemed a mile to him. "Restrain your warmth, my son," said Oswald; "compose your mind, and recover your breath, before you enter upon a business of such consequence." Margery met them at the door, and asked Edmund, what wind blew him thither?

"Is it so very surprising," said he, "that I should visit my parents?"

"Yes, it is," said she, "considering the treatment you have met with from us; but since Andrew is not in the house, I may say I am glad to see you; Lord bless you, what a fine youth you be grown! 'Tis a long time since I saw you; but that is not my fault; many a cross word, and many a blow, have I had on your account; but I may now venture to embrace my dear child."

Edmund came forward and embraced her fervently; the starting tears, on both sides, evinced their affection. "And why," said he, "should my father forbid you to embrace your child? what have I ever done to deserve his hatred?"

"Nothing, my dear boy! you were always good and tender-hearted, and deserved the love of every body."

"It is not common," said Edmund, "for a parent to hate his first-born son without his having deserved it."

"That is true," said Oswald; "it is uncommon, it is unnatural; nay, I am of opinion it is almost impossible. I am so convinced of this truth, that I believe the man who thus hates and abuses Edmund, cannot be his father." In saying this, he observed her countenance attentively; she changed colour apparently. "Come," said he, "let us sit down; and do you, Margery, answer to what I have said."

"Blessed Virgin!" said Margery, "what does your reverence mean? what do you suspect?"

"I suspect," said he, "that Edmund is not the son of Andrew your husband."

"Lord bless me!" said she, "what is it you do suspect?"

"Do not evade my question, woman! I am come here by authority to examine you upon this point."

The woman trembled every joint. "Would to Heaven!" said she, "that Andrew was at home!"

"It is much better as it is," said Oswald; "you are the person we are to examine."

"Oh, father," said she, "do you think that I — that I — that I am to blame in this matter? what have I done?"

"Do you, sir," said he, "ask your own questions."

Upon this, Edmund threw himself at her feet, and embraced her knees. "O my mother!" said he, "for as such my heart owns you, tell me for the love of Heaven! tell me, who was my father?"

"Gracious Heaven!" said she, "what will become of me?"

"Woman!" said Oswald, "confess the truth, or you shall be compelled to do it; by whom had you this youth?"

"Who, I?" said she; "I had him! No, father, I am not guilty of the black crime of adultery; God, He knows my innocence; I am not worthy to be the mother of such a sweet youth as that is."

"You are not his mother, then, nor Andrew his father?"

"Oh, what shall I do?" said Margery; "Andrew will be the death of me!"

"No, he shall not," said Edmund; "you shall be protected and rewarded for the discovery."

"Goody," said Oswald, "confess the whole truth, and I will protect you from harm and from blame; you may be the means of making Edmund's fortune, in which case he will certainly provide for you; on the other hand, by an obstinate silence you will deprive yourself of all advantages you might receive from the discovery; and, beside, you will soon be examined in a different manner, and be obliged to confess all you know, and nobody will thank you for it."

"Ah," said she, "but Andrew beat me the last time I spoke to Edmund; and told me he would break every bone in my skin, if ever I spoke to him again."

"He knows it then?" said Oswald.

"He know it! Lord help you, it was all his own doing."

"Tell us then," said Oswald; "for Andrew shall never know it, till it is out of his power to punish you."

"'Tis a long story," said she, "and cannot be told in a few

words."

"It will never be told at this rate," said he; "sit down and begin it instantly."

"My fate depends upon your words," said Edmund; "my soul is impatient of the suspense! If ever you loved me and cherished me, shew it now, and tell while I have breath to ask it."

He sat in extreme agitation of mind; his words and actions were equally expressive of his inward emotions.

"I will," said she; "but I must try to recollect all the circumstances. You must know, young man, that you are just one-and-twenty years of age."

"On what day was he born," said Oswald?

"The day before yesterday," said she, "the 21st of September."

"A remarkable era," said he.

"'Tis so, indeed," said Edmund; "Oh, that night! that apartment!"

"Be silent," said Oswald; "and do you, Margery, begin your story."

"I will," said she. "Just one-and-twenty years ago, on that very day, I lost my first-born son; I got a hurt by over-reaching myself, when I was near my time, and so the poor child died. And so, as I was sitting all alone, and very melancholy, Andrew came home from work; 'See, Margery,' said he, 'I have brought you a child instead of that you have lost.' So he gave me a bundle, as I thought; but sure enough it was a child; a poor helpless babe just born, and only rolled up in a fine handkerchief, and over that a rich velvet cloak, trimmed with gold lace. 'And where did you find this?' says I. 'Upon the foot-bridge,' says he, 'just below the clayfield. This child,' said he, 'belongs to some great folk, and perhaps it may be enquired after one day, and may make our fortunes; take care of it,' said he, 'and bring it up as if it was your own.' The poor infant was cold, and it cried, and looked up at me so pitifully, that I loved it; beside, my milk was troublesome to me, and I was glad to be eased of it; so I gave it the breast, and from that hour I loved the child as if it were my own, and so I do still if I dared to own it."

"And this is all you know of Edmund's birth?" said Oswald.

"No, not all," said Margery; "but pray look out and see whether Andrew is coming, for I am all over in a twitter."

"He is not," said Oswald; "go on, I beseech you!"

"This happened," said she, "as I told you, on the 21st. On the morrow, my Andrew went out early to work, along with one Robin Rouse, our neighbour; they had not been gone above an hour, when they both came back seemingly very much frightened. Says Andrew, 'Go you, Robin, and borrow a pickaxe at neighbour Styles's.' What is the matter now?' said I. 'Matter enough!' quoth Andrew; 'we may come to be hanged, perhaps, as many an innocent man has before us.' 'Tell me what is the matter,' said I. 'I will,' said he; 'but if ever you open your mouth about it, woe be to you!' 'I never will,' said I; but he made me swear by all the blessed saints in the Calendar; and then he told me, that, as Robin and he were going over the foot-bridge, where he found the child the evening before, they saw something floating upon the water; so they followed it, till it stuck against a stake, and found it to be the dead body of a woman; 'as sure as you are alive, Madge,' said he, 'this was the mother of the child I brought home.'"

"Merciful God!" said Edmund; "am I the child of that hapless mother?"

"Be composed," said Oswald; "proceed, good woman, the time is precious."

"And so," continued she, "Andrew told me they dragged the body out of the river, and it was richly dressed, and must be somebody of consequence. 'I suppose,' said he, 'when the poor Lady had taken care of her child, she went to find some help; and, the night being dark, her foot slipped, and she fell into the river, and was drowned.'

"'Lord have mercy!' said Robin, 'what shall we do with the dead body? we may be taken up for the murder; what had we to do to meddle with it?' 'Ay, but,' says Andrew, 'we must have something to do with it now; and our wisest way is to bury it.' Robin was sadly frightened, but at last they agreed to carry it into the wood, and bury it there; so they came home for a pickaxe and shovel. 'Well,' said I, 'Andrew, but will you bury all the rich clothes you speak of?' 'Why,' said he, 'it would be both a sin and a shame to strip the dead.' 'So it would,' said I; 'but I will give you a sheet to wrap the body in, and you may take off her upper garments, and any thing of value; but do not strip her to the skin for any thing.' 'Well said, wench!' said he; 'I will do as you say.' So I fetched a sheet, and by that time Robin was come back, and away they went together.

"They did not come back again till noon, and then they sat down and ate a morsel together. Says Andrew, 'Now we may sit down and eat in peace.' 'Aye,' says Robin, 'and sleep in peace too, for we have done no harm.' 'No, to be sure,' said I; 'but yet I am much concerned that the poor Lady had not Christian burial.' 'Never trouble thyself about that,' said Andrew; 'we have done the best we could for her; but let us see what we have got in our bags; we must divide them.' So they opened their bags, and took out a fine gown and a pair of rich shoes; but, besides these, there was a fine necklace with a golden locket, and a pair of earrings. Says Andrew, and winked at me, 'I will have these, and you may take the rest.' Robin said, he was satisfied, and so he went his way. When he was gone, 'Here, you fool,' says Andrew, 'take these, and keep them as safe as the bud of your eye; If ever young master is found, these will make our fortune.'"

"And have you them now?" said Oswald.

"Yes, that I have," answered she; "Andrew would have sold them long ago, but I always put him off it."

"Heaven be praised!" said Edmund.

"Hush," said Oswald, "let us not lose time; proceed, Goody!"

"Nay," said Margery, "I have not much more to say. We looked every day to hear some enquiries after the child, but nothing passed, nobody was missing."

"Did nobody of note die about that time?" said Oswald.

"Why yes," said Margery, "the widow Lady Lovel died that same week; by the same token, Andrew went to the funeral, and brought home a scutcheon, which I keep unto this day."

"Very well; go on."

"My husband behaved well enough to the boy, till such time as he had two or three children of his own; and then he began to grumble, and say, it was hard to maintain other folks' children, when he found it hard enough to keep his own; I loved the boy quite as well as my own; often and often have I pacified Andrew, and made him to hope that he should one day or other be paid for his trouble; but at last he grew out of patience, and gave over all hopes of that kind.

"As Edmund grew up, he grew sickly and tender, and could not bear hard labour; and that was another reason why my husband could not bear with him. 'If,' quoth he, 'the boy could earn his living, I did not care; but I must bear all the expence.['] There came an old pilgrim into our parts; he was a scholar, and had been a soldier, and he taught Edmund to read; then he told him histories of wars, and knights, and lords, and great men; and Edmund took such delight in hearing him, that he would not take to any thing else.

"To be sure, Edwin was a pleasant companion; he would tell old stories, and sing old songs, that one could have sat all night to hear him; but, as I was a saying, Edmund grew more and more fond of reading, and less of work; however, he would run of errands, and do many handy turns for the neighbours; and he was so courteous a lad, that people took notice of him. Andrew once catched him alone reading, and then told him, that if he did not find some way to earn his bread, he would turn him out of doors in a very short time; and so he would have done, sure enough, if my Lord Fitz-Owen had not taken him into his service just in the nick."

"Very well, Goody," said Oswald; "you have told your story very well; I am glad, for Edmund's sake, that you can do it so properly. But now, can you keep a secret?"

"Why, an't please your reverence, I think I have shewed you that I can."

"But can you keep it from your husband?"

"Aye," said she, "surely I can; for I dare not tell it him."

"That is a good security," said he; "but I must have a better. You must swear upon this book not to disclose any thing that has passed between us three, till we desire you to do it. Be assured you will soon be called upon for this purpose; Edmund's birth is near the discovery; He is the son of parents of high degree; and it will be in his power to make your fortune, when he takes possession of his own."

"Holy Virgin! what is it you tell me? How you rejoice me to hear, that what I have so long prayed for will come to pass!"

She took the oath required, saying it after Oswald.

"Now," said he, "go and fetch the tokens you have mentioned."

When she was gone, Edmund's passions, long suppressed, broke out in tears and exclamations; he kneeled down, and, with his hands clasped together, returned thanks to Heaven for the discovery. Oswald begged him to be composed, lest Margery should perceive his agitation, and misconstrue the cause. She soon returned with the necklace and ear-rings; They were pearls of great value; and the necklace had a locket, on which the cypher of Lovel was engraved.

"This," said Oswald, "is indeed a proof of consequence. Keep it, sir, for it belongs to you."

"Must he take it away?" said she.

"Certainly," returned Oswald; "we can do nothing without it; but if Andrew should ask for it, you must put him off for the present, and hereafter he will find his account in it."

Margery consented reluctantly to part with the jewels; and, after some further conversation, they took leave of her.

Edmund embraced her affectionately. "I thank you with my whole heart," said he, "for all your goodness to me! Though I confess, I never felt much regard for your husband, yet for you I had always the tender affection of a son. You will, I trust, give your evidence in my behalf when called upon; and I hope it will one day be in my power to reward your kindness; In that case, I will own you as my foster-mother, and you shall always be treated as such."

Margery wept. "The Lord grant it!" said she; "and I pray him to have you in his holy keeping. Farewell, my dear child!"

Oswald desired them to separate for fear of intrusion; and they returned to the castle. Margery stood at the door of her cottage, looking every way to see if the coast was clear.

"Now, Sir," said Oswald, "I congratulate you as the son of Lord and Lady Lovel; the proofs are strong and indisputable."

"To us they are so," said Edmund; "but how shall we make them so to others? and what are we to think of the funeral of Lady Lovel?"

"As of a fiction," said Oswald; "the work of the present lord, to secure his title and fortune."

"And what means can we use to dispossess him?" said Edmund; "He is not a man for a poor youth like me to contend with."

"Doubt not," said Oswald, "but Heaven, who has evidently conducted you by the hand thus far, will complete its own work; for my part, I can only wonder and adore!"

"Give me your advice then," said Edmund; "for Heaven assists us by natural means."

"It seems to me," said Oswald, "that your first step must be to make a friend of some great man, of consequence enough to espouse your cause, and to get this affair examined into by authority."

Edmund started, and crossed himself; he suddenly exclaimed, "A friend! Yes; I have a friend! a powerful one too; one sent by Heaven to be my protector, but whom I have too long neglected."

"Who can that be?" said Oswald.

"Who should it be," said Edmund, "but that good Sir Philip Harclay, the chosen friend of him, whom I shall from henceforward call my father."

"'Tis true indeed," said Oswald; "and this is a fresh proof of what I before observed, that Heaven assists you, and will complete its own work."

"I think so myself," said Edmund, "and rely upon its direction. I have already determined on my future conduct, which I will communicate to you. My first step shall be to leave the castle; my lord has this day given me a horse, upon which I purpose to set out this very night, without the knowledge of any of the family. I will go to Sir Philip Harclay; I will throw myself at his feet, relate my strange story, and implore his protection; With him I will consult on the most proper way of bringing this murderer to public justice; and I will be guided by his advice and direction in everything."

"Nothing can be better," said Oswald, "than what you propose; but give me leave to offer an addition to your scheme. You shall set off in the dead of night, as you intend; Joseph and

I, will favour your departure in such a manner as to throw a mystery over the circumstances of it. Your disappearing at such a time from the haunted apartment will terrify and confound all the family; they will puzzle themselves in vain to account for it, and they will be afraid to pry into the secrets of that place."

"You say well, and I approve your addition," replied Edmund. "Suppose, likewise, there was a letter written in a mysterious manner, and dropt in my lord's way, or sent to him afterwards; it would forward our design, and frighten them away from that apartment." "That shall be my care," said Oswald; "and I will warrant you that they will not find themselves disposed to inhabit it presently."

"But how shall I leave my dear friend Mr. William, without a word of notice of this separation?"

"I have thought of that too," said Oswald; "and I will so manage, as to acquaint him with it in such a manner as he shall think out of the common course of things, and which shall make him wonder and be silent."

"How will you do that," said Edmund?

"I will tell you hereafter," said Oswald; "for here comes old Joseph to meet us."

He came, indeed, as fast as his age would permit him. As soon as he was within hearing, he asked them what news? They related all that had passed at Twyford's cottage; he heard them with the greatest eagerness of attention, and as soon as they came to the great event, "I knew it! I knew it!" exclaimed Joseph; "I was sure it would prove so! Thank God for it! But I will be the first to acknowledge my young lord, and I will live and die his faithful servant!" Here Joseph attempted to kneel to him, but Edmund prevented him with a warm embrace.

"My friend! my dear friend!" said he, "I cannot suffer a man of your age to kneel to me; are you not one of my best and truest friends? I will ever remember your disinterested affection for me; and if heaven restores me to my rights, it shall be one of my first cares to render your old age easy and happy." Joseph wept over him, and it was some time before he could utter a word.

Oswald gave them both time to recover their emotion, by acquainting

Joseph with Edmund's scheme for his departure. Joseph

wiped his eyes and spoke. "I have thought," said he, "of something that will be both agree and useful to my dear master. John Wyatt, Sir Philip Harclay's servant, is now upon a visit at his father's; I have heard that he goes home soon; now he would be both a guide and companion, on the way."

"That is, indeed, a happy circumstance," said Edmund; "but how shall we know certainly the time of his departure?"

"Why, Sir, I will go to him, and enquire; and bring you word directly."

"Do so," said Edmund, "and you will oblige me greatly."

"But, Sir," said Oswald, "I think it will be best not to let John Wyatt know who is to be his companion; only let Joseph tell him that a gentleman is going to visit his master, and, if possible, prevail upon him to set out this night."

"Do so, my good friend," said Edmund; "and tell him, further, that this person has business of great consequence to communicate to his master, and cannot delay his journey on any account."

"I will do this, you may depend," said Joseph, "and acquaint you with my success as soon as possible; but, sir, you must not go without a guide, at any rate."

"I trust I shall not," said Edmund, "though I go alone; he that has received such a call as I have, can want no other, nor fear any danger."

They conversed on these points till they drew near the castle, when Joseph left them to go on his errand, and Edmund attended his Lord at dinner. The Baron observed that he was silent and reserved; the conversation languished on both sides. As soon as dinner was ended, Edmund asked permission to go up into his own apartment; where he packed up some necessaries, and made a hasty preparation for his departure.

Afterwards he walked into the garden, revolving in his mind the peculiarity of his situation, and the uncertainty of his future prospects; lost in thought, he walked to and fro in a covered walk, with his arms crossed and his eyes cast down, without perceiving that he was observed by two females who stood at a distance watching his motions. It was the Lady Emma, and her attendant, who were thus engaged. At length, he lifted up his eyes and saw them; he stood still, and was irresolute whether to advance or retire. They approached him; and, as they drew near, fair Emma spoke.

"You have been so wrapt in meditation, Edmund, that I am apprehensive of some new vexation that I am yet a stranger to. Would it were in my power to lessen those you have already! But tell me if I guess truly?"

He stood still irresolute, he answered with hesitation. "O, lady—I am—I am grieved, I am concerned, to be the cause of so much confusion in this noble family, to which I am so much indebted; I see no way to lessen these evils but to remove the cause of them."

"Meaning yourself?" said she.

"Certainly, Madam; and I was meditating on my departure."

"But," said she, "by your departure you will not remove the cause."

"How so, madam?"

"Because you are not the cause, but those you will leave behind you."

"Lady Emma!"

"How can you affect this ignorance, Edmund? You know well enough it is that odious Wenlock, your enemy and my aversion, that has caused all this mischief among us, and will much more, if he is not removed."

"This, madam, is a subject that it becomes me to be silent upon. Mr. Wenlock is your kinsman; he is not my friend; and for that reason I ought not to speak against him, nor you to hear it from me. If he has used me ill, I am recompensed by the generous treatment of my lord your father, who is all that is great and good; he has allowed me to justify myself to him, and he has restored me to his good opinion, which I prize among the best gifts of heaven. Your amiable brother William thinks well of me, and his esteem is infinitely dear to me; and you, excellent Lady, permit me to hope that you honour me with your good opinion. Are not these ample amends for the ill-will Mr. Wenlock bears me?"

"My opinion of you, Edmund," said she, "is fixed and settled. It is not founded upon events of yesterday, but upon long knowledge and experience; upon your whole conduct and character."

"You honour me, lady! Continue to think well of me, it will excite me to deserve it. When I am far distant from this place, the remembrance of your goodness will be a cordial to my heart."

"But why will you leave us, Edmund? Stay and defeat the designs of your enemy; you shall have my wishes and assistance."

"Pardon me, Madam, that is among the things I cannot do, even if it were in my power, which it is not. Mr. Wenlock loves you, lady, and if he is so unhappy as to be your aversion, that is a punishment severe enough. For the rest, I may be unfortunate by the wickedness of others, but if I am unworthy, it must be by my own fault."

"So then you think it is an unworthy action to oppose Mr. Wenlock! Very well, sir. Then I suppose you wish him success; you wish that I may be married to him?"

"I, Madam!" said Edmund, confused; "what am I that I should give my opinion on an affair of so much consequence? You distress me by the question. May you be happy! may you enjoy your own wishes!"

He sighed, he turned away. She called him back; he trembled, and kept silence.

She seemed to enjoy his confusion; she was cruel enough to repeat the question.

"Tell me, Edmund, and truly, do you wish to see me give my hand to Wenlock? I insist upon your answer."

All on a sudden he recovered both his voice and courage; he stepped forward, his person erect, his countenance assured, his voice resolute and intrepid.

"Since Lady Emma insists upon my answer, since she avows a dislike to Wenlock, since she condescends to ask my opinion, I will tell her my thoughts, my wishes."

The fair Emma now trembled in her turn; she blushed, looked down, and was ashamed to have spoken so freely.

Edmund went on. "My most ardent wishes are, that the fair Emma may reserve her heart and hand till a certain person, a friend of mine, is at liberty to solicit them; whose utmost ambition is, first to deserve, and then to obtain them."

"Your friend, Sir!" said Lady Emma! her brow clouded, her eye disdainful.

Edmund proceeded. "My friend is so particularly circumstanced that he cannot at present with propriety ask for Lady Emma's favour; but as soon as he has gained a cause that is yet in suspence, he will openly declare his pretensions, and if he is unsuccessful, he will then condemn himself to eternal silence."

Lady Emma knew not what to think of this declaration; she hoped, she feared, she meditated; but her attention was too strongly excited to be satisfied without some gratification; After a pause, she pursued the subject.

"And this friend of yours, sir, of what degree and fortune is he?"

Edmund smiled; but, commanding his emotion, he replied, "His birth is noble, his degree and fortune uncertain."

Her countenance fell, she sighed; he proceeded. "It is utterly impossible," said he, "for any man of inferior degree to aspire to Lady Emma's favour; her noble birth, the dignity of her beauty and virtues, must awe and keep at their proper distance, all men of inferior degree and merit; they may admire, they may revere; but they must not presume to approach too near, lest their presumption should meet with its punishment."

"Well, sir," said she, suddenly; "and so this friend of yours has commissioned you to speak in his behalf?"

"He has, Madam."

"Then I must tell you, that I think his assurance is very great, and yours not much less."

"I am sorry for that, Madam."

"Tell him, that I shall reserve my heart and hand for the man to whom my father shall bid me give them."

"Very well, Lady; I am certain my lord loves you too well to dispose of them against your inclination."

"How do you know that, sir? But tell him, that the man that hopes for my favour must apply to my lord for his."

"That is my friend's intention — his resolution, I should say — as soon as he can do it with propriety; and I accept your permission for him to do so."

"My permission did you say? I am astonished at your assurance! tell me no more of your friend; But perhaps you are pleading for Wenlock all this time; It is all one to me; only, say no more."

"Are you offended with me, madam?"

"No matter, sir."

"Yes, it is."

"I am surprised at you, Edmund."

"I am surprised at my own temerity; but, forgive me."

"It does not signify; good bye ty'e, sir."

"Don't leave me in anger, madam; I cannot bear that. Perhaps I may not see you again for a long time."

He looked afflicted; she turned back. "I do forgive you, Edmund; I was concerned for you; but, it seems, you are more concerned for every body than for yourself." She sighed; "Farewell!" said she.

Edmund gazed on her with tenderness; he approached her, he just touched her hand; his heart was rising to his lips, but he recollected his situation; he checked himself immediately; he retired back, he sighed deeply, bowed low, and hastily quitted her.

The lady turning into another walk, he reached the house first, and went up again to his chamber; he threw himself upon his knees; prayed for a thousand blessings upon every one of the family of his benefactor, and involuntarily wept at mentioning the name of the charming Emma, whom he was about to leave abruptly, and perhaps for ever. He then endeavoured to compose himself, and once more attended the Baron; wished him a good night; and withdrew to his chamber, till he was called upon to go again to the haunted apartment.

He came down equipped for his journey, and went hastily for fear of observation; he paid his customary devotions, and soon after Oswald tapped at the door. They conferred together upon the interesting subject that engrossed their attention, until Joseph came to them, who brought the rest of Edmund's baggage, and some refreshment for him before he set out. Edmund promised to give them the earliest information of his situation and success. At the hour of twelve they heard the same groans as the night before in the lower apartment; but, being somewhat familiarized to it, they were not so strongly affected. Oswald crossed himself, and prayed for the departed soul; he also prayed for Edmund, and recommended him to the Divine protection. He then arose, and embraced that young man; who, also, took a tender leave of his friend Joseph. They then went, with silence and caution, through a long gallery; they descended the stairs in the same manner; they crossed the hall in profound silence, and hardly dared to breathe, lest they should be overheard; they found some difficulty in opening one of the folding doors, which at last they accomplished; they were again in jeopardy at the outward gate. At length they conveyed him safely into the stables; there they again embraced him, and prayed for his prosperity.

He then mounted his horse, and set forward to Wyatt's cottage; he hallooed at the door, and was answered from within. In a few minutes John came out to him.

"What, is it you, Master Edmund?"

"Hush!" said he; "not a word of who I am; I go upon private business, and would not wish to be known."

"If you will go forward, sir, I will soon overtake you." He did so; and they pursued their journey to the north. In the mean time, Oswald and Joseph returned in silence into the house; they retired to their respective apartments without hearing or being heard by any one.

About the dawn of day Oswald intended to lay his packets in the way of those to whom they were addressed; after much contrivance he determined to take a bold step, and, if he were discovered, to frame some excuse. Encouraged by his late success, he went on tip-toe into Master William's chamber, placed a letter upon his pillow, and withdrew unheard. Exulting in his heart, he attempted the Baron's apartment, but found it fastened within. Finding this scheme frustrated, he waited till the hour the Baron was expected down to breakfast, and laid the letter and the key of the haunted apartment upon the table. Soon after, he saw the Baron enter the breakfast room; he got out of sight, but staid within call, preparing himself for a summons. The Baron sat down to breakfast; he saw a letter directed to himself—he opened it, and to his great surprise, read as follows:—

"The guardian of the haunted apartment to Baron Fitz-Owen. To thee I remit the key of my charge, until the right owner shall come, who will both discover and avenge my wrongs; then, woe be to the guilty!—But let the innocent rest in peace. In the mean time, let none presume to explore the secrets of my apartment, lest they suffer for their temerity."

The Baron was struck with amazement at the letter. He took up the key, examined it, then laid it down, and took up the letter; he was in such confusion of thought, he knew not what to do or say for several minutes. At length he called his servants about him; the first question he asked was—

"Where is Edmund?"

"They could not tell.

"Has he been called?"

"Yes, my Lord, but nobody answered, and the key was not in the door."

"Where is Joseph?"

"Gone into the stables."

"Where is father Oswald?"

"In his study."

"Seek him, and desire him to come hither."

By the time the Baron had read the letter over again, he came.

He had been framing a steady countenance to answer to all interrogatories. As he came in he attentively observed the Baron, whose features were in strong agitation; as soon as he saw Oswald, he spoke as one out of breath.

"Take that key, and read this letter!"

He did so, shrugged up his shoulders, and remained silent.

"Father," said my lord, "what think you of this letter?"

"It is a very surprising one."

"The contents are alarming. Where is Edmund?"

"I do not know."

"Has nobody seen him?"

"Not that I know of."

"Call my sons, my kinsmen, my servants."

The servants came in.

"Have any of you seen or heard of Edmund?"

"No," was the answer.

"Father, step upstairs to my sons and kinsmen, and desire them to come down immediately."

Oswald withdrew; and went, first, to Mr. William's chamber.

"My dear sir, you must come to my lord now directly—he has something extraordinary to communicate to you."

"And so have I, father—see what I have found upon my pillow!"

"Pray, sir, read it to me before you shew it to any body; my lord is alarmed too much already, and wants nothing to increase his consternation."

William read his letter, while Oswald looked as if he was an utter stranger to the contents, which were these:—

"Whatever may be heard or seen, let the seal of friendship be upon thy lips. The peasant Edmund is no more; but there still lives a man who hopes to acknowledge, and repay, the Lord Fitz-Owen's generous care and protection; to return his beloved William's vowed affection, and to claim his friendship on terms of equality."

"What," said William, "can this mean?"

"It is not easy to say," replied Oswald.

"Can you tell what is the cause of this alarm?"

"I can tell you nothing, but that my lord desires to see you directly—pray make haste down; I must go up to your brothers and kinsmen, nobody knows what to think, or believe."

Master William went down stairs, and Father Oswald went to the malcontents. As soon as he entered the outward door of their apartment, Mr. Wenlock called out. "Here comes the friend—now for some new proposal!"

"Gentlemen," said Oswald, "my lord desires your company immediately in the breakfast parlour."

"What! to meet your favourite Edmund, I suppose?" said Mr. Wenlock.

"No, sir."

"What, then, is the matter?" said Sir Robert.

"Something very extraordinary has happened, gentlemen. Edmund is not to be found—he disappeared from the haunted apartment, the key of which was conveyed to my lord in a strange manner, with a letter from an unknown hand; my lord is both surprised and concerned, and wishes to have your opinion and advice on the occasion."

"Tell him," said Sir Robert, "we will wait upon him immediately."

As Oswald went away, he heard Wenlock say, "So Edmund is gone, it is no matter how, or whither."

Another said, "I hope the ghost has taken him out of the way." The rest laughed at the conceit, as they followed Oswald down stairs. They found the Baron, and his son William,

171

commenting upon the key and the letter. My lord gave them to Sir Robert, who looked on them with marks of surprise and confusion.

The Baron addressed him—

"Is not this a very strange affair? Son Robert, lay aside your ill humours, and behave to your father with the respect and affection his tenderness deserves from you, and give me your advice and opinion on this alarming subject."

"My Lord," said Sir Robert, "I am as much confounded as yourself—I can give no advice—let my cousins see the letter—let us have their opinion."

They read it in turn—they were equally surprised; but when it came into Wenlock's hand, he paused and meditated some minutes.

At length—"I am indeed surprised, and still more concerned, to see my lord and uncle the dupe of an artful contrivance; and, if he will permit me, I shall endeavour to unriddle it, to the confusion of all that are concerned in it."

"Do so, Dick," said my lord, "and you shall have my thanks for it."

"This letter," said he, "I imagine to be the contrivance of Edmund, or some ingenious friend of his, to conceal some designs they have against the peace of this family, which has been too often disturbed upon that rascal's account."

"But what end could be proposed by it?" said the Baron.

"Why, one part of the scheme is to cover Edmund's departure, that is clear enough; for the rest, we can only guess at it—perhaps he may be concealed somewhere in that apartment, from whence he may rush out in the night, and either rob or murder us; or, at least, alarm and terrify the family."

The Baron smiled.

"You shoot beyond the mark, sir, and overshoot yourself, as you have done before now; you shew only your inveteracy against that poor lad, whom you cannot mention with temper. To what purpose should he shut himself up there, to be starved?"

"Starved! no, no! he has friends in this house (looking at Oswald), who will not suffer him to want anything; those who have always magnified his virtues, and extenuated his faults, will lend a hand to help him in time of need; and, perhaps, to assist his ingenious contrivances."

Oswald shrugged up his shoulders, and remained silent.

"This is a strange fancy of yours, Dick," said my lord; "but I am willing to pursue it,—first, to discover what you drive at; and, secondly, to satisfy all that are here present of the truth or falsehood of it, that they may know what value to set upon your sagacity hereafter. Let us all go over that apartment together; and let Joseph be called to attend us thither."

Oswald offered to call him, but Wenlock stopped him. "No, father," said he, "you must stay with us; we want your ghostly counsel and advice; Joseph shall have no private conference with you."

"What mean you," said Oswald, "to insinuate to my lord against me or Joseph? But your ill-will spares nobody. It will one day be known who is the disturber of the peace of this family; I wait for that time, and am silent."

Joseph came; when he was told whither they were going, he looked hard at Oswald. Wenlock observed them.

"Lead the way, father," said he, "and Joseph shall follow us."

Oswald smiled.

"We will go where Heaven permits us," said he; "alas! the wisdom of man can neither hasten, nor retard, its decrees."

They followed the father up stairs, and went directly to the haunted apartment. The Baron unlocked the door; he bid Joseph open the shutters, and admit the daylight, which had been excluded for many years. They went over the rooms above stairs, and then descended the staircase, and through the lower rooms in the same manner. However, they overlooked the closet, in which the fatal secret was concealed; the door was covered with tapestry, the same as the room, and united so well that it seemed but one piece. Wenlock tauntingly desired Father Oswald to introduce them to the ghost. The father, in reply, asked them where they should find Edmund. "Do you think," said he, "that he lies hid in my pocket, or in Joseph's?"

"'Tis no matter," answered he; "thoughts are free."

"My opinion of you, Sir," said Oswald, "is not founded upon thoughts—I judge of men by their actions,—a rule, I believe, it will not suit you to be tried by."

"None of your insolent admonitions, father!" returned Wenlock; "this is neither the time nor the place for them."

"That is truer than you are aware of, sir; I meant not to enter into the subject just now."

"Be silent," said my Lord.

"I shall enter into this subject with you hereafter—then look you be prepared for it. In the mean time, do you, Dick Wenlock, answer to my questions:—Do you think Edmund is concealed in this apartment?"

"No, sir."

"Do you think there is any mystery in it?"

"No, my lord."

"Is it haunted, think you?"

"No, I think not."

"Should you be afraid to try?"

"In what manner, my lord?"

"Why, you have shewn your wit upon the subject, and I mean to show your courage;—you, and Jack Markham your confident, shall sleep here three nights, as Edmund has done before."

"Sir," said Sir Robert, "for what purpose? I should be glad to understand why."

"I have my reasons, sir, as well as your kinsmen there. No reply, Sirs! I insist upon being obeyed in this point. Joseph, let the beds be well aired, and every thing made agreeable to the gentlemen; If there is any contrivance to impose upon me, they, I am sure, will have pleasure in detecting it; and, if not, I shall obtain my end in making these rooms habitable. Oswald, come with me; and the rest may go where they list till dinner-time."

The Baron went with Oswald into the parlour.

"Now tell me, father," said he, "do you disapprove what I have done?"

"Quite the contrary, my lord," said he; "I entirely approve it."

"But you do not know all my reasons for it. Yesterday Edmund's behaviour was different from what I have ever seen it—he is naturally frank and open in all his ways; but he was then silent, thoughtful, absent; he sighed deeply, and once I saw tears stand in his eyes. Now, I do suspect there is something uncommon in that apartment—that Edmund has discovered the secret; and, fearing to disclose it, he is fled away from the house. As to this letter, perhaps he may have written it to hint that there is more than he dares reveal; I tremble at the hints contained in it, though I shall appear to make light of it. But I and mine are innocent; and if Heaven discloses the guilt of others, I ought to adore and submit to its decrees."

"That is prudently and piously resolved, my lord; let us do our duty, and leave events to Heaven."

"But, father, I have a further view in obliging my kinsmen to sleep there:—if any thing should appear to them, it is better that it should only be known to my own family; if there is nothing in it, I shall put to the proof the courage and veracity of my two kinsmen, of whom I think very indifferently. I mean shortly to enquire into many things I have heard lately to their disadvantage; and, if I find them guilty, they shall not escape with impunity."

"My lord," said Oswald, "you judge like yourself; I wish you to make enquiry concerning them, and believe the result will be to their confusion, and your Lordship will be enabled to re-establish the peace of your family."

During this conversation, Oswald was upon his guard, lest any thing should escape that might create suspicion. He withdrew as soon as he could with decency, and left the Baron meditating what all these things should mean; he feared there was some misfortune impending over his house, though he knew not from what cause.

He dined with his children and kinsmen, and strove to appear cheerful; but a gloom was perceivable through his deportment. Sir Robert was reserved and respectful; Mr.

William was silent and attentive; the rest of the family dutifully assiduous to my Lord; only Wenlock and Markham were sullen and chagrined. The Baron detained the young men the whole afternoon; he strove to amuse and to be amused; he shewed the greatest affection and parental regard to his children, and endeavoured to conciliate their affections, and engage their gratitude by kindness. Wenlock and Markham felt their courage abate as the night approached; At the hour of nine, old Joseph came to conduct them to the haunted apartment; they took leave of their kinsmen, and went up stairs with heavy hearts.

They found the chamber set in order for them, and a table spread with provision and good liquor to keep up their spirits.

"It seems," said Wenlock, "that your friend Edmund was obliged to you for his accommodations here."

"Sir," said Joseph, "his accommodations were bad enough the first night; but, afterwards, they were bettered by my lord's orders."

"Owing to your officious cares?" said Wenlock.

"I own it," said Joseph, "and I am not ashamed of it."

"Are you not anxious to know what is become of him?" said Markham.

"Not at all, sir; I trust he is in the best protection; so good a young man as he is, is safe everywhere."

"You see, cousin Jack," said Wenlock, "how this villain has stole the hearts of my uncle's servants; I suppose this canting old fellow knows where he is, if the truth were known."

"Have you any further commands for me, gentlemen?" said the old man.

"No, not we."

"Then I am ordered to attend my lord, when you have done with me."

"Go, then, about your business."

Joseph went away, glad to be dismissed.

"What shall we do, cousin Jack," said Wenlock, "to pass

away the time? — it is plaguy dull sitting here."

"Dull enough," said Markham, "I think the best thing we can do, is to go to bed and sleep it away."

"Faith!" says Wenlock, "I am in no disposition to sleep. Who would have thought the old man would have obliged us to spend the night here?"

"Don't say us, I beg of you; it was all your own doing," replied Markham.

"I did not intend he should have taken me at my word."

"Then you should have spoken more cautiously. I have always been governed by you, like a fool as I am; you play the braggart, and I suffer for it; But they begin to see through your fine-spun arts and contrivances, and I believe you will meet with your deserts one day or other."

"What now? do you mean to affront me, Jack? Know, that some are born to plan, others to execute; I am one of the former, thou of the latter. Know your friend, or —"

"Or what?" replied Markham; "do you mean to threaten me? If you do!"

"What then?" said Wenlock.

"Why, then, I will try which of us two is the best man, sir!"

Upon this Markham arose, and put himself into a posture of defence. Wenlock perceiving he was serious in his anger, began to soothe him; he persuaded, he flattered, he promised great things if he would be composed. Markham was sullen, uneasy, resentful; whenever he spoke, it was to upbraid Wenlock with his treachery and falsehood. Wenlock tried all his eloquence to get him into a good humour, but in vain; he threatened to acquaint his uncle with all that he knew, and to exculpate himself at the other's expence. Wenlock began to find his choler rise; they were both almost choaked with rage; and, at length, they both rose with a resolution to fight.

As they stood with their fists clenched, on a sudden they were alarmed with a dismal groan from the room underneath. They stood like statues petrified by fear, yet listening with trembling expectation. A second groan increased their consternation; and, soon after, a third completed it. They staggered to a seat, and sunk down upon it, ready to faint. Presently, all the doors flew open, a pale glimmering light appeared at the door, from the staircase, and a man in complete armour entered the room. He stood, with one hand extended, pointing to the outward door; they took the hint, and crawled away as fast as fear would let them; they staggered along the gallery, and from thence to the Baron's apartment, where Wenlock sunk down in a swoon, and Markham had just strength enough to knock at the door.

The servant who slept in the outward room alarmed his lord.

Markham cried out, "For Heaven's sake, let us in!"

Upon hearing his voice, the door was opened, and Markham approached his Uncle in such an attitude of fear, as excited a degree of it in the Baron. He pointed to Wenlock, who was with some difficulty recovered from the fit he was fallen into; the servant was terrified, he rung the alarm-bell; the servants came running from all parts to their Lord's apartment; The young gentlemen came likewise, and presently all was confusion, and the terror was universal. Oswald, who guessed the business, was the only one that could question them. He asked several times,

"What is the matter?"

Markham, at last, answered him, "We have seen the ghost!"

All regard to secrecy was now at an end; the echo ran through the whole family — "They have seen the ghost!"

The Baron desired Oswald to talk to the young men, and endeavour to quiet the disturbance. He came forward; he comforted some, he rebuked others; he had the servants retire into the outward room. The Baron, with his sons and kinsmen, remained in the bed-chamber.

"It is very unfortunate," said Oswald, "that this affair should be made so public; surely these young men might have related what they had seen, without alarming the whole family. I am very much concerned upon my lord's account."

"I thank you, father," said the Baron; "but prudence was quite overthrown here. Wenlock was half dead, and Markham half distracted; the family were alarmed without my being able to prevent it. But let us hear what these poor terrified creatures say."

Oswald demanded, "What have you seen, gentlemen?"

"The ghost!" said Markham.

"In what form did it appear?"

"A man in armour."

"Did it speak to you?"

"No."

"What did it do to terrify you so much?"

"It stood at the farthest door, and pointed to the outward door, as if to have us leave the room; we did not wait for a second notice, but came away as fast as we could."

"Did it follow you?"

"No."

"Then you need not have raised such a disturbance."

Wenlock lifted up his head, and spoke—

"I believe, father, if you had been with us, you would not have stood upon ceremonies any more than we did. I wish my lord would send you to parley with the ghost; for, without doubt, you are better qualified than we."

"My Lord," said Oswald, "I will go thither, with your permission; I will see that every thing is safe, and bring the key back to you; Perhaps this may help to dispel the fears that have been raised—at least, I will try to do it."

"I thank you, father, for your good offices—do as you please."

Oswald went into the outward room. "I am going," said he, "to shut up the apartment. The young gentlemen have been more frightened than they had occasion for; I will try to account for it. Which of you will go with me?"

They all drew back, except Joseph, who offered to bear him company. They went into the bedroom in the haunted apartment, and found every thing quiet there. They put out the fire, extinguished the lights, locked the door, and brought away the key. As they returned, "I thought how it would be," said Joseph.

"Hush! not a word," said Oswald; "you find we are suspected of something, though they know not what. Wait till you are called upon, and then we will both speak to purpose." They carried the key to the Baron.

"All is quiet in the apartment," said Oswald, "as we can testify."

"Did you ask Joseph to go with you," said the Baron, "or did he offer himself?"

"My Lord, I asked if any body would go with me, and they all declined it but he; I thought proper to have a witness beside myself, for whatever might be seen or heard."

"Joseph, you were servant to the late Lord Lovel; what kind of man was he?"

"A very comely man, please your lordship."

"Should you know him if you were to see him?"

"I cannot say, my lord."

"Would you have any objection to sleep a night in that apartment?"

"I beg," — "I hope," — "I beseech your lordship not to command me to do it!"

"You are then afraid; why did you offer yourself to go thither?"

"Because I was not so much frightened as the rest."

"I wish you would lie a night there; but I do not insist upon it."

"My lord, I am a poor ignorant old man, not fit for such an undertaking; beside, if I should see the ghost, and if it should be the person of my master, and if it should tell me any thing, and bid me keep it secret, I should not dare to disclose it; and then, what service should I do your lordship?"

"That is true, indeed," said the Baron.

"This speech," said Sir Robert, "is both a simple and an artful one. You see, however, that Joseph is not a man for us to depend upon; he regards the Lord Lovel, though dead, more than Lord Fitz-Owen, living; he calls him his master, and promises to keep his secrets. What say you, father, Is the ghost your master, or your friend? Are you under any obligation to keep his secrets?"

"Sir," said Oswald, "I answer as Joseph does; I would sooner die than discover a secret revealed in that manner."

"I thought as much," said Sir Robert; "there is a mystery in Father Oswald's behaviour, that I cannot comprehend."

"Do not reflect upon the father," said the Baron; "I have no cause to complain of him; perhaps the mystery may be too soon explained; but let us not anticipate evils. Oswald and Joseph have spoken like good men; I am satisfied with their answers; let us, who are innocent, rest in peace; and let us endeavour to restore peace in the family; and do you, father, assist us."

"With my best services," said Oswald. He called the servants in. "Let nothing be mentioned out of doors," said he, "of what has lately passed within, especially in the east apartment; the young gentlemen had not so much reason to be frightened as they apprehended; a piece of furniture fell down in the rooms underneath, which made the noise that alarmed them so much; but I can certify that all things in the rooms are in quiet, and there is nothing to fear. All of you attend me in the chapel in an hour; do your duties, put your trust in God, and obey your Lord, and you will find every thing go right as it used to do."

They dispersed; the sun rose, the day came on, and every thing went on in the usual course; but the servants were not so easily satisfied; they whispered that something was wrong, and expected the time that should set all right. The mind of the Baron was employed in meditating upon these circumstances, that seemed to him the forerunners of some great events; he sometimes thought of Edmund; he sighed for his expulsion, and lamented the uncertainty of his fate; but, to his family, he appeared easy and satisfied.

From the time of Edmund's departure, the fair Emma had many uneasy hours; she wished to enquire after him, but feared to shew any solicitude concerning him. The next day, when her brother William came into her apartment, she took courage to ask a question.

"Pray, brother, can you give any guess what is become of Edmund?"

"No," said he, with a sigh; "why do you ask me?"

"Because, my dear William, I should think if any body knew, it must be you; and I thought he loved you too well to leave you in ignorance. But don't you think he left the castle in a very strange manner?"

"I do, my dear; there is a mystery in every circumstance of his departure; Nevertheless (I will trust you with a secret), he did not leave the castle without making a distinction in my favour."

"I thought so," said she; "but you might tell me what you know about him."

"Alas, my dear Emma! I know nothing. When I saw him last, he seemed a good deal affected, as if he were taking leave of me; and I had a foreboding that we parted for a longer time than usual."

"Ah! so had I," said she, "when he parted from me in the garden."

"What leave did he take of you, Emma?"

She blushed, and hesitated to tell him all that passed between them; but he begged, persuaded, insisted; and, at length, under the strongest injunctions of secrecy, she told him all.

He said, "That Edmund's behaviour on that occasion was as mysterious as the rest of his conduct; but, now you have revealed your secret, you have a right to know mine."

He then gave her the letter he found upon his pillow; she read it with great emotion.

"Saint Winifred assist me!" said she; "what can I think? 'The peasant Edmund is no more, but there lives one,'—that is to my thinking, Edmund lives, but is no peasant."

"Go on, my dear," said William; "I like your explanation."

"Nay, brother, I only guess; but what think you?"

"I believe we think alike in more than one respect, that he meant to recommend no other person than himself to your favour; and, if he were indeed of noble birth, I would prefer him to a prince for a husband to my Emma!"

"Bless me!" said she, "do you think it possible that he should be of either birth or fortune?"

"It is hard to say what is impossible! we have proof that the east apartment is haunted. It was there that Edmund was made acquainted with many secrets, I doubt not: and, perhaps, his own fate may be involved in that of others. I am confident that what he saw and heard there, was the cause of his departure. We must wait with patience the unravelling this intricate affair; I believe I need not enjoin your secrecy as to what I have said; your heart will be my security."

"What mean you, brother?"

"Don't affect ignorance, my dear; you love Edmund, so do I; it is nothing to be ashamed of. It would have been strange, if a girl of your good sense had not distinguished a swan among a flock of geese."

"Dear William, don't let a word of this escape you; but you have taken a weight off my heart. You may depend that I will not dispose of my hand or heart till I know the end of this affair."

William smiled: "Keep them for Edmund's friend; I shall rejoice to see him in a situation to ask them."

"Hush, my brother! not a word more; I hear footsteps."

They were her eldest brother's, who came to ask Mr. William to ride out with him, which finished the conference.

The fair Emma from this time assumed an air of satisfaction; and William frequently stole away from his companions to talk with his sister upon their favourite subject.

While these things passed at the castle of Lovel, Edmund and his companion John Wyatt proceeded on their journey to Sir Philip Harclay's seat; they conversed together on the way, and Edmund found him a man of understanding, though not improved by education; he also discovered that John loved his master, and respected him even to veneration; from him he learned many particulars concerning that worthy knight. Wyatt told him, "That Sir Philip maintained twelve old soldiers who had been maimed and disabled in the wars, and had no provision made for them; also six old officers, who had been unfortunate, and were grown grey without preferment; he likewise mentioned the Greek gentleman, his master's captive and friend, as a man eminent for valour and piety; but, beside these," said Wyatt, "there are many others who eat of my master's bread and drink of his cup, and who join in blessings and prayers to Heaven for their noble benefactor; his ears are ever open to distress, his hand to relieve it, and he shares in every good man's joys and blessings."

"Oh, what a glorious character!" said Edmund; "how my heart throbs with wishes to imitate such a man! Oh, that I might resemble him, though at ever so great a distance!"

Edmund was never weary of hearing the actions of this truly great man, nor Wyatt with relating them; and, during three days journey, there were but few pauses in their conversation.

The fourth day, when they came within view of the house, Edmund's heart began to raise doubts of his reception. "If," said he, "Sir Philip should not receive me kindly, if he should resent my long neglect, and disown my acquaintance, it would be no more than justice."

He sent Wyatt before, to notify his arrival to Sir Philip, while he waited at the gate, full of doubts and anxieties concerning his reception. Wyatt was met and congratulated on his return by most of his fellow-servants. He asked —

"Where is my master?"

"In the parlour."

"Are any strangers with him?"

"No, only his own family."

"Then I will shew myself to him."

He presented himself before Sir Philip.

"So, John," said he, "you are welcome home! I hope you left your parents and relations well?"

"All well, thank God! and send their humble duty to your honour, and they pray for you every day of their lives. I hope your honour is in good health."

"Very well."

"Thank God for that! but, sir, I have something further to tell you; I have had a companion all the way home, a person who comes to wait on your honour, on business of great consequence, as he says."

"Who is that, John?"

"It is Master Edmund Twyford, from the castle of Lovel."

"Young Edmund!" says Sir Philip, surprised; "where is he?"

"At the gate, sir."

"Why did you leave him there?"

"Because he bade me come before, and acquaint your honour, that he waits your pleasure."

"Bring him hither," said Sir Philip; "tell him I shall be glad to see him."

John made haste to deliver his message, and Edmund followed him in silence into Sir Philip's presence.

He bowed low, and kept at a distance. Sir Philip held out his hand, and bad him approach. As he drew near, he was seized with an universal trembling; he kneeled down, took his hand, kissed it, and pressed it to his heart in silence.

"You are welcome, young man!" said Sir Philip; "take courage, and speak for yourself."

Edmund sighed deeply; he at length broke silence with difficulty. "I am come thus far, noble sir, to throw myself at your feet, and implore your protection. You are, under God, my only reliance."

"I receive you," said Sir Philip, "with all my heart! Your person is greatly improved since I saw you last, and I hope your mind is equally so; I have heard a great character of you from some that knew you in France. I remember the promise I made you long ago, and am ready now to fulfil it, upon condition that you have done nothing to disgrace the good opinion I formerly entertained of you; and am ready to serve you in any thing consistent with my own honour."

Edmund kissed the hand that was extended to raise him. "I accept your favour, sir, upon this condition only; and if ever you find me to impose upon your credulity, or incroach on your goodness, may you renounce me from that moment!"

"Enough," said Sir Philip; "rise, then, and let me embrace you; You are truly welcome!"

"Oh, noble sir!" said Edmund, "I have a strange story to tell you; but it must be by ourselves, with only heaven to bear witness to what passes between us."

"Very well," said Sir Philip; "I am ready to hear you; but first, go and get some refreshment after your journey, and then come to me again. John Wyatt will attend you."

"I want no refreshment," said Edmund; "and I cannot eat or drink till I have told my business to your honour."

"Well then," said Sir Philip, "come along with me." He took the youth by the hand, and led him into another parlour, leaving his friends in great surprise, what this young man's errand could be; John Wyatt told them all that he knew relating to Edmund's birth, character, and situation.

When Sir Philip had seated his young friend, he listened in silence to the surprising tale he had to tell him. Edmund told him briefly the most remarkable circumstances of his life, from the time when he first saw and liked him, till his return from France; but from that era, he related at large every thing that had happened, recounting every interesting particular, which was imprinted on his memory in strong and lasting characters. Sir Philip grew every moment more affected by the recital; sometimes he clasped his hands together, he lifted them up to heaven, he smote his breast, he sighed, he exclaimed aloud; when Edmund related his dream, he breathed short, and seemed to devour him with attention; when he described the fatal closet, he trembled, sighed, sobbed, and was almost suffocated with his agitation. But when he related all that passed between his supposed mother and himself, and finally produced the jewels, the proofs of his birth, and the death of his unfortunate mother, he flew to him, he pressed him to his bosom, he strove to speak, but speech was for some minutes denied. He wept aloud; and, at length, his words found their way in broken exclamations.

"Son of my dearest friend! Dear and precious relic of a noble house! child of Providence! the beloved of heaven! welcome! thrice welcome to my arms! to my heart! I will be thy parent from henceforward, and thou shalt be indeed my child, my heir! My mind told me from the first moment I beheld thee, that thou wert the image of my friend! my heart then opened itself to receive thee, as his offspring. I had a strange foreboding that I was to be thy protector. I would then have made thee my own; but heaven orders things for the best; it made thee the instrument of this discovery, and in its own time and manner conducted thee to my arms. Praise be to God for his wonderful doings towards the children of men! every thing that has befallen thee is by his direction, and he will not leave his work unfinished; I trust that I shall be his instrument to do justice on the guilty, and to restore the orphan of my friend to his rights and title. I devote myself to this service, and will make it the business of my life to effect it."

Edmund gave vent to his emotions, in raptures of joy and gratitude. They spent several hours in this way, without thinking of the time that passed; the one enquiring, the other explaining, and repeating, every particular of the interesting story.

At length they were interrupted by the careful John Wyatt, who was anxious to know if any thing was likely to give trouble to his master.

"Sir," said John, "it grows dark—do you want a light?"

"We want no light but what heaven gives us," said Sir Philip; "I knew not whether it was dark or light."

"I hope," said John, "nothing has happened, I hope your honour has heard no bad tidings; I—I—I hope no offence."

"None at all," said the good knight; "I am obliged to your solicitude for me; I have heard some things that grieve me, and others that give me great pleasure; but the sorrows are past, and the joys remain."

"Thank God!" said John; "I was afraid something was the matter to give your honour trouble."

"I thank you, my good servant! You see this young gentleman; I would have you, John, devote yourself to his service; I give you to him for an attendant on his person, and would have you show your affection to me by your attachment to him."

"Oh, Sir!" said John in a melancholy voice, "what have I done to be turned out of your service?"

"No such matter, John," said Sir Philip; "you will not leave my service."

"Sir," said John, "I would rather die than leave you."

"And, my lad, I like you too well to part with you; but in serving my friend you will serve me. Know, that this young man is my son."

"Your son, sir!" said John.

"Not my natural son, but my relation; my son by adoption, my heir!"

"And will he live with you, sir?"

"Yes, John; and I hope to die with him."

"Oh, then, I will serve him with all my heart and soul; and I will do my best to please you both."

"I thank you, John, and I will not forget your honest love and duty. I have so good an opinion of you, that I will tell you of some things concerning this gentleman that will entitle him to your respect."

"'Tis enough for me," said John, "to know that your honour respects him, to make me pay him as much duty as yourself."

"But, John, when you know him better, you will respect him still more; at present, I shall only tell you what he is not; for you think him only the son of Andrew Twyford."

"And is he not?" said John.

"No, but his wife nursed him, and he passed for her son."

"And does old Twyford know it, sir?"

"He does, and will bear witness to it; but he is the son of a near friend of mine, of quality superior to my own, and as such you must serve and respect him."

"I shall, to be sure, sir; but what name shall I call him?"

"You shall know that hereafter; in the mean time bring a light, and wait on us to the other parlour."

When John was withdrawn, Sir Philip said, "That is a point to be considered and determined immediately; It is proper that you should assume a name till you can take that of your father; for I choose you should drop that of your foster-father; and I would have you be called by one that is respectable."

"In that, and every other point, I will be wholly governed by you, sir," said Edmund.

"Well then, I will give you the name of Seagrave; I shall say that you are a relation of my own; and my mother was really of that family."

John soon returned, and attended them into the other parlour; Sir Philip entered, with Edmund in his hand.

"My friends," said he, "this gentleman is Mr. Edward Seagrave, the son of a dear friend and relation of mine. He was lost in his infancy, brought up by a good woman out of pure humanity, and is but lately restored to his own family. The circumstances shall be made known hereafter; In the meantime, I have taken him under my care and protection, and will use all my power and interest to see him restored to his fortune, which is enjoyed by the usurper who was the cause of his expulsion, and the death of his parents. Receive him as my relation, and friend; Zadisky, do you embrace him first. Edmund, you and this gentleman must love each other for my sake; hereafter you will do it for your own.["] They all rose; each embraced and congratulated the young man.

Zadisky said, "Sir, whatever griefs and misfortunes you may have endured, you may reckon them at an end, from the hour you are beloved and protected by Sir Philip Harclay."

"I firmly believe it, sir," replied Edmund; "and my heart enjoys, already, more happiness than I ever yet felt, and promises me all that I can wish in future; his friendship is the earnest Heaven gives me of its blessings hereafter."

They sat down to supper with mutual cheerfulness; and Edmund enjoyed the repast with more satisfaction than he had felt a long time. Sir Philip saw his countenance brighten up, and looked on him with heart-felt pleasure.

"Every time I look on you," said he, "reminds me of your father; you are the same person I loved twenty-three years ago—I rejoice to see you under my roof. Go to your repose early, and to-morrow we will consult farther."

Edmund withdrew, and enjoyed a night of sweet undisturbed repose.

The next morning Edmund arose in perfect health and spirits: he waited on his benefactor. They were soon after joined by Zadisky, who shewed great attention and respect to the youth, and offered him his best services without reserve. Edmund accepted them with equal respect and modesty; and finding himself at ease, began to display his amiable qualities. They breakfasted together; afterwards, Sir Philip desired Edmund to walk out with him.

As soon as they were out of hearing, Sir Philip said, "I could not sleep last night for thinking of your affairs; I laid schemes for you, and rejected them again. We must lay our plan before we begin to act. What shall be done with this treacherous kinsman! this inhuman monster! this assassin of his nearest relation? I will risk my life and fortune to bring him to justice. Shall I go to court, and demand justice of the king? or shall I accuse him of the murder, and make him stand a public trial? If I treat him as a baron of the realm, he must be tried by his peers; if as a commoner, he must be tried at the county assize; but we must shew reason why he should be degraded from his title. Have you any thing to propose?"

"Nothing, sir; I have only to wish that it might be as private as possible, for the sake of my noble benefactor, the Lord Fitz-Owen, upon whom some part of the family disgrace would naturally fall; and that would be an ill return for all his kindness and generosity to me."

"That is a generous and grateful consideration on your part; but you owe still more to the memory of your injured parents. However, there is yet another way that suits me better than any hitherto proposed; I will challenge the traitor to meet me in the field; and, if he has spirit enough to answer my call, I will there bring him to justice; if not, I will bring him to a public trial."

"No, sir," said Edmund, "that is my province. Should I stand by and see my noble, gallant friend expose his life for me, I should be unworthy to bear the name of that friend whom you so much lament. It will become his son to vindicate his name, and revenge his death. I will be the challenger, and no other."

"And do you think he will answer the challenge of an unknown youth, with nothing but his pretensions to his name and title? Certainly not. Leave this matter to me; I will think of a way that will oblige him to meet me at the house of a third person who is known to all the parties concerned, and where we will have authentic witnesses of all that passes between him and me. I will devise the time, place, and manner, and satisfy all your scruples."

Edmund offered to reply; but Sir Philip bad him be silent, and let him proceed in his own way.

He then led him over his estate, and shewed him every thing deserving his notice; he told him all the particulars of his domestic economy, and they returned home in time to meet their friends at dinner.

They spent several days in consulting how to bring Sir Walter to account, and in improving their friendship and confidence in each other. Edmund endeared himself so much to his friend and patron, that he declared him his adopted son and heir before all his friends and servants, and ordered them to respect him as such. He every day improved their love and regard for him, and became the darling of the whole family.

After much consideration, Sir Philip fixed his resolutions, and began to execute his purposes. He set out for the seat of the Lord Clifford, attended by Edmund, M. Zadisky, and two servants. Lord Clifford received them with kindness and hospitality.

Sir Philip presented Edmund to Lord Clifford and his family, as his near relation and presumptive heir; They spent the evening in the pleasures of convivial mirth and hospitable entertainment. The next day Sir Philip began to open his mind to Lord Clifford, informing him that both his young friend and himself had received great injuries from the present Lord Lovel, for which they were resolved to call him to account; but that, for many reasons, they were desirous to have proper witnesses of all that should pass between them, and begging the favour of his Lordship to be the principal one. Lord Clifford acknowledged the confidence placed in him; and besought Sir Philip to let him be the arbitrator between them. Sir Philip assured him, that their wrongs would not admit of arbitration, as he should hereafter judge; but that he was unwilling to explain them further till he knew certainly whether or not the Lord Lovel would meet him; for, if he refused, he must take another method with him.

Lord Clifford was desirous to know the grounds of the quarrel; but Sir Philip declined entering into particulars at present, assuring him of a full information hereafter. He then sent M. Zadisky, attended by John Wyatt, and a servant of Lord Clifford, with a letter to Lord Lovel; the contents were as follow: —

"My Lord Lovel, — Sir Philip Harclay earnestly desires to see you at the house of Lord Clifford, where he waits to call you to account for the injuries done by you to the late Arthur Lord Lovel, your kinsman; If you accept his demand, he will make the Lord Clifford a witness and a judge of the cause; if not, he will expose you publicly as a traitor and a coward. Please to answer this letter, and he will acquaint you with the time, place, and manner of the meeting.

"PHILIP HARCLAY."

Zadisky presented the letter to Lord Lovel, informing him that he was the friend of Sir Philip Harclay. He seemed surprised and confounded at the contents; but, putting on an haughty air, "I know nothing," said he, "of the business this letter hints at; but wait a few hours, and I will give you an answer." He gave orders to treat Zadisky as a gentleman in every respect, except in avoiding his company; for the Greek had a shrewd and penetrating aspect, and he observed every turn of his countenance. The next day he came and apologized for his absence, and gave him the answer; sending his respects to the Lord Clifford. The messengers returned with all speed, and Sir Philip read the answer before all present.

"Lord Lovel knows not of any injuries done by him to the late Arthur Lord Lovel, whom he succeeded by just right of inheritance; nor of any right Sir Philip Harclay has, to call to account a man to whom he is barely known, having seen him only once, many years ago, at the house of his uncle, the old Lord Lovel: Nevertheless, Lord Lovel will not suffer any man to call his name and honour into question with impunity; for which reason he will meet Sir Philip Harclay at any time, place, and in what manner he shall appoint, bringing the same number of friends and dependents, that justice may be done to all parties.

"LOVEL."

"'Tis well," said Sir Philip; "I am glad to find he has the spirit to meet me; he is an enemy worthy of my sword."

Lord Clifford then proposed that both parties should pass the borders, and obtain leave of the warden of the Scottish marches to decide the quarrel in his jurisdiction, with a select number of friends on both sides. Sir Philip agreed to the proposal; and Lord Clifford wrote in his own name to ask permission of the Lord Graham, that his friends might come there; and obtained it, on condition that neither party should exceed a limited number of friends and followers.

Lord Clifford sent chosen messengers to Lord Lovel, acquainting him with the conditions, and appointing the time, place, and manner of their meeting, and that he had been desired to accept the office of judge of the field. Lord Lovel accepted the conditions, and promised to be there without fail. Lord Clifford notified the same to Lord Graham, warden of the marches, who caused a piece of ground to be inclosed for the lists, and made preparations against the day appointed.

In the interim, Sir Philip Harclay thought proper to settle his worldly affairs. He made Zadisky acquainted with every circumstance of Edmund's history, and the obligation that lay upon him to revenge the death of his friend, and see justice done to his heir. Zadisky entered into the cause with an ardour that spoke the affection he bore to his friend.

"Why," said he, "would you not suffer me to engage this traitor? Your life is of too much consequence to be staked against his; but though I trust that the justice of your cause must succeed, yet, if it should happen otherwise, I vow to revenge you; he shall never go back from us both. However, my hope and trust is, to see your arm the minister of justice."

Sir Philip then sent for a lawyer and made his will, by which he appointed Edmund his chief heir, by the name of

Lovel, alias Seagrave, alias Twyford; he ordered that all his old friends, soldiers, and servants, should be maintained in the same manner during their lives; he left to Zadisky an annuity of an hundred a year, and a legacy of two hundred pounds; one hundred pounds to a certain monastery; the same sum to be distributed among disbanded soldiers, and the same to the poor and needy in his neighbourhood.

He appointed Lord Clifford joint executor with Edmund, and gave his will into that nobleman's care, recommending Edmund to his favour and protection.

"If I live," said he, "I will make him appear to be worthy of it; if I die, he will want a friend. I am desirous your lordship, as a judge of the field, should be unprejudiced on either side, that you may judge impartially. If I die, Edmund's pretensions die with me; but my friend Zadisky will acquaint you with the foundation of them. I take these precautions, because I ought to be prepared for every thing; but my heart is warm with better hopes, and I trust I shall live to justify my own cause, as well as that of my friend, who is a person of more consequence than he appears to be."

Lord Clifford accepted the trust, and expressed the greatest reliance upon Sir Philip's honour and veracity.

While these preparations were making for the great event that was to decide the pretensions of Edmund, his enemies at the Castle of Lovel were brought to shame for their behaviour to him.

The disagreement between Wenlock and Markham had by degrees brought on an explanation of some parts of their conduct. Father Oswald had often hinted to the Baron, Wenlock's envy of Edmund's superior qualities, and the artifices by which he had obtained such an influence with Sir Robert, as to make him take his part upon all occasions. Oswald now took advantage of the breach between these two incendiaries, to persuade Markham to justify himself at Wenlock's expence, and to tell all he knew of his wickedness; at length, he promised to declare all he knew of Wenlock's conduct, as well in France as since their return, when he should be called upon; and, by him, Oswald was enabled to unravel the whole of his contrivances, against the honour, interest, and even life of Edmund.

He prevailed on Hewson, and Kemp, his associate, to add their testimony to the others. Hewson confessed that he was touched in his conscience, when he reflected on the cruelty and injustice of his behaviour to Edmund, whose behaviour towards him, after he had laid a snare for his life, was so noble and generous, that he was cut to the heart by it, and had suffered so much pain and remorse, that he longed for nothing so much as an opportunity to unburden his mind; but the dread of Mr. Wenlock's anger, and the effects of his resentment, had hitherto kept him silent, always hoping there would come a time, when he might have leave to declare the whole truth.

Oswald conveyed this information to the Baron's ear, who waited for an opportunity to make the proper use of it. Not long after, the two principal incendiaries came to an open rupture, and Markham threatened Wenlock that he would shew his uncle what a serpent he had harboured in his bosom. The Baron arrested his words, and insisted upon his telling all he knew; adding, —

"If you speak the truth, I will support you; but if you prove false, I will punish you severely. As to Mr. Wenlock, he shall have a fair trial; and, if all the accusations I have heard are made good, it is high time that I should put him out of my family."

The Baron, with a stern aspect, bade them follow him into the great hall; and sent for all the rest of the family together.

He then, with great solemnity, told them he was ready to hear all sides of the question. He declared the whole substance of his informations, and called upon the accusers to support the charge. Hewson and Kemp gave the same account they had done to Oswald, offering to swear to the truth of their testimony; several of the other servants related such circumstances as had come to their knowledge. Markham then spoke of every thing, and gave a particular account of all that had passed on the night they spent in the east apartment; he accused himself of being privy to Wenlock's villany, called himself fool and blockhead for being the instrument of his malignant disposition, and asked pardon of his uncle for concealing it so long.

The Baron called upon Wenlock to reply to the charge; who, instead of answering, flew into a passion, raged, swore, threatened, and finally denied every thing. The witnesses persisted in their assertions. Markham desired leave to make known the reason why they were all afraid of him.

"He gives it out," said he, "that he is to be my lord's son-in-law; and they, supposing him to stand first in his favour, are afraid of his displeasure."

"I hope," said the Baron, "I shall not be at such a loss for a son-in-law, as to make choice of such a one as him; he never but once hinted at such a thing, and then I gave him no encouragement. I have long seen there was something very wrong in him; but I did not believe he was of so wicked a disposition; It is no wonder that princes should be so frequently deceived, when I, a private man, could be so much imposed upon within the circle of my own family. What think you, son Robert?"

"I, sir, have been much more imposed on; and I take shame to myself on the occasion."

"Enough, my son," said the Baron; "a generous confession is only a proof of growing wisdom. You are now sensible, that the best of us are liable to imposition. The artifices of this unworthy kinsman have set us at variance with each other, and driven away an excellent youth from this house, to go I know not whither; but he shall no longer triumph in his wickedness; he shall feel what it is to be banished from the house of his protector. He shall set out for his mother's this very day; I will write to her in such a manner as shall inform her that he has offended me, without particularising the nature of his faults; I will give him an opportunity of recovering his credit with his own family, and this shall be my security against his doing further mischief. May he repent, and be forgiven.

"Markham deserves punishment, but not in the same degree."

"I confess it," said he, "and will submit to whatever your lordship shall enjoin."

"You shall only be banished for a time, but he for ever. I will send you abroad on a business that shall put you in a way to do credit to yourself, and service to me. Son Robert, have you any objection to my sentence?"

"My Lord," said he, "I have great reason to distrust myself; I am sensible of my own weakness, and your superior wisdom, as well as goodness; and I will henceforward submit to you in all things."

The Baron ordered two of his servants to pack up Wenlock's clothes and necessaries, and to set out with him that very day; he bade some others keep an eye upon him lest he should escape; As soon as they were ready, my Lord wished him a good journey, and gave him a letter for his mother. He departed without saying a word, in a sullen kind of resentment, but his countenance shewed the inward agitations of his mind.

As soon as he was gone, every mouth was opened against him; a thousand stories came out that they never heard before; The Baron and his sons were astonished that he should go on so long without detection. My lord sighed deeply at the thoughts of Edmund's expulsion, and ardently wished to know what was become of him.

Sir Robert took the opportunity of coming to an explanation with his brother William; he took shame to himself for some part of his past behaviour. Mr. William owned his affection to Edmund, and justified it by his merit and attachment to him, which were such that he was certain no time or distance could alter them. He accepted his brother's acknowledgement, as a full amends for all that had passed, and begged that henceforward an entire love and confidence might ever subsist between them. These new regulations restored peace, confidence, and harmony, in the Castle of Lovel.

At length, the day arrived for the combatants to meet. The Lord Graham, with twelve followers gentlemen, and twelve servants, was ready at the dawn of day to receive them.

The first that entered the field, was Sir Philip Harclay, knight, armed completely, excepting his head-piece; Hugh Rugby, his esquire, bearing his lance; John Barnard, his page, carrying his helmet and spurs; and two servants in his proper livery. The next came Edmund, the heir of Lovel, followed by his servant John Wyatt; Zadisky, followed by his servant.

At a short distance came the Lord Clifford, as judge of the field, with his esquire, two pages, and two livery-servants; followed by his eldest son, his nephew, and a gentleman his friend, each attended by one servant; He also brought a surgeon of note to take care of the wounded.

The Lord Graham saluted them; and, by his order, they took their places without the lists, and the trumpet sounded for the challenger. It was answered by the defendant, who soon after appeared, attended by three gentlemen his friends, with each one servant, beside his own proper attendants.

A place was erected for the Lord Clifford, as judge of the field; he desired Lord Graham would share the office, who accepted it, on condition that the combatants should make no objection, and they agreed to it with the greatest courtesy and respect. They consulted together on many points of honour and ceremony between the two combatants.

They appointed a marshal of the field, and other inferior officers, usually employed on these occasions. The Lord Graham sent the marshal for the challenger, desiring him to declare the cause of his quarrel before his enemy. Sir Philip Harclay then advanced, and thus spoke:

"I, Philip Harclay, knight, challenge Walter, commonly called Lord Lovel, as a base, treacherous, and bloody man, who, by his wicked arts and devices, did kill, or cause to be killed, his kinsman, Arthur Lord Lovel, my dear and noble friend. I am called upon, in an extraordinary manner, to revenge his death; and I will prove the truth of what I have affirmed at the peril of my life."

Lord Graham then bade the defendant answer to the charge. Lord Lovel stood forth before his followers, and thus replied:

"I, Walter, Baron of Lovel, do deny the charge against me, and affirm it to be a base, false, and malicious accusation of this Sir Philip Harclay, which I believe to be invented by himself, or else framed by some enemy, and told to him for wicked ends; but, be that as it may, I will maintain my own honour, and prove him to be a false traitor, at the hazard of my own life, and to the punishment of his presumption."

Then said the Lord Graham, "will not this quarrel admit of arbitration?"

"No," replied Sir Philip; "when I have justified this charge, I have more to bring against him. I trust in God and the justice of my cause, and defy that traitor to the death!"

Lord Clifford then spoke a few words to Lord Graham, who immediately called to the marshal, and bade him open the lists, and deliver their weapons to the combatants.

While the marshal was arranging the combatants and their followers, Edmund approached his friend and patron; he put one knee to the ground, he embraced his knees with the strongest emotions of grief and anxiety. He was dressed in complete armour, with his visor down; his device was a hawthorn, with a graft of the rose upon it, the motto—This is not my true parent; but Sir Philip bade him take these words—E fructu arbor cognoscitur.

Sir Philip embraced the youth with strong marks of affection. "Be composed, my child!" said he; "I have neither guilt, fear, nor doubt in me; I am so certain of success, that I bid you be prepared for the consequence."

Zadisky embraced his friend, he comforted Edmund, he suggested every thing that could confirm his hopes of success.

The marshal waited to deliver the spear to Sir Philip; he now presented it with the usual form.

"Sir, receive your lance, and God defend the right!"

Sir Philip answered, "Amen!" in a voice that was heard by all present.

He next presented his weapon to Lord Lovel with the same sentence, who likewise answered "Amen!" with a good courage. Immediately the lists were cleared, and the combatants began to fight.

They contended a long time with equal skill and courage; at length Sir Philip unhorsed his antagonist. The judges ordered, that either he should alight, or suffer his enemy to remount; he chose the former, and a short combat on foot ensued. The sweat ran off their bodies with the violence of the exercise. Sir Philip watched every motion of his enemy, and strove to weary him out, intending to wound, but not to kill him, unless obliged for his own safety.

He thrust his sword through his left arm, and demanded, whether he would confess the fact? Lord Lovel enraged, answered, he would die sooner. Sir Philip then passed the sword through his body twice, and Lord Lovel fell, crying out that he was slain.

"I hope not," said Sir Philip, "for I have a great deal of business for you to do before you die: confess your sins, and endeavour to atone for them, as the only ground to hope for pardon."

Lord Lovel replied, "You are the victor, use your good fortune generously!"

Sir Philip took away his sword, and then waved it over his head, and beckoned for assistance. The judges sent to beg Sir Philip to spare the life of his enemy.

"I will," said he, "upon condition that he will make an honest confession."

Lord Lovel desired a surgeon and a confessor.

"You shall have both," said Sir Philip; "but you must first answer me a question or two. Did you kill your kinsman or not?"

"It was not my hand that killed him," answered the wounded man.

"It was done by your own order, however? You shall have no assistance till you answer this point."

"It was," said he, "and Heaven is just!"

"Bear witness all present," said Sir Philip; "he confesses the fact!"

He then beckoned Edmund, who approached.

"Take off your helmet," said he; "look on that youth, he is the son of your injured kinsman."

"It is himself!" said the Lord Lovel, and fainted away.

Sir Philip then called for a surgeon and a priest, both of which Lord Graham had provided; the former began to bind up his wounds, and his assistants poured a cordial into his mouth. "Preserve his life, if it be possible," said Sir Philip; "for much depends upon it."

He then took Edmund by the hand, and presented him to all the company. "In this young man," said he, "you see the true heir of the house of Lovel! Heaven has in its own way made him the instrument to discover the death of his parents. His father was assassinated by order of that wicked man, who now receives his punishment; his mother was, by his cruel treatment, compelled to leave her own house; she was delivered in the fields, and perished herself in seeking a shelter for her infant. I have sufficient proofs of every thing I say, which I am ready to communicate to every person who desires to know the particulars. Heaven, by my hand, has chastised him; he has confessed the fact I accuse him of, and it remains that he make restitution of the fortune and honours he hath usurped so long."

Edmund kneeled, and with uplifted hands returned thanks to Heaven, that his noble friend and champion was crowned with victory. The lords and gentlemen gathered round them, they congratulated them both; while Lord Lovel's friends and followers were employed in taking care of him. Lord Clifford took Sir Philip's hand.

"You have acted with so much honour and prudence, that it is presumptuous to offer you advice; but what mean you to do with the wounded man?"

"I have not determined," said he; "I thank you for the hint, and beg your advice how to proceed."

"Let us consult Lord Graham," replied he.

Lord Graham insisted upon their going all to his castle: "There," said he, "you will have impartial witnesses of all that passes." Sir Philip was unwilling to give so much trouble. The Lord Graham protested he should be proud to do any service to so noble a gentleman. Lord Clifford enforced his request, saying, it was better upon all accounts to keep their prisoner on this side the borders till they saw what turn his health would take, and to keep him safely till he had settled his worldly affairs.

This resolution being taken, Lord Graham invited the wounded man and his friends to his castle, as being the nearest place where he could be lodged and taken proper care of, it being dangerous to carry him further. They accepted the proposal with many acknowledgements; and, having made a kind of litter of boughs, they all proceeded to Lord Graham's castle, where they put Lord Lovel to bed, and the surgeon dressed his wounds, and desired he might be kept quiet, not knowing at present whether they were dangerous or not.

About an hour after, the wounded man complained of thirst; he asked for the surgeon, and enquired if his life was in danger? The surgeon answered him doubtfully. He asked—

"Where is Sir Philip Harclay?"

"In the castle."

"Where is that young man whom he calls the heir of Lovel?"

"He is here, too."

"Then I am surrounded with my enemies. I want to speak to one of my own servants, without witnesses; let one be sent to me."

The surgeon withdrew, and acquainted the gentlemen below. "He shall not speak to any man," said Sir Philip, "but in my presence." He went with him into the sick man's room. Upon the sight of Sir Philip, he seemed in great agitation.

"Am I not allowed to speak with my own servant?" said he.

"Yes, sir, you may; but not without witnesses."

"Then I am a prisoner, it seems?"

"No, not so, sir; but some caution is necessary at present. But compose yourself, I do not wish for your death."

"Then why did you seek it? I never injured you."

"Yes, you have, in the person of my friend, and I am only the instrument of justice in the hand of Heaven; endeavour to make atonement while life is spared to you. Shall I send the priest to you? perhaps he may convince you of the necessity of restitution, in order to obtain forgiveness of your sins."

Sir Philip sent for the priest and the surgeon, and obliged the servant to retire with him. "I leave you, sir, to the care of these gentlemen; and whenever a third person is admitted, I will be his attendant; I will visit you again within an hour."

He then retired, and consulted his friends below; they were of opinion that no time should be lost. "You will then," said he, "accompany me into the sick man's apartment in an hour's time."

Within the hour, Sir Philip, attended by Lord Clifford and Lord Graham, entered the chamber. Lord Lovel was in great emotion; the priest stood on one side of the bed, the surgeon on the other; the former exhorted him to confess his sins, the other desired he might be left to his repose. Lord Lovel seemed in great anguish of mind; he trembled, and was in the utmost confusion. Sir Philip intreated him, with the piety of a confessor, to consider his soul's health before that of his body. He then asked Sir Philip, by what means he knew that he was concerned in the death of his kinsman?

"Sir," replied he, "it was not merely by human means this fact was discovered. There is a certain apartment in the Castle of Lovel, that has been shut up these one and twenty years, but has lately been opened and examined into."

"O Heaven!" exclaimed he, "then Geoffry must have betrayed me!"

"No, sir, he has not; it was revealed in a very extraordinary manner to that youth whom it most concerns."

"How can he be the heir of Lovel?"

"By being the son of that unfortunate woman, whom you cruelly obliged to leave her own house, to avoid being compelled to wed the murderer of her husband: we are not ignorant, moreover, of the fictitious funeral you made for her. All is discovered, and you will not tell us any more than we know already; but we desire to have it confirmed by your confession."

"The judgments of Heaven are fallen upon me!" said Lord Lovel. "I am childless, and one is arisen from the grave to claim my inheritance."

"Nothing, then, hinders you to do justice and make restitution; it is for the ease of your conscience; and you have no other way of making atonement for all the mischief you have done."

"You know too much," said the criminal, "and I will relate what you do not know."

"You may remember," proceeded he, "that I saw you once at my uncle's house?"

"I well remember it."

"At that time my mind was disturbed by the baleful passion of envy; it was from that root all my bad actions sprung."

"Praise be to God!" said the good priest; "he hath touched your heart with true contrition, and you shew the effect of his mercies; you will do justice, and you will be rewarded by the gift of repentance unto salvation."

Sir Philip desired the penitent to proceed.

"My kinsman excelled me in every kind of merit, in the graces of person and mind, in all his exercises, and in every accomplishment. I was totally eclipsed by him, and I hated to be in his company; but what finished my aversion, was his addressing the lady upon whom I had fixed my affections. I strove to rival him there, but she gave him the preference that, indeed, was only his due; but I could not bear to see, or acknowledge, it.

"The most bitter hatred took possession of my breast, and I vowed to revenge the supposed injury as soon as opportunity should offer. I buried my resentment deep in my heart, and outwardly appeared to rejoice at his success. I made a merit of resigning my pretensions to him, but I could not bear to be present at his nuptials; I retired to my father's seat, and brooded over my revenge in secret. My father died this year, and soon after my uncle followed him; within another year my kinsman was summoned to attend the king on his Welch expedition.

"As soon as I heard he was gone from home, I resolved to prevent his return, exulting in the prospect of possessing his title, fortune, and his lady. I hired messengers, who were constantly going and coming to give me intelligence of all that passed at the castle; I went there soon after, under pretence of visiting my kinsman. My spies brought me an account of all that happened; one informed me of the event of the battle, but could not tell whether my rival was living or dead; I hoped the latter, that I might avoid the crime I meditated. I reported his death to his Lady, who took it very heavily.

"Soon after a messenger arrived with tidings that he was alive and well, and had obtained leave to return home immediately.

"I instantly dispatched my two emissaries to intercept him on the way. He made so much haste to return, that he was met within a mile of his own castle; he had out-rode his servants, and was alone. They killed him, and drew him aside out of the highway. They then came to me with all speed, and desired my orders; it was then about sunset. I sent them back to fetch the dead body, which they brought privately into the castle: they tied it neck and heels, and put it into a trunk, which they buried under the floor in the closet you mentioned. The sight of the body stung me to the heart; I then felt the pangs of remorse, but it was too late; I took every precaution that prudence suggested to prevent the discovery; but nothing can be concealed from the eye of Heaven.

"From that fatal hour I have never known peace, always in fear of something impending to discover my guilt, and to bring me to shame; at length I am overtaken by justice. I am brought to a severe reckoning here, and I dread to meet one more severe hereafter."

"Enough," said the priest; "you have done a good work, my son! trust in the Lord; and, now this burden is off your mind, the rest will be made easy to you."

Lord Lovel took a minute's repose, and then went on.

"I hope by the hint you gave, Sir Philip, the poor lady is yet alive?"

"No, sir, she is not; but she died not till after she brought forth a son, whom Heaven made its instrument to discover and avenge the death of both his parents."

"They are well avenged!" said he. "I have no children to lament for me; all mine have been taken from me in the bloom of youth; only one daughter lived to be twelve years old; I intended her for a wife for one of my nephews, but within three months I have buried her." He sighed, wept, and was silent.

The gentlemen present lifted up their hands and eyes to Heaven in silence.

"The will of Heaven be obeyed!" said the priest. "My penitent hath confessed all; what more would you require?"

"That he make atonement," said Sir Philip; "that he surrender the title and estate to the right heir, and dispose of his own proper fortune to his nearest relations, and resign himself to penitence and preparation for a future state. For this time I leave him with you, father, and will join my prayers with yours for his repentance."

So saying, he left the room, and was followed by the Barons and the surgeon; the priest alone remaining with him. As soon as they were out of hearing, Sir Philip questioned the surgeon concerning his patient's situation; who answered, that at present he saw no signs of immediate danger, but he could not yet pronounce that there was none.

"If he were mortally wounded," said he, "he could not be so well, nor speak so long without faintness; and it is my opinion that he will soon recover, if nothing happens to retard the cure."

"Then," said Sir Philip, "keep this opinion from him; for I would suffer the fear of death to operate on him until he hath performed some necessary acts of justice. Let it only be known to these noblemen, upon whose honour I can rely, and I trust they will approve my request to you, sir."

"I join in it," said Lord Clifford, "from the same motives."

"I insist upon it," said Lord Graham; "and I can answer for my surgeon's discretion."

"My lords," said the surgeon, "you may depend on my fidelity; and, after what I have just heard, my conscience is engaged in this noble gentleman's behalf, and I will do every thing in my power to second your intentions."

"I thank you, sir," said Sir Philip, "and you may depend on my gratitude in return. I presume you will sit up with him to-night; if any danger should arise, I desire to be called immediately; but, otherwise, I would suffer him to rest quietly, that he may be prepared for the business of the following day."

"I shall obey your directions, sir; my necessary attendance will give me a pretence not to leave him, and thus I shall hear all that passes between him and all that visit him."

"You will oblige me highly," said Sir Philip, "and I shall go to rest with confidence in your care."

The surgeon returned to the sick man's chamber, Sir Philip and the Barons to the company below: they supped in the great hall, with all the gentlemen that were present at the combat. Sir Philip and his Edmund retired to their repose, being heartily fatigued; and the company staid to a late hour, commenting upon the action of the day, praising the courage and generosity of the noble knight, and wishing a good event to his undertaking.

Most of Lord Lovel's friends went away as soon as they saw him safely lodged, being ashamed of him, and of their appearance in his behalf; and the few that stayed were induced by their desire of a further information of the base action he had committed, and to justify their own characters and conduct.

The next morning Sir Philip entered into consultation with the two Barons, on the methods he should take to get Edmund received, and acknowledged, as heir of the house of Lovel. They were all of opinion, that the criminal should be kept in fear till he had settled his worldly affairs, and they had resolved how to dispose of him. With this determination they entered his room, and enquired of the surgeon how he had passed the night. He shook his head, and said but little.

Lord Lovel desired that he might be removed to his own house. Lord Graham said, he could not consent to that, as there was evident danger in removing him; and appealed to the surgeon, who confirmed his opinion. Lord Graham desired he would make himself easy, and that he should have every kind of assistance there.

Sir Philip then proposed to send for the Lord Fitz-Owen, who would see that all possible care was taken of his brother-in-law, and would assist him in settling his affairs. Lord Lovel was against it; he was peevish and uneasy, and desired to be left with only his own servants to attend him. Sir Philip quitted the room with a significant look; and the two Lords endeavoured to reconcile him to his situation. He interrupted them. "It is easy for men in your situation to advise, but it is difficult for one in mine to practise; wounded in body and mind, it is natural that I should strive to avoid the extremes of shame and punishment; I thank you for your kind offices, and beg I may be left with my own servants."

"With them, and the surgeon, you shall," said Lord Graham; and they both retired.

Sir Philip met them below. "My lords," said he, "I am desirous that my Lord Fitz-Owen should be sent for, and that he may hear his brother's confession; for I suspect that he may hereafter deny, what only the fear of death has extorted from him; with your permission I am determined to send messengers to-day."

They both expressed approbation, and Lord Clifford proposed to write to him, saying, a letter from an impartial person will have the more weight; I will send one of my principal domestics with your own. This measure being resolved upon, Lord Clifford retired to write, and Sir Philip to prepare his servants for instant departure. Edmund desired leave to write to father Oswald, and John Wyatt was ordered to be the bearer of his letter. When the Lord Clifford had finished his letter, he read it to Sir Philip and his chosen friends, as follows:—

"RIGHT HON. MY GOOD LORD,—I have taken upon me to acquaint your Lordship, that there has been a solemn combat at arms between your brother-in-law, the Lord Lovel, and Sir Philip Harclay, Knt. of Yorkshire. It was fought in the jurisdiction of the Lord Graham, who, with myself, was appointed judge of the field; it was fairly won, and Sir Philip is the conqueror. After he had gained the victory he declared at large the cause of the quarrel, and that he had revenged the death of Arthur Lord Lovel his friend, whom the present Lord Lovel had assassinated, that he might enjoy his title and estate. The wounded man confessed the fact; and Sir Philip gave him his life, and only carried off his sword as a trophy of his victory. Both the victor and the vanquished were conveyed to Lord Graham's castle, where the Lord Lovel now lies in great danger. He is desirous to settle his worldly affairs, and to make his peace with God and man. Sir Philip Harclay says there is a male heir of the house of Lovel, for whom he claims the title and estate; but he is very desirous that your Lordship should be present at the disposal of your brother's property that of right belongs to him, of which your children are the undoubted heirs. He also wants to consult you in many other points of honour and equity. Let me intreat you, on the receipt of this letter, to set out immediately for Lord Graham's castle, where you will be received with the utmost respect and hospitality. You will hear things that will surprise you as much as they do me; you will judge of them with that justice and honour that speaks your character; and you will unite with us in wondering at the ways of Providence, and submitting to its decrees, in punishing the guilty, and doing justice to the innocent and oppressed. My best wishes and prayers attend you and your hopeful family. My lord, I remain your humble servant,

"CLIFFORD."

Every one present expressed the highest approbation of this letter. Sir Philip gave orders to John Wyatt to be very circumspect in his behaviour, to give Edmund's letter privately to father Oswald, and to make no mention of him, or his pretensions to Lovel Castle.

Lord Clifford gave his servant the requisite precautions. Lord Graham added a note of invitation, and sent it by a servant of his own. As soon as all things were ready, the messengers set out with all speed for the Castle of Lovel.

They stayed no longer by the way than to take some refreshment, but rode night and day till they arrived there.

Lord Fitz-Owen was in the parlour with his children; Father Oswald was walking in the avenue before the house, when he saw three messengers whose horses seemed jaded, and the riders fatigued, like men come a long journey. He came up, just as the first had delivered his message to the porter. John Wyatt knew him; he dismounted, and made signs that he had something to say to him; he retired back a few steps, and John, with great dexterity, slipped a letter into his hand. The father gave him his blessing, and a welcome.

"Who do you come from?" said he aloud.

"From the Lords Graham and Clifford to the Lord Fitz-Owen; and we bring letters of consequence to the Baron."

Oswald followed the messengers into the hall; a servant announced their arrival. Lord Fitz-Owen received them in the parlour; Lord Clifford's servant delivered his master's letter, Lord Graham's his, and they said they would retire and wait his Lordship's answer. The Baron ordered them some refreshment. They retired, and he opened his letters. He read them with great agitations, he struck his hand upon his heart, he exclaimed, "My fears are all verified! the blow is struck, and it has fallen upon the guilty!"

Oswald came in a minute after.

"You are come in good time," said the Baron. "Read that letter, that my children may know the contents."

He read it, with faultering voice, and trembling limbs. They were all in great surprise. William looked down, and kept a studied silence. Sir Robert exclaimed—

"Is it possible? can my uncle be guilty of such an action?"

"You hear," said the Baron, "he has confessed it!"

"But to whom?" said Sir Robert.

His father replied, "Lord Clifford's honour is unquestionable, and I cannot doubt what he affirms."

Sir Robert leaned his head upon his hand, as one lost in thought; at length he seemed to awake.

"My Lord, I have no doubt that Edmund is at the bottom of this business. Do you not remember that Sir Philip Harclay long ago promised him his friendship? Edmund disappears; and, soon after, this man challenges my Uncle. You know what passed here before his departure; He has suggested this affair to Sir Philip, and instigated him to this action. This is the return he has made for the favours he has received from our family, to which he owes every thing!"

"Softly, my son!" said the Baron; "let us be cautious of reflecting upon Edmund; there is a greater hand in this business. My conjecture was too true; It was in that fatal apartment that he was made acquainted with the circumstances of Lord Lovel's death; he was, perhaps, enjoined to reveal them to Sir Philip Harclay, the bosom friend of the deceased. The mystery of that apartment is disclosed, the woe to the guilty is accomplished! There is no reflection upon any one; Heaven effects its purposes in its own time and manner. I and mine are innocent; let us worship, and be silent!"

"But what do you propose to do?" said Sir Robert.

"To return with the messengers," answered the Baron. "I think it highly proper that I should see your Uncle, and hear what he has to say; my children are his heirs; in justice to them, I ought to be acquainted with every thing that concerns the disposal of his fortune."

"Your Lordship is in the right," answered Sir Robert, "it concerns us all. I have only to ask your permission to bear you company."

"With all my heart," said the Baron; "I have only to ask of you in return, that you will command yourself, and not speak your mind hastily; wait for the proofs before you give judgment, and take advice of your reason before you decide upon any thing; if you reflect upon the past, you will find reason to distrust yourself. Leave all to me, and be assured I will protect your honour and my own."

"I will obey you in all things, my lord; and will make immediate preparation for our departure." So saying, he left the room.

As soon as he was gone, Mr. William broke silence.

"My Lord," said he, "if you have no great objection, I beg leave also to accompany you both."

"You shall, my son, if you desire it; I think I can see your motives, and your brother's also; your coolness will be a good balance to his warmth; you shall go with us. My son Walter shall be his sister's protector in our absence, and he shall be master here till we return."

"I hope, my dear father, that will not be long; I shall not be happy till you come home," said the fair Emma.

"It shall be no longer, my dearest, than till this untoward affair is settled."

The Baron desired to know when the messengers were expected to return. Oswald took this opportunity to retire; he went to his own apartment, and read the letter, as follows:—

"The Heir of Lovel, to his dear and reverend friend, father Oswald.

"Let my friends at the Castle of Lovel know that I live in hopes one day to see them there. If you could by any means return with the messengers, your testimony would add weight to mine; perhaps you might obtain permission to attend the Baron; I leave it to you to manage this. John Wyatt will inform you of all that has passed here, and that hitherto my success has outrun my expectation, and, almost, my wishes. I am in the high road to my inheritance; and trust that the Power who hath conducted me thus far, will not leave his work unfinished. Tell my beloved William, that I live, and hope to embrace him before long. I recommend myself to your holy prayers and blessing, and remain your son and servant, Edmund."

Oswald then went to the messengers; he drew John Wyatt to a distance from the rest, and got the information he wanted. He stayed with him till he was sent for by the Baron, to whom he went directly, and prevented his questions, by saying, "I have been talking with the messengers; I find they have travelled night and day to bring the letters with all speed; they only require one night's rest, and will be ready to set out with you to-morrow."

"'Tis well," said the Baron; "we will set out as soon as they are ready."

"My Lord," said Oswald, "I have a favour to beg of you; it is, that I may attend you; I have seen the progress of this wonderful discovery, and I have a great desire to see the conclusion of it; perhaps my presence may be of service in the course of your business."

"Perhaps it may," said the Baron; "I have no objection, if you desire to go."

They then separated, and went to prepare for their journey.

Oswald had a private interview with Joseph, whom he informed of all that he knew, and his resolution to attend the Baron in his journey to the north.

"I go," said he, "to bear witness in behalf of injured innocence. If it be needful, I shall call upon you; therefore hold yourself in readiness in case you should be sent for."

"That I will," said Joseph, "and spend my last remains of life and strength, to help my young lord to his right and title. But do they not begin to suspect who is the heir of Lovel?"

"Not in the least," said Oswald; "they think him concerned in the discovery, but have no idea of his being interested in the event."

"Oh, father!" said Joseph, "I shall think every day a week till your return; but I will no longer keep you from your repose."

"Good night," said Oswald; "but I have another visit to pay before I go to rest."

He left Joseph, and went on tip-toe to Mr. William's room, and tapped at his door. He came and opened it. "What news, father?"

"Not much; I have only orders to tell you that Edmund is well, and as much your friend as ever."

"I guessed," said William, "that we should hear something of him. I have still another guess."

"What is that, my child?"

"That we shall see or hear of him where we are going."

"It is very likely," said Oswald; "and I would have you be prepared for it;—I am confident we shall hear nothing to his discredit."

"I am certain of that," said William, "and I shall rejoice to see him; I conclude that he is under the protection of Sir Philip Harclay."

"He is so," said Oswald; "I had my information from Sir Philip's servant, who is one of the messengers, and was guide to the others in their way hither."

After some farther conversation they separated, and each went to his repose.

The next morning the whole party set out on their journey; they travelled by easy stages on account of the Baron's health, which began to be impaired, and arrived in health and spirits at the castle of Lord Graham, where they were received with the utmost respect and kindness by the noble master.

The Lord Lovel had recovered his health and strength as much as possible in the time, and was impatient to be gone from thence to his own house. He was surprised to hear of the arrival of his brother and nephews, and expressed no pleasure at the thoughts of seeing them. When Sir Philip Harclay came to pay his respects to Baron Fitz-Owen, the latter received him with civility, but with a coldness that was apparent. Sir Robert left the room, doubting his resolution. Sir Philip advanced, and took the Baron by the hand.

"My Lord," said he, "I rejoice to see you here. I cannot be satisfied with the bare civilities of such a man as you. I aspire to your esteem, to your friendship, and I shall not be happy till I obtain them. I will make you the judge of every part of my conduct, and where you shall condemn me, I will condemn myself."

The Baron was softened, his noble heart felt its alliance with its counterpart, but he thought the situation of his brother demanded some reserve towards the man who sought his life; but, in spite of himself, it wore off every moment. Lord Clifford related all that had passed, with the due regard to Sir Philip's honour; he remarked how nobly he concealed the cause of his resentment against the Lord Lovel till the day of combat, that he might not prepossess the judges against him. He enlarged on his humanity to the vanquished, on the desire he expressed to have justice done to his heirs; finally, he mentioned his great respect for the Lord Fitz-Owen, and the solicitude he shewed to have him come to settle the estate of the sick man in favour of his children. Lord Clifford also employed his son to soften Sir Robert, and to explain to him every doubtful part of Sir Philip's behaviour.

213

After the travellers had taken some rest, the Lord Graham proposed that they should make a visit to the sick man's chamber. The lords sent to acquaint him they were coming to visit him, and they followed the messenger. The Lord Fitz-Owen went up to the bedside; he embraced his brother with strong emotions of concern. Sir Robert followed him; then Mr. William.

Lord Lovel embraced them, but said nothing; his countenance shewed his inward agitations. "Lord Fitz-Owen first broke silence.

"I hope," said he, "I see my brother better than I expected?"

Lord Lovel bit his fingers, he pulled the bed-clothes, he seemed almost distracted; at length he broke out—

"I owe no thanks to those who sent for my relations! Sir Philip Harclay, you have used ungenerously the advantage you have gained over me! you spared my life, only to take away my reputation. You have exposed me to strangers, and, what is worse, to my dearest friends; when I lay in a state of danger, you obliged me to say any thing, and now you take advantage of it, to ruin me in my friends' affection. But, if I recover, you may repent it!"

Sir Philip then came forward.

"My Lords, I shall take no notice of what this unhappy man has just now said; I shall appeal to you, as to the honourable witnesses of all that has passed; you see it was no more than necessary. I appeal to you for the motives of my treatment of him, before, at, and after our meeting. I did not take his life, as I might have done; I wished him to repent of his sins, and to make restitution of what he unjustly possesses. I was called out to do an act of justice; I had taken the heir of Lovel under my protection, my chief view was to see justice done to him;—what regarded this man was but a secondary motive. This was my end, and I will never, never lose sight of it."

Lord Lovel seemed almost choaked with passion, to see every one giving some mark of approbation and respect to Sir Philip. He called out—

"I demand to know who is this pretended heir, whom he brings out to claim my title and fortune?"

"My noble auditors," said Sir Philip, "I shall appeal to your

214

judgment, in regard to the proofs of my ward's birth and family; every circumstance shall be laid before you, and you shall decide upon them.

"Here is a young man, supposed the son of a peasant, who, by a train of circumstances that could not have happened by human contrivance, discovers not only who were his real parents, but that they came to untimely deaths. He even discovers the different places where their bones are buried, both out of consecrated ground, and appeals to their ashes for the truth of his pretensions. He has also living proofs to offer, that will convince the most incredulous. I have deferred entering into particulars, till the arrival of Baron Fitz-Owen. I know his noble heart and honourable character, from one that has long been an eye-witness of his goodness; such is the opinion I have of his justice, that I will accept him as one of the judges in his brother's cause. I and my ward will bring our proofs before him, and the company here present; in the course of them, it will appear that he is the best qualified of any to judge of them, because he can ascertain many of the facts we shall have occasion to mention. I will rest our cause upon their decision."

Lord Graham applauded Sir Philip's appeal, affirming his own impartiality, and calling upon Lord Clifford and his son, and also his own nephews who were present. Lord Clifford said—

"Sir Philip offers fairly, and like himself; there can be no place nor persons more impartial than the present, and I presume the Lord Lovel can have no objection."

"No objection!" answered he; "what, to be tried like a criminal, to have judges appointed over me, to decide upon my right to my own estate and title? I will not submit to such a jurisdiction!"

"Then," said Sir Philip, "you had rather be tried by the laws of the land, and have them pronounce sentence upon you? Take your choice, sir; if you refuse the one, you shall be certain of the other."

Lord Clifford then said—"You will allow Lord Lovel to consider of the proposal; he will consult his friends, and be determined by their advice."

Lord Fitz-Owen said—"I am very much surprised at what I have heard. I should be glad to know all that Sir Philip Harclay has to say for his ward, that I may judge what my brother has to hope or fear; I will then give my best advice, or offer my mediation, as he may stand in need of them."

"You say well," replied Lord Graham, "and pray let us come directly to the point; Sir Philip, you will introduce your ward to this company, and enter upon your proofs."

Sir Philip bowed to the company; he went out and brought in Edmund, encouraging him by the way; he presented him to Baron Fitz-Owen, who looked very serious.

"Edmund Twyford," said he, "are you the heir of the house of Lovel?"

"I am, my Lord," said Edmund, bowing to the ground; "the proofs will appear; but I am, at the same time, the most humble and grateful of all your servants, and the servant of your virtues."

Sir Robert rose up, and was going to leave the room.

"Son Robert, stay," said the Baron; "if there is any fraud, you will be pleased to detect it, and, if all that is affirmed be true, you will not shut your eyes against the light; you are concerned in this business; hear it in silence, and let reason be arbiter in your cause."

He bowed to his father, bit his lip, and retired to the window. William nodded to Edmund, and was silent. All the company had their eyes fixed on the young man, who stood in the midst, casting down his eyes with modest respect to the audience; while Sir Philip related all the material circumstances of his life, the wonderful gradation by which he came to the knowledge of his birth, the adventures of the haunted apartment, the discovery of the fatal closet, and the presumptive proofs that Lord Lovel was buried there. At this part of his narration, Lord Fitz-Owen interrupted him.

"Where is this closet you talk of? for I and my sons went over the apartment since Edmund's departure, and found no such place as you describe."

"My Lord," said Edmund, "I can account for it: the door is covered with tapestry, the same as the room, and you might easily overlook it; but I have a witness here," said he, and putting his hand into his bosom, he drew out the key. "If this is not the key of that closet, let me be deemed an impostor, and all I say a falsehood; I will risk my pretensions upon this proof."

"And for what purpose did you take it away?" said the Baron.

"To prevent any person from going into it," replied Edmund; "I have vowed to keep it till I shall open that closet before witnesses appointed for that purpose."

"Proceed, sir," said the Baron Fitz-Owen.

Sir Philip then related the conversation between Edmund and Margery Twyford, his supposed mother.

Lord Fitz-Owen seemed in the utmost surprise. He exclaimed, "Can this be true? strange discovery! unfortunate child!"

Edmund's tears bore witness to his veracity. He was obliged to hide his face, he lifted up his clasped hands to heaven, and was in great emotions during all this part of the relation; while Lord Lovel groaned, and seemed in great agitation.

Sir Philip then addressed himself to Lord Fitz-Owen.

"My Lord, there was another person present at the conversation between Edmund and his foster-mother, who can witness to all that passed; perhaps your lordship can tell who that was?"

"It was father Oswald," replied the Baron; "I well remember that he went with him at his request; let him be called in."

He was sent for, and came immediately. The Baron desired him to relate all that passed between Edmund and his mother.

Oswald then began—

"Since I am now properly called upon to testify what I know concerning this young man, I will speak the truth, without fear or favour of any one; and I will swear, by the rules of my holy order, to the truth of what I shall relate."

He then gave a particular account of all that passed on that occasion, and mentioned the tokens found on both the infant and his mother.

"Where are these tokens to be seen?" said the Lord Clifford.

"I have them here, my lord," said Edmund, "and I keep

them as my greatest treasures."

He then produced them before all the company.

"There is no appearance of any fraud or collusion," said Lord Graham; "if any man thinks he sees any, let him speak."

"Pray, my lord, suffer me to speak a word," said Sir Robert. "Do you remember that I hinted my suspicions concerning father Oswald, the night our kinsmen lay in the east apartment?"

"I do," said the Baron.

"Well, sir, it now appears that he did know more than he would tell us; you find he is very deep in all Edmund's secrets, and you may judge what were his motives for undertaking this journey."

"I observe what you say," answered his father, "but let us hear all that Oswald has to say; I will be as impartial as possible."

"My lord," returned Oswald, "I beg you also to recollect what I said, on the night your son speaks of, concerning secrecy in certain matters."

"I remember that also," said the Baron; "but proceed."

"My lord," continued Oswald, "I knew more than I thought myself at liberty to disclose at that time; but I will now tell you every thing. I saw there was something more than common in the accidents that befell this young man, and in his being called out to sleep in the east apartment; I earnestly desired him to let me be with him on the second night, to which he consented reluctantly; we heard a great noise in the rooms underneath, we went down stairs together; I saw him open the fatal closet, I heard groans that pierced me to the heart, I kneeled down and prayed for the repose of the spirit departed; I found a seal, with the arms of Lovel engraven upon it, which I gave to Edmund, and he now has it in his possession. He enjoined me to keep secret what I had seen and heard, till the time should come to declare it. I conceived that I was called to be a witness of these things; besides, my curiosity was excited to know the event; I, therefore, desired to be present at the interview between him and his mother, which was affecting beyond expression. I heard what I have now declared as nearly as my memory permits me. I hope no impartial person will blame me for any part of my conduct; but if they should, I do not repent it. If I should forfeit the favour of the rich and great, I shall have acquitted myself to God and my conscience. I have no worldly ends to answer; I plead the cause of the injured orphan; and I think, also, that I second the designs of Providence."

"You have well spoken, father," said the Lord Clifford; "your testimony is indeed of consequence."

"It is amazing and convincing," said Lord Graham; "and the whole story is so well connected, that I can see nothing to make us doubt the truth of it; but let us examine the proofs."

Edmund gave into their hands the necklace and earrings; he showed them the locket with the cypher of Lovel, and the seal with the arms; he told them the cloak, in which he was wrapped, was in the custody of his foster-mother, who would produce it on demand. He begged that some proper persons might be commissioned to go with him to examine whether or no the bodies of his parents were buried where he affirmed; adding, that he put his pretensions into their hands with pleasure, relying entirely upon their honour and justice.

During this interesting scene, the criminal covered his face, and was silent; but he sent forth bitter sighs and groans that denoted the anguish of his heart. At length, Lord Graham, in compassion to him, proposed that they should retire and consider of the proofs; adding, "Lord Lovel must needs be fatigued; we will resume the subject in his presence, when he is disposed to receive us."

Sir Philip Harclay approached the bed; "Sir," said he, "I now leave you in the hands of your own relations; they are men of strict honour, and I confide in them to take care of you and of your concerns."

They then went out of the room, leaving only the Lord Fitz-Owen and his sons with the criminal. They discoursed of the wonderful story of Edmund's birth, and the principal events of his life.

After dinner, Sir Philip requested another conference with the Lords, and their principal friends. There were present also Father Oswald, and Lord Graham's confessor, who had taken the Lord Lovel's confession, Edmund, and Zadisky. "Now, gentlemen," said Sir Philip, "I desire to know your opinion of our proofs, and your advice upon them."

Lord Graham replied, "I am desired to speak for the rest. We think there are strong presumptive proofs that this young man is the true heir of Lovel; but they ought to be confirmed and authenticated. Of the murder of the late Lord there is no doubt; the criminal hath confessed it, and the circumstances confirm it; the proofs of his crime are so connected with those of the young man's birth, that one cannot be public without the other. We are desirous to do justice; and yet are unwilling, for the Lord Fitz-Owen's sake, to bring the criminal to public shame and punishment. We wish to find out a medium; we therefore desire Sir Philip to make proposals for his ward, and let Lord Fitz-Owen answer for himself and his brother, and we will be moderators between them."

Here every one expressed approbation, and called upon Sir Philip to make his demands.

"If," said he, "I were to demand strict justice, I should not be satisfied with any thing less than the life of the criminal; but I am a Christian soldier, the disciple of Him who came into the world to save sinners; — for His sake," continued he, crossing himself, "I forego my revenge, I spare the guilty. If Heaven gives him time for repentance, man should not deny it. It is my ward's particular request, that I will not bring shame upon the house of his benefactor, the Lord Fitz-Owen, for whom he hath a filial affection and profound veneration. My proposals are these: — First, that the criminal make restitution of the title and estate, obtained with so much injustice and cruelty, to the lawful heir, whom he shall acknowledge such before proper witnesses. Secondly, that he shall surrender his own lawful inheritance and personal estate into the hands of the Lord Fitz-Owen, in trust for his sons, who are his heirs of blood. Thirdly, that he shall retire into a religious house, or else quit the kingdom in three months time; and, in either case, those who enjoy his fortune shall allow him a decent annuity, that he may not want the comforts of life. By the last, I disable him from the means of doing further mischief, and enable him to devote the remainder of his days to penitence. These are my proposals, and I give him four-and-twenty hours to consider of them; if he refuses to comply with them, I shall be obliged to proceed to severer measures, and to a public prosecution. But the goodness of the Lord Fitz-Owen bids me expect, from his influence with his brother, a compliance with proposals made out of respect to his honourable character."

Lord Graham applauded the humanity, prudence, and piety of Sir Philip's proposals. He enforced them with all his influence and eloquence. Lord Clifford seconded him; and the rest gave tokens of approbation.

Sir Robert Fitz-Owen then rose up. "I beg leave to observe to the company, who are going to dispose so generously of another man's property, that my father purchased the castle and estate of the house of Lovel; who is to repay him the money for it?"

Sir Philip then said, "I have also a question to ask. Who is to pay the arrears of my ward's estate, which he has unjustly been kept out of these one-and-twenty years? Let Lord Clifford answer to both points, for he is not interested in either."

Lord Clifford smiled.

"I think," returned he, "the first question is answered by the second, and that the parties concerned should set one against the other, especially as Lord Fitz-Owen's children will inherit the fortune, which includes the purchase-money."

Lord Graham said, "This determination is both equitable and generous, and I hope will answer the expectations on all sides."

"I have another proposal to make to my Lord Fitz-Owen," said Sir Philip; "but I first wait for the acceptance of those already made."

Lord Fitz-Owen replied, "I shall report them to my brother, and acquaint the company with his resolution to-morrow."

They then separated; and the Baron, with his sons, returned to the sick man's chamber; there he exhorted his brother, with the piety of a confessor, to repent of his sins and make atonement for them. He made known Sir Philip's proposals, and observed on the wonderful discovery of his crime, and the punishment that followed it. "Your repentance," continued he, "may be accepted, and your crime may yet be pardoned. If you continue refractory, and refuse to make atonement, you will draw down upon you a severer punishment."

The criminal would not confess, and yet could not deny, the truth and justice of his observations. The Baron spent several hours in his brother's chamber. He sent for a priest, who took his confession; and they both sat up with him all night, advising, persuading, and exhorting him to do justice, and to comply with the proposals. He was unwilling to give up the world, and yet more so to become the object of public shame, disgrace, and punishment.

The next day, Lord Fitz-Owen summoned the company into his brother's chamber, and there declared, in his name, that he accepted Sir Philip Harclay's proposals; that, if the young man could, as he promised, direct them to the places where his parents were buried, and if his birth should be authenticated by his foster-parents, he should be acknowledged the heir of the house of Lovel. That to be certified of these things, they must commission proper persons to go with him for this purpose; and, in case the truth should be made plain, they should immediately put him in possession of the castle and estate, in the state it was. He desired Lord Graham and Lord Clifford to chuse the commissioners, and gave Sir Philip and Edmund a right to add to them, each, another person. [sic]

Lord Graham named the eldest son of Lord Clifford, and the other, in return, named his nephew; they also chose the priest, Lord Graham's confessor, and the eldest son of Baron Fitz-Owen, to his great mortification. Sir Philip appointed Mr. William Fitz-Owen, and Edmund named father Oswald; they chose out the servants to attend them, who were also to be witnesses of all that should pass. Lord Clifford proposed to Baron Fitz-Owen, that, as soon as the commissioners were set out, the remainder of the company should adjourn to his seat in Cumberland, whither Lord Graham should be invited to accompany them, and to stay till this affair was decided. After some debate, this was agreed to; and, at the same time, that the criminal should be kept with them till every thing was properly settled.

Lord Fitz-Owen gave his son William the charge to receive and entertain the commissioners at the castle; But, before they set out, Sir Philip had a conference with Lord Fitz-Owen, concerning the surrender of the castle; in which he insisted on the furniture and stock of the farm, in consideration of the arrears. Lord Fitz-Owen slightly mentioned the young man's education and expences. Sir Philip answered, "You are right, my Lord; I had not thought of this point; we owe you, in this respect, more than we can ever repay. But you know not half the respect and affection Edmund bears for you. When restitution of his title and fortune are fully made, his happiness will still depend on you."

"How on me?" said the Baron.

"Why, he will not be happy unless you honour him with your notice and esteem; but this is not all, I must hope that you will do still more for him."

"Indeed," said the Baron, "he has put my regard for him to a severe proof; what further can he expect from me?"

"My dear Lord, be not offended, I have only one more proposal to make to you; if you refuse it, I can allow for you; and I confess it requires a greatness of mind, but not more than you possess, to grant it."

"Well, sir, speak your demand."

"Say rather my request; it is this: Cease to look upon Edmund as the enemy of your house; look upon him as a son, and make him so indeed."

"How say you, Sir Philip? my son!"

"Yes, my lord, give him your daughter. He is already your son in filial affection; your son William and he are sworn brothers; what remains but to make him yours? He deserves such a parent, you such a son; and you will, by this means, ingraft into your family, the name, title, and estate of Lovel, which will be entailed on your posterity for ever."

"This offer requires much consideration," returned the Baron.

"Suffer me to suggest some hints to you," said Sir Philip. "This match is, I think, verily pointed out by Providence, which hath conducted the dear boy through so many dangers, and brought him within view of his happiness; look on him as the precious relic of a noble house, the son of my dearest friend! or look on him as my son and heir, and let me, as his father, implore you to consent to his marriage with your daughter."

The Baron's heart was touched, he turned away his face.

"Oh, Sir Philip Harclay, what a friend are you! why should such a man be our enemy?"

"My lord," said Sir Philip, "we are not, cannot be enemies; our hearts are already allied; and I am certain we shall one day be dear friends."

The Baron suppressed his emotions, but Sir Philip saw into his heart.

"I must consult my eldest son," returned he.

"Then," replied Sir Philip, "I foresee much difficulty; he is prejudiced against Edmund, and thinks the restitution of his inheritance an injury to your family. Hereafter he will see this alliance in a different light, and will rejoice that such a brother is added to the family; but, at present, he will set his face against it. However, we will not despair; virtue and resolution will surmount all obstacles. Let me call in young Lovel."

He brought Edmund to the Baron, and acquainted him with the proposal he had been making in his name, my Lord's answers, and the objections he feared on the part of Sir Robert. Edmund kneeled to the Baron; he took his hand and pressed it to his lips.

"Best of men! of parents! of patrons!" said he, "I will ever be your son in filial affection, whether I have the honour to be legally so or not; not one of your own children can feel a stronger sense of love and duty."

"Tell me," said the Baron, "do you love my daughter?"

"I do, my lord, with the most ardent affection; I never loved any woman but her; and, if I am so unfortunate as to be refused her, I will not marry at all. Oh, my Lord, reject not my honest suit! Your alliance will give me consequence with myself, it will excite me to act worthy of the station to which I am exalted; if you refuse me, I shall seem an abject wretch, disdained by those whom my heart claims relation to; your family are the whole world to me. Give me your lovely daughter! give me also your son, my beloved William; and let me share with them the fortune Providence bestows upon me. But what is title or fortune, if I am deprived of the society of those I love?"

"Edmund," said the Baron, "you have a noble friend; but you have a stronger in my heart, which I think was implanted there by Heaven to aid its own purposes. I feel a variety of emotions of different kinds, and am afraid to trust my own heart with you. But answer me a question: Are you assured of my daughter's consent? have you solicited her favour? have you gained her affections?"

"Never, my lord. I am incapable of so base an action; I have loved her at an humble distance; but, in my situation, I should have thought it a violation of all the laws of gratitude and hospitality to have presumed to speak the sentiments of my heart."

"Then you have acted with unquestionable honour on this, and, I must say, on all other occasions."

"Your approbation, my lord, is the first wish of my life; it is the seal of my honour and happiness."

Sir Philip smiled: "My Lord Fitz-Owen, I am jealous of Edmund's preferable regard for you; it is just the same now as formerly."

Edmund came to Sir Philip, he threw himself into his arms, he wept, he was overpowered with the feelings of his heart; he prayed to Heaven to strengthen his mind to support his inexpressible sensations.

"I am overwhelmed with obligation," said he; "oh, best of friends, teach me, like you, to make my actions speak for me!"

"Enough, Edmund; I know your heart, and that is my security. My lord, speak to him, and bring him to himself, by behaving coldly to him, if you can."

The Baron said, "I must not trust myself with you, you make a child of me. I will only add, gain my son Robert's favour, and be assured of mine; I owe some respect to the heir of my family; he is brave, honest, and sincere; your enemies are separated from him, you have William's influence in your behalf; make one effort, and let me know the result."

Edmund kissed his hand in transports of joy and gratitude.

"I will not lose a moment," said he; "I fly to obey your commands."

Edmund went immediately to his friend William, and related all that had passed between the Baron, Sir Philip, and himself. William promised him his interest in the warmest manner; he recapitulated all that had passed in the castle since his departure; but he guarded his sister's delicacy, till it should be resolved to give way to his address. They both consulted young Clifford, who had conceived an affection to Edmund for his amiable qualities, and to William for his generous friendship for him. He promised them his assistance, as Sir Robert seemed desirous to cultivate his friendship. Accordingly, they both attacked him with the whole artillery of friendship and persuasion. Clifford urged the merits of Edmund, and the advantages of his alliance. William enforced his arguments by a retrospect of Edmund's past life; and observed, that every obstacle thrown in his way had brought his enemies to shame, and increase of honour to himself. "I say nothing," continued he, "of his noble qualities and affectionate heart; those who have been so many years his companions, can want no proofs of it."

"We know your attachment to him, sir," said Sir Robert; "and, in consequence, your partiality."

"Nay," replied William, "you are sensible of the truth of my assertions; and, I am confident, would have loved him yourself, but for the insinuations of his enemies. But if he should make good his assertions, even you must be convinced of his veracity."

"And you would have my father give him your sister upon this uncertainty?"

"No, sir, but upon these conditions."

"But suppose he does not make them good?"

"Then I will be of your party, and give up his interest."

"Very well, sir; my father may do as he pleases; but I cannot agree to give my sister to one who has always stood in the way of our family, and now turns us out of our own house."

"I am sorry, brother, you see his pretensions in so wrong a light; but if you think there is any imposture in the case, go with us, and be a witness of all that passes."

"No, not I; if Edmund is to be master of the castle, I will never more set my foot in it."

"This matter," said Mr. Clifford, "must be left to time, which has brought stranger things to pass. Sir Robert's honour and good sense will enable him to subdue his prejudices, and to judge impartially."

They took leave, and went to make preparations for their journey. Edmund made his report of Sir Robert's inflexibility to his father, in presence of Sir Philip; who, again, ventured to urge the Baron on his favourite subject.

"It becomes me to wait for the further proofs," said he; "but, if they are as clear as I expect, I will not be inexorable to your wishes; Say nothing more on this subject till the return of the commissioners."

They were profuse in their acknowledgments of his goodness.

Edmund took a tender leave of his two paternal friends.

"When," said he, "I take possession of my inheritance, I must hope for the company of you both to complete my happiness."

"Of me," said Sir Philip, "you may be certain; and, as far as my influence reaches, of the Baron."

He was silent. Edmund assured them of his constant prayers for their happiness.

Soon after, the commissioners, with Edmund, set out for Lovel Castle; and the following day the Lord Clifford set out for his own house, with Baron Fitz-Owen and his son. The nominal Baron was carried with them, very much against his will. Sir Philip Harclay was invited to go with them by Lord Clifford, who declared his presence necessary to bring things to a conclusion. They all joined in acknowledging their obligations to Lord Graham's generous hospitality, and besought him to accompany them. At length he consented, on condition they would allow him to go to and fro, as his duty should call him.

Lord Clifford received them with the greatest hospitality, and presented them to his lady, and three daughters, who were in the bloom of youth and beauty. They spent their time very pleasantly, excepting the criminal, who continued gloomy and reserved, and declined company.

In the mean time, the commissioners proceeded on their journey. When they were within a day's distance from the castle, Mr. William and his servant put forward, and arrived several hours before the rest, to make preparations for their reception. His sister and brother received them with open arms, and enquired eagerly after the event of the journey to the North. He gave them a brief account of every thing that had happened to their uncle; adding, "But this is not all: Sir Philip Harclay has brought a young man who he pretends is the son of the late Lord Lovel, and claims his estate and title. This person is on his journey hither, with several others who are commissioned to enquire into certain particulars, to confirm his pretensions. If he make good his claim, my father will surrender the castle and estate into his hands. Sir Philip and my lord have many points to settle; and he has proposed a compromise, that you, my sister, ought to know, because it nearly concerns you."

"Me! brother William; pray explain yourself."

"Why, he proposes that, in lieu of arrears and other expectations, my father shall give his dear Emma to the heir of Lovel, in full of all demands."

She changed colour.

"Holy Mary!" said she; "and does my father agree to this proposal?"

"He is not very averse to it; but Sir Robert refuses his consent. However, I have given him my interest with you."

"Have you indeed? What! a stranger, perhaps an impostor, who comes to turn us out of our dwelling?"

"Have patience, my Emma! see this young man without prejudice, and perhaps you will like him as well as I do."

"I am surprised at you, William."

"Dear Emma, I cannot bear to see you uneasy. Think of the man who of all others you would with to see in a situation to ask you of your father, and expect to see your wishes realized."

"Impossible!" said she.

"Nothing is impossible, my dear; let us be prudent, and all will end happily. You must help me to receive and entertain these commissioners. I expect a very solemn scene; but when that is once got over, happier hours than the past will succeed. We shall first visit the haunted apartment; you, my sister, will keep in your own till I shall send for you. I go now to give orders to the servants."

He went and ordered them to be in waiting; and himself, and his youngest brother, stood in readiness to receive them.

The sound of the horn announced the arrival of the commissioners; at the same instant a sudden gust of wind arose, and the outward gates flew open. They entered the court-yard, and the great folding-doors into the hall were opened without any assistance. The moment Edmund entered the hall, every door in the house flew open; the servants all rushed into the hall, and fear was written on their countenances; Joseph only was undaunted. "These doors," said he, "open of their own accord to receive their master! this is he indeed!"

Edmund was soon apprized of what had happened.

"I accept the omen!" said he. "Gentlemen, let us go forward to the apartment! let us finish the work of fate! I will lead the way." He went on to the apartment, followed by all present. "Open the shutters," said he, "the daylight shall no longer be excluded here; the deeds of darkness shall now be brought to light."

They descended the staircase; every door was open, till they came to the fatal closet. Edmund called to Mr. William: "Approach, my friend, and behold the door your family overlooked!"

They came forward; he drew the key out of his bosom, and unlocked the door; he made them observe that the boards were all loose; he then called to the servants, and bid them remove every thing out of the closet. While they were doing this, Edmund shewed them the breastplate all stained with blood. He then called to Joseph: —

"Do you know whose was this suit of armour?"

"It was my Lord's," said Joseph; "the late Lord Lovel; I have seen him wear it."

Edmund bade them bring shovels and remove the earth. While they were gone, he desired Oswald to repeat all that passed the night they sat up together in that apartment, which he did till the servants returned. They threw out the earth, while the by-standers in solemn silence waited the event. After some time and labour they struck against something. They proceeded till they discovered a large trunk, which with some difficulty they drew out. It had been corded round, but the cords were rotted to dust. They opened it, and found a skeleton which appeared to have been tied neck and heels together, and forced into the trunk.

"Behold," said Edmund, "the bones of him to whom I owe my birth!"

The priest from Lord Graham's advanced. "This is undoubtedly the body of the Lord Lovel; I heard his kinsman confess the manner in which he was interred. Let this awful spectacle be a lesson to all present, that though wickedness may triumph for a season, a day of retribution will come!"

Oswald exclaimed. "Behold the day of retribution! of triumph to the innocent, of shame and confusion to the wicked!"

The young gentlemen declared that Edmund had made good his assertions.

"What then," said they, "remains?"

"I propose," said Lord Graham's priest, "that an account be written of this discovery, and signed by all the witnesses present; that an attested copy be left in the hands of this gentleman, and the original be sent to the Barons and Sir Philip Harclay, to convince them of the truth of it."

Mr. Clifford then desired Edmund to proceed in his own way.

"The first thing I propose to do," said he, "is to have a coffin made for these honoured remains. I trust to find the bones of my other parent, and to inter them all together in consecrated ground. Unfortunate pair! you shall at last rest together! your son shall pay the last duties to your ashes!"

He stopped to shed tears, and none present but paid this tribute to their misfortunes. Edmund recovered his voice and proceeded.

"My next request is, that Father Oswald and this reverend father, with whoever else the gentlemen shall appoint, will send for Andrew and Margery Twyford, and examine them concerning the circumstances of my birth, and the death and burial of my unfortunate mother."

"It shall be done," said Mr. William; "but first let me intreat you to come with me and take some refreshment after your journey, for you must be fatigued; after dinner we will proceed in the enquiry."

They all followed him into the great hall, where they were entertained with great hospitality, and Mr. William did the honours in his father's name. Edmund's heart was deeply affected, and the solemnity of his deportment bore witness to his sincerity; but it was a manly sorrow, that did not make him neglect his duty to his friends or himself. He enquired after the health of the lady Emma.

"She is well," said William, "and as much your friend as ever."

Edmund bowed in silence.

After dinner the commissioners sent for Andrew and his wife. They examined them separately, and found their accounts agreed together, and were in substance the same as Oswald and Edmund had before related, separately also. The commissioners observed, that there could be no collusion between them, and that the proofs were indisputable. They kept the foster parents all night; and the next day Andrew directed them to the place where the Lady Lovel was buried, between two trees which he had marked for a memorial. They collected the bones and carried them to the Castle, where Edmund caused a stately coffin to be made for the remains of the unfortunate pair. The two priests obtained leave to look in the coffin buried in the church, and found nothing but stones and earth in it. The commissioners then declared they were fully satisfied of the reality of Edmund's pretensions.

The two priests were employed in drawing up a circumstantial account of these discoveries, in order to make their report to the Barons at their return. In the mean time Mr. William took an opportunity to introduce Edmund to his sister.

"My Emma," said he, "the heir of Lovel is desirous to pay his respects to you."

They were both in apparent confusion; but Edmund's wore off, and Emma's increased.

"I have been long desirous," said he, "to pay my respects to the lady whom I most honour, but unavoidable duties have detained me; when these are fully paid, it is my wish to devote the remainder of my life to Lady Emma!"

"Are you, then, the heir of Lovel?"

"I am, madam; and am also the man in whose behalf I once presumed to speak."

"'Tis very strange indeed!"

"It is so, madam, to myself; but time that reconciles us to all things, will, I hope, render this change in my situation familiar to you."

William said, "You are both well acquainted with the wishes of my heart; but my advice is, that you do not encourage a farther intimacy till my lord's determination be fully known."

"You may dispose of me as you please," said Edmund; "but I cannot help declaring my wishes; yet I will submit to my Lord's sentence, though he should doom me to despair."

From this period, the young pair behaved with solemn respect to each other, but with apparent reserve. The young lady sometimes appeared in company, but oftener chose to be in her own apartment, where she began to believe and hope for the completion of her wishes. The uncertainty of the Baron's determination, threw an air of anxiety over Edmund's face. His friend William, by the most tender care and attention, strove to dispel his fears, and encourage his hopes; but he waited with impatience for the return of the commissioners, and the decision of his fate.

While these things passed at the Castle of Lovel, the nominal Baron recovered his health and strength at the house of Lord Clifford. In the same proportion he grew more and more shy and reserved, avoided the company of his brother and nephew, and was frequently shut up with his two servants. Sir Robert Fitz-Owen made several attempts to gain his confidence, but in vain; he was equally shy to him as the rest. M. Zadisky observed his motions with the penetration for which his countrymen have been distinguished in all ages; he communicated his suspicions to Sir Philip and the Barons, giving it as his opinion, that the criminal was meditating an escape. They asked, what he thought was to be done? Zadisky offered to watch him in turn with another person, and to lie in wait for him; he also proposed, that horses should be kept in readiness, and men to mount them, without knowledge of the service they were to be employed in. The Barons agreed to leave the whole management of this affair to Zadisky. He took his measures so well, that he intercepted the three fugitives in the fields adjoining to the house, and brought them all back prisoner. They confined them separately, while the Lords and Gentlemen consulted how to dispose of them.

Sir Philip applied to Lord Fitz-Owen, who begged leave to be silent. "I have nothing," said he, "to offer in favour of this bad man; and I cannot propose harsher measures with so near a relation."

Zadisky then begged to be heard.

"You can no longer have any reliance upon the word of a man who has forfeited all pretensions to honour and sincerity. I have long wished to revisit once more my native country, and to enquire after some very dear friends I left there. I will undertake to convey this man to a very distant part of the world, where it will be out of his power to do further mischief, and free his relations from an ungrateful charge, unless you should rather chuse to bring him to punishment here."

Lord Clifford approved of the proposal; Lord Fitz-Owen remained silent, but shewed no marks of disapprobation.

Sir Philip objected to parting with his friend; but Zadisky assured him he had particular reasons for returning to the Holy Land, of which he should be judge hereafter. Sir Philip desired the Lord Fitz-Owen to give him his company to the criminal's apartment, saying, "We will have one more conversation with him, and that shall decide his fate."

They found him silent and sullen, and he refused to answer their questions.

Sir Philip then bespoke him: "After the proofs you have given of your falsehood and insincerity, we can no longer have any reliance upon you, nor faith in your fulfilling the conditions of our agreement; I will, therefore, once more make you a proposal that shall still leave you indebted to our clemency. You shall banish yourself from England for ever, and go in pilgrimage to the Holy Land, with such companions as we shall appoint; or, secondly, you shall enter directly into a monastery, and there be shut up for life; or, thirdly, if you refuse both these offers, I will go directly to court, throw myself at the feet of my Sovereign, relate the whole story of your wicked life and actions, and demand vengeance on your head. The King is too good and pious to let such villany go unpunished; he will bring you to public shame and punishment; and be you assured, if I begin this prosecution, I will pursue it to the utmost. I appeal to your worthy brother for the justice of my proceeding. I reason no more with you, I only declare my resolution. I wait your answer one hour, and the next I put in execution whatever you shall oblige me to determine."

So saying, they retired, and left him to reflect and to resolve. At the expiration of the hour they sent Zadisky to receive his answer; he insinuated to him the generosity and charity of Sir Philip and the Lords, and the certainty of their resolutions, and begged him to take care what answer he returned, for that his fate depended on it. He kept silent several minutes, resentment and despair were painted on his visage. At length he spoke:—

"Tell my proud enemies that I prefer banishment to death, infamy, or a life of solitude."

"You have chosen well," said Zadisky. "To a wise man all countries are alike; it shall be my care to make mine agreeable to you."

"Are you, then, the person chosen for my companion?"

"I am, sir; and you may judge by that circumstance, that those whom you call your enemies, are not so in effect. Farewell, sir—I go to prepare for our departure."

Zadisky went and made his report, and then set immediately about his preparations. He chose two active young men for his attendants; and gave them directions to keep a strict eye upon their charge, for that they should be accountable if he should escape them.

In the meantime the Baron Fitz-Owen had several conferences with his brother; he endeavoured to make him sensible of his crimes, and of the justice and clemency of his conqueror; but he was moody and reserved to him as to the rest. Sir Philip Harclay obliged him to surrender his worldly estates into the hands of Lord Fitz-Owen. A writing was drawn up for that purpose, and executed in the presence of them all. Lord Fitz-Owen engaged to allow him an annual sum, and to advance money for the expences of his voyage. He spoke to him in the most affectionate manner, but he refused his embrace.

"You will have nothing to regret," said he, haughtily, "for the gain is yours."

Sir Philip conjured Zadisky to return to him again, who answered:

"I will either return, or give such reasons for my stay, as you shall approve. I will send a messenger to acquaint you with my arrival in Syria, and with such other particulars as I shall judge interesting to you and yours. In the meantime remember me in your prayers, and preserve for me those sentiments of friendship and esteem, that I have always deemed one of the chief honours and blessings of my life. Commend my love and duty to your adopted son; he will more than supply my absence, and be the comfort of your old age. Adieu, best and noblest of friends!"

They took a tender leave of each other, not without tears on both sides.

The travellers set out directly for a distant seaport where they heard of a ship bound for the Levant, in which they embarked and proceeded on their voyage.

The Commissioners arrived at Lord Clifford's a few days after the departure of the adventurers. They gave a minute account of their commission, and expressed themselves entirely satisfied of the justice of Edmund's pretensions; they gave an account in writing of all that they had been eyewitnesses to, and ventured to urge the Baron Fitz-Owen on the subject of Edmund's wishes. The Baron was already disposed in his favour; his mind was employed in the future establishment of his family. During their residence at Lord Clifford's, his eldest son Sir Robert had cast his eye upon the eldest daughter of that nobleman, and he besought his father to ask her in marriage for him. The Baron was pleased with the alliance, and took the first opportunity to mention it to Lord Clifford; who answered him, pleasantly:

"I will give my daughter to your son, upon condition that you will give yours to the Heir of Lovel." The Baron looked serious; Lord Clifford went on:

"I like that young man so well, that I would accept him for a son-in-law, if he asked me for my daughter; and if I have any influence with you, I will use it in his behalf."

"A powerful solicitor indeed!" said the Baron; "but you know my eldest son's reluctance to it; if he consents, so will I."

"He shall consent," said Lord Clifford, "or he shall have no daughter of mine. Let him subdue his prejudices, and then I will lay aside my scruples."

"But, my Lord," replied the Baron, "if I can obtain his free consent, it will be the best for all; I will try once more, and if he will not, I will leave it wholly to your management."

When the noble company were all assembled, Sir Philip Harclay revived the subject, and besought the Lord Fitz-Owen to put an end to the work he had begun, by confirming Edmund's happiness. The Baron rose up, and thus spoke:

"The proofs of Edmund's noble birth, the still stronger ones of his excellent endowments and qualities, the solicitations of so many noble friends in his behalf, have altogether determined me in his favour; and I hope to do justice to his merit, without detriment to my other children; I am resolved to make them all as happy as my power will allow me to do. Lord Clifford has been so gracious to promise his fair daughter to my son Robert, upon certain conditions, that I will take upon me to ratify, and which will render my son worthy of the happiness that awaits him. My children are the undoubted heirs of my unhappy brother, Lovel; you, my son, shall therefore immediately take possession of your uncle's house and estate, only obliging you to pay to each of your younger brothers, the sum of one thousand pounds; on this condition, I will secure that estate to you and your heirs for ever. I will by my own act and deed surrender the castle and estate of Lovel to the right owner, and at the same time marry him to my daughter. I will settle a proper allowance upon my two younger sons, and dispose of what remains by a will and testament; and then I shall have done all my business in this world, and shall have nothing to do but prepare for the next."

"Oh, my father!" said Sir Robert, "I cannot bear your generosity! you would give away all to others, and reserve nothing for yourself."

"Not so, my son," said the Baron; "I will repair my old castle in Wales, and reside there. I will visit my children, and be visited by them; I will enjoy their happiness, and by that means increase my own; whether I look backwards or forwards, I shall have nothing to do but rejoice, and be thankful to Heaven that has given me so many blessings; I shall have the comfortable reflection of having discharged my duties as a citizen, a husband, a father, a friend; and, whenever I am summoned away from this world, I shall die content."

Sir Robert came forward with tears on his cheeks; he kneeled to his father.

"Best of parents, and of men!" said he; "you have subdued a heart that has been too refractory to your will; you have this day made me sensible how much I owe to your goodness and forbearance with me. Forgive me all that is past, and from henceforward dispose of me; I will have no will but yours, no ambition but to be worthy of the name of your son."

"And this day," said the Baron, "do I enjoy the true happiness of a father! Rise, my son, and take possession of the first place in my affection without reserve." They embraced with tears on both sides; The company rose, and congratulated both father and son. The Baron presented his son to Lord Clifford, who embraced him, and said:

"You shall have my daughter, for I see that you deserve her."

Sir Philip Harclay approached — the Baron gave his son's hand to the knight.

"Love and respect that good man," said he; "deserve his friendship, and you will obtain it."

Nothing but congratulations were heard on all sides.

When their joy was in some degree reduced to composure, Sir Philip proposed that they should begin to execute the schemes of happiness they had planned. He proposed that my Lord Fitz-Owen should go with him to the Castle of Lovel, and settle the family there. The Baron consented; and both together invited such of the company, as liked it, to accompany them thither. It was agreed that a nephew of Lord Graham's, another of Lord Clifford's, two gentlemen, friends of Sir Philip Harclay, and father Oswald, should be of the party; together with several of Sir Philip's dependants and domestics, and the attendants on the rest. Lord Fitz Owen gave orders for their speedy departure. Lord Graham and his friends took leave of them, in order to return to his own home; but, before he went, he engaged his eldest nephew and heir to the second daughter of the Lord Clifford; Sir Robert offered himself to the eldest, who modestly received his address, and made no objection to his proposal. The fathers confirmed their engagement.

Lord Fitz-Owen promised to return to the celebration of the marriage; in the mean time he ordered his son to go and take possession of his uncle's house, and to settle his household; He invited young Clifford, and some other gentlemen, to go with him. The company separated with regret, and with many promises of friendship on all sides; and the gentlemen of the North were to cultivate the good neighbourhood on both sides of the borders.

Sir Philip Harclay and the Baron Fitz-Owen, with their friends and attendants, set forwards for the Castle of Lovel; a servant went before, at full speed, to acquaint the family of their approach. Edmund was in great anxiety of mind, now the crisis of his fate was near at hand; He enquired of the messenger, who were of the party? and finding that Sir Philip Harclay was there, and that Sir Robert Fitz-Owen stayed in the North, his hopes rose above his fears. Mr. William, attended by a servant, rode forward to meet them; he desired Edmund to stay and receive them. Edmund was under some difficulty with regard to his behaviour to the lovely Emma; a thousand times his heart rose to his lips, as often he suppressed his emotions; they both sighed frequently, said little, thought much, and wished for the event. Master Walter was too young to partake of their anxieties, but he wished for the arrival of his father to end them.

Mr. William's impatience spurred him on to meet his father; as soon as he saw him, he rode up directly to him.

"My dear father, you are welcome home!" said he.

"I think not, sir," said the Baron, and looked serious.

"Why so, my lord?" said William.

"Because it is no longer mine, but another man's home," answered he, "and I must receive my welcome from him."

"Meaning Edmund?" said William.

"Whom else can it be?"

"Ah, my Lord! he is your creature, your servant; he puts his fate into your hands, and will submit to your pleasure in all things!"

"Why comes he not to meet us?" said the Baron.

"His fears prevent him," said William; "but speak the word, and I will fetch him."

"No," said the Baron, "we will wait on him."

William looked confused.

"Is Edmund so unfortunate," said he, "as to have incurred your displeasure?"

Sir Philip Harclay advanced, and laid his hand on William's saddle.

"Generous impatience! noble youth!" said he; "look round you, and see if you can discover in this company one enemy of your friend! Leave to your excellent father the time and manner of explaining himself; he only can do justice to his own sentiments."

The Baron smiled on Sir Philip; William's countenance cleared up; they went forward, and soon arrived at the Castle of Lovel.

Edmund was walking to and fro in the hall, when he heard the horn that announced their arrival; his emotions were so great that he could hardly support them. The Baron and Sir Philip entered the hall hand in hand; Edmund threw himself at their feet, and embraced their knees, but could not utter a word. They raised him between them, and strove to encourage him; but he threw himself into the arms of Sir Philip Harclay, deprived of strength, and almost of life. They supported him to a seat, where he recovered by degrees, but had no power to speak his feelings; he looked up to his benefactors in the most affecting manner, he laid his hand upon his bosom, but was still silent.

"Compose yourself, my dear son," said Sir Philip; "you are in the arms of your best friends. Look up to the happiness that awaits you — enjoy the blessings that Heaven sends you — lift up your heart in gratitude to the Creator, and think left of what you owe to the creature! You will have time enough to pay us your acknowledgments hereafter."

The company came round them, the servants flocked into the hall: shouts of joy were heard on all sides; the Baron came and took Edmund's hand.

"Rise, sir," said he, "and do the honours of your house! it is yours from this day: we are your guests, and expect from you our welcome!"

Edmund kneeled to the Baron, he spoke with a faltering voice:

"My Lord, I am yours! all that I have is at your devotion! dispose of me as it pleases you best."

The Baron embraced him with the greatest affection.

"Look round you," said he, "and salute your friends; these gentlemen came hither to do you honour."

Edmund revived, he embraced and welcomed the

gentlemen. Father Oswald received his embrace with peculiar affection, and gave him his benediction in a most affecting manner.

Edmund exclaimed, "Pray for me, father! that I may bear all these blessings with gratitude and moderation!"

He then saluted and shook hands with all the servants, not omitting the meanest; he distinguished Joseph by a cordial embrace; he called him his dear friend.

"Now," said he, "I can return your friendship, and I am proud to acknowledge it!"

The old man, with a faltering voice, cried out:

"Now I have lived long enough! I have seen my master's son acknowledged for the heir of Lovel!"

The hall echoed with his words, "Long live the heir of Lovel!"

The Baron took Edmund's hands in his own:

"Let us retire from this crowd," said he; "we have business of a more private nature to transact."

He led to the parlour, followed by Sir Philip and the other gentlemen.

"Where are my other children?" said he.

William retired, and presently returned with his brother and sister. They kneeled to their father, who raised and embraced them. He then called out, "William! — Edmund! — come and receive my blessing also."

They approached hand in hand, they kneeled, and he gave them a solemn benediction.

"Your friendship deserves our praise, my children! love each other always! and may Heaven pour down its choicest blessings upon your heads!"

They rose, and embraced in silent raptures of joy. Edmund presented his friend to Sir Philip.

"I understand you," said he; "this gentleman was my first

acquaintance of this family; he has a title to the second place in my heart; I shall tell him, at more leisure, how much I love and honour him for his own sake as well as yours."

He embraced the youth, and desired his friendship.

"Come hither, my Emma!" said the Baron.

She approached with tears on her check, sweetly blushing, like the damask rose wet with the dew of the morning.

"I must ask you a serious question, my child; answer me with the same sincerity you would to Heaven. You see this young man, the heir of Lovel! You have known him long; consult your own heart, and tell me whether you have any objection to receive him for your husband. I have promised to all this company to give you to him; but upon condition that you approve him: I think him worthy of you; and, whether you accept him or not, he shall ever be to me a son; but Heaven forbid that I should compel my child to give her hand, where she cannot bestow her heart! Speak freely, and decide this point for me and for yourself."

The fair Emma blushed, and was under some confusion; her virgin modesty prevented her speaking for some moments. Edmund trembled; he leaned upon William's shoulder to support himself. Emma cast her eye upon him, she saw his emotion, and hastened to relieve him; and thus spoke in a soft voice which gathered strength as she proceeded:

"My lord and father's goodness has always prevented my wishes; I am the happiest of all children, in being able to obey his commands, without offering violence to my own inclinations. As I am called upon in this public manner, it is but justice to this gentleman's merit to declare, that, were I at liberty to chuse a husband from all the world, he only should be my choice, who I can say, with joy, is my father's also."

Edmund bowed low, he advanced towards her; the Baron took his daughter's hand, and presented it to him; he kneeled upon one knee, he took her hand, kissed it, and pressed it to his bosom. The Baron embraced and blessed them; he presented them to Sir Philip Harclay — "Receive and acknowledge your children!" said he.

"I do receive them as the gift of Heaven!" said the noble knight; "they are as much mine as if I had begotten them: all that I have is theirs, and shall descend to their children for ever." A fresh scene of congratulation ensued; and the hearts of all the auditors were too much engaged to be able soon to return to the ease and tranquillity of common life.

After they had refreshed themselves, and recovered from the emotions they had sustained on this interesting occasion, Edmund thus addressed the Baron:

"On the brink of happiness I must claim your attention to a melancholy subject. The bones of both my parents lie unburied in this house; permit me, my honoured lord, to perform my last duties to them, and the remainder of my life shall be devoted to you and yours."

"Certainly," said the Baron; "why have you not interred them?"

"My lord, I waited for your arrival, that you might be certified of the reality, and that no doubts might remain."

"I have no doubts," said the Baron; "Alas! both the crime and punishment of the offender leave no room for them!" He sighed. "Let us now put an end to this affair; and, if possible, forget it for ever."

"If it will not be too painful to you, my lord, I would intreat you, with these gentlemen our friends, to follow me into the east apartment, the scene of my parents' woes, and yet the dawning of my better hopes."

They rose to attend him; he committed the Lady Emma to the care of her youngest brother, observing that the scene was too solemn for a lady to be present at it. They proceeded to the apartment; he showed the Baron the fatal closet, and the place where the bones were found, also the trunk that contained them; he recapitulated all that passed before their arrival; he shewed them the coffin where the bones of the unfortunate pair were deposited: he then desired the Baron to give orders for their interment.

"No," replied he, "it belongs to you to order, and every one here is ready to perform it."

Edmund then desired father Oswald to give notice to the friars of the monastery of St. Austin, that with their permission the funeral should be solemnized there, and the bones interred in the church. He also gave orders that the closet should be floored, the apartment repaired and put in order. He then returned to the other side of the Castle.

Preparations being made for the funeral, it was performed a few days after. Edmund attended in person as chief mourner, Sir Philip Harclay as the second; Joseph desired he might assist as servant to the deceased. They were followed by most people of the village. The story was now become public, and every one blessed Edmund for the piety and devotion with which he performed the last duties to his parents. — Edmund appeared in deep mourning; the week after, he assisted at a mass for the repose of the deceased.

Sir Philip Harclay ordered a monument to be erected to the memory of his friends, with the following inscription:

"Praye for the soules of Arthur Lord Lovele and Marie his wife, who were cut off in the flowere of theire youthe, by the trecherye and crueltie of theire neare kinnesmanne. Edmunde theire onlie sonne, one and twentie yeares after theire deathe, by the direction of heavene, made the discoverye of the mannere of theire deathe, and at the same time proved his owne birthe. He collected theire bones together, and interred them in this place: A warning and proofe to late posteritie, of the justice of Providence, and the certaintie of Retribution."

The Sunday after the funeral Edmund threw off his mourning, and appeared in a dress suitable to his condition. He received the compliments of his friends with ease and cheerfulness, and began to enjoy his happiness. He asked an audience of his fair mistress, and was permitted to declare the passion he had so long stifled in his own bosom. She gave him a favourable hearing, and in a short time confessed that she had suffered equally in that suspense that was so grievous to him. They engaged themselves by mutual vows to each other, and only waited the Baron's pleasure to complete their happiness; every cloud was vanished from their brows, and sweet tranquillity took possession of their bosoms. Their friends shared their happiness; William and Edmund renewed their vows of everlasting friendship, and promised to be as much together as William's other duties would permit.

The Baron once more summoned all his company together; he told Edmund all that had passed relating to his brother in-law, his exile, and the pilgrimage of Zadisky; he then related the circumstances of Sir Robert's engagement to Lord Clifford's daughter, his establishment in his uncle's seat, and his own obligations to return time enough to be present at the marriage: "But before I go," said he, "I will give my daughter to the heir of

Lovel, and then I shall have discharged my duty to him, and my promise to Sir Philip Harclay."

"You have nobly performed both," said Sir Philip, "and whenever you depart I shall be your companion."

"What," said Edmund, "am I to be deprived of both my fathers at once? My honoured lord, you have given away two houses — where do you intend to reside?"

"No matter," said the Baron; "I know I shall be welcome to both."

"My dear Lord," said Edmund, "stay here and be still the master; I shall be proud to be under your command, and to be your servant as well as your son!"

"No, Edmund," said the Baron, "that would not now be proper; this is your castle, you are its lord and master, and it is incumbent on you to shew yourself worthy of the great things Providence has done for you."

"How shall I, a young man, acquit myself of so many duties as will be upon me, without the advice and assistance of my two paternal friends? Oh, Sir Philip! will you too leave me? once you gave me hopes —"

He stopped greatly affected.

Sir Philip said, "Tell me truly, Edmund, do you really desire that I should live with you?"

"As truly, sir, as I desire life and happiness!"

"Then, my dear child, I will live and die with you!"

They embraced with tears of affection, and Edmund was all joy and gratitude.

"My good Lord," said Sir Philip, "you have disposed of two houses, and have none ready to receive you; will you accept of mine? It is much at your service, and its being in the same county with your eldest son, will be an inducement to you to reside there."

The Baron caught Sir Philip's hand.

"Noble sir, I thank you, and I will embrace your kind offer; I will be your tenant for the present; my castle in Wales shall be put in repair, in the meantime; if I do not reside there, it will be an establishment for one of my younger sons."

"But what will you do with your old soldiers and dependants?"

"My lord, I will never cast them off. There is another house on my estate that has been shut up many years; I will have it repaired and furnished properly for the reception of my old men: I will endow it with a certain sum to be paid annually, and will appoint a steward to manage their revenue; I will continue it during the lives of the first inhabitants, and after that I shall leave it to my son here, to do as he pleases."

"Your son," said Edmund, "will make it the business of his life to act worthy of such a father."

"Enough," said Sir Philip, "I am satisfied that you will. I purpose to reside myself in that very apartment which my dear friend your father inhabited; I will tread in his footsteps, and think he sees me acting his part in his son's family. I will be attended by my own servants; and, whenever you desire it, I will give you my company; your joys, your griefs shall be mine; I shall hold your children in my arms, and their prattle shall amuse my old age; and, as my last earthly wish, your hands shall close my eyes."

"Long, very long," said Edmund, with eyes and hands lifted up, "may it be ere I perform so sad a duty!"

"Long and happily may you live together!" said the Baron; "I will hope to see you sometimes, and to claim a share in your blessings. But let us give no more tears to sorrow, the rest shall be those of joy and transport. The first step we take shall be to marry our Edmund; I will give orders for the celebration, and they shall be the last orders I shall give in this house." They then separated, and went to prepare for the approaching solemnity.

Sir Philip and the Baron had a private conference concerning Edmund's assuming the name and title of Lovel. "I am resolved," said Sir Philip, "to go to the king; to acquaint him briefly with Edmund's history; I will request that he may be called up to parliament by a writ, for there is no need of a new patent, he being the true inheritor; in the mean time he shall assume the name, arms, and title, and I will answer any one that shall dispute his right to them.["] Sir Philip then declared his resolution to set out with the Baron at his departure, and to settle all his other affairs before he returned to take up his residence at the Castle.

A few days after, the marriage was celebrated, to the entire satisfaction of all parties. The Baron ordered the doors to be thrown open, and the house free for all comers; with every other token of joy and festivity. Edmund appeared full of joy without levity, of mirth without extravagance; he received the congratulations of his friends, with ease, freedom, and vivacity. He sent for his foster father and mother, who began to think themselves neglected, as he had been so deeply engaged in affairs of more consequence that he had not been particularly attentive to them; he made them come into the great hall, and presented them to his lady.

"These," said he, "are the good people to whom I am, under God, indebted for my present happiness; they were my first benefactors; I was obliged to them for food and sustenance in my childhood, and this good woman nourished my infancy at her own breast." The lady received them graciously, and saluted Margery. Andrew kneeled down, and, with great humility, begged Edmund's pardon for his treatment of him in his childhood. "I heartily forgive you," said he, "and I will excuse you to yourself; it was natural for you to look upon me as an intruder that was eating your children's bread; you saved my life, and afterwards you sustained it by your food and raiment: I ought to have maintained myself, and to have contributed to your maintenance. But besides this, your treatment of me was the first of my preferment; it recommended me to the notice of this noble family. Everything that happened to me since, has been a step to my present state of honour and happiness. Never man had so many benefactors as myself; but both they, and myself, have been only instruments in the hands of Providence, to bring about its own purposes; let us praise God for all! I shared your poverty, and you will share my riches; I will give you the cottage where you dwell, and the ground about it; I will also pay you the annual sum of ten pounds for the lives of you both; I will put out your children to manual trades, and assist you to provide for them in their own station; and you are to look upon this as paying a debt, and not bestowing a gift; I owe you more than I can ever pay; and, if there be any thing further in my power that will contribute to your happiness, you can ask nothing in reason that I will deny you."

Andrew hid his face; "I cannot bear it!" said he; "oh what a brute was I, to abuse such a child as this! I shall never forgive myself!"

"You must indeed, my friend; for I forgive and thank you."

Andrew retired back, but Margery came forward; she looked earnestly on Edmund, she then threw her arms about his neck, and wept aloud.

"My precious child! my lovely babe! thank God, I have lived to see this day! I will rejoice in your good fortune, and your bounty to us, but I must ask one more favour yet; that I may sometimes come hither and behold that gracious countenance, and thank God that I was honoured so far as to give thee food from my own breast, and to bring thee up to be a blessing to me, and to all that know thee!"

Edmund was affected, he returned her embrace; he bade her come to the Castle as often as she pleased, and she should always be received as his mother; the bride saluted her, and told her the oftener she came, the more welcome she should be.

Margery and her husband retired, full of blessings and prayers for their happiness; she gave vent to her joy, by relating to the servants and neighbours every circumstance of Edmund's birth, infancy, and childhood. Many a tear was dropped by the auditors, and many a prayer wafted to Heaven for his happiness. Joseph took up the story where she left it: he told the rising dawn of youth and virtue, darting its ray through the clouds of obscurity, and how every stroke of envy and malignity brushed away some part of the darkness that veiled its lustre. He told the story of the haunted apartment, and all the consequences of it; how he and Oswald conveyed the youth away from the Castle, no more to return till he came as master of it. He closed the tale with praise to Heaven for the happy discovery, that gave such an heir to the house of Lovel; to his dependants such a Lord and Master; to mankind a friend and benefactor. There was truly a house of joy; not that false kind, in the midst of which there is heaviness, but that of rational creatures, grateful to the Supreme Benefactor, raising their minds by a due enjoyment of earthly blessings to a preparation for a more perfect state hereafter.

A few days after the wedding, the Lord Fitz-Owen began to prepare for his journey to the north. He gave to Edmund the plate, linen, and furniture of the Castle, the farming stock and utensils; he would have added a sum of money, but Sir Philip stopped his hand.

"We do not forget," said he, "that you have other children, we will not suffer you to injure them; give us your blessing and paternal affection, and we have nothing more to ask. I told you, my Lord, that you and I should one day be sincere friends."

"We must be so," answered the Baron; "it is impossible to be long your enemy. We are brothers, and shall be to our lives' end."

They regulated the young man's household; the Baron gave leave to the servants to choose their master; the elder ones followed him (except Joseph, who desired to live with Edmund, as the chief happiness of his life); most of the younger ones chose the service of the youthful pair. There was a tender and affectionate parting on all sides. Edmund besought his beloved William not to leave him. The Baron said, he must insist on his being at his brother's wedding, as a due attention to him, but after that he should return to the Castle for some time.

The Baron and Sir Philip Harclay, with their train, set forward. Sir Philip went to London and obtained all he desired for his Edmund; from thence he went into Yorkshire, and settled his affairs there, removing his pensioners to his other house, and putting Lord Fitz-Owen in possession of his own. They had a generous contention about the terms; but Sir Philip insisted on the Baron's accepting the use of everything there.

"You hold it in trust for a future grandchild," said he, "whom I hope to live to endow with it."

During Sir Philip's absence, the young Lord Lovel caused the haunted apartment to be repaired and furnished for the reception of his father by adoption. He placed his friend Joseph over all his men-servants, and ordered him to forbear his attendance; but the old man would always stand at the side-board, and feast his eyes with the countenance of his own master's son, surrounded with honour and happiness. John Wyatt waited upon the person of his lord, and enjoyed his favour without abatement. Mr. William Fitz-Owen accompanied Sir Philip Harclay from the north country, when he returned to take up his residence at the Castle of Lovel.

Edmund, in the arms of love and friendship, enjoyed with true relish the blessings that surrounded him, with an heart overflowing with benevolence to his fellow creatures, and raptures of gratitude to his Creator. His lady and himself were examples of conjugal affection and happiness. Within a year from his marriage she brought him a son and heir, whose birth renewed the joy and congratulations of all his friends. The Baron Fitz-Owen came to the baptism, and partook of his children's blessings. The child was called Arthur, after the name of his grandfather.

The year following was born a second son, who was called Philip Harclay; upon him the noble knight of that name settled his estate in Yorkshire; and by the king's permission, he took the name and arms of that family.

The third son was called William; he inherited the fortune of his uncle of that name, who adopted him, and he made the Castle of Lovel his residence, and died a bachelor.

The fourth son was called Edmund; the fifth Owen; and there was also a daughter, called Emma.

When time had worn out the prejudices of Sir Robert Fitz-Owen, the good old Baron of that name proposed a marriage between his eldest son and heir, and the daughter of Edmund Lord Lovel, which was happily concluded. The nuptials were honoured with the presence of both families; and the old Baron was so elevated with this happy union of his descendants, that he cried out, "Now I am ready to die — I have lived long enough — this is the band of love that unites all my children to me, and to each other!" He did not long survive this happy event; he died full of years and honours, and his name was never mentioned but with the deepest marks of gratitude, love and veneration. Sweet is the remembrance of the virtuous, and happy are the descendants of such a father! they will think on him and emulate his virtues — they will remember him, and be ashamed to degenerate from their ancestor.

Many years after Sir Philip Harclay settled at the Castle, he received tidings from his friend Zadisky, by one of the two servants who attended him to the Holy Land. From him he learned that his friend had discovered, by private advices, that he had a son living in Palestine, which was the chief motive of his leaving England; that he had met with various adventures in pursuit of him; that at length he found him, converted him to the Christian religion, and then persuaded him to retire from the world into a monastery by the side of Mount Libanus, where he intended to end his days.

That Walter, commonly called Lord Lovel, had entered into the service of the Greek emperor, John Paleologus, not bearing to undergo a life of solitude and retirement; that he made up a story of his being compelled to leave his native country by his relations, for having accidentally killed one of them, and that he was treated with great cruelty and injustice; that he had accepted a post in the emperor's army, and was soon after married to the daughter of one of the chief officers of it.

Zadisky foresaw, and lamented the downfall of that Empire, and withdrew from the storm he saw approaching. Finally, he bade the messenger tell Sir Philip Harclay and his adopted son, that he should not cease to pray for them, and desired their prayers in return.

Sir Philip desired Lord Lovel to entertain this messenger in his service. That good knight lived to extreme old age in honour and happiness, and died in the arms of his beloved Edmund, who also performed the last duties to his faithful Joseph.

Father Oswald lived many years in the family as chaplain; he retired from thence at length, and died in his own monastery.

Edmund Lord Lovel lived to old age, in peace, honour and happiness; and died in the arms of his children.

Sir Philip Harclay caused the papers relating to his son's history to be collected together; the first part of it was written under his own eye in Yorkshire, the subsequent parts by Father Oswald at the Castle of Lovel. All these, when together, furnish a striking lesson to posterity, of the over-ruling hand of Providence, and the certainty of RETRIBUTION.

Vathek;
An Arabian Tale

By William Beckford, Esq.

MEMOIR.

BY WILLIAM NORTH.

William Beckford, the author of the following celebrated Eastern tale, was born in 1760, and died in the spring of 1844, at the advanced age of eighty-four years. It is to be regretted, that a man of so remarkable a character, did not leave the world some record of a life offering points of interest different from that of any of his contemporaries, from the peculiarly studious retirement and eccentric avocations in which it was chiefly passed. Such a memoir would have formed a curious contrast with that of the late M. de Chateaubriand, who, born nearly at the same period, outlived but by a few years, the strange Englishman, whose famous romance forms a brilliant ornament to French literature, which even Atala is unlikely to outlive in the memory of Chateaubriand's countrymen. All men of genius should write autobiographies. Such works are inestimable lessons to posterity. As it is, there are few men, of whom it is more difficult to compose an elaborate and detailed history than the author of "Vathek." From such scanty sources as are open to us, the reader must be content with a few striking facts and illustrations, which may serve to convey some idea of the idiosyncrasy of a man, whose whole life was a sort of mystery, even to his personal acquaintances.

His great-great-grandfather was lieutenant-governor and commander of the forces in Jamaica; and his grandfather president of the council in the same island. His father, though not a merchant, as has been represented, but a large landed proprietor, both in England and the West Indies, was lord mayor of London, and distinguished himself in presenting an address to the king, George the Third,—by a spirited retort to his majesty,—who had the ill-breeding to treat discourteously a deputation which the lord mayor headed. The portraits of Alderman Beckford, and his more celebrated son, were painted by Sir Joshua Reynolds. The former died in 1770, leaving the subject of this memoir the wealthiest commoner in England.

No pains were spared on the education of the young Croesus—the lords Chatham and Camden being consulted by his father on that subject. Besides Latin and Greek, he spoke five modern languages, and wrote three with facility and elegance. He read Persian and Arabic, designed with great skill, and studied the science of music under the great Mozart.

At the age of eighteen he visited Paris, and was introduced to Voltaire. "On taking leave of me," said Beckford, "he placed his hand on my head, saying, 'There, young Englishman, I give you the blessing of a very old man.' Voltaire was a mere skeleton—a bony anatomy. His countenance I shall never forget."

His first literary production, "Memoirs of Extraordinary Painters," was written at the early age of seventeen. It would appear, that the old housekeeper at Fonthill, was in the habit of edifying visitors to its picture gallery by a description of the paintings, mainly derived from her own fertile imagination. This suggested to our author, the humorous idea of composing a catalogue of supposititious painters with histories of each, equally fanciful and grotesque. Henceforward, the old housekeeper had a printed guide (or rather, mis-guider) to go by, and could discourse at large on the merits of Og of Bashan! Waterslouchy of Amsterdam! and Herr Sucrewasser of Vienna! their wives and styles! As for the country squires, etc., "they," Beckford tells us, "took all for gospel."

"Vathek,"—the superb "Vathek," which Lord Byron so much admired, and on which he so frequently complimented the author,—"Vathek," the finest of Oriental romances, as "Lallah Rookh" is the first of Oriental poems, by the pen of a "Frank," was written and published before our author had completed his twentieth year, it having been composed at a single sitting! Yes, for three days and two nights did the indefatigable author persevere in his task. He completed it, and a serious illness was the result. What other literary man ever equalled this feat of rapidity and genius?

"Vathek" was originally written in French, of which its style is a model. The translation which follows, is not by the author himself, though he expressed perfect satisfaction with it. It was originally published in 1786. For splendour of description, exquisite humour, and supernatural interest and grandeur, it stands without a rival in romance. In as thoroughly Oriental keeping, Hope's "Anastasius, or Memoirs of a Modern Greek," which Beckford himself highly admired, can alone be compared with it.

252

Much of the description of Vathek's palace, and even the renowned "Hall of Eblis," was afterwards visibly embodied in the real Fonthill Abbey, of which wonders, almost as fabulous, were at one time reported and believed.

Fonthill Abbey, which had been destroyed by fire, and re-built during the life-time of the elder Beckford, was on account of its bad site demolished, and again re-built under the superintendence of our author himself, assisted by James Wyatt, Esq., the architect, with a magnificence that excited the greatest attention and wonder at the time. The total outlay of building Fonthill, including furniture, articles of virtu, etc., must have been enormous, not much within the million, as estimated by the "Times." A writer in the "Athenæum" mentions £400,000 as the sum. Beckford informed Mr. Cyrus Redding, that the exact cost of building Fonthill was £273,000.

The distinguishing architectural peculiarity of Fonthill Abbey, was a lofty tower, 280 feet in height. This tower was prominently shadowed forth in "Vathek," and shows how strong a hold the idea had upon his mind. Such was his impatience to see Fonthill completed, that he had the works continued by torchlight, with relays of workmen. During the progress of the building, the tower caught fire, and was partly destroyed. The owner, however, was present, and enjoyed the magnificent burning spectacle. It was soon restored; but a radical fault in laying the foundation, caused it eventually to fall down, and leave Fonthill a ruin in the life-time of its founder.

Not so much his extravagant mode of life, which is the common notion, as the loss of two large estates in a law suit (the value of which may be inferred from the fact, that fifteen hundred slaves were upon them) induced our author to quit Fonthill, and offer it and its contents for public sale. There was a general desire to see the interior of the palace, in which its lord had lived in a luxurious seclusion, so little admired by the curious of the fashionable world. "He is fortunate," says the "Times" of 1822, "who finds a vacant chair within twenty miles of Fonthill; the solitude of a private apartment is a luxury which few can hope for." . . . "Falstaff himself could not take his ease at this moment within a dozen leagues of Fonthill." . . . "The beds through the county are (literally) doing double duty — people who come in from a distance during the night must wait to go to bed until others get up in the morning." . . . "Not a farm-house, however humble, — not a cottage near Fonthill, but gives shelter to fashion, to beauty, and rank; ostrich plumes, which, by their very waving, we can trace back to Piccadilly, are seen nodding at a casement window over a depopulated poultry-yard."

The costly treasures of art and virtu, as well as the furniture of the rich mansion, were scattered far and wide; and one of its tables served the writer of this memoir to scribble upon, when first stern necessity, or yet sterner ambition, urged him to add his mite to the Babel tower of literature. At that table I first read "Vathek." I have read it often since, and every perusal has increased my admiration.

Nearly fifty years after the publication of "Vathek," in 1835, Mr. Beckford published his "Recollections of an Excursion to the Monasteries of Alcobaca and Batalha," which he had taken in 1795, together with an epistolatory record of his observations in Italy, Spain and Portugal, between the years 1780 and 1794. These are marked, as he himself intimates, "with the bloom and heyday of youthful spirits and youthful confidence, at a period when the older order of things existed with all its picturesque pomps and absurdities; when Venice enjoyed her Piombi and sub-marine dungeons; Prance her Bastille; the Peninsula her Holy Inquisition." With none of those subjects, however, are the letters occupied—but with delineations of landscape, and the effects of natural phenomena. These literary efforts appear to have exhausted their author's productive powers; in a word, he seems soon to have been "used-up," and then to have discontinued his search after new sensations, or to have been content to live without them.

After the sale of Fonthill, our author lived a considerable time in Portugal, and hence Lord Byron, who was fond of casting the shadow of his own imagination over every object, penned the well-known lines at Cintra:

"There thou, too, Vathek, England's wealthiest son,

Once formed thy paradise; as not aware

Where wanton wealth her mightiest deeds hath done,

Meek peace, voluptuous lures, was ever wont to shun.

Here didst thou dwell; here scenes of pleasure plan,

Beneath yon mountain's ever beauteous brow;

But now, as if a thing unblest by man,

Thy fairy dwelling is as lone as thou!

Here giant weeds a passage scarce allow

To halls deserted; portals gaping wide

Fresh lessons to the thinking bosom; how

Vain are the pleasaunces on earth supplied,

Swept into wrecks anon by time's ungentle tide."

These sombre verses contrast strangely with Beckford's saying to Mr. Cyrus Redding, in his seventy-sixth year, "that he had never felt a moments' ennui in his life."

Beckford was in person scarcely above the middle height, slender, and well formed, with features indicating great intellectual power. He was exactly one year younger than Pitt, the companion of his minority. His political principles were popular, though it is recorded, that at a court ball on the Queen's birth-day, in 1782, he, with Miss North, led up a country dance. He sat in parliament, in his early years, both for Wells and Hendon, but retired on account of bad health. This, however, he overcame by careful diet and exercise, as testified by his great bodily activity almost to the last. He was a man of most extensive reading, and cultivated taste.

The last years of his life were passed at Bath—where he united two houses in Lansdown Crescent, by an arch thrown across the street, and containing his library, which was well selected, and very extensive. Not far off, he again erected a tower, 180 feet high, of which the following description was given at the time of his decease, by a correspondent of the Athenæum:—

"Mr. Beckford, at an early period of his residence there, erected a lofty tower, in the apartments of which were placed many of his choicest paintings and articles of virtu. Asiatic in its style, with gilded lattices and blinds, or curtains, of crimson cloth, its striped ceilings, its minaret, and other accessories, conveyed the idea that the being who designed the place and endeavoured to carry out the plan, was deeply imbued with the spirit of that lonely grandeur and strict solitariness which obtains through all countries and among all people of the East. The building was surrounded by a high wall, and entrance afforded to the garden in which the tower stood, by a door of small dimensions. The garden itself was Eastern in its character. Though comparatively circumscribed in its size, nevertheless were to be found within it, solitary walks and deep retiring shades, such as could be supposed Vathek, the mournful and the magnificent, loved, and from the bowers of which might be expected would suddenly fall upon the ear, sounds of the cymbal and the dulcimer. The building contained several apartments crowded with the finest paintings. At the time I made my inspection the walls were crowded with the choicest productions of the easel. The memory falls back upon ineffaceable impressions of Old Franks, Breughel, Cuyp, Titian, (a Holy Family), Hondekooter, Polemberg, and a host of other painters whose works have immortalized Art. Ornaments of the most exquisite gold fillagree, carvings in ivory and wood, Raphaelesque china, goblets formed of gems, others fashioned by the miraculous hands of Benvenuto Cellini, filled the many cabinets and recherché receptacles created for such things. The doors of the rooms were of finely polished wood — the windows of single sweeps of plate glass — the cornices of gilded silver; every part, both within and without, bespeaking the wealth, the magnificence, and the taste of him who had built this temple in dedication to grandeur, solitariness, and the arts."

From the summit of this tower, Mr. Beckford, and he alone without a telescope, — could behold that other tower of his youthful magnificence, Fonthill; on which he loved to gaze, with feelings which it would be difficult to describe. His eyesight was wonderful; he could gaze upon the sun like an eagle; and on the day that the great tower at Fonthill fell he missed it in the landscape long before the news of the catastrophe reached Bath.

In conclusion, we have only to add, that our author, in his life-time, had all that wealth can give, and in his grave his memory will retain that which no wealth can purchase. Whatever may have been his errors, they have died with him. His genius yet lives, and "Vathek," now for the first time presented to the public in a popular form, will, whilst English literature lasts, never want readers, and, while good taste flourishes, admirers.

PREFACE.

The original of the following story, with some others of a similar kind, collected in the east by a man of letters, was communicated to the editor above three years ago. The pleasure he received from the perusal of it induced him at that time to transcribe, and since to translate it. How far the copy may be a just representation it becomes not him to determine. He presumes however to hope that if the difficulty of accommodating our English idioms to the Arabic, preserving the correspondent tones of a diversified narration, and discriminating the nicer touches of character through the shades of foreign manners be duly considered, a failure in some points will not preclude him from all claim to indulgence; especially if those images, sentiments, and passions, which being independent of local peculiarities, may be expressed in every language, shall be found to retain their native energy in our own.

VATHEK.

Vathek, ninth Caliph [7a] of the race of the Abassides, was the son of Motassem, and the grandson of Haroun Al Raschid. From an early accession to the throne, and the talents he possessed to adorn it, his subjects were induced to expect that his reign would be long and happy. His figure was pleasing and majestic; but when he was angry, one of his eyes became so terrible [7b] that no person could bear to behold it; and the wretch upon whom it was fixed instantly fell backward, and sometimes expired. For fear, however, of depopulating his dominions, and making his palace desolate, he but rarely gave way to his anger.

Being much addicted to women, and the pleasures of the table, he sought by his affability to procure agreeable companions; and he succeeded the better, as his generosity was unbounded and his indulgences unrestrained; for he was by no means scrupulous: nor did he think, with the Caliph Omar Ben Abdalaziz, [8a] that it was necessary to make a hell of this world to enjoy Paradise in the next.

He surpassed in magnificence all his predecessors. The palace of Alkoremmi, which his father Motassem had erected on the hill of Pied Horses, and which commanded the whole city of Samarah, [8b] was in his idea far too scanty: he added, therefore, five wings, or rather other palaces, which he destined for the particular gratification of each of his senses.

257

In the first of these were tables continually covered with the most exquisite dainties, which were supplied both by night and by day according to their constant consumption; whilst the most delicious wines, and the choicest cordials, flowed forth from a hundred fountains, that were never exhausted. This palace was called "The Eternal, or Unsatiating Banquet."

The second was styled "The Temple of Melody, or the Nectar of the Soul." It was inhabited by the most skilful musicians and admired poets of the time, who not only displayed their talents within, but dispersing in bands without, caused every surrounding scene to reverberate their songs, which were continually varied in the most delightful succession.

The palace named "The Delight of the Eyes, or the Support of Memory," was one entire enchantment. Rarities collected from every corner of the earth were there found in such profusion as to dazzle and confound, but for the order in which they were arranged. One gallery exhibited the pictures of the celebrated Mani; and statues that seemed to be alive. Here a well-managed perspective attracted the sight; there, the magic of optics agreeably deceived it; whilst the naturalist, on his part, exhibited in their several classes the various gifts that heaven had bestowed on our globe. In a word, Vathek omitted nothing in this particular that might gratify the curiosity of those who resorted to it, although he was not able to satisfy his own; for he was, of all men, the most curious.

"The Palace of Perfumes," which was termed likewise, "The Incentive to Pleasure," consisted of various halls, where the different perfumes which the earth produces were kept perpetually burning in censers of gold. Flambeaus and aromatic lamps were here lighted in open day; but the too powerful effects of this agreeable delirium might be avoided by descending into an immense garden, where an assemblage of every fragrant flower diffused through the air the purest odours.

The fifth palace, denominated "The Retreat of Joy, or the Dangerous," was frequented by troops of young females, beautiful as the Houris, [9] and not less seducing, who never failed to receive with caresses all whom the Caliph allowed to approach them; for he was by no means disposed to be jealous, as his own women were secluded within the palace he inhabited himself.

Notwithstanding the sensuality in which Vathek indulged, he experienced no abatement in the love of his people, who thought that a sovereign immersed in pleasure was not less tolerable to his subjects than one that employed himself in creating them foes. But the unquiet and impetuous disposition of the Caliph would not allow him to rest there: he had studied so much for his amusement in the life-time of his father as to acquire a great deal of knowledge, though not a sufficiency to satisfy himself; for he wished to know everything; even sciences that did not exist. He was fond of engaging in disputes with the learned, but liked them not to push their opposition with warmth. He stopped the mouths of those with presents, whose mouths could be stopped; whilst others, whom his liberality was unable to subdue, he sent to prison to cool their blood; a remedy that often succeeded.

Vathek discovered also a predilection for theological controversy; but it was not with the orthodox that he usually held. By this means he induced the zealots to oppose him, and then persecuted them in return; for he resolved, at any rate, to have reason on his side.

The great prophet Mahomet, whose vicars the Caliphs are, beheld with indignation from his abode in the seventh heaven the irreligious conduct of such a vicegerent.

"Let us leave him to himself," said he to the Genii, [10] who are always ready to receive his commands; "let us see to what lengths his folly and impiety will carry him; if he run into excess we shall know how to chastise him. Assist him, therefore, to complete the tower which, in imitation of Nimrod, he hath begun; not, like that great warrior, to escape being drowned, but from the insolent curiosity of penetrating the secrets of heaven: he will not divine the fate that awaits him."

The Genii obeyed; and when the workmen had raised their structure a cubit in the day time, two cubits more were added in the night. The expedition with which the fabric arose was not a little flattering to the vanity of Vathek. He fancied that even insensible matter showed forwardness to subserve his designs; not considering that the successes of the foolish and wicked form the first rod of their chastisement.

His pride arrived at its height when, having ascended, for the first time, the eleven thousand stairs of his tower, he cast his eyes below and beheld men not larger than pismires; mountains than shells; and cities than bee-hives. The idea which such an elevation inspired of his own grandeur completely bewildered him; he was almost ready to adore himself; till lifting his eyes upwards, he saw the stars as high above him as they appeared when he stood on the surface of the earth. He consoled himself, however, for this transient perception of his littleness with the thought of being great in the eyes of the others, and flattered himself that the light of his mind would extend beyond the reach of his sight, and transfer to the stars the decrees of his destiny.

With this view the inquisitive prince passed most of his nights on the summit of his tower, till he became an adept in the mysteries of astrology, and imagined that the planets had disclosed to him the most marvellous adventures, which were to be accomplished by an extraordinary personage, from a country altogether unknown. Prompted by motives of curiosity, he had always been courteous to strangers; but from this instant he redoubled his attention, and ordered it to be announced by sound of trumpet, through all the streets of Samarah, that no one of his subjects, on peril of his displeasure, should either lodge or detain a traveller, but forthwith bring him to the palace.

Not long after this proclamation, there arrived in his metropolis, a man so hideous that the very guards who arrested him were forced to shut their eyes as they led him along. The Caliph himself appeared startled at so horrible a visage; but joy succeeded to this emotion of terror when the stranger displayed to his view such rarities as he had never before seen, and of which he had no conception.

In reality, nothing was ever so extraordinary as the merchandise this stranger produced. Most of his curiosities, which were not less admirable for their workmanship than their splendour, had besides, their several virtues described on a parchment fastened to each. There were slippers which enabled the feet to walk; knives that cut without the motion of a hand; sabres which dealt the blow at the person they were wished to strike; and the whole enriched with gems that were hitherto unknown.

The sabres, whose blades emitted a dazzling radiance, fixed more than all the Caliph's attention, who promised himself to decipher at his leisure the uncouth characters engraven on their sides. Without, therefore, demanding their price, he ordered all the coined gold to be brought from his treasury, and commanded the merchant to take what he pleased. The stranger complied with modesty and silence.

Vathek, imagining that the merchant's taciturnity was occasioned by the awe which his presence inspired, encouraged him to advance, and asked him, with an air of condescension, "Who he was? whence he came? and where he obtained such beautiful commodities?"

The man, or rather monster, instead of making a reply, thrice rubbed his forehead, which, as well as his body, was blacker than ebony; four times clapped his paunch, the projection of which was enormous; opened wide his huge eyes, which glowed like firebrands; began to laugh with a hideous noise, and discovered his long amber coloured teeth bestreaked with green.

The Caliph, though a little startled, renewed his enquiries, but without being able to procure a reply. At which, beginning to be ruffled, he exclaimed, "knowest thou, varlet, who I am? and at whom thou art aiming thy gibes?" Then addressing his guards, "have ye heard him speak? is he dumb?"

"He hath spoken," they replied, "though but little."

"Let him speak then again," said Vathek, "and tell me who he is, from whence he came, and where he procured these singular curiosities, or I swear, by the ass of Balaam, that I will make him rue his pertinacity."

This menace was accompanied by the Caliph with one of his angry and perilous glances, which the stranger sustained without the slightest emotion, although his eyes were fixed on the terrible eye of the prince.

No words can descibe the amazement of the courtiers, when they beheld this rude merchant withstand the encounter unshocked. They all fell prostrate with their faces on the ground, to avoid the risk of their lives, and continued in the same abject posture till the Caliph exclaimed in a furious tone:

"Up, cowards! seize the miscreant! see that he be committed to prison, and guarded by the best of my soldiers! Let him, however, retain the money I gave him; it is not my intent to take from him his property, I only want him to speak."

No sooner had he uttered these words than the stranger was surrounded, pinioned with strong fetters, and hurried away to the prison of the great tower, which was encompassed by seven empalements of iron bars, and armed with spikes in every direction, longer and sharper than spits.

The Caliph, nevertheless, remained in the most violent agitation. He sat down indeed to eat, but of the three hundred covers that were daily placed before him, could taste of no more than thirty-two.

A diet to which he had been so little accustomed, was sufficient of itself to prevent him from sleeping, what then must be its effect when joined to the anxiety that prayed upon his spirits? At the first glimpse of dawn he hastened to the prison, again to importune this intractable stranger; but the rage of Vathek exceeded all bounds on finding the prison empty, the gates burst asunder, and his guards lying lifeless around him. In the paroxysm of his passion he fell furiously on the poor carcases, and kicked them till evening without intermission. His courtiers and viziers exerted their efforts to soothe his extravagance, but finding every expedient ineffectual, they all united in one vociferation:

"The Caliph is gone mad! the Caliph is out of his senses!"

This outcry, which was soon resounded through the streets of Samarah, at length reached the ears of Carathis, his mother: she flew in the utmost consternation to try her ascendency on the mind of her son. Her tears and caresses called off his attention; and he was prevailed upon by her entreaties to be brought back to the palace.

Carathis, apprehensive of leaving Vathek to himself, caused him to be put to bed; and seating herself by him, endeavoured by her conversation to heal and compose him. Nor could any one have attempted it with better success; for the Caliph not only loved her as a mother but respected her as a person of superior genius. It was she who had induced him, being a Greek herself, to adopt all the sciences and systems of her country, which good Mussulmans hold in such thorough abhorrence.

Judicial astrology was one of those systems in which Carathis was a perfect adept. She began, therefore, with reminding her son of the promise which the stars had made him; and intimated an intention of consulting them again.

"Alas!" sighed the Caliph, as soon at he could speak, "what a fool have I been! not for the kicks bestowed on my guards, who so tamely submitted to death, but for never considering that this extraordinary man was the same the planets had foretold; whom, instead of ill-treating, I should have conciliated by all the arts of persuasion."

"The past," said Carathis, "cannot be recalled; but it behoves us to think of the future: perhaps you may again see the object you so much regret: it is possible the inscriptions on the sabres will afford information. Eat, therefore, and take thy repose, my dear son. We will consider, to-morrow, in what manner to act."

Vathek yielded to her counsel as well as he could, and arose in the morning with a mind more at ease. The sabres he commanded to be instantly brought; and poring upon them through a green glass, that their glittering might not dazzle, he set himself in earnest to decipher the inscriptions; but his reiterated attempts were all of them nugatory: in vain did he beat his head and bite his nails; not a letter of the whole was he able to ascertain. So unlucky a disappointment would have undone him again, had not Carathis, by good fortune, entered the apartment.

"Have patience, son!" said she. "You certainly are possessed of every important science, but the knowledge of languages is a trifle, at best; and the accomplishment of none but a pedant. Issue forth a proclamation that you will confer such rewards as become your greatness upon any one that shall interpret what you do not understand, and what it is beneath you to learn. You will soon find your curiosity gratified."

"That may be," said the Caliph; "but in the mean time I shall be horribly disgusted by a crowd of smatterers, who will come to the trial as much for the pleasure of retailing their jargon as from the hope of gaining the reward. To avoid this evil, it will be proper to add that I will put every candidate to death who shall fail to give satisfaction; for, thank heaven, I have skill enough to distinguish between one that translates and one that invents."

"Of that I have no doubt," replied Carathis, "but to put the ignorant to death is somewhat severe, and may be productive of dangerous effects. Content yourself with commanding their beards to be burnt: beards, in a state, are not quite so essential as men."

The Caliph submitted to the reasons of his mother, and sending for Morakanabad, his prime vizier, said:

"Let the common criers proclaim, not only in Samarah, but throughout every city in my empire, that whosoever will repair hither, and decipher certain characters which appear to be inexplicable, shall experience the liberality for which I am renowned; but that all who fail upon trial shall have their beards burnt off to the last hair. Let them add also, that I will bestow fifty beautiful slaves, and as many jars of apricots from the isle of Kirmith, upon any man that shall bring me intelligence of the stranger."

The subjects of the Caliph, like their sovereign, being great admirers of women, and apricots from Kirmith, felt their mouths water at these promises, but were totally unable to gratify their hankering, for no one knew which way the stranger had gone.

As to the Caliph's other requisition the result was different: the learned, the half-learned, and those who were neither, but fancied themselves equal to both, came boldly to hazard their beards, and all shamefully lost them.

The exaction of these forfeitures, which found sufficient employment for the Eunuchs, gave them such a smell of singed hair as greatly to disgust the ladies of the seraglio, and make it necessary that this new occupation of their guardians should be transferred into other hands.

At length, however, an old man presented himself, whose beard was a cubit-and-a-half longer than any that had appeared before him. The officers of the palace whispered to each other, as they ushered him in:

"What a pity such a beard should be burnt!"

Even the Caliph, when he saw it, concurred with them in opinion; but his concern was entirely needless. This venerable personage read the characters with facility, and explained them verbatim, as follows:

"We were made where everything good is made; we are the least of the wonders of a place where all is wonderful; and deserving the sight of the first potentate on earth."

"You translate admirably!" cried Vathek. "I know to what these marvellous characters allude. Let him receive as many robes of honour, and thousands of sequins of gold, as he hath spoken words. I am in some measure relieved from the perplexiy that embarrassed me!"

Vathek invited the old man to dine, and even to remain some days in the palace. Unluckily for him, he accepted the offer; for the Caliph having ordered him next morning to be called, said:

"Read again to me what you have read already; I cannot hear too often the promise that is made me, the completion of which I languish to obtain."

The old man forthwith put on his green spectacles; but they instantly dropped from his nose, on perceiving that the characters he had read the day preceding, had given place to others of different import.

"What ails you?" asked the Caliph; "and why these symptoms of wonder?"

"Sovereign of the world," replied the old man, "these sabres hold another language to-day, from that they yesterday held."

"How say you?" returned Vathek. "But it matters not! tell me, if you can, what they mean."

"It is this, my lord," rejoined the old man: "'Woe to the rash mortal who seeks to know that of which he should remain ignorant and to undertake that which surpasseth his power!'"

"And woe to thee!" cried the Caliph, in a burst of indignation: "to-day thou art void of understanding: begone from my presence, they shall burn but the half of thy beard, because thou wert yesterday fortunate in guessing. My gifts I never resume."

The old man, wise enough to perceive he had luckily escaped, considering the folly of disclosing so disgusting a truth, immediately withdrew, and appeared not again.

But it was not long before Vathek discovered abundant reason to regret his precipitation; for though he could not decipher the characters himself, yet, by constantly poring upon them, he plainly perceived that they every day changed; and unfortunately no other candidate offered to explain them. This perplexing occupation inflamed his blood, dazzled his sight, and brought on a giddiness and debility that he could not support. He failed not, however, though in so reduced a condition, to be often carried to his tower, as he flattered himself that he might there read in the stars, which he went to consult, something more congruous to his wishes. But in this his hopes were deluded; for his eyes, dimmed by the vapours of his head, began to subserve his curiosity so ill, that he beheld nothing but a thick dun cloud, which he took for the most direful of omens.

265

Agitated with so much anxiety, Vathek entirely lost all firmness; a fever seized him and his appetite failed. Instead of being one of the greatest eaters, he became as distinguished for drinking. So insatiable was the thirst which tormented him, that his mouth, like a funnel, was always open to receive the various liquors that might be poured into it and especially cold water, which calmed him more than every other.

This unhappy prince being thus incapacitated for the enjoyment of any pleasure, commanded the palaces of the five senses to be shut up; forebore to appear in public, either to display his magnificence or administer justice; and retired to the inmost apartment of his harem. As he had ever been an indulgent husband, his wives, overwhelmed with grief at his deplorable situation, incessantly offered their prayers for his health, and unremittingly supplied him with water.

In the mean time, the Princess Carathis, whose affliction no words can describe, instead of restraining herself to sobbing and tears, was closeted daily with the Vizier Morakanabad, to find out some cure or mitigation of the Caliph's disease. Under the persuasion that it was caused by enchantment, they turned over together leaf by leaf, all the books of magic that might point out a remedy; and caused the horrible stranger, whom they accused as the enchanter, to be everywhere sought for with the strictest diligence.

At the distance of a few miles from Samarah stood a high mountain, whose sides were swarded with wild thyme and basil, and its summit overspread with so delightful a plain that it might be taken for the Paradise destined for the faithful. Upon it grew a hundred thickets of eglantine and other fragrant shrubs; a hundred arbours of roses, jessamine, and honeysuckle; as many clumps of orange trees, cedar, and citron; whose branches, interwoven with the palm, the pomegranate, and the vine, presented every luxury that could regale the eye or the taste. The ground was strewed with violets, harebells, and pansies; in the midst of which sprung forth tufts of jonquils, hyacinths, and carnations, with every other perfume that impregnates the air. Four fountains, not less clear than deep, and so abundant as to slake the thirst of ten armies, seemed purposely placed here to make the scene more resemble the garden of Eden, which was watered by the four sacred rivers. Here the nightingale sang the birth of the rose, her well-beloved, and at the same time lamented its short-lived beauty; whilst the turtle deplored the loss of more substantial pleasures and the wakeful lark hailed the rising light that reanimates the whole creation. Here, more than anywhere, the mingled melodies of birds expressed the various passions they inspired; as if the exquisite fruits, which they pecked at pleasure, had given them a double energy.

To this mountain Vathek was sometimes brought, for the sake of breathing a purer air; and especially, to drink at will of the four fountains, which were reputed in the highest degree salubrious, and sacred to himself. His attendants were his mother, his wives, and some eunuchs, who assiduously employed themselves in filling capacious bowls of rock crystal, and emulously presenting them to him. But it frequently happened that his avidity exceeded their zeal; insomuch that he would prostrate himself upon the ground to lap up the water, of which he could never have enough.

One day when this unhappy prince had been long lying in so debasing a posture, a voice, hoarse but strong, thus addressed him:

"Why assumest thou the function of a dog, oh Caliph, so proud of thy dignity and power?"

At this apostrophe he raised up his head and beheld the stranger that had caused him so much affliction. Inflamed with anger at the sight, he exclaimed:

"Accursed Giaour! [23] what comest thou hither to do? is it not enough to have transformed a prince, remarkable for his agility, into one of those leather barrels which the Bedouin Arabs carry on their camels when they traverse the deserts? Perceivest thou not that I may perish by drinking to excess, no less than by a total abstinence?"

"Drink then this draught," said the stranger, as he presented to him a phial of a red and yellow mixture; "and to satiate the thirst of thy soul as well as of thy body, know that I am an Indian, but from a region of India which is wholly unknown."

The Caliph, delighted to see his desires accomplished in part, and flattering himself with the hope of obtaining their entire fulfilment, without a moment's hesitation swallowed the potion, and instantaneously found his health restored, his thirst appeased, and his limbs as agile as ever.

In the transports of his joy, Vathek leaped upon the neck of the frightful Indian, and kissed his horrid mouth and hollow cheeks, as though they had been the coral lips, and the lilies and roses of his most beautiful wives; whilst they, less terrified than jealous at the sight, dropped their veils to hide the blush of mortification that suffused their foreheads.

Nor would the scene have closed here, had not Carathis, with all the art of insinuation, a little repressed the raptures of her son. Having prevailed upon him to return to Samarah, she caused a herald to precede him, whom she commanded to proclaim as loudly as possible:

"The wonderful stranger hath appeared again; he hath healed the Caliph; he hath spoken! he hath spoken!"

Forthwith all the inhabitants of this vast city quitted their habitations, and ran together in crowds to see the procession of Vathek and the Indian, whom they now blessed as much as they had before execrated, incessantly shouting,

"He hath healed our sovereign; he hath spoken! he hath spoken!"

Nor were these words forgotten in the public festivals, which were celebrated the same evening to testify the general joy, for the poets applied them as a chorus to all the songs they composed.

The Caliph, in the mean while caused the palaces of the senses to be again set open, and as he found himself prompted to visit that of taste, in preference to the rest, immediately ordered a splendid entertainment, to which his great officers and favourite courtiers were all invited. The Indian, who was placed near the prince, seemed to think that as a proper acknowledgment of so distinguished a privilege, he could neither eat, drink, nor talk too much. The various dainties were no sooner served up than they vanished, to the great mortification of Vathek, who piqued himself on being the greatest eater alive, and at this time in particular had an excellent appetite.

The rest of the company looked round at each other in amazement, but the Indian without appearing to observe it, quaffed large bumpers to the health of each of them: sung in a style altogether extravagant; related stories at which he laughed immoderately; and poured forth extemporaneous verses which would not have been thought bad, but for the strange grimaces with which they were uttered. In a word, his loquacity was equal to that of a hundred astrologers; he ate as much as a hundred porters, and caroused in proportion.

The Caliph, notwithstanding the table had been thirty times covered, found himself incommoded by the voraciousness of his guest, who was now considerably declined in the prince's esteem. Vathek, however, being unwilling to betray the chagrin he could hardly disguise, said in a whisper to Bababalouk, [26a] the chief of his eunuchs:

"You see how enormous his performances in every way are; what would be the consequence should he get at my wives? Go! redouble your vigilance, and be sure look well to my Circassians, who would be more to his taste than all of the rest."

The bird of the morning had thrice renewed his song, when the hour of the divan [26b] sounded. Vathek, in gratitude to his subjects, having promised to attend, immediately arose from table and repaired thither leaning upon his vizier, who could scarcely support him, so disordered was the poor prince by the wine he had drank, and still more by the extravagant vagaries of his boisterous guest.

The viziers, the officers of the crown, and of the law, arranged themselves in a semi-circle about their sovereign, and preserved a respectful silence, whilst the Indian, who looked as cool as if come from a fast, sat down without ceremony on a step of the throne, laughing in his sleeve at the indignation with which his temerity had filled the spectators.

The Caliph, however, whose ideas were confused and his head embarrassed, went on administering justice at hap-hazard, till at length the prime vizier [27] perceiving his situation, hit upon a sudden expedient to interrupt the audience, and rescue the honour of his master, to whom he said in a whisper:

"My lord, the princess Carathis, who hath passed the night in consulting the planets, informs you that they portend you evil; and the danger is urgent. Beware, lest this stranger whom you have so lavishly recompensed for his magical gewgaws, should make some attempt on your life: his liquor, which at first had the appearance of effecting your cure, may be no more than a poison of a sudden operation. Slight not this surmise; ask him, at least, of what it was compounded; whence he procured it; and mention the sabres, which you seem to have forgotten."

Vathek, to whom the insolent airs of the stranger became every moment less supportable, intimated to his vizier by a wink of acquiescence, that he would adopt his advice, and at once turning towards the Indian, said:

"Get up and declare in full divan of what drugs the liquor was compounded you enjoined me to take, for it is suspected to be poison; add also the explanation I have so earnestly desired concerning the sabres you sold me, and thus show your gratitude for the favours heaped on you."

Having pronounced these words in as moderate a tone as a Caliph well could, he waited in silent expectation for an answer; but the Indian, still keeping his seat, began to renew his loud shouts of laughter, and exhibit the same horrid grimaces he had shown them before, without vouchsafing a word in reply. Vathek, no longer able to brook such insolence, immediately kicked him from the steps, instantly descending repeated his blow, and persisted with such assiduity, as incited all who were present to follow his example. Every foot was aimed at the Indian, and no sooner had any one given him a kick than he felt himself constrained to reiterate the stroke.

The stranger afforded them no small entertainment; for being both short and plump, he collected himself into a ball and rolled round on all sides at the blows of his assailants, who pressed after him wherever he turned, with an eagerness beyond conception, whilst their numbers were every moment increasing. The ball, indeed, in passing from one apartment to another, drew every person after it that came in its way, insomuch that the whole palace was thrown into confusion, and resounded with a tremendous clamour. The women of the harem, amazed at the uproar, flew to their blinds to discover the cause, but no sooner did they catch a glimpse of the ball than feeling themselves unable to refrain, they broke from the clutches of their eunuchs, who to stop their flight pinched them till they bled, but in vain; whilst themselves, though trembling with terror at the escape of their charge, were as incapable of resisting the attraction.

The Indian, after having traversed the halls, galleries, chambers, kitchens, gardens, and stables of the palace, at last took his course through the courts, whilst the Caliph, pursuing him closer than the rest, bestowed as many kicks as he possibly could, yet not without receiving now and then one, which his competitors, in their eagerness, designed for the ball.

Carathis, Morakanabad, and two or three old viziers whose wisdom had hitherto withstood the attraction, wishing to prevent Vathek from exposing himself in the presence of his subjects, fell down in his way to impede the pursuit, but he, regardless of their obstruction, leaped over their heads, and went on as before. They then ordered the muezzins to call the people to prayers, both for the sake of getting them out of the way, and of endeavouring by their petitions to avert the calamity; but neither of these expedients was a whit more successful. The sight of this fatal ball was alone sufficient to draw after it every beholder. The muezzins themselves, though they saw it but at a distance, hastened down from their minarets and mixed with the crowd, which continued to increase in so surprising a manner, that scarce an inhabitant was left in Samarah, except the aged, the sick confined to their beds, and infants at the breast, whose nurses could run more nimbly without them. Even Carathis, Morakanabad, and the rest, were all become of the party.

The shrill screams of the females who had broken from their apartments, and were unable to extricate themselves from the pressure of the crowd, together with those of the eunuchs jostling after them, terrified lest their charge should escape from their sight, increased by the execrations of husbands urging forward and menacing both, kicks given and received, stumblings and overthrows at every step, in a word, the confusion that universally prevailed, rendered Samarah like a city taken by storm, and devoted to absolute plunder.

At last the cursed Indian, who still preserved his rotundity of figure, after passing through all the streets and public places, and leaving them empty, rolled onwards to the plain of Catoul, and traversed the valley at the foot of the mountain of the four fountains.

As a continual fall of water had excavated an immense gulph in the valley, whose opposite side was closed in by a steep acclivity, the Caliph and his attendants were apprehensive lest the ball should bound into the chasm, and to prevent it, redoubled their efforts, but in vain. The Indian persevered in his onward direction, and as had been apprehended, glancing from the precipice with the rapidity of lightning, was lost in the gulph below.

Vathek would have followed the perfidious Giaour, had not an invisible agency arrested his progress. The multitude that pressed after him were at once checked in the same manner, and a calm instantaneously ensued. They all gazed at each other with an air of astonishment; and notwithstanding that the loss of veils and turbans, together with torn habits, and dust blended with sweat, presented a most laughable spectacle, there was not one smile to be seen; on the contrary, all with looks of confusion and sadness returned in silence to Samarah, and retired to their inmost apartments, without ever reflecting that they had been impelled by an invisible power into the extravagance for which they reproached themselves: for it is but just, that men who so often arrogate to their own merit the good of which they are but instruments, should attribute to themselves the absurdities which they could not prevent.

The Caliph was the only person that refused to leave the valley. He commanded his tents to be pitched there, and stationed himself on the very edge of the precipice, in spite of the representations of Carathis and Morakanabad, who pointed out the hazard of its brink giving way, and the vicinity to the magician that had so severely tormented him. Vathek derided all their remonstrances; and having ordered a thousand flambeaus to be lighted, and directed his attendants to proceed in lighting more, lay down on the slippery margin, and attempted, by the help of this artificial splendour, to look through that gloom which all the fires of the empyrean had been insufficient to pervade. One while he fancied to himself voices arising from the depth of the gulph, at another he seemed to distinguish the accents of the Indian, but all was no more than the hollow murmur of waters, and the din of the cataracts that rushed from steep to steep, down the sides of the mountain.

Having passed the night in this cruel perturbation, the Caliph at day-break retired to his tent, where, without taking the least sustenance, he continued to doze till the dusk of evening began to come on; he then resumed his vigils as before, and persevered in observing them for many nights together. At length, fatigued with so successless an employment, he sought relief from change. To this end he sometimes paced with hasty strides across the plain; and as he wildly gazed at the stars, reproached them with having deceived him; but lo! on a sudden the clear blue sky appeared streaked over with streams of blood, which reached from the valley even to the city of Samarah. As this awful phenomenon seemed to touch his tower, Vathek at first thought of repairing thither to view it more distinctly, but feeling himself unable to advance, and being overcome with apprehension, he muffled up his face in his robe.

Terrifying as these prodigies were, this impression upon him was no more than momentary, and served only to stimulate his love of the marvellous. Instead, therefore, of returning to his palace, he persisted in the resolution of abiding where the Indian vanished from his view. One night, however, while he was walking as usual on the plain, the moon and the stars at once were eclipsed, and a total darkness ensued. The earth trembled beneath him, and a voice came forth, the voice of the

Giaour, who in accents more sonorous than thunder, thus addressed him:

"Would'st thou devote thyself to me? adore then the terrestrial influences, and abjure Mahomet. On these conditions I will bring thee to the palace of subterranean fire: there shalt thou behold, in immense depositories, the treasures which the stars have promised thee, and which will be conferred by those intelligences whom thou shalt thus render propitious. It was from thence I brought my sabres; and it is there that Soliman Ben Daoud reposes, surrounded by the talismans that control the world."

The astonished Caliph trembled as he answered, yet in a style that showed him to be no novice in preternatural adventures:

"Where art thou? Be present to my eyes; dissipate the gloom that perplexes me, and of which I deem thee the cause. After the many flambeaus I have burnt to discover thee, thou mayest at least grant a glimpse of thy horrible visage."

"Abjure then Mahomet," replied the Indian, "and promise me full proofs of thy sincerity; otherwise thou shalt never behold me again."

The unhappy Caliph, instigated by insatiable curiosity, lavished his promises in the utmost profusion. The sky immediately brightened; and by the light of the planets, which seemed almost to blaze, Vathek beheld the earth open, and at the extremity of a vast black chasm a portal of ebony, before which stood the Indian, still blacker, holding in his hand a golden key, that caused the lock to resound.

"How," cried Vathek, "can I descend to thee, without the certainty of breaking my neck? Come take me, and instantly open the portal."

"Not so fast," replied the Indian, "impatient Caliph! Know that I am parched with thirst, and cannot open this door till my thirst be thoroughly appeased. I require the blood of fifty of the most beautiful sons of thy viziers and great men, or neither can my thirst nor thy curiosity be satisfied. Return to Samarah; procure for me this necessary libation; come back hither; throw it thyself into this chasm; and then shalt thou see!"

Having thus spoken, the Indian turned his back on the Caliph, who, incited by the suggestion of demons, resolved on the direful sacrifice. He now pretended to have regained his tranquillity, and set out for Samarah amidst the acclamations of a people who still loved him, and forbore not to rejoice when they believed him to have recovered his reason. So successfully did he conceal the emotion of his heart, that even Carathis and Morakanabad were equally deceived with the rest. Nothing was heard of but festivals and rejoicings. The ball, which no tongue had hitherto ventured to mention, was again brought on the tapis. A general laugh went round; though many, still smarting under the hands of the surgeon, from the hurts received in that memorable adventure, had no great reason for mirth.

The prevalence of this gay humour was not a little grateful to Vathek, as perceiving how much it conduced to his project. He put on the appearance of affability to every one; but especially to his viziers, and the grandees of his court, whom he failed not to regale with a sumptuous banquet, during which he insensibly inclined the conversation to the children of his guests. Having asked, with a good-natured air, who of them were blessed with the handsomest boys, every father at once asserted the pretensions of his own; and the contest imperceptibly grew so warm, that nothing could have withholden them from coming to blows but their profound reverence for the person of the Caliph. Under the pretence, therefore, of reconciling the disputants, Vathek took upon him to decide; and with this view commanded the boys to be brought.

It was not long before a troop of these poor children made their appearance, all equipped by their fond mothers with such ornaments as might give the greatest relief to their beauty, or most advantageously display the graces of their age. But whilst this brilliant assemblage attracted the eyes and hearts of every one besides, the Caliph scrutinized each in his turn with a malignant avidity that passed for attention, and selected from their number the fifty whom he judged the Giaour would prefer.

With an equal show of kindness as before, he proposed to celebrate a festival on the plain, for the entertainment of his young favourites, who he said ought to rejoice still more than all at the restoration of his health, on account of the favours he intended for them.

The Caliph's proposal was received with the greatest delight, and soon published through Samarah. Litters, camels, and horses were prepared. Women and children, old men and young—every one placed himself in the station he chose. The cavalcade set forward, attended by all the confectioners in the city and its precincts. The populace, following on foot, composed an amazing crowd, and occasioned no little noise. All was joy; nor did any one call to mind what most of them had suffered when they first travelled the road they were now passing so gaily.

The evening was serene, the air refreshing, the sky clear, and the flowers exhaled their fragrance. The beams of the declining sun, whose mild splendour reposed on the summit of the mountain, shed a glow of ruddy light over its green declivity, and the white flocks sporting upon it. No sounds were audible, save the murmurs of the four fountains, and the reeds and voices of shepherds, calling to each other from different eminences.

The lovely innocents, proceeding to the destined sacrifice, added not a little to the hilarity of the scene. They approached the plain full of sportiveness; some coursing butterflies, others culling flowers, or picking up the shining little pebbles that attracted their notice. At intervals, they nimbly started from each other, for the sake of being caught again, and mutually imparting a thousand caresses.

The dreadful chasm, at whose bottom the portal of ebony was placed, began to appear at a distance. It looked like a black streak that divided the plain. Morakanabad and his companions took it for some work which the Caliph had ordered. Unhappy men! little did they surmise for what it was destined.

Vathek, not liking that they should examine it too nearly, stopped the procession, and ordered a spacious circle to be formed on this side, at some distance from the accursed chasm. The body-guard of eunuchs was detached, to measure out the lists intended for the games, and prepare ringles for the lines to keep off the crowd. The fifty competitors were soon stripped, and presented to the admiration of the spectators the suppleness and grace of their delicate limbs. Their eyes sparkled with a joy which those of their fond parents reflected. Every one offered wishes for the little candidate nearest his heart, and doubted not of his being victorious. A breathless suspense awaited the contest of these amiable and innocent victims.

The Caliph, availing himself of the first moment to retire from the crowd, advanced towards the chasm, and there heard, yet not without shuddering, the voice of the Indian; who, gnashing his teeth, eagerly demanded:

"Where are they? Where are they? perceivest thou not how my mouth waters?"

"Relentless Giaour!" answered Vathek, with emotion, "can nothing content thee but the massacre of these lovely victims? Ah! wert thou to behold their beauty, it must certainly move thy compassion."

"Perdition on thy compassion, babbler!" cried the Indian. "Give them me! instantly give them, or my portal shall be closed against thee for ever!"

"Not so loudly," replied the Caliph, blushing.

"I understand thee," returned the Giaour, with the grin of an ogre: "thou wantest to summon up more presence of mind. I will for a moment forbear."

During this exquisite dialogue the games went forward with all alacrity, and at length concluded, just as the twilight began to overcast the mountains. Vathek, who was still standing on the edge of the chasm, called out with all his might:

"Let my fifty little favourites approach me, separately; and let them come in the order of their success. To the first I will give my diamond bracelet; to the second my collar of emeralds; to the third my aigret of rubies; to the fourth my girdle of topazes; and to the rest, each a part of my dress, even down to my slippers."

This declaration was received with reiterated acclamations; and all extolled the liberality of a prince who would thus strip himself for the amusement of his subjects and the encouragement of the rising generation.

The Caliph in the mean while undressed himself by degrees; and raising his arm as high as he was able, made each of the prizes glitter in the air; but, whilst he delivered it with one hand to the child, who sprang forward to receive it, he with the other pushed the poor innocent into the gulph, where the Giaour, with a sullen muttering, incessantly repeated "More! more!"

This dreadful device was executed with so much dexterity, that the boy who was approaching him remained unconscious of the fate of his forerunner; and as to the spectators, the shades of evening, together with their distance, precluded them from perceiving any object distinctly. Vathek, having in this manner thrown in the last of the fifty, and expecting that the Giaour on receiving him would have presented the key, already fancied himself as great as Soliman, and consequently above being amenable for what he had done; when, to his utter amazement, the chasm closed, and the ground became as entire as the rest of the plain.

No language could express his rage and despair. He execrated the perfidy of the Indian; loaded him with the most infamous invectives; and stamped with his foot as resolving to be heard. He persisted in this demeanour till his strength failed him, and then fell on the earth like one void of sense. His viziers and grandees, who were nearer than the rest, supposed him at first to be sitting on the grass at play with their amiable children; but at length, prompted by doubt, they advanced towards the spot, and found the Caliph alone, who wildly demanded what they wanted.

"Our children! our children!" cried they.

"It is assuredly pleasant," said he, "to make me accountable for accidents. Your children, while at play, fell from the precipice that was here; and I should have experienced their fate had I not been saved by a sudden start back."

At these words, the fathers of the fifty boys cried out aloud: the mothers repeated their exclamations an octave higher; whilst the rest, without knowing the cause, soon drowned the voices of both, with still louder lamentations of their own.

"Our Caliph," said they, and the report soon circulated, "Our Caliph has played us this trick, to gratify his accursed Giaour. Let us punish him for his perfidy! let us avenge ourselves! let us avenge the blood of the innocent! let us throw this cruel Prince into the gulph that is near, and let his name be mentioned no more!"

At this rumour, and these menaces, Carathis, full of consternation, hastened to Morakanabad, and said:

"Vizier, you have lost two beautiful boys, and must necessarily be the most afflicted of fathers; but you are virtuous; save your master!"

"I will brave every hazard," replied the Vizier, "to rescue him from his present danger; but afterwards will abandon him to his fate. Bababalouk," continued he, "put yourself at the head of your Eunuchs, disperse the mob, and if possible bring back this unhappy Prince to his palace."

Bababalouk and his fraternity, felicitating each other in a low voice on their disability of ever being fathers, obeyed the mandate of the Vizier; who, seconding their exertions to the utmost of his power, at length accomplished his generous enterprise, and retired, as he resolved, to lament at his leisure.

No sooner had the Caliph re-entered his palace, than Carathis commanded the doors to be fastened; but perceiving the tumult to be still violent, and hearing the imprecations which resounded from all quarters, she said to her son:

"Whether the populace be right or wrong, it behoves you to provide for your safety: let us retire to your own apartment, and from thence, through the subterranean passage known only to ourselves, into your tower; there, with the assistance of the mutes who never leave it, we may be able to make some resistance. Bababalouk, supposing us to be still in the palace, will guard its avenues for his own sake; and we shall soon find, without the counsels of that blubberer Morakanabad, what expedient may be the best to adopt."

Vathek, without making the least reply, acquiesced in his mother's proposal, and repeated as he went:

"Nefarious Giaour! where art thou? hast thou not yet devoured those poor children? where are thy sabres? thy golden key? thy talismans?"

Carathis, who guessed from these interrogations a part of the truth, had no difficulty to apprehend in getting at the whole, as soon as he should be a little composed in his tower. This Princess was so far from being influenced by scruples that she was as wicked as woman could be, which is not saying a little, for the sex pique themselves on their superiority in every competition. The recital of the Caliph therefore occasioned neither terror nor surprise to his mother; she felt no emotion but from the promises of the Giaour; and said to her son:

"This Giaour, it must be confessed, is somewhat sanguinary in his taste, but the terrestrial powers are always terrible: nevertheless, what the one has promised and the others can confer, will prove a sufficient indemnification. No crimes should be thought too dear for such a reward. Forbear then to revile the Indian: you have not fulfilled the conditions to which his services are annexed. For instance, is not a sacrifice to the subterranean Genii required? and should we not be prepared to offer it as soon as the tumult is subsided? This charge I will take on myself, and have no doubt of succeeding by means of your treasures; which, as there are now so many others in store, may without fear be exhausted."

Accordingly, the Princess, who possessed the most consummate skill in the art of persuasion, went immediately back through the subterranean passage, and presenting herself to the populace from a window of the palace, began to harangue them with all the address of which she was mistress, whilst Bababalouk showered money from both hands amongst the crowd, who by these united means were soon appeased. Every person retired to his home, and Carathis returned to the tower.

Prayer at break of day was announced, when Carathis and Vathek ascended the steps which led to the summit of the tower, where they remained for some time, though the weather was lowering and wet. This impending gloom corresponded with their malignant dispositions; but when the sun began to break through the clouds, they ordered a pavilion to be raised as a screen from the intrusion of his beams. The Caliph, overcome with fatigue, sought refreshment from repose, at the same time hoping that significant dreams might attend on his slumbers; whilst the indefatigable Carathis, followed by a party of her mutes, descended to prepare whatever she judged proper for the oblation of the approaching night.

By secret stairs, known only to herself and her son, she first repaired to the mysterious recesses in which were deposited the mummies that had been brought from the catacombs of the ancient Pharaohs. Of these she ordered several to be taken. From thence she resorted to a gallery, where, under the guard of fifty female negroes, mute, and blind of the right eye, were preserved the oil of the most venomous serpents, rhinoceros' horns, and woods of a subtle and penetrating odour, procured from the interior of the Indies, together with a thousand other horrible rarieties. This collection had been formed for a purpose like the present, by Carathis herself, from a presentiment that she might one day enjoy some intercourse with the infernal powers, to whom she had ever been passionately attached, and to whose taste she was no stranger.

To familiarize herself the better with the horrors in view, the Princess remained in the company of her negresses, who squinted in the most amiable manner from the only eye they had, and leered with exquisite delight at the skulls and skeletons which Carathis had drawn forth from her cabinets, whose key she entrusted to no one; all of them making contortions, and uttering a frightful jargon, but very amusing to the Princess till at last, being stunned by their gibbering, and suffocated by the potency of their exhalations, she was forced to quit the gallery, after stripping it of a part of its treasures.

Whilst she was thus occupied, the Caliph, who instead of the visions he expected, had acquired in these insubstantial regions a voracious appetite, was greatly provoked at the negresses: for, having totally forgotten their deafness, he had impatiently asked them for food; and seeing them regardless of his demand, he began to cuff, pinch, and push them, till Carathis arrived to terminate a scene so indecent, to the great content of these miserable creatures, who having been brought up by her, understood all her signs, and communicated in the same way their thoughts in return.

"Son! what means all this?" said she, panting for breath. "I thought I heard as I came up, the shrieks of a thousand bats, tearing from their crannies in the recesses of a cavern, and it was the outcry only of these poor mutes, whom you were so unmercifully abusing. In truth you but ill deserve the admirable provision I have brought you."

"Give it me instantly!" exclaimed the Caliph: "I am perishing for hunger!"

"As to that," answered she, "you must have an excellent stomach if it can digest what I have been preparing."

"Be quick," replied the Caliph. "But oh, heavens! what horrors! What do you intend?"

"Come, come," returned Carathis, "be not so squeamish, but help me to arrange every thing properly, and you shall see that what you reject with such symptoms of disgust will soon complete your felicity. Let us get ready the pile for the sacrifice of to-night, and think not of eating till that is performed. Know you not that all solemn rites are preceded by a rigorous abstinence?"

The Caliph, not daring to object, abandoned himself to grief, and the wind that ravaged his entrails, whilst his mother went forward with the requisite operations. Phials of serpents' oil, mummies, and bones, were soon set in order on the balustrade of the tower. The pile began to rise; and in three hours was as many cubits high. At length, darkness approached, and Carathis having stripped herself to her inmost garment, clapped her hands in an impulse of ecstasy, and struck light with all her force. The mutes followed her example: but Vathek, extenuated with hunger and impatience, was unable to support himself, and fell down in a swoon. The sparks had already kindled the dry wood; the venomous oil burst into a thousand blue flames; the mummies, dissolving, emitted a thick dun vapour; and the rhinoceros' horns beginning to consume; all together diffused such a stench, that the Caliph, recovering, started from his trance and gazed wildly on the scene in full blaze around him. The oil gushed forth in a plentitude of streams; and the negresses, who supplied it without intermission, united their cries to those of the Princess. At last the fire became so violent, and the flames reflected from the polished marble so dazzling, that the Caliph, unable to withstand the heat and the blaze, effected his escape, and clambered up the imperial standard.

In the mean time, the inhabitants of Samarah, scared at the light which shone over the city, arose in haste, ascended their roofs, beheld the tower on fire, and hurried half-naked to the square. Their love to their sovereign immediately awoke; and apprehending him in danger of perishing in his tower, their whole thoughts were occupied with the means of his safety. Morakanabad flew from his retirement, wiped away his tears, and cried out for water like the rest. Bababalouk, whose olfactory nerves were more familiarized to magical odours, readily conjecturing that Carathis was engaged in her favourite amusements, strenuously exhorted them not to be alarmed. Him, however, they treated as an old poltroon; and forbore not to style him a rascally traitor. The camels and dromedaries were advancing with water, but no one knew by which way to enter the tower. Whilst the populace was obstinate in forcing the doors, a violent east wind drove such a volume of flame against them, as at first forced them off; but afterwards, rekindled their zeal. At the same time, the stench of the horns and mummies increasing, most of the crowd fell backward in a state of suffocation. Those that kept their feet mutually wondered at the cause of the smell, and admonished each other to retire. Morakanabad, more sick than the rest, remained in a piteous condition. Holding his nose with one hand, he persisted in his efforts with the other to burst open the doors, and obtain admission. A hundred and forty of the strongest and most resolute at length accomplished their purpose. Having gained the staircase by their violent exertions, they attained a great height in a quarter of an hour.

Carathis, alarmed at the signs of her mutes, advanced to the staircase, went down a few steps, and heard several voices calling out from below:

"You shall in a moment have water!"

Being rather alert, considering her age, she presently regained the top of the tower, and bade her son suspend the sacrifice for some minutes, adding:

"We shall soon be enabled to render it more grateful. Certain dolts of your subjects, imagining, no doubt, that we were on fire, have been rash enough to break through those doors, which had hitherto remained inviolate, for the sake of bringing up water. They are very kind, you must allow, so soon to forget the wrongs you have done them: but that is of little moment. Let us offer them to the Giaour. Let them come up: our mutes, who neither want strength nor experience, will soon despatch them, exhausted as they are with fatigue."

"Be it so," answered the Caliph, "provided we finish, and I dine."

In fact, these good people, out of breath from ascending eleven thousand stairs in such haste, and chagrined at having spilt, by the way, the water they had taken, were no sooner arrived at the top than the blaze of the flames and the fumes of the mummies at once overpowered their senses. It was a pity! for they beheld not the agreeable smile with which the mutes and the negresses adjusted the cord to their necks: these amiable personages rejoiced, however, no less at the scene. Never before had the ceremony of strangling been performed with so much facility. They all fell without the least resistance or struggle; so that Vathek, in the space of a few moments, found himself surrounded by the dead bodies of his most faithful subjects, all of which were thrown on the top of the pile.

Carathis, whose presence of mind never forsook her, perceiving that she had carcases sufficient to complete her oblation, commanded the chains to be stretched across the staircase, and the iron doors barricaded, that no more might come up.

No sooner were these orders obeyed, than the tower shook; the dead bodies vanished in the flames; which at once changed from a swarthy crimson to a bright rose colour. An ambient vapour emitted the most exquisite fragrance; the marble columns rang with harmonious sounds, and the liquefied horns diffused a delicious perfume. Carathis, in transports, anticipated the success of her enterprise; whilst the mutes and negresses, to whom these sweets had given the cholic, retired to their cells grumbling.

Scarcely were they gone, when, instead of the pile, horns, mummies, and ashes, the Caliph both saw and felt, with a degree of pleasure which he could not express, a table, covered with the most magnificent repast: flaggons of wine, and vases of exquisite sherbet, floating on snow. He availed himself, without scruple, of such an entertainment; and had already laid hands on a lamb stuffed with pistachios, whilst Carathis was privately drawing from a fillagreen urn, a parchment that seemed to be endless; and which had escaped the notice of her son. Totally occupied, in gratifying an importunate appetite, he left her to peruse it, without interruption; which having finished, she said to him, in an authoritative tone,

"Put an end to your gluttony, and hear the splendid promises with which you are favoured!" She then read, as follows:

"Vathek, my well-beloved, thou hast surpassed my hopes: my nostrils have been regaled by the savour of thy mummies, thy horns; and, still more, by the lives devoted on the pile. At the full of the moon, cause the bands of thy musicians, and thy tymbals, to be heard; depart from thy palace surrounded by all the pageants of majesty; thy most faithful slaves, thy best beloved wives; thy most magnificent litters; thy richest loaden camels; and set forward on thy way to Istakar. There await I thy coming. That is the region of wonders. There shalt thou receive the diadem of Gian Ben Gian, [50] the talismans of Soliman, and the treasures of the preadimite Sultans: there shalt thou be solaced with all kinds of delight. But, beware how thou enterest any dwelling on thy route, or thou shalt feel the effects of my anger."

The Caliph, who, notwithstanding his habitual luxury, had never before dined with so much satisfaction, gave full scope to the joy of these golden tidings, and betook himself to drinking anew. Carathis, whose antipathy to wine was by no means insuperable, failed not to supply a reason for every bumper, which they ironically quaffed to the health of Mahomet. This infernal liquor completed their impious temerity, and prompted them to utter a profusion of blasphemies. They gave a loose to their wit, at the expense of the ass of Balaam, the dog of the seven sleepers, and the other animals admitted into the paradise of Mahomet. In this sprightly humour they descended the eleven thousand stairs, diverting themselves as they went at the anxious faces they saw on the square, through the oilets of the tower, and at length arrived at the royal apartments by the subterranean passage. Bababalouk was parading to and fro, and issuing his mandates with great pomp to the eunuchs, who were snuffing the lights and painting the eyes of the Circassians. No sooner did he catch sight of the Caliph and his mother than he exclaimed,

"Hah! you have then, I perceive, escaped from the flames; I was not, however, altogether out of doubt."

"Of what moment is it to us what you thought or think?" cried Carathis "go, speed, tell Morakanabad that we immediately want him; and take care how you stop by the way to make your insipid reflections."

Morakanabad delayed not to obey the summons, and was received by Vathek and his mother with great solemnity. They told him with an air of composure and commiseration that the fire at the top of the tower was extinguished, but that it had cost the lives of the brave people who sought to assist them.

"Still more misfortunes!" cried Morakanabad with a sigh. "Ah, commander of the faithful, our holy prophet is certainly irritated against us! it behoves you to appease him."

"We will appease him hereafter," replied the Caliph, with a smile that augured nothing of good. "You will have leisure sufficient for your supplications during my absence; for this country is the bane of my health. I am disgusted with the mountain of the Four Fountains, and am resolved to go and drink of the stream of Rocnabad. [51] I long to refresh myself in the delightful valleys which it waters. Do you, with the advice of my mother, govern my dominions; and take care to supply whatever her experiments may demand; for you well know that our tower abounds in materials for the advancement of science."

The tower but ill suited Morakanabad's taste. Immense treasures had been lavished upon it, and nothing had he ever seen carried thither but female negroes, mutes, and abominable drugs. Nor did he know well what to think of Carathis, who like a chamelion could assume all possible colours. Her cursed eloquence had often driven the poor Mussulman to his last shifts. He considered, however, that if she possessed but few good qualities, her son had still fewer, and that the alternative, on the whole, would be in her favour. Consoled, therefore, with this reflection, he went in good spirits to soothe the populace, and make the proper arrangements for his master's journey.

Vathek, to conciliate the spirits of the subterranean palace, resolved that his expedition should be uncommonly splendid. With this view he confiscated on all sides the property of his subjects, whilst his worthy mother stripped the seraglios she visited of the gems they contained. She collected all the sempstresses and embroiderers of Samarah, and other cities, to the distance of sixty leagues, to prepare pavilions, palanquins, sofas, canopies, and litters, for the train of the monarch. There was not left in Masulipatan a single piece of chintz; and so much muslin had been bought up to dress out Bababalouk and the other black eunuchs, that there remained not an ell in the whole Irak of Babylon.

During these preparations, Carathis, who never lost sight of her great object, which was to obtain favour with the powers of darkness, made select parties of the fairest and most delicate ladies of the city; but in the midst of their gaiety she contrived to introduce serpents amongst them, and to break pots of scorpions under the table. They all bit to a wonder, and Carathis would have left them to bite, were it not that to fill up the time, she now and then amused herself in curing their wounds with an excellent anodyne of her own invention; for this good princess abhorred being indolent.

Vathek, who was not altogether so active as his mother, devoted his time to the sole gratification of his senses, in the palaces which were severally dedicated to them. He disgusted himself no more with the divan or the mosque. One half of Samarah followed his example, whilst the other lamented the progress of corruption.

In the midst of these transactions, the embassy returned which had been sent in pious times to Mecca. It consisted of the most reverend moullahs, [53] who had fulfilled their commission, and brought back one of those precious besoms which are used to sweep the sacred caaba; a present truly worthy of the greatest potentate on earth!

The Caliph happened at this instant to be engaged in an apartment by no means adapted to the reception of embassies, though adorned with a certain magnificence, not only to render it agreeable, but also because he resorted to it frequently, and staid a considerable time together. Whilst occupied in this retreat, he heard the voice of Bababalouk calling out from between the door and the tapestry that hung before it:

"Here are the excellent Mahomet Ebn Edris al Shafei, and the seraphic Al Mouhadethin, who have brought the besom from Mecca, and with tears of joy entreat they may present it to your majesty in person."

"Let them bring the besom hither, it may be of use," said Vathek, who was still employed, not having quite racked off his wine.

"How!" answered Bababalouk, half aloud and amazed.

"Obey," replied the Caliph, "for it is my sovereign will; go instantly! vanish! for here will I receive the good folk who have thus filled thee with joy."

The eunuch departed muttering, and bade the venerable train attend him. A sacred rapture was diffused amongst these reverend old men. Though fatigued with the length of their expedition, they followed Bababalouk with an alertness almost miraculous, and felt themselves highly flattered as they swept along the stately porticos, that the Caliph would not receive them like ambassadors in ordinary, in his hall of audience. Soon reaching the interior of the harem (where, through blinds of persian they perceived large soft eyes, dark and blue, that went and came like lightning) penetrated with respect and wonder, and full of their celestial mission, they advanced in procession towards the small corridors that appeared to terminate in nothing, but nevertheless led to the cell where the Caliph expected their coming.

"What! is the commander of the faithful sick?" said Ebn Edris al Shafei, in a low voice to his companion.

"I rather think he is in his oratory," answered Al Mouhadethin.

Vathek, who heard the dialogue, cried out "What imports it you how I am employed? approach without delay."

They advanced, and Bababalouk almost sunk with confusion, [55] whilst the Caliph, without showing himself, put forth his hand from behind the tapestry that hung before the door, and demanded of them the besom.

Having prostrated themselves as well as the corridor would permit, and even in a tolerable semi-circle, the venerable Al Shafei, drawing forth the besom from the embroidered and perfumed scarfs in which it had been enveloped, and secured from the profane gaze of vulgar eyes, arose from his associates and advanced with an air of the most awful solemnity towards the supposed oratory; but with what astonishment! with what horror was he seized!

Vathek, bursting out into a villainous laugh, snatched the besom from his trembling hand, and fixing upon it some cobwebs that hung suspended from the ceiling, gravely brushed away till not a single one remained.

The old men, overpowered with amazement, were unable to lift their beards from the ground; for as Vathek had carelessly left the tapestry between them half drawn, they were witnesses to the whole transaction. Their tears gushed forth on the marble. Al Mouhadethin swooned through mortification and fatigue, whilst the Caliph, throwing himself backward on his seat, shouted and clapped his hands without mercy. At last, addressing himself to Bababalouk:

"My dear black," said he, "go, regale these pious poor souls with my good wine from Shiraz; and as they can boast of having seen more of my palace than any one besides, let them also visit my office courts, and lead them out by the back steps that go to my stables." Having said this, he threw the besom in their face, and went to enjoy the laugh with Carathis.

Bababalouk did all in his power to console the ambassadors, but the two most infirm expired on the spot; the rest were carried to their beds, from whence, being heart-broken with sorrow and shame, they never arose.

The succeeding night, Vathek, attended by his mother, ascended the tower to see if everything were ready for his journey, for he had great faith in the influence of the stars. The planets appeared in their most favourable aspects. The Caliph, to enjoy so flattering a sight, supped gaily on the roof, and fancied that he heard, during his repast, loud shouts of laughter resound through the sky, in a manner that inspired the fullest assurance.

All was in motion at the palace; lights were kept burning through the whole of the night; the sound of implements, and of artisans finishing their work; the voices of women and their guardians who sung at their embroidery; all conspired to interrupt the stillness of nature, and infinitely delight the heart of Vathek, who imagined himself going in triumph to sit upon the throne of Soliman.

The people were not less satisfied than himself; all assisted to accelerate the moment which should rescue them from the wayward caprices of so extravagant a master.

The day preceding the departure of this infatuated prince was employed by Carathis in repeating to him the decrees of the mysterious parchment, which she had thoroughly gotten by heart; and in recommending him not to enter the habitation of any one by the way; "for well thou knowest," added she, "how liquorish thy taste is after good dishes and young damsels; let me therefore enjoin thee to be content with thy old cooks, who are the best in the world; and not to forget that in thy ambulatory seraglio there are three dozen pretty faces, which Bababalouk hath not yet unveiled. I, myself, have a great desire to watch over thy conduct, and visit the subterranean palace, which no doubt contains whatever can interest persons like us. There is nothing so pleasing as retiring to caverns; my taste for dead bodies and everything like mummy is decided; and I am confident thou wilt see the most exquisite of their kind. Forget me not then, but the moment thou art in possession of the talismans which are to open to thee the mineral kingdoms, and the centre of the earth itself, fail not to dispatch some trusty genius to take me and my cabinet, for the oil of the serpents I have pinched to death will be a pretty present to the Giaour, who cannot but be charmed with such dainties."

Scarcely had Carathis ended this edifying discourse, when the sun, setting behind the mountain of the Four Fountains, gave place to the rising moon. This planet being that evening at full, appeared of unusual beauty and magnitude in the eyes of the women, the eunuchs, and the pages, who were all impatient to set forward. The city re-echoed with shouts of joy and flourishing of trumpets. Nothing was visible but plumes nodding on pavilions, and aigrets shining in the mild lustre of the moon. The spacious square resembled an immense parterre, variegated with the most stately tulips of the east.

Arrayed in the robes which were only worn at the most distinguished ceremonials, and supported by his vizier and Bababalouk, the Caliph descended the grand staircase of the tower in the sight of all his people. He could not forbear pausing at intervals to admire the superb appearance which everywhere courted his view, whilst the whole multitude, even to the camels with their sumptuous burdens, knelt down before him. For some time a general stillness prevailed, which nothing happened to disturb, but the shrill screams of some eunuchs in the rear. These vigilant guards having remarked certain cages of the ladies swagging somewhat awry, and discovered that a few adventurous gallants had contrived to get in, soon dislodged the enraptured culprits, and consigned them with good commendations, to the surgeons of the serail. The majesty of so magnificent a spectacle was not, however, violated by incidents like these. Vathek, meanwhile, saluted the moon with an idolatrous air, that neither pleased Morakanabad nor the doctors of the law, any more than the viziers and grandees of his court, who were all assembled to enjoy the last view of their sovereign.

At length the clarions and trumpets from the top of the tower announced the prelude of departure. Though the instruments were in unison with each other, yet a singular dissonance was blended with their sounds. This proceeded from Carathis, who was singing her direful orisons to the Giaour, whilst the negresses and mutes supplied thorough bass without articulating a word. The good Mussulmans fancied that they heard the sullen hum of those nocturnal insects which presage evil, and importuned Vathek to beware how he ventured his sacred person.

On a given signal the great standard of the Califat was displayed; twenty thousand lances shone around it; and the Caliph, treading royally on the cloth of gold which had been spread for his feet, ascended his litter amidst the general awe that possessed his subjects.

The expedition commenced with the utmost order, and so entire a silence, that even the locusts were heard from the thickets on the plain of Catoul. Gaiety and good humour prevailing, six good leagues were past before the dawn; and the morning star was still glittering in the firmament when the whole of this numerous train had halted on the banks of the Tigris, where they encamped to repose for the rest of the day.

The three days that followed were spent in the same manner, but on the fourth the heavens looked angry, lightnings broke forth in frequent flashes, re-echoing peals of thunder succeeded, and the trembling Circassians clung with all their might to their ugly guardians. The Caliph himself was greatly inclined to take shelter in the large town of Gulchissar, the governor of which came forth to meet him, and tendered every kind of refreshment the place could supply. But having examined his tablets, he suffered the rain to soak him almost to the bone, notwithstanding the importunity of his first favourites. Though he began to regret the palace of the senses, yet he lost not sight of his enterprise, and his sanguine expectations confirmed his resolution. His geographers were

289

ordered to attend him, but the weather proved so terrible, that these poor people exhibited a lamentable appearance; and as no long journeys had been undertaken since the time of Haroun al Raschid, their maps of the different countries were in a still worse plight than themselves. Every one was ignorant which way to turn; for Vathek, though well versed in the course of the heavens, no longer knew his situation on earth. He thundered even louder than the elements, and muttered forth certain hints of the bowstring which were not very soothing to literary ears. Disgusted at the toilsome weariness of the way, he determined to cross over the craggy heights, and follow the guidance of a peasant, who undertook to bring him, in four days, to Rocnabad. Remonstrances were all to no purpose, his resolution was fixed, and an invasion commenced on the province of the goats, who sped away in large troops before them. It was curious to view on these half calcined rocks camels richly caparisoned, and pavilions of gold and silk waving on their summits, which till then had never been covered, but with sapless thistles and fern.

The females and eunuchs uttered shrill wailings at the sight of the precipices below them, and the dreary prospects that opened in the vast gorges of the mountains. Before they could reach the ascent of the steepest rock night overtook them, and a boisterous tempest arose, which having rent the awnings of the palanquins and cages, exposed to the raw gusts the poor ladies within, who had never before felt so piercing a cold. The dark clouds that overcast the face of the sky deepened the horrors of this disastrous night, insomuch that nothing could be heard distinctly but the mewling of pages, and lamentations of sultanas.

To increase the general misfortune, the frightful uproar of wild beasts resounded at a distance, and there were soon perceived in the forest they were skirting the glaring of eyes which could belong only to devils or tigers. The pioneers, who as well as they could, had marked out a track, and a part of the advanced guard were devoured before they had been in the least apprised of their danger. The confusion that prevailed was extreme. Wolves, tigers, and other carnivorous animals, invited by the howling of their companions, flocked together from every quarter. The crushing of bones was heard on all sides, and a fearful rush of wings over head, for now vultures also began to be of the party.

The terror at length reached the main body of the troops which surrounded the monarch and his harem, at the distance of two leagues from the scene. Vathek (voluptuously reposed in his capacious litter upon cushions of silk, with two little pages beside him, of complexions more fair than the enamel of Franguestan, who were occupied in keeping off flies) was soundly asleep, and contemplating in his dreams the treasures of Soliman. The shrieks, however, of his wives awoke him with a start, and instead of the Giaour with his key of gold, he beheld Bababalouk full of consternation.

"Sire," exclaimed this good servant of the most potent of monarchs, "misfortune has arrived at its height; wild beasts, who entertain no more reverence for your sacred person than for that of a dead ass, have beset your camels and their drivers: thirty of the richest laden are already become their prey, as well as all your confectioners, your cooks, and purveyors, and unless our holy prophet should protect us, we shall have all eaten our last meal."

At the mention of eating, the Caliph lost all patience. He began to bellow, and even beat himself, for there was no seeing in the dark. The rumour every instant increased, and Bababalouk finding no good could be done with his master stopped both his ears against the hurly-burly of the harem, and called out aloud:

"Come, ladies and brothers! all hands to work! strike light in a moment! never shall it be said that the commander of the faithful served to regale these infidel brutes."

Though there wanted not in this bevy of beauties a sufficient number of capricious and wayward, yet, on the present occasion they were all compliance. Fires were visible in a twinkling in all their cages. Ten thousand torches were lighted at once. The Caliph himself seized a large one of wax; every person followed his example; and by kindling ropes ends dipped in oil and fastened on poles, an amazing blaze was spread. The rocks were covered with the splendour of sunshine. The trails of sparks wafted by the wind, communicated to the dry fern, of which there was plenty. Serpents were observed to crawl forth from their retreats with amazement and hissings, whilst the horses snorted, stamped the ground, tossed their noses in the air, and plunged about without mercy.

One of the forests of cedar that bordered their way took fire, and the branches that overhung the path extending their flames to the muslins and chintzes which covered the cages of the ladies, obliged them to jump out at the peril of their necks. Vathek, who vented on the occasion a thousand blasphemies, was himself compelled to touch with his sacred feet the naked earth.

Never had such an incident happened before. Full of mortification, shame and despondence, and not knowing how to walk, the ladies fell into the dirt.

"Must I go on foot," said one.

"Must I wet my feet," cried another.

"Must I soil my dress," asked a third.

"Execrable Bababalouk," exclaimed all; "Outcast of hell! what hadst thou to do with torches? Better were it to be eaten by tigers than to fall into our present condition; we are for ever undone. Not a porter is there in the army, nor a currier of camels but hath seen some part of our bodies, and what is worse, our very faces!"

On saying this, the most bashful amongst them hid their foreheads on the ground, whilst such as had more boldness flew at Bababalouk, but he, well apprised of their humour, and not wanting in shrewdness, betook himself to his heels along with his comrades, all dropping their torches and striking their tymbals.

It was not less light than in the brightest of the dog-days, and the weather was hot in proportion; but how degrading was the spectacle, to behold the Caliph bespattered like an ordinary mortal! As the exercise of his faculties seemed to be suspended, one of his Ethiopian wives (for he delighted in variety) clasped him in her arms, threw him upon her shoulder like a sack of dates, and finding that the fire was hemming them in, set off with no small expedition, considering the weight of her burden. The other ladies who had just learned the use of their feet followed her; their guards galloped after; and the camel drivers brought up the rear as fast as their charge would permit.

They soon reached the spot where the wild beasts had commenced the carnage, and which they had too much spirit to leave, notwithstanding the approaching tumult, and the luxurious supper they had made. Bababalouk nevertheless seized on a few of the plumpest, which were unable to budge from the place, and began to flay them with admirable adroitness. The cavalcade being got so far from the conflagration as that the heat felt rather grateful than violent, it was immediately resolved on to halt. The tattered chintzes were picked up; the scraps left by the wolves and tigers interred; and vengeance was taken on some dozens of vultures that were too much glutted to rise on the wing. The camels which had been left unmolested to make sal-ammoniac being numbered, and the ladies once more inclosed in their cages, the imperial tent was pitched on the levellest ground they could find.

Vathek, reposing upon a matress of down, and tolerably recovered from the jolting of the Ethiopian, who, to his feelings seemed the roughest trotting jade he had hitherto mounted, called out for something to eat; but alas! those delicate cakes which had been baked in silver ovens for his royal mouth, those rich manchets, amber comfits, flaggons of Schiraz wine, porcelain vases of snow, and grapes from the banks of the Tigris, were all irremediably lost; and nothing had Bababalouk to present in their stead, but a roasted wolf, vultures à la daube, aromatic herbs of the most acrid poignancy, rotten truffles, boiled thistles, and such other wild plants as must ulcerate the throat and parch up the tongue. Nor was he better provided in the article of drink, for he could procure nothing to accompany these irritating viands but a few phials of abominable brandy, which had been secreted by the scullions in their slippers.

Vathek made wry faces at so savage a repast, and Bababalouk answered them with shrugs and contortions. The Caliph however ate with tolerable appetite, and fell into a nap that lasted six hours. The splendour of the sun, reflected from the white cliffs of the mountains in spite of the curtains that inclosed him, at length disturbed his repose. He awoke terrified, and stung to the quick by those wormwood-coloured flies which emit from their wings a suffocating stench. The miserable monarch was perplexed how to act, though his wits were not idle in seeking expedients, whilst Bababalouk lay snoring amidst a swarm of those insects, that busily thronged to pay court to his nose. The little pages, famished with hunger, had dropped their fans on the ground, and exerted their dying voices in bitter reproaches on the Caliph, who now for the first time heard the language of truth.

Thus stimulated, he renewed his imprecations against the Giaour, and bestowed upon Mahomet some soothing expressions.

"Where am I?" cried he; "What are these dreadful rocks; these valleys of darkness? Are we arrived at the horrible Kaf? [67a] Is the Simurgh [67b] coming to pluck out my eyes as a punishment for undertaking this impious enterprise?"

Having said this, he bellowed like a calf, and turned himself towards an outlet in the side of his pavilion. But alas! what objects occurred to his view! on one side a plain of black sand that appeared to be unbounded, and on the other perpendicular crags bristled over with those abominable thistles which had so severely lacerated his tongue. He fancied, however, that he perceived amongst the brambles and briars some gigantic flowers, but was mistaken, for these were only the dangling palampores and variegated tatters of his gay retinue. As there were several clefts in the rock from whence water seemed to have flowed, Vathek applied his ear with the hope of catching the sound of some latent runnel, but could only distinguish the low murmurs of his people, who were repining at their journey, and complaining for the want of water.

"To what purpose," asked they, "have we been brought hither? Hath our Caliph another tower to build? or have the relentless Afrits [67c] whom Carathis so much loves, fixed in this place their abode?"

At the name of Carathis, Vathek recollected the tablets he had received from his mother, who assured him they were fraught with preternatural qualities, and advised him to consult them as emergencies might require. Whilst he was engaged in turning them over, he heard a shout of joy, and a loud clapping of hands. The curtains of his pavilion were soon drawn back, and he beheld Bababalouk, followed by a troop of his favourites, conducting two dwarfs, each a cubit high, who brought between them a large basket of melons, oranges, and pomegranites. They were singing in the sweetest tones the words that follow:

"We dwell on the top of these rocks, in a cabin of rushes and canes; the eagles envy us our nest; a small spring supplies us with abdest, and we daily repeat prayers which the prophet approves. We love you, O commander of the faithful! our master, the good emir Fakreddin, loves you also; he reveres in your person the vicegerent of Mahomet. Little as we are, in us he confides; he knows our hearts to be good, as our bodies are contemptible, and hath placed us here to aid those who are bewildered on these dreary mountains. Last night, whilst we were occupied within our cell in reading the holy koran, a sudden hurricane blew out our lights and rocked our habitation. For two whole hours a palpable darkness prevailed: but we heard sounds at a distance which we conjectured to proceed from the bells of a cafila, passing over the rocks. Our ears were soon filled with deplorable shrieks, frightful roarings, and the sound of tymbals. Chilled with terror, we concluded that the

Deggial [68] with his exterminating angels had sent forth their plagues on the earth. In the midst of these melancholy reflections, we perceived flames of the deepest red glow in the horizon, and found ourselves in a few moments covered with flakes of fire. Amazed at so strange an appearance, we took up the volume dictated by the blessed intelligence, and kneeling by the light of the fire that surrounded us, we recited the verse which says: 'Put no trust in any thing but the mercy of heaven; there is no help save in the holy prophet; the mountain of Kaf itself may tremble; it is the power of Alla only that cannot be moved.' After having pronounced these words, we felt consolation, and our minds were hushed into a sacred repose. Silence ensued, and our ears clearly distinguished a voice in the air, saying: 'Servants of my faithful servant, go down to the happy valley of Fakreddin; tell him that an illustrious opportunity now offers to satiate the thirst of his hospitable heart. The commander of true believers is this day bewildered amongst these mountains, and stands in need of thy aid.' We obeyed with joy the angelic mission, and our master, filled with pious zeal, hath culled with his own hands these melons, oranges, and pomegranites. He is following us with a hundred dromedaries laden with the purest waters of his fountains, and is coming to kiss the fringe of your consecrated robe, and implore you to enter his humble habitation, which, placed amidst these barren wilds, resembles an emerald set in lead."

The dwarfs having ended their address, remained still standing, and with hands crossed upon their bosoms, preserved a respectful silence.

Vathek, in the midst of this curious harangue seized the basket, and long before it was finished, the fruits had dissolved in his mouth. As he continued to eat, his piety increased, and in the same breath which recited his prayers, he called for the koran and sugar.

Such was the state of his mind when the tablets, which were thrown by at the approach of the dwarfs, again attracted his eye. He took them up, but was ready to drop on the ground when he beheld, in large red characters, these words inscribed by Carathis, which were indeed enough to make him tremble.

"Beware of thy old doctors, and their puny messengers of but one cubit high; distrust their pious frauds; and instead of eating their melons, impale on a spit the bearers of them. Shouldst thou be such a fool as to visit them, the portal of the subterranean palace will be shut in thy face, and with such force as shall shake thee asunder; thy body shall be spit upon, and bats will engender in thy belly."

"To what tends this ominous rhapsody?" cries the Caliph; "and must I then perish in these deserts with thirst, whilst I may refresh myself in the valley of melons and cucumbers? Accursed be the Giaour with his portal of ebony! he hath made me dance attendance too long already. Besides, who shall prescribe laws to me? I, forsooth, must not enter any one's habitation! Be it so, but what one can I enter that is not my own."

Bababalouk, who lost not a syllable of this soliloquy, applauded it with all his heart; and the ladies, for the first time, agreed with him in opinion. The dwarfs were entertained, caressed, and seated with great ceremony on little cushions of satin. The symmetry of their persons was the subject of criticism; not an inch of them was suffered to pass unexamined. Nick-nacks and dainties were offered in profusion, but all were declined with respectful gravity. They clambered up the sides of the Caliph's seat, and placing themselves each on one of his shoulders, began to whisper prayers in his ears. Their tongues quivered like the leaves of a poplar, and the patience of Vathek was almost exhausted, when the acclamations of the troops announced the approach of Fakreddin, who was come with a hundred old grey-beards, and as many korans and dromedaries. They instantly set about their ablutions, and began to repeat the Bismillah. Vathek, to get rid of these officious monitors, followed their example, for his hands were burning.

The good Emir, who was punctiliously religious, and likewise a great dealer in compliments, made an harangue five times more prolix and insipid than his harbingers had already delivered. The Caliph, unable any longer to refrain, exclaimed:

"For the love of Mahomet, my dear Fakreddin, have done! let us proceed to your valley, and enjoy the fruits that heaven hath vouchsafed you." The hint of proceeding put all into motion. The venerable attendants of the emir set forward somewhat slowly, but Vathek having ordered his little pages, in private, to goad on the dromedaries, loud fits of laughter broke forth from the cages, for the unwieldy curvetting of these poor beasts, and the ridiculous distress of their superannuated riders afforded the ladies no small entertainment.

They descended, however, unhurt into the valley, by the large steps which the emir had cut in the rock; and already the murmuring of streams and the rustling of leaves began to catch their attention. The cavalcade soon entered a path, which was skirted by flowering shrubs, and extended to a vast wood of palm-trees whose branches overspread a building of hewn stone. This edifice was crowned with nine domes, and adorned with as many portals of bronze, on which was engraven the following inscription:

"This is the asylum of pilgrims, the refuge of travellers, and the depository of secrets for all parts of the world."

Nine pages beautiful as the day, and clothed in robes of Egyptian linen, very long and very modest, were standing at each door. They received the whole retinue with an easy and inviting air. Four of the most amiable placed the Caliph on a magnificent taktrevan; four others, somewhat less graceful, took charge of Bababalouk, who capered for joy at the snug little cabin that fell to his share; the pages that remained, waited on the rest of the train.

When every thing masculine was gone out of sight, the gate of a large inclosure on the right turned on its harmonious hinges, and a young female of a slender form came forth. Her light brown hair floated in the hazy breeze of the twilight. A troop of young maidens, like the Pleiades, attended her on tip-toe. They hastened to the pavilions that contained the sultanas; and the young lady gracefully bending said to them:

"Charming princesses, every thing is ready; we have prepared beds for your repose, and strewed your apartments with jasamine; no insects will keep off slumber from visiting your eyelids; we will dispel them with a thousand plumes. Come then, amiable ladies! refresh your delicate feet and your ivory limbs in baths of rose water, and by the light of perfumed lamps your servants will amuse you with tales."

The sultanas accepted with pleasure these obliging offers, and followed the young lady to the emir's harem, where we must for a moment leave them and return to the Caliph.

Vathek found himself beneath a vast dome illuminated by a thousand lamps of rock crystal, as many vases of the same material filled with excellent sherbet sparkled on a large table, where a profusion of viands were spread. Amongst others were sweetbreads stewed in milk of almonds, saffron soups, and lamb à la crême, of all of which the Caliph was amazingly fond. He took of each as much as he was able; testified his sense of the emir's friendship by the gaiety of his heart; and made the dwarfs dance against their will; for these little devotees durst not refuse the commander of the faithful. At last he spread himself on the sofa and slept sounder than he had ever before.

Beneath this dome a general silence prevailed, for there was nothing to disturb it but the jaws of Bababalouk, who had untrussed himself to eat with greater advantage, being anxious to make amends for his fast in the mountains. As his spirits were too high to admit of his sleeping, and not loving to be idle, he proposed with himself to visit the harem, and repair to his charge of the ladies, to examine if they had been properly lubricated with the balm of Mecca, if their eye-brows and tresses were in order, and in a word, to perform all the little offices they might need. He sought for a long time together, but without being able to find out the door. He durst not speak aloud for fear of disturbing the Caliph, and not a soul was stirring in the precincts of the palace. He almost despaired of effecting his purpose, when a low whispering just reached his ear: it came from the dwarfs, who were returned to their old occupation, and for the nine hundred and ninety-ninth time in their lives were reading over the koran. They very politely invited Bababalouk to be of their party, but his head was full of other concerns. The dwarfs, though scandalized at his dissolute morals, directed him to the apartments he wanted to find. His way thither lay through a hundred dark corridors, along which he groped as he went, and at last began to catch, from the extremity of a passage, the charming gossiping of women, which not a little delighted his heart.

"Ah, ah! what not yet asleep?" cried he, and taking long strides as he spoke, "did you not suspect me of abjuring my charge? I stayed but to finish what my master had left."

Two of the black eunuchs on hearing a voice so loud detached a party in haste, sabre in hand, to discover the cause, but presently was repeated on all sides:

"'Tis only Bababalouk, no one but Bababalouk!"

This circumspect guardian having gone up to a thin veil of carnation colour silk that hung before the doorway, distinguished by means of a softened splendour that shone through it, an oval bath of dark porphyry surrounded by curtains festooned in large folds. Through the apertures between them, as they were not drawn close, groups of young slaves were visible, amongst whom Bababalouk perceived his pupils indulgingly expanding their arms, as if to embrace the perfumed water, and refresh themselves after their fatigues. The looks of tender languor, their confidential whispers, and the enchanting smiles with which they were imparted, the exquisite fragrance of the roses, all combined to inspire a voluptuousness which even Bababalouk himself was scarce able to withstand.

He summoned up, however, his usual solemnity, and in the peremptory tone of authority commanded the ladies instantly to leave the bath. Whilst he was issuing these mandates, the young Nouronihar, daughter of the emir, who was sprightly as an antelope, and full of wanton gaiety, beckoned one of her slaves to let down the great swing, which was suspended to the ceiling by cords of silk, and whilst this was doing winked to her companions in the bath, who chagrined to be forced from so soothing a state of indolence, began to twist it round Bababalouk, and teaze him with a thousand vagaries.

When Nouronihar perceived that he was exhausted with fatigue, she accosted him with an arch air of respectful concern, and said:

"My lord, it is not by any means decent that the chief eunuch of the Caliph our sovereign should thus continue standing, deign but to recline your graceful person upon this sofa, which will burst with vexation if it have not the honour to receive you."

Caught by these flattering accents, Bababalouk gallantly replied:

"Delight of the apple of my eye! I accept the invitation of thy honied lips, and to say truth, my senses are dazzled with the radiance that beams from thy charms."

"Repose, then, at your ease," replied the beauty, and placed him on the pretended sofa, which, quicker than lightning, gave way all at once. The rest of the women having aptly conceived her design, sprang naked from the bath and plied the swing with such unmerciful jerks, that it swept through the whole compass of a very lofty dome, and took from the poor victim all power of respiration. Sometimes his feet rased the surface of the water, and at others the skylight almost flattened his nose. In vain did he pierce the air with the cries of a voice that resembled the ringing of a cracked basin, for their peals of laughter were still more predominant.

Nouronihar in the inebriety of youthful spirits being used only to eunuchs of ordinary harems, and having never seen any thing so royal and disgusting, was far more diverted than all of the rest. She began to parody some Persian verses, and sung with an accent most demurely piquant:

"O gentle white dove as thou soar'st through the air,

Vouchsafe one kind glance on the mate of thy love:

Melodious Philomel I am thy rose;

Warble some couplet to ravish my heart!"

The sultanas and their slaves stimulated by these pleasantries persevered at the swing with such unremitted assiduity, that at length the cord which had secured it snapped suddenly asunder, and Bababalouk fell floundering like a turtle to the bottom of the bath. This accident occasioned a universal shout. Twelve little doors till now unobserved flew open at once, and the ladies in an instant made their escape, after throwing all the towels on his head, and putting out the lights that remained.

The deplorable animal, in water to the chin, overwhelmed with darkness, and unable to extricate himself from the warp that embarrassed him, was still doomed to hear for his further consolation, the fresh bursts of merriment his disaster occasioned. He bustled but in vain to get from the bath, for the margin was become so slippery with the oil spilt in breaking the lamps, that at every effort he slid back with a plunge, which resounded aloud through the hollow of the dome. These cursed peals of laughter at every relapse were redoubled, and he, who thought the place infested rather by devils than women, resolved to cease groping, and abide in the bath, where he amused himself with soliloquies interspersed with imprecations, of which his malicious neighbours, reclining on down, suffered not an accent to escape. In this delectable plight the morning surprised him. The Caliph, wondering at his absence, had caused him to be everywhere sought for. At last he was drawn forth almost smothered from the whisp of linen, and wet even to the marrow. Limping, and chattering his teeth, he appeared before his master, who inquired what was the matter, and how he came soused in so strange a pickle.

"And why did you enter this cursed lodge?" answered Bababalouk, gruffly. "Ought a monarch like you to visit with his harem the abode of a grey bearded emir who knows nothing of life? And with what gracious damsels does the place too abound! Fancy to yourself how they have soaked me like a burnt crust, and made me dance like a jack-pudding the live-long night through on their damnable swing. What an excellent lesson for your sultanas to follow, into whom I have instilled such reserve and decorum!"

Vathek, comprehending not a syllable of all this invective, obliged him to relate minutely the transaction; but instead of sympathising with the miserable sufferer, he laughed immoderately at the device of the swing, and the figure of Bababalouk mounting upon it. The stung eunuch could scarcely preserve the semblance of respect.

"Aye, laugh my lord! laugh," said he, "but I wish this Nouronihar would play some trick on you; she is too wicked to spare even majesty itself."

These words made for the present but a slight impression on the Caliph, but they not long after recurred to his mind.

This conversation was cut short by Fakreddin, who came to request that Vathek would join in the prayers and ablutions to be solemnized on a spacious meadow, watered by innumerable streams. The Caliph found the waters refreshing, but the prayers abominably irksome. He diverted himself however with the multitude of Calenders, [79a] Santons, [79b] and Dervises [79c] who were continually coming and going, but especially with the Brahmins, [79d] Faquirs, [79e] and other enthusiasts, who had travelled from the heart of India, and halted on their way with the emir. These latter had each of them some mummery peculiar to himself. One dragged a huge chain where ever he went, another an ourang-outang, whilst a third was furnished with scourges, and all performed to a charm. Some clambered up trees, holding one foot in the air; others poised themselves over a fire, and without mercy fillipped their noses. There were some amongst them that cherished vermin, which were not ungrateful in requiting their caresses. These rambling fanatics revolted the hearts of the Dervises, the Calenders, and Santons; however the vehemence of their aversion soon subsided under the hope that the presence of the Caliph would cure their folly, and convert them to the Mussulman faith. But alas! how great was their disappointment! for Vathek, instead of preaching to them, treated them as buffoons; bade them present his compliments to Visnow and Ixhora, and discovered a predilection for a squat old man from the Isle of Serendib, who was more ridiculous than any of the rest.

"Come," said he, "for the love of your gods, bestow a few slaps on your chops to amuse me."

The old fellow offended at such an address began loudly to weep; but as he betrayed a villainous drivelling in his tears, the Caliph turned his back and listened to Bababalouk, who whispered, whilst he held the umbrella over him:

"Your majesty should be cautious of this odd assembly, which hath been collected I know not for what. Is it necessary to exhibit such spectacles to a mighty potentate, with interludes of talapoins more mangy than dogs? Were I you, I would command a fire to be kindled, and at once purge the earth of the emir, his harem, and all his menagery."

"Tush, dolt," answered Vathek, "and know that all this infinitely charms me. Nor shall I leave the meadow till I have visited every hive of these pious mendicants."

Where ever the Caliph directed his course, objects of pity were sure to swarm round him: the blind, the purblind, smarts without noses, damsels without ears, each to extol the munificence of Fakreddin, who, as well as his attendant grey-beards, dealt about gratis plasters and cataplasms to all that applied. At noon a superb corps of cripples made its appearance; and soon after advanced by platoons on the plain the completest association of invalids that had ever been embodied till then. The blind went groping with the blind; the lame limped on together; and the maimed made gestures to each other with the only arm that remained. The sides of a considerable waterfall were crowded by the deaf, amongst whom were some from Pegu, with ears uncommonly handsome and large, but were still less able to hear than the rest. Nor were there wanting others in abundance with hump backs, wenny necks, and even horns of an exquisite polish.

The emir, to aggrandize the solemnity of the festival in honour of his illustrious visitant, ordered the turf to be spread on all sides with skins and table cloths, upon which were served up for the good mussulmans pilaus of every hue, with other orthodox dishes, and by the express order of Vathek, who was shamefully tolerant, small plates of abominations for regaling the rest. This prince on seeing so many mouths put in motion began to think it time for employing his own. In spite, therefore, of every remonstrance from the chief of his eunuchs, he resolved to have a dinner dressed on the spot. The complaisant emir immediately gave orders for a table to be placed in the shade of the willows. The first service consisted of fish, which they drew from a river flowing over sands of gold, at the foot of a lofty hill: these were broiled as fast as taken, and served up with a sauce of vinegar and small herbs that grew on

Mount Sinai; for everything with the emir was excellent and pious.

The dessert was not quite set on when the sound of lutes from the hill was repeated by the echoes of the neighbouring mountains. The Caliph with an emotion of pleasure and surprise, had no sooner raised up his head than a handful of jasmine dropped on his face. An abundance of tittering succeeded this frolic, and instantly appeared through the bushes the elegant forms of several young females, skipping and bounding like roes. The fragrance diffused from their hair struck the sense of Vathek, who in an ecstasy, suspending his repast, said to Bababalouk:

"Are the Peries [82] come down from their spheres? Note her in particular whose form is so perfect, venturously running on the brink of the precipice, and turning back her head as regardless of nothing but the graceful flow of her robe. With what captivating impatience doth she contend with the bushes for her veil? Could it be she who threw the jasmine at me?"

"Aye, she it was; and you too would she throw from the top of the rock," answered Bababalouk, "for that is my good friend Nouronihar, who so kindly lent me her swing. My dear lord and master," added he, twisting a twig that hung by the rind from a willow, "let me correct her for her want of respect: the emir will have no reason to complain, since (bating what I owe to his piety) he is much to be censured for keeping a troop of girls on the mountains, whose sharp air gives their blood too brisk a circulation."

"Peace, blasphemer!" said the Caliph: "speak not thus of her who over her mountains leads my heart a willing captive. Contrive, rather, that my eyes may be fixed upon hers—that I may respire her sweet breath, as she bounds panting along these delightful wilds!"

On saying these words, Vathek extended his arms towards the hill, and directing his eyes with an anxiety unknown to him before, endeavoured to keep within view the object that enthralled his soul; but her course was as difficult to follow as the flight of one of those beautiful blue butterflies of Cachmere, which are at once so volatile and rare.

The Caliph, not satisfied with seeing, wished also to hear Nouronihar, and eagerly turned to catch the sound of her voice. At last he distinguished her whispering to one of her companions behind the thicket from whence she had thrown the jasamine:

"A Caliph, it must be owned, is a fine thing to see, but my little Gulchenrouz is much more amiable; one lock of his hair is of more value to me than the richest embroidery of the Indies. I had rather that his teeth should mischievously press my finger, than the richest ring of the imperial treasure. Where have you left him, Sutlememe? and why is he now not here?"

The agitated Caliph still wished to hear more, but she immediately retired with all her attendants. The fond monarch pursued her with his eyes till she was gone out of sight, and then continued like a bewildered and benighted traveller, from whom the clouds had obscured the constellation that guided his way. The curtain of night seemed dropped before him — everything appeared discoloured. The falling waters filled his soul with dejection, and his tears trickled down the jasamines he had caught from Nouronihar, and placed in his inflamed bosom. He snatched up a shining pebble to remind him of the scene where he felt the first tumults of love. Two hours were elapsed, and evening drew on before he could resolve to depart from the place. He often, but in vain, attempted to go: a soft languor enervated the powers of his mind. Extending himself on the brink of the stream, he turned his eyes towards the blue summits of the mountain, and exclaimed:

"What concealest thou behind thee? what is passing in thy solitudes? Whither is she gone? O heaven! perhaps she is now wandering in the grottoes with her happy Gulchenrouz!"

In the mean time the damps began to descend, and the emir, solicitous for the health of the Caliph, ordered the imperial litter to be brought. Vathek, absorbed in his reveries, was imperceptibly removed and conveyed back to the saloon that received him the evening before.

But let us leave the Caliph immersed in his new passion, and attend Nouronihar beyond the rocks, where she had again joined her beloved Gulchenrouz. This Gulchenrouz was the son of Ali Hassan, brother to the emir, and the most delicate and lovely creature in the world. Ali Hassan, who had been absent ten years on a voyage to the unknown seas, committed at his departure this child, the only survivor of many, to the care and protection of his brother. Gulchenrouz could write in various characters with precision, and paint upon vellum the most elegant arabesques that fancy could devise. His sweet voice accompanied the lute in the most enchanting manner; and when he sung the loves of Megnoun and Leileh, or some unfortunate lovers of ancient days, tears insensibly overflowed the cheeks of his auditors. The verses he composed (for like Megnoun, he too was a poet) inspired that unresisting languor so frequently fatal to the female heart. The women all doated upon him, for though he had passed his thirteenth year, they still detained him in the harem. His dancing was light as the gossamer waved by the zephyrs of spring; but his arms which twined so gracefully with those of the young girls in the dance, could neither dart the lance in the chase, nor curb the steeds that pastured his uncle's domains. The bow, however, he drew with a certain aim, and would have excelled his competitors in the race, could he have broken the ties that bound him to Nouronihar.

The two brothers had mutually engaged their children to each other; and Nouronihar loved her cousin more than her eyes. Both had the same tastes and amusements; the same long languishing looks; the same tresses; the same fair complexions; and when Gulchenrouz appeared in the dress of his cousin, he seemed to be more feminine than even herself. If at any time he left the harem to visit Fakreddin, it was with all the bashfulness of a fawn that consciously ventures from the lair of its dam; he was however wanton enough to mock the solemn old grey-beards to whom he was subject, though sure to be rated without mercy in return. Whenever this happened, he would plunge into the recesses of the harem, and sobbing take refuge in the arms of Nouronihar, who loved even his faults beyond the virtues of others.

It fell out this evening that after leaving the Caliph in the meadow, she ran with Gulchenrouz over the green sward of the mountain that sheltered the vale, where Fakreddin had chosen to reside. The sun was dilated on the edge of the horizon; and the young people, whose fancies were lively and inventive, imagined they beheld in the gorgeous clouds of the west the domes of Shadukiam and Ambreabad, where the Peries have fixed their abode. Nouronihar, sitting on the slope of the hill, supported on her knees the perfumed head of Gulchenrouz. The air was calm, and no sound stirred but the voices of other young girls who were drawing cool water from the streams below. The unexpected arrival of the Caliph, and the splendour that marked his appearance, had already filled with emotion the ardent soul of Nouronihar. Her vanity irresistibly prompted her to pique the prince's attention, and this she before took good care to effect whilst he picked up the jasmine she had thrown upon him. But when Gulchenrouz asked after the flowers he had culled for her bosom, Nouronihar was all in confusion. She hastily kissed his forehead, arose in a flutter, and walked with unequal steps on the border of the precipice. Night advanced, and the pure gold of the setting sun had yielded to a sanguine red, the glow of which, like the reflection of a burning furnace, flushed Nouronihar's animated countenance. Gulchenrouz alarmed at the agitation of his cousin, said to her with a supplicating accent:

"Let us be gone; the sky looks portentious: the tamarisks tremble more than common; and the raw wind chills my very heart. Come, let us be gone, 'tis a melancholy night."

Then taking hold of her hand he drew it towards the path he besought her to go. Nouronihar unconsciously followed the attraction, for a thousand strange imaginations occupied her spirit. She passed the large round of honeysuckles, her favourite resort, without ever vouchsafing it a glance, yet Gulchenrouz could not help snatching off a few shoots in his way, though he ran as if a wild beast were behind.

The young females seeing him approach in such haste, and according to custom expecting a dance, instantly assembled in a circle and took each other by the hand, but Gulchenrouz coming up out of breath, fell down at once on the grass. This accident struck with consternation the whole of this frolicsome party, whilst Nouronihar, half distracted, and overcome both by the violence of her exercise and the tumult of her thoughts, sunk feebly down at his side, cherished his cold hands in her bosom, and chafed his temples with a fragrant unguent. At length he came to himself, and wrapping up his head in the robe of his cousin, entreated that she would not return to the harem. He was afraid of being snapped at by Shaban his tutor, a wrinkled old eunuch of a surly disposition, for having interrupted the stated walk of Nouronihar, he dreaded lest the churl should take it amiss. The whole of this sprightly group, sitting round upon a mossy knole, began to entertain themselves with various pastimes, whilst their superintendents the eunuchs were gravely conversing at a distance. The nurse of the emir's daughter observing her pupil sit ruminating with her eyes on the ground, endeavoured to amuse her with diverting tales, to which Gulchenrouz, who had already forgotten his inquietudes, listened with a breathless attention. He laughed; he clapped his hands; and passed a hundred little tricks on the whole of the company, without omitting the eunuchs, whom he provoked to run after him, in spite of their age and decrepitude.

During these occurrences the moon arose, the wind subsided, and the evening became so serene and inviting that a resolution was taken to sup on the spot. Sutlememe, who excelled in dressing a salad, having filled large bowls of porcelain with eggs of small birds, curds turned with citron juice, slices of cucumber, and the inmost leaves of delicate herbs, handed it round from one to another, and gave each their shares in a large spoon of cocknos. Gulchenrouz nestling as usual in the bosom of Nouronihar, pouted out his vermillion little lips against the offer of Sutlememe, and would take it only from the hand of his cousin, on whose mouth he hung like a bee inebriated with the quintessence of flowers. One of the eunuchs ran to fetch melons, whilst others were employed in showering down almonds from the branches that overhung this amiable party.

In the midst of this festive scene there appeared a light on the top of the highest mountain, which attracted the notice of every eye. This light was not less bright than the moon when at full, and might have been taken for her had it not been that the moon was already risen. The phenomenon occasioned a general surprise, and no one could conjecture the cause. It could not be a fire, for the light was clear and bluish; nor had meteors ever been seen of that magnitude or splendour. This strange light faded for a moment, and immediately renewed its brightness. It first appeared motionless at the foot of the rock, whence it darted in an instant to sparkle in a thicket of palm trees, from thence it glided along the torrent, and at last fixed in a glen that was narrow and dark. The moment it had taken its direction, Gulchenrouz, whose heart always trembled at any thing sudden or rare, drew Nouronihar by the robe, and anxiously requested her to return to the harem. The women were importunate in seconding the entreaty, but the curiosity of the emir's daughter prevailed. She not only refused to go back, but resolved at all hazards to pursue the appearance. Whilst they were debating what was best to be done, the light shot forth so dazzling a blaze that they all fled away shrieking. Nouronihar followed them a few steps, but coming to the turn of a little bye path stopped, and went back alone. As she ran with an alertness peculiar to herself, it was not long before she came to the place where they had just been supping. The globe of fire now appeared stationary in the glen, and burned in majestic stillness. Nouronihar compressing her hands upon her bosom, hesitated for some moments to advance. The solitude of her situation was new; the silence of the night awful; and every object inspired sensations which till then she never had felt. The affright of Gulchenrouz recurred to her mind; and she a thousand times turned to go back, but this luminous appearance was always before her. Urged on by an irresistible impulse, she continued to approach it in defiance of every obstacle that opposed her progress.

At length she arrived at the opening of the glen, but instead of coming up to the light, she found herself surrounded by darkness, except that at a considerable distance a faint spark glimmered by fits. She stopped a second time: the sound of waterfalls mingling their murmurs, the hollow rustlings amongst the palm branches, and the funereal screams of the birds from their rifted trunks, all conspired to fill her with terror. She imagined every moment that she trod on some venomous reptile. All the stories of malignant Dives, and dismal Goules thronged into her memory, but her curiosity was notwithstanding more predominant than her fears. She therefore firmly entered a winding track that led towards the spark, but being a stranger to the path, she had not gone far till she began to repent of her rashness.

"Alas!" said she, "that I were but in those secure and illuminated apartments where my evenings glided on with Gulchenrouz! Dear child, how would thy heart flutter with terror wert thou wandering in these wild solitudes like me."

At the close of this apostrophe she regained her road, and coming to steps hewn out in the rock ascended them undismayed. The light, which was now gradually enlarging, appeared above her on the summit of the mountain. At length she distinguished a plaintive and melodious union of voices proceeding from a sort of cavern, that resembled the dirges which are sung over tombs. A sound likewise like that which arises from the filling of baths, at the same time struck her ear. She continued ascending, and discovered large wax torches in full blaze planted here and there in the fissures of the rock. This preparation filled her with fear, whilst the subtle and potent odour which the torches exhaled caused her to sink almost lifeless at the entrance of the grot.

Casting her eyes within in this kind of trance, she beheld a large cistern of gold filled with a water, whose vapour distilled on her face a dew of the essence of roses. A soft symphony resounded through the grot. On the sides of the cistern she noticed appendages of royalty; diadems and feathers of the heron, all sparkling with carbuncles. Whilst her attention was fixed on this display of magnificence, the music ceased, and a voice instantly demanded:

"For what monarch were these torches kindled, this bath prepared, and these habiliments? which belong not only to the sovereigns of the earth, but even to the talismanic powers!"

To which a second voice answered:

"They are for the charming daughter of the emir Fakreddin."

"What," replied the first, "for that trifler who consumes her time with a giddy child, immersed in softness, and who at best can make but an enervated husband?"

"And can she," rejoined the other voice, "be amused with such empty trifles, whilst the Caliph, the sovereign of the world, he who is destined to enjoy the treasures of the preadimite sultans, a prince six feet high, and whose eyes pervade the inmost soul of a female, is inflamed with the love of her? no, she will be wise enough to answer that passion alone that can aggrandize her glory. No doubt she will, and despise the puppet of her fancy; then all the riches this place contains, as well as the carbuncle of Giamschid shall be hers."

"You judge right," returned the first voice, "and I haste to Istakar to prepare the palace of subterranean fire for the reception of the bridal pair."

The voices ceased, the torches were extinguished, the most entire darkness succeeded, and Nouronihar recovering with a start, found herself reclined on a sofa in the harem of her father. She clapped her hands, and immediately came together Gulchenrouz and her women, who, in despair at having lost her, had despatched eunuchs to seek her in every direction. Shaban appeared with the rest, and began to reprimand her with an air of consequence:

"Little impertinent," said he, "whence got you false keys? or are you beloved of some genius that hath given you a picklock? I will try the extent of your power; come, to your chamber! through the two sky-lights, and expect not the company of Gulchenrouz. Be expeditious! I will shut you up in the double tower."

At these menaces Nouronihar indignantly raised her head, opened on Shaban her black eyes, which since the important dialogue of the enchanted grot were considerably enlarged, and said:

"Go, speak thus to slaves! but learn to reverence her who is born to give laws, and subject all to her power."

She was proceeding in the same style, but was interrupted by a sudden exclamation of,

"The Caliph! the Caliph!"

The curtains at once were thrown open, and the slaves prostrate in double rows, whilst poor little Gulchenrouz hid himself beneath the elevation of a sofa. At first appeared a file of black eunuchs trailing after them long trains of muslin embroidered with gold, and holding in their hands censers, which dispensed as they passed the grateful perfume of the wood of aloes. Next marched Bababalouk with a solemn strut, and tossing his head as not over pleased at the visit. Vathek came close after superbly robed; his gait was unembarrassed and noble, and his presence would have engaged admiration, though he had not been the sovereign of the world. He approached Nouronihar with a throbbing heart, and seemed enraptured at the full effulgence of her radiant eyes, of which he had before caught but a few glimpses; but she instantly depressed them, and her confusion augmented her beauty.

Bababalouk, who was a thorough adept in coincidences of this nature, and knew that the worst game should be played with the best face, immediately made a signal for all to retire, and no sooner did he perceive beneath the sofa the little one's feet, than he drew him forth without ceremony, set him upon his shoulders, and lavished on him as he went off a thousand odious caresses. Gulchenrouz cried out, and resisted till his cheeks became the colour of the blossom of the pomegranite, and the tears that started into his eyes shot forth a gleam of indignation. He cast a significant glance at Nouronihar, which the Caliph noticing, asked:

"Is that then your Gulchenrouz?"

"Sovereign of the world," answered she, "spare my cousin, whose innocence and gentleness deserve not your anger!"

"Take comfort," said Vathek with a smile, "he is in good hands. Bababalouk is fond of children, and never goes without sweetmeats and comfits."

The daughter of Fakreddin was abashed; and suffered Gulchenrouz to be borne away without adding a word. The tumult of her bosom betrayed her confusion; and Vathek becoming still more impassioned, gave a loose to his frenzy, which had only not subdued the last faint strugglings of reluctance, when the emir suddenly bursting in, threw his face upon the ground at the feet of the Caliph, and said:

"Commander of the faithful, abase not yourself to the meanness of your slave."

"No, emir," replied Vathek, "I raise her to an equality with myself; I declare her my wife; and the glory of your race shall extend from one generation to another."

"Alas! my lord," said Fakreddin, as he plucked off the honours of his beard, "cut short the days of your faithful servant rather than force him to depart from his word. Nouronihar, as her hands evince, is solemnly promised to Gulchenrouz, the son of my bother, Ali Hassan; they are united also in heart; their faith is mutually plighted; and affiances so sacred cannot be broken."

"What, then," replied the Caliph bluntly, "would you surrender this divine beauty to a husband more womanish than herself? And can you imagine that I will suffer her charms to decay in hands so inefficient and nerveless? No! she is destined to live out her life within my embraces: such is my will: retire, and disturb not the night I devote to the homage of her charms."

The irritated emir drew forth his sabre, presented it to Vathek, and stretching out his neck, said in a firm tone of voice:

"Strike your unhappy host my lord! he has lived long enough, since he hath seen the prophet's vicegerent violate the rights of hospitality."

At his uttering these words, Nouronihar unable to support any longer the conflict of her passions, sunk down in a swoon. Vathek, both terrified for her life, and furious at an opposition to his will, bade Fakreddin assist his daughter, and withdrew, darting his terrible look at the unfortunate emir, who suddenly fell backward bathed in a sweat, cold as the damp of death.

Gulchenrouz, who had escaped from the hands of Bababalouk, and was that instant returned, called out for help as loudly as he could, not having strength to afford it himself. Pale and panting, the poor child attempted to revive Nouronihar by caresses, and it happened that the thrilling warmth of his lips restored her to life. Fakreddin beginning also to recover from the look of the Caliph, with difficulty tottered to a seat, and after warily casting round his eye to see if this dangerous prince were gone, sent for Shaban and Sutlememe, and said to them apart —

"My friends, violent evils require as violent remedies; the Caliph has brought desolation and horror into my family, and how shall we resist his power? Another of his looks will send me to my grave. Fetch then that narcotic powder which the Dervise brought me from Aracan. A dose of it, the effect of which will continue three days, must be administered to each of these children. The Caliph will believe them to be dead, for they will have all the appearance of death. We shall go as if to inter them in the cave of Meimoune, at the entrance of the great desert of sand, and near the cabin of my dwarfs. When all the spectators shall be withdrawn, you, Shaban, and four select eunuchs shall convey them to the lake, where provision shall be ready to support them a month; for, one day allotted to the surprise this event will occasion, five to the tears, a fortnight to reflection, and the rest to prepare for renewing his progress, will, according to my calculation, fill up the whole time that Vathek will tarry, and I shall then be freed from his intrusion."

"Your plan," said Sutlememe, "is a good one, if it can but be effected. I have remarked that Nouronihar is well able to support the glances of the Caliph, and that he is far from being sparing of them to her; be assured therefore, notwithstanding her fondness for Gulchenrouz, she will never remain quiet while she knows him to be here, unless we can persuade her that both herself and Gulchenrouz are really dead, and that they were conveyed to those rocks for a limited season to expiate the little faults of which their love was the cause. We will add that we killed ourselves in despair, and that your dwarfs whom they never yet saw will preach to them delectable sermons. I will engage that every thing shall succeed to the bent of your wishes."

"Be it so," said Fakreddin; "I approve your proposal; let us lose not a moment to give it effect." They forthwith hastened to seek for the powder, which being mixed in a sherbet was immediately drunk by Gulchenrouz and Nouronihar. Within the space of an hour both were seized with violent palpitations, and a general numbness gradually ensued. They arose from the floor, where they had remained ever since the Caliph's departure, and ascending to the sofa, reclined themselves at full length upon it, clasped in each other's embraces.

"Cherish me, my dear Nouronihar," said Gulchenrouz; "put thy hand upon my heart, for it feels as if it were frozen. Alas! thou art as cold as myself! hath the Caliph murdered us both with his terrible look?"

"I am dying," cried she in a faltering voice; "press me closer, I am ready to expire!"

"Let us die then together," answered the little Gulchenrouz, whilst his breast laboured with a convulsive sigh; "let me at least breathe forth my soul on thy lips."

They spoke no more, and became as dead.

Immediately the most piercing cries were heard through the harem, whilst Shaban and Sutlememe personated with great adroitness the parts of persons in despair. The emir, who was sufficiently mortified to be forced into such untoward expedients, and had now for the first time made a trial of his powder, was under no necessity of counterfeiting grief. The slaves, who had flocked together from all quarters, stood motionless at the spectacle before them. All lights were extinguished save two lamps, which shed a wan glimmering over the faces of these lovely flowers, that seemed to be faded in the spring-time of life. Funeral vestments were prepared; their bodies were washed with rose water; their beautiful tresses were braided and incensed; and they were wrapped in symars whiter than alabaster. At the moment that their attendants were placing two wreaths of their favourite jasamines on their brows, the Caliph, who had just heard the tragical catastrophe, arrived. He looked not less pale and haggard than the goules that wander at night among graves. Forgetful of himself and every one else, he broke through the midst of the slaves, fell prostrate at the foot of the sofa, beat his bosom, called himself "atrocious murderer," and invoked upon his head a thousand imprecations. With a trembling hand he raised the veil that covered the countenance of Nouronihar, and uttering a loud shriek fell lifeless on the floor. The chief of the eunuchs dragged him off with horrible grimaces, and repeated as he went:

"Aye, I foresaw she would play you some ungracious turn."

No sooner was the Caliph gone than the emir commanded biers to be brought, and forbade that any one should enter the harem. Every window was fastened; all instruments of music were broken; and the Imams began to recite their prayers. Towards the close of this melancholy day Vathek sobbed in silence, for they had been forced to compose with anodynes his convulsions of rage and desperation.

At the dawn of the succeeding morning the wide folding doors of the palace were set open, and the funeral procession moved forward for the mountain. The wailful cries of "La Ilah illa Alla," reached to the Caliph, who was eager to cicatrize himself and attend the ceremonial; nor could he have been dissuaded, had not his excessive weakness disabled him from walking. At the few first steps he fell on the ground, and his people were obliged to lay him on a bed, where he remained many days in such a state of insensibility as excited compassion in the emir himself.

When the procession was arrived at the grot of Meimoune, Shaban and Sutlememe dismissed the whole of the train excepting the four confidential eunuchs who were appointed to remain. After resting some moments near the biers which had been left in the open air, they caused them to be carried to the brink of a small lake whose banks were overgrown with a hoary moss. This was the great resort of herons and storks, which preyed continually on little blue fishes. The dwarfs, instructed by the emir, soon repaired thither, and with the help of the eunuchs began to construct cabins of rushes and reeds, a work in which they had admirable skill. A magazine also was contrived for provisions, with a small oratory for themselves, and a pyramid of wood neatly piled, to furnish the necessary fuel, for the air was bleak in the hollows of the mountains.

At evening two fires were kindled on the brink of the lake, and the two lovely bodies taken from their biers were carefully deposited upon a bed of dried leaves within the same cabin. The dwarfs began to recite the koran with their clear shrill voices, and Shaban and Sutlememe stood at some distance anxiously waiting the effects of the powder. At length Nouronihar and Gulchenrouz faintly stretched out their arms, and gradually opening their eyes began to survey with looks of increasing amazement every object around them. They even attempted to rise, but for want of strength fell back again. Sutlememe on this administered a cordial which the emir had taken care to provide.

Gulchenrouz thoroughly aroused sneezed out aloud, and raising himself with an effort that expressed his surprise, left the cabin, and inhaled the fresh air with the greatest avidity.

"Yes," said he, "I breathe again! again do I exist! I hear sounds! I behold a firmament spangled over with stars!"

Nouronihar catching these beloved accents extricated herself from the leaves, and ran to clasp Gulchenrouz to her bosom. The first objects she remarked were their long symars, their garlands of flowers, and their naked feet: she hid her face in her hands to reflect. The vision of the enchanted bath, the despair of her father, and more vividly than both, the majestic figure of Vathek recurred to her memory. She recollected also, that herself and Gulchenrouz had been sick and dying; but all these images bewildered her mind. Not knowing where she was, she turned her eyes on all sides, as if to recognise the surrounding scene. This singular lake, those flames reflected from its glassy surface, the pale hues of its banks, the romantic cabins, the bull-rushes that sadly waved their drooping heads, the storks whose melancholy cries blended with the shrill voices of the dwarfs, every thing conspired to persuade them that the angel of death had opened the portal of some other world.

Gulchenrouz on his part, lost in wonder, clung to the neck of his cousin. He believed himself in the region of phantoms, and was terrified at the silence she preserved. At length addressing her:

"Speak," said he; "where are we! do you not see those spectres that are stirring the burning coals? Are they the Monker and Nakir, come to throw us into them? Does the fatal bridge cross this lake, whose solemn stillness perhaps conceals from us an abyss, in which for whole ages we shall be doomed incessantly to sink?"

"No my children," said Sutlememe going towards them; "take comfort, the exterminating angel who conducted our souls hither after yours, hath assured us that the chastisement of your indolent and voluptuous life shall be restricted to a certain series of years, which you must pass in this dreary abode, where the sun is scarcely visible, and where the soil yields neither fruits nor flowers. These," continued she, pointing to the dwarfs, "will provide for our wants; for souls so mundane as ours retain too strong a tincture of their earthly extraction. Instead of meats, your food will be nothing but rice, and your bread shall be moistened in the fogs that brood over the surface of the lake."

At this desolating prospect the poor children burst into tears, and prostrated themselves before the dwarfs, who perfectly supported their characters, and delivered an excellent discourse of a customary length upon the sacred camel, which after a thousand years was to convey them to the paradise of the faithful.

The sermon being ended and ablutions performed, they praised Alla and the prophet, supped very indifferently, and retired to their withered leaves. Nouronihar and her little cousin consoled themselves on finding that, though dead, they yet lay in one cabin. Having slept well before, the remainder of the night was spent in conversation on what had befallen them; and both, from a dread of apparitions, betook themselves for protection to one another's arms.

In the morning, which was lowering and rainy, the dwarfs mounted high poles like minarets, and called them to prayers. The whole congregation, which consisted of Sutlememe, Shaban, the four eunuchs, and some storks, were already assembled. The two children came forth from their cabin with a slow and dejected pace. As their minds were in a tender and melancholy mood, their devotions were performed with fervour. No sooner were they finished than Gulchenrouz demanded of Sutlememe and the rest, "how they happened to die so opportunely for his cousin and himself."

"We killed ourselves," returned Sutlememe, "in despair at your death."

On this, said Nouronihar, who notwithstanding what was past, had not yet forgotten her vision:

"And the Caliph, is he also dead of his grief? and will he likewise come hither?"

The dwarfs, who were prepared with an answer, most demurely replied:

"Vathek is damned beyond all redemption!"

"I readily believe so," said Gulchenrouz; "and am glad from my heart to hear it, for I am convinced it was his horrible look that sent us hither, to listen to sermons and mess upon rice."

One week passed away on the side of the lake unmarked by any variety; Nouronihar ruminating on the grandeur of which death had deprived her, and Gulchenrouz applying to prayers and to panniers along with the dwarfs, who infinitely pleased him. Whilst this scene of innocence was exhibiting in the mountains, the Caliph presented himself to the emir in a new light. The instant he recovered the use of his senses, with a voice that made Bababalouk quake, he thundered out:

"Perfidious Giaour! I renounce thee for ever! it is thou who hast slain my beloved Nouronihar! and I supplicate the pardon of Mahomet, who would have preserved her to me had I been more wise. Let water be brought to perform my ablutions, and let the pious Fakreddin be called to offer up his prayers with mine, and reconcile me to him. Afterwards we will go together and visit the sepulchre of the unfortunate Nouronihar. I am resolved to become a hermit, and consume the residue of my days on this mountain, in hope of expiating my crimes."

Nouronihar was not altogether so content, for though she felt a fondness for Gulchenrouz, who to augment the attachment, had been left at full liberty with her, yet she still regarded him as but a bauble that bore no competition with the carbuncle of Giamschid. At times she indulged doubts on the mode of her being, and scarcely could believe that the dead had all the wants and the whims of the living. To gain satisfaction, however, on so perplexing a topic, she arose one morning whilst all were asleep with a breathless caution from the side of Gulchenrouz, and after having given him a soft kiss, began to follow the windings of the lake till it terminated with a rock whose top was accessible though lofty. This she clambered up with considerable toil, and having reached the summit, set forward in a run like a doe that unwittingly follows her hunter. Though she skipped along with the alertness of an antelope, yet at intervals she was forced to desist, and rest beneath the tamarisks to recover her breath. Whilst she, thus reclined, was occupied with her little reflections on the apprehension that she had some knowledge of the place, Vathek, who finding himself that morning but ill at ease, had gone forth before the dawn, presented himself on a sudden to her view. Motionless with surprise, he durst not approach the figure before him, which lay shrouded up in a symar extended on the ground, trembling and pale, but yet lovely to behold. At length Nouronihar, with a mixture of pleasure and affliction, raising her fine eyes to him, said:

"My lord, are you come hither to eat rice and hear sermons with me?"

"Beloved phantom!" cried Vathek, "dost thou speak? hast thou the same graceful form? the same radiant features? art thou palpable likewise?" and eagerly embracing her he added, "here are limbs and a bosom animated with a gentle warmth! what can such a prodigy mean?"

Nouronihar with diffidence answered:

"You know my lord that I died on the night you honoured me with your visit; my cousin maintains it was from one of your glances, but I cannot believe him, for to me they seem not so dreadful. Gulchenrouz died with me, and we were both brought into a region of desolation, where we are fed with a wretched diet. If you be dead also, and are come hither to join us, I pity your lot, for you will be stunned with the clang of the dwarfs and the storks. Besides, it is mortifying in the extreme that you as well as myself should have lost the treasures of the subterranean palace."

At the mention of the subterranean palace, the Caliph suspended his caresses, which indeed had proceeded pretty far, to seek from Nouronihar an explanation of her meaning. She then recapitulated her vision—what immediately followed—and the history of her pretended death; adding also a description of the palace of expiation from whence she had fled; and all in a manner that would have extorted his laughter, had not the thoughts of Vathek been too deeply engaged. No sooner, however, had she ended, than he again clasped her to his bosom, and said:

"Light of my eyes! the mystery is unravelled; we both are alive! Your father is a cheat, who for the sake of dividing hath deluded us both; and the Giaour, whose design, as far as I can discover, is that we shall proceed together, seems scarce a whit better. It shall be some time at least before he find us in his palace of fire. Your lovely little person in my estimation is far more precious than all the treasures of the preadimite sultans, and I wish to possess it at pleasure, and in open day for many a moon, before I go to burrow under ground like a mole."

"Forget this little trifler Gulchenrouz, and"—

"Ah, my lord," interposed Nouronihar, "let me entreat that you do him no evil."

"No, no," replied Vathek, "I have already bid you forbear to alarm yourself for him. He has been brought up too much on milk and sugar to stimulate my jealousy. We will leave him with the dwarfs, who by the bye are my old acquaintances; their company will suit him far better than yours. As to other matters, I will return no more to your father's. I want not to have my ears dinned by him and his dotards with the violation of the rights of hospitality; as if it were less an honour for you to espouse the sovereign of the world, than a girl dressed up like a boy."

Nouronihar could find nothing to oppose in a discourse so eloquent. She only wished the amorous monarch had discovered more ardour for the carbuncle of Giamschid; but flattered herself it would gradually increase, and therefore yielded to his will with the most bewitching submission.

When the Caliph judged it proper he called for Bababalouk, who was asleep in the cave of Meimoune, and dreaming that the phantom of Nouronihar having mounted him once more on her swing, had just given him such a jerk that he one moment soared above the mountains, and the next sunk into the abyss. Starting from his sleep at the voice of his master, he ran gasping for breath, and had nearly fallen backward at the sight, as he believed, of the spectre, by whom he had so lately been haunted in his dream.

"Ah my lord," cried he, recoiling ten steps, and covering his eyes with both hands, "do you then perform the office of a goule? 'Tis true you have dug up the dead, yet hope not to make her your prey; for after all she hath caused me to suffer, she is even wicked enough to prey upon you."

"Cease thy folly," said Vathek, "and thou shalt soon be convinced that it is Nouronihar herself, alive and well, whom I clasp to my breast. Go only, and pitch my tents in the neighbouring valley. There will I fix my abode with this beautiful tulip, whose colours I soon shall restore. There exert thy best endeavours to procure whatever can augment the enjoyments of life, till I shall disclose to thee more of my will."

The news of so unlucky an event soon reached the ears of the emir, who abandoned himself to grief and despair, and began, as did all his old greybeards, to begrime his visage with ashes. A total supineness ensued; travellers were no longer entertained, no more plasters were spread, and instead of the charitable activity that had distinguished this asylum, the whole of its inhabitants exhibited only faces of a half cubit long, and uttered groans that accorded with their forlorn situation.

Though Fakreddin bewailed his daughter as lost to him for ever, yet Gulchenrouz was not forgotten. He despatched immediate instruction to Sutlememe, Shaban, and the dwarfs, enjoining them not to undeceive the child in respect to his state, but under some pretence to convey him far from the lofty rock at the extremity of the lake, to a place which he should appoint, as safer from danger; for he suspected that Vathek intended him evil.

Gulchenrouz in the mean while was filled with amazement at not finding his cousin; nor were the dwarfs at all less surprised; but Sutlememe, who had more penetration, immediately guessed what had happened. Gulchenrouz was amused with the delusive hope of once more embracing Nouronihar in the interior recesses of the mountains, where the ground, strewed over with orange blossoms and jasamines, offered beds much more inviting than the withered leaves in their cabin, where they might accompany with their voices the sounds of their lutes, and chase butterflies in concert. Sutlememe was far gone in this sort of description when one of the four eunuchs beckoned her aside to apprise her of the arrival of a messenger from their fraternity, who had explained the secret of the flight of Nouronihar, and brought the commands of the emir. A council with Shaban and the dwarfs was immediately held. Their baggage being stowed in consequence of it, they embarked in a shallop and quietly sailed with the little one, who acquiesced in all their proposals. Their voyage proceeded in the same manner, till they came to the place where the lake sinks beneath the hollow of the rock, but as soon as the bark had entered it, and Gulchenrouz found himself surrounded with darkness, he was seized with a dreadful consternation, and incessantly uttered the most piercing outcries; for he now was persuaded he should actually be damned for having taken too many little freedoms in his life-time with his cousin.

But let us return to the Caliph, and her who ruled over his heart. Bababalouk had pitched the tents, and closed up the extremities of the valley with magnificent screens of India cloth, which were guarded by Ethiopian slaves with their drawn sabres. To preserve the verdure of this beautiful enclosure in its natural freshness, the white eunuchs went continually round it with their red water vessels. The waving of fans was heard near the imperial pavilion, where by the voluptuous light that glowed through the muslins, the Caliph enjoyed at full view all the attractions of Nouronihar. Inebriated with delight, he was all ear to her charming voice which accompanied the lute; while she was not less captivated with his descriptions of Samarah and the tower full of wonders, but especially with his relation of the adventure of the ball, and the chasm of the Giaour with its ebony portal.

In this manner they conversed for a day and a night; they bathed together in a basin of black marble, which admirably relieved the fairness of Nouronihar. Bababalouk, whose good graces this beauty had regained, spared no attention that their repasts might be served up with the minutest exactness: some exquisite rariety was ever placed before them; and he sent even to Schiraz for that fragrant and delicious wine which had been hoarded up in bottles prior to the birth of Mahomet. He had excavated little ovens in the rock to bake the nice manchets which were prepared by the hands of Nouronihar, from whence they had derived a flavour so grateful to Vathek, that he regarded the ragouts of his other wives as entirely maukish; whilst they would have died at the emir's of chagrin at finding themselves so neglected, if Fakreddin, notwithstanding his resentment, had not taken pity upon them.

The sultana Dilara, who till then had been the favourite, took this dereliction of the Caliph to heart with a vehemence natural to her character; for during her continuance in favour she had imbibed from Vathek many of his extravagant fancies, and was fired with impatience to behold the superb tombs of Istakar, and the palace of forty columns; besides, having been brought up amongst the magi, she had fondly cherished the idea of the Caliph's devoting himself to the worship of fire; thus his voluptuous and desultory life with her rival was to her a double source of affliction. The transient piety of Vathek had occasioned her some serious alarms, but the present was an evil of far greater magnitude. She resolved therefore without hesitation to write to Carathis, and acquaint her that all things went ill; that they had eaten, slept, and revelled at an old emir's, whose sanctity was very formidable, and that after all the prospect of possessing the treasures of the preadimite sultans was no less remote than before. This letter was entrusted to the care of two woodmen who were at work on one of the great forests of the mountains, and being acquainted with the shortest cuts, arrived in ten days at Samarah.

The princess Carathis was engaged at chess with Morakanabad, when the arrival of these wood-fellers was announced. She, after some weeks of Vathek's absence, had forsaken the upper regions of her tower, because everything appeared in confusion among the stars, whom she consulted relative to the fate of her son. In vain did she renew her fumigations, and extend herself on the roof to obtain mystic visions, nothing more could she see in her dreams than pieces of brocade, nosegays of flowers, and other unmeaning gewgaws. These disappointments had thrown her into a state of dejection which no drug in her power was sufficient to remove. Her only resource was in Morakanabad, who was a good man, and endowed with a decent share of confidence, yet whilst in her company he never thought himself on roses.

No person knew aught of Vathek, and a thousand ridiculous stories were propagated at his expense. The eagerness of Carathis may be easily guessed at receiving the letter, as well as her rage at reading the dissolute conduct of her son.

"Is it so," said she; "either I will perish, or Vathek shall enter the palace of fire. Let me expire in flames, provided he may reign on the throne of Soliman!"

Having said this, and whirled herself round in a magical manner, which struck Morakanabad with such terror as caused him to recoil, she ordered her great camel Alboufaki to be brought, and the hideous Nerkes with the unrelenting Cafour to attend.

"I require no other retinue," said she to Morakanabad: "I am going on affairs of emergency, a truce therefore to parade! Take you care of the people, fleece them well in my absence, for we shall expend large sums, and one knows not what may betide."

The night was uncommonly dark, and a pestilential blast ravaged the plain of Catoul that would have deterred any other traveller however urgent the call; but Carathis enjoyed most whatever filled others with dread. Nerkes concurred in opinion with her, and Cafour had a particular predilection for a pestilence. In the morning this accomplished caravan, with the wood-fellers who directed their route, halted on the edge of an extensive marsh, from whence so noxious a vapour arose as would have destroyed any animal but Alboufaki, who naturally inhaled these malignant fogs. The peasants entreated their convoy not to sleep in this place.

"To sleep," cried Carathis, "what an excellent thought! I never sleep but for visions; and as to my attendants, their occupations are too many to close the only eye they each have."

The poor peasants, who were not over pleased with their party, remained open-mouthed with surprise.

Carathis alighted as well as her negresses, and severally stripping off their outer garments, they all ran in their drawers to cull from those spots where the sun shone fiercest, the venomous plants that grew on the marsh. This provision was made for the family of the emir, and whoever might retard the expedition to Istakar. The woodmen were overcome with fear when they beheld these three horrible phantoms run, and not much relishing the company of Alboufaki, stood aghast at the command of Carathis to set forward, notwithstanding it was noon, and the heat fierce enough to calcine even rocks. In spite, however, of every remonstrance, they were forced implicitly to submit.

Alboufaki, who delighted in solitude, constantly snorted whenever he perceived himself near a habitation, and Carathis, who was apt to spoil him with indulgence, as constantly turned him aside; so that the peasants were precluded from procuring subsistence; for the milch goats and ewes which Providence had sent towards the district they traversed, to refresh travellers with their milk, all fled at the sight of the hideous animal and his strange riders. As to Carathis, she needed no common aliment; for her invention had previously furnished her with an opiate to stay her stomach, some of which she imparted to her mutes.

At the fall of night Alboufaki making a sudden stop, stamped with his foot, which to Carathis, who understood his paces, was a certain indication that she was near the confines of some cemetery. The moon shed a bright light on the spot, which served to discover a long wall with a large door in it standing a-jar, and so high that Alboufaki might easily enter. The miserable guides, who perceived their end approaching, humbly implored Carathis, as she had now so good an opportunity, to inter them, and immediately gave up the ghost. Nerkes and Cafour, whose wit was of a style peculiar to themselves, were by no means parsimonious of it on the folly of these poor people, nor could any thing have been found more suited to their taste than the site of the burying ground, and the sepulchres which its precincts contained. There were at least two thousand of them on the declivity of a hill; some in the form of pyramids, others like columns, and in short the variety of their shapes was endless. Carathis was too much immersed in her sublime contemplations to stop at the view, charming as it appeared in her eyes. Pondering the advantages that might accrue from her present situation, she could not forbear to exclaim:

"So beautiful a cemetery must be haunted by Gouls, and they want not for intelligence! having heedlessly suffered my guides to expire, I will apply for directions to them, and as an inducement, will invite them to regale on these fresh corpses."

After this short soliloquy, she beckoned to Nerkes and Cafour, and made signs with her fingers, as much as to say:

"Go, knock against the sides of the tombs, and strike up your delightful warblings, that are so like to those of the guests whose company I wish to obtain."

323

The negresses, full of joy at the behests of their mistress, and promising themselves much pleasure from the society of the Gouls, went with an air of conquest, and began their knockings at the tombs. As their strokes were repeated, a hollow noise was heard in the earth, the surface hove up into heaps, and the Gouls on all sides protruded their noses to inhale the effluvia which the carcasses of the woodmen began to emit.

They assembled before a sarcophagus of white marble, where Carathis was seated between the bodies of her miserable guides. The princess received her visitants with distinguished politeness, and when supper was ended, proceeded with them to business. Having soon learnt from them every thing she wished to discover, it was her intention to set forward forthwith on her journey, but her negresses, who were forming tender connections with the Gouls, importuned her with all their fingers to wait, at least till the dawn. Carathis, however, being chastity in the abstract, and an implacable enemy to love and repose, at once rejected their prayer, mounted Alboufaki, and commanded them to take their seats in a moment. Four days and four nights she continued her route, without turning to the right hand or left; on the fifth she traversed the mountains and half-burnt forests, and arrived on the sixth before the beautiful screens which concealed from all eyes the voluptuous wanderings of her son.

It was day-break, and the guards were snoring on their posts in careless security, when the rough trot of Alboufaki awoke them in consternation. Imagining that a group of spectres ascended from the abyss was approaching, they all without ceremony took to their heels. Vathek was at that instant with Nouronihar in the bath, hearing tales and laughing at Bababalouk who related them; but no sooner did the outcry of his guards reach him, than he flounced from the water like a carp, and as soon threw himself back at the sight of Carathis, who advancing with her negresses upon Alboufaki, broke through the muslin awnings and veils of the pavilion. At this sudden apparition Nouronihar (for she was not at all times free from remorse) fancied that the moment of celestial vengeance was come, and clung about the Caliph in amorous despondence.

Carathis, still seated on her camel, foamed with indignation at the spectacle which obtruded itself on her chaste view. She thundered forth without check or mercy:

"Thou double-headed and four legged monster! what means all this winding and writhing? art thou not ashamed to be seen grasping this limber sapling, in preference to the sceptre of the preadimite sultans? Is it then for this paltry doxy that thou hast violated the conditions in the parchment of our Giaour? Is it on her thou hast lavished thy precious moments? Is this the fruit of the knowledge I have taught thee? Is this the end of thy journey? Tear thyself from the arms of this little simpleton; drown her in the water before me, and instantly follow my guidance."

In the first ebullition of his fury, Vathek resolved to make a skeleton of Alboufaki, and to stuff the skins of Carathis and her blacks; but the ideas of the Giaour, the palace of Istakar, the sabres, and the talismans, flashing before his imagination with the simultaneousness of lightning, he became more moderate, and said to his mother in a civil but decisive tone:

"Dread lady, you shall be obeyed; but I will not drown Nouronihar; she is sweeter to me than a Myrabolan comfit, and is enamoured of carbuncles, especially that of Giamschid, which hath also been promised to be conferred upon her; she therefore shall go along with us, for I intend to repose with her beneath the canopies of Soliman; I can sleep no more without her."

"Be it so," replied Carathis alighting, and at the same time committing Alboufaki to the charge of her women.

Nouronihar, who had not yet quitted her hold, began to take courage, and said with an accent of fondness to the Caliph:

"Dear sovereign of my soul! I will follow thee, if it be thy will beyond the Kaf, in the land of the Afrits. I will not hesitate to climb for thee the nest of the Simurgh, who, this lady excepted, is the most awful of created existences."

"We have here then," subjoined Carathis, "a girl both of courage and science."

Nouronihar had certainly both; but notwithstanding all her firmness, she could not help casting back a look of regret upon the graces of her little Gulchenrouz, and the days of tenderness she had participated with him. She even dropped a few tears, which Carathis observed, and inadvertently breathed out with a sigh:

"Alas! my gentle cousin, what will become of him!"

Vathek at this apostrophe knitted up his brows, and Carathis enquired what it could mean.

"She is preposterously sighing after a stripling with languishing eyes and soft hair who loves her," said the Caliph.

"Where is he?" asked Carathis. "I must be acquainted with this pretty child; for," added she, lowering her voice, "I design before I depart to regain the favour of the Giaour. There is nothing so delicious in his estimation as the heart of a delicate boy, palpitating with the first tumults of love."

Vathek as he came from the bath commanded Bababalouk to collect the women and other moveables of his harem, embody his troops, and hold himself in readiness to march in three days; whilst Carathis retired alone to a tent, where the Giaour solaced her with encouraging visions; but at length waking, she found at her feet Nerkes and Cafour, who informed her by their signs, that having led Alboufaki to the borders of a lake, to browse on some moss that looked tolerably venomous, they had discovered certain blue fishes of the same kind with those in the reservoir on the top of the tower.

"Ah, ah," said she, "I will go thither to them. These fish are past doubt of a species that by a small operation I can render oracular. They may tell me where this little Gulchenrouz is, whom I am bent upon sacrificing."

Having thus spoken, she immediately set out with her swarthy retinue.

It being but seldom that time is lost in the accomplishment of a wicked enterprise, Carathis and her negresses soon arrived at the lake, where, after burning the magical drugs with which they were always provided, they, stripping themselves naked, waded to their chins, Nerkes and Cafour waving torches around them, and Carathis pronouncing her barbarous incantations. The fishes with one accord thrust forth their heads from the water, which was violently rippled by the flutter of their fins, and at length finding themselves constrained by the potency of the charm, they opened their piteous mouths, said:

"From gills to tail we are yours; what seek ye to know?"

"Fishes," answered she, "I conjure you by your glittering scales, tell me where now is Gulchenrouz?"

"Beyond the rock," replied the shoal in full chorus: "will this content you? for we do not delight in expanding our mouths."

"It will," returned the princess: "I am not to learn that you like not long conversations; I will leave you therefore to repose, though I had other questions to propound."

The instant she had spoken the water became smooth, and the fishes at once disappeared.

Carathis, inflated with the venom of her projects, strode hastily over the rock, and found the amiable Gulchenrouz asleep in an arbour, whilst the two dwarfs were watching at his side, and ruminating their accustomed prayers. These diminutive personages possessed the gift of divining whenever an enemy to good Mussulmans approached; thus they anticipated the arrival of Carathis, who stopping short, said to herself:

"How placidly doth he recline his lovely little head! how pale and languishing are his looks! it is just the very child of my wishes!"

The dwarfs interrupted this delectable soliloquy by leaping instantly upon her, and scratching her face with their utmost zeal. But Nerkes and Cafour betaking themselves to the succour of their mistress, pinched the dwarfs so severely in return, that they both gave up the ghost, imploring Mahomet to inflict his sorest vengeance upon this wicked woman and all her household.

At the noise which this strange conflict occasioned in the valley, Gulchenrouz awoke, and bewildered with terror sprung impetuously upon an old fig-tree that rose against the acclivity of the rocks, from thence gained their summits, and ran for two hours without once looking back. At last, exhausted with fatigue, he fell as if dead into the arms of a good old Genius, whose fondness for the company of children had made it his sole occupation to protect them, and who, whilst performing his wonted rounds through the air, happening on the cruel Giaour at the instant of his growling in the horrible chasm, rescued the fifty little victims which the impiety of Vathek had devoted to his maw. These the Genius brought up in nests still higher than the clouds, and himself fixed his abode in a nest more capacious than the rest, from which he had expelled the possessors that had built it.

These inviolable asylums were defended against the Dives and the Afrits by waving streamers, on which were inscribed in characters of gold that flashed like lightning, the names of Alla and the prophet. It was there that Gulchenrouz, who as yet remained undeceived with respect to his pretended death, thought himself in the mansions of eternal peace. He admitted without fear the congratulations of his little friends, who were all assembled in the nest of the venerable Genius, and vied with each other in kissing his serene forehead and beautiful eye-lids. This he found to be the state congenial to his soul — remote from the inquietudes of earth — the impertinence of harems — the brutality of eunuchs — and the lubricity of women. In this peaceable society his days, months, and years glided on, nor was he less happy than the rest of his companions, for the Genius, instead of burdening his pupils with perishable riches, and the vain sciences of the world, conferred upon them the boon of perpetual childhood.

Carathis, unaccustomed to the loss of her prey, vented a thousand execrations on her negresses for not seizing the child, instead of amusing themselves with pinching to death the dwarfs, from which they could gain no advantage. She returned into the valley murmuring, and finding that her son was not risen from the arms of Nouronihar, discharged her ill-humour upon both. The idea, however, of departing next day for Istakar, and cultivating, through the good offices of the Giaour, an intimacy with Eblis himself, at length consoled her chagrin: but fate had ordained it otherwise.

In the evening, as Carathis was conversing with Dilara, who through her contrivance had become of the party, and whose taste resembled her own, Bababalouk came to acquaint her "that the sky towards Samarah looked of a fiery red, and seemed to portend some alarming disaster." Immediately recurring to her astrolabes and instruments of magic, she took the altitude of the planets, and discovered by her calculations, to her great mortification, that a formidable revolt had taken place at Samarah; that Motavakel, availing himself of the disgust which was inveterate against his brother had incited commotions amongst the populace, made himself master of the palace, and actually invested the great tower, to which Morakanabad had retired with a handful of the few that still remained faithful to Vathek.

"What," exclaimed she, "must I lose then my tower, my mutes, my negresses, my mummies, and worse than all, the laboratory, in which I have spent so many a night, without knowing, at least, if my hair-brained son will complete his adventure? No! I will not be the dupe! Immediately will I speed to support Morakanabad. By my formidable art the clouds shall sleet hail-stones in the faces of the assailants, and shafts of red-hot iron on their heads. I will spring mines of serpents and torpedoes from beneath them, and we shall soon see the stand they will make against such an explosion!"

Having thus spoken, Carathis hasted to her son, who was tranquilly banqueting with Nouronihar in his superb carnation coloured tent.

"Glutton that thou art," cried she, "were it not for me, thou wouldst soon find thyself the commander only of pies. Thy faithful subjects have abjured the faith they swore to thee. Motavakel thy brother now reigns on the hill of pied horses; and had I not some slight resources in the tower, would not be easily persuaded to abdicate. But that time may not be lost, I shall only add four words: strike tent to-night; set forward; and beware how thou loiterest again by the way. Though thou hast forfeited the conditions of the parchment, I am not yet without hope; for it cannot be denied that thou hast violated to admiration the laws of hospitality by seducing the daughter of the emir, after having partaken of his bread and his salt. Such a conduct cannot but be delightful to the Giaour; and if on thy march thou canst signalize thyself by an additional crime, all will still go well, and thou shalt enter the palace of Soliman in triumph. Adieu! Alboufaki and my negresses are waiting."

The Caliph had nothing to offer in reply: he wished his mother a prosperous journey, and eat on till he had finished his supper. At midnight the camp broke up, amidst the flourishing of trumpets and other martial instruments; but loud indeed must have been the sound of the tymbals, to overpower the blubbering of the emir and his long-beards, who by an excessive profusion of tears had so far exhausted the radical moisture, that their eyes shrivelled up in their sockets, and their hairs dropped off by the roots. Nouronihar, to whom such a symphony was painful, did not grieve to get out of hearing. She accompanied the Caliph in the imperial litter, where they amused themselves with imagining the splendour which was soon to surround them. The other women, overcome with dejection, were dolefully rocked in their cages, whilst Dilara consoled herself with anticipating the joy of celebrating the rites of fire on the stately terraces of Istakar.

In four days they reached the spacious valley of Rocnabad. The season of spring was in all its vigour, and the grotesque branches of the almond trees in full blossom fantastically chequered the clear blue sky. The earth, variegated with hyacinths and jonquils, breathed forth a fragrance which diffused through the soul a divine repose. Myriads of bees, and scarce fewer of Santons had there taken up their abode. On the banks of the stream hives and oratories were alternately ranged, and their neatness and whiteness were set off by the deep green of the cypresses that spired up amongst them. These pious personages amused themselves with cultivating little gardens that abounded with flowers and fruits, especially musk-melons of the best flavour that Persia could boast. Sometimes dispersed over the meadow they entertained themselves with feeding peacocks whiter than snow, and turtles more blue than the sapphire. In this manner were they occupied when the harbingers of the imperial procession began to proclaim:

"Inhabitants of Rocnabad, prostrate yourselves on the brink of your pure waters, and tender your thanksgivings to heaven that vouchsafeth to shew you a ray of its glory; for lo! the commander of the faithful draws near."

The poor Santons, filled with holy energy, having bustled to light up wax torches in their oratories, and expand the koran on their ebony desks, went forth to meet the Caliph with baskets of honeycomb, dates, and melons. But whilst they were advancing in solemn procession and with measured steps, the horses, camels, and guards wantoned over their tulips and other flowers, and made a terrible havoc amongst them. The Santons could not help casting from one eye a look of pity on the ravages committing around them, whilst the other was fixed upon the Caliph and heaven. Nouronihar, enraptured with the scenery of a place which brought back to her remembrance the pleasing solitudes where her infancy had passed, entreated Vathek to stop, but he, suspecting that each oratory might be deemed by the Giaour a distinct habitation, commanded his pioneers to level them all. The Santons stood motionless with horror at the barbarous mandate, and at last broke out into lamentations, but these were uttered with so ill a grace, that Vathek bade his eunuchs to kick them from his presence. He then descended from the litter with Nouronihar. They sauntered together in the meadow, and amused themselves with culling flowers, and passing a thousand pleasantries on each other. But the bees, who were staunch Mussulmans, thinking it their duty to revenge the insult on their dear masters the Santons, assembled so zealously to do it with effect, that the Caliph and Nouronihar were glad to find their tents prepared to receive them.

Bababalouk, who in capacity of purveyor, had acquitted himself with applause, as to peacocks and turtles, lost no time in consigning some dozens to the spit, and as many more to be fricasseed. Whilst they were feasting, laughing, carousing, and blaspheming at pleasure on the banquet so liberally furnished, the Moullahs, the Sheiks, the Cadis, and Imans of Schiraz (who seemed not to have met the Santons) arrived, leading by bridles of ribband, inscribed from the koran, a train of asses which were loaded with the choicest fruits the country could boast. Having presented their offerings to the Caliph, they petitioned him to honour their city and mosques with his presence.

"Fancy not," said Vathek, "that you can detain me. Your presents I condescend to accept, but beg you will let me be quiet, for I am not over fond of resisting temptation. Retire then. Yet, as it is not decent for personages so reverend to return on foot, and as you have not the appearance of expert riders, my eunuchs shall tie you on your asses with the precaution that your backs be not turned towards me, for they understand etiquette."

In this deputation were some high-stomached Sheiks, who taking Vathek for a fool, scrupled not to speak their opinion. These Bababalouk girded with double cords; and having well disciplined their asses with nettles behind, they all started with a preternatural alertness, plunging, kicking, and running foul of each other in the most ludicrous manner imaginable.

Nouronihar and the Caliph mutually contended who should most enjoy so degrading a sight. They burst out in volleys of laughter to see the old men and their asses fall into the stream. The leg of one was fractured, the shoulder of another dislocated, the teeth of a third dashed out, and the rest suffered still worse.

Two days more, undisturbed by fresh embassies, having been devoted to the pleasures of Rocnabad, the expedition proceeded, leaving Schiraz on the right, and verging towards a large plain, from whence were discernible on the edge of the horizon the dark summits of the mountains of Istakar.

At this prospect the Caliph and Nouronihar were unable to repress their transports. They bounded from their litter to the ground, and broke forth into such wild exclamations as amazed all within hearing. Interrogating each other, they shouted,

"Are we not approaching the radiant palace of light, or gardens more delightful than those of Sheddad?"

Infatuated mortals! they thus indulged delusive conjecture, unable to fathom the decrees of the Most High!

The good Genii who had not totally relinquished the superintendence of Vathek, repairing to Mahomet in the seventh heaven, said:

"Merciful Prophet! stretch forth thy propitious arms towards thy vicegerent, who is ready to fall irretrievably into the snare which his enemies the Dives have prepared to destroy him. The Giaour is awaiting his arrival in the abominable palace of fire, where if he once set his foot his perdition will be inevitable."

Mahomet answered with an air of indignation:

"He hath too well deserved to be resigned to himself; but I permit you to try if one effort more will be effectual to divert him from pursuing his ruin."

One of these beneficent Genii, assuming without delay the exterior of a shepherd, more renowned for his piety than all the Dervises and Santons of the region, took his station near a flock of white sheep on the slope of a hill, and began to pour forth from his flute such airs of pathetic melody, as subdued the very soul; and awakening remorse, drove far from it every frivolous fancy. At these energetic sounds, the sun hid himself beneath a gloomy cloud; and the waters of two little lakes, that were naturally clearer than chrystal, became a colour like blood. The whole of this superb assembly, was involuntarily drawn towards the declivity of the hill. With downcast eyes, they all stood abashed; each upbraiding himself with the evil he had done. The heart of Dilara palpitated; and the chief of the eunuchs, with a sigh of contrition, implored pardon of the women, whom, for his own satisfaction, he had so often tormented.

Vathek and Nouronihar turned pale in their litter; and, regarding each other with haggard looks, reproached themselves—the one with a thousand of the blackest crimes, a thousand projects of impious ambition; the other, with the desolation of her family, and the perdition of the amiable Gulchenrouz. Nouronihar persuaded herself that she heard in the fatal music the groans of her dying father; and Vathek, the sobs of the fifty children he had sacrificed to the Giaour. Amidst these complicated pangs of anguish, they perceived themselves impelled towards the shepherd, whose countenance was so commanding, that Vathek, for the first time, felt overawed; whilst Nouronihar concealed her face with her hands. The music paused, and the Genius, addressing the Caliph, said:

"Deluded Prince! to whom Providence hath confided the care of innumerable subjects, is it thus that thou fulfillest thy mission? Thy crimes are already completed; and, art thou now hastening towards thy punishment? Thou knowest, that beyond these mountains, Eblis and his accursed Dives hold their infernal empire; and seduced by a malignant phantom, thou art proceeding to surrender thyself to them! This moment is the last of grace allowed thee! Abandon thy atrocious purpose. Return. Give back Nouronihar to her father, who still retains a few sparks of life. Destroy thy tower, with all its abominations. Drive Carathis from thy councils. Be just to thy subjects. Respect the ministers of the Prophet. Compensate for thy impieties by an exemplary life; and, instead of squandering thy days in voluptuous indulgence, lament thy crimes on the sepulchres of thy ancestors. Thou beholdest the clouds that obscure the sun; at the instant he recovers his splendour, if thy heart be not changed, the time of mercy assigned thee will be past for ever."

Vathek, depressed with fear, was on the point of prostrating himself at the feet of the shepherd, whom he perceived to be of a nature superior to man, but his pride prevailing, he audaciously lifted his head, and glancing at him one of his terrible looks, said:

"Whoever thou art, withhold thy useless admonitions. Thou wouldst either delude me, or art thyself deceived. If what I have done be so criminal as thou pretendest, there remains not for me a moment of grace. I have traversed a sea of blood, to acquire a power which will make thy equals tremble; deem not that I shall retire when in view of the port; or that I will relinquish her who is dearer to me than either my life or thy mercy. Let the sun appear! Let him illumine my career! It matters not where it may end."

On uttering these words, which made even the Genius shudder, Vathek threw himself into the arms of Nouronihar, and commanded that his horses should be forced back to the road.

There was no difficulty in obeying these orders, for the attraction had ceased, the sun shone forth in all his glory, and the shepherd vanished with a lamentable scream.

The fatal impression of the music of the Genius remained, notwithstanding, in the hearts of Vathek's attendants. They viewed each other with looks of consternation. At the approach of night, almost all of them escaped; and, of this numerous assemblage, there only remained the chief of the eunuchs, some idolatrous slaves, Dilara, and a few other women, who, like herself, were votaries of the religion of the Magi.

The Caliph, fired with the ambition of prescribing laws to the Intelligences of Darkness, was but little embarrassed at this dereliction. The impetuosity of his blood prevented him from sleeping; nor did he encamp any more as before. Nouronihar, whose impatience, if possible, exceeded his own, importuned him to hasten his march, and lavished on him a thousand caresses, to beguile all reflection. She fancied herself already more potent than Balkis; [134] and pictured to her imagination the Genii falling prostrate at the foot of her throne. In this manner they advanced by moonlight, till they came within view of the two towering rocks, that form a kind of portal to the valley, at whose extremity rose the vast ruins of Istakar. Aloft on the mountain, glimmered the fronts of various royal mausoleums, the horror of which was deepened by the shadows of night. They passed through two villages, almost deserted; the only inhabitants remaining being a few feeble old men, who at the sight of horses and litters fell upon their knees, and cried out:

"O heaven! is it then by these phantoms that we have been for six months tormented! Alas! it was from the terror of these spectres, and the noise beneath the mountains, that our people have fled, and left us at the mercy of maleficent spirits!"

The Caliph, to whom these complaints were but unpromising auguries, drove over the bodies of these wretched old men, and at length arrived at the foot of the terrace of black marble. There he descended from his litter, handing down Nouronihar; both, with beating hearts, stared wildly around them, and expected, with an apprehensive shudder, the approach of the Giaour. But nothing as yet announced his appearance.

A deathlike stillness reigned over the mountain, and through the air. The moon dilated, on a vast platform, the shades of the lofty columns, which reached from the terrace almost to the clouds. The gloomy watch-towers, whose number could not be counted, were veiled by no roof: and their capitals, of an architecture unknown in the records of the earth, served as an asylum for the birds of darkness, which, alarmed at the approach of such visitants, fled away croaking.

The chief of the eunuchs, trembling with fear, besought Vathek that a fire might be kindled.

"No!" replied he, "there is no time left to think of such trifles; abide where thou art, and expect my commands."

Having thus spoken, he presented his hand to Nouronihar, and ascending the steps of a vast staircase, reached the terrace, which was flagged with squares of marble, and resembled a smooth expanse of water, upon whose surface not a leaf ever dared to vegetate. On the right rose the watch-towers, ranged before the ruins of an immense palace, whose walls were embossed with various figures. In front stood forth the colossal forms of four creatures, composed of the leopard and the griffin; and though but of stone, inspired emotions of terror. Near these were distinguished by the splendour of the moon, which streamed full on the place, characters like those on the sabres of the Giaour, that possessed the same virtue of changing every moment. These, after vacillating for some time, at last fixed in Arabic letters, and prescribed to the Caliph the following words:

"Vathek! thou hast violated the conditions of my parchment, and deservest to be sent back; but in favour to thy companion, and as the meed for what thou hast done to obtain it, Eblis permitteth that the portal of his palace shall be opened, and the subterranean fire will receive thee into the number of its adorers."

He scarcely had read these words before the mountain, against which the terrace was reared, trembled; and the watch-towers were ready to topple headlong upon them. The rock yawned, and disclosed within it a staircase of polished marble, that seemed to approach the abyss. Upon each stair were planted two large torches, like those Nouronihar had seen in her vision, the camphorated vapour ascending from which gathered into a cloud under the hollow of the vault.

This appearance, instead of terrifying, gave new courage to the daughter of Fakreddin. Scarcely deigning to bid adieu to the moon and the firmament, she abandoned without hesitation the pure atmosphere, to plunge into these infernal exhalations. The gait of those impious personages was haughty and

335

determined. As they descended, by the effulgence of the torches, they gazed on each other with mutual admiration, and both appeared so resplendent, that they already esteemed themselves spiritual intelligences. The only circumstance that perplexed them, was their not arriving at the bottom of the stairs. On hastening their descent, with an ardent impetuosity, they felt their steps accelerated to such a degree, that they seemed not walking, but falling from a precipice. Their progress, however, was at length impeded by a vast portal of ebony, which the Caliph without difficulty recognized. Here the Giaour awaited them, with the key in his hand,

"Ye are welcome!" said he to them, with a ghastly smile, "in spite of Mahomet, and all his dependents. I will now admit you into that palace, where you have so highly merited a place."

Whilst he was uttering these words, he touched the enamelled lock with his key, and the doors at once expanded with a noise still louder than the thunder of mountains, and as suddenly recoiled the moment they had entered.

The Caliph and Nouronihar beheld each other with amazement, at finding themselves in a place which, though roofed with a vaulted ceiling, was so spacious and lofty, that at first they took it for an immeasurable plain. But their eyes at length growing to the grandeur of the objects at hand, they extended their view to those at a distance, and discovered rows of columns and arcades, which gradually diminished, till they terminated in a point, radiant as the sun, when he darts his last beams athwart the ocean. The pavement, strewed over with gold dust and saffron, exhaled so subtile an odour, as almost overpowered them. They, however, went on, and observed an infinity of censers, in which ambergris and the wood of aloes were continually burning. Between the several columns were placed tables, each spread with a profusion of viands, and wines of every species, sparkling in vases of chrystal. A throng of Genii, and other phantastic spirits, of each sex, danced lasciviously in troops, at the sound of music which issued from beneath.

In the midst of this immense hall, a vast multitude was incessantly passing, who severally kept their right hands on their hearts, without once regarding any thing around them. They had all the livid paleness of death. Their eyes, deep sank in their sockets, resembled those phosphoric meteors, that glimmer by night in places of interment. Some stalked slowly on, absorbed in profound reverie; some shrieking with agony, ran furiously about, like tigers wounded with poisoned arrows;

whilst others, grinding their teeth in rage, foamed along, more frantic than the wildest maniac. They all avoided each other, and though surrounded by a multitude that no one could number, each wandered at random unheedful of the rest, as if alone on a desert which no foot had trodden.

Vathek and Nouronihar, frozen with terror at a sight so baleful, demanded of the Giaour what these appearances might mean, and why these ambulating spectres never withdrew their hands from their hearts.

"Perplex not yourselves," replied he bluntly, "with so much at once, you will soon be acquainted with all; let us haste and present you to Eblis."

They continued their way through the multitude, but notwithstanding their confidence at first, they were not sufficiently composed to examine with attention the various perspectives of halls, and of galleries, that opened on the right hand and left, which were all illuminated by torches and braziers, whose flames rose in pyramids, to the centre of the vault. At length they came to a place where long curtains, brocaded with crimson and gold, fell from all parts, in striking confusion. Here the choirs and dances were heard no longer. The light which glimmered came from afar.

After some time Vathek and Nouronihar perceived a gleam brightening through the drapery, and entered a vast tabernacle, carpeted with the skins of leopards. An infinity of elders, with streaming beards, and afrits, in complete armour, had prostrated themselves before the ascent of a lofty eminence, on the top of which, upon a globe of fire, sat the formidable Eblis. His person was that of a young man, whose noble and regular features seemed to have been tarnished by malignant vapours. In his large eyes appeared both pride and despair; his flowing hair retained some resemblance to that of an angel of light. In his hand, which thunder had blasted, he swayed the iron sceptre, that causes the monster Ouranabad, [140] the afrits, and all the powers of the abyss to tremble. At his presence the heart of the Caliph sank within him, and, for the first time, he fell prostrate on his face. Nouronihar, however, though greatly dismayed, could not help admiring the person of Eblis, for she expected to have seen some stupendous giant. Eblis, with a voice more mild than might be imagined, but such as transfused through the soul the deepest melancholy, said:

"Creatures of clay, I receive you into mine empire. Ye are numbered amongst my adorers. Enjoy whatever this palace affords — the treasures of the preadimite sultans, their bickering sabres, and those talismans that compel the Dives to open the subterranean expanses of the mountain of Kaf, which communicate with these. There, insatiable as your curiosity may be, shall you find sufficient to gratify it. You shall possess the exclusive privilege of entering the fortress of Aherman, and the halls of Argenk, where are portrayed all creatures endowed with intelligence, and the various animals that inhabited the earth prior to the creation of that contemptible being, whom ye denominate the Father of Mankind."

Vathek and Nouronihar feeling themselves revived and encouraged by this harangue, eagerly said to the Giaour:

"Bring us instantly to the place which contains these precious talismans."

"Come," answered this wicked Dive, with his malignant grin, "come, and possess all that my sovereign hath promised, and more."

He then conducted them into a long aisle adjoining the tabernacle, preceding them with hasty steps, and followed by his disciples with the utmost alacrity. They reached at length a hall of great extent, and covered with a lofty dome, around which appeared fifty portals of bronze, secured with as many fastenings of iron. A funereal gloom prevailed over the whole scene. Here, upon two beds of incorruptible cedar, lay recumbent the fleshless forms of the preadimite kings, who had been monarchs of the whole earth. They still possessed enough of life to be conscious of their deplorable condition. Their eyes retained a melancholy motion; they regarded each other with looks of the deepest dejection, each holding his right hand motionless on his heart. At their feet were inscribed the events of their several reigns, their power, their pride, and their crimes. Soliman Raad, Soliman Daki, and Soliman Di Gian Ben Gian, who, after having chained up the Dives in the dark caverns of Kaf, became so presumptuous, as to doubt of the Supreme Power. All these maintained great state, though not to be compared with the eminence of Soliman Ben Daoud.

This king, so renowned for his wisdom, was on the loftiest elevation, and placed immediately under the dome. He appeared to possess more animation than the rest, though, from time to time, he laboured with profound sighs, and, like his companions, kept his right hand on his heart; yet his countenance was more composed, and he seemed to be listening to the sullen roar of a vast cataract, visible in part through the grated portals. This was the only sound that intruded on the silence of these doleful mansions. A range of brazen vases surrounded the elevation.

"Remove the covers from these cabalistic depositaries," said the Giaour to Vathek, "and avail thyself of the talismans, which will break asunder all these gates of bronze, and not only render thee master of the treasures contained within them, but also of the spirits by which they are guarded."

The Caliph, whom this ominous preliminary had entirely disconcerted, approached the vases with faltering footsteps, and was ready to sink with terror, when he heard the groans of Soliman. As he proceeded, a voice from the livid lips of the prophet articulated these words:

"In my lifetime, I filled a magnificent throne, having on my right hand twelve thousand seats of gold, where the patriarchs and prophets heard my doctrines; on my left the sages and doctors, upon as many thrones of silver, were present at all my decisions. Whilst I thus administered justice to innumerable multitudes, the birds of the air librating over me, served as a canopy from the rays of the sun. My people flourished, and my palace rose to the clouds. I erected a temple to the Most High, which was the wonder of the universe; but I basely suffered myself to be seduced by the love of women, and a curiosity that could not be restrained by sub-lunary things. I listened to the counsels of Aherman, and the daughter of Pharaoh; and adored fire, and the host of heaven. I forsook the holy city, and commanded the Genii to rear the stupendous palace of Istakar, and the terrace of the watch-towers, each of which was consecrated to a star. There for a while I enjoyed myself in the zenith of glory and pleasure. Not only men, but supernatural existences were subject also to my will. I began to think, as these unhappy monarchs around had already thought, that the vengeance of heaven was asleep, when at once the thunder burst my structures asunder, and precipitated me hither; where, however, I do not remain like the other inhabitants totally destitute of hope, for an angel of light hath revealed, that in consideration of the piety of my early youth, my woes shall come to an end when this cataract shall for ever cease to flow. Till then I am in torments, ineffable torments, an unrelenting fire preys on my heart."

Having uttered this exclamation, Soliman raised his hands towards heaven, in token of supplication, and the Caliph discerned through his bosom, which was transparent as crystal, his heart enveloped in flames. At a sight so full of horror, Nouronihar fell back like one petrified, into the arms of Vathek, who cried out with a convulsive sob:

"O Giaour! whither hast thou brought us! Allow us to depart, and I will relinquish all thou hast promised. O Mahomet! remains there no more mercy!"

"None! none!" replied the malicious Dive. "Know, miserable prince, thou art now in the abode of vengeance, and despair. Thy heart, also, will be kindled, like those of the other votaries of Eblis. A few days are allotted thee previous to this fatal period: employ them as thou wilt. Recline on these heaps of gold: command the Infernal Potentates: range at thy pleasure through these immense subterranean domains. No barrier shall be shut against thee. As for me, I have fulfilled my mission. I now leave thee to thyself."

At these words he vanished.

The Caliph and Nouronihar remained in the most abject affliction. Their tears unable to flow, scarcely could they support themselves. At length, taking each other despondingly by the hand, they went faltering from this fatal hall, indifferent which way they turned their steps. Every portal opened at their approach. The Dives fell prostrate before them. Every reservoir of riches was disclosed to their view, but they no longer felt the incentives of curiosity, pride, or avarice. With like apathy they heard the chorus of Genii, and saw the stately banquets prepared to regale them. They went wandering on from chamber to chamber, hall to hall, and gallery to gallery; all without bounds or limit; all distinguishable by the same lowering gloom; all adorned with the same awful grandeur; all traversed by persons in search of repose and consolation, but who sought them in vain, for every one carried within him a heart tormented in flames. Shunned by these various sufferers, who seemed by their looks to be upbraiding the partners of their guilt, they withdrew from them, to wait in direful suspense the moment which should render them to each other the like objects of terror.

"What," exclaimed Nouronihar, "will the time come, when I shall snatch my hand from thine!"

"Ah!" said Vathek, "and shall my eyes ever cease to drink from thine long draughts of enjoyment! Shall the moments of our reciprocal ecstasies be reflected on with horror! It was not thou that broughtest me hither; the principles by which Carathis perverted my youth have been the sole cause of my perdition!"

Having given vent to these painful expressions, he called to an Afrit, who was stirring up one of the braziers, and bade him fetch the Princess Carathis from the palace of Samarah.

After issuing these orders, the Caliph and Nouronihar continued walking amidst the silent crowd, till they heard voices at the end of the gallery. Presuming them to proceed from some unhappy beings, who like themselves were awaiting their final doom, they followed the sound, and found it to come from a small square chamber, where they discovered sitting on sofas, five young men of goodly figure, and a lovely female, who were all holding a melancholy conversation, by the glimmering of a lonely lamp. Each had a gloomy and forlorn air, and two of them were embracing each other with great tenderness. On seeing the Caliph and the daughter of Fakreddin enter they arose, saluted, and gave them place. Then he who had appeared the most considerable of the group, addressed himself thus to Vathek:

"Strangers! who doubtless are in the same state of suspense as ourselves, as you do not yet bear your hand on your heart, if you are come hither to pass the interval allotted previous to the infliction of our common punishment, condescend to relate the adventures that have brought you to this fatal place; and we in return will acquaint you with ours; which deserves but too well to be heard. We will trace back our crimes to their source, though we are not permitted to repent. This is the only employment suited to wretches like us."

The Caliph and Nouronihar assented to the proposal, and Vathek began, not without tears and lamentations, a sincere recital of every circumstance that had passed. When the afflicting narrative was closed, the young man entered on his own. Each person proceeded in order, and when the fourth prince had reached the midst of his adventures, a sudden noise interrupted him, which caused the vault to tremble, and to open.

Immediately a cloud descended, which gradually dissipating, discovered Carathis, on the back of an Afrit, who grievously complained of his burden. She, instantly springing to the ground, advanced towards her son, and said:

"What dost thou here, in this little square chamber? As the Dives are become subject to thy beck, I expected to have found thee on the throne of the preadimite kings."

"Execrable woman!" answered the Caliph; "cursed be the day thou gavest me birth! Go! follow this Afrit; let him conduct thee to the hall of the Prophet Soliman; there thou wilt learn to what these palaces are destined, and how much I ought to abhor the impious knowledge thou hast taught me."

"The height of power to which thou art arrived, has certainly turned thy brain," answered Carathis; "but I ask no more, than permission to show my respect for the prophet. It is, however, proper thou shouldst know, that, as the Afrit has informed me neither of us shall return to Samarah, I requested his permission to arrange my affairs, and he politely consented. Availing myself, therefore, of the few moments allowed me, I set fire to the tower, and consumed in it the mutes, negresses, and serpents, which have rendered me so much good service; nor should I have been less kind to Morakanabad, had he not prevented me, by deserting at last to thy brother. As for Bababalouk, who had the folly to return to Samarah, and all the good brotherhood to provide husbands for thy wives, I undoubtedly would have put them to the torture, could I but have allowed them the time. Being, however, in a hurry, I only hung him, after having caught him in a snare with thy wives; whilst them I buried alive by the help of my negresses, who thus spent their last moments, greatly to their satisfaction. With respect to Dilara, who ever stood high in my favour, she hath evinced the greatness of her mind, by fixing herself near, in the service of one of the Magi, and, I think, will soon be our own."

Vathek, too much cast down to express the indignation excited by such a discourse, ordered the Afrit to remove Carathis from his presence, and continued immersed in thought, which his companions durst not disturb.

Carathis, however, eagerly entered the dome of Soliman, and, without regarding in the least the groans of the Prophet, undauntedly removed the covers of the vases, and violently seized on the talismans. Then, with a voice more loud than had hitherto been heard in these mansions, she compelled the Dives to disclose to her the most secret treasures, the most profound stores, which the Afrit himself had not seen. She passed by rapid descents known only to Eblis and his most favoured Potentates, and thus penetrated the very entrails of the earth, where breathes the Sansar, or icy wind of death. Nothing appalled her dauntless soul. She perceived, however, in all the inmates who bore their hands on their heart, a little singularity not much to her taste. As she was emerging from one of the abysses, Eblis stood forth to her view, but, notwithstanding he displayed the full effulgence of his infernal majesty, she preserved her countenance unaltered, and even paid her compliments with considerable firmness.

This superb monarch thus answered:

"Princess, whose knowledge and whose crimes have merited a conspicuous rank in my empire, thou doest well to employ the leisure that remains, for the flames and torments which are ready to seize on thy heart, will not fail to provide thee with full employment."

He said this, and was lost in the curtains of his tabernacle.

Carathis paused for a moment with surprise, but, resolved to follow the advice of Eblis, she assembled all the choirs of Genii, and all the Dives, to pay her homage. Thus marched she in triumph through a vapour of perfumes, amidst the acclamations of all the malignant spirits; with most of whom she had formed a previous acquaintance. She even attempted to dethrone one of the Solimans, for the purpose of usurping his place, when a voice, proceeding from the Abyss of Death, proclaimed:

"All is accomplished!"

Instantaneously, the haughty forehead of the intrepid princess became corrugated with agony; she uttered a tremendous yell, and fixed — no more to be withdrawn — her right hand upon her heart, which was become a receptacle of eternal fire.

In this delirium, forgetting all ambitious projects, and her thirst for that knowledge which should ever be hidden from mortals, she overturned the offerings of the Genii; and, having execrated the hour she was begotten, and the womb that had borne her, glanced off in a whirl that rendered her invisible, and continued to revolve without intermission.

At almost the same instant, the same voice announced to the Caliph, Nouronihar, the five princes, and the princess, the awful and irrevocable decree. Their hearts immediately took fire, and they at once lost the most precious of the gifts of heaven — hope. These unhappy beings recoiled, with looks of the most furious distraction. Vathek beheld in the eyes of Nouronihar nothing but rage and vengeance; nor could she discern ought in his but aversion and despair. The two princes who were friends, and till that moment had preserved their attachment, shrunk back, gnashing their teeth with mutual and unchangeable hatred. Kalilah and his sister made reciprocal gestures of imprecation; whilst the two other princes testified their horror for each other by the most ghastly convulsions, and screams that could not be smothered. All severally plunged themselves into the accursed multitude, there to wander in an eternity of unabating anguish.

Such was, and such should be, the punishment of unrestrained passions, and atrocious actions. Such is, and such should be, the chastisement of blind ambition, that would transgress those bounds which the Creator hath prescribed to human knowledge, and by aiming at discoveries reserved for pure intelligence, acquire that infatuated pride, which perceives not the condition appointed to man is, to be ignorant and humble.

Thus the Caliph Vathek who, for the sake of empty pomp and forbidden power, hath sullied himself with a thousand crimes, became a prey to grief without end, and remorse without mitigation; whilst the humble and despised Gulchenrouz passed whole ages in undisturbed tranquillity, and the pure happiness of childhood.

NOTES.

[7a] Caliph. This title amongst the Mahometans comprehends the concrete character of prophet, priest, and king; and is used to signify the Vicar of God on earth. — Habesci's State of the Ottoman Empire, p. 9. Herbelot, p. 985.

[7b] One of his eyes became so terrible. The author of Nighiaristan hath preserved a fact that supports this account; and there is no history of Vathek, in which his terrible eye is not mentioned.

[8a] Omar Ben Abdalaziz. This Caliph was eminent above all others for temperance and self-denial; insomuch, that he is believed to have been raised to Mahomet's bosom, as a reward for his abstinence in an age of corruption. Herbelot, p. 690.

[8b] Samarah. A city of the Babylonian Irak, supposed to have stood on the site where Nimrod erected his tower. Khondemir relates, in his life of Motassem, that this prince, to terminate the disputes which were perpetually happening between the

inhabitants of Bagdat and his Turkish slaves, withdrew from thence; and, having fixed on a situation in the plain of Catoul, there founded Samarah. He is said to have had in the stables of this city a hundred and thirty thousand pied horses; each of which carried, by his order, a sack of earth to a place he had chosen. By this accumulation, an elevation was formed that commanded a view of all Samarah, and served for the foundation of his magnificent palace. Herbelot, p. 752, 808, 985. Anecdotes Arabes, p. 413.

[9] Houris. The Virgins of Paradise, called, from their large black eyes, Hur al oyun. An intercourse with these, according to the institution of Mahomet, is to constitute the principal felicity of the faithful. Not formed of clay, like mortal women, they are deemed in the highest degree beautiful, and exempt from every inconvenience incident to the sex. Al Koran; passim.

[10] Genii. Genn or Ginn, in the Arabic, signifies a Genius or Demon—a being of a higher order, and formed of more subtile matter than man. According to Oriental mythology, the Genii governed the world long before the creation of Adam. The Mahometans regarded them as an intermediate race between angels and men, and capable of salvation: whence Mahomet pretended a commission to convert them. Consonant to this, we read that, "When the servant of God stood up to invoke him, it wanted little but that the Genii had pressed on him in crowds, to hear him rehearse the Koran." Herbelot, p. 357. Al Koran ch. 72.

[23] Accursed Giaour. Dives of this kind are frequently mentioned by Eastern writers. Consult their tales in general, and especially those of "The Fisherman," "Aladdin," and "The Princess of China."

[26a] Bababalouk, the Chief of his Eunuchs. As it was the employment of the black eunuchs to wait upon, and guard the sultanas, to the general superintendence of the Harem was particularly committed to their chief. Habesci's State of the Ottoman Empire, p. 155–6.

[26b] The Divan. This was both the supreme council, and court of justice, at which the Caliphs of the race of the Abassides assisted in person to redress the injuries of every appellant. Herbelot, p. 298.

[27] The Prime Vizier. Vazir, Vezir, or as we express it, Vizier, literally signifies a porter; and by metaphor, the minister who bears the principal burden of the state.

[50] Gian Ben Gian. By this appellation was distinguished the monarch of that species of beings, whom the Arabians denominate Gian or Ginn, that is, Genii; and the Tarik Thabari, Peres, Feez, or Faeries.

[51] Rocnabad. The stream thus denominated flows near the city of Schiraz. Its waters are uncommonly pure and limpid, and their banks swarded with the finest verdure.

[53] Moullahs. Those among the Mahometans who were bred to the law had this title; and from their order the judges of cities and provinces were taken.

[55] Bababalouk almost sunk with confusion, whilst, etc. The heinousness of Vathek's profanation can only be judged of by an orthodox Mussulman; or one who recollects the ablution and prayer indispensably required on the exoneration of nature. Sale's Prelim. Disc. p. 139. Al Koran, ch. 4. Habesci's State of the Ottoman Empire, p. 93.

[67a] Horrible Kaf. This mountain, which in reality is no other than Caucasus, was supposed to surround the earth, like a ring encompassing a finger. The sun was believed to rise from one of its eminences (as over Octa, by the Latin poets) and to set on the opposite; whence "from Kaf to Kaf," signified from one extremity of the earth to the other.

[67b] The Simurgh. This is that wonderful bird of the East concerning which so many marvels are told. It was not only endowed with reason, but possessed also the knowledge of every language. This creature relates of itself, that it had seen the great revolution of seven thousand years, twelve times, commence and close; and, that in its duration, the world had been seven times void of inhabitants, and as often replenished. The Simurgh is represented as a great friend to the race of Adam, and not less inimical to the Dives.

[67c] Afrits. These were a kind of Medusa, or Lamia, supposed to be the most terrible and cruel of all the orders of the Dives. Herbelot, p. 66.

[68] Deggial. This word signifies properly a liar and imposter, but is applied by Mahometan writers to their Antichrist. He is described as having but one eye and eyebrow, and on his forehead the radicals of cafer, or infidel, are said to be impressed.

[79a] Calenders. These were a sort of men amongst the

Mahometans who abandoned father and mother, wife and children, relations and possessions, to wander through the world, under a pretence of religion, entirely subsisting on the fortuitous bounty of those they had the address to dupe. Herbelot, Suppl. p. 204.

[79b] Santons. A body of religionists who were also called Abdals, and pretended to be inspired with the most enthusiastic raptures of divine love. They were regarded by the vulgar as saints. Olearius, Tom. I. p. 971. Herbelot, p. 5.

[79c] Dervises. The term dervise signifies a poor man, and is the general appellation by which a religious sect amongst the Mahometans is named.

[79d] Brahmins. These constituted the principal caste of the Indians, according to whose doctrines Brahma, from whom they are called, is the first of the three created beings by whom the world was made. This Brahma is said to have communicated to the Indians four books, in which all the sciences and ceremonies of their religion are comprised.

[79e] Faquirs. This sect were a kind of religious anchorites, who spent their whole lives in the severest austerities and mortification.

[82] Peries. The word Peri, in the Persian language, signifies that beautiful race of creatures which constitutes the link between angels and men.

[134] Balkis. This was the Arabian name of the Queen of Sheba, who went from the South to hear the wisdom and admire the glory of Solomon. The Koran represents her as a worshipper of fire. Solomon is said not only to have entertained her with the greatest magnificence, but also to have raised her to his bed and his throne. Al Koran, ch. 27, and Sale's notes. Herbelot, p. 182.

[140] Ouranabad. This monster is represented as a fierce flying hydra, and belongs to the same class with the Rakshe, whose ordinary food was serpents and dragons; the Soham, which had the head of a horse, with four eyes, and the body of a flame-coloured dragon; the Syl, a basilisk with a face resembling the human, but so tremendous that no mortal could bear to behold it; the Ejder, and others. See these respective titles in Richardson's Dictionary, Persian, Arabic and English.

The Castles of Athlin and Dunbayne

By Ann Radcliffe

CHAPTER I.

ON the north-east coast of Scotland, in the most romantic part of the Highlands, stood the Castle of Athlin; an edifice built on the summit of a rock whose base was in the sea. This pile was venerable from its antiquity, and from its Gothic structure; but more venerable from the virtues which it enclosed. It was the residence of the still beautiful widow, and the children of the noble Earl of Athlin, who was slain by the hand of Malcolm, a neighbouring chief, proud, oppressive, revengeful; and still residing in all the pomp of feudal greatness, within a few miles of the castle of Athlin. Encroachment on the domain of Athlin, was the occasion of the animosity which subsisted between the chiefs. Frequent broils had happened between their clans, in which that of Athlin had generally been victorious. Malcolm, whose pride was touched by the defeat of his people; whose ambition was curbed by the authority, and whose greatness was rivalled by the power of the Earl, conceived for him that deadly hatred which opposition to its favourite passions naturally excites in a mind like his, haughty and unaccustomed to controul; and he meditated his destruction. He planned his purpose with all that address which so eminently marked his character, and in a battle which was attended by the chiefs of each party in person, he contrived, by a curious finesse, to entrap the Earl, accompanied by a small detachment, in his wiles, and there slew him. A general rout of his clan ensued, which was followed by a dreadful slaughter; and a few only escaped to tell the horrid catastrophe to Matilda. Overwhelmed by the news, and deprived of those numbers which would make revenge successful, Matilda forbore to sacrifice the lives of her few remaining people to a feeble attempt at retaliation, and she was constrained to endure in silence her sorrows and her injuries.

Inconsolable for his death, Matilda had withdrawn from the public eye, into this ancient seat of feudal government, and there, in the bosom of her people and her family, had devoted herself to the education of her children. One son and one daughter were all that survived to her care, and their growing virtues promised to repay all her tenderness. Osbert was in his nineteenth year: nature had given him a mind ardent and susceptible, to which education had added refinement and expansion. The visions of genius were bright in his imagination, and his heart, unchilled by the touch of disappointment, glowed with all the warmth of benevolence.

When first we enter on the theatre of the world, and begin to notice its features, young imagination heightens every scene, and the warm heart expands to all around it. The happy benevolence of our feelings prompts us to believe that every body is good, and excites our wonder why every body is not happy. We are fired with indignation at the recital of an act of injustice, and at the unfeeling vices of which we are told. At a tale of distress our tears flow a full tribute to pity: at a deed of virtue our heart unfolds, our soul aspires, we bless the action, and feel ourselves the doer. As we advance in life, imagination is compelled to relinquish a part of her sweet delirium; we are led reluctantly to truth through the paths of experience; and the objects of our fond attention are viewed with a severer eye. Here an altered scene appears; — frowns where late were smiles; deep shades where late was sunshine: mean passions, or disgusting apathy stain the features of the principal figures. We turn indignant from a prospect so miserable, and court again the sweet illusions of our early days; but ah! they are fled for ever! Constrained, therefore, to behold objects in their more genuine hues, their deformity is by degrees less painful to us. The fine touch of moral susceptibility, by frequent irritation becomes callous; and too frequently we mingle with the world, till we are added to the number of its votaries.

Mary, who was just seventeen, had the accomplishments of riper years, with the touching simplicity of youth. The graces of her person were inferior only to those of her mind, which illumined her countenance with inimitable expression.

Twelve years had now elapsed since the death of the Earl, and time had blunted the keen edge of sorrow. Matilda's grief had declined into a gentle, and not unpleasing melancholy, which gave a soft and interesting shade to the natural dignity of her character. Hitherto her attention had been solely directed towards rearing those virtues which nature had planted with so liberal a hand in her children, and which, under the genial

349

influence of her eye, had flourished and expanded into beauty and strength. A new hope, and new solicitudes, now arose in her breast; these dear children were arrived at an age, dangerous from its tender susceptibility, and from the influence which imagination has at that time over the passions. Impressions would soon be formed which would stamp their destiny for life. The anxious mother lived but in her children, and she had yet another cause of apprehension.

When Osbert learned the story of his father's death, his young heart glowed to avenge the deed. The late Earl, who had governed with the real dignity of power, was adored by his clan; they were eager to revenge his injuries; but oppressed by the generous compassion of the Countess, their murmurs sunk into silence: yet they fondly cherished the hope that their young Lord would one day lead them on to conquest and revenge. The time was now come when they looked to see this hope, the solace of many a cruel moment, realized. The tender fears of a mother would not suffer Matilda to risque the chief of her last remaining comforts. She forbade Osbert to engage. He submitted in silence, and endeavored by application to his favourite studies, to stifle the emotions which roused him to aims. He excelled in the various accomplishments of his rank, but chiefly in the martial exercises, for they were congenial to the nobility of his soul, and he had a secret pleasure in believing that they would one time assist him to do justice to the memory of his dead father. His warm imagination directed him to poetry, and he followed where she led. He loved to wander among the romantic scenes of the Highlands, where the wild variety of nature inspired him with all the enthusiasm of his favourite art. He delighted in the terrible and in the grand, more than in the softer landscape; and, wrapt in the bright visions of fancy, would often lose himself in awful solitudes.

It was in one of these rambles, that having strayed for some miles over hills covered with heath, from whence the eye was presented with only the bold outlines of uncultivated nature, rocks piled on rocks, cataracts and vast moors unmarked by the foot of traveller, he lost the path which he had himself made; he looked in vain for the objects which had directed him, and his heart, for the first time, felt the repulse of fear. No vestige of a human being was to be seen, and the dreadful silence of the place was interrupted only by the roar of distant torrents, and by the screams of the birds which flew over his head. He shouted, and his voice was answered only by the deep echoes of the mountains. He remained for some time in a silent dread not wholly unpleasing, but which was soon heightened to a degree of terror not to be endured; and he turned his steps backward, forlorn, and dejected. His memory gave him back no image of the past; having wandered some time, he came to a narrow pass, which he entered, overcome with fatigue and fruitless search: he had not advanced far, when an abrupt opening in the rock suddenly presented him with a view of the most beautifully romantic spot he had ever seen. It was a valley almost surrounded by a barrier of wild rocks, whose base was shaded with thick woods of pine and fir. A torrent, which tumbled from the heights, and was seen between the woods, rushed with amazing impetuosity into a fine lake which flowed through the vale, and was lost in the deep recesses of the mountains. Herds of cattle grazed in the bottom, and the delighted eyes of Osbert were once more blessed with the sight of human dwellings. Far on the margin of the stream were scattered a few neat cottages. His heart was so gladdened at the prospect, that he forgot he had yet the way to find which led to this Elysian vale. He was just awakened to this distressing reality, when his attention was once more engaged by the manly figure of a young Highland peasant, who advanced towards him with an air of benevolence, and, having learned his distress, offered to conduct him to his cottage. Osbert accepted the invitation, and they wound down the hill, through an obscure and intricate path, together. They arrived at one of the cottages which the Earl had observed from the height; they entered, and the peasant presented his guest to a venerable old Highlander, his father. Refreshments were spread on the table by a pretty young girl, and Osbert, after having partook of them and rested awhile, departed, accompanied by Alleyn, the young peasant, who had offered to be his guide. The length of the walk was beguiled by conversation. Osbert was interested by discovering in his companion a dignity of thought, and a course of sentiment similar to his own. On their way, they passed at some distance the castle of Dunbayne. This object gave to Osbert a bitter reflection, and drew from him a deep sigh. Alleyn made observations on the bad policy of oppression in a chief, and produced as an instance the Baron Malcolm. These lands, said he, are his, and they are scarcely sufficient to support his wretched people, who, sinking under severe exactions, suffer to lie uncultivated, tracts which would otherwise add riches to their Lord. His clan, oppressed by their burdens, threaten to rise and do justice to themselves by force of arms. The Baron, in haughty confidence, laughs at their defiance, and is insensible to his danger: for should an insurrection happen, there are other clans who would eagerly join in his destruction, and punish with the same weapon the tyrant and the murderer. Surprized at the bold independence of these words, delivered with uncommon energy, the heart of Osbert beat quick, and "O God! my father!" burst from his lips. Alleyn stood aghast!

uncertain of the effect which his speech had produced; in an instant the whole truth flashed upon his mind: he beheld the son of the Lord whom he had been taught to love, and whose sad story had been impressed upon his heart in the early days of childhood; he sunk at his feet, and embraced his knees with a romantic ardor. The young Earl raised him from the ground, and the following words relieved him from his astonishment, and filled his eyes with tears of mingled joy and sorrow: "There are other clans as ready as your own to avenge the wrongs of the noble Earl of Athlin; the Fitz–Henrys were ever friends to virtue." The countenance of the youth, while he spoke, was overspread with the glow of conscious dignity, and his eyes were animated with the pride of virtue. — The breast of Osbert kindled with noble purpose, but the image of his weeping mother crossed his mind, and checked the ardor of the impulse. "A time may come my friend," said he, "when your generous zeal will be accepted with the warmth of gratitude it deserves. Particular circumstances will not suffer me, at present, to say more." The warm attachment of Alleyn to his father sunk deep in his heart.

It was evening before they reached the castle, and Alleyn remained the Earl's guest for that night.

CHAPTER II.

THE following day was appointed for the celebration of an annual festival given by the Earl to his people, and he would not suffer Alleyn to depart. The hall was spread with tables; and dance and merriment resounded through the castle. It was usual on that day for the clan to assemble in arms, on account of an attempt, the memory of which it was meant to perpetuate, made, two centuries before, by an hostile clan to surprize them in their festivity.

In the morning were performed the martial exercises, in which emulation was excited by the honorary rewards bestowed on excellence. The Countess and her lovely daughter beheld, from the ramparts of the castle, the feats performed on the plains below. Their attention was engaged, and their curiosity excited, by the appearance of a stranger who managed the lance and the bow with such exquisite dexterity, as to bear off each prize of chivalry. It was Alleyn. He received the palm of victory, as was usual, from the hands of the Earl; and the modest dignity with which he accepted it, charmed the beholders.

The Earl honoured the feast with his presence, at the conclusion of which, each guest arose, and seizing his goblet with his left hand, and with his right striking his sword, drank to the memory of their departed Lord. The hall echoed with the general voice. Osbert felt it strike upon his heart the alarum of war. The people then joined hands, and drank to the honour of the son of their late master. Osbert understood the signal, and overcome with emotion, every consideration yielded to that of avenging his father. He arose, and harangued the clan with all the fire of youth and indignant virtue. As he spoke, the countenance of his people flashed with impatient joy; a deep murmur of applause ran through the assembly: and when he was silent each man, crossing his sword with that of his neighbour, swore that sacred pledge of union, never to quit the cause in which they now engaged, till the life of their enemy had paid the debt of justice and of revenge.

In the evening, the wives and daughters of the peasantry came to the castle, and joined in the festivity. It was usual for the Countess and her ladies to observe from a gallery of the hall, the various performances of dance and song; and it had been a custom of old for the daughter of the castle to grace the occasion by performing a Scotch dance with the victor of the morning. This victor now was Alleyn, who beheld the lovely Mary led by the Earl into the hall, and presented to him as his partner in the dance. She received his homage with a sweet grace. She was dressed in the habit of a Highland lass, and her fine auburn tresses, which waved in her neck, were ornamented only with a wreath of roses. She moved in the dance with the light steps of the Graces. Profound silence reigned through the hall during the performance, and a soft murmur of applause arose on its conclusion. The admiration of the spectators was divided between Mary and the victorious stranger. She retired to the gallery, and the night concluded in joy to all but the Earl, and to Alleyn; but very different was the source and the complexion of their inquietude. The mind of Osbert revolved the chief occurrences of the day, and his soul burned with impatience to accomplish the purposes of filial piety; yet he dreaded the effect which the communication of his designs might have on the tender heart of Matilda: on the morrow, however, he resolved to acquaint her with them, and in a few days to rise and prosecute his cause with arms.

Alleyn, whose bosom, till now, had felt only for others' pains, began to be conscious of his own. His mind, uneasy and restless, gave him only the image of the high-born Mary; he endeavoured to exclude her idea, but with an effort so faint, that it would still intrude! Pleased, yet sad, he would not acknowledge, even to himself, that he loved; so ingenious are we to conceal every appearance of evil from ourselves. He arose with the dawn, and departed from the castle full of gratitude and secret love, to prepare his friends for the approaching war.

The Earl awoke from broken slumbers, and summoned all his fortitude to encounter the tender opposition of his mother. He entered her apartment with faultering steps, and his countenance betrayed the emotions of his soul. Matilda was soon informed of what her heart had foreboded, and overcome with dreadful sensation, sunk lifeless in her chair. Osbert flew to her assistance, and Mary and the attendants soon recovered her to sense and wretchedness.

The mind of Osbert was torn by the most cruel conflict: filial duty, honour, revenge, commanded him to go; filial love, regret, and pity, entreated him to stay. Mary fell at his feet, and clasping his knees with all the wild energy of grief besought him to relinquish his fatal purpose, and save his last surviving parent. Her tears, her sighs, and the soft simplicity of her air, spoke a yet stronger language than her tongue: but the silent grief of the Countess was still more touching, and in his endeavours to sooth her, he was on the point of yielding his resolution, when the figure of his dying father arose to his imagination, and stamped his purpose irrevocably. The anxiety of a fond mother, presented Matilda with the image of her son bleeding and ghastly; and the death of her Lord was revived in her memory with all the agonizing grief that sad event had impressed upon her heart, the harsher characters of which, the lenient hand of time had almost obliterated. So lovely is Pity in all her attitudes, that fondness prompts us to believe she can never transgress; but she changes into a vice, when she overcomes the purposes of stronger virtue. Sterner principles now nerved the breast of Osbert against her influence and impelled him on to deeds of arms. He summoned a few of the most able and trusty of the clan, and held a council of war; in which it was resolved that Malcolm should be attacked with all the force they could assemble, and with all the speed which the importance of the preparation would allow. To prevent suspicion and alarm to the Baron, it was agreed it should be given out, that these preparations were intended for assistance to the Chief of a distant part. That when they set out on the expedition, they should pursue, for some time, a contrary way, but under favour of the night should suddenly change their route, and turn upon the castle of Dunbayne.

In the mean time, Alleyn was strenuous in exciting his friends to the cause, and so successful in the undertaking, as to have collected, in a few days, a number of no inconsiderable consequence. To the warm enthusiasm of virtue was now added a new motive of exertion. It was no longer simply an attachment to the cause of justice, which roused him to action; the pride of distinguishing himself in the eyes of his mistress, and of deserving her esteem by his zealous services, gave combined force to the first impulse of benevolence. The sweet thought of deserving her thanks, operated secretly on his soul, for he was yet ignorant of its influence there. In this state he again appeared at the castle, and told the Earl, that himself and his friends were ready to follow him whenever the signal should be given. His offer was accepted with the warmth of kindness it claimed, and he was desired to hold himself in readiness for the onset.

In a few days the preparations were completed, Alleyn and his friends were summoned, the clan assembled in arms, and, with the young Earl at their head, departed on their expedition. The parting between Osbert and his family may be easily conceived; nor could all the pride of expected conquest suppress a sigh which escaped from Alleyn when his eyes bade adieu to Mary who, with the Countess, stood on the terrace of the castle, pursuing with aching sight the march of her beloved brother, till distance veiled him from her view; she then turned into the castle weeping, and foreboding future calamity. She endeavoured, however, to assume an appearance of tranquillity, that she might deceive the fears of Matilda, and sooth her sorrow. Matilda, whose mind was strong as her heart was tender, since she could not prevent this hazardous undertaking, summoned all her fortitude to resist the impressions of fruitless grief, and to search for the good which the occasion might present. Her efforts were not vain; she found it in the prospect which the enterprize afforded of honour to the memory of her murdered Lord, and of retribution on the head of the murderer.

It was evening when the Earl departed from the castle; he pursued a contrary route till night favoured his designs, when he wheeled towards the castle of Dunbayne. The extreme darkness of the night assisted their plan, which was to scale the walls, surprize the centinels; burst their way into the inner courts sword in hand, and force the murderer from his retreat. They had trod many miles the dreary wilds, unassisted by the least gleam of light, when suddenly their ears were struck with the dismal note of a watch-bell, which chimed the hour of the night. Every heart beat to the sound. They knew they were near the abode of the Baron. They halted to consult concerning their proceedings, when it was agreed, that the Earl with Alleyn and a chosen few, should proceed to reconnoitre the castle, while the rest should remain at a small distance awaiting the signal of approach. The Earl and his party pursued their march with silent steps; they perceived a faint light, which they guessed to proceed from the watch-tower of the castle, and they were now almost under its walls. They paused awhile in silence to give breath to expectation, and to listen if any thing was stirring. All was involved in the gloom of night, and the silence of death prevailed. They had now time to examine, as well as the darkness would permit, the situation of the castle, and the height of the walls; and to prepare for the assault. The edifice was built with Gothic magnificence upon a high and dangerous rock. Its lofty towers still frowned in proud sublimity, and the immensity of the pile stood a record of the ancient consequence of its possessors. The rock was surrounded by a ditch, broad, but not deep, over which were two draw-bridges, one on the north side, the other on the east; they were both up, but as they separated in the center, one half of the bridge remained on the side of the plains. The bridge on the north led to the grand gateway of the castle; that on the east to a small watch-tower: these were all the entrances. The rock was almost perpendicular with the walls, which were strong and lofty. After surveying the situation, they pitched upon a spot where the rock appeared most accessible, and which was contiguous to the principal gate, and gave signal to the clan. They approached in silence, and gently throwing down the bundles of faggot, which they had brought for the purpose, into the ditch, made themselves a bridge over which they passed in safety, and prepared to ascend the heights. It had been resolved that a party, of which Alleyn was one, should scale the walls, surprize the centinels, and open the gates to the rest of the clan, which, with the Earl, were to remain without. Alleyn was the first who fixed his ladder and mounted; he was instantly followed by the rest of his party, and with much difficulty, and some hazard, they gained the ramparts in safety. They traversed a part of the platform without hearing the sound of a voice or a step; profound sleep seemed to bury all. A number of the party approached some centinels who were asleep on their post; them they seized; while Alleyn, with a few others, flew to open the nearest gate, and to let down the draw-bridge. This they accomplished; but in the mean time the signal of surprize was given, and instantly the alarm bell rang out, and the castle resounded with the clang of arms. All was tumult and confusion. The Earl, with part of his people, entered the gate; the rest were following, when suddenly the portcullis was dropped, the bridge drawn up, and the Earl and his people found themselves surrounded by an armed multitude, which poured in torrents from every recess of the castle. Surprized, but not daunted, the Earl rushed forward sword in hand, and fought with a desperate valour. The soul of Alleyn seemed to acquire new vigour from the conflict; he fought like a man panting for honour, and certain of victory; wherever he rushed, conquest flew before him. He, with the Earl, forced his way into the inner courts, in search of the Baron, and hoped to have satisfied a just revenge, and to have concluded the conflict with the death of the murderer; but the moment in which they entered the courts, the gates were closed upon them; they were environed by a band of guards; and, after a short resistance, in which Alleyn received a slight wound, they were seized as prisoners of war. The slaughter without was great and dreadful: the people of the Baron inspired with fury, were insatiate for death: many of the Earl's followers were killed in the courts and on the platform; many, in attempting to escape, were thrown from the ramparts, and many were destroyed by the sudden raising of the bridge. A small part, only of the brave and adventurous band who had engaged in the cause of justice, and who were driven back from the walls, survived to carry the dreadful tidings to the Countess. The fate of the Earl remained unknown. The consternation among the friends of the slain is not to be described, and it was heightened by the unaccountable manner in which the victory had been obtained; for it was well known that Malcolm had never, but when war made it necessary, more soldiers in his garrison than feudal pomp demanded; yet on this occasion, a number of armed men rushed from the recesses of his castle, sufficient to overpower the force of a whole clan. But they knew not the secret means of intelligence which the Baron possessed; the jealousy of conscience had armed him with apprehension for his safety; and for some years he had planted spies near the castle of Athlin, to observe all that passed within it, and to give him immediate intelligence of every war-like preparation. A transaction so striking, and so public as that which had occurred on the day of the festival, when the whole people swore to avenge the murder of their Chief, it was not probable would escape the valiant eye of his mercenaries: the circumstance had been communicated to him with all the exaggerations of fear and wonder, and had given him the signal for defence. The accounts sent him of the military preparations which were forming, convinced him that this defence would soon be called for; and, laughing at the idle tales which were told him of distant wars, he hastened to store his garrison with arms and with men, and held himself in readiness to receive the assailants. The Baron had conducted his plans with all that power of contrivance which the secrecy of the business demanded; and it was his design to suffer the enemy to mount his walls, and to put them to the sword, when the purpose of this deep-laid stratagem had been nearly defeated by the drowsiness of the centinels who were posted to give signal of their approach.

The fortitude of Matilda fainted under the pressure of so heavy a calamity; she was attacked with a violent illness, which had nearly terminated her sorrows and her life; and had rendered unavailing all the tender cares of her daughter. These tender cares, however, were not ineffectual; she revived, and they assisted to support her in the severe hours of affliction, which the unknown fate of the Earl occasioned. Mary, who felt all the horrors of the late event, was ill qualified for the office of a comforter; but her generous heart, susceptible of the deep sufferings of Matilda, almost forgot its own distress in the remembrance of her mother's. Yet the idea of her brother, surrounded with the horrors of imprisonment and death, would often obtrude itself on her imagination, with an emphasis which almost overcame her reason. She had also a strong degree of pity for the fate of the brave young Highlander who had assisted, with a disinterestedness so noble, in the cause of her house; she wished to learn his further destiny, and her heart often melted in compassion at the picture which her fancy drew of his sufferings.

CHAPTER III.

THE Earl, after being loaded with fetters, was conducted to the chief prison of the castle, and left alone to the bitter reflections of defeat and uncertain destiny; but misfortune, though it might shake, could not overcome his firmness; and hope had not yet entirely forsaken him. It is the peculiar attribute of great minds, to bear up with increasing force against the shock of misfortune; with them the nerves of resistance strengthen with attack; and they may be said to subdue adversity with her own weapons.

Reflection, at length, afforded him time to examine his prison: it was a square room, which formed the summit of a tower built on the east side of the castle, round which the bleak winds howled mournfully; the inside of the apartment was old and falling to decay: a small mattrass, which lay in one corner of the room, a broken matted chair, and a tottering table, composed its furniture; two small and strongly grated windows, which admitted a sufficient degree of light and air, afforded him on one side a view into an inner court, and on the other a dreary prospect of the wild and barren Highlands.

Alleyn was conveyed through dark and winding passages to a distant part of the castle, where at length a small door, barred with iron, opened, and disclosed to him an abode, whence light and hope were equally excluded. He shuddered as he entered, and the door was closed upon him.

The mind of the Baron, in the mean time, was agitated with all the direful passions of hate, revenge, and exulting pride. He racked imagination for the invention of tortures equal to the force of his feelings; and he at length discovered that the sufferings of suspense are superior to those of the most terrible evils, when once ascertained, of which the contemplation gradually affords to strong minds the means of endurance. He determined, therefore, that the Earl should remain confined in the tower, ignorant of his future destiny; and in the mean while should be allowed food only sufficient to keep him sensible of his wretchedness.

Osbert was immersed in thought, when he heard the door of his prison unbarred, and the Baron Malcolm stood before him. The heart of Osbert swelled high with indignation, and defiance flashed in his eyes. "I am come," said the insulting victor, "to welcome the Earl of Athlin to my castle; and to shew that I can receive my friends with the hospitality they deserve; but I am yet undetermined what kind of festival I shall bestow on his arrival."

"Weak tyrant," returned Osbert, his countenance impressed with the firm dignity of virtue, "to insult the vanquished, is congenial with the cruel meanness of the murderer; nor do I expect, that the man who slew the father, will spare the son; but know, that son is nerved against your wrath, and welcomes all that your fears or your cruelty can impose."

"Rash youth," replied the Baron; "your words are air; they fade from sense, and soon your boasted strength shall sink beneath my power. I go to meditate your destiny." With these words he quitted the prison, enraged at the unbending virtue of the Earl.

The sight of the Baron, roused in the soul of Osbert all those opposite emotions of furious indignation and tender pity which the glowing image of his father could excite, and produced a moment of perfect misery. The dreadful energy of these sensations exasperated his brain almost to madness; the cool fortitude in which he had so lately gloried, disappeared; and he was on the point of resigning his virtue and his life, by means of a short dagger, which he wore concealed under his vest, when the soft notes of a lute surprized his attention. It was accompanied by a voice so enchantingly tender and melodious, that its sounds fell on the heart of Osbert in balmy comfort: it seemed sent by Heaven to arrest his fate: — the storm of passion was hushed within him, and he dissolved in kind tears of pity and contrition. The mournful tenderness of the air declared the person from whom it came to be a sufferer; and Osbert suspected it to proceed from a prisoner like himself. The music ceased. Absorbed in wonder, he went to the grates, in quest of the sweet musician, but no one was to be seen; and he was uncertain whether the sounds arose from within or from without the castle. Of the guard, who brought him his small allowance of food, he inquired concerning what he had heard; but from him he could not obtain the information he sought, and he was constrained to remain in a state of suspense.

In the mean time the castle of Athlin, and its neighbourhood, was overwhelmed with distress. The news of the earl's imprisonment at length reached the ears of the countess, and hope once more illumined her mind. She immediately sent offers of immense ransom to the baron, for the restoration of her son, and the other prisoners; but the ferocity of his nature disdained an incomplete triumph. Revenge subdued his avarice; and the offers were rejected with the spurn of contempt. An additional motive, however, operated in his mind, and confirmed his purpose. The beauty of Mary had been often reported to him in terms which excited his curiosity; and an incidental view he once obtained of her, raised a passion in his soul, which the turbulence of his character would not suffer to be extinguished. Various were the schemes he had projected to obtain her, none of which had ever been executed: the possession of the earl was a circumstance the most favourable to his wishes; and he resolved to obtain Mary, as the future ransom of her brother. He concealed, for the present, his purpose, that the tortures of anxiety and despair might operate on the mind of the countess, to grant him an easy consent to the exchange, and to resign the victim the wife of her enemy.

The small remains of the clan, unsubdued by misfortune, were eager to assemble; and, hazardous as was the enterprize, to attempt the rescue of their Chief. The hope which this undertaking afforded, once more revived the Countess; but alas! a new source of sorrow was now opened for her: the health of Mary visibly declined; she was silent and pensive; her tender frame was too susceptible of the sufferings of her mind; and these sufferings were heightened by concealment. She was prescribed amusement and gentle exercise, as the best restoratives of peace and health. One day, as she was seeking on horseback these lost treasures, she was tempted by the fineness of the evening to prolong her ride beyond its usual limits: the sun was declining when she entered a wood, whose awful glooms so well accorded with the pensive tone of her mind. The soft serenity of evening, and the still solemnity of the scene, conspired to lull her mind into a pleasing forgetfulness of its troubles; from which she was, ere long, awakened by the approaching sound of horses' feet. The thickness of the foliage limited her view; but looking onward, she thought she perceived through the trees, a glittering of arms; she turned her palfry, and sought the entrance of the wood. The clattering of hoofs advanced in the breeze! her heart, misgave her, and she quickened her pace. Her fears were soon justified; she looked back, and beheld three horsemen armed and disguised advancing with the speed of pursuit. Almost fainting, she flew on the wings of terror; all her efforts were vain; the villains came up; one seized her horse, the others fell upon her two attendants: a stout scuffle ensued, but the strength of her servants soon yielded to the weapons of their adversaries; they were brought to the ground, dragged into the wood, and there left bound to the trees. In the mean time, Mary, who had fainted in the arms of the villain who seized her, was borne away through the intricate mazes of the woods; and her terrors may be easily imagined, when she revived, and found herself in the hands of unknown men. Her dreadful screams, her tears, her supplications, were ineffectual; the wretches were deaf alike to pity and to enquiry; they preserved an inflexible silence, and she saw herself conveying towards the mouth of a horrible cavern, when despair seized her mind, and she lost all signs of existence: in this state she remained some time; but it is impossible to describe her situation, when she unclosed her eyes, and beheld Alleyn, who was watching with the most trembling anxiety her return to life, and whose eyes, on seeing her revive, swam in joy and tenderness. Wonder; fearful joy, and the various shades of mingled emotions, passed in quick succession over her countenance; her surprize was increased, when she observed her own servants standing by, and could discover no one but friends. She scarcely dared to trust her senses, but the voice of Alleyn, tremulous with tenderness, dissolved in a moment the illusions of fear, and confirmed her in the surprising reality. When she was sufficiently recovered, they quitted this scene of gloom: they travelled on in a slow pace, and the shades of night were fallen long before they reached the castle; there distress and confusion appeared. The Countess, alarmed with the most dreadful apprehensions, had dispatched her servants various ways in search of her child, and her transports on again beholding her in safety, prevented her observing immediately that it was Alleyn who accompanied her. Joy, however, soon yielded to its equal wonder, when she perceived him, and in the tumult of contending emotions, she scarce knew which first to interrogate. When she had been told the escape of her daughter, and by whom effected, she prepared to hear, with impatient solicitude, news of her beloved son, and the means by which the brave young Highlander had eluded the vigilance of the Baron. Of the Earl, Alleyn could only inform the Countess, that he was taken prisoner with himself, within the walls of the fortress, as they fought side by side; that he was conducted unwounded, to a tower, situated on the east angle of the castle, where he was still confined. Himself had been imprisoned in a distant part of the pile, and had been able to collect no other particulars of the Earl's situation, than those he had related. Of himself he gave a brief relation of the following circumstances:

After having lain some weeks in the horrible dungeon allotted him, his mind involved in the gloom of despair, and filled with the momentary expectation of death, desperation furnished him with invention, and he concerted the following plan of escape: — He had observed, that the guard who brought him his allowance of food, on quitting the dungeon, constantly sounded his spear against the pavement near the entrance. This circumstance excited his surprize and curiosity. A ray of hope beamed through the gloom of his dungeon. He examined the spot, as well as the obscurity of the place would permit; it was paved with flag stones like the other parts of the cell, and the paving was everywhere equally firm. He, however, became certain, that some means of escape was concealed beneath that part, for the guard was constant in examining it by striking that spot, and treading more firmly on it; and this he endeavoured to do without being observed. One day, immediately after the departure of the guard, Alleyn set himself to unfasten the pavement; this, with much patience and industry, he effected, by means of a small knife which had escaped the search of the soldiers. He found the earth beneath hard, and without any symptoms of being lately disturbed; but after digging a few feet, he arrived at a trap; he trembled with eagerness. It was now almost night, and he overcome with weariness; he doubted whether he should be able to penetrate through the door, and what other obstructions were behind it, before the next day. He therefore, threw the earth again into the hole, and endeavoured to close the pavement; with much difficulty, he trod the earth into the opening, but the pavement he was unable exactly to replace. It was too dark to examine the stones; and he found, that even if he should be able to make them fit, the pavement could not be made firm. His mind and body were now overcome, and he threw himself on the ground in an agony of despair. It was midnight, when the return of his strength and spirits produced another effort. He tore the earth up with hasty violence, cut round the lock of the trap door, and raising it, unwilling to hesitate or consider, sprung through the aperture. The vault was of considerable depth, and he was thrown down by the violence of the fall; an hollow echo, which seemed to murmur at a distance, convinced him that the place was of considerable extent. He had no light to direct him, and was therefore obliged to walk with his arms extended, in silent and fearful examination. After having wandered through the void a considerable time, he came to a wall, along which he groped with anxious care; it conducted him onward for a length of way: it turned; he followed, and his hand touched the cold iron work of a barred window. He felt the gentle undulation of the air upon his face; and to him, who had been so long confined among the damp vapours of a dungeon, this was a moment of luxury. The air gave him strength; and the means of escape, which now seemed presented to him, renewed his courage. He set his foot against the wall, and grasping a bar with his hand, found it gradually yield to his strength, and by successive efforts, he entirely displaced it. He attempted another but, it was more firmly fixed, and every effort to loosen it was ineffectual; he found that it was fastened in a large stone of the wall, and to remove this stone, was his only means of displacing the bar; he set himself, therefore, again to work with his knife, and with much patience, loosened the mortar sufficiently to effect his purpose. After some hours, for the darkness made his labour tedious, and sometimes ineffectual, he had removed several of the bars, and had made an opening almost sufficient to permit his escape, when the dawn of light appeared; he now discovered, with inexpressible anguish, that the grate opened into an inner court of the castle, and even while he hesitated, he could perceive soldiers descending slowly into the court, from the narrow staircases which led to their apartments. His heart sickened at the sight. He rested against the wall in a pause of despair, and was on the point of springing into the court, to make a desperate effort at escape, or die in the attempt, when he perceived, by the increasing light which fell across the vault, a massy door in the wall; he ran towards it, and endeavoured to open it; it was fastened by a lock and several bolts. He struck against it with his foot, and the hollow sound which was returned, convinced him that there were vaults beyond; and by the direction of these vaults, he was certain that they must extend to the outer walls of the castle; if he could gain these vaults, and penetrate beyond them in the darkness of the ensuing night, it would be easy to leap the wall, and cross the ditch; but it was impossible to cut away the lock, before the return of his guard, who regularly visited the cell soon after the dawn of day. After some consideration, therefore, he determined to secrete himself in a dark part of the vault, and there await the entrance of the guard, who on observing the deranged bars of the grate, would conclude, that he had escaped through the aperture. He had scarcely placed himself according to his plan, when he heard the door of the dungeon unbolted; this was instantly followed by a loud, voice, which founded down the opening, and "Alleyn" was shouted in a tone of fright and consternation. After repeating the call, a man jumped into the vault. Alleyn, though himself concealed in darkness, could perceive, by the faint light which fell upon the spot, a soldier with a drawn sword in his hand. He approached the grate with execrations, examined it, and proceeded to the door; it was fast, he returned to the grate, and then proceeded along the walls, tracing them with the point of his sword. He at length approached the spot where Alleyn was concealed, who felt the sword strike upon his arm, and instantly grasping the hand which held it, the weapon fell to the ground. A short scuffle ensued. Alleyn threw down his adversary, and standing over him, seized the sword, and presented it to his breast; the soldier called for mercy. Alleyn, always unwilling to take the life of another, and considering that if the soldier was slain, his comrades would certainly follow to the vault, returned him his sword. "Take your life," said he, "your death can avail me nothing; — take it, and if you can, go tell Malcolm, that an innocent man has endeavoured to escape destruction." The guard, struck with his conduct, arose from the ground in silence, he received his sword, and followed Alleyn to the trap door. They returned into the dungeon, where Alleyn was once more left alone. The soldier, undetermined how to act, went to find his comrades; on the way he met Malcolm, who, ever restless and vigilant frequently walked the ramparts at an early hour. He enquired if all was well. The soldier, fearful of discovery, and unaccustomed to dissemble, hesitated at the question; and the stern air assumed by Malcolm, compelled him to relate what had happened. The Baron, with much harshness, reprobated his neglect, and immediately followed him to the dungeon, where he loaded Alleyn with insult. He examined the cell, descended into the vault, and returning to the dungeon stood by, while a chain, which had been fetched from a distant part of the castle, was fixed into the wall; — to this Alleyn was fastened. "We will not long confine you thus," said Malcolm as he quitted the cell, "a few days shall restore you to the liberty you are so fond of; but as a conqueror ought to have spectators of his triumph, you must wait till a number is collected sufficient to witness the death of so great an hero." "I disdain your insults," returned Alleyn, "and am equally able to support misfortune, and to despise a tyrant." Malcolm retired enraged at the boldness of his prisoner, and uttering menaces on the carelessness of the guard, who vainly endeavoured to justify himself. "His safety be upon your head," said the Baron. The soldier was shocked, and turned away in sullen silence. Dread of his prisoner's effecting an escape, now seized his mind; the words of Malcolm filled him with resentment, while gratitude towards Alleyn, for the life he had spared, operated with these sentiments, and he hesitated whether he should obey the Baron, or deliver Alleyn, and fly his oppressor. At noon, he carried him his customary food; Alleyn was not so lost in misery, but that he observed the gloom which hung upon his features; his heart foreboded impending evil: the soldier bore on his tongue the sentence of death. He told Alleyn, that the Baron had appointed the following day for his execution; and his people were ordered to attend. Death, however long contemplated, must be dreadful when it arrives; this was no more than what Alleyn had expected, and on what he had brought his mind to gaze without terror; but his fortitude now sunk before its immediate presence, and every nerve of his frame thrilled with agony. "Be comforted," said the soldier, in a tone of pity, "I, too, am no stranger to misery; and if you are willing to risque the danger of double torture, I will attempt to release both you and myself from the hands of a tyrant." At these words, Alleyn started from the ground in a transport of delightful wonder: "Tell me not of torture," cried he, "all tortures are equal if death is the end, and from death I may now escape; lead me but beyond these walls, and the small possessions I have, shall be yours for ever." "I want them not," replied the generous soldier, "it is enough for me, that I save a fellow creature from destruction." These words overpowered the heart of Alleyn, and tears of gratitude swelled in his eyes. Edric told him, that the door he had seen in the vault below, opened into a chain of vaults, which stretched beyond the wall of the castle, and communicated with a subterraneous way, anciently formed as a retreat from the fortress, and which terminated in the cavern of a forest at some distance. If this door could be opened, their escape was almost certain. They consulted on the measures necessary to be taken. The soldier gave Alleyn a knife larger than the one he had, and directed him to cut round the lock, which was all that with-held their passage. Edric's office of centinel was propitious to their scheme, and it was agreed that at midnight they should descend the vaults. Edric, after having unfastened the chain, left the cell, and Alleyn set himself again to remove the pavement, which had been already re-placed by order of the Baron. The near prospect of deliverance now gladdened his spirits; his knife was better formed for his purpose; and he worked with alacrity and ease. He arrived at the trap door, and once more leaped into the vault. He applied himself to the lock of the door, which was extremely thick, and it was with difficulty he separated them; with trembling hands he undrew the bolts, the door unclosed, and discovered to him the vaults. It was evening when he finished his work. He was but just returned to the dungeon, and had thrown himself on the ground to rest, when the sound of a distant step caught his ear; he listened to its advance with trembling eagerness. At length the door was unbolted; Alleyn, breathless with expectation, started up, and beheld not his soldier, but another; the opening was again discovered, and all was now over. The soldier brought a pitcher of water, and casting round the place a look of sullen scrutiny, departed in silence. The stretch of human endurance was now exceeded, and Alleyn sunk down in a state of torpidity. On recovering, he found himself again enveloped in the horrors of darkness, silence, and despair. Yet amid all his sufferings, he disdained to doubt the integrity of his soldier: we naturally recoil from painful sensations, and it is one of the most exquisite tortures of a noble mind, to doubt the sincerity of those in whom it has confided. Alleyn concluded, that the conversation of the morning had been overheard, and that this guard had been sent to examine the cell, and to watch his movements. He believed that Edric was now, by his own generosity, involved in destruction; and in the energy of this thought, he forgot for a moment his own situation.

Midnight came, but Edric did not appear; his doubts were now confirmed into certainty, and he resigned himself to the horrid tranquillity of mute despair. He heard, from a distance, the clock of the castle strike one; it seemed to sound the knell of death; it roused his benumbed senses, and he rose from the ground in an agony of acutest recollection. Suddenly he heard the steps of two persons advancing down the avenue; he started, and listened. Malcolm and murder arose to his mind; he doubted not that the soldier had reported what he had seen in the evening, and that the persons whom he now heard, were coming to execute the final orders of the Baron. They now drew near the dungeon, when suddenly he remembered the door in the vault. His senses had been so stunned by the appearance of the stranger, and his mind so occupied with a feeling of despair, as to exclude every idea of escape; and in the energy of his sufferings he had forgot this last resource. It now flashed like lightning upon his mind; he sprung to the trap door, and his feet had scarcely touched the bottom of the vault, when he heard the bolts of the dungeon undraw; he had just reached the entrance of the inner vault, when a voice sounded from above. He paused, and knew it to be Edric's. Apprehension so entirely possessed his mind, that he hesitated whether he should discover himself; but a moment of recollection dissipated every ignoble suspicion of Edric's fidelity, and he answered the call. Immediately Edric descended, followed by the soldier whose former appearance had filled Alleyn with despair, and whom Edric now introduced as his faithful friend and comrade, who, like himself, was weary of the oppression of Malcolm, and who had resolved to fly with them, and escape his rigour. This was a moment of happiness too great for thought! Alleyn, in the confusion of his joy, and in his impatience to seize the moment of deliverance, scarcely heard the words of Edric. Edric having returned to fasten the door of the dungeon, to delay pursuit, and given Alleyn a sword which he had brought for him, led the way through the vaults. The profound silence of the place was interrupted only by the echoes of their footsteps, which running through the dreary chasms in confused whisperings, filled their imaginations with terror. In traversing these gloomy and desolate recesses they often paused to listen, and often did their fears give them the distant sounds of pursuit. On quitting the vaults, they entered an avenue, winding, and of considerable length, from whence branched several passages into the rock. It was closed by a low and narrow door, which opened upon a flight of steps, that led to the subterraneous way under the ditch of the castle. Edric knew the intricacies of the place: they entered, and closing the door began to descend, when the lamp which Edric carried in his hand was blown out by the current of the wind, and they were left in total darkness.

Their feelings may be more easily imagined than described; they had, however, no way but to proceed, and grope with cautious steps the dark abyss. Having continued to descend for some time, their feet reached the bottom, and they found themselves once more on even ground; but Edric knew they had yet another flight to encounter, before they could gain the subterraneous passage under the fosse, and for which it required their utmost caution to search. They were proceeding with slow and wary steps, when the foot of Alleyn stumbled upon something which clattered like broken armour, and endeavouring to throw it from him, he felt the weight resist his effort: he stooped to discover what it was, and found in his grasp the cold hand of a dead person. Every nerve thrilled with horror at the touch, and he started back in an agony of terror. They remained for some time in silent dismay, unable to return, yet fearful to proceed, when a faint light which seemed to issue from the bottom of the last descent, gleamed upon the walls, and discovered to them the second staircase, and at their feet the pale and disfigured corpse of a man in armour, while at a distance they could distinguish the figures of men. At this sight their hearts died within them, and they gave themselves up for lost. They doubted not but the men whom they saw were the murderers; that they belonged to the Baron; and were in search of some fugitives from the castle. Their only chance of concealment was to remain where they were; but the light appeared to advance, and the faces of the men to turn towards them. Winged with terror, they sought the first ascent, and flying up the steps, reached the door, which they endeavoured to open, that they might hide themselves from pursuit among the intricacies of the rock; their efforts, however, were vain, for the door was fastened by a spring lock, and the key was on the other side. Compelled to give breath to their fears, they ventured to look back, and found themselves again in total darkness; they paused upon the steps, and listening, all was silent. They rested here a considerable time; no footsteps startled them; no ray of light darted through the gloom; every thing seemed hushed in the silence of death: they resolved once more to venture forward; they gained again the bottom of the first descent, and shuddering as they approached the spot where they knew the corpse was laid, they groped to avoid its horrid touch, when suddenly the light again appeared, and in the same place where they had first seen it. They stood petrified with despair. The light, however, moved slowly onward, and disappeared in the windings of the avenue. After remaining a long time in silent suspense, and finding no further obstacle, they ventured to proceed. The light had discovered to them their situation, and the staircase, and they now moved with greater certainty. They reached the bottom in safety, and without any fearful interruption; they listened, and again the silence of the place was undisturbed. Edric knew they were now under the fosse, their way was plain before them, and their hopes were renewed in the belief, that the light and the people they had seen, had taken a different direction, Edric knowing there were various passages branching from the main avenue which led to different openings in the rock. They now stepped on with alacrity, the prospect of deliverance was near, for Edric judged they were now not far from the cavern. An abrupt turning in the passage confirmed at once this supposition, and extinguished the hope which had attended it; for the light of a lamp burst suddenly upon them, and exhibited to their sickening eyes, the figures of four men in an attitude of menace, with their swords pointed ready to receive them. Alleyn drew his sword, and advanced: "We will die hardly," cried he. At the sound of his voice, the weapons instantly dropped from the hands of his adversaries, and they advanced to meet him in a transport of joy. Alleyn recognized with astonishment, in the faces of the three strangers, his faithful friends and followers; and Edric in that of the fourth, a fellow soldier. The same purpose had assembled them all in the same spot. They quitted the cave together; and Alleyn, in the joyful experience of unexpected deliverance, resolved never more to admit despair. They concluded, that the body which they had passed in the avenue, was that of some person who had perished either by hunger or by the sword in those subterranean labyrinths.

They marched in company till they came within a few miles in of the castle of Athlin, when Alleyn made known his design of collecting his friends, and joining the clan in an attempt to release the Earl; Edric, and the other soldier, having solemnly enlisted in the cause, they parted; Alleyn and Edric pursuing the road to the castle, and the others striking off to a different part of the country. Alleyn and Edric had not proceeded far, when the groans of the wounded servants of Matilda drew them into the wood, in which the preceding dreadful scene had been acted. The surprize of Alleyn was extreme, when he discovered the servants of the Earl in this situation; but surprize soon yielded to a more poignant sensation, when he heard that Mary had been carried off by armed men. He scarcely waited to release the servants, but seized one of their horses which was grazing near, instantly mounted, ordering the rest to follow, and took the way which had been pointed as the course of the ravishers. Fortunately it was the right direction; and Alleyn and the soldier came up with them as they were hastening to the mouth of that cavern, whose frightful aspect had chilled the heart of Mary with a temporary death. Their endeavours to fly were vain; they were overtaken at the entrance; a sharp conflict ensued in which one of the ruffians was wounded and fled: his comrades seeing the servants of the Earl approaching relinquished their prize, and escaped through the recesses of the cave. The eyes of Alleyn were now fixed in horror on the lifeless form of Mary, who had remained insensible during the whole of the affray; he was exerting every effort for her recovery, when she unclosed her eyes, and joy once more illumined his soul.

During the recital of these particulars, which Alleyn delivered with a modest brevity, the mind of Mary had suffered a variety of emotions sympathetic to all the vicissitudes of his situation. She endeavoured to conceal from herself the particular interest she felt in his adventures; but so unequal were her efforts to the strength of her emotions, that when Alleyn related the scene of Dunbayne cavern, her cheek grew pale and she relapsed into a fainting fit. This circumstance alarmed the penetration of the Countess; but the known weakness of her daughter's frame appeared a probable cause of the disorder, and repressed her first apprehension. It gave to Alleyn a mixed delight of hope and fear, such as he had never known before; for the first time he dared to acknowledge to his own heart that he loved, and that heart for the first time thrilled with the hope of being loved again.

He received from the Countess the warm overflowings of a heart grateful for the preservation of her child, and from Mary a blush which spoke more than her tongue could utter. But the minds of all were involved in the utmost perplexity concerning the rank and the identity of the author of the plan, nor could they discover any clue which would lead them through this intricate maze of wonder, to the villain who had fabricated so diabolical a scheme. Their suspicions, at length, rested upon the Baron Malcolm, and this supposition was confirmed by the appearance of the horsemen, who evidently acted only as the agents of superior power. Their conjectures were indeed just. Malcolm was the author of the scheme. It had been planned, and he had given orders to his people to execute it long before the Earl fell into his hands. They had, however, found no opportunity of accomplishing the design when the castle was surprized, and in the consequent tumult of his mind, the Baron had forgot to withdraw his orders.

Alleyn expressed his design of collecting the small remnant of his friends, and uniting with the clan in attempting the rescue of the Earl. "Noble youth," exclaimed the Countess, unable longer to repress her admiration, "how can I ever repay your generous services! Am I then to receive both my children at your hands? Go-my clan are now collecting for a second attempt upon the walls of Dunbayne, — go! lead them to conquest, and restore to me my son." The languid eyes of Mary rekindled at these words, she glowed with the hope of clasping once more to her bosom her long lost brother; but the suffusions of hope were soon chased by the chilly touch of fear, for it was Alleyn who was to lead the enterprize, and it was Alleyn who might fall in the attempt. These contrary emotions unveiled to her at once the state of her affections, and she saw in the eye of fancy, the long train of inquietudes and sorrows which were likely to ensue. She sought to obliterate from her mind every remembrance of the past, and of the fatal knowledge which was now disclosed; but she sought in vain, for the monitor in her breast constantly presented to her mind the image of Alleyn, adorned with those brave and manly virtues which had so eminently distinguished his conduct; the insignificance of the peasant was lost in the nobility of the character, and every effort at forgetfulness was baffled.

Alleyn passed that night at the castle, and the next morning, after taking leave of the Countess and her daughter, to whom his eyes bade a respectful and mournful adieu, he departed with Edric for his father's cottage, impatient to acquaint the good old man with his safety, and to rouse to arms his slumbering friends. The breath of love had now raised into flame those sparks of ambition which had so long been kindling in his breast; he was not only eager to avenge the cause of injured virtue, and to rescue from misery and death, the son of the Chief whom he had been ever taught to reverence, but he panted to avenge the insult offered to his mistress, and to achieve some deed of valour worthy her admiration and her thanks.

Alleyn found his father at breakfast, with his niece at his side; his face was darkened with sorrow, and he did not perceive Alleyn, when he entered. The joy of the old man almost overcame him when he beheld his son in safety, for he was the solace of his declining years; and Edric was welcomed with the heartiness of an old friend.

CHAPTER IV.

MEANWHILE the Earl remained a solitary prisoner in the tower; uncertain fate was yet suspended over him; he had, however, a magnanimity in his nature which baffled much of the cruel effort of the Baron. He had prepared his mind by habitual contemplation for the worst, and although that worst was death, he could now look to it even with serenity. Those violent transports which had assailed him on sight of the Baron, were, since he was no longer subject to his presence, reduced within their proper limits; yet he anxiously avoided dwelling on the memory of his father, lest those dreadful sensations should threaten him with returning torture. Whenever he permitted himself to think of the sufferings of the Countess and his sister, his heart melted with a sorrow that almost unnerved him; much he wished to know how they supported this trial, and much he wished that he could convey to them intelligence of his state. He endeavoured to abstract his mind from his situation, and sought to make himself artificial comforts even from the barren objects around him; his chief amusement was in observing the manners and customs of the birds of prey which lodged themselves in the battlements of his tower, and the rapacity of their nature furnished him with too just a parallel to the habits of men.

As he was one day standing at the grate which looked upon the castle, observing the progress of these birds, his ear caught the sound of that sweet lute whose notes had once saved him from destruction; it was accompanied by the same melodious voice he had formerly heard, and which now sung with impassioned tenderness the following air:

When first the vernal morn of life

Beam'd on my infant eye,

Fond I survey'd the smiling scene,

Nor saw the tempest nigh.

Hope's bright illusions touch'd my soul,

My young ideas led;

And Fancy's vivid tints combin'd,

And fairy prospect spread.

My guileless heart expanded wide,
With filial fondness fraught;
Paternal love that heart supplied
With all its fondness sought.

But O! the cruel quick reverse!
Fate all I loved involv'd;
Pale Grief Hope's trembling rays dispers'd,
And Fancy's dreams dissolv'd.

Lost in surprize, Osbert stood for some time looking down upon an inner court, whence the sounds seemed to arise; after a few minutes he observed a young lady enter from that side on which the tower arose; on her arm rested an elder one, in whose face might be traced the lines of decaying beauty; but it was visible, from the melancholy which clouded her features, that the finger of affliction had there anticipated the ravages of time. She was dressed in the habit of a widow, and the black veil which shaded her forehead, and gave a fine expression to her countenance, devolved upon the ground in a length of train, and heightened the natural majesty of her figure; she moved with slow steps, and was supported by the young lady whose veil half disclosed a countenance where beauty was touched with sorrow and inimitable expression; the elegance of her form and the dignity of her air, proclaimed her to be of distinguished rank. On her arm was hung that lute, whose melody had just charmed the attention of the Earl, who was now fixed in wonder at what he beheld, that was equalled only by his admiration. They retired through a gate on the opposite side of the court, and were seen no more. Osbert followed them with his eyes, which for some time remained fixed upon the door through which they had disappeared, almost insensible of their departure. When he returned to himself, he discovered, as if for the first time, that he was in solitude. He conjectured that these strangers were confined by the oppressive power of the Baron, and his eyes were suffused with tears of pity. When he considered that so much beauty and dignity were the unresisting victims of a tyrant, his heart swelled high with indignation, his prison became intolerable to him, and he longed to become at once the champion of virtue, and the deliverer of oppressed innocence. The character of Malcolm arose to his mind black with accumulated guilt, and aggravated the detestation with which he had ever contemplated it: the hateful idea nerved his soul with a confidence of revenge. Of the guard, who entered, he enquired concerning the strangers, but could obtain no positive information; he came to impart other news; to prepare the Earl for death; the morrow was appointed for his execution. He received the intelligence with the firm hardihood of indignant virtue, disdaining to solicit, and disdaining to repine; and his mind yet grasped the idea of revenge. He drove from his thoughts, with precipitation, the tender ideas of his mother and sister; remembrances which would subdue his fortitude without effecting any beneficial purpose. He was told of the escape of Alleyn; this intelligence gave him inexpressible pleasure, and he knew this faithful youth would undertake to avenge his death.

When the news of Alleyn's flight had reached the Baron, his soul was stung with rage, and he called for the guards of the dungeon; they were no where to be found; and after a long search it was known that they were fled with their prisoner; the flight of the other captives was also discovered. This circumstance exasperated the passion of Malcolm to the utmost, and he gave orders that the life of the remaining centinel should be forfeited for the treachery of his comrades, and his own negligence; when recollecting the Earl, whom in the heat of his resentment he had forgot, his heart exulted in the opportunity he afforded of complete revenge; and in the fullness of joy with which he pronounced his sentence, he retracted the condemnation of the trembling guard. The moment after he had dispatched the messenger with his resolve to the Earl, his heart faultered from its purpose. Such is the alternate violence of evil passions, that they never suffer their subjects to act with consistency, but, torn by conflicting energies, the gratification of one propensity is destruction to the enjoyment of another; and the moment in which they imagine happiness in their grasp, is to them the moment of disappointment. Thus it was with the Baron; his soul seemed to attain its full enjoyment in the contemplation of revenge, till the idea of Mary inflamed his heart with an opposite passion; his wishes had caught new ardor from disappointment, for he had heard that Mary had been once in the power of his emissaries; and perhaps the pain which recoils upon the mind from every fruitless effort of wickedness, served to increase the energies of his desires. He spurned the thought of relinquishing the pursuit, yet there appeared to be no method of obtaining its object, but by sacrificing his favourite passion; for he had little doubt of obtaining Mary, when it should be known that he resolved not to grant the life of the Earl upon any other ransom. The balance of these passions hung in his mind in such nice equilibrium, that it was for some time uncertain which would preponderate; revenge, at length, yielded to love; but he resolved to preserve the torture of expected death, by keeping the Earl ignorant of his reprieve till the last moment.

The Earl awaited death with the same stern fortitude with which he received its sentence, and was led from the tower to the platform of the castle, silent and unmoved. He beheld the preparations for his execution, the instruments of death, the guards arranged in files, with an undaunted mind. The glare of externals had no longer power over his imagination. He beheld every object with indifference, but that on which his eye now rested; it was on the murderer, who exhibited himself in all the pride of exulting conquest: he started at the sight, and his soul shrunk back upon itself. Disdaining, however, to appear disconcerted, he endeavoured to resume his dignity, when the remembrance of his mother, overwhelmed with sorrow, rushed upon his mind, and quite unmanned him; the tears started in his eyes, and he sunk senseless on the ground.

On recovering, he found himself in his prison, and he was informed that the Baron had granted him a respite. Malcolm mistaking the cause of disorder in the Earl, thought he had stretched his sufferings to their utmost limits; he therefore had ordered him to be re-conveyed to the tower.

A scene so striking and so public as that which had just been performed at the castle of Dunbayne, was a subject of discourse to the whole country; it was soon reported to the Countess with a variety of additional circumstances, among which it was affirmed, that the Earl had been really executed. Overwhelmed with this intelligence, Matilda relapsed into her former disorder. Sickness had rendered Mary less able to support the shock, and to apply that comfort to the ambitions of her mother, which had once been so successfully administered. The physician pronounced the malady of the Countess to be seated in the mind, and beyond the reach of human skill, when one day a letter was brought to her, the superscription of which was written in the hand of Osbert; she knew the characters, and bursting the seal, read that her son was yet alive, and did not despair of throwing himself once more at her feet. He requested that the remains of his clan might immediately attempt his release. He described in what part of the castle his prison was situated, and thought, that by the assistance of long scaling-ladders and ropes, contrived in the manner he directed, he might be able to effect his escape through the grate. This letter was a reviving cordial to the Countess and to Mary.

375

Alleyn was indefatigable in collecting followers for the enterprize he had engaged in. On receiving intelligence of the safety of the Earl, he visited the clan, and was strenuous in exhorting them to immediate action. They required little incitement to a cause in which every heart was so much interested, and for which every hand was already busied in preparation. These preparations were at length completed; Alleyn, at the head of his party, joined the assembled clan. The Countess for a second time beheld from the ramparts the departure of her people upon the same hazardous enterprize; the present scene revived in her mind a sad membrance of the past: the same tender fears, and the same prayers for success she now gave to their departure; and when they faded in distance from her sight, she returned into the castle dissolved in tears. The heart of Mary was torn by a complex sorrow, and incapable of longer concealing from herself the interest she took in the departure of Alleyn, her agitation became more apparent. The Countess in vain endeavoured to compose her mind. Mary, affected by her tender concern, and prompted by the natural ingenuousness of her disposition, longed to make her the confidant of her weakness, if weakness that can be termed which arises from gratitude, and from admiration of great and generous qualities; but delicacy and timidity arrested the half-formed sentence, and closed her lips in silence. Her health gradually declined under the secret agitation of her mind; her physician knew her disorder to originate in suppressed sorrow; and advised, as the best cordial, a confidential friend. Matilda now perceived the cause of her grief; her former passing observations recurred to her memory, and justified her discernment. She strove by every soothing effort to win her to her confidence. Mary, oppressed by the idea of ungenerous concealment, resolved at length to unveil her heart to a mother so tender of her happiness. She told her all her sentiments. The Countess suffered a distress almost equal to that of her daughter; her affectionate heart swelled with equal wishes for her happiness; she admired with warmest gratitude the noble and aspiring virtues of the young Highlander; but the proud nobility of her soul repelled with quick vivacity every idea of union with a youth of such ignoble birth: she regarded the present attachment as the passing impression of youthful fancy, and believed that gentle reasoning, aided by time and endeavour, would conquer the enthusiasm of love. Mary listened with attention to the reasonings of the Countess; her judgment acknowledged their justness, while her heart regretted their force. She resolved, however, to overcome an attachment which would produce so much distress to her family and to herself. Notwithstanding her endeavours to exclude Alleyn from her thoughts, the generous and heroic qualities of his mind burst upon her memory in all their splendor, she could not but be conscious that he loved her; she saw the struggles of his soul, and the delicacy of his passion, which made him ever retire in the most profound and respectful silence from its object. She solicited her mother to assist in expelling the destructive image from her mind. The Countess exerted every effort to amuse her to forgetfulness; every hour, except those which were given to exercises necessary for her health, was devoted to the cultivation of her mind, and the improvement of her various accomplishments. These endeavours were not unsuccessful; the Countess with joy observed the returning health and tranquillity of her daughter; and Mary almost believed she had taught herself to forget. These engagements served also to beguile the tedious moments which must intervene, ere news could arrive from Alleyn concerning the probable success of the enterprize.

Misery yet dwelt in the castle of Dunbayne; for there the virtues were captive, while the vices reigned despotic. The mind of the Baron, ardent and restless, knew no peace: torn by conflicting passions, he was himself the victim of their power.

The Earl knew that his life hung upon the caprice of a tyrant; his mind was nerved for the worst; yet the letter which the compassion of one of his guards, at the risque of his life, had undertaken to convey to the Countess, afforded him a faint hope that his people might yet effect his escape. In this expectation, he spent hour after hour at his grate, wishing, with trembling anxiety, to behold his clan advancing over the distant hills. These hills became at length, in a situation so barren of real comforts, a source of ideal pleasure to him. He was always at the grate, and often, in the fine evenings of summer saw the ladies, whose appearance had so strongly excited his admiration and pity, walk on a terrace below the tower. One very fine evening, under the pleasing impressions of hope for himself, and compassion for them, his sufferings for a time lost their acuteness. He longed to awaken their sympathy, and make known to them that they had a fellow-prisoner. The parting sun trembled on the tops of the mountains, and a softer shade fell upon the distant landscape. The sweet tranquillity of evening threw an air of tender melancholy over his mind: his sorrows for a while were hushed; and under the enthusiasm of the hour, he composed the following stanzas, which, having committed them to paper, he the next evening dropp'd upon the terrace.

SONNET

Hail! to the hallow'd hill, the circling lawn,
The breezy upland, and the mountain stream!
The last tall pine that earliest meets the dawn,
And glistens latest to the western gleam!

Hail! every distant hill, and downland plain!
Your dew-hid beauties Fancy oft unveils;
What time to shepherd's reed, or poet's strain,
Sorrowing my heart its destin'd woe bewails.

Blest are the fairy hour, the twilight shade
Of Ev'ning, wand'ring thro' her woodlands dear,
Sweet the still sound that steals along the glade;
'Tis fancy wafts it, and her vot'ries hear.

'Tis fancy wafts it! — and how sweet the sound!
I hear it now the distant hills uplong;
While fairy echos from their dells around,
And woods, and wilds, the feeble notes prolong!

He had the pleasure to observe that the paper was taken up by the ladies, who immediately retired into the castle.

CHAPTER V.

ONE morning early, the Earl discerned a martial band emerging from the verge of the horizon; his heart welcomed his hopes, which were soon confirmed into certainty. It was his faithful people, led on by Alleyn. It was their design to surround and attack the castle; and though their numbers gave them but little hopes of conquest, they yet believed that, in the tumult of the engagement, they might procure the deliverance of the Earl. With this view they advanced to the walls. The centinels had descried them at a distance; the alarm was given; the trumpets sounded, and the walls of the castle were filled with men. The Baron was present, and directed the preparations. The secret purpose of his soul was fixed. The clan surrounded the fosse, into which they threw bundles of faggots, and gave the signal of attack. Scaling ladders were thrown up to the window of the tower. The Earl, invigorated with hope and joy, had by the force of his arm, almost wrenched from its fastening, one of the iron bars of the grate; his foot was lifted to the stanchion, ready to aid him in escaping through the opening, when he was seized by the guards of the Baron, and conveyed precipitately from the prison. He was led, indignant and desperate, to the lofty ramparts of the castle, from whence he beheld Alleyn and his clan, whose eager eyes were once more blessed with the sight of their Chief; — they were blessed but for a moment; they beheld their Lord in chains, surrounded with guards, and with the instruments of death. Animated, however, with a last hope, they renewed the attack with redoubled fury, when the trumpets of the Baron sounded a parley, and they suspended their arms. The Baron appeared on the ramparts; Alleyn advanced to hear him. "The moment of attack," cried the Baron, "is the moment of death to your Chief. If you wish to preserve his life, desist from the assault, and depart in peace; and bear this message to the Countess your mistress: — the Baron Malcolm will accept no other ransom for the life and the liberty of the Earl, than her beauteous daughter, whom he now sues to become his wife. If she accedes to these terms, the Earl is instantly liberated, — if she refuses, he dies." The emotions of the Earl, and of Alleyn on hearing these words, were inexpressible. The Earl spurned, with haughty virtue, the base concession. "Give me death," cried he with loud impatience; "the house of Athlin shall not be dishonoured by alliance with a murderer: renew the attack, my brave people; since you cannot save the life, revenge the death of your Chief; he dies contented, since his death preserves his family from dishonour." The guards instantly surrounded the Earl.

Alleyn, whose heart, torn by contending emotions, was yet true to the impulse of honour, on observing this, instantly threw down his arms, refusing to obey the commands of the Earl; a hostage for whose life he demanded, while he hastened to the castle of Athlin with the conditions of the Baron. The clan, following the example of Alleyn, rested on their arms, while a few prepared to depart with him on the embassy. In vain were the remonstrances and the commands of the Earl; his people loved him too well to obey them, and his heart was filled with anguish when he saw Alleyn depart from the walls.

The situation of Alleyn was highly pitiable; all the firm virtues of his soul were called upon to support it. He was commissioned on an embassy, the alternate conditions of which would bring misery on the woman he adored, or death to the friend whom he loved.

When the arrival of Alleyn was announced to the Countess, impatient joy thrilled in her bosom; for she had no doubt that he brought offers of accommodation; and no ransom was presented to her imagination, which she would not willingly give for the restoration of her son. At the sound of Alleyn's voice, those tumults which had began to subside in the heart of Mary, were again revived, and she awoke to the mournful certainty of hopeless endeavour. Yet she could not repress a strong emotion of joy on again beholding him. The soft blush of her cheek shewed the colours of her mind, while, in endeavouring to shade her feelings, she impelled them into stronger light.

The agitations of Alleyn almost subdued his strength, when he entered the presence of the Countess; and his visage, on which was impressed deep distress, and the paleness of fear, betrayed the inward workings of his soul. Matilda was instantly seized with apprehension for the safety of her son, and in a tremulous voice, enquired his fate. Alleyn told her he was well, proceeding with tender caution to acquaint her with the business of his embassy, and with the scene to which he had lately been witness. The sentence of the Baron fell like the stroke of death upon the heart of Mary, who fainted at the words. Alleyn flew to support her. In endeavouring to revive her daughter, the Countess was diverted for a time from the anguish which this intelligence must naturally impart. It was long ere Mary returned to life, and she returned only to a sense of wretchedness. The critical situation of Matilda can scarcely be felt in its full extent. Torn by the conflict of opposite interests, her brain was the seat of tumult, and wild dismay. Which ever way she looked, destruction closed the view. The murderer of the husband, now sought to murder the happiness of the daughter. On the sentence of the mother hung the final fate of the son. In rejecting these terms, she would give him instant death; in accepting them, her conduct would be repugnant to the feelings of indignant virtue, and to the tender injured memory of her murdered Lord. She would destroy for ever the peace of her daughter, and the honour of her house. To effect his deliverance by force of arms was utterly impracticable, since the Baron had declared, that "the moment of attack should be the moment of death to the Earl." Honour, humanity, parental tenderness, bade her save her son; yet, by a strange contrariety of interests, the same virtues pleaded with a voice equally powerful, for the reverse of the sentence. Hitherto hope had still illumined her mind with a distant ray; she now found herself suddenly involved in the darkness of despair, whose glooms were interrupted only by the gleams of horror which arose from the altar, on which was to be sacrificed one of her beloved children. Her mind shrunk from the idea of uniting her daughter to the murderer of her father. The ferocious character of Malcolm was alone sufficient to blight for ever the happiness of the woman whose fate should be connected with his. To give to the murderer the child of the murdered was a thought too horrid to rest upon. The Countess rejected with force the Baron's offer of exchange, when the bleeding figure of her beloved son, pale and convulsed in death, started on her imagination, and stretched her brain almost to frenzy.

Meanwhile Mary suffered a conflict equally dreadful. Nature had bestowed on her a heart susceptible of all the fine emotions of delicate passion; a heart which vibrated in unison with the sweetest feelings of humanity; a mind, quick in perceiving the nicest lines of moral rectitude, and strenuous in endeavouring to act up to its perceptions. These gifts were unnecessary to make her sensible of the wretchedness of her present situation; of which a common mind would have felt the misery; they served, however, to sharpen the points of affliction, to increase their force, and to disclose, in stronger light, the various horrors of her situation. Fraternal love and pity called loudly upon her to resign herself into the power of the man whom, from the earliest dawn of perception, she had contemplated with trembling aversion and horror. The memory of her murdered parent, every feeling dear to virtue, the tremulous, but forceful voice of love awakened her heart, and each opposed, with wild impetuosity, every other sentiment. Her soul shrunk back with terror from the idea of union with the Baron. Could she bear to receive, in marriage, that hand which was stained with the blood of her father? — The polluted touch would freeze her heart in horror! — could she bear to pass her life with the man, who had for ever blasted the smiling days of him who gave her being? — With the man who would stand before her eyes a perpetual monument of misery to herself, and of dishonour to her family? whose chilling aspect would repel every amiable and generous affection, and strike them back upon her heart only to wound it? To cherish the love of the noble virtues, would be to cherish the remembrance of her dead father, and of her living lover. How wretched must be her situation, when to obliterate from her memory the image of virtue, could alone afford her a chance of obtaining a horrid tranquillity; virtue which is so dear to the human heart, that when her form forsakes us, we pursue her shadow. Wherever in search of comfort she directed her aching sight, Misery's haggard countenance obtruded on her view. Here she beheld herself entombed in the arms of the murderer; — there, the spectacle of her beloved brother, encircled with chains, and awaiting the stroke of death, arose to her imagination; the scene was too affecting; fancy gave her the horrors of reality. The reflection, that through her he suffered, that she yet might save him from destruction, broke with irresistible force upon her mind, and instantly bore away every opposing feeling. — She resolved, that since she must be wretched, she would be nobly wretched; since misery demanded one sacrifice, she would devote herself the victim.

With these thoughts, she entered the apartment of the Countess, whose concurrence was necessary to ratify her resolves, and, having declared them, awaited in trembling expectation her decision. Matilda had suffered a distraction of mind, which the nature of no former trial had occasioned her. On the unfortunate death of a husband tenderly beloved, she had suffered all the sorrow which tenderness, and all the shock which the manner of his death could occasion. The event, however, shocking as it was, did not hang upon circumstances over which she had an influence; it was decided by an higher power; — it was decided, and never could be recalled; she had there no dreadful choice of horrors, no evil ratified by her own voice, to taint with deadly recollections her declining days. This choice, though forced upon her by the power of a tyrant, she would still consider as in part her own; and the thought that she was compelled to doom to destruction one of her children, harrowed up her soul almost to frenzy.

Her mind, at length exhausted with excess of feeling, was now fallen into a state of cold and silent despair; she became insensible to the objects around her, almost to the sense of her own sufferings, and the voice, and the proposal of her daughter, scarcely awakened her powers of perception. "He shall live," said Mary, in a voice broken and tender; "He shall live, I am ready to become the sacrifice." Tears prevented her proceeding. At the word "live," the Countess raised her eyes, and threw round her a look of wildness, which settling on the features of Mary, softened into an expression of ineffable tenderness, she waved her head, and turned to the window. A few tears bedewed her cheek; they fell like the drops of Heaven upon the withered plant, reviving and expanding its dying foliage; they were the first her eyes had known since the fatal news had reached her. Recovering herself a little, she sent for Alleyn, who was still in the castle. She wished to consult with him, whether there was not yet a possibility of effecting the escape of the Earl. In afflictions of whatever degree, where death has not already fixed the events in certainty, the mind shoots almost beyond the sphere of possibility in search of hope, and seldom relinquishes the fond illusion, till the stroke of reality dissolves the enchantment. Thus it was with Matilda; after the grief produced by the first stroke of this disaster was somewhat abated, she was inclined to think that her situation might not prove so desperate as she imagined; and her heart was warmed by a remote hope, that there might yet be devised some method of procuring the escape of the Earl. Alleyn came; he came in the trembling expectation of receiving the decision of the Countess, and in the intention of offering to engage in any enterprize, however hazardous, for the enlargement of the Earl. He repelled, with instant force, every idea of Mary's becoming the wife of Malcolm; the thought was too full of agony to be endured, and he threw the sensation from his heart as a poison which would destroy the pulse of life. To preserve Mary from a misery so exquisite, and to save the life of the Earl, he was willing to encounter any hazard; to meet death itself as an evil which appeared less dreadful than either of the former. He came prepared with this resolution, and it served to support that fortitude which affliction had disturbed, though it could not subdue. When he came again to the Countess, his distress was heightened by the scene before him; he beheld her leaning on a sofa, pale and silent; her unconscious eyes were fixed on an opposite window; her countenance was touched with a wildness expressive of the disorder of her mind, and she remained for some time insensible of his approach. Such is the fluctuation of a mind overcome by distress, that if for a moment a ray of hope cheers its darkness, it vanishes at the touch of recollection. Mary was standing near the Countess, whose hand she held to her bosom. Her present sorrow had heightened the natural pensiveness of her countenance, and shaded her features with an interesting langour, more enchanting than the vivacity of blooming health; her eyes sought to avoid Alleyn, as an object dangerous to the resolution she had formed. Matilda remained absorbed in thought. Mary wished to repeat the purpose of her soul, but her voice trembled, and the half-formed sentence died away on her lips. Alleyn enquired the commands of the Countess. "I am ready," said Mary, at length, in a low and tremulous voice, "to give myself the victim to the Baron's revenge. — I will save my brother." At these words, the heart of Alleyn grew cold. Mary, overcome by the effort which they had occasioned her, scarcely finished the sentence; her nerves shook, a mist fell over her eyes, and she sunk on the sofa by which she had stood. Alleyn hung over the couch in silent agony, watching her return to life. By the assistance of those about her, she soon revived. Alleyn, in the joy which he felt at her recovery, forgot for a moment his situation, and pressed with ardor her hand to his bosom. Mary, whose senses were yet scarcely recollected, yielded unconsciously to the softness of her heart, and betrayed its situation by a smile so tender, as to thrill the breast of Alleyn with the sweet certainty of being loved. Hitherto his passion had been chilled by the despair which the vast superiority of her birth occasioned, and by the modesty which forbade him to imagine that he had merit sufficient to arrest the eye of the accomplished Mary. Perhaps, too, the diffidence natural to genuine love, might contribute to deceive him. It was not till this moment, that he experienced that certainty which awakened in his heart a sense of delight hitherto unknown to him. For a moment he forgot the distresses of the castle, and his own situation; every idea faded from his mind, but the one he had so lately acquired; and in that moment he seemed to taste perfect felicity. Recollection, however, with all its train of black dependancies soon returned, and plunged him in a misery as poignant as the joy from which he was now precipitated.

The Countess was now sufficiently composed to enter on the subject nearest her heart. Alleyn caught, with eagerness, her mention of attempting the deliverance of the Earl, for the possibility of accomplishing which, he declared himself willing to encounter any danger: he seconded so warmly the design, and spoke with such flattering probability of success, that the spirits of Matilda began once more to revive; yet she trembled to encourage hopes which hung on such perilous uncertainty. It was agreed, that Alleyn should consult with the most able and trusty of the clan, whom age or infirmity had detained from battle, on the means most likely to ensure success, and then proceed immediately on the expedition: having first delivered to the Baron a message from the Countess, requiring time for deliberation upon a choice so important, and importing that an answer should be returned at the expiration of a fortnight.

Alleyn accordingly assembled those whom he judged most worthy of the council: various schemes were proposed, none of which appeared likely to succeed; when it was recollected that the Earl might possibly have been removed from the tower to some new place of confinement, which it would be necessary first to discover, that the plan might be adapted to the situation. It was therefore concluded to suspend further consultation till Alleyn had obtained the requisite information; and that in the mean time he should deliver to Malcolm the message of the Countess: for these purposes Alleyn immediately set out for the castle.

CHAPTER VI.

THE castle of Dunbayne was still the scene of triumph, and of wretchcdness. Malcolm, exulting in his scheme, already beheld Mary at his feet, and the Earl retiring in an anguish more poignant than that of death. He was surprized that his invention had not before supplied him with this means of torture: for the first time he welcomed love, as the instrument of his revenge; and the charms of Mary were heightened to his imagination by the ardent colours of this passion. He was confirmed in his resolves, never to relinquish the Earl, but on the conditions he had offered; and thus for ever would he preserve the house of Athlin a monument of his triumph.

Osbert, for greater security, was conveyed from the tower into a more centrical part of the castle, to an apartment spacious but gloomy, whose gothic windows partly excluding light, threw a solemnity around, which chilled the heart almost to horror. He heeded not this; his heart was occupied with horrors of its own. He was now involved in a misery more intricate, and more dreadful, than his imagination had yet painted. To die, was to him, who had so long contemplated the near approach of death, a familiar and transient evil; but to see, even in idea, his family involved in infamy, and in union with the murderer, was the stroke which pierced his heart to its center. He feared that the cruel tenderness of the mother would tempt Matilda to accept the offers of the Baron; and he scarcely doubted, that the noble Mary would resign herself the price of his life. He would have written to the Countess to have forbidden her acceptance of the terms, and to have declared his fixed resolution to die, but that he had no means of conveying to her a letter; the soldier who had so generously undertaken the conveyance of his former one, having soon after disappeared from his station. The manly fortitude which had supported him through his former trials, did not desert him in this hour of darkness; habituated so long to struggle with opposing feelings, he had acquired the art of managing them; his mind attained a confidence in its powers; resistance served only to increase its strength, and to confirm the magnanimity of its nature.

Alleyn had now joined the clan, and was ardent in pursuit of the necessary intelligence. He learned that the Earl had been removed from the tower, but in what part of the castle he was now confined he could not discover; on this point all was vague conjecture. That he was alive, was only judged from the policy of the Baron, whose ardent passion for Mary was now well understood. Alleyn employed every stratagem his invention could suggest, to discover the prison of the Earl, but without success: at length compelled to deliver to Malcolm the message of the Countess, he demanded as a preliminary, that the Earl should be shewn to his people from the ramparts, that they might be certain he was still alive. Alleyn hoped that his appearance would lead to a discovery of the place of his imprisonment, purposing to observe narrowly the way by which he should retire.

The Earl appeared in safety on the ramparts, amid the shouts and acclamations of his people; the Baron frowning defiance, was seen at his side. Alleyn advanced to the walls, and delivered the message of Matilda. Osbert started at its purpose; he foresaw that deliberation portended compliance: − stung with the thought, he swore aloud he never would survive the infamy of the concession; and addressing himself to Alleyn, commanded him instantly to return to the Countess, and bid her spurn the base compliance, as she feared to sacrifice both her children to the murderer of their father. At these words, a smile of haughty triumph marked the features of the Baron, and he turned from Osbert in silent joy and exultation. The Earl was led off by the guards. Alleyn endeavoured in vain to mark the way they took; the lofty walls soon concealed them from his view.

Alleyn now experienced how strenuously a vigorous mind protects its favourite hope; wayward circumstances may shock, disappointment may check it; but it rises superior to opposition and traverses the sphere of possibility to accomplish its purpose. Alleyn did not yet despair, but he was perplexed in what manner to proceed.

On his way from the ramparts, Osbert was surprized by the appearance of two ladies at a window near which he passed: the agitation of his mind did not prevent his recognizing them as the same he had observed from the grates of the tower, with such lively admiration, and who had excited in his mind so much pity and curiosity: In the midst of his distress, his thoughts had often dwelt on the sweet graces of the younger, and he had sighed to obtain the story of her sorrows; for the melancholy which hung upon her features proclaimed her to be unfortunate. They now stood observing Osbert as he passed, and their eyes expressed the pity which his situation inspired. He gazed earnestly and mournfully upon them, and when he entered his prison, again enquired concerning them, but the same inflexible silence was preserved on the subject.

As the Earl sat one day musing in his prison, his eyes involuntarily fixed upon a pannel in the opposite wainscot; — he observed that it was differently formed from the rest, and that its projection was somewhat greater; a hope started into his mind, and he quitted his seat to examine it. He perceived that it was surrounded by a small crack, and on pushing it with his hands it shook under them. Certain that it was something more than a pannel, he exerted all his strength against it, but without producing any new effect. Having tried various means to move it without success, he gave up the experiment, and returned to his seat melancholy and disappointed. Several days passed without any further notice being taken of the wainscot; unwilling, however, to relinquish a last hope, he returned to the examination, when, in endeavouring to remove the pannel, his foot accidentally hit against one corner, and it suddenly flew open. It had been contrived that a spring which was concealed within, and which fastened the partition, should receive its impulse from the pressure of a certain part of the pannel, which was now touched by the foot of the Earl. His joy on the discovery cannot be expressed. An apartment wide and forlorn, like that which formed his prison, now lay before him; the windows, which were high and arched, were decorated with painted glass; the floor was paved with marble; and it seemed to be the deserted remains of a place of worship. Osbert traversed, with hesitating steps, its dreary length, towards a pair of folding doors, large and of oak, which closed the apartment: these he opened; a gallery, gloomy and vast, appeared beyond; the windows, which were in the same style of Gothic architecture with the former, were shaded by thick ivy that almost excluded the light. Osbert stood at the entrance uncertain whether to proceed; he listened, but heard no footstep in his prison, and determined to go on. The gallery terminated on the left in a large winding stair-case, old and apparently neglected, which led to a hall below; on the right was a door, low, and rather obscure. Osbert, apprehensive of discovery, passed the staircase, and opened the door, when a suite of noble apartments, magnificently furnished, was disclosed to his wondering eyes. He proceeded onward without perceiving any person, but having passed the second room, heard the faint sobs of a person weeping; he stood for a moment, undetermined whether to proceed; but an irresistible curiosity impelled him forward, and he entered an apartment, in which were seated the beautiful strangers, whose appearance had so much interested his feelings. The elder of the ladies was dissolved in tears and a casket and some papers lay open on a table beside her. The younger was so intent upon a drawing, which she seemed to be finishing, as not to observe the entrance of the Earl; the elder lady, on perceiving him, arose in some confusion, and the surprize in her eyes seemed to demand an explanation of so unaccountable a visit. The Earl, surprized at what he beheld, stepped back with an intention of retiring; but recollecting that the intrusion demanded an apology, he returned. The grace with which he excused himself, confirmed the impression which his figure had already made on the mind of Laura, which was the name of the younger lady; who on looking up, discovered a countenance in which dignity and sweetness were happily blended. She appeared to be about twenty, her person was of the middle stature, extremely delicate, and very elegantly formed. The bloom of her youth was shaded by a soft and pensive melancholy, which communicated an expression to her fine blue eyes, extremely interesting. Her features were partly concealed by the beautiful luxuriance of her auburn hair, which curling round her face, descended in tresses on her bosom; every feminine grace played around her; and the simple dignity of her air declared the purity and the nobility of her mind. On perceiving the Earl, a faint blush animated her cheek, and she involuntarily quitted the drawing upon which she had been engaged.

If the former imperfect view he had caught of Laura had given an impression to the heart of Osbert, it now received a stronger character from the opportunity afforded him of contemplating her beauty. He concluded that the Baron, attracted by her charms, had entrapped her into his power, and detained her in the castle an unwilling prisoner. In this conjecture he was confirmed by the mournful cast of her countenance, and by the mystery which appeared to surround her. Fired by this idea, he melted in compassion for her sufferings; which compassion was tinctured and increased by the passion which now glowed in his heart. At that moment he forgot the danger of his present situation; he forgot even that he was a prisoner; and awake only to the wish of alleviating her sorrows, he rejected cold and useless delicacy, and resolved, if possible, to learn the cause of her misfortunes. Addressing himself to the Baroness, "if, Madam," said he, "I could by any means soften the affliction which I cannot affect not to perceive, and which has so warmly interested my feelings, I should regard this as one of the most happy moments of my life; a life marked alas! too strongly with misery! but misery has not been useless, since it has taught me sympathy." The Baroness was no stranger to the character and the misfortunes of the Earl. Herself the victim of oppression, she knew how to commiserate the sufferings of others. She had ever felt a tender compassion for the misfortunes of Osbert, and did not now with-hold sincere expressions of sympathy, and of gratitude, for the interest which he felt in her sorrow. She expressed her surprise at seeing him thus at liberty; but observing the chains which encircled his hands, she shuddered, and guessed a part of the truth. He explained to her the discovery of the pannel, by which circumstance he had found his way into that apartment. The idea of aiding him to escape, rushed upon the mind of the Baroness, but was repressed by the consideration of her own confined situation; and she was compelled, with mournful reluctance, to resign that thought which reverence for the character of the late Earl, and compassion for the misfortunes of the present, had inspired. She lamented her inability to assist him, and informed him that herself and her daughter were alike prisoners with himself; that the walls of the castle were the limits of their liberty; and that they had suffered the pressure of tyranny for fifteen years. The Earl expressed the indignation which he felt at this recital, and solicited the Baroness to confide in his integrity; and, if the relation would not be too painful to her, to honour him so far as to acquaint him by what cruel means she fell into the power of Malcolm. The Baroness, apprehensive for his safety reminded him of the risk of discovery by a longer absence from his prison; and, thanking him again for the interest he took in her sufferings, assured him of her warmest wishes for his deliverance, and that if an opportunity ever offered, she would acquaint him with the sad particulars of her story. The eyes of Osbert made known that gratitude which it was difficult for his tongue to utter. Tremulously he solicited the consolation of sometimes revisiting the apartments of the Baroness; a permission which would give him some intervals of comfort amid the many hours of torment to which he was condemned. The Baroness, in compassion to his sufferings, granted the request. The Earl departed, gazing on Laura with eyes of mournful tenderness; yet he was pleased with what had passed, and retired to his prison in one of those peaceful intervals which are known even to the wretched. He found all quiet, and closing the pannel in safety, sat down to consider the past, and anticipate the future. He was flattered with hopes, that the discovery of the pannel might aid him to escape; the glooms of despondence which had lately enveloped his mind, gradually disappeared, and joy once more illumined his prospects; but it was the sunshine of an April morn, deceitful and momentary. He recollected that the castle was beset with guards, whose vigilance was insured by the severity of the Baron; he remembered that the strangers, who had taken so kind an interest in his fate, were prisoners like himself; and that he had no generous soldier to teach him the secret windings of the castle, and to accompany him in flight. His imagination was haunted by the image of Laura; vainly he strove to disguise from himself the truth; his heart constantly belied the sophistry of his reasonings. Unwarily he had drank the draught of love, and he was compelled to acknowledge the fatal indiscretion. He could not, however, resolve to throw from his heart the delicious poison; he could not resolve to see her no more.

The painful apprehension for his safety, which his forbearing to renew the visit he had so earnestly solicited, would occasion the Baroness; the apparent disrespect it would convey; the ardent curiosity with which he longed to obtain the history of her misfortunes; the lively interest he felt in learning the situation of Laura, with respect to the Baron; and the hope, — the wild hope, with which he deluded his reason, that he might be able to assist them, determined him to repeat the visit. Under these illusions, the motive which principally impelled him to the interview was concealed.

In the mean time Alleyn had returned to the castle of Athlin with the resolutions of the Earl; whose resolves served only to aggravate the distress of its fair inhabitants. Alleyn, however, unwilling to crush a last hope, tenderly concealed from them the circumstance of the Earl's removal from the tower: silently and almost hopelessly meditating to discover his prison; and administered that comfort to the Countess, and to Mary, which his own expectation would not suffer him to participate. He retired in haste to the veterans whom he had before assembled, and acquainted them with the removal of the Earl; which circumstance must for the present suspend their consultations. He left them, therefore, and instantly returned to the clan: there to prosecute his enquiries. Every possible exertion was made to obtain the necessary intelligence, but without success. The moment in which the Baron would demand the answer of the Countess, was now fast approaching, and every heart sunk in despair, when one night the centinels of the camp were alarmed by the approach of men, who hailed them in unknown voices; fearful of surprize, they surrounded the strangers, and led them to Alleyn; to whom they related, that they fled from the capricious tyranny of Malcolm, and sought refuge in the camp of his enemy; whose misfortunes they bewailed, and in whose cause they enlisted. Rejoiced at the circumstance, yet doubtful of its truth, Alleyn interrogated the soldiers concerning the prison of the Earl. From them he learned, that Osbert was confined in a part of the castle extremely difficult of access; and that any plan of escape must be utterly impracticable without the assistance of one well acquainted with the various intricacies of the pile. An opportunity of success was now presented, with which the most sanguine hopes of Alleyn had never flattered him. He received from the soldiers strong assurance of assistance; from them, likewise, he learned, that discontent reigned, among the people of the Baron; who, impatient of the yoke of tyranny, only waited a favourable opportunity to throw it off, and resume the rights of nature. That the vigilant suspicions of Malcolm excited him to punish with the harshest severity every appearance of inattention; that being condemned to suffer a very heavy punishment for a slight offence, they had eluded the impending misery, and the future oppression of their Chief, by desertion.

Alleyn immediately convened a council, before whom the soldiers were brought; they repeated their former assertions; and one of the fugitives added, that he had a brother, whose place of guard over the person of the Earl on that night, had made it difficult to elude observation, and had prevented his escaping with them; that on the night of the morrow he stood guard at the gate of the lesser draw-bridge, where the centinels were few; that he was himself willing to risque the danger of conversing with him; and had little doubt of gaining him to assist in the deliverance of the Earl. At these words, the heart of Alleyn throbbed with joy. He promised large rewards to the brave soldier and to his brother, if they undertook the enterprize. His companion was well acquainted with the subterraneous passages of the rock, and expressed himself desirous of being useful. The hopes of Alleyn every instant grew stronger; and he vainly wished, at that moment, to communicate to the Earl's unhappy family the joy which dilated his heart.

The eve of the following day was fixed upon to commence their designs; when James should endeavour to gain his brother to their purpose. Having adjusted these matters, they retired to rest for the remainder of the night; but sleep had fled the eyes of Alleyn; anxious expectation filled his mind; and he saw, in the waking visions of fancy, the meeting of the Earl with his family: he anticipated the thanks he should receive from the lovely Mary; and sighed at the recollection, that thanks were all for which he could ever dare to hope.

At length the dawn appeared, and waked the clan to hopes and prospects far different from those of the preceding morn. The hours hung heavily on the expectation of Alleyn, whose mind was filled with solicitude for the event of the meeting between the brothers. Night at length came to his wishes. The darkness was interrupted only by the faint light of the moon moving through the watery and broken clouds, which enveloped the horizon. Tumultuous gusts of wind broke at intervals the silence of the hour. Alleyn watched the movements of the castle; he observed the lights successively disappear. The bell from the watch-tower chimed one; all was still within the walls; and James ventured forth to the draw-bridge. The draw-bridge divided in the center, and the half next the plains was down; he mounted it, and in a low yet firm voice called on Edmund. No answer was returned; and he began to fear that his brother had already quitted the castle. He remained some time in silent suspense before he repeated the call, when he heard the gate of the draw-bridge gently unbarred, and Edmund appeared. He was surprized to see James, and bade him instantly fly the danger that surrounded him. The Baron, incensed at the frequent desertion of his soldiers, had sent out people in pursuit, and had promised considerable rewards for the apprehension of the fugitives. James, undaunted by what he heard, kept his ground, resolved to urge his purpose to the point. Happily the centinels who stood guard with Edmund, overcome with the effect of a potion he had administered to favour his escape, were sunk in sleep, and the soldiers conducted their discourse in a low voice without interruption.

Edmund was unwilling to defer his flight, and possessed not resolution sufficient to encounter the hazard of the enterprize, till the proffered reward consoled his self-denial, and roused his slumbering courage. He was well acquainted with the subterraneous avenues of the castle; the only remaining difficulty, was that of deceiving the vigilance of his fellow-centinels, whose watchfulness made it impossible for the Earl to quit his prison unperceived. The soldiers who were to mount guard with him on the following night, were stationed in a distant part of the castle, till the hour of their removal to the door of the prison; it was, therefore, difficult to administer to them that draught which had steeped in forgetfulness the senses of his present associates. To confide to their integrity, and endeavour to win them to his purpose, was certainly to give his life into their hands, and probably to aggravate the disastrous fate of the Earl. This scheme was beset too thick with dangers to be hazarded, and their invention could furnish them with none more promising. It was, however, agreed, that on the following night, Edmund should seize the moment of opportunity to impart to the Earl the designs of his friends, and to consult on the means of accomplishing them. Thus concluding, James returned in safety to the tent of Alleyn, where the most considerable of the clan were assembled, there awaiting with impatient solicitude, his arrival. The hopes of Alleyn were somewhat chilled by the report of the soldier; from the vigilance which beset the doors of the prison, escape from thence appeared impracticable. He was condemned, however, to linger in suspense till the third night from the present, when the return of Edmund to his station at the bridge would enable him again

393

to commune with his brother. But Alleyn was unsuspicious of a circumstance which would utterly have defeated his hopes, and whose consequence threatened destruction to all their schemes. A centinel on duty upon that part of the rampart which surmounted the draw-bridge, had been alarmed by hearing the gate unbar, and approaching the wall, had perceived a man standing on the half of the bridge which was dropped, and in converse with some person on the castle walls. He drew as near as the wall would permit, and endeavoured to listen to their discourse. The gloom of night prevented his recognizing the person on the bridge; but he could clearly distinguish the voice of Edmund in that of the man who was addressed. Excited by new wonder, he gave all his attention to discover the subject of their conversation. The distance occasioned between the brothers by the suspended half of the bridge, obliged them to speak in a somewhat higher tone than they would otherwise have done; and the centinel gathered sufficient from their discourse, to learn that they were concerting the rescue of the Earl; that the night of Edmund's watch at the prison was to be the night of enterprize; and that some friends of the Earl were to await him in the environs of the castle. All this he carefully treasured up, and the next morning communicated it to his comrades.

On the following evening the Earl, yielding to the impulse of his heart, once more unclosed his partition, and sought the apartments of the Baroness. She received him with expressions of satisfaction; while the artless pleasure which lighted up the countenance of Laura, awakened the pulse of rapture in that heart which had long throbbed only to misery. The Earl reminded the Baroness of her former promise, which the desire of exciting sympathy in those we esteem, and the melancholy pleasure which the heart finds in lingering among the scenes of former happiness, had induced her to give. She endeavoured to compose her spirits, which were agitated by the remembrance of past sufferings, and gave him a relation of the following circumstances.

CHAPTER VII.

THLOUISA, Baroness Malcolm, was the descendant of an ancient and honourable house in Switzerland. Her father, the Marquis de St. Claire, inherited all those brave qualities, and that stern virtue, which had so eminently distinguished his ancestors. Early in life he lost a wife whom he tenderly loved, and he seemed to derive his sole consolation from the education of the dear children she had left behind. His son, whom he had brought up to the arms himself so honourably bore, fell before he reached his nineteenth year, in the service of his country; an elder daughter died in infancy; Louisa was his sole surviving child. His chateau was situated in one of those delightful vallies of the Swiss cantons, in which the beautiful and the sublime are so happily united; where the magnificent features of the scenery are contrasted, and their effect heightened by the blooming luxuriance of woods and pasturage, by the gentle winding of the stream, and the peaceful aspect of the cottage. The Marquis was now retired from the service, for grey age had overtaken him. His residence was the resort of foreigners of distinction, who, attracted by the united talents of the soldier and the philosopher, under his roof partook of the hospitality so characteristic of his country. Among the visitors of this description was the late Baron Malcolm, brother to the present Chief, who then travelled through Switzerland. The beauty of Louisa, embellished by the elegance of a mind highly cultivated, touched his heart, and he solicited her hand in marriage. The manly sense of the Baron, and the excellencies of his disposition, had not passed unobserved, or unapproved by the Marquis; while the graces of his person, and of his mind, had anticipated for him, in the heart of Louisa, a pre-eminence over every other suitor. The Marquis had but one objection to the marriage; this was likewise the objection of Louisa: neither the one nor the other could endure the idea of the distance which was to separate them. Louisa was to the Marquis the last prop of his declining years; the Marquis was to Louisa the father and the friend to whom her heart had hitherto been solely devoted, and from whom it could not now be torn but with an anguish equal to its attachment. This remained an insurmountable obstacle, till it was removed by the tenderness of the Baron, who entreated the Marquis to quit Switzerland, and reside with his daughter in Scotland. The attachment of the Marquis to his natal land, and the pride of hereditary dominion, was too powerful to suffer him to acquiesce in the proposal without much struggle of contending feelings. The desire of securing the happiness of his child, by a union with a character so excellent as the Baron's, and of seeing her settled before death should deprive her of the protection of a father, at length subdued every other

395

consideration, and he resigned the hand of his daughter to the Baron Malcolm. The Marquis adjusted his affairs, and consigning his estates to the care of trusty agents, bade a last adieu to his beloved country; that country which, during sixty years, had been the principal scene of his happiness, and of his regrets. The course of years had not obliterated from his heart the early affections of his youth: he took a sad farewell of that grave which enclosed the reliques of his wife, from which it was not his least effort to depart, and whither he ordered that his remains should be conveyed. Louisa quitted Switzerland with a concern scarcely less acute than that of her father; the poignancy of which, however, was greatly softened by the tender assiduities of her Lord, whose affectionate attentions hourly heightened her esteem, and encreased her love.

They arrived at Scotland without any accident, where the Baron welcomed Louisa as the mistress of his domains. The Marquis de St. Claire had apartments in the castle, where the evening of his days declined in peaceful happiness. Before his death, he had the pleasure of seeing his race renewed in the children of the Baroness, in a son who was called by the name of the Marquis, and in a daughter who now shared with her mother the sorrows of confinement. On the death of the Marquis it was necessary for the Baron to visit Switzerland, in order to take possession of his estates, and to adjust some affairs which a long absence had deranged. He attended the remains of the Marquis to their last abode. The Baroness, desirous of once more beholding her native country, and anxious to pay a last respect to the memory of her father, entrusted her children to the care of a faithful old servant, whom she had brought with her from the Vallois, and who had been the nurse of her early childhood, and accompanied the Baron to the continent. Having deposited the remains of the Marquis according to his wish in the tomb of his wife, and arranged their affairs, they returned to Scotland, where the first intelligence they received on their arrival at the castle, was of the death of their son, and of the old nurse his attendant. The servant had died soon after their departure; the child only a fortnight before their return. This disastrous event affected equally the Baron and his lady, who never ceased to condemn herself for having entrusted her son to the care of servants. Time, however subdued the poignancy of this affliction, but came fraught with another yet more acute; this was the death of the Baron, who, in the pride of youth, constituting the felicity of his family, and of his people, was killed by a fall from his horse, which he received in hunting. He left the Baroness and an only daughter to bewail with unceasing sorrow his loss.

The paternal estates devolved of course to his only brother, the present Baron, whose character formed a mournful and striking contrast to that of the deceased Lord. All his personal property, which was considerable, with the estates in Switzerland, he bequeathed to his beloved wife and daughter. The new Baron, immediately on the demise of his brother, took possession of the castle, but allowed the Baroness, with a part of her suit, to remain its inhabitant till the expiration of the year. The Baroness, absorbed in grief, still loved to recall, in the scene of her late felicity, the image of her Lord, and to linger in his former haunts. This motive, together with the necessity of preparation for a journey to Switzerland, induced her to accept the offer of the Baron.

The memory of his brother had quickly faded from the mind of Malcolm, whose attention appeared to be wholly occupied by schemes of avarice and ambition. His arrogance, and boundless love of power, embroiled him with the neighbouring Chiefs, and engaged him in continual hostility. He seldom visited the Baroness; when he did, his manner was cold, and even haughty. The Baroness, shocked to receive such treatment from the brother of her deceased Lord, and reduced to feel herself an unwelcome guest in that castle which she had been accustomed to consider as her own, determined to set off for the continent immediately, and seek, in the solitudes of her native mountains, an asylum from the frown of insulting power. The contrast of character between the brothers drew many a sigh of bitter recollection from her heart, and added weight to the sorrows which already oppressed it. She gave orders, therefore, to her domestics, to prepare for immediate departure; but was soon after told that the Baron had forbade them to obey the command. Astonished at this circumstance, she had not time to demand an explanation, ere a message from Malcolm required a few moments private conversation. The messenger was followed almost instantly by the Baron, who entered the apartment with hurried steps, his countenance overspread with the dark purposes of his soul. "I come, Madam," said he, in a voice stern and determined, "to inform you, that you quit not this castle. The estates which you call yours, are mine; and; think not that I shall neglect to prosecute my claim. The frequent and ill-timed generosities of my brother, have diminished the value of the lands which are mine by inheritance; and I have therefore an indispensable right to repay myself from those estates which he acquired with you. In point of justice, he possessed not the right of devising these estates, and I shall not suffer myself to be deceived by the evasions of the law; resign, therefore, the will, which remains only a record of unjust wishes, and ineffectual claims. When the receipts from your estates have satisfied my demands, they shall again be yours. The apartments you now inhabit shall remain your own; but beyond the wall of this castle you shall not pass; for I will not, by suffering your departure, afford you an opportunity of contesting those rights which I can enforce without opposition."

Overcome with astonishment and dread, the Baroness was for some time deprived of all power of reply. At length, roused by the spirit of indignation, "I am too well informed, my Lord," said she, "of my just claims to the lands in question; and know also too well the value of that integrity which is now no more, to credit your bold assertions; they serve only to unveil to me the darkness of a character, cruel and rapacious; whose boundless avarice, trampling on the barriers of justice and humanity, seizes on the right of the defenceless widow, and on the portion of the unresisting orphan. This, my Lord, you are permitted to do; they have no means of resistance; but think not to impose on me by a sophistical assertion of right, or to gloss the villainy of your conduct with the colours of justice; the artifice is beneath the desperate force of your character, and is not sufficiently specious to deceive the discernment of virtue. From being your prisoner I have no means of escaping; but never, my Lord, will I resign into your hands that will which is the efficient bond of my rights, and the last sad record of the affection of my departed Lord." Grief closed her lips. The Baron denouncing vengeance on her resistance, his features inflamed with rage, quitted the apartment. The Baroness was left to lament, with deepening anguish, the stroke which had deprived her of a beloved husband; and reflection gave her the wretchedness of her situation in yet more lively colours. She was now a stranger in a foreign land, deprived by him, of whom she had a right to demand protection, of all her possessions; a prisoner in his castle, without one friend to vindicate her cause, and far remote from any means of appeal to the laws of the country. She wept over the youthful Laura, and while she pressed her with mournful fondness to her bosom, she was confirmed in her resolution never to relinquish that will, by which alone the rights of her injured child could ever be ascertained.

The Baron, bold in iniquity, obtained, by forged powers, the revenues of the foreign estates; and by this means, effectually kept the Baroness in his power, and deprived her of her last resource. Secure in the possession of the estates, and of the Baroness, he no longer regarded the will as an object of importance; and as she did not attempt any means of escape, or the recovery of her rights, he suffered her to remain undisturbed, and in quiet possession of the will.

The Baroness now passed her days in unvaried sorrow, except in those intervals when she forced her mind from its melancholy subject, and devoted herself to the education of her daughter. The artless efforts of Laura, to assuage the sorrows of her mother, only fixed them in her heart in deeper impression, since they gave to her mind, in stronger tints, the cruelty and oppression to which her tender years were condemned. The progress which she made in music and drawing, and in the lighter subjects of literature, while it pleased the Baroness, who was her sole instructress, brought with it the bitter apprehension, that these accomplishments would probably be buried in the obscurity of a prison; still, however, they were not useless, since they served at present to cheat affliction of many a weary moment, and would in future delude the melancholy hours of solitude. Laura was particularly fond of the lute, which she touched with exquisite sensibility, and whose tender notes were so sweetly in unison with the chords of sorrow, and with those plaintive tones with which she loved to accompany it. While she sung, the Baroness would sit absorbed in recollection, the tears fast falling from her eyes, and she might be said to taste in those moments the luxury of woe.

Malcolm, stung with a sense of guilt, avoided the presence of his injured captive, and sought an asylum from conscience in the busy scenes of war.

Eighteen years had now elapsed since the death of the Baron, and the confinement of Louisa. Time had blunted the point of affliction, though it still retained its venom; but she seldom dared to hope for that which for eighteen years had been with-held. She derived her only consolation from the improvement and the tender sympathy of her daughter, who endeavoured, by every soothing attention, to alleviate the sorrows of her parent.

It was at this period that the Baroness communicated to the Earl the story of her calamities.

The Earl listened with deep attention to the recital. His soul burned with indignation against the Baron, while his heart gave to the sufferings of the fair mourners all that sympathy could ask. Yet he was relieved from a very painful sensation, when he learned that the beauty of Laura had not influenced the conduct of the Baron. Her oppressed situation struck upon his heart the finest touch of pity; and the passion which her beauty and her simplicity had inspired, was strengthened and meliorated by her misfortunes. The fate of his father, and the idea of his own injuries, rushed upon his mind; and, combining with the

399

sufferings of the victims now before him, roused in his soul a storm of indignation, little inferior to that he had suffered in his first interview with the Baron. Every consideration sunk before the impulse of a just revenge; his mind, occupied with the hateful image of the murderer was hardened against danger, and in the first energies of his resentment he would have rushed to the apartment of Malcolm, and striking the sword of justice in his heart, have delivered the earth from a monster, and have resigned himself the willing sacrifice of the action. "Shall the monster live?" cried he, rising from his seat. His step was hurried, and his countenance was stamped with a stern virtue. The Baroness was alarmed, and following him to the door of her apartment, which he had half opened, conjured him to pause for a moment on the dangers that surrounded him. The voice of reason, in the accents of the Baroness, interrupted the hurried tumult of his soul; the illusions of passion disappeared; he recollected that he was ignorant of the apartment of the Baron, and that he had no weapon to assist his purpose; and he found himself as a traveller on enchanted ground, when the wand of the magician suddenly dissolves the airy scene, and leaves him environed with the horrors of solitude and of darkness.

The Earl returned to his seat hopeless and dejected, and lost to every thing but to the bitterness of disappointment. He forgot where he was, and the lateness of the hour, till reminded by the Baroness of the dangers of a longer stay, when he mournfully bade her good night; and advancing to Laura with timid respect, pressed her hand tenderly to his lips, and retired to his prison.

CHAPTER VIII.

HE had now opened the partition, and was entering the room, when by the faint gleam which the fire threw across the apartment, he perceived indistinctly the figure of a man, and in the same instant heard the sound of approaching armour. Surprize and horror thrilled through every nerve; he remained fixed to the spot, and for some moments hesitated whether to retire. A fearful silence ensued; the person whom he thought he had seen, disappeared in the darkness of the room; the noise of armour was heard no more; and he began to think that the figure he had seen, and the sound he had heard were the phantoms of a sick imagination, which the agitation of his spirits, the solemnity of the hour, and the wide desolation of the place, had conjured up. The low sounds of an unknown voice now started upon his ear; it seemed to be almost close beside him; he sprung onward, and his hand grasped the steely coldness of armour, while the arm it enclosed struggled to get free. "Speak! what wretch art thou?" cried Osbert, when a sudden blaze of light from the fire discovered to him a soldier of the Baron. His agitation for some time prevented his observing that there was more of alarm than of design expressed in the countenance of the man; but the apprehension of the Earl was quickly lost in astonishment, when he beheld the guard at his feet. It was Edmund who had entered the prison under pretense of carrying fuel to the fire, but secretly for the purpose of conferring with Osbert. When the Earl understood he came from Alleyn, his bosom glowed with gratitude towards that generous youth, whose steady and active zeal had never relaxed since the hour in which he first engaged in his cause. The transport of his heart may be easily imagined, when he learned the schemes that were planning for his deliverance. The circumstance which had nearly defeated the warm hopes of his friends, was by him disregarded, since the knowledge of the secret door opened to him, with the assistance of a guide through the intricacies of the castle, a certain means of escape. Edmund was well acquainted with all these. The Earl told him of the discovery of the false panel; bade him return to Alleyn with the joyful intelligence, and on his next night of watch prepare to aid him in escape. Edmund knew well the apartments which Osbert described, and the great staircase which led into a part of the castle that had long been totally forsaken, and from whence it was easy to pass unobserved into the vaults which communicated with the subterraneous passages in the rock.

Alleyn heard the report of James with a warm and generous joy, which impelled him to hasten immediately to the castle of Athlin, and dispel the sorrows that inhabited there; but the consideration that his sudden absence from the camp might create suspicion, and invite discovery, checked the impulse; and he yielded with reluctance to the necessity which condemned the Countess and Mary to the horrors of a lengthened suspense.

The Countess, meanwhile, whose designs, strengthened by the steady determination of Mary, were unshaken by the message of the Earl, which she considered as only the effect of a momentary impulse, watched the gradual departure of those days which led to that which enveloped the fate of her children, with agony and fainting hope. She received no news from the camp; no words of comfort from Alleyn; and she saw the confidence which had nourished her existence slowly sinking in despair. Mary sought to administer that comfort to the afflictions of her mother, which her own equally demanded; she strove, by the fortitude with which she endeavoured to resign herself, to soften the asperity of the sufferings which threatened the Countess, and she contemplated the approaching storm with the determined coolness of a mind aspiring to virtue as the chief good. But she sedulously sought to exclude Alleyn from her mind; his disinterested and noble conduct excited emotions dangerous to her fortitude, and which rendered yet more poignant the tortures of the approaching sacrifice.

Anxious to inform the Baroness of his approaching deliverance, to assure her of his best services, to bid adieu to Laura, and to seize the last opportunity he might ever possess of disclosing to her his admiration and his love, the Earl revisited the apartments of the Baroness. She felt a lively pleasure on the prospect of his escape; and Laura, in the joy which animated her on hearing this intelligence, forgot the sorrows of her own situation; forgot that of which her heart soon reminded her-that Osbert was leaving the place of her confinement, and that she should probably see him no more. This thought cast a sudden shade over her features, and from the enlivening expression of joy, they resumed their wonted melancholy. Osbert marked the momentary change, and his heart spoke to him the occasion. "My cup of joy is dashed with bitterness," said he, "for amid the happiness of approaching deliverance, I quit not my prison without some pangs of keen regret; — pangs which it were probably useless to make known, yet which my feeling will not suffer me at this moment to conceal. Within these walls, from whence I fly with eagerness, I leave a heart fraught with the most tender passion; a heart which, while it beats with life, must ever unite the image of Laura with the fondness of love. Could I hope that she were not insensible to my attachment I should depart in peace, and would defy the obstacles which bid me despair. Were I even certain that she would repel my love with cold indifference, I would yet, if she accept my services, effect her rescue, or give my life the forfeiture." Laura was silent; she wished to speak her gratitude, yet feared to tell her love; but the soft timidity of her eye, and the tender glow of her cheek, revealed the secret that trembled on her lips. The Baroness observed her confusion, and thanking the Earl for the noble service he offered, declined accepting it. She besought him to involve no further the peace of his family and of himself, by attempting an enterprize so crowded with dangers, and which might probably cost him his life. The arguments of the Baroness fell forceless when opposed to the feelings of the Earl; so warmly he urged his suit, and dwelt so forcibly on his approaching departure, that the Baroness ceased to oppose, and the silence of Laura yielded acquiescence. After a tender farewell, with many earnest wishes for his safety, the Earl quitted the apartment elated with hope. But the Baron had been informed of his projected escape, and had studied the means of counteracting it. The centinel had communicated his discovery to some of his comrades, who, without virtue or courage sufficient to quit the service of the Baron, were desirous of obtaining his favour and failed not to seize on an opportunity so flattering as the present, to accomplish their purpose they communicated to their Chief the intelligence they had received.

Malcolm, careful to conceal his knowledge of the scheme, from a design to entrap those of the clan who were to meet the Earl, had suffered Edmund to return to his station at the prison, where he had placed the informers as secret guards, and had taken such other precautions as were necessary to intercept their flight, should they elude the vigilance of the soldiers, and likewise to secure those of his people who should be drawn toward the castle in expectation of their Chief. Having done this, he prided himself in security, and in the certainty of exulting over his enemies, thus entangled in their own stratagem.

After many weary moments of impatience to Alleyn, and of expectation to the Earl, the night at length arrived on which hung the event of all their hopes. It was agreed that Alleyn, with a chosen few, should await the arrival of the Earl in the cavern where terminated the subterraneous avenue. Alleyn parted from James with extreme agitation, and returned to his tent to compose his mind.

It was now the dead of night; profound sleep reigned through the castle of Dunbayne, when Edmund gently unbolted the prison door, and hailed the Earl. He sprung forward, and instantly unclosed the pannel, which they fastened after them to prevent discovery, and passing with fearful steps the cold and silent apartments, descended the great staircase into the hall, whose wide and dark desolation was rendered visible only by the dim light of the taper which Edmund carried in his hand, and whose vaulted ceiling re-echoed their steps. After various windings they descended into the vaults; in passing their dreary length they often paused in fearful silence, listening to the hollow blasts which burst suddenly through the passages, and which seemed to bear in the sound the footsteps of pursuit. At length they reached the extremity of the vaults, where Edmund searched for a trapdoor which lay almost concealed in the dirt and darkness; after some time they found, and with difficulty raised it, for it was long since it had been opened; and it was besides heavy with iron work. They entered, and letting the door fall after them, descended a narrow flight of steps which conducted them to a winding passage closed by a door that opened into the main avenue whence Alleyn had before made his escape. Having gained this, they stepped on with confidence, for they were now not far from the cavern where Alleyn and his companions were awaiting their arrival. The heart of Alleyn now swelled with joy, for he perceived a gleam of distant light break upon the walls of the avenue, and at the same time thought he heard the faint sound of approaching footsteps. Impatient to throw himself at the feet of the Earl, he entered the avenue. The light grew stronger upon the walls; but a point of rock, whose projection caused a winding in the passage, concealed from his view the persons his eyes so eagerly sought. The sound of steps was now fast approaching, and Alleyn gaining the rock, suddenly turned upon three soldiers of the Baron. They instantly seized him their prisoner. Astonishment for a while overcame every other sensation; but as they led him along, the horrid reverse of the moment struck upon his heart with all its consequences, and he had no doubt that the Earl had been seized and carried back to his prison. As he marched along, absorbed in this reflection, a light appeared at some distance, from a door that opened upon the avenue, and discovered the figures of two men, who on perceiving the party, they retreated with precipitation, and closed the door after them. Alleyn knew the Earl in the person of one of them. Two of the soldiers quitting Alleyn, pursued the fugitives, and quickly disappeared through a door. Alleyn finding himself alone with the guard, seized the moment of opportunity, and made a desperate effort to regain his sword. He succeeded; and in the suddenness of the attack, obtained also the weapon of his adversary, who, unarmed, fell at his feet, and called for mercy. Alleyn gave him his life. The soldier, grateful for the gift, and fearful of the Baron's vengeance, desired to fly with him, and enlist in his service. They quitted the subterraneous way together. On entering the cavern, Alleyn found it vacated by his friends, who on hearing the clash of armour, and the loud and menacing voices of the soldiers, understood his fate, and apprehensive of numbers, had fled to avoid a similar disaster. Alleyn returned to his tent, shocked with disappointment, and lost in despair. Every effort which he had made for the deliverance of the Earl, had proved unsuccessful; and this scheme, on which was suspended his last hope, had been defeated at the very moment when he exulted in its completion. He threw himself on the ground, and lost in bitter thought, observed not the curtain of his tent undraw, till recalled by a sudden noise, he looked up, and beheld the Earl. Terror fixed him to the spot, and for a moment he involuntarily acknowledged the traditionary visions of his nation. The well-known voice of Osbert, however, awakened him to truth, and the ardor with which he embraced his knees, immediately convinced him that he clasped reality.

The soldiers, in the eagerness of pursuit, had mistaken the door by which Osbert had retired, and had entered one below it, which, after engaging them in a fruitless search through various intricate passages, had conducted them to a remote part of the castle, from whence, after much perplexity and loss of time, they were at length extricated. The Earl, who had retreated on sight of the soldiers, had fled in the mean time to regain the trap-door; but the united strength of himself and of Edmund was in vain exerted to open it. Compelled to encounter the approaching evil, the Earl took the sword of his companion, resolving to meet the approach of his adversaries, and to effect his deliverance, or yield his life and his misfortunes to the attempt. With this design he advanced deliberately along the passage, and arriving at the door, stopped to discover the motions of his pursuers: all was profoundly silent. After remaining some time in this situation, he opened the door, and examining the avenue with a firm yet anxious eye as far as the light of his taper threw its beams, discovered no human being. He proceeded with cautious firmness towards the cavern, every instant expecting the soldiers to start suddenly upon him from some dark recess. — With astonishment he reached the cave without interruption; and unable to account for his unexpected deliverance, hastened with Edmund to join his faithful people.

The soldiers who watched the prison, being ignorant of any other way by which the Earl could escape, than the door which they guarded, had suffered Edmund to enter the apartment without fear. It was some time before they discovered their error; surprized at the length of his stay, they opened the door of the prison, which to their utter astonishment, they found empty. The grates were examined; they remained as usual; every corner was explored; but the false pannel remained unknown; and having finished their examination without discovering any visible means by which the Earl had quitted the prison, they were seized with terror, concluding it to be the work of a supernatural power, and immediately alarmed the castle. The Baron, roused by the tumult, was informed of the fact, and dubious of the integrity of his guards, ascended to the apartment; which having himself examined without discovering any means of escape, he no longer hesitated to pronounce the centinels accessary to the Earl's enlargement. The unfeigned terror which they exhibited was mistaken for artifice, and their supposed treachery was admitted and punished in the same moment. They were thrown into the dungeon of the castle. Soldiers were immediately dispatched in pursuit; but the time which had elapsed ere the guards had entered the prison, had given the Earl an opportunity of escape. When the certainty of this was communicated to the Baron, every passion whose single force is misery, united in his breast to torture him; and his brain, exasperated almost to madness, gave him only direful images of revenge.

The Baroness and Laura, awakened by the tumult, had been filled with apprehension for the Earl, till they were informed of the cause of the general confusion; and hope and dubious joy were ere long confirmed into certainty, for they were told of the fruitless search of the pursuers.

It was now the last day of the term in which the Countess had stipulated to return her answer; she had yet heard nothing from Alleyn; for Alleyn had been busied in schemes, of the event of which he could send no account, for their success had been yet undetermined. Every hope of the Earl's deliverance was now expired, and in the anguish of her heart, the Countess prepared to give that answer which would send the devoted Mary to the arms of the murderer. Mary, who assumed a fortitude not her own, strove to abate the rigor of her mother's sufferings, but vainly strove; they were of a nature which defied consolation. She wrote the fatal agreement, but delayed till the last moment delivering it into the hands of the messenger. It was necessary, however, that the Baron should receive it on the following morn, lest the impatience of revenge should urge him to seize on the life of the Earl as the forfeiture of delay. She sent, therefore, for the messenger, who was a veteran of the clan, and with extreme agitation delivered to him her answer; grief interrupted her voice; she was unable to speak to him; and he was awaiting her orders, when the door of the apartment was thrown open, and the Earl, followed by Alleyn, threw himself at her feet. A faint scream was uttered by the Countess, and she sunk in her chair. Mary, not daring to trust herself with the delightful vision, endeavoured to restrain the tide of joy, which hurried to her heart, and, threatened to overwhelm her.

The castle of Athlin resounded with tumultuous joy on this happy event; the courts were filled with those of the clan who had been disabled from attending the field, and whom the report of the Earl's return, which had circulated with astonishing rapidity, had brought thither. The hall re-echoed with voices; and the people could hardly be restrained from rushing into the presence of their Chief, to congratulate him on his escape.

When the first transports of the meeting were subsided, the Earl presented Alleyn to his family as his friend and deliverer; whose steady attachment he could never forget, and whose zealous service he could never repay. The cheek of Mary glowed with pleasure and gratitude at this tribute to the worth of Alleyn; and the smiling approbation of her eyes rewarded him for his noble deeds. The Countess received him as the deliverer of both her children, and related to Osbert the adventure in the wood. The Earl embraced Alleyn, who received the united acknowledgments of the family, with unaffected modesty. Osbert hesitated not to pronounce the Baron the author of the plot; his heart swelled to avenge the repeated injuries of his family, and he secretly resolved to challenge the enemy to single combat. To renew the siege he considered as a vain project; and this challenge, though a very inadequate mode of revenge, was the only honourable one that remained for him. He forbore to mention his design to the Countess, well knowing that her tenderness would oppose the measure, and throw difficulties in his way, which would embarrass, without preventing his purpose. He mentioned the misfortunes of the Baroness, and the loveliness of her daughter, and excited the esteem and the commiseration of his hearers.

The clamours of the people to behold their Lord, now arose to the apartment of the Countess, and he descended into the hall, accompanied by Alleyn, to gratify their zeal. An universal shout of joy resounded through the walls on his appearance. A noble pleasure glowed on the countenance of the Earl at sight of

407

his faithful people; and in the delight of that moment his heart bore testimony to the superior advantages of an equitable government. The Earl, impatient to testify his gratitude, introduced Alleyn to the clan, as his friend and deliverer, and immediately presented his father with a lot of land, where he might end his days in peace and plenty. Old Alleyn thanked the Earl for his offered kindness, but declined accepting it; alleging, that he was attached to his old cottage, and that he had already sufficient for the comforts of his age.

On the following morning, a messenger was privately dispatched to the Baron, with the challenge of the Earl. The challenge was couched in terms of haughty indignation, and expressed, that nothing but the failure of all other means could have urged him to the condescension of meeting the assassin of his father, on terms of equal combat.

Happiness was once more restored to Athlin. The Countess, in the unexpected preservation of her children, seemed to be alive only to joy. The Earl was now for a time secure in the bosom of his family, and, though his impatience to avenge the injuries of those most dear to him, and to snatch from the hand of oppression the fair sufferers at Dunbayne, would not allow him to be tranquil, yet he assumed a gaiety unknown to his heart, and the days were spent in festivals and joy.

CHAPTER IX.

IT was at this period, that, one stormy evening, the Countess was sitting with her family in a room, the windows of which looked upon the sea. The winds burst in sudden squalls over the deep, and dashed the foaming waves against the rocks with inconceivable fury. The spray, notwithstanding the high situation of the castle, flew up with violence against the windows. The Earl went out upon the terrace beneath to contemplate the storm. The moon shone faintly by intervals, through broken clouds upon the waters, illumining the white foam which burst around, and enlightening the scene sufficiently to render it visible. The surges broke on the distant shores in deep resounding murmurs, and the solemn pauses between the stormy gusts filled the mind with enthusiastic awe. As the Earl stood wrapt in the sublimity of the scene, the moon, suddenly emerging from a heavy cloud, shewed him at some distance a vessel driven by the fury of the blast towards the coast. He presently heard the signals of distress; and soon after shrieks of terror, and a confused uproar of voices were borne on the wind. He hastened from the terrace to order his people to go out with boats to the assistance of the crew, for he doubted not that the vessel was wrecked; but the sea ran so high as to make the adventure impracticable. The sound of voices ceased, and he concluded that the wretched mariners were lost, when the screams of distress again struck his ear, and again were lost in the tumult of the storm; in a moment after, the vessel struck upon the rock beneath the castle; an universal shriek ensued. The Earl, with his people, hastened to the assistance of the crew; the fury of the gust was now abated, and the Earl, jumping into a boat with Alleyn and some others, rowed to the ship, where they rescued a part of the drowning people. They were conducted to the castle, and every comfort was liberally administered to them. Among those, whom the Earl had received into his boat, was a stranger, whose dignified aspect and manners bespoke him to be of rank; he had several people belonging to him, but they were foreigners, and ignorant of the language of the country. He thanked his deliverer with a noble frankness, that charmed him. In the hall they were met by the Countess and her daughter, who received the stranger with the warm welcome, which compassion for his situation had inspired. He was conducted to the supper room, where the magnificence of the board exhibited only the usual hospitality of his host. The stranger spoke English fluently, and displayed in his conversation a manly and vigorous mind, acquainted with the sciences, and with life; and the cast of his observations seemed to characterize the benevolence of his heart. The Earl was so much pleased with his guest, that he pressed him to remain at his castle till another vessel could be procured; his guest equally pleased with the Earl, and a stranger to the country, accepted the invitation.

New distress now broke upon the peace of Athlin; several days had expired, and the messenger, who had been sent to Malcolm, did not appear. It was almost evident, that the Baron, disappointed and enraged at the escape of his prisoner, and eager for a sacrifice, had seized this man as the subject of a paltry revenge. The Earl, however, resolved to wait a few days, and watch the event.

The struggles of latent tenderness and assumed indifference, banished tranquillity from the bosom of Mary, and pierced it with many sorrows. The friendship and honours bestowed by the Earl on Alleyn, who now resided solely at the castle, touched her heart with a sweet pride; but alas! these distinctions served only to confirm her admiration of that worth, which had already attached her affections, and afforded him opportunities of exhibiting, in brighter colours, the various excellencies of a heart noble and expansive, and of a mind, whose native elegance meliorated and adorned the bold vigour of its flights. The langour of melancholy, notwithstanding the efforts of Mary, would at intervals steal from beneath the disguise of cheerfulness, and diffuse over her beautiful features an expression extremely interesting. The stranger was not insensible to its charms, and it served to heighten the admiration, with which he had first beheld her, into something more tender and more powerful. The modest dignity, with which she delivered her sentiments, which breathed the purest delicacy and benevolence, touched his heart, and he felt an interest concerning her, which he had never before experienced.

Alleyn, whose heart amid the anxieties and tumults of the past scenes, had still sighed to the image of Mary; — that image, which fancy had pictured in all the charms of the original, and whose glowing tints were yet softened and rendered more interesting by the shade of melancholy with which absence and a hopeless passion had surrounded them, found, amid the leisure of peace, and the frequent opportunities which were afforded him of beholding the object of his attachment, his sighs redouble, and the glooms of sorrow thicken. In the presence of Mary, a soft sadness clouded his brow; he endeavoured to assume a cheerfulness foreign to his heart; but endeavoured in vain. Mary perceived the change in his manners; and the observation did not contribute to enliven her own. The Earl, too, observed that Alleyn had lost much of his wonted spirits, and bantered him on the change, but thought not of his sister.

Alleyn wished to quit a place so destructive to his peace as the castle of Athlin; he formed repeated resolutions of withdrawing himself from those walls, which held him in a sort of fascination, and rendered ineffectual every half-formed wish, and every weak endeavour. When he could no longer behold Mary, he would frequently retire to the terrace, which was overlooked by the windows of her apartment, and spend half the night in traversing, with silent, mournful steps, that spot, which afforded him the melancholy pleasure of being near the object of his love.

Matilda wished to question Alleyn concerning some circumstances of the late events, and for this purpose ordered him one day to attend her in her closet. As he passed the outer apartment of the Countess, he perceived something lying near the door, through which she had before gone, and, examining it, discovered a bracelet, to which was attached a miniature of Mary. His heart beat quick at the sight; the temptation was too powerful to be resisted; he concealed it in his bosom, and passed on. On quitting the closet, he sought, with breathless impatience, a spot, where he might contemplate at leisure that precious portrait, which chance had so kindly thrown in his way. He drew it trembling from his bosom, and beheld again that countenance, whose sweet expression had touched his heart with all the delightful agonies of love. As he pressed it with impassioned tenderness to his lips, the tear of rapture trembled in his eye, and the romantic ardour of the moment was scarcely heightened by the actual presence of the beloved object, whose light step now stole upon his ear, and half turning he beheld not the picture, but the reality! — Surprized! — confused! — The picture fell from his hand. Mary, who had accidentally strolled to that spot, on observing the agitation of Alleyn, was retiring, when he, in whose heart had been awakened every tender sensation, losing in the temptation of the moment the fear of disdain, and forgetting the resolution which he had formed of eternal silence, threw himself at her feet, and pressed her hand to his trembling lips. His tongue would have told her that he loved, but his emotion, and the repulsive look of Mary, prevented him. She instantly disengaged herself with an air of offended dignity, and casting on him a look of mingled anger and concern, withdrew in silence. Alleyn remained fixed to the spot; his eyes pursuing her retiring steps, insensible to every feeling but those of love and despair. So absorbed was he in the transition of the moment, that he almost doubted whether a visionary illusion had not crossed his sight to blast his only remaining comfort-the consciousness of deserving, and of possessing the esteem of her he loved. He left the place with anguish in his heart, and, in the

411

perturbation of his mind, forgot the picture.

Mary had observed her mother's bracelet fall from his hand, and was no longer in perplexity concerning her miniature; but in the confusion which his behavior occasioned her, she forgot to demand it of him. The Countess had missed it almost immediately after his departure from the closet, and had caused a search to be made, which proving fruitless, her suspicions wavered upon him. The Earl, who soon after passed the spot whence Alleyn had just departed, found the miniature. It was not long ere Alleyn recollected the treasure he had dropped, and returned in search of it. Instead of the picture, he found the Earl: a conscious blush crossed his cheek; the confusion of his countenance informed Osbert of a part of the truth; who, anxious to know by what means he had obtained it, presented him the picture, and demanded if he knew it. The soul of Alleyn knew not to dissemble; he acknowledged that he had found, and concealed it; prompted by that passion, the confession of which, no other circumstance than the present could have wrung from his heart. The Earl listened to him with a mixture of concern and pity; but hereditary pride chilled the warm feelings of friendship and of gratitude, and extinguished the faint spark of hope which the discovery had kindled in the bosom of Alleyn. "Fear not, my Lord," said he, "the degradation of your house from one who would sacrifice his life in its defence; never more shall the passion which glows in my heart escape from my lips. I will retire from the spot where I have buried my tranquillity." "No," replied the Earl, "you shall remain here; I can confide in your honour. O! that the only reward which is adequate to your worth and to your services, it should be impossible for me to bestow." His voice faultered, and he turned away to conceal his emotion, with a suffering little inferior to that of Alleyn.

The discovery which Mary had made, did not contribute to restore peace to her mind. Every circumstance conspired to assure her of that ardent passion which filled the bosom of him whom all her endeavours could not teach her to forget; and this conviction served only to heighten her malady, and consequently her wretchedness.

The interest which the stranger discovered, and the attention he paid to Mary, had not passed unobserved by Alleyn. Love pointed to him the passion which was rising in his heart, and whispered that the vows of his rival would be propitious. The words of Osbert confirmed him in the torturing apprehension; for though his humble birth had never suffered him to hope, yet he thought he discovered in the speech of the Earl, something more than mere hereditary pride.

The stranger had contemplated the lovely form of Mary with increasing admiration, since the first hour he beheld her; this admiration was now confirmed into love; — and he resolved to acquaint the Earl with his birth, and with his passion. For this purpose, he one morning drew him aside to the terrace of the castle, where they could converse without interruption; and pointing to the ocean, over which he had so lately been borne, thanked the Earl, who had thus softened the horrors of shipwreck, and the desolation of a foreign land, by the kindness of his hospitality. He informed him that he was a native of Switzerland, where he possessed considerable estates, from which he bore the title of Count de Santmorin; that enquiry of much moment to his interests had brought him to Scotland, to a neighbouring port of which he was bound, when the disaster from which he had been so happily rescued, arrested the progress of his designs. He then related to the Earl, that his voyage was undertaken upon a report of the death of some relations, at whose demise considerable estates in Switzerland became his inheritance. That the income of these estates had been hitherto received upon the authority of powers, which, if the report was true, were become invalid.

The Earl listened to this narrative in silent astonishment, and enquired, with much emotion, the name of the Count's relations. "The Baroness Malcolm," returned he. The Earl clasped his hands in extasy. The Count, surprized at his agitation, began to fear that the Earl was disagreeably interested in the welfare of his adversaries, and regretted that he had disclosed the affair, till he observed the pleasure which was diffused through his features. Osbert explained the cause of his emotion, by relating his knowledge of the Baroness; in the progress of whose story, the character of Malcolm was sufficiently elucidated. He told the cause of his hatred towards the Baron, and the history of his imprisonment; and also confided to his honour the secret of his challenge.

The indignation of the Count was strongly excited; he was, however, prevailed on by Osbert to forego any immediate effort of revenge, awaiting for awhile the movements of Malcolm.

The Count was so absorbed in wonder and in new sensations, that he had almost forgot the chief object of the interview. Recollecting himself, he discovered his passion, and requested permission of the Earl to throw himself at the feet of Mary. The Earl listened to the declaration with a mixture of pleasure and concern; the remembrance of Alleyn saddened his mind; but the wish of an equal connection, made him welcome the offers of the Count, whose alliance, he told him, would do honour to the first nobility of his nation. If he found the sentiments of his sister in sympathy with his own on this point, he would welcome him to his family with the affection of a brother; but he wished to discover the situation of her heart, ere his noble friend disclosed to her his prepossession.

The Earl on his return to the castle enquired for Mary, whom he found in the apartment of her mother. He opened to them the history of the Count; his relationship with the Baroness Malcolm, with the object of his expedition, and closed the narrative with discovering the attachment of his friend to Mary, and his offers of alliance with his family. Mary grew pale at this declaration; there was a pang in her heart which would not suffer her to speak; she threw her eyes on the ground, and burst into tears. The Earl took her hand tenderly in his; "My beloved sister," said he, "knows me too well to doubt my affection, or to suppose I can wish to influence her upon a subject so material to her future happiness; and where her heart ought to be the principal directress. Do me the justice to believe, that I make known to you the offers of the Count as a friend, not as a director. He is a man, who from the short period of our acquaintance, I have judged to be deserving of particular esteem. His mind appears to be noble; his heart expansive; his rank is equal with your own; and he loves you with an attachment warm and sincere. But with all these advantages, I would not have my sister give herself to the man who does not meet an interest in her heart to plead his cause."

The gentle soul of Mary swelled with gratitude towards her brother; she would have thanked him for the tenderness of these sentiments, but a variety of emotions were struggling at her heart, and suppressed her utterance; tears and a smile, softly clouded with sorrow, were all she could give him in reply. He could not but perceive that some secret cause of grief preyed upon her mind, and he solicited to know, and to remove it. "My dear brother will believe the gratitude which his kindness-" She would have finished the sentence, but the words died away upon her lips, and she threw herself on the bosom of her mother, endeavouring to conceal her distress, and wept in silence. The Countess too well understood the grief of her daughter; she had witnessed the secret struggles of her heart, which all her endeavours were not able to overcome, and which rendered the offers of the Count disgusting, and dreadful to her imagination. Matilda knew how to feel for her sufferings; but the affection of the mother extended her views beyond the present temporary evil, to the future welfare of her child; and in the long perspective of succeeding years, she beheld her united to the Count, whose character diffused happiness, and the mild dignity of virtue to all around him: she received the thanks of Mary for her gentle guidance to the good she possessed; the artless looks of the little ones around her, smiled their thanks; and the luxury of that scene recalled the memory of times for ever passed, and mingled with the tear of rapture the sigh of fond regret. The surest method of erasing that impression which threatened serious evil to the peace of her child if suffered to continue, and to secure her permanent felicity, was to unite her to the Count; whose amiable disposition would soon win her affections, and obliterate from her heart every improper remembrance of Alleyn. She determined, therefore, to employ argument and gentle persuasion, to guide her to her purpose. She knew the mind of Mary to be delicate and candid; easy of conviction, and firm to pursue what her judgment approved; and she did not despair of succeeding.

The Earl still pressed to know the cause of that emotion which afflicted her. "I am unworthy of your solicitude," said Mary, "I cannot teach my heart to submit." "To submit! — Can you suppose your friends can wish your heart to submit on a point so material to its happiness, to aught that is repugnant to its feelings? If the offers of the Count are displeasing to you, tell me so; and I will return him his answer. Believe that my first wish is to see you happy." "Generous Osbert! How can I repay the goodness of such a brother! I would accept in gratitude the hand of the Count, did not my feelings assure me I should be miserable. I admire his character, and esteem his goodness; but alas! — why should I conceal it from you? — My heart is another's-is another's, whose noble deeds have won its involuntary regards; and who is yet unconscious of my distinction, one who shall for ever remain in ignorance of it." The idea of Alleyn flashed into the mind of the Earl, and he no longer doubted to whom her heart was engaged. "My own sentiments," said he, "sufficiently inform me of the object of your admiration. You do well to remember the dignity of your sex and of your rank; though I must lament with you, that worth like Alleyn's is not empowered by fortune to take its standard with nobility." At Alleyn's name, the blushes of Mary confirmed Osbert in his discovery. "My child," said the Countess, "will not resign her tranquillity to a vain and ignoble attachment. She may esteem merit wherever it is found, but she will remember the duty which she owes to her family and to herself, in contracting an alliance which is to support or diminish the ancient consequence of her house. The offers of a man endowed with so much apparent excellence as the Count, and whose birth is equal to your own, affords a prospect too

415

promising of felicity, to be hastily rejected. We will hereafter converse more largely on this subject." "Never shall you have reason to blush for your daughter," said Mary, with a modest pride; "but pardon me, Madam, if I entreat that we no more renew a subject so painful to my feelings, and which cannot be productive of good; — for never will I give my hand where my heart does not accompany it." This was not a time to press the topic; the Countess for the present desisted, and the Earl left the apartment with a heart divided between pity and disappointment. Hope, however, whispered to his wishes, that Mary might in time be induced to admit the addresses of the Count, and he determined not wholly to destroy his hopes.

CHAPTER X.

THE Count was walking on the ramparts of the castle, involved in thought, when Osbert approached; whose lingering step and disappointed air spoke to his heart the rejection of his suit. He told the Count that Mary did not at present feel for him those sentiments of affection which would justify her in accepting his proposals. This information, though it shocked the hopes of the Count, did not entirely destroy them; for he yet believed that time and assiduity might befriend his wishes. While these Noblemen were leaning on the walls of the castle, engaged in earnest conversation, they observed on a distant hill a cloud emerging from the verge of the horizon, whose dusky hue glittered with sudden light; in an instant they descried the glance of arms, and a troop of armed men poured in long succession over the hill, and hurried down its side to the plains below. The Earl thought he recognized the clan of the Baron. It was the Baron himself who now advanced at the head of his people, in search of that revenge which had been hitherto denied him; and who, determined on conquest, had brought with him an host which he thought more than sufficient to overwhelm the castle of his enemy.

The messenger, who had been sent with the challenge, had been detained a prisoner by Malcolm; who in the mean time had hastened his preparations to surprize the castle of Athlin. The detention of his servant had awakened the suspicions of the Earl, and he had taken precautions to guard against the designs of his enemy. He had summoned his clan to hold themselves in readiness for a sudden attack, and had prepared his castle for the worst emergency. He now sent a messenger to the clan with such orders as he judged expedient, arranged his plans within the walls, and took his station on the ramparts to observe the movements of his enemy. The Count, clad in arms, stood by his side. Alleyn was posted with a party within the great gate of the castle.

The Baron advanced with his people, and quickly surrounded the walls. Within all was silent; the castle seemed to repose in security; and the Baron, certain of victory, congratulated himself on the success of the enterprize, when observing the Earl, whose person was concealed in armour, he called to him to surrender himself and his Chief to the arms of Malcolm. The Earl answered the summons with an arrow from his bow, which missing the Baron, pierced one of his attendants. The archers who had been planted behind the walls, now discovered themselves, and discharged a shower of arrows; at the same time every part of the castle appeared thronged with the soldiers of the Earl, who hurled on the heads of the astonished besiegers, lances and other missile weapons with unceasing rapidity. The alarum bell now rung out the signal to that part of the clan without the walls, and they immediately poured upon the enemy, who, confounded by this unexpected attack, had scarcely time to defend themselves. The clang of arms resounded through the air, with the shouts of the victors, and the groans of the dying. The fear of the Baron, which had principally operated on the minds of his people, was now overcome by surprize, and the fear of death; and on the first repulse, they deserted from the ranks in great numbers, and fled to the distant hills. In vain the Baron endeavoured to rally his soldiers, and keep them to the charge; they yielded to a stronger impulse than the menace of their Chief, who was now left with less than half his number at the foot of the walls. The Baron, to whom cowardice was unknown, disdaining to retreat, continued the attack. At length the gates of the castle were thrown open, and a party issued upon the assailants, headed by the Earl and the Count, who divided in quest of Malcolm. The Count fought in vain, and the search of Osbert was equally fruitless; their adversary was no where to be found. Osbert, apprehensive of his gaining admittance to the castle by stratagem, was returning in haste to the gates, when he received the stroke of a sword upon his shoulder; his armour had broke the force of the blow, and the wound it had given was slight. He turned his sword, and facing his enemy, discovered a soldier of Malcolm's who attacked him with a desperate courage. The encounter was furious and long; dexterity and equal valour seemed to animate both the combatants. Alleyn, who observed from his post the danger of the Earl, flew instantly to his assistance; but the crisis of the scene was past ere he arrived; the weapon of Osbert had pierced the side of his adversary, and he fell to the ground. The Earl disarmed him, and holding over him his sword, bade him ask his life. "I have no life to ask," said Malcolm, whose fainting voice the Earl now discovered, "if I had, 'tis death only I would accept from you. O! cursed-" He would have finished the sentence, but his wound flowed apace, and he fainted with loss of blood. The Earl threw down his sword, and calling a party of his people, he committed to them the care of the Baron, and ordered them to proceed and seize the castle of Dunbayne. Understanding their Chief was mortally wounded, the remains of Malcolm's army had fled from the walls. The people of the Earl proceeded without interruption, and took possession of the castle without opposition.

The wounds of the Baron were examined when he reached Dunbayne, and a dubious sentence of the event was pronounced. His countenance marked the powerful workings of his mind, which seemed labouring with an unknown evil; he threw his eyes eagerly round the apartment, as if in search of some object which was not present. After several attempts to speak, "Flatter me not," said he, "with hopes of life; it is flitting fast away; but while I have breath to speak, let me see the Baroness." She came, and hanging over his couch in silent horror, received his words: "I have injured you, Madam, I fear beyond reparation. In these last few moments let me endeavour to relieve my conscience by discovering to you my guilt and my remorse." The Baroness started, fearful of the coming sentence. "You had a son." "What of my son?" "You had a son, whom my boundless ambition doomed to exile from his parents and his heritage, and who I caused you to believe died in your absence." "Where is my child!" exclaimed the Baroness. "I know not," resumed Malcolm, "I committed him to the care of a man and woman who then lived on a remote part of my lands, but a few years after they disappeared, and I have never heard of them since. The boy passed for a foundling whom I had saved from perishing. One servant only I entrusted with the secret; the rest were imposed upon. Thus far I tell you, Madam, to prompt you to enquiry, and to assuage the agonies of a bleeding conscience. I have other deeds-" The Baroness could hear no more; she was carried insensible from the apartment. Laura, shocked at her condition, was informed of its cause, and filial tenderness watched over her with unwearied attention.

In the mean time the Earl, on quitting Malcolm, had returned immediately to the castle, and was the first messenger of that event which would probably avenge the memory of his father, and terminate the distresses of his family. The sight of Osbert, and the news he brought, revived the Countess and Mary, who had retired during the assault into an inner apartment of the castle for greater security, and who had suffered, during that period, all the terrors which their situation could inspire. They were soon after joined by the Count and by Alleyn, whose conduct did not pass unnoticed by the Earl. The cheek of Mary glowed at the relation of this new instance of his worth; and it was Alleyn's sweet reward to observe her emotion. There was a sentiment in the heart of Osbert which struggled against the pride of birth; he wished to reward the services and the noble spirit of the youth, with the virtues of Mary; but the authority of early prejudice silenced the grateful impulse, and swept from his heart the characters of truth.

The Earl, accompanied by the Count, now hastened to the castle of Dunbayne, to cheer the Baroness and her daughter with their presence. As they approached the castle, the stillness and desolation of the scene bespoke the situation of its lord; his people were entirely dispersed, a few only of his centinels wandered before the eastern gate; who, having made no opposition, were suffered by the Earl's people to remain. Few of the Baron's people were to be seen; those few were unarmed, and appeared the effigies of fallen greatness. As the Earl crossed the platform, the remembrance of the past crowded upon his mind. The agonies which he had there suffered, — the image of death which glared upon his sight, aggravated by the bitter and ignominious circumstances which attended his fate; the figure of Malcolm, mighty in injustice, and cruel in power; whose countenance, smiling horribly in triumphant revenge, sent to his heart the stroke of anguish; — each circumstance of torture arose to his imagination in the glowing colours of truth; he shuddered as he passed; and the contrast of the present scene touched his heart with the most affecting sentiments. He saw the innate and active power of justice, which pervades all the circumstances even of this life like vital principle, and shines through the obscurity of human actions to the virtuous, the pure ray of Heaven; — to the guilty, the destructive glare of lightning.

On enquiring for the Baroness, they were told she was in the apartment of Malcolm, whose moment of dissolution was now approaching. The name of the Count was delivered to the Baroness, and overheard by the Baron, who desired to see him. Louisa went out to receive her noble relation with all the joy which a meeting so desirable and so unlooked for, could inspire. On seeing Osbert, her tears flowed fast, and she thanked him for his generous care, in a manner that declared a deep sense of his services. Leaving him, she conducted the Count to Malcolm, who lay on his couch surrounded with the stillness and horrors of death. He raised his languid head, and discovered a countenance wild and terrific, whose ghastly aspect was overspread with the paleness of death. The beauteous Laura, overcome by the scene, hung like a drooping lily over his couch, dropping fast her tears. "My lord," said Malcolm, in a low tone, "you see before you a wretch, anxious to relieve the agony of a guilty mind. My vices have destroyed the peace of this lady, — have robbed her of a son-but she will disclose to you the secret guilt, which I have now no time to tell: I have for some years received, as you now well know, the income of those foreign lands which are her due; as a small reparation for the injuries she has sustained, I bequeath to her all the possessions which I lawfully inherit, and resign her into your protection. To ask oblivion of the past of you, Madam, and of you, my Lord, is what I dare not do; yet it would be some consolation to my departing spirit, to be assured of your forgiveness." The Baroness was too much affected to reply but by a look of assent; the Count assured him of forgiveness, and besought him to compose his mind for his approaching fate. "Composure, my Lord, is not for me; my Life has been marked with vice, and my death with the bitterness of fruitless remorse. I have understood virtue, but I have loved vice. I do not now lament that I am punished, but that I have deserved punishment." The Baron sunk on his couch, and in a few moments after expired in a strong sigh. Thus terminated the life of a man, whose understanding might have reached the happiness of virtue, but whose actions displayed the features of vice.

From this melancholy scene, the Baroness, with the Count and Laura, retired to her apartment, where the Earl awaited their return with anxious solicitude. The sternness of justice for a moment relaxed when he heard of Malcolm's death; his heart would have sighed with compassion, had not the remembrance of his father crossed his mind, and checked the impulse. "I can now, Madam," said he, addressing the Baroness, "restore you a part of those possessions which were once your Lord's, and which ought to have been the inheritance of your son; this castle from henceforth is yours; I resign it to its lawful owner." The Baroness was overcome with the remembrance of his services, and could scarcely thank him but with her tears. The servant whom the Baron had mentioned as the confidant of his iniquities, was sent for, and interrogated concerning the infant he had charge of. From him, however, little comfort was received; for he could only tell that he had conveyed the child, by the orders of his master, to a cottage on the furthest borders of his estates, where he had delivered it to the care of a woman, who there lived with her husband. These people received at the same time a sum of money for its support, with a promise of future supplies. For some years he had been punctual in the payment of the sums entrusted to him by the Baron, but at length he yielded to the temptation of withholding them for his own use; and on enquiring for the people some years after, he found they were gone from the place. The conditions of the Baroness's pardon to the man depended on his endeavours to repair the injury he had promoted, by a strict search for the people to whom he had committed her child. She now consulted with her friends on the best means to be pursued in this business, and immediately sent off messengers to different parts of the country to gather information.

The Baroness was now released from oppression and imprisonment; she was reinstated in her ancient possessions, to which were added all the hereditary lands of Malcolm, together with his personal fortune: she was surrounded by those whom she most loved, and in the midst of a people who loved her; yet the consequence of the Baron's guilt had left in her heart one drop of gall which embittered each source of happiness, and made her life melancholy and painful.

The Count was now her visitor; she was much consoled by his presence; and Laura's hours were often enlivened by the conversation of the Earl, to whom her heart was tenderly attached, and whose frequent visits to the castle were devoted to love and her.

The felicity of Matilda now appeared as perfect and as permanent as is consistent with the nature of sublunary beings. Justice was done to the memory of her Lord, and her beloved son was spared to bless the evening of her days. The father of Laura had ever been friendly to the house of Athlin, and her delicacy felt no repugnance to the union which Osbert solicited. But her happiness, whatever it might appear, was incomplete; she saw the settled melancholy of Mary, for love still corroded her heart and notwithstanding her efforts, shaded her countenance. The Countess wished to produce those nuptials with the Count which she thought would re-establish the peace of her child, and insure her future felicity. She omitted no opportunity of pressing his suit, which she managed with a delicacy that rendered it less painful to Mary; whose words, however, were few in reply, and who could seldom bear that the subject should ever be long continued. Her settled aversion to the addresses of the Count, at length baffled the expectations of Matilda, and shewed her the fallacy of her efforts. She thought it improper to suffer the Count any longer to nourish in his heart a vain hope; and she reluctantly commissioned the Earl to undeceive him on this point.

With the Baroness, month after month still elapsed in fruitless search of her son; the people with whom he had been placed were no where to be found, and no track was discovered which might lead to the truth. The distress of the Baroness can only be imagined; she resigned herself, in calm despair, to mourn in silence the easy confidence which had entrusted her child to the care of those who had betrayed him. Though happiness was denied her, she was unwilling to withhold it from those whom it awaited; and at length yielded to the entreaties of the Earl, and became its advocate with Laura, for the nuptials which were to unite their fate.

The Earl introduced the Countess and Mary to the castle of Dunbayne. Similarity of sentiment and disposition united Matilda and the Baroness in a lasting friendship. Mary and

Laura were not less pleased with each other. The dejection of the Count at sight of Mary, declared the ardour of his passion, and would have awakened in her breast something more than compassion, had not her heart been pre-occupied. Alleyn, who could think of Mary only, wandered through the castle of Athlin a solitary being, who fondly haunts the spot where his happiness lies buried. His prudence formed resolutions, which his passion as quickly broke; and cheated by love, though followed by despair, he delayed his departure from day to day, and the illusion of yesterday continued to be the illusion of the morrow. The Earl, attached to his virtues, and grateful for his services, would have bestowed on him every honour but that alone which could give him happiness, and which his pride would have suffered him to accept. Yet the honours which he refused, he refused with a grace so modest, as to conciliate kindness rather than wound generosity.

In a gallery on the North side of the castle, which was filled with pictures of the family, hung a portrait of Mary. She was drawn in the dress which she wore on the day of the festival, when she was led by the Earl into the hall, and presented as the partner of Alleyn. The likeness was striking, and expressive of all the winning grace of the original. As often as Alleyn could steal from observation, he retired to this gallery, to contemplate the portrait of her who was ever present to his imagination: here he could breath that sigh which her presence restrained, and shed those tears which her presence forbade to flow. As he stood one day in this place wrapt in melancholy musing, his ear was struck with the notes of sweet music; they seemed to issue from the bottom of the gallery. The instrument was touched with an exquisite expression, and in a voice whose tones floated on the air in soft undulations, he distinguished the following words, which he remembered to be an ode composed by the Earl, and presented to Mary, who had set it to music the day before.

MORNING

Darkness! through thy chilling glooms
Weakly trembles twilight grey;
Twilight fades-and Morning comes,
And melts thy shadows swift away!

She comes in her Atherial car,
Involv'd in many a varying hue;
And thro' the azure shoots afar,
Spirit-light-and life anew!

Her breath revives the drooping flowers,
Her ray dissolves the dews of night;
Recalls the sprightly-moving hours.
And the green scene unveils in light!

Her's the fresh gale that wanders wild
O'er mountain top, and dewy glade;
And fondly steals the breath, beguil'd,
Of ev'ry flow'r in every shade.

Mother of Roses-bright Aurora! — hail!
Thee shall the chorus of the hours salute,
And song of early birds from ev'ry vale,
And blithesome horn, and fragrant zephyr mute!

And oft as rising o'er the plain,
Thou and thy roseate Nymphs appear,
This simple song in choral strain,
From rapturing Bards shall meet thine ear.

CHORUS

Dance ye lightly-lightly on!
'Tis the bold lark thro' the air,
Hails your beauties with his song;
Lightly-lightly fleeting fair!

Entranced in the sweet sounds, he had proceeded some steps down the gallery, when the music ceased. He stopped. After a short pause it returned, and as he advanced he distinguished these words, sung in a low voice mournfully sweet:

In solitude I mourn thy reign,

Ah! youth beloved-but loved in vain!

The voice was broken and lost in sobs; the chords of the lute were wildly struck: and in a few moments silence ensued. He stepped on towards the spot whence the sounds had proceeded, and through a door which was left open, he discovered Mary hanging over her lute dissolved in tears. He stood for some moments absorbed in mute admiration, and unobserved by Mary, who was lost in her tears, till a sigh which escaped him, recalled her to reality; she raised her eyes, and beheld the object of her secret sorrows. She arose in confusion; the blush on her cheek betrayed her heart; she was retiring in haste from Alleyn, who remained at the entrance of the room the statue of despair, when she was intercepted by the Earl, who entered by the door she was opening; her eyes were red with weeping; he glanced on her a look of surprize and displeasure, and passed on to the gallery followed by Alleyn, who was now awakened from his trance. "From you Alleyn," said the Earl, in a tone of displeasure, "I expected other conduct; on your word I relied, and your word has deceived me." "Hear me, my Lord," returned the youth, "your confidence I have never abused; hear me." "I have now no time for parley," replied Osbert, "my moments are precious; some future hour of leisure may suffice." So saying, he walked away, with an abrupt haughtiness, which touched the soul of Alleyn, who disdained to pursue him with further explanation. He was now completely wretched. The same accident which had unveiled to him the heart of Mary, and the full extent of that happiness which fate with-held, confirmed him in despair. The same accident had exposed the delicacy of her he loved to a cruel shock, and had subjected his honour to suspicion; and to a severe rebuke from him, by whom it was his pride to be respected, and for whose safety he had suffered imprisonment, and encountered death.

Mary had quitted the closet distressed and perplexed. She perceived the mistake of the Earl, and it shocked her. She wished to undeceive him; but he was gone to the castle of Dunbayne, to pay one of those visits which were soon to conclude in the nuptials, and whence he did not return till evening. The scene which he had witnessed in the morning, involved him in tumult of distress. He considered the mutual passion which filled the bosom of his sister and Alleyn; he had surprized them in a solitary apartment; he had observed the tender and melancholy air of Alleyn, and the tears and confusion of Mary; and he at first did not hesitate to believe that the interview had been appointed. In the heat of his displeasure he had rejected the explanation of Alleyn with a haughty resentment, which the late scene alone could have excited, and which the delusion it had occasioned alone could excuse. Cooler consideration however, brought to his mind the delicacy and the amiable pride of Mary, and the integrity of Alleyn; and he accused himself of a too hasty decision. The zealous services of Alleyn came to his heart; he repented that he had treated him so rigorously; and on his return enquired for him, that he might hear an explanation, and that he might soften the asperity of his former behaviour.

CHAPTER XI.

ALLEYN was no where to be found. The Earl went himself in quest of him, but without success. As he returned from the terrace, chagrined and disappointed, he observed two persons cross the platform at some distance before him; and he could perceive by the dim moon-light which fell upon the spot, that they were not of the castle. He called to them: no answer was returned; but at the sound of his voice they quickened their pace and almost instantly disappeared in the darkness of the ramparts. Surprized at this phenomenon, the Earl followed with hasty steps, and endeavoured to pursue the way they had taken. He walked on silently, but there was no sound to direct his steps. When he came to the extremity of the rampart, which formed the North angle of the castle, he stopped to examine the spot, and to listen if any thing was stirring. No person was to be seen, and all was hushed. After he had stood some time surveying the rampart, he heard the low restrained voice of a person unknown, but the distance prevented his distinguishing the subject of the conversation. The voice seemed to approach the place where he stood. He drew his sword, and watched in silence their motions. They continued to advance, till, suddenly stopping, they turned, and took a long survey of the fabric. Their discourse was conducted in a low tone; but the Earl could discover by the vehemence of their gesture, and the caution of their steps, that they were upon some design dangerous to the peace of the castle. Having finished their examination, they turned again towards the place where the Earl still remained; the shade of a high turret concealed him from their view, and they continued to approach till they arrived within a short space of him, when they turned through a ruined arch-way of the castle, and were lost in the dark recesses of the pile. Astonished at what he had seen, Osbert hastened to the castle, whence he dispatched some of his people in search of the unknown fugitives; he accompanied some of his domestics to the spot where they had last disappeared. They entered the arch-way, which led to a decayed part of the castle; they followed over broken pavement the remains of a passage, which was closed by a low obscure door almost concealed from sight by the thick ivy which overshadowed it. On opening this door, they descended a flight of steps which led under the castle, so extremely narrow and broken as to make the descent both difficult and dangerous. The powerful damps of long pent-up vapours extinguished their light, and the Earl and his attendants were compelled to remain in utter darkness, while one of them went round to the habitable part of the castle to relume the lamp. While they awaited in silence the return of light, a short breathing was distinctly heard at intervals, near the place where they stood.

427

The servants shook with fear, and the Earl was not wholly unmoved. They remained entirely silent, listening its return, when a sound of footsteps slowly stealing through the vault, startled them. The Earl demanded who passed; — he was answered only by the deep echoes of his voice. They clashed their swords and had advanced, when the steps hastily retired before them. The Earl rushed forward, pursuing the sound, till overtaking the person who fled, he seized him; a short scuffle ensued; the strength of Osbert was too powerful for his antagonist, who was nearly overcome, when the point of a sword from an unknown hand pierced his side, he relinquished his grasp, and fell to the ground. His domestics, whom the activity of their master had outran, now came up; but the assassins, whoever they were, had accomplished their escape, for the sound of their steps was quickly lost in the distance of the vaults. They endeavored to raise the Earl, who lay speechless on the ground; but they knew not how to convey him from that place of horror, for they were yet in total darkness, and unacquainted with the place. In this situation, every moment of delay seemed an age. Some of them tried to find their way to the entrance, but their efforts were defeated by the darkness, and the ruinous situation of the place. The light at length appeared, and discovered the Earl insensible, and weltering in his blood. He was conveyed into the castle, where the horror of the Countess on seeing him borne into the hall, may be easily imagined. By the help of proper applications he was restored to life; his wound was examined, and found to be dangerous; he was carried to bed in a state which gave very faint hopes of recovery. The astonishment of the Countess, on hearing the adventure, was equalled only by her distress. All her conjectures concerning the designs, and the identity of the assassin, were vague and uncertain. She knew not on whom to fix the stigma; nor could discover any means by which to penetrate this mysterious affair. The people who had remained in the vaults to pursue the search, now returned to Matilda. Every recess of the castle, and every part of the ramparts, had been explored, yet no one could be found; and the mystery of the proceeding was heightened by the manner in which the men had effected their escape.

Mary watched over her brother in silent anguish, yet she strove to conceal her distress, that she might encourage the Countess to hope. The Countess endeavoured to resign herself to the event with a kind of desperate fortitude. There is a certain point of misery, beyond which the mind becomes callous, and acquires a sort of artificial calm. Excess of misery may be said to blast the vital powers of feeling, and by a natural consequence consumes its own principle. Thus it was with Matilda; a long succession of trials had reduced her to a state of horrid tranquillity, which followed the first shock of the present event. It was not so with Laura; young in misfortune, and gay in hope, she saw happiness fade from her grasp, with a warmth of feeling untouched by the chill of disappointment. When the news of the Earl's situation reached her, she was overcome with affliction, and pined in silent anguish. The Count hastened to Osbert, but grief sat heavy at his heart, and he had no power to offer to others the comfort which he wanted himself.

A fever, which was the consequence of his wounds, added to the danger of the Earl, and to the despair of his family. During this period, Alleyn had not been seen at the castle; and his absence at this time, raised in Mary a variety of distressing apprehensions. Osbert enquired for him, and wished to see him. The servant who had been sent to his father's cottage, brought word that it was some days since he had been there, and that nobody knew whither he was gone. The surprize was universal; but the effect it produced was various and opposite. A collection of strange and concomitant circumstances, now forced a suspicion on the mind of the Countess, which her heart, and the remembrance of the former conduct of Alleyn, at once condemned. She had heard of what passed between the Earl and him in the gallery; his immediate absence, the event which followed, and his subsequent flight, formed a chain of evidence which compelled her, with the utmost reluctance, to believe him concerned in the affair which had once more involved her house in misery. Mary had too much confidence in her knowledge of his character, to admit a suspicion of this nature. She rejected, with instant disdain, the idea of uniting Alleyn with dishonour; and that he should be guilty of an action so base as the present, soared beyond all the bounds of possibility. Yet she felt a strange solicitude concerning him, and apprehension for his safety tormented her incessantly. The anguish in which he had quitted the apartment, her brother's injurious treatment, and his consequent absence, all conspired to make her fear that despair had driven him to commit some act of violence on himself.

The Earl, in the delirium of the fever, raved continually of Laura and of Alleyn; they were the sole subjects of his ramblings. Seizing one day the hand of Mary, who sat mournfully by his bed-side, and looking for some time pensively in her face, "weep not, my Laura," said he, "Malcolm, nor all the powers on earth shall tear you from me; his walls-his guards-what are they? I'll wrest you from his hold, or perish. I have a friend whose valour will do much for us; — a friend-O! name him not; these are strange times; beware of trusting. I could have given him my very life-but not-I will not name him."

429

Then starting to the other side of the bed, and looking earnestly towards the door with an expression of sorrow not to be described, "not all the miseries which my worst enemy has heaped upon me; not all the horrors of imprisonment and death, have ever touched my soul with a sting so sharp as thy unfaithfulness." Mary was so much shocked by this scene, that she left the room and retired to her own apartment to indulge the agony of grief it occasioned.

The situation of the Earl grew daily more alarming; and the fever, which had not yet reached its crisis, kept the hopes and fears of his family suspended. In one of his lucid intervals, addressing himself to the Countess in the most pathetic manner, he requested, that as death might probably soon separate him for ever from her he most loved, he might see Laura once again before he died. She came, and weeping over him, a scene of anguish ensued too poignant for description. He gave her his last vows; she took of him a last look; and with a breaking heart tearing herself away, was carried to Dunbayne in a state of danger little inferior to his.

The agitation he had suffered during this interview, caused a return of phrenzy more violent than any fit he had yet suffered; exhausted by it, he at length sunk into a sleep, which continued without interruption for near four and twenty hours. During this time his repose was quiet and profound, and afforded the Countess and Mary, who watched him alternately, the consolations of hope. When he awoke he was perfectly sensible, and in a very altered state from that he had been in a few hours before. The crisis of the disorder was now past, and from that time it rapidly declined till he was restored to perfect health.

The joy of Laura, whose health gradually returned with returning peace, and that of his family, was such as the merits of the Earl deserved. This joy, however, suffered a short interruption from the Count of Santmorin, who, entering one morning the apartment of the Baroness, with letters in his hand, came to acquaint her that he had just received news of the death of a distant relation, who had bequeathed him some estates of value, to which it was necessary he should immediately lay claim; and that he was, therefore, obliged, however reluctantly, to set off for Switzerland without delay. Though the Baroness rejoiced with all his friends, at his good fortune, she regretted, with them, the necessity of his abrupt departure. He took leave of them, and particularly of Mary, for whom his passion was still the same, with much emotion; and it was some time ere the space he had left in their society was filled up, and ere they resumed their wonted cheerfulness.

Preparations were now making for the approaching nuptials, and the day of their celebration was at length fixed. The ceremony was to be performed in a chapel belonging to the castle of Dunbayne, by the chaplain of the Baroness. Mary only was to attend as bride-maid; and the Countess also, with the Baroness, was to be present. The absence of the Count was universally regretted; for from his hand the Earl was to have received his bride. The office was now to be supplied by a neighbouring Laird, whom the family of the Baroness had long esteemed. At the earnest request of Laura, Mary consented to spend the night preceding the day of marriage, at the castle of Dunbayne. The day so long and so anxiously expected by the Earl at length arrived. The morning was extremely fine, and the joy which glowed in his heart seemed to give additional splendour to the scene around him. He set off, accompanied by the Countess, for the castle of Dunbayne. He anticipated the joy with which he should soon retrace the way he then travelled, with Laura by his side, whom death alone could then separate from him. On their arrival they were received by the Baroness, who enquired for Mary; and the Countess and Osbert were thrown into the utmost consternation, when they learned that she had not been seen at the castle. The nuptials were again deferred; the castle was a scene of universal confusion. The Earl returned home instantly to dispatch his people in search of Mary. On enquiry, he learned that the servants who had attended her, had not been heard of since their departure with their lady. Still more alarmed by this intelligence he rode himself in pursuit, yet not knowing which course to take. Several days were employed in a fruitless search; no footstep of her flight could be traced.

CHAPTER XII.

MARY, in the mean time, suffered all the terror which her situation could excite. On her way to Dunbayne, she had been overtaken by a party of armed men, who seized her bridle, and after engaging her servants in a feigned resistance, carried her off senseless. On recovering, she found herself travelling through a forest, whose glooms were deepened by the shades of night. The moon, which was now up, glancing through the trees, served to shew the dreary aspect of the place, and the number of men who surrounded her; and she was seized with a terror that almost deprived her of reason. They travelled all night, during which a profound silence was observed. At the dawn of day she found herself on the skirts of a heath, to whose wide desolation her eye could discover no limits. Before they entered on the waste, they halted at the entrance of a cave, formed in a rock, which was overhung with pine and fir; where, spreading their breakfast on the grass, they offered refreshments to Mary, whose mind was too much distracted to suffer her to partake of them. She implored them in the most moving accents, to tell her from whom they came, and whither they were carrying her; but they were insensible to her tears and her entreaties, and she was compelled to await, in silent terror, the extremity of her fate. They pursued their journey over the wilds, and towards the close of day approached the ruins of an abbey, whose broken arches and lonely towers arose in gloomy grandeur through the obscurity of evening. It stood the solitary inhabitant of the waste, — a monument of mortality and of ancient superstition, and the frowning majesty of its aspect seemed to command silence and veneration. The chilly dews fell thick, and Mary, fatigued in body, and harassed in mind, lay almost expiring on her horse, when they stopped under an arch of the ruin. She was not so ill as to be insensible to the objects around her; the awful solitude of the place and the solemn aspect of the fabric, whose effect was heightened by the falling glooms of evening, chilled her heart with horror; and when they took her from the horse, she shrieked in the agonies of a last despair. They bore her over loose stones to a part of the building, which had been formerly the cloisters of the abbey, but which was now fallen to decay, and overgrown with ivy. There was, however, at the extremity of these cloisters a nook, which had withstood with hardier strength the ravages of time; the roof was here entire, and the shattered stanchions of the casements still remained. Hither they carried Mary, and laid her almost lifeless on the grassy pavement, while some of the ruffians hastened to light a fire of the heath and sticks they could pick up. They took out their provisions, and placed themselves round the fire, where they had not long been seated, when the sound of distant thunder foretold an approaching storm. A violent storm, accompanied with peals which shook the pile, came on. They were sheltered from the heaviness of the rain; but the long and vivid flashes of lightning which glanced through the casements, alarmed them all. The shrieks of Mary were loud and continued; and the fears of the ruffians did not prevent their uttering dreadful imprecations at her distress. One of them, in the fury of his resentment, swore she should be gagged; and seizing her resistless hands to execute the purpose, her cries redoubled. The servants who had betrayed her, were not yet so entirely lost to the feelings of humanity, as to stand regardless of her present distress; though they could not resist the temptations of a bribe, they were unwilling their lady should be loaded with unnecessary misery. They opposed the ruffians; a dispute ensued; and the violence of the contest arose so high, that they determined to fight for the decision. Amid the peals of thunder, the oaths and execrations of the combatants, added terror to the scene. The strength of the ruffians were superior to that of their opponents; and Mary; beholding victory deciding against herself, uttered a loud scream, when the attention of the whole party was surprized by the sound of a footstep in the cloister. Immediately after a man rushed into the place, and drawing his sword, demanded the cause of the tumult. Mary, who lay almost expiring on the ground, now raised her eyes; but what were her sensations, when she raised them to Alleyn-who now stood before her petrified with horror. Before he could fly to her assistance, the attacks of the ruffians obliged him to defend himself; he parried their blows for some time, but he must inevitably have yielded to the force of numbers, had not the trampling of feet, which fast approached, called off for a moment their attention. In an instant the place was filled with men. The astonishment of Alleyn was, if possible, now increased; for the Earl, followed by a party, now entered. The Earl, when he perceived Alleyn, stood at the entrance, aghast. — But resuming his firmness, he bade him defend himself. The loud voice of Osbert re-called Mary, and observing their menacing attitudes, she collected just strength sufficient to throw herself between them. Alleyn dropped his sword, and raised her from the ground; when the Earl rudely pushed him away, and snatched her to his heart. "Hear me, Osbert," was all she could say. "Declare who brought her hither," said the Earl sternly to Alleyn. "I know not," replied he, "you must ask those men whom your people have secured. If my life is hateful to you, strike! and spare me the anguish of defending it against the brother of Mary." The Earl hesitated in surprize, and the generosity of Alleyn called a blush into his face. He was going to have replied, but was interrupted by some of his men, who had been engaged in a sharp contest with the ruffians, two of whom they had secured, and now brought to their lord; the rest were fled. In the person of one of them, the Earl discovered his own servant, who sinking in his presence with conscious guilt, fell on his knees imploring mercy. "Wretch," said the Earl, seizing him, and holding his sword over his head, "declare by whose authority you have acted, and all you know of the affair; — remember your life depends on the truth of your assertions." "I'll tell the truth, my Lord," replied the trembling wretch, "and nothing else as I hope for mercy. About three weeks ago, — no, it is not so much; about a fortnight ago, when I was sent on a message to the lady Malcolm, the Count de Santmorin's gentleman-" "The Count de Santmorin!" re-echoed the whole company. "But proceed," said Osbert. "The Count de Santmorin's gentleman called me into a private room, where he told me to wait for his master, who would soon be there." "Be quick," said the Earl, "proceed to facts." "I will, my lord; the Count came, and said to me, 'Robert, I have observed you, and I think you can be faithful,' he said so, my lord, — God forgive me!" "Well-well, proceed." "Where was I?" — 'Oh! he said, "I think you can be faithful."' — "Good God! this is beyond endurance; you trifle, rascal, with my patience, to give your associates time for escape; be brief, or you die." "I will, my lord, as I hope for life. He took from his pocket a handful of gold, which he gave me; — 'can you be secret, Robert?' said he, — 'yes, my lord Count,' said I, God forgive me! — 'Then observe what I say to you. You often attend your young lady in her rides to Dunbayne.'" — "What, then it was the Count de Santmorin who commissioned you to undertake this scheme!" "Not me only, my lord." "Answer my question; was the Count the author of this plot?" "He was, my lord." "And where is he?" said Osbert, in a stern voice. "I know not, as I am a living creature. He embarked, as you know, my lord, not far from the castle of Dunbayne, and we were travelling to a distant part of the coast to meet him, when we were all to have set sail for Switzerland." "You cannot be ignorant of the place of your destination," said the Earl, turning to the other prisoner; "where is your employer?" "That is not for me to tell," said he, in a sullen tone. "Reveal the truth," said the Earl, turning towards him the point of his sword, "or we will find a way to make you." "The place where we were to meet the Count, had no name." "You know the way to it." "I do." "Then lead me thither." "Never!" — "Never! Your life shall answer the refusal," said Osbert, pointing the sword to his breast. "Strike!" said the Count, throwing off the cloak which had concealed him; "strike! and rid me of a being which passion has made hateful to me; — strike! — and make the first moment of my entering this place, the last of my guilt." A faint scream was uttered by Mary; the small remains of her strength forsook her, and she sunk on the pavement. The Earl started a few steps back, and stood suspended in wonder. The looks of the whole group defy description. "Take a sword," said the Earl, recovering himself, "and defend your life." "Never, my lord, never! Though I have been hurried by the force of passion to rob you of a sister, I will not aggravate my guilt by the murder of the brother. Your life has already been once endangered through my means, though not by my design; Heaven knows the anguish which that accident cost me. The impetuosity of passion impelled me onward with irresistible fury; it urged me to violate the sacred duties of gratitude, of friendship-and of humanity. To live in shame, and in the consciousness of guilt, is a living death. With your sword do justice to yourself and virtue; and spare me the misery of long comparing what I am, with what I was." "Away, you trifle," said the Earl, "defend yourself." The Count repeated his refusal. "And you, villain," said Osbert, turning to the man who had confessed the plot, "you pretended ignorance of the presence of the Count; your perfidy shall be rewarded." "As I now plead for mercy, my lord, I knew not he was here." "The fellow speaks truth," said the Count, "he was ignorant of the place where he was to meet me. I was approaching this spot to discover myself to the dear object of my passion, when your people surprized and took me." Mary confirmed the testimony of the Count, by declaring that she had not till that moment seen him since she quitted the castle of Dunbayne. She pleaded for his life, and also for the servants, who had opposed the cruelty of their comrades. "I am no assassin," said the Earl, "let the Count take a sword, and fight me on equal terms." — "Shall virtue be reduced to an equality with vice?" said the Count, "No, my lord, — plunge your sword in my heart, and expiate my guilt." The Earl still urged him to defence; and the Count still persisted in refusal. Touched by the recollection of past friendship, and grieved that a soul like the Count's should ever be under the dominion of vice, Osbert threw down his sword, and, overcome with a sort of tenderness-"Go, my lord, your person is safe; and if it is necessary to your peace, — stretching forth his hand, — take my forgiveness." The Count, overcome by his generosity, and by a sense of his own unworthiness, shrunk back: "Forbear, my lord, to wound by your goodness, a mind already too sensible of its own debasement; nor excite, by your generosity, a remorse too keen to be endured. Your reproaches I can bear, — your vengeance I solicit! — but your kindness inflicts a torture too exquisite for my soul." "Never, my lord," continued he, the big tear swelling in his eye, "never more shall your friendship be polluted by my unworthiness. Since you will not satisfy justice, by taking my life, I go to lose it in the obscurity of distant regions. Yet, ere I go, suffer me to make one last request to you, and to that dear lady whom I have thus injured, and on whom my eyes now gaze for the last time, — suffer me to hope that you will blot from your memory the existence of Santmorin." He concluded the sentence with a groan, which vibrated upon the hearts of all present; and without waiting for a reply, hurried from the scene. The Earl had turned away his head in pity, and when he again looked round to reply, perceived that the Count was departed; he followed his steps through the cloister, — he called-but he was gone.

Alleyn had observed the Count with a mixture of pity and admiration; and he sighed for the weakness of human nature. "How," said the Earl, returning eagerly to Alleyn, — "how can I recompense you for my injurious suspicions, and my injurious treatment? — How can you forgive, or I forget, my injustice? But the mystery of this affair, and the doubtful appearance of circumstances, must speak for me." "O! let us talk no more of this, my lord," replied Alleyn; with emotion; "let us only rejoice at the safety of our dear lady, and offer her the comfort she is so much in want of." The fire was re-kindled, and the Earl's servants laid before him some wine, and other provisions. Mary, who had not tasted any food since she left the castle, now took some wine; it revived her, and enabled her to take other nourishment. She enquired, what happy circumstance had enabled the Earl to trace her route. "Ever since I discovered your flight," said he, "I have been in pursuit of you. Chance directed me over these wilds, when I was driven by the storm to seek shelter among these ruins. The light, and an uproar of voices, drew me to the cloister, where, to my unutterable astonishment, I discovered you and Alleyn: Spare me the remembrance of what followed." Mary wished to enquire what brought Alleyn to the place; but delicacy kept her silent. Osbert, however, whose anxiety for his sister had hitherto allowed him to attend only to her, now relieved her from the pain of lengthened suspense. "By what strange accident was you brought hither?" said he to Alleyn, "and what motive has induced you so long to absent yourself from the castle?" At the last question, Alleyn blushed, and an involuntary sigh escaped him. Mary understood the blush and the sigh, and awaited his reply in trembling emotion. "I fled, my lord, from your displeasure, and to tear myself from an object too dangerous, alas! for my peace. I sought to wear away in absence, a passion which must ever be hopeless, but which, I now perceive, is interwoven with my existence. — But forgive, my lord, the intrusion of a subject which is painful to us all. With some money, and a few provisions, I left my father's cottage; and since that time have wandered over the country a forlorn and miserable being, passing my nights in the huts which chance threw in my way, and designing to travel onward, and to enlist myself in the service of my country. Night overtook me on these wastes, and as I walked on comfortless and bewildered, I was alarmed by distant cries of distress. I quickened my pace; but the sound which should have directed my steps was ceased, and chilling silence ensued. As I stood musing, and uncertain which course to take, I observed a feeble light break through the gloom; I endeavoured to follow its rays; it led me to these ruins, whose solemn appearance struck me with a momentary dread. A confused murmur of voices from within struck my ear; as I stood hesitating whether to enter, I again heard those shrieks which had alarmed me. I followed the sound; it led me to the entrance of this cloister, at the extremity of which I discovered a party of men engaged in fight; I drew my sword and rushed forward; and the sensations which I felt, on perceiving the lady Mary, cannot be expressed!" "Still-still Heaven destines you the deliverer of Mary!" said the Earl, gratitude swelling in his eyes; "O! that I could remove that obstacle which withholds you from your just reward." A responsive sigh stole from Alleyn, and he remained silent. Never was the struggle of opposing feelings more violent, than that which now agitated the bosom of the Earl. The worth of Alleyn arose more conspicuously bright from every shade with which misfortune had veiled it. His noble and disinterested enthusiasm in the cause of justice, had attached him to the Earl, and had engaged him in a course of enterprizes and of dangers, which it required valour to undertake, and skill and perseverance to perform; and which had produced services for which no adequate reward could be found. He had rescued the Earl from captivity and death; and had twice preserved Mary in dangers. All these circumstances arose in strong reflection to the mind of Osbert; but the darkness of prejudice and ancient pride, opposed their influence, and weakened their effect.

The joy which Mary felt on seeing Alleyn in safety, and still worthy of the esteem she had ever bore him, was dashed by the bitterness of reflection; and reflection imparted a melancholy which added to the langour of illness. At the dawn of day they quitted the abbey, and set forward on their return to the castle; the Earl insisting upon Alleyn's accompanying them. On the way, the minds of the party were variously and silently engaged. The Earl ruminated on the conduct of Alleyn, and the late scene. Mary dwelt chiefly on the virtues of her lover, and on the dangers she had escaped; and Alleyn mused on his defeated purposes, and anticipated future trials. The Earl's thoughts, however, were not so wholly occupied, as to prevent his questioning the servant who had been employed by the Count, concerning the further particulars of his scheme. The words of the Count, importing that he had once already endangered his life, had not escaped the notice of the Earl; though they were uttered in a moment of too much distraction to suffer him to demand an explanation. He now enquired of the man, concerning the mysterious scene of the vaults. "You, I suppose, are not ignorant who were the persons from whom I received my wound." "I, my lord, had no concern in that affair; wicked as I am, I could not raise my hands against your life." "But you know who did." "I — I — ye-yes, my lord, I was afterwards told. But they did not mean to hurt your lordship." "Not mean to hurt me! — What then were their designs, and who were the people?" "That accident happened long before the Count ever spoke to me of his purpose. Indeed, my lord, I had no hand in it; and Heaven knows how I grieved for your lordship; and-" "Well-well, inform me, who were the persons in the vaults, and what were their design." "I was told by a fellow servant; but he made me promise to be secret; but it is proper your lordship should know all; and I hope your lordship will forgive me for having listened to it, — 'Robert,' said he, as we were talking one day of what had happened, — 'Robert,' said he, 'there is more in this matter than you, or any body thinks; but it is not for me to tell all I know.' With that, I begged he would tell me what he knew; he still kept refusing. I promised him faithfully I would not tell; and so at last he told me-'Why, there is my lord Count there, he is in love with our young lady; and to be sure as sweet a lady she is, as ever eyes looked upon; but she don't like him; and so finding himself refused, he is determined to marry her at any rate; and means some night to get into the castle, and carry her off.'" "What, then! — was it the Count who wounded me? — Be quick in your relation." "No, my lord, it was not the Count himself-but two of his people, whom he had sent to examine the castle; and particularly the windows of my young lady's apartment, from whence he designed to have carried her, when every thing was ready for execution. Those men were let within the walls through a way under ground, which leads into the vaults, by my fellow servant, as I afterwards was told; and they escaped through the same way. Their meeting with your lordship was accidental, and they fought only in self-defence; for they had no orders to attack any body." "And who is the villain that connived at this scheme!" "It was my fellow servant, who fled with the Count's people, whom he himself let within the ramparts. Forgive me, my lord; but I did not dare tell; he threatened my life, if I betrayed the secret."

After a journey of fatigue and unpleasant reflections, they arrived, on the second morning at the castle of Athlin. The Countess, during the absence of her son, had endured a state of dreadful suspense. The Baroness, in her friendship, had endeavoured to soothe her distress, by her constant presence; she was engaged in this amiable office when the trampling of horses in the court reached the ears of Matilda. "It is my son," said she, rising from her chair! — "it is my son; he brings me life or death!" She said no more, but rushed into the hall, and in a moment after clasped her almost expiring daughter to her bosom. The transport of the scene repelled utterance; sobs and tears were all that could be given. The general joy, however, was suddenly interrupted by the Baroness, who had followed Matilda into the hall; and who now fell senseless to the ground; delight yielded to surprize, and to the business of assisting the object of it. On recovering, the Baroness looked wildly round her; — "Was it a vision that I saw, or a reality?" The whole company moved their eyes round the hall, but could discover nothing extraordinary. "It was himself; his very air, his features; that benign countenance which I have so often contemplated in imagination!" Her eyes still seemed in search of some ideal object; and they began to doubt whether a sudden phrenzy had not seized her brain. "Ah! again!" said she, and instantly relapsed. Their eyes were now turned towards the door, on which she had gazed; it was Alleyn who entered, with water which he had brought for the Countess, and on whom the attention of all present was centered. He approached ignorant of what had happened; and his surprize was great, when the Baroness, reviving, fixed her eyes mournfully upon him, and asked him to uncover his arm. — "It is, — it is my Philip!" said she, with strong emotion; "I have, indeed, found my long lost child; that strawberry on his arm confirms the decision. Send for the man who calls himself your father, and for my servant Patrick." The sensations of the mother and the son may be more easily conceived than described; those of Mary were little inferior to theirs; and the whole company awaited with trembling eagerness the arrival of the two persons whose testimony was to decide this interesting affair. They came. "This young man you call your son?" said the Baroness. "I do, an' please your ladyship," he replied, with a degree of confusion which belied his words. When Patrick came, his instant surprize on seeing the old man, declared the truth. "Do you know this person?" said the Baroness to Patrick. "Yes, my lady, I know him too well; it was to him I gave your infant son." The old man started with surprize-"Is that youth the son of your ladyship?" "Yes!" "Then God forgive me for having thus long detained him from you! but I was ignorant of his birth, and received him into my cottage as a foundling succoured by lord Malcolm's compassion." The whole company crowded round them. Alleyn fell at the feet of his mother, and bathed her hand with his tears. — "Gracious God; for what hast thou reserved me!" He could say no more. The Baroness raised him, and again pressed him in transport to her heart. It was some time before either of them could speak; and all present were too much affected to interrupt the silence. At length, the Baroness presented Laura to her brother. "Such a mother! and have I such a sister!" said he. Laura wept silently upon his neck the joy of her heart. The Earl was the first who recovered composure sufficient to congratulate Alleyn; and embracing him-"O happy moment, when I can indeed embrace you as my brother!" The whole company now poured forth their joy and their congratulations; — all but Mary, whose emotions almost overcame her, and were too powerful for utterance.

The company now adjourned to the drawing-room; and Mary withdrew to take that repose she so much required. She was sufficiently recovered in a few hours to join her friends in the banquetting-room.

After the transports of the scene were subsided-"I have yet much to hope, and much to fear," said Philip Malcolm, who was yet Alleyn in every thing but in name, "You madam," addressing the Baroness, — "you will willingly become my advocate with her whom I have so long and so ardently loved." "May I hope," continued he, taking tenderly the hand of Mary, who stood trembling by, — "that you have not been insensible to my long attachment, and that you will confirm the happiness which is now offered me?" A smile of ineffable sweetness broke through the melancholy which had long clouded her features, and which even the present discovery had not been able entirely to dissipate, and her eye gave the consent which her tongue refused to utter.

The conversation, for the remainder of the day, was occupied by the subject of the discovery, and with a recital of Mary's adventure. It was determined that on the morrow the marriage of the Earl should be concluded.

On this happy discovery, the Earl ordered the gates of the castle to be thrown open; mirth and festivity resounded through the walls, and the evening closed in universal rejoicings.

On the following morn, the chapel of the castle was decorated for the marriage of the Earl; who with Laura, came attended by Philip, now Baron Malcolm, by Mary, and the whole family. When they approached the altar, the Earl, addressing himself to his bride, — "Now, my Laura," said he, "we may celebrate those nuptials which have twice been so painfully interrupted, and which are to crown me with felicity. This day shall unite our families in a double marriage, and

440

reward the worth of my friend. It is now seen, that those virtues which stimulated him to prosecute for another the cause of justice mysteriously urged him to the recovery of his rights. Virtue may for a time be pursued by misfortune, — and justice be obscured by the transient triumphs of vice, — but the power whose peculiar attributes they are, clears away the clouds of error, and even in this world reveals his THRONE OF JUSTICE."

The Earl stepped forward, and joining the hands of Philip and Mary, — "Surely," said he, "this is a moment of perfect happiness! — I can now reward those virtues which I have ever loved; and those services to which every gift must be inadequate, but this I now bestow."

FINISH

A Sicilian Romance

By Ann Radcliffe

On the northern shore of Sicily are still to be seen the magnificent remains of a castle, which formerly belonged to the noble house of Mazzini. It stands in the centre of a small bay, and upon a gentle acclivity, which, on one side, slopes towards the sea, and on the other rises into an eminence crowned by dark woods. The situation is admirably beautiful and picturesque, and the ruins have an air of ancient grandeur, which, contrasted with the present solitude of the scene, impresses the traveller with awe and curiosity. During my travels abroad I visited this spot. As I walked over the loose fragments of stone, which lay scattered through the immense area of the fabrick, and surveyed the sublimity and grandeur of the ruins, I recurred, by a natural association of ideas, to the times when these walls stood proudly in their original splendour, when the halls were the scenes of hospitality and festive magnificence, and when they resounded with the voices of those whom death had long since swept from the earth. 'Thus,' said I, 'shall the present generation — he who now sinks in misery — and he who now swims in pleasure, alike pass away and be forgotten.' My heart swelled with the reflection; and, as I turned from the scene with a sigh, I fixed my eyes upon a friar, whose venerable figure, gently bending towards the earth, formed no uninteresting object in the picture. He observed my emotion; and, as my eye met his, shook his head and pointed to the ruin. 'These walls,' said he, 'were once the seat of luxury and vice. They exhibited a singular instance of the retribution of Heaven, and were from that period forsaken, and abandoned to decay.' His words excited my curiosity, and I enquired further concerning their meaning.

'A solemn history belongs to this castle, said he, 'which is too long and intricate for me to relate. It is, however, contained in a manuscript in our library, of which I could, perhaps, procure you a sight. A brother of our order, a descendant of the noble house of Mazzini, collected and recorded the most striking incidents relating to his family, and the history thus formed, he left as a legacy to our convent. If you please, we will walk thither.'

I accompanied him to the convent, and the friar introduced me to his superior, a man of an intelligent mind and benevolent heart, with whom I passed some hours in interesting conversation. I believe my sentiments pleased him; for, by his indulgence, I was permitted to take abstracts of the history before me, which, with some further particulars obtained in conversation with the abate, I have arranged in the following pages.

CHAPTER I

Towards the close of the sixteenth century, this castle was in the possession of Ferdinand, fifth marquis of Mazzini, and was for some years the principal residence of his family. He was a man of a voluptuous and imperious character. To his first wife, he married Louisa Bernini, second daughter of the Count della Salario, a lady yet more distinguished for the sweetness of her manners and the gentleness of her disposition, than for her beauty. She brought the marquis one son and two daughters, who lost their amiable mother in early childhood. The arrogant and impetuous character of the marquis operated powerfully upon the mild and susceptible nature of his lady: and it was by many persons believed, that his unkindness and neglect put a period to her life. However this might be, he soon afterwards married Maria de Vellorno, a young lady eminently beautiful, but of a character very opposite to that of her predecessor. She was a woman of infinite art, devoted to pleasure, and of an unconquerable spirit. The marquis, whose heart was dead to paternal tenderness, and whose present lady was too volatile to attend to domestic concerns, committed the education of his daughters to the care of a lady, completely qualified for the undertaking, and who was distantly related to the late marchioness.

He quitted Mazzini soon after his second marriage, for the gaieties and splendour of Naples, whither his son accompanied him. Though naturally of a haughty and overbearing disposition, he was governed by his wife. His passions were vehement, and she had the address to bend them to her own purpose; and so well to conceal her influence, that he thought himself most independent when he was most enslaved. He paid an annual visit to the castle of Mazzini; but the marchioness seldom attended him, and he staid only to give such general directions concerning the education of his daughters, as his pride, rather than his affection, seemed to dictate.

Emilia, the elder, inherited much of her mother's disposition. She had a mild and sweet temper, united with a clear and comprehensive mind. Her younger sister, Julia, was of a more lively cast. An extreme sensibility subjected her to frequent uneasiness; her temper was warm, but generous; she was quickly irritated, and quickly appeased; and to a reproof, however gentle, she would often weep, but was never sullen. Her imagination was ardent, and her mind early exhibited symptoms of genius. It was the particular care of Madame de Menon to counteract those traits in the disposition of her young pupils, which appeared inimical to their future happiness; and for this task she had abilities which entitled her to hope for success. A series of early misfortunes had entendered her heart, without weakening the powers of her understanding. In retirement she had acquired tranquillity, and had almost lost the consciousness of those sorrows which yet threw a soft and not unpleasing shade over her character. She loved her young charge with maternal fondness, and their gradual improvement and respectful tenderness repaid all her anxiety. Madame excelled in music and drawing. She had often forgot her sorrows in these amusements, when her mind was too much occupied to derive consolation from books, and she was assiduous to impart to Emilia and Julia a power so valuable as that of beguiling the sense of affliction. Emilia's taste led her to drawing, and she soon made rapid advances in that art. Julia was uncommonly susceptible of the charms of harmony. She had feelings which trembled in unison to all its various and enchanting powers.

The instructions of madame she caught with astonishing quickness, and in a short time attained to a degree of excellence in her favorite study, which few persons have ever exceeded. Her manner was entirely her own. It was not in the rapid intricacies of execution, that she excelled so much in as in that delicacy of taste, and in those enchanting powers of expression, which seem to breathe a soul through the sound, and which take captive the heart of the hearer. The lute was her favorite instrument, and its tender notes accorded well with the sweet and melting tones of her voice.

The castle of Mazzini was a large irregular fabrick, and seemed suited to receive a numerous train of followers, such as, in those days, served the nobility, either in the splendour of peace, or the turbulence of war. Its present family inhabited only a small part of it; and even this part appeared forlorn and almost desolate from the spaciousness of the apartments, and the length of the galleries which led to them. A melancholy stillness reigned through the halls, and the silence of the courts, which were shaded by high turrets, was for many hours together undisturbed by the sound of any foot-step. Julia, who discovered an early taste for books, loved to retire in an evening to a small closet in which she had collected her favorite authors. This room formed the western angle of the castle: one of its windows looked upon the sea, beyond which was faintly seen, skirting the horizon, the dark rocky coast of Calabria; the other opened towards a part of the castle, and afforded a prospect of the neighbouring woods. Her musical instruments were here deposited, with whatever assisted her favorite amusements. This spot, which was at once elegant, pleasant, and retired, was

445

embellished with many little ornaments of her own invention, and with some drawings executed by her sister. The cioset was adjoining her chamber, and was separated from the apartments of madame only by a short gallery. This gallery opened into another, long and winding, which led to the grand staircase, terminating in the north hall, with which the chief apartments of the north side of the edifice communicated.

Madame de Menon's apartment opened into both galleries. It was in one of these rooms that she usually spent the mornings, occupied in the improvement of her young charge. The windows looked towards the sea, and the room was light and pleasant. It was their custom to dine in one of the lower apartments, and at table they were always joined by a dependant of the marquis's, who had resided many years in the castle, and who instructed the young ladies in the Latin tongue, and in geography. During the fine evenings of summer, this little party frequently supped in a pavilion, which was built on an eminence in the woods belonging to the castle. From this spot the eye had an almost boundless range of sea and land. It commanded the straits of Messina, with the opposite shores of Calabria, and a great extent of the wild and picturesque scenery of Sicily. Mount Etna, crowned with eternal snows, and shooting from among the clouds, formed a grand and sublime picture in the background of the scene. The city of Palermo was also distinguishable; and Julia, as she gazed on its glittering spires; would endeavour in imagination to depicture its beauties, while she secretly sighed for a view of that world, from which she had hitherto been secluded by the mean jealousy of the marchioness, upon whose mind the dread of rival beauty operated strongly to the prejudice of Emilia and Julia. She employed all her influence over the marquis to detain them in retirement; and, though Emilia was now twenty, and her sister eighteen, they had never passed the boundaries of their father's domains.

Vanity often produces unreasonable alarm; but the marchioness had in this instance just grounds for apprehension; the beauty of her lord's daughters has seldom been exceeded. The person of Emilia was finely proportioned. Her complexion was fair, her hair flaxen, and her dark blue eyes were full of sweet expression. Her manners were dignified and elegant, and in her air was a feminine softness, a tender timidity which irresistibly attracted the heart of the beholder. The figure of Julia was light and graceful—her step was airy—her mien animated, and her smile enchanting. Her eyes were dark, and full of fire, but tempered with modest sweetness. Her features were finely turned—every laughing grace played round her mouth, and her countenance quickly discovered all the various emotions of her soul. The dark auburn hair, which curled in beautiful profusion in her neck, gave a finishing charm to her appearance.

Thus lovely, and thus veiled in obscurity, were the daughters of the noble Mazzini. But they were happy, for they knew not enough of the world seriously to regret the want of its enjoyments, though Julia would sometimes sigh for the airy image which her fancies painted, and a painful curiosity would arise concerning the busy scenes from which she was excluded. A return to her customary amusements, however, would chase the ideal image from her mind, and restore her usual happy complacency. Books, music, and painting, divided the hours of her leisure, and many beautiful summer-evenings were spent in the pavilion, where the refined conversation of madame, the poetry of Tasso, the lute of Julia, and the friendship of Emilia, combined to form a species of happiness, such as elevated and highly susceptible minds are alone capable of receiving or communicating. Madame understood and practised all the graces of conversation, and her young pupils perceived its value, and caught the spirit of its character.

Conversation may be divided into two classes—the familiar and the sentimental. It is the province of the familiar, to diffuse cheerfulness and ease—to open the heart of man to man, and to beam a temperate sunshine upon the mind.—Nature and art must conspire to render us susceptible of the charms, and to qualify us for the practice of the second class of conversation, here termed sentimental, and in which Madame de Menon particularly excelled. To good sense, lively feeling, and natural delicacy of taste, must be united an expansion of mind, and a refinement of thought, which is the result of high cultivation. To render this sort of conversation irresistibly attractive, a knowledge of the world is requisite, and that enchanting case, that elegance of manner, which is to be acquired only by frequenting the higher circles of polished life. In sentimental conversation, subjects interesting to the heart, and to the imagination, are brought forward; they are discussed in a kind of sportive way, with animation and refinement, and are never continued longer than politeness allows. Here fancy flourishes, —the sensibilities expand—and wit, guided by delicacy and embellished by taste—points to the heart.

Such was the conversation of Madame de Menon; and the pleasant gaiety of the pavilion seemed peculiarly to adapt it for the scene of social delights. On the evening of a very sultry day, having supped in their favorite spot, the coolness of the hour, and the beauty of the night, tempted this happy party to remain

447

there later than usual. Returning home, they were surprised by the appearance of a light through the broken window-shutters of an apartment, belonging to a division of the castle which had for many years been shut up. They stopped to observe it, when it suddenly disappeared, and was seen no more. Madame de Menon, disturbed at this phaenomenon, hastened into the castle, with a view of enquiring into the cause of it, when she was met in the north hall by Vincent. She related to him what she had seen, and ordered an immediate search to be made for the keys of those apartments. She apprehended that some person had penetrated that part of the edifice with an intention of plunder; and, disdaining a paltry fear where her duty was concerned, she summoned the servants of the castle, with an intention of accompanying them thither. Vincent smiled at her apprehensions, and imputed what she had seen to an illusion, which the solemnity of the hour had impressed upon her fancy. Madame, however, persevered in her purpose; and, after along and repeated search, a massey key, covered with rust, was produced. She then proceeded to the southern side of the edifice, accompanied by Vincent, and followed by the servants, who were agitated with impatient wonder. The key was applied to an iron gate, which opened into a court that separated this division from the other parts of the castle. They entered this court, which was overgrown with grass and weeds, and ascended some steps that led to a large door, which they vainly endeavoured to open. All the different keys of the castle were applied to the lock, without effect, and they were at length compelled to quit the place, without having either satisfied their curiosity, or quieted their fears. Everything, however, was still, and the light did not reappear. Madame concealed her apprehensions, and the family retired to rest.

This circumstance dwelt on the mind of Madame de Menon, and it was some time before she ventured again to spend an evening in the pavilion. After several months passed, without further disturbance or discovery, another occurrence renewed the alarm. Julia had one night remained in her closet later than usual. A favorite book had engaged her attention beyond the hour of customary repose, and every inhabitant of the castle, except herself, had long been lost in sleep. She was roused from her forgetfulness, by the sound of the castle clock, which struck one. Surprised at the lateness of the hour, she rose in haste, and was moving to her chamber, when the beauty of the night attracted her to the window. She opened it; and observing a fine effect of moonlight upon the dark woods, leaned forwards. In that situation she had not long remained, when she perceived a light faintly flash through a casement in the uninhabited part of the castle. A sudden tremor seized her, and she with difficulty supported herself. In a few moments it disappeared, and soon after a figure, bearing a lamp, proceeded from an obscure door belonging to the south tower; and stealing along the outside of the castle walls, turned round the southern angle, by which it was afterwards hid from the view. Astonished and terrified at what she had seen, she hurried to the apartment of Madame de Menon, and related the circumstance. The servants were immediately roused, and the alarm became general. Madame arose and descended into the north hall, where the domestics were already assembled. No one could be found of courage sufficient to enter into the courts; and the orders of madame were disregarded, when opposed to the effects of superstitious terror. She perceived that Vincent was absent, but as she was ordering him to be called, he entered the hall. Surprised to find the family thus assembled, he was told the occasion. He immediately ordered a party of the servants to attend him round the castle walls; and with some reluctance, and more fear, they obeyed him. They all returned to the hall, without having witnessed any extraordinary appearance; but though their fears were not confirmed, they were by no means dissipated. The appearance of a light in a part of the castle which had for several years been shut up, and to which time and circumstance had given an air of singular desolation, might reasonably be supposed to excite a strong degree of surprise and terror. In the minds of the vulgar, any species of the wonderful is received with avidity; and the servants did not hesitate in believing the southern division of the castle to be inhabited by a supernatural power. Too much agitated to sleep, they agreed to watch for the remainder of the night. For this purpose they arranged themselves in the east gallery, where they had a view of the south tower from which the light had issued. The night, however, passed without any further disturbance; and the morning dawn, which they beheld with inexpressible pleasure, dissipated for a while the glooms of apprehension. But the return of evening renewed the general fear, and for several successive nights the domestics watched the southern tower. Although nothing remarkable was seen, a report was soon raised, and believed, that the southern side of the castle was haunted. Madame de Menon, whose mind was superior to the effects of superstition, was yet disturbed and perplexed, and she determined, if the light reappeared, to inform the marquis of the circumstance, and request the keys of those apartments.

The marquis, immersed in the dissipations of Naples, seldom remembered the castle, or its inhabitants. His son, who had been educated under his immediate care, was the sole object of his pride, as the marchioness was that of his affection. He loved her with romantic fondness, which she repaid with seeming tenderness, and secret perfidy. She allowed herself a free indulgence in the most licentious pleasures, yet conducted herself with an art so exquisite as to elude discovery, and even suspicion. In her amours she was equally inconstant as ardent, till the young Count Hippolitus de Vereza attracted her attention. The natural fickleness of her disposition seemed then to cease, and upon him she centered all her desires.

The count Vereza lost his father in early childhood. He was now of age, and had just entered upon the possession of his estates. His person was graceful, yet manly; his mind accomplished, and his manners elegant; his countenance expressed a happy union of spirit, dignity, and benevolence, which formed the principal traits of his character. He had a sublimity of thought, which taught him to despise the voluptuous vices of the Neapolitans, and led him to higher pursuits. He was the chosen and early friend of young Ferdinand, the son of the marquis, and was a frequent visitor in the family. When the marchioness first saw him, she treated him with great distinction, and at length made such advances, as neither the honor nor the inclinations of the count permitted him to notice. He conducted himself toward her with frigid indifference, which served only to inflame the passion it was meant to chill. The favors of the marchioness had hitherto been sought with avidity, and accepted with rapture; and the repulsive insensibility which she now experienced, roused all her pride, and called into action every refinement of coquetry.

It was about this period that Vincent was seized with a disorder which increased so rapidly, as in a short time to assume the most alarming appearance. Despairing of life, he desired that a messenger might be dispatched to inform the marquis of his situation, and to signify his earnest wish to see him before he died. The progress of his disorder defied every art of medicine, and his visible distress of mind seemed to accelerate his fate. Perceiving his last hour approaching, he requested to have a confessor. The confessor was shut up with him a considerable time, and he had already received extreme unction, when Madame de Menon was summoned to his bedside. The hand of death was now upon him, cold damps hung upon his brows, and he, with difficulty, raised his heavy eyes to madame as she entered the apartment. He beckoned her towards him, and desiring that no person might be permitted to enter the room, was for a few moments silent. His mind appeared to labour under oppressive remembrances; he made several attempts to speak, but either resolution or strength failed him. At length, giving madame a look of unutterable anguish, 'Alas, madam,' said he, 'Heaven grants not the prayer of such a wretch as I am. I must expire long before the marquis can arrive. Since I shall see him no more, I would impart to you a secret which lies heavy at my heart, and which makes my last moments dreadful, as they are without hope.' 'Be comforted,' said madame, who was affected by the energy of his manner, 'we are taught to believe that forgiveness is never denied to sincere repentance.' 'You, madam, are ignorant of the enormity of my crime, and of the secret—the horrid secret which labours at my breast. My guilt is beyond remedy in this world, and I fear will be without pardon in the next; I therefore hope little from confession even to a priest. Yet some good it is still in my power to do; let me disclose to you that secret which is so mysteriously connected with the southern apartments of this castle.'—'What of them!' exclaimed madame, with impatience. Vincent returned no answer; exhausted by the effort of speaking, he had fainted. Madame rung for assistance, and by proper applications, his senses were recalled. He was, however, entirely speechless, and in this state he remained till he expired, which was about an hour after he had conversed with madame.

The perplexity and astonishment of madame, were by the late scene heightened to a very painful degree. She recollected the various particulars relative to the southern division of the castle, the many years it had stood uninhabited—the silence which had been observed concerning it—the appearance of the light and the figure—the fruitless search for the keys, and the reports so generally believed; and thus remembrance presented her with a combination of circumstances, which served only to increase her wonder, and heighten her curiosity. A veil of mystery enveloped that part of the castle, which it now seemed impossible should ever be penetrated, since the only person who could have removed it, was no more.

The marquis arrived on the day after that on which Vincent had expired. He came attended by servants only, and alighted at the gates of the castle with an air of impatience, and a countenance expressive of strong emotion. Madame, with the young ladies, received him in the hall. He hastily saluted his daughters, and passed on to the oak parlour, desiring madame to follow him. She obeyed, and the marquis enquired with great agitation after Vincent. When told of his death, he paced the room with hurried steps, and was for some time silent. At length seating himself, and surveying madame with a scrutinizing eye, he asked some questions concerning the particulars of Vincent's death. She mentioned his earnest desire to see the marquis, and repeated his last words. The marquis remained silent, and madame proceeded to mention those circumstances relative to the southern division of the castle, which she thought it of so much importance to discover. He treated the affair very lightly, laughed at her conjectures, represented the appearances she described as the illusions of a weak and timid mind, and broke up the conversation, by going to visit the chamber of Vincent, in which he remained a considerable time.

On the following day Emilia and Julia dined with the marquis. He was gloomy and silent; their efforts to amuse him seemed to excite displeasure rather than kindness; and when the repast was concluded, he withdrew to his own apartment, leaving his daughters in a state of sorrow and surprise.

Vincent was to be interred, according to his own desire, in the church belonging to the convent of St Nicholas. One of the servants, after receiving some necessary orders concerning the funeral, ventured to inform the marquis of the appearance of the lights in the south tower. He mentioned the superstitious reports that prevailed amongst the household, and complained that the servants would not cross the courts after it was dark. 'And who is he that has commissioned you with this story?' said the marquis, in a tone of displeasure; 'are the weak and ridiculous fancies of women and servants to be obtruded upon my notice? Away—appear no more before me, till you have learned to speak what it is proper for me to hear.' Robert withdrew abashed, and it was some time before any person ventured to renew the subject with the marquis.

The majority of young Ferdinand now drew near, and the marquis determined to celebrate the occasion with festive magnificence at the castle of Mazzini. He, therefore, summoned the marchioness and his son from Naples, and very splendid preparations were ordered to be made. Emilia and Julia dreaded the arrival of the marchioness, whose influence they had long been sensible of, and from whose presence they anticipated a painful restraint. Beneath the gentle guidance of Madame de Menon, their hours had passed in happy tranquillity, for they were ignorant alike of the sorrows and the pleasures of the world. Those did not oppress, and these did not inflame them. Engaged in the pursuits of knowledge, and in the attainment of elegant accomplishments, their moments flew lightly away, and the flight of time was marked only by improvement. In madame was united the tenderness of the mother, with the sympathy of a friend; and they loved her with a warm and inviolable affection.

The purposed visit of their brother, whom they had not seen for several years, gave them great pleasure. Although their minds retained no very distinct remembrance of him, they looked forward with eager and delightful expectation to his virtues and his talents; and hoped to find in his company, a consolation for the uneasiness which the presence of the marchioness would excite. Neither did Julia contemplate with indifference the approaching festival. A new scene was now opening to her, which her young imagination painted in the warm and glowing colours of delight. The near approach of pleasure frequently awakens the heart to emotions, which would fail to be excited by a more remote and abstracted observance. Julia, who, in the distance, had considered the splendid gaieties of life with tranquillity, now lingered with impatient hope through the moments which withheld her from their enjoyments. Emilia, whose feelings were less lively, and whose imagination was less powerful, beheld the approaching festival with calm consideration, and almost regretted the interruption of those tranquil pleasures, which she knew to be more congenial with her powers and disposition.

In a few days the marchioness arrived at the castle. She was followed by a numerous retinue, and accompanied by Ferdinand, and several of the Italian noblesse, whom pleasure attracted to her train. Her entrance was proclaimed by the sound of music, and those gates which had long rusted on their hinges, were thrown open to receive her. The courts and halls, whose aspect so lately expressed only gloom and desolation, now shone with sudden splendour, and echoed the sounds of gaiety and gladness. Julia surveyed the scene from an obscure window; and as the triumphal strains filled the air, her breast throbbed; her heart beat quick with joy, and she lost her apprehensions from the marchioness in a sort of wild delight hitherto unknown to her. The arrival of the marchioness seemed indeed the signal of universal and unlimited pleasure. When the marquis came out to receive her, the gloom that lately clouded his countenance, broke away in smiles of welcome, which the whole company appeared to consider as invitations to joy.

The tranquil heart of Emilia was not proof against a scene so alluring, and she sighed at the prospect, yet scarcely knew why. Julia pointed out to her sister, the graceful figure of a young man who followed the marchioness, and she expressed her wishes that he might be her brother. From the contemplation of the scene before them, they were summoned to meet the marchioness. Julia trembled with apprehension, and for a few moments wished the castle was in its former state. As they advanced through the saloon, in which they were presented, Julia was covered with blushes; but Emilia, tho' equally timid, preserved her graceful dignity. The marchioness received them

453

with a mingled smile of condescension and politeness, and immediately the whole attention of the company was attracted by their elegance and beauty. The eager eyes of Julia sought in vain to discover her brother, of whose features she had no recollection in those of any of the persons then present. At length her father presented him, and she perceived, with a sigh of regret, that he was not the youth she had observed from the window. He advanced with a very engaging air, and she met him with an unfeigned welcome. His figure was tall and majestic; he had a very noble and spirited carriage; and his countenance expressed at once sweetness and dignity. Supper was served in the east hall, and the tables were spread with a profusion of delicacies. A band of music played during the repast, and the evening concluded with a concert in the saloon.

CHAPTER II

The day of the festival, so long and so impatiently looked for by Julia, was now arrived. All the neighbouring nobility were invited, and the gates of the castle were thrown open for a general rejoicing. A magnificent entertainment, consisting of the most luxurious and expensive dishes, was served in the halls. Soft music floated along the vaulted roofs, the walls were hung with decorations, and it seemed as if the hand of a magician had suddenly metamorphosed this once gloomy fabric into the palace of a fairy. The marquis, notwithstanding the gaiety of the scene, frequently appeared abstracted from its enjoyments, and in spite of all his efforts at cheerfulness, the melancholy of his heart was visible in his countenance.

In the evening there was a grand ball: the marchioness, who was still distinguished for her beauty, and for the winning elegance of her manners, appeared in the most splendid attire. Her hair was ornamented with a profusion of jewels, but was so disposed as to give an air rather of voluptuousness than of grace, to her figure. Although conscious of her charms, she beheld the beauty of Emilia and Julia with a jealous eye, and was compelled secretly to acknowledge, that the simple elegance with which they were adorned, was more enchanting than all the studied artifice of splendid decoration. They were dressed alike in light Sicilian habits, and the beautiful luxuriance of their flowing hair was restrained only by bandellets of pearl. The ball was opened by Ferdinand and the lady Matilda Constanza. Emilia danced with the young Marquis della Fazelli, and acquitted herself with the ease and dignity so natural to her. Julia experienced a various emotion of pleasure and fear when the Count de Vereza, in whom she recollected the cavalier she had observed from the window, led her forth. The grace of her step, and the elegant symmetry of her figure, raised in the assembly a gentle murmur of applause, and the soft blush which now stole over her cheek, gave an additional charm to her appearance. But when the music changed, and she danced to the soft Sicilian measure, the airy grace of her movement, and the unaffected tenderness of her air, sunk attention into silence, which continued for some time after the dance had ceased. The marchioness observed the general admiration with seeming pleasure, and secret uneasiness. She had suffered a very painful solicitude, when the Count de Vereza selected her for his partner in the dance, and she pursued him through the evening with an eye of jealous scrutiny. Her bosom, which before glowed only with love, was now torn by the agitation of other passions more violent and destructive. Her thoughts were restless, her mind wandered from the scene before her, and it required all her address to preserve an apparent ease. She saw, or fancied she saw, an impassioned air in the count, when he addressed himself to Julia, that corroded her heart with jealous fury.

At twelve the gates of the castle were thrown open, and the company quitted it for the woods, which were splendidly illuminated. Arcades of light lined the long vistas, which were terminated by pyramids of lamps that presented to the eye one bright column of flame. At irregular distances buildings were erected, hung with variegated lamps, disposed in the gayest and most fantastic forms. Collations were spread under the trees; and music, touched by unseen hands, breathed around. The musicians were placed in the most obscure and embowered spots, so as to elude the eye and strike the imagination. The scene appeared enchanting. Nothing met the eye but beauty and romantic splendour; the ear received no sounds but those of mirth and melody. The younger part of the company formed themselves into groups, which at intervals glanced through the woods, and were again unseen. Julia seemed the magic queen of the place. Her heart dilated with pleasure, and diffused over her features an expression of pure and complacent delight. A generous, frank, and exalted sentiment sparkled in her eyes, and animated her manner. Her bosom glowed with benevolent affections; and she seemed anxious to impart to all around her, a happiness as unmixed as that she experienced. Wherever she moved, admiration followed her steps. Ferdinand was as gay as the scene around him. Emilia was pleased; and the marquis seemed to have left his melancholy in the castle. The marchioness alone was wretched. She supped with a select party, in a pavilion on the sea-shore, which was fitted up with peculiar elegance. It was hung with white silk, drawn up in festoons, and richly fringed with gold. The sofas were of the same materials, and alternate wreaths of lamps and of roses entwined the columns. A row of small lamps placed about the cornice, formed an edge of light round the roof which, with the other numerous lights, was reflected in a blaze of splendour from the large mirrors that adorned the room. The Count Muriani was of the party; — he complimented the marchioness on the beauty of her daughters; and after lamenting with gaiety the captives which their charms would enthral, he mentioned the Count de Vereza. 'He is certainly of all others the man most deserving the lady Julia. As they danced, I thought they exhibited a perfect model of the beauty of either sex; and if I mistake not, they are inspired with a mutual admiration.' The marchioness, endeavouring to conceal her uneasiness, said, 'Yes, my lord, I allow the count all the merit you adjudge him, but from the little I have seen of his disposition, he is too volatile for a serious attachment.' At that instant the count entered the pavilion: 'Ah,' said Muriani, laughingly, 'you was the subject of our conversation, and seem to be come in good time to receive the honors allotted you. I was interceding with the marchioness for her interest in your favor, with the lady Julia; but she absolutely refuses it; and though she allows you merit, alleges, that you are by nature fickle and inconstant. What say you — would not the beauty of lady Julia bind your unsteady heart?'.

'I know not how I have deserved that character of the marchioness,' said the count with a smile, 'but that heart must be either fickle or insensible in an uncommon degree, which can boast of freedom in the presence of lady Julia.' The marchioness, mortified by the whole conversation, now felt the full force of Vereza's reply, which she imagined he pointed with particular emphasis.

The entertainment concluded with a grand firework, which was exhibited on the margin of the sea, and the company did not part till the dawn of morning. Julia retired from the scene with regret. She was enchanted with the new world that was now exhibited to her, and she was not cool enough to distinguish the vivid glow of imagination from the colours of real bliss. The pleasure she now felt she believed would always be renewed, and in an equal degree, by the objects which first excited it. The weakness of humanity is never willingly perceived by young minds. It is painful to know, that we are operated upon by objects whose impressions are variable as they are indefinable — and that what yesterday affected us strongly, is to-day but imperfectly felt, and to-morrow perhaps shall be disregarded. When at length this unwelcome truth is received into the mind, we at first reject, with disgust, every appearance of good, we disdain to partake of a happiness which we cannot always command, and we not unfrequently sink into a temporary despair. Wisdom or accident, at length, recal us from our error, and offers to us some object capable of producing a pleasing, yet lasting effect, which effect, therefore, we call happiness. Happiness has this essential difference from what is commonly called pleasure, that virtue forms its basis, and virtue being the offspring of reason, may be expected to produce uniformity of effect.

The passions which had hitherto lain concealed in Julia's heart, touched by circumstance, dilated to its power, and afforded her a slight experience of the pain and delight which flow from their influence. The beauty and accomplishments of Vereza raised in her a new and various emotion, which reflection made her fear to encourage, but which was too pleasing to be wholly resisted. Tremblingly alive to a sense of delight, and unchilled by disappointment, the young heart welcomes every feeling, not simply painful, with a romantic expectation that it will expand into bliss.

Julia sought with eager anxiety to discover the sentiments of Vereza towards her; she revolved each circumstance of the day, but they afforded her little satisfaction; they reflected only a glimmering and uncertain light, which instead of guiding, served only to perplex her. Now she remembered some instance of particular attention, and then some mark of apparent indifference. She compared his conduct with that of the other young noblesse; and thought each appeared equally desirous of the favor of every lady present. All the ladies, however, appeared to her to court the admiration of Vereza, and she trembled lest he should be too sensible of the distinction. She drew from these reflections no positive inference; and though distrust rendered pain the predominate sensation, it was so exquisitely interwoven with delight, that she could not wish it exchanged for her former ease. Thoughtful and restless, sleep fled from her eyes, and she longed with impatience for the morning, which should again present Vereza, and enable her to pursue the enquiry. She rose early, and adorned herself with unusual care. In her favorite closet she awaited the hour of breakfast, and endeavoured to read, but her thoughts wandered from the subject. Her lute and favorite airs lost half their power to please; the day seemed to stand still—she became melancholy, and thought the breakfast-hour would never arrive. At length the clock struck the signal, the sound vibrated on every nerve, and trembling she quitted the closet for her sister's apartment. Love taught her disguise. Till then Emilia had shared all her thoughts; they now descended to the breakfast-room in silence, and Julia almost feared to meet her eye. In the breakfast-room they were alone. Julia found it impossible to support a conversation with Emilia, whose observations interrupting the course of her thoughts, became uninteresting and tiresome. She was therefore about to retire to her closet, when the marquis entered. His air was haughty, and his look severe. He coldly saluted his daughters, and they had scarcely time to reply to his general enquiries, when the marchioness entered, and the company soon after assembled. Julia, who had awaited with so painful an impatience for the moment which should present Vereza to her sight, now sighed that it was arrived. She scarcely dared to lift her timid eyes from the ground, and when by accident they met his, a soft tremour seized her; and apprehension lest he should discover her sentiments, served only to render her confusion conspicuous. At length, a glance from the marchioness recalled her bewildered thoughts; and other fears superseding those of love, her mind, by degrees, recovered its dignity. She could distinguish in the behaviour of Vereza no symptoms of particular admiration, and she resolved to conduct herself towards him with the most scrupulous care.

This day, like the preceding one, was devoted to joy. In the evening there was a concert, which was chiefly performed by the nobility. Ferdinand played the violoncello, Vereza the German flute, and Julia the piana-forte, which she touched with a delicacy and execution that engaged every auditor. The confusion of Julia may be easily imagined, when Ferdinand, selecting a beautiful duet, desired Vereza would accompany his sister. The pride of conscious excellence, however, quickly overcame her timidity, and enabled her to exert all her powers. The air was simple and pathetic, and she gave it those charms of expression so peculiarly her own. She struck the chords of her piana-forte in beautiful accompaniment, and towards the close of the second stanza, her voice resting on one note, swelled into a tone so exquisite, and from thence descended to a few simple notes, which she touched with such impassioned tenderness that every eye wept to the sounds. The breath of the flute trembled, and Hippolitus entranced, forgot to play. A pause of silence ensued at the conclusion of the piece, and continued till a general sigh seemed to awaken the audience from their enchantment. Amid the general applause, Hippolitus was silent. Julia observed his behaviour, and gently raising her eyes to his, there read the sentiments which she had inspired. An exquisite emotion thrilled her heart, and she experienced one of those rare moments which illuminate life with a ray of bliss, by which the darkness of its general shade is contrasted. Care, doubt, every disagreeable sensation vanished, and for the remainder of the evening she was conscious only of delight. A timid respect marked the manner of Hippolitus, more flattering to Julia than the most ardent professions. The evening concluded with a ball, and Julia was again the partner of the count.

When the ball broke up, she retired to her apartment, but not to sleep. Joy is as restless as anxiety or sorrow. She seemed to have entered upon a new state of existence;—those fine springs of affection which had hitherto lain concealed, were now touched, and yielded to her a happiness more exalted than any her imagination had ever painted. She reflected on the tranquillity of her past life, and comparing it with the emotions of the present hour, exulted in the difference. All her former pleasures now appeared insipid; she wondered that they ever had power to affect her, and that she had endured with content the dull uniformity to which she had been condemned. It was now only that she appeared to live. Absorbed in the single idea of being beloved, her imagination soared into the regions of romantic bliss, and bore her high above the possibility of evil. Since she was beloved by Hippolitus, she could only be happy.

From this state of entranced delight, she was awakened by the sound of music immediately under her window. It was a lute touched by a masterly hand. After a wild and melancholy symphony, a voice of more than magic expression swelled into an air so pathetic and tender, that it seemed to breathe the very soul of love. The chords of the lute were struck in low and sweet accompaniment. Julia listened, and distinguished the following words;

SONNET

Still is the night-breeze! — not a lonely sound

Steals through the silence of this dreary hour;

O'er these high battlements Sleep reigns profound,

And sheds on all, his sweet oblivious power.

On all but me — I vainly ask his dews

To steep in short forgetfulness my cares.

Th' affrighted god still flies when Love pursues,

Still — still denies the wretched lover's prayers.

An interval of silence followed, and the air was repeated; after which the music was heard no more. If before Julia believed that she was loved by Hippolitus, she was now confirmed in the sweet reality. But sleep at length fell upon her senses, and the airy forms of ideal bliss no longer fleeted before her imagination. Morning came, and she arose light and refreshed. How different were her present sensations from those of the preceding day. Her anxiety had now evaporated in joy, and she experienced that airy dance of spirits which accumulates delight from every object; and with a power like the touch of enchantment, can transform a gloomy desert into a smiling Eden. She flew to the breakfast-room, scarcely conscious of motion; but, as she entered it, a soft confusion overcame her; she blushed, and almost feared to meet the eyes of Vereza. She was presently relieved, however, for the Count was not there. The company assembled — Julia watched the entrance of every person with painful anxiety, but he for whom she looked did not appear. Surprised and uneasy, she fixed her eyes on the door, and whenever it opened, her heart beat with an expectation which was as often checked by disappointment. In spite of all her efforts, her vivacity sunk into languor, and she then perceived that love may produce other sensations than those of delight. She found it possible to be unhappy, though loved by Hippolitus; and acknowledged with a sigh of regret, which was yet new to her, how tremblingly her peace depended upon him. He neither appeared nor was mentioned at breakfast; but though delicacy prevented her enquiring after him, conversation soon became irksome to her, and she retired to the apartment of Madame de Menon. There she employed herself in painting, and endeavoured to beguile the time till the hour of dinner, when she hoped to see Hippolitus. Madame was, as usual, friendly and cheerful, but she perceived a reserve in the conduct of Julia, and penetrated without difficulty into its cause. She was, however, ignorant of the object of her pupil's admiration. The hour so eagerly desired by Julia at length arrived, and with a palpitating heart she entered the hall. The Count was not there, and in the course of conversation, she learned that he had that morning sailed for Naples. The scene which so lately appeared enchanting to her eyes, now changed its hue; and in the midst of society, and surrounded by gaiety, she was solitary and dejected. She accused herself of having suffered her wishes to mislead her judgment; and the present conduct of Hippolitus convinced her, that she had mistaken admiration for a sentiment more tender. She believed, too, that the musician who had addressed her in his sonnet, was not the Count; and thus at once was dissolved all the ideal fabric of her happiness. How short a period often reverses the character of our sentiments, rendering that which yesterday we despised, to-day desirable. The tranquil state which she had so lately delighted to quit, she now reflected upon with regret. She had, however, the consolation of believing that her sentiments towards the Count were unknown, and the sweet consciousness that her conduct had been governed by a nice sense of propriety.

The public rejoicings at the castle closed with the week; but the gay spirit of the marchioness forbade a return to tranquillity; and she substituted diversions more private, but in splendour scarcely inferior to the preceding ones. She had observed the behaviour of Hippolitus on the night of the concert with chagrin, and his departure with sorrow; yet, disdaining to perpetuate misfortune by reflection, she sought to lose the sense of disappointment in the hurry of dissipation. But her efforts to erase him from her remembrance were ineffectual.

Unaccustomed to oppose the bent of her inclinations, they now maintained unbounded sway; and she found too late, that in order to have a due command of our passions, it is necessary to subject them to early obedience. Passion, in its undue influence, produces weakness as well as injustice. The pain which now recoiled upon her heart from disappointment, she had not strength of mind to endure, and she sought relief from its pressure in afflicting the innocent. Julia, whose beauty she imagined had captivated the count, and confirmed him in indifference towards herself, she incessantly tormented by the exercise of those various and splenetic little arts which elude the eye of the common observer, and are only to be known by those who have felt them. Arts, which individually are inconsiderable, but in the aggregate amount to a cruel and decisive effect.

From Julia's mind the idea of happiness was now faded. Pleasure had withdrawn her beam from the prospect, and the objects no longer illumined by her ray, became dark and colourless. As often as her situation would permit, she withdrew from society, and sought the freedom of solitude, where she could indulge in melancholy thoughts, and give a loose to that despair which is so apt to follow the disappointment of our first hopes.

Week after week elapsed, yet no mention was made of returning to Naples. The marquis at length declared it his intention to spend the remainder of the summer in the castle. To this determination the marchioness submitted with decent resignation, for she was here surrounded by a croud of flatterers, and her invention supplied her with continual diversions: that gaiety which rendered Naples so dear to her, glittered in the woods of Mazzini, and resounded through the castle.

The apartments of Madame de Menon were spacious and noble. The windows opened upon the sea, and commanded a view of the straits of Messina, bounded on one side by the beautiful shores of the isle of Sicily, and on the other by the high mountains of Calabria. The straits, filled with vessels whose gay streamers glittered to the sun-beam, presented to the eye an ever-moving scene. The principal room opened upon a gallery that overhung the grand terrace of the castle, and it commanded a prospect which for beauty and extent has seldom been equalled. These were formerly considered the chief apartments of the castle; and when the Marquis quitted them for Naples, were allotted for the residence of Madame de Menon, and her young charge. The marchioness, struck with the prospect which the windows afforded, and with the pleasantness of the gallery, determined to restore the rooms to their former splendour. She signified this intention to madame, for whom other apartments were provided. The chambers of Emilia and Julia forming part of the suite, they were also claimed by the marchioness, who left Julia only her favorite closet. The rooms to which they removed were spacious, but gloomy; they had been for some years uninhabited; and though preparations had been made for the reception of their new inhabitants, an air of desolation reigned within them that inspired melancholy sensations. Julia observed that her chamber, which opened beyond madame's, formed a part of the southern building, with which, however, there appeared no means of communication. The late mysterious circumstances relating to this part of the fabric, now arose to her imagination, and conjured up a terror which reason could not subdue. She told her emotions to madame, who, with more prudence than sincerity, laughed at her fears. The behaviour of the marquis, the dying words of Vincent, together with the preceding circumstances of alarm, had sunk deep in the mind of madame, but she saw the necessity of confining to her own breast doubts which time only could resolve.

Julia endeavoured to reconcile herself to the change, and a circumstance soon occurred which obliterated her present sensations, and excited others far more interesting. One day that she was arranging some papers in the small drawers of a cabinet that stood in her apartment, she found a picture which fixed all her attention. It was a miniature of a lady, whose countenance was touched with sorrow, and expressed an air of dignified resignation. The mournful sweetness of her eyes, raised towards Heaven with a look of supplication, and the melancholy languor that shaded her features, so deeply affected Julia, that her eyes were filled with involuntary tears. She sighed and wept, still gazing on the picture, which seemed to engage her by a kind of fascination. She almost fancied that the portrait breathed, and that the eyes were fixed on hers with a look of penetrating softness. Full of the emotions which the miniature had excited, she presented it to madame, whose mingled sorrow and surprise increased her curiosity. But what were the various sensations which pressed upon her heart, on learning that she had wept over the resemblance of her mother! Deprived of a mother's tenderness before she was sensible of its value, it was now only that she mourned the event which lamentation could not recall. Emilia, with an emotion as exquisite, mingled her tears with those of her sister. With eager impatience they pressed madame to disclose the cause of that sorrow which so emphatically marked the features of their mother.

463

'Alas! my dear children,' said madame, deeply sighing, 'you engage me in a task too severe, not only for your peace, but for mine; since in giving you the information you require, I must retrace scenes of my own life, which I wish for ever obliterated. It would, however, be both cruel and unjust to withhold an explanation so nearly interesting to you, and I will sacrifice my own ease to your wishes.

'Louisa de Bernini, your mother, was, as you well know, the only daughter of the Count de Bernini. Of the misfortunes of your family, I believe you are yet ignorant. The chief estates of the count were situated in the Val di Demona, a valley deriving its name from its vicinity to Mount AEtna, which vulgar tradition has peopled with devils. In one of those dreadful eruptions of AEtna, which deluged this valley with a flood of fire, a great part of your grandfather's domains in that quarter were laid waste. The count was at that time with a part of his family at Messina, but the countess and her son, who were in the country, were destroyed. The remaining property of the count was proportionably inconsiderable, and the loss of his wife and son deeply affected him. He retired with Louisa, his only surviving child, who was then near fifteen, to a small estate near Cattania. There was some degree of relationship between your grandfather and myself; and your mother was attached to me by the ties of sentiment, which, as we grew up, united us still more strongly than those of blood. Our pleasures and our tastes were the same; and a similarity of misfortunes might, perhaps, contribute to cement our early friendship. I, like herself, had lost a parent in the eruption of AEtna. My mother had died before I understood her value; but my father, whom I revered and tenderly loved, was destroyed by one of those terrible events; his lands were buried beneath the lava, and he left an only son and myself to mourn his fate, and encounter the evils of poverty. The count, who was our nearest surviving relation, generously took us home to his house, and declared that he considered us as his children. To amuse his leisure hours, he undertook to finish the education of my brother, who was then about seventeen, and whose rising genius promised to reward the labours of the count. Louisa and myself often shared the instruction of her father, and at those hours Orlando was generally of the party. The tranquil retirement of the count's situation, the rational employment of his time between his own studies, the education of those whom he called his children, and the conversation of a few select friends, anticipated the effect of time, and softened the asperities of his distress into a tender complacent melancholy. As for Louisa and myself, who were yet new in life, and whose spirits possessed the happy elasticity of youth, our minds gradually shifted from suffering to tranquillity, and from tranquillity to happiness. I have sometimes thought that when my brother has been reading to her a delightful passage, the countenance of Louisa discovered a tender interest, which seemed to be excited rather by the reader than by the author. These days, which were surely the most enviable of our lives, now passed in serene enjoyments, and in continual gradations of improvement.

'The count designed my brother for the army, and the time now drew nigh when he was to join the Sicilian regiment, in which he had a commission. The absent thoughts, and dejected spirits of my cousin, now discovered to me the secret which had long been concealed even from herself; for it was not till Orlando was about to depart, that she perceived how dear he was to her peace. On the eve of his departure, the count lamented, with fatherly yet manly tenderness, the distance which was soon to separate us. "But we shall meet again," said he, "when the honors of war shall have rewarded the bravery of my son." Louisa grew pale, a half suppressed sigh escaped her, and, to conceal her emotion, she turned to her harpsichord.

'My brother had a favorite dog, which, before he set off, he presented to Louisa, and committing it to her care, begged she would be kind to it, and sometimes remember its master. He checked his rising emotion, but as he turned from her, I perceived the tear that wetted his cheek. He departed, and with him the spirit of our happiness seemed to evaporate. The scenes which his presence had formerly enlivened, were now forlorn and melancholy, yet we loved to wander in what were once his favorite haunts. Louisa forbore to mention my brother even to me, but frequently, when she thought herself unobserved, she would steal to her harpsichord, and repeat the strain which she had played on the evening before his departure.

'We had the pleasure to hear from time to time that he was well: and though his own modesty threw a veil over his conduct, we could collect from other accounts that he had behaved with great bravery. At length the time of his return approached, and the enlivened spirits of Louisa declared the influence he retained in her heart. He returned, bearing public testimony of his valour in the honors which had been conferred upon him. He was received with universal joy; the count welcomed him with the pride and fondness of a father, and the villa became again the seat of happiness. His person and manners were much improved; the elegant beauty of the youth was now exchanged for the graceful dignity of manhood, and some knowledge of the world was added to that of the sciences. The joy which illumined his countenance when he met Louisa, spoke at once his admiration and his love; and the blush which her observation of it brought upon her cheek, would have discovered, even to an uninterested spectator, that this joy was mutual.

'Orlando brought with him a young Frenchman, a brother officer, who had rescued him from imminent danger in battle, and whom he introduced to the count as his preserver. The count received him with gratitude and distinction, and he was for a considerable time an inmate at the villa. His manners were singularly pleasing, and his understanding was cultivated and refined. He soon discovered a partiality for me, and he was indeed too pleasing to be seen with indifference. Gratitude for the valuable life he had preserved, was perhaps the groundwork of an esteem which soon increased into the most affectionate love. Our attachment grew stronger as our acquaintance increased; and at length the chevalier de Menon asked me of the count, who consulted my heart, and finding it favorable to the connection, proceeded to make the necessary enquiries concerning the family of the stranger. He obtained a satisfactory and pleasing account of it. The chevalier was the second son of a French gentleman of large estates in France, who had been some years deceased. He had left several sons; the family-estate, of course, devolved to the eldest, but to the two younger he had bequeathed considerable property. Our marriage was solemnized in a private manner at the villa, in the presence of the count, Louisa, and my brother. Soon after the nuptials, my husband and Orlando were remanded to their regiments. My brother's affections were now unalterably fixed upon Louisa, but a sentiment of delicacy and generosity still kept him silent. He thought, poor as he was, to solicit the hand of Louisa, would be to repay the kindness of the count with ingratitude. I have seen the inward struggles of his heart, and mine has bled for him. The count and Louisa so earnestly solicited me to remain at the villa during the campaign, that at length my husband consented. We parted—O! let me forget that period!—Had I accompanied him, all might have been well; and the long, long years of affliction which followed had been spared me.'

The horn now sounded the signal for dinner, and interrupted the narrative of Madame. Her beauteous auditors wiped the tears from their eyes, and with extreme reluctance descended to the hall. The day was occupied with company and diversions, and it was not till late in the evening that they were suffered to retire. They hastened to madame immediately upon their being released; and too much interested for sleep, and too importunate to be repulsed, solicited the sequel of her story. She objected the lateness of the hour, but at length yielded to their entreaties. They drew their chairs close to hers; and every sense being absorbed in the single one of hearing, followed her through the course of her narrative.

'My brother again departed without disclosing his sentiments; the effort it cost him was evident, but his sense of honor surmounted every opposing consideration. Louisa again drooped, and pined in silent sorrow. I lamented equally for my friend and my brother; and have a thousand times accused that delicacy as false, which withheld them from the happiness they might so easily and so innocently have obtained. The behaviour of the count, at least to my eye, seemed to indicate the satisfaction which this union would have given him. It was about this period that the marquis Mazzini first saw and became enamoured of Louisa. His proposals were very flattering, but the count forbore to exert the undue authority of a father; and he ceased to press the connection, when he perceived that Louisa was really averse to it. Louisa was sensible of the generosity of his conduct, and she could scarcely reject the alliance without a sigh, which her gratitude paid to the kindness of her father.

'But an event now happened which dissolved at once our happiness, and all our air-drawn schemes for futurity. A dispute, which it seems originated in a trifle, but soon increased to a serious degree, arose between the Chevalier de Menon and my brother. It was decided by the sword, and my dear brother fell by the hand of my husband. I shall pass over this period of my life. It is too painful for recollection. The effect of this event upon Louisa was such as may be imagined. The world was now become indifferent to her, and as she had no prospect of happiness for herself, she was unwilling to withhold it from the father who had deserved so much of her. After some time, when the marquis renewed his addresses, she gave him her hand. The characters of the marquis and his lady were in their nature too opposite to form a happy union. Of this Louisa was very soon sensible; and though the mildness of her disposition made her tamely submit to the unfeeling authority of her husband, his behaviour sunk deep in her heart, and she pined in secret. It was impossible for her to avoid opposing the character of the marquis to that of him upon whom her affections had been so fondly and so justly fixed. The comparison increased her sufferings, which soon preyed upon her constitution, and very visibly affected her health. Her situation deeply afflicted the count, and united with the infirmities of age to shorten his life.

'Upon his death, I bade adieu to my cousin, and quitted Sicily for Italy, where the Chevalier de Menon had for some time expected me. Our meeting was very affecting. My resentment towards him was done away, when I observed his pale and altered countenance, and perceived the melancholy which preyed upon his heart. All the airy vivacity of his former manner was fled, and he was devoured by unavailing grief and remorse. He deplored with unceasing sorrow the friend he had murdered, and my presence seemed to open afresh the wounds which time had begun to close. His affliction, united with my own, was almost more than I could support, but I was doomed to suffer, and endure yet more. In a subsequent engagement my husband, weary of existence, rushed into the heat of battle, and there obtained an honorable death. In a paper which he left behind him, he said it was his intention to die in that battle; that he had long wished for death, and waited for an opportunity of obtaining it without staining his own character by the cowardice of suicide, or distressing me by an act of butchery. This event gave the finishing stroke to my afflictions; — yet let me retract; — another misfortune awaited me when I least expected one. The Chevalier de Menon died without a will, and his brothers refused to give up his estate, unless I could produce a witness of my marriage. I returned to Sicily, and, to my inexpressible sorrow, found that your mother had died during my stay abroad, a prey, I fear, to grief. The priest who performed the ceremony of my marriage, having been threatened with punishment for some ecclesiastical offences, had secretly left the country; and thus was I deprived of those proofs which were necessary to authenticate my claims to the estates of my husband. His brothers, to whom I was an utter stranger, were either too prejudiced to believe, or believing, were too dishonorable to acknowledge the justice of my claims. I was therefore at once abandoned to sorrow and to poverty; a small legacy from the count de Bernini being all that now remained to me.

'When the marquis married Maria de Vellorno, which was about this period, he designed to quit Mazzini for Naples. His son was to accompany him, but it was his intention to leave you, who were both very young, to the care of some person qualified to superintend your education. My circumstances rendered the office acceptable, and my former friendship for your mother made the duty pleasing to me. The marquis was, I believe, glad to be spared the trouble of searching further for what he had hitherto found it difficult to obtain — a person whom inclination as well as duty would bind to his interest.'

Madame ceased to speak, and Emilia and Julia wept to the memory of the mother, whose misfortunes this story recorded. The sufferings of madame, together with her former friendship for the late marchioness, endeared her to her pupils, who from this period endeavoured by every kind and delicate attention to obliterate the traces of her sorrows. Madame was sensible of this tenderness, and it was productive in some degree of the effect desired. But a subject soon after occurred, which drew off their minds from the consideration of their mother's fate to a subject more wonderful and equally interesting.

One night that Emilia and Julia had been detained by company, in ceremonial restraint, later than usual, they were induced, by the easy conversation of madame, and by the pleasure which a return to liberty naturally produces, to defer the hour of repose till the night was far advanced. They were engaged in interesting discourse, when madame, who was then speaking, was interrupted by a low hollow sound, which arose from beneath the apartment, and seemed like the closing of a door. Chilled into a silence, they listened and distinctly heard it repeated. Deadly ideas crowded upon their imaginations, and inspired a terror which scarcely allowed them to breathe. The noise lasted only for a moment, and a profound silence soon ensued. Their feelings at length relaxed, and suffered them to move to Emilia's apartment, when again they heard the same sounds. Almost distracted with fear, they rushed into madame's apartment, where Emilia sunk upon the bed and fainted. It was a considerable time ere the efforts of madame recalled her to sensation. When they were again tranquil, she employed all her endeavours to compose the spirits of the young ladies, and dissuade them from alarming the castle. Involved in dark and fearful doubts, she yet commanded her feelings, and endeavoured to assume an appearance of composure. The late behaviour of the marquis had convinced her that he was nearly connected with the mystery which hung over this part of the edifice; and she dreaded to excite his resentment by a further mention of alarms, which were perhaps only ideal, and whose reality she had certainly no means of proving.

Influenced by these considerations, she endeavoured to prevail on Emilia and Julia to await in silence some confirmation of their surmises; but their terror made this a very difficult task. They acquiesced, however, so far with her wishes, as to agree to conceal the preceding circumstances from every person but their brother, without whose protecting presence they declared it utterly impossible to pass another night in the apartments. For the remainder of this night they resolved to watch. To beguile the tediousness of the time they endeavoured to converse, but the minds of Emilia and Julia were too much affected by the late occurrence to wander from the subject. They compared this with the foregoing circumstance of the figure and the light which had appeared; their imaginations kindled wild conjectures, and they submitted their opinions to madame, entreating her to inform them sincerely, whether she believed that disembodied spirits were ever permitted to visit this earth.

'My children,' said she, 'I will not attempt to persuade you that the existence of such spirits is impossible. Who shall say that any thing is impossible to God? We know that he has made us, who are embodied spirits; he, therefore, can make unembodied spirits. If we cannot understand how such spirits exist, we should consider the limited powers of our minds, and that we cannot understand many things which are indisputably true. No one yet knows why the magnetic needle points to the north; yet you, who have never seen a magnet, do not hesitate to believe that it has this tendency, because you have been well assured of it, both from books and in conversation. Since, therefore, we are sure that nothing is impossible to God, and that such beings may exist, though we cannot tell how, we ought to consider by what evidence their existence is supported. I do not say that spirits have appeared; but if several discreet unprejudiced persons were to assure me that they had seen one, I should not be proud or bold enough to reply — 'it is impossible.' Let not, however, such considerations disturb your minds. I have said thus much, because I was unwilling to impose upon your understandings; it is now your part to exercise your reason, and preserve the unmoved confidence of virtue. Such spirits, if indeed they have ever been seen, can have appeared only by the express permission of God, and for some very singular purposes; be assured that there are no beings who act unseen by him; and that, therefore, there are none from whom innocence can ever suffer harm.'

No further sounds disturbed them for that time; and before the morning dawned, weariness insensibly overcame apprehension, and sunk them in repose.

When Ferdinand learned the circumstances relative to the southern side of the castle, his imagination seized with avidity each appearance of mystery, and inspired him with an irresistible desire to penetrate the secrets of his desolate part of the fabric. He very readily consented to watch with his sisters in Julia's apartment; but as his chamber was in a remote part of the castle, there would be some difficulty in passing unobserved to her's. It was agreed, however, that when all was hushed, he should make the attempt. Having thus resolved, Emilia and

Julia waited the return of night with restless and fearful impatience.

At length the family retired to rest. The castle clock had struck one, and Julia began to fear that Ferdinand had been discovered, when a knocking was heard at the door of the outer chamber.

Her heart beat with apprehensions, which reason could not justify. Madame rose, and enquiring who was there, was answered by the voice of Ferdinand. The door was cheerfully opened. They drew their chairs round him, and endeavoured to pass the time in conversation; but fear and expectation attracted all their thoughts to one subject, and madame alone preserved her composure. The hour was now come when the sounds had been heard the preceding night, and every ear was given to attention. All, however, remained quiet, and the night passed without any new alarm.

The greater part of several succeeding nights were spent in watching, but no sounds disturbed their silence. Ferdinand, in whose mind the late circumstances had excited a degree of astonishment and curiosity superior to common obstacles, determined, if possible, to gain admittance to those recesses of the castle, which had for so many years been hid from human eye. This, however, was a design which he saw little probability of accomplishing, for the keys of that part of the edifice were in the possession of the marquis, of whose late conduct he judged too well to believe he would suffer the apartments to be explored. He racked his invention for the means of getting access to them, and at length recollected that Julia's chamber formed a part of these buildings, it occurred to him, that according to the mode of building in old times, there might formerly have been a communication between them. This consideration suggested to him the possibility of a concealed door in her apartment, and he determined to survey it on the following night with great care.

CHAPTER III

The castle was buried in sleep when Ferdinand again joined his sisters in madame's apartment. With anxious curiosity they followed him to the chamber. The room was hung with tapestry. Ferdinand carefully sounded the wall which communicated with the southern buildings. From one part of it a sound was returned, which convinced him there was something less solid than stone. He removed the tapestry, and behind it appeared, to his inexpressible satisfaction, a small door. With a hand trembling through eagerness, he undrew the bolts, and was rushing forward, when he perceived that a lock withheld his passage. The keys of madame and his sisters were applied in vain, and he was compelled to submit to disappointment at the very moment when he congratulated himself on success, for he had with him no means of forcing the door.

He stood gazing on the door, and inwardly lamenting, when a low hollow sound was heard from beneath. Emilia and Julia seized his arm; and almost sinking with apprehension, listened in profound silence. A footstep was distinctly heard, as if passing through the apartment below, after which all was still. Ferdinand, fired by this confirmation of the late report, rushed on to the door, and again tried to burst his way, but it resisted all the efforts of his strength. The ladies now rejoiced in that circumstance which they so lately lamented; for the sounds had renewed their terror, and though the night passed without further disturbance, their fears were very little abated.

Ferdinand, whose mind was wholly occupied with wonder, could with difficulty await the return of night. Emilia and Julia were scarcely less impatient. They counted the minutes as they passed; and when the family retired to rest, hastened with palpitating hearts to the apartment of madame. They were soon after joined by Ferdinand, who brought with him tools for cutting away the lock of the door. They paused a few moments in the chamber in fearful silence, but no sound disturbed the stillness of night. Ferdinand applied a knife to the door, and in a short time separated the lock. The door yielded, and disclosed a large and gloomy gallery. He took a light. Emilia and Julia, fearful of remaining in the chamber, resolved to accompany him, and each seizing an arm of madame, they followed in silence. The gallery was in many parts falling to decay, the ceiling was broke, and the window-shutters shattered, which, together with the dampness of the walls, gave the place an air of wild desolation.

They passed lightly on, for their steps ran in whispering echoes through the gallery, and often did Julia cast a fearful glance around.

The gallery terminated in a large old stair-case, which led to a hall below; on the left appeared several doors which seemed to lead to separate apartments. While they hesitated which course to pursue, a light flashed faintly up the stair-case, and in a moment after passed away; at the same time was heard the sound of a distant footstep. Ferdinand drew his sword and sprang forward; his companions, screaming with terror, ran back to madame's apartment.

Ferdinand descended a large vaulted hall; he crossed it towards a low arched door, which was left half open, and through which streamed a ray of light. The door opened upon a narrow winding passage; he entered, and the light retiring, was quickly lost in the windings of the place. Still he went on. The passage grew narrower, and the frequent fragments of loose stone made it now difficult to proceed. A low door closed the avenue, resembling that by which he had entered. He opened it, and discovered a square room, from whence rose a winding stair-case, which led up the south tower of the castle. Ferdinand paused to listen; the sound of steps was ceased, and all was profoundly silent. A door on the right attracted his notice; he tried to open it, but it was fastened. He concluded, therefore, that the person, if indeed a human being it was that bore the light he had seen, had passed up the tower. After a momentary hesitation, he determined to ascend the stair-case, but its ruinous condition made this an adventure of some difficulty. The steps were decayed and broken, and the looseness of the stones rendered a footing very insecure. Impelled by an irresistible curiosity, he was undismayed, and began the ascent. He had not proceeded very far, when the stones of a step which his foot had just quitted, loosened by his weight, gave way; and dragging with them those adjoining, formed a chasm in the stair-case that terrified even Ferdinand, who was left tottering on the suspended half of the steps, in momentary expectation of falling to the bottom with the stone on which he rested. In the terror which this occasioned, he attempted to save himself by catching at a kind of beam which projected over the stairs, when the lamp dropped from his hand, and he was left in total darkness. Terror now usurped the place of every other interest, and he was utterly perplexed how to proceed. He feared to go on, lest the steps above, as infirm as those below, should yield to his weight; — to return was impracticable, for the darkness precluded the possibility of discovering a means. He determined, therefore, to remain in this situation till light

473

should dawn through the narrow grates in the walls, and enable him to contrive some method of letting himself down to the ground.

He had remained here above an hour, when he suddenly heard a voice from below. It seemed to come from the passage leading to the tower, and perceptibly drew nearer. His agitation was now extreme, for he had no power of defending himself, and while he remained in this state of torturing expectation, a blaze of light burst upon the stair-case beneath him. In the succeeding moment he heard his own name sounded from below. His apprehensions instantly vanished, for he distinguished the voices of madame and his sisters.

They had awaited his return in all the horrors of apprehension, till at length all fear for themselves was lost in their concern for him; and they, who so lately had not dared to enter this part of the edifice, now undauntedly searched it in quest of Ferdinand. What were their emotions when they discovered his perilous situation!

The light now enabled him to take a more accurate survey of the place. He perceived that some few stones of the steps which had fallen still remained attached to the wall, but he feared to trust to their support only. He observed, however, that the wall itself was partly decayed, and consequently rugged with the corners of half-worn stones. On these small projections he contrived, with the assistance of the steps already mentioned, to suspend himself, and at length gained the unbroken part of the stairs in safety. It is difficult to determine which individual of the party rejoiced most at this escape. The morning now dawned, and Ferdinand desisted for the present from farther enquiry.

The interest which these mysterious circumstances excited in the mind of Julia, had withdrawn her attention from a subject more dangerous to its peace. The image of Vereza, notwithstanding, would frequently intrude upon her fancy; and, awakening the recollection of happy emotions, would call forth a sigh which all her efforts could not suppress. She loved to indulge the melancholy of her heart in the solitude of the woods. One evening she took her lute to a favorite spot on the seashore, and resigning herself to a pleasing sadness, touched some sweet and plaintive airs. The purple flush of evening was diffused over the heavens. The sun, involved in clouds of splendid and innumerable hues, was setting o'er the distant waters, whose clear bosom glowed with rich reflection. The beauty of the scene, the soothing murmur of the high trees,

waved by the light air which overshadowed her, and the soft
shelling of the waves that flowed gently in upon the shores,
insensibly sunk her mind into a state of repose. She touched the
chords of her lute in sweet and wild melody, and sung the
following ode:

EVENING

Evening veil'd in dewy shades,
   Slowly sinks upon the main;
See th'empurpled glory fades,
   Beneath her sober, chasten'd reign.

Around her car the pensive Hours,
   In sweet illapses meet the sight,
Crown'd their brows with closing flow'rs
   Rich with chrystal dews of night.

Her hands, the dusky hues arrange
   O'er the fine tints of parting day;
Insensibly the colours change,
   And languish into soft decay.

Wide o'er the waves her shadowy veil she draws.
   As faint they die along the distant shores;
Through the still air I mark each solemn pause,
   Each rising murmur which the wild wave pours.

A browner shadow spreads upon the air,
   And o'er the scene a pensive grandeur throws;
The rocks — the woods a wilder beauty wear,
   And the deep wave in softer music flows;

And now the distant view where vision fails,
   Twilight and grey obscurity pervade;
Tint following tint each dark'ning object veils,
   Till all the landscape sinks into the shade.

Oft from the airy steep of some lone hill,

> While sleeps the scene beneath the purple glow:

And evening lives o'er all serene and still,

> Wrapt let me view the magic world below!

And catch the dying gale that swells remote,

> That steals the sweetness from the shepherd's flute:

The distant torrent's melancholy note

> And the soft warblings of the lover's lute.

Still through the deep'ning gloom of bow'ry shades

> To Fancy's eye fantastic forms appear;

Low whisp'ring echoes steal along the glades

> And thrill the ear with wildly-pleasing fear.

Parent of shades! — of silence! — dewy airs!

> Of solemn musing, and of vision wild!

To thee my soul her pensive tribute bears,

> And hails thy gradual step, thy influence mild.

Having ceased to sing, her fingers wandered over the lute in melancholy symphony, and for some moments she remained lost in the sweet sensations which the music and the scenery had inspired. She was awakened from her reverie, by a sigh that stole from among the trees, and directing her eyes whence it came, beheld — Hippolitus! A thousand sweet and mingled emotions pressed upon her heart, yet she scarcely dared to trust the evidence of sight. He advanced, and throwing himself at her feet: 'Suffer me,' said he, in a tremulous voice, 'to disclose to you the sentiments which you have inspired, and to offer you the effusions of a heart filled only with love and admiration.' 'Rise, my lord,' said Julia, moving from her seat with an air of dignity, 'that attitude is neither becoming you to use, or me to suffer. The evening is closing, and Ferdinand will be impatient to see you.'

'Never will I rise, madam,' replied the count, with an impassioned air, 'till' — He was interrupted by the marchioness, who at this moment entered the grove. On observing the position of the count she was retiring. 'Stay, madam,' said Julia, almost sinking under her confusion. 'By no means,' replied the marchioness, in a tone of irony, 'my presence would only interrupt a very agreeable scene. The count, I see, is willing to pay you his earliest respects.' Saying this she disappeared, leaving Julia distressed and offended, and the count provoked at the intrusion. He attempted to renew the subject, but Julia hastily followed the steps of the marchioness, and entered the castle.

The scene she had witnessed, raised in the marchioness a tumult of dreadful emotions. Love, hatred, and jealousy, raged by turns in her heart, and defied all power of controul. Subjected to their alternate violence, she experienced a misery more acute than any she had yet known. Her imagination, invigorated by opposition, heightened to her the graces of Hippolitus; her bosom glowed with more intense passion, and her brain was at length exasperated almost to madness.

In Julia this sudden and unexpected interview excited a mingled emotion of love and vexation, which did not soon subside. At length, however, the delightful consciousness of Vereza's love bore her high above every other sensation; again the scene more brightly glowed, and again her fancy overcame the possibility of evil.

During the evening a tender and timid respect distinguished the behaviour of the count towards Julia, who, contented with the certainty of being loved, resolved to conceal her sentiments till an explanation of his abrupt departure from Mazzini, and subsequent absence, should have dissipated the shadow of mystery which hung over this part of his conduct. She observed that the marchioness pursued her with steady and constant observation, and she carefully avoided affording the count an opportunity of renewing the subject of the preceding interview, which, whenever he approached her, seemed to tremble on his lips.

Night returned, and Ferdinand repaired to the chamber of Julia to pursue his enquiry. Here he had not long remained, when the strange and alarming sounds which had been heard on the preceding night were repeated. The circumstance that now sunk in terror the minds of Emilia and Julia, fired with new wonder that of Ferdinand, who seizing a light, darted through the discovered door, and almost instantly disappeared.

He descended into the same wild hall he had passed on the preceding night. He had scarcely reached the bottom of the stair-case, when a feeble light gleamed across the hall, and his eye caught the glimpse of a figure retiring through the low

477

arched door which led to the south tower. He drew his sword and rushed on. A faint sound died away along the passage, the windings of which prevented his seeing the figure he pursued. Of this, indeed, he had obtained so slight a view, that he scarcely knew whether it bore the impression of a human form. The light quickly disappeared, and he heard the door that opened upon the tower suddenly close. He reached it, and forcing it open, sprang forward; but the place was dark and solitary, and there was no appearance of any person having passed along it. He looked up the tower, and the chasm which the stair-case exhibited, convinced him that no human being could have passed up. He stood silent and amazed; examining the place with an eye of strict enquiry, he perceived a door, which was partly concealed by hanging stairs, and which till now had escaped his notice. Hope invigorated curiosity, but his expectation was quickly disappointed, for this door also was fastened. He tried in vain to force it. He knocked, and a hollow sullen sound ran in echoes through the place, and died away at a distance. It was evident that beyond this door were chambers of considerable extent, but after long and various attempts to reach them, he was obliged to desist, and he quitted the tower as ignorant and more dissatisfied than he had entered it. He returned to the hall, which he now for the first time deliberately surveyed. It was a spacious and desolate apartment, whose lofty roof rose into arches supported by pillars of black marble. The same substance inlaid the floor, and formed the stair-case. The windows were high and gothic. An air of proud sublimity, united with singular wildness, characterized the place, at the extremity of which arose several gothic arches, whose dark shade veiled in obscurity the extent beyond. On the left hand appeared two doors, each of which was fastened, and on the right the grand entrance from the courts. Ferdinand determined to explore the dark recess which terminated his view, and as he traversed the hall, his imagination, affected by the surrounding scene, often multiplied the echoes of his footsteps into uncertain sounds of strange and fearful import.

He reached the arches, and discovered beyond a kind of inner hall, of considerable extent, which was closed at the farther end by a pair of massy folding-doors, heavily ornamented with carving. They were fastened by a lock, and defied his utmost strength.

As he surveyed the place in silent wonder, a sullen groan arose from beneath the spot where he stood. His blood ran cold at the sound, but silence returning, and continuing unbroken, he attributed his alarm to the illusion of a fancy, which terror had impregnated. He made another effort to force the door, when a groan was repeated more hollow, and more dreadful than the first. At this moment all his courage forsook him; he quitted the door, and hastened to the stair-case, which he ascended almost breathless with terror.

He found Madame de Menon and his sisters awaiting his return in the most painful anxiety; and, thus disappointed in all his endeavours to penetrate the secret of these buildings, and fatigued with fruitless search, he resolved to suspend farther enquiry.

When he related the circumstances of his late adventure, the terror of Emilia and Julia was heightened to a degree that overcame every prudent consideration. Their apprehension of the marquis's displeasure was lost in a stronger feeling, and they resolved no longer to remain in apartments which offered only terrific images to their fancy. Madame de Menon almost equally alarmed, and more perplexed, by this combination of strange and unaccountable circumstances, ceased to oppose their design. It was resolved, therefore, that on the following day madame should acquaint the marchioness with such particulars of the late occurrence as their purpose made it necessary she should know, concealing their knowledge of the hidden door, and the incidents immediately dependant on it; and that madame should entreat a change of apartments.

Madame accordingly waited on the marchioness. The marchioness having listened to the account at first with surprise, and afterwards with indifference, condescended to reprove madame for encouraging superstitious belief in the minds of her young charge. She concluded with ridiculing as fanciful the circumstances related, and with refusing, on account of the numerous visitants at the castle, the request preferred to her.

It is true the castle was crowded with visitors; the former apartments of Madame de Menon were the only ones unoccupied, and these were in magnificent preparation for the pleasure of the marchioness, who was unaccustomed to sacrifice her own wishes to the comfort of those around her. She therefore treated lightly the subject, which, seriously attended to, would have endangered her new plan of delight.

But Emilia and Julia were too seriously terrified to obey the scruples of delicacy, or to be easily repulsed. They prevailed on Ferdinand to represent their situation to the marquis.

Meanwhile Hippolitus, who had passed the night in a state of sleepless anxiety, watched, with busy impatience, an opportunity of more fully disclosing to Julia the passion which glowed in his heart. The first moment in which he beheld her, had awakened in him an admiration which had since ripened into a sentiment more tender. He had been prevented formally declaring his passion by the circumstance which so suddenly called him to Naples. This was the dangerous illness of the Marquis de Lomelli, his near and much-valued relation. But it was a task too painful to depart in silence, and he contrived to inform Julia of his sentiments in the air which she heard so sweetly sung beneath her window.

When Hippolitus reached Naples, the marquis was yet living, but expired a few days after his arrival, leaving the count heir to the small possessions which remained from the extravagance of their ancestors.

The business of adjusting his rights had till now detained him from Sicily, whither he came for the sole purpose of declaring his love. Here unexpected obstacles awaited him. The jealous vigilance of the marchioness conspired with the delicacy of Julia, to withhold from him the opportunity he so anxiously sought.

When Ferdinand entered upon the subject of the southern buildings to the marquis, he carefully avoided mentioning the hidden door. The marquis listened for some time to the relation in gloomy silence, but at length assuming an air of displeasure, reprehended Ferdinand for yielding his confidence to those idle alarms, which he said were the suggestions of a timid imagination. 'Alarms,' continued he, 'which will readily find admittance to the weak mind of a woman, but which the firmer nature of man should disdain. — Degenerate boy! Is it thus you reward my care? Do I live to see my son the sport of every idle tale a woman may repeat? Learn to trust reason and your senses, and you will then be worthy of my attention.'

The marquis was retiring, and Ferdinand now perceived it necessary to declare, that he had himself witnessed the sounds he mentioned. 'Pardon me, my lord,' said he, 'in the late instance I have been just to your command — my senses have been the only evidences I have trusted. I have heard those sounds which I cannot doubt.' The marquis appeared shocked. Ferdinand perceived the change, and urged the subject so vigorously, that the marquis, suddenly assuming a look of grave importance, commanded him to attend him in the evening in his closet.

Ferdinand in passing from the marquis met Hippolitus. He was pacing the gallery in much seeming agitation, but observing Ferdinand, he advanced to him. 'I am ill at heart,' said he, in a melancholy tone, 'assist me with your advice. We will step into this apartment, where we can converse without interruption.'

'You are not ignorant,' said he, throwing himself into a chair, 'of the tender sentiments which your sister Julia has inspired. I entreat you by that sacred friendship which has so long united us, to afford me an opportunity of pleading my passion. Her heart, which is so susceptible of other impressions, is, I fear, insensible to love. Procure me, however, the satisfaction of certainty upon a point where the tortures of suspence are surely the most intolerable.'

'Your penetration,' replied Ferdinand, 'has for once forsaken you, else you would now be spared the tortures of which you complain, for you would have discovered what I have long observed, that Julia regards you with a partial eye.'

'Do not,' said Hippolitus, 'make disappointment more terrible by flattery; neither suffer the partiality of friendship to mislead your judgment. Your perceptions are affected by the warmth of your feelings, and because you think I deserve her distinction, you believe I possess it. Alas! you deceive yourself, but not me!'

'The very reverse,' replied Ferdinand; 'tis you who deceive yourself, or rather it is the delicacy of the passion which animates you, and which will ever operate against your clear perception of a truth in which your happiness is so deeply involved. Believe me, I speak not without reason:—she loves you.'

At these words Hippolitus started from his seat, and clasping his hands in fervent joy, 'Enchanting sounds!' cried he, in a voice tenderly impassioned; 'could I but believe ye!—could I but believe ye-this world were paradise!'

During this exclamation, the emotions of Julia, who sat in her closet adjoining, can with difficulty be imagined. A door which opened into it from the apartment where this conversation was held, was only half closed. Agitated with the pleasure this declaration excited, she yet trembled with apprehension lest she should be discovered. She hardly dared to breathe, much less to move across the closet to the door, which opened upon the gallery, whence she might probably have

481

escaped unnoticed, lest the sound of her step should betray her. Compelled, therefore, to remain where she was, she sat in a state of fearful distress, which no colour of language can paint.

'Alas!' resumed Hippolitus, 'I too eagerly admit the possibility of what I wish. If you mean that I should really believe you, confirm your assertion by some proof.' — 'Readily,' rejoined Ferdinand.

The heart of Julia beat quick.

'When you was so suddenly called to Naples upon the illness of the Marquis Lomelli, I marked her conduct well, and in that read the sentiments of her heart. On the following morning, I observed in her countenance a restless anxiety which I had never seen before. She watched the entrance of every person with an eager expectation, which was as often succeeded by evident disappointment. At dinner your departure was mentioned: — she spilt the wine she was carrying to her lips, and for the remainder of the day was spiritless and melancholy. I saw her ineffectual struggles to conceal the oppression at her heart. Since that time she has seized every opportunity of withdrawing from company. The gaiety with which she was so lately charmed — charmed her no longer; she became pensive, retired, and I have often heard her singing in some lonely spot, the most moving and tender airs. Your return produced a visible and instantaneous alteration; she has now resumed her gaiety; and the soft confusion of her countenance, whenever you approach, might alone suffice to convince you of the truth of my assertion.'

'O! talk for ever thus!' sighed Hippolitus. 'These words are so sweet, so soothing to my soul, that I could listen till I forgot I had a wish beyond them. Yes! — Ferdinand, these circumstances are not to be doubted, and conviction opens upon my mind a flow of extacy I never knew till now. O! lead me to her, that I may speak the sentiments which swell my heart.'

They arose, when Julia, who with difficulty had supported herself, now impelled by an irresistible fear of instant discovery, rose also, and moved softly towards the gallery. The sound of her step alarmed the count, who, apprehensive lest his conversation had been overheard, was anxious to be satisfied whether any person was in the closet. He rushed in, and discovered Julia! She caught at a chair to support her trembling frame; and overwhelmed with mortifying sensations, sunk into it, and hid her face in her robe. Hippolitus threw himself at her feet, and seizing her hand, pressed it to his lips in expressive silence. Some moments passed before the confusion of either would suffer them to speak. At length recovering his voice, 'Can you, madam,' said he, 'forgive this intrusion, so unintentional? or will it deprive me of that esteem which I have but lately ventured to believe I possessed, and which I value more than existence itself. O! speak my pardon! Let me not believe that a single accident has destroyed my peace for ever.'—'If your peace, sir, depends upon a knowledge of my esteem,' said Julia, in a tremulous voice, 'that peace is already secure. If I wished even to deny the partiality I feel, it would now be useless; and since I no longer wish this, it would also be painful.' Hippolitus could only weep his thanks over the hand he still held. 'Be sensible, however, of the delicacy of my situation,' continued she, rising, 'and suffer me to withdraw.' Saying this she quitted the closet, leaving Hippolitus overcome with this sweet confirmation of his wishes, and Ferdinand not yet recovered from the painful surprize which the discovery of Julia had excited. He was deeply sensible of the confusion he had occasioned her, and knew that apologies would not restore the composure he had so cruelly yet unwarily disturbed.

Ferdinand awaited the hour appointed by the marquis in impatient curiosity. The solemn air which the marquis assumed when he commanded him to attend, had deeply impressed his mind. As the time drew nigh, expectation increased, and every moment seemed to linger into hours. At length he repaired to the closet, where he did not remain long before the marquis entered. The same chilling solemnity marked his manner. He locked the door of the closet, and seating himself, addressed Ferdinand as follows:—

'I am now going to repose in you a confidence which will severely prove the strength of your honour. But before I disclose a secret, hitherto so carefully concealed, and now reluctantly told, you must swear to preserve on this subject an eternal silence. If you doubt the steadiness of your discretion—now declare it, and save yourself from the infamy, and the fatal consequences, which may attend a breach of your oath;—if, on the contrary, you believe yourself capable of a strict integrity—now accept the terms, and receive the secret I offer.' Ferdinand was awed by this exordium—the impatience of curiosity was for a while suspended, and he hesitated whether he should receive the secret upon such terms. At length he signified his consent, and the marquis arising, drew his sword from the scabbard.—'Here,' said he, offering it to Ferdinand, 'seal your vows—swear by this sacred pledge of honor never to repeat what I shall now reveal.' Ferdinand vowed upon the sword, and raising his eyes to heaven, solemnly swore. The marquis then resumed his seat, and proceeded.

'You are now to learn that, about a century ago, this castle was in the possession of Vincent, third marquis of Mazzini, my grandfather. At that time there existed an inveterate hatred between our family and that of della Campo. I shall not now revert to the origin of the animosity, or relate the particulars of the consequent feuds — suffice it to observe, that by the power of our family, the della Campos were unable to preserve their former consequence in Sicily, and they have therefore quitted it for a foreign land to live in unmolested security. To return to my subject. — My grandfather, believing his life endangered by his enemy, planted spies upon him. He employed some of the numerous banditti who sought protection in his service, and after some weeks past in waiting for an opportunity, they seized Henry della Campo, and brought him secretly to this castle. He was for some time confined in a close chamber of the southern buildings, where he expired; by what means I shall forbear to mention. The plan had been so well conducted, and the secrecy so strictly preserved, that every endeavour of his family to trace the means of his disappearance proved ineffectual. Their conjectures, if they fell upon our family, were supported by no proof; and the della Campos are to this day ignorant of the mode of his death. A rumour had prevailed long before the death of my father, that the southern buildings of the castle were haunted. I disbelieved the fact, and treated it accordingly. One night, when every human being of the castle, except myself, was retired to rest, I had such strong and dreadful proofs of the general assertion, that even at this moment I cannot recollect them without horror. Let me, if possible, forget them. From that moment I forsook those buildings; they have ever since been shut up, and the circumstance I have mentioned, is the true reason why I have resided so little at the castle.'

Ferdinand listened to this narrative in silent horror. He remembered the temerity with which he had dared to penetrate those apartments — the light, and figure he had seen — and, above all, his situation in the stair-case of the tower. Every nerve thrilled at the recollection; and the terrors of remembrance almost equalled those of reality.

The marquis permitted his daughters to change their apartments, but he commanded Ferdinand to tell them, that, in granting their request, he consulted their ease only, and was himself by no means convinced of its propriety. They were accordingly reinstated in their former chambers, and the great room only of madame's apartments was reserved for the marchioness, who expressed her discontent to the marquis in terms of mingled censure and lamentation. The marquis privately reproved his daughters, for what he termed the idle fancies of a weak mind; and desired them no more to disturb the peace of the castle with the subject of their late fears. They received this reproof with silent submission—too much pleased with the success of their suit to be susceptible of any emotion but joy.

Ferdinand, reflecting on the late discovery, was shocked to learn, what was now forced upon his belief, that he was the descendant of a murderer. He now knew that innocent blood had been shed in the castle, and that the walls were still the haunt of an unquiet spirit, which seemed to call aloud for retribution on the posterity of him who had disturbed its eternal rest. Hippolitus perceived his dejection, and entreated that he might participate his uneasiness; but Ferdinand, who had hitherto been frank and ingenuous, was now inflexibly reserved. 'Forbear,' said he, 'to urge a discovery of what I am not permitted to reveal; this is the only point upon which I conjure you to be silent, and this even to you, I cannot explain.' Hippolitus was surprized, but pressed the subject no farther.

Julia, though she had been extremely mortified by the circumstances attendant on the discovery of her sentiments to Hippolitus, experienced, after the first shock had subsided, an emotion more pleasing than painful. The late conversation had painted in strong colours the attachment of her lover. His diffidence—his slowness to perceive the effect of his merit—his succeeding rapture, when conviction was at length forced upon his mind; and his conduct upon discovering Julia, proved to her at once the delicacy and the strength of his passion, and she yielded her heart to sensations of pure and unmixed delight. She was roused from this state of visionary happiness, by a summons from the marquis to attend him in the library. A circumstance so unusual surprized her, and she obeyed with trembling curiosity. She found him pacing the room in deep thought, and she had shut the door before he perceived her. The authoritative severity in his countenance alarmed her, and prepared her for a subject of importance. He seated himself by her, and continued a moment silent. At length, steadily observing her, 'I sent for you, my child,' said he, 'to declare the honor which awaits you. The Duke de Luovo has solicited your hand. An alliance so splendid was beyond my expectation. You will receive the distinction with the gratitude it claims, and prepare for the celebration of the nuptials.'

This speech fell like the dart of death upon the heart of Julia. She sat motionless—stupified and deprived of the power of utterance. The marquis observed her consternation; and mistaking its cause, 'I acknowledge,' said he, 'that there is somewhat abrupt in this affair; but the joy occasioned by a distinction so unmerited on your part, ought to overcome the little feminine weakness you might otherwise indulge. Retire and compose yourself; and observe,' continued he, in a stern voice, 'this is no time for finesse.' These words roused Julia from her state of horrid stupefaction. 'O! sir,' said she, throwing herself at his feet, 'forbear to enforce authority upon a point where to obey you would be worse than death; if, indeed, to obey you were possible.'—'Cease,' said the marquis, 'this affectation, and practice what becomes you.'—'Pardon me, my lord,' she replied, 'my distress is, alas! unfeigned. I cannot love the duke.'—'Away!' interrupted the marquis, 'nor tempt my rage with objections thus childish and absurd.'—'Yet hear me, my lord,' said Julia, tears swelling in her eyes, 'and pity the sufferings of a child, who never till this moment has dared to dispute your commands.'

'Nor shall she now,' said the marquis. 'What—when wealth, honor, and distinction, are laid at my feet, shall they be refused, because a foolish girl—a very baby, who knows not good from evil, cries, and says she cannot love! Let me not think of it—My just anger may, perhaps, out-run discretion, and tempt me to chastise your folly.—Attend to what I say—accept the duke, or quit this castle for ever, and wander where you will.' Saying this, he burst away, and Julia, who had hung weeping upon his knees, fell prostrate upon the floor. The violence of the fall completed the effect of her distress, and she fainted. In this state she remained a considerable time. When she recovered her senses, the recollection of her calamity burst upon her mind with a force that almost again overwhelmed her. She at length raised herself from the ground, and moved towards her own apartment, but had scarcely reached the great gallery, when Hippolitus entered it. Her trembling limbs would no longer support her; she caught at a bannister to save herself; and Hippolitus, with all his speed, was scarcely in time to prevent her falling. The pale distress exhibited in her countenance terrified him, and he anxiously enquired concerning it. She could answer him only with her tears, which she found it impossible to suppress; and gently disengaging herself, tottered to her closet. Hippolitus followed her to the door, but desisted from further importunity. He pressed her hand to his lips in tender silence, and withdrew, surprized and alarmed.

Julia, resigning herself to despair, indulged in solitude the excess of her grief. A calamity, so dreadful as the present, had never before presented itself to her imagination. The union proposed would have been hateful to her, even if she had no prior attachment; what then must have been her distress, when she had given her heart to him who deserved all her admiration, and returned all her affection.

The Duke de Luovo was of a character very similar to that of the marquis. The love of power was his ruling passion; — with him no gentle or generous sentiment meliorated the harshness of authority, or directed it to acts of beneficence. He delighted in simple undisguised tyranny. He had been twice married, and the unfortunate women subjected to his power, had fallen victims to the slow but corroding hand of sorrow. He had one son, who some years before had escaped the tyranny of his father, and had not been since heard of. At the late festival the duke had seen Julia; and her beauty made so strong an impression upon him, that he had been induced now to solicit her hand. The marquis, delighted with the prospect of a connection so flattering to his favorite passion, readily granted his consent, and immediately sealed it with a promise.

Julia remained for the rest of the day shut up in her closet, where the tender efforts of Madame and Emilia were exerted to soften her distress. Towards the close of evening Ferdinand entered. Hippolitus, shocked at her absence, had requested him to visit her, to alleviate her affliction, and, if possible, to discover its cause. Ferdinand, who tenderly loved his sister, was alarmed by the words of Hippolitus, and immediately sought her. Her eyes were swelled with weeping, and her countenance was but too expressive of the state of her mind. Ferdinand's distress, when told of his father's conduct, was scarcely less than her own. He had pleased himself with the hope of uniting the sister of his heart with the friend whom he loved. An act of cruel authority now dissolved the fairy dream of happiness which his fancy had formed, and destroyed the peace of those most dear to him. He sat for a long time silent and dejected; at length, starting from his melancholy reverie, he bad Julia good-night, and returned to Hippolitus, who was waiting for him with anxious impatience in the north hall.

Ferdinand dreaded the effect of that despair, which the intelligence he had to communicate would produce in the mind of Hippolitus. He revolved some means of softening the dreadful truth; but Hippolitus, quick to apprehend the evil which love taught him to fear, seized at once upon the reality. 'Tell me all,' said he, in a tone of assumed firmness. 'I am

prepared for the worst.' Ferdinand related the decree of the
marquis, and Hippolitus soon sunk into an excess of grief which
defied, as much as it required, the powers of alleviation.

Julia, at length, retired to her chamber, but the sorrow which
occupied her mind withheld the blessings of sleep. Distracted
and restless she arose, and gently opened the window of her
apartment. The night was still, and not a breath disturbed the
surface of the waters. The moon shed a mild radiance over the
waves, which in gentle undulations flowed upon the sands. The
scene insensibly tranquilized her spirits. A tender and pleasing
melancholy diffused itself over her mind; and as she mused, she
heard the dashing of distant oars. Presently she perceived upon
the light surface of the sea a small boat. The sound of the oars
ceased, and a solemn strain of harmony (such as fancy wafts
from the abodes of the blessed) stole upon the silence of night.
A chorus of voices now swelled upon the air, and died away at
a distance. In the strain Julia recollected the midnight hymn to
the virgin, and holy enthusiasm filled her heart. The chorus was
repeated, accompanied by a solemn striking of oars. A sigh of
exstacy stole from her bosom. Silence returned. The divine
melody she had heard calmed the tumult of her mind, and she
sunk in sweet repose.

She arose in the morning refreshed by light slumbers; but
the recollection of her sorrows soon returned with new force,
and sickening faintness overcame her. In this situation she
received a message from the marquis to attend him instantly.
She obeyed, and he bade her prepare to receive the duke, who
that morning purposed to visit the castle. He commanded her to
attire herself richly, and to welcome him with smiles. Julia
submitted in silence. She saw the marquis was inflexibly
resolved, and she withdrew to indulge the anguish of her heart,
and prepare for this detested interview.

The clock had struck twelve, when a flourish of trumpets
announced the approach of the duke. The heart of Julia sunk at
the sound, and she threw herself on a sopha, overwhelmed with
bitter sensations. Here she was soon disturbed by a message
from the marquis. She arose, and tenderly embracing Emilia,
their tears for some moments flowed together. At length,
summoning all her fortitude, she descended to the hall, where
she was met by the marquis. He led her to the saloon in which
the duke sat, with whom having conversed a short time, he
withdrew. The emotion of Julia at this instant was beyond any
thing she had before suffered; but by a sudden and strange
exertion of fortitude, which the force of desperate calamity
sometimes affords us, but which inferior sorrow toils after in

vain, she recovered her composure, and resumed her natural dignity. For a moment she wondered at herself, and she formed the dangerous resolution of throwing herself upon the generosity of the duke, by acknowledging her reluctance to the engagement, and soliciting him to withdraw his suit.

The duke approached her with an air of proud condescension; and taking her hand, placed himself beside her. Having paid some formal and general compliments to her beauty, he proceeded to profess himself her admirer. She listened for some time to his professions, and when he appeared willing to hear her, she addressed him — 'I am justly sensible, my lord, of the distinction you offer me, and must lament that respectful gratitude is the only sentiment I can return. Nothing can more strongly prove my confidence in your generosity, than when I confess to you, that parental authority urges me to give my hand whither my heart cannot accompany it.'

She paused — the duke continued silent. — ''Tis you only, my lord, who can release me from a situation so distressing; and to your goodness and justice I appeal, certain that necessity will excuse the singularity of my conduct, and that I shall not appeal in vain.'

The duke was embarrassed — a flush of pride overspread his countenance, and he seemed endeavouring to stifle the feelings that swelled his heart. 'I had been prepared, madam,' said he, 'to expect a very different reception, and had certainly no reason to believe that the Duke de Luovo was likely to sue in vain. Since, however, madam, you acknowledge that you have already disposed of your affections, I shall certainly be very willing, if the marquis will release me from our mutual engagements, to resign you to a more favored lover.'

'Pardon me, my lord,' said Julia, blushing, 'suffer me to' — 'I am not easily deceived, madam,' interrupted the duke, — 'your conduct can be attributed only to the influence of a prior attachment; and though for so young a lady, such a circumstance is somewhat extraordinary, I have certainly no right to arraign your choice. Permit me to wish you a good morning.' He bowed low, and quitted the room. Julia now experienced a new distress; she dreaded the resentment of the marquis, when he should be informed of her conversation with the duke, of whose character she now judged too justly not to repent the confidence she had reposed in him.

The duke, on quitting Julia, went to the marquis, with whom he remained in conversation some hours. When he had left the castle, the marquis sent for his daughter, and poured forth his resentment with all the violence of threats, and all the acrimony of contempt. So severely did he ridicule the idea of her disposing of her heart, and so dreadfully did he denounce vengeance on her disobedience, that she scarcely thought herself safe in his presence. She stood trembling and confused, and heard his reproaches without the power to reply. At length the marquis informed her, that the nuptials would be solemnized on the third day from the present; and as he quitted the room, a flood of tears came to her relief, and saved her from fainting.

Julia passed the remainder of the day in her closet with Emilia. Night returned, but brought her no peace. She sat long after the departure of Emilia; and to beguile recollection, she selected a favorite author, endeavouring to revive those sensations his page had once excited. She opened to a passage, the tender sorrow of which was applicable to her own situation, and her tears flowed wean. Her grief was soon suspended by apprehension. Hitherto a deadly silence had reigned through the castle, interrupted only by the wind, whose low sound crept at intervals through the galleries. She now thought she heard a footstep near her door, but presently all was still, for she believed she had been deceived by the wind. The succeeding moment, however, convinced her of her error, for she distinguished the low whisperings of some persons in the gallery. Her spirits, already weakened by sorrow, deserted her: she was seized with an universal terror, and presently afterwards a low voice called her from without, and the door was opened by Ferdinand.

She shrieked, and fainted. On recovering, she found herself supported by Ferdinand and Hippolitus, who had stolen this moment of silence and security to gain admittance to her presence. Hippolitus came to urge a proposal which despair only could have suggested. 'Fly,' said he, 'from the authority of a father who abuses his power, and assert the liberty of choice, which nature assigned you. Let the desperate situation of my hopes plead excuse for the apparent boldness of this address, and let the man who exists but for you be the means of saving you from destruction. Alas! madam, you are silent, and perhaps I have forfeited, by this proposal, the confidence I so lately flattered myself I possessed. If so, I will submit to my fate in silence, and will to-morrow quit a scene which presents only images of distress to my mind.'

Julia could speak but with her tears. A variety of strong and contending emotions struggled at her breast, and suppressed the power of utterance. Ferdinand seconded the proposal of the count. 'It is unnecessary,' my sister, said he, 'to point out the misery which awaits you here. I love you too well tamely to suffer you to be sacrificed to ambition, and to a passion still more hateful. I now glory in calling Hippolitus my friend—let me ere long receive him as a brother. I can give no stronger testimony of my esteem for his character, than in the wish I now express. Believe me he has a heart worthy of your acceptance—a heart noble and expansive as your own.'—'Ah, cease,' said Julia, 'to dwell upon a character of whose worth I am fully sensible. Your kindness and his merit can never be forgotten by her whose misfortunes you have so generously suffered to interest you.' She paused in silent hesitation. A sense of delicacy made her hesitate upon the decision which her heart so warmly prompted. If she fled with Hippolitus, she would avoid one evil, and encounter another. She would escape the dreadful destiny awaiting her, but must, perhaps, sully the purity of that reputation, which was dearer to her than existence. In a mind like hers, exquisitely susceptible of the pride of honor, this fear was able to counteract every other consideration, and to keep her intentions in a state of painful suspense. She sighed deeply, and continued silent. Hippolitus was alarmed by the calm distress which her countenance exhibited. 'O! Julia,' said he, 'relieve me from this dreadful suspense!—speak to me—explain this silence.' She looked mournfully upon him—her lips moved, but no sounds were uttered. As he repeated his question, she waved her hand, and sunk back in her chair. She had not fainted, but continued some time in a state of stupor not less alarming. The importance of the present question, operating upon her mind, already harassed by distress, had produced a temporary suspension of reason. Hippolitus hung over her in an agony not to be described, and Ferdinand vainly repeated her name. At length uttering a deep sigh, she raised herself, and, like one awakened from a dream, gazed around her. Hippolitus thanked God fervently in his heart. 'Tell me but that you are well,' said he, 'and that I may dare to hope, and we will leave you to repose.'—'My sister,' said Ferdinand, 'consult only your own wishes, and leave the rest to me. Suffer a confidence in me to dissipate the doubts with which you are agitated.'—'Ferdinand,' said Julia, emphatically, 'how shall I express the gratitude your kindness has excited?'—'Your gratitude,' said he, 'will be best shown in consulting your own wishes; for be assured, that whatever procures your happiness, will most effectually establish mine. Do not suffer the prejudices of education to render you miserable. Believe me, that a choice which involves the happiness or misery of your whole life, ought to be decided only by yourself.'

'Let us forbear for the present,' said Hippolitus, 'to urge the subject. Repose is necessary for you,' addressing Julia, 'and I will not suffer a selfish consideration any longer to with-hold you from it. — Grant me but this request — that at this hour to-morrow night, I may return hither to receive my doom.' Julia having consented to receive Hippolitus and Ferdinand, they quitted the closet. In turning into the grand gallery, they were surprised by the appearance of a light, which gleamed upon the wall that terminated their view. It seemed to proceed from a door which opened upon a back stair-case. They pushed on, but it almost instantly disappeared, and upon the stair-case all was still. They then separated, and retired to their apartments, somewhat alarmed by this circumstance, which induced them to suspect that their visit to Julia had been observed.

Julia passed the night in broken slumbers, and anxious consideration. On her present decision hung the crisis of her fate. Her consciousness of the influence of Hippolitus over her heart, made her fear to indulge its predilection, by trusting to her own opinion of its fidelity. She shrunk from the disgraceful idea of an elopement; yet she saw no means of avoiding this, but by rushing upon the fate so dreadful to her imagination.

On the following night, when the inhabitants of the castle were retired to rest, Hippolitus, whose expectation had lengthened the hours into ages, accompanied by Ferdinand, revisited the closet. Julia, who had known no interval of rest since they last left her, received them with much agitation. The vivid glow of health had fled her cheek, and was succeeded by a languid delicacy, less beautiful, but more interesting. To the eager enquiries of Hippolitus, she returned no answer, but faintly smiling through her tears, presented him her hand, and covered her face with her robe. 'I receive it,' cried he, 'as the pledge of my happiness; — yet — yet let your voice ratify the gift.' 'If the present concession does not sink me in your esteem,' said Julia, in a low tone, 'this hand is yours.' — 'The concession, my love, (for by that tender name I may now call you) would, if possible, raise you in my esteem; but since that has been long incapable of addition, it can only heighten my opinion of myself, and increase my gratitude to you: gratitude which I will endeavour to shew by an anxious care of your happiness, and by the tender attentions of a whole life. From this blessed moment,' continued he, in a voice of rapture, 'permit me, in thought, to hail you as my wife. From this moment let me banish every vestige of sorrow; — let me dry those tears,' gently pressing her cheek with his lips, 'never to spring again.' — The gratitude and joy which Ferdinand expressed upon this occasion, united with the tenderness of Hippolitus to soothe the agitated spirits of Julia, and she gradually recovered her complacency.

They now arranged their plan of escape; in the execution of which, no time was to be lost, since the nuptials with the duke were to be solemnized on the day after the morrow. Their scheme, whatever it was that should be adopted, they, therefore, resolved to execute on the following night. But when they descended from the first warmth of enterprize, to minuter examination, they soon found the difficulties of the undertaking. The keys of the castle were kept by Robert, the confidential servant of the marquis, who every night deposited them in an iron chest in his chamber. To obtain them by stratagem seemed impossible, and Ferdinand feared to tamper with the honesty of this man, who had been many years in the service of the marquis. Dangerous as was the attempt, no other alternative appeared, and they were therefore compelled to rest all their hopes upon the experiment. It was settled, that if the keys could be procured, Ferdinand and Hippolitus should meet Julia in the closet; that they should convey her to the seashore, from whence a boat, which was to be kept in waiting, would carry them to the opposite coast of Calabria, where the marriage might be solemnized without danger of interruption. But, as it was necessary that Ferdinand should not appear in the affair, it was agreed that he should return to the castle immediately upon the embarkation of his sister. Having thus arranged their plan of operation, they separated till the following night, which was to decide the fate of Hippolitus and Julia.

Julia, whose mind was soothed by the fraternal kindness of Ferdinand, and the tender assurances of Hippolitus, now experienced an interval of repose. At the return of day she awoke refreshed, and tolerably composed. She selected a few clothes which were necessary, and prepared them for her journey. A sentiment of generosity justified her in the reserve she preserved to Emilia and Madame de Menon, whose faithfulness and attachment she could not doubt, but whom she disdained to involve in the disgrace that must fall upon them, should their knowledge of her flight be discovered.

In the mean time the castle was a scene of confusion. The magnificent preparations which were making for the nuptials, engaged all eyes, and busied all hands. The marchioness had the direction of the whole; and the alacrity with which she acquitted herself, testified how much she was pleased with the alliance, and created a suspicion, that it had not been concerted without some exertion of her influence. Thus was Julia designed the joint victim of ambition and illicit love.

The composure of Julia declined with the day, whose hours had crept heavily along. As the night drew on, her anxiety for the success of Ferdinand's negociation with Robert increased to a painful degree. A variety of new emotions pressed at her heart, and subdued her spirits. When she bade Emilia good night, she thought she beheld her for the last time. The ideas of the distance which would separate them, of the dangers she was going to encounter, with a train of wild and fearful anticipations, crouded upon her mind, tears sprang in her eyes, and it was with difficulty she avoided betraying her emotions. Of madame, too, her heart took a tender farewell. At length she heard the marquis retire to his apartment, and the doors belonging to the several chambers of the guests successively close. She marked with trembling attention the gradual change from bustle to quiet, till all was still.

She now held herself in readiness to depart at the moment in which Ferdinand and Hippolitus, for whose steps in the gallery she eagerly listened, should appear. The castle clock struck twelve. The sound seemed to shake the pile. Julia felt it thrill upon her heart. 'I hear you,' sighed she, 'for the last time.' The stillness of death succeeded. She continued to listen; but no sound met her ear. For a considerable time she sat in a state of anxious expectation not to be described. The clock chimed the successive quarters; and her fear rose to each additional sound. At length she heard it strike one. Hollow was that sound, and dreadful to her hopes; for neither Hippolitus nor Ferdinand appeared. She grew faint with fear and disappointment. Her mind, which for two hours had been kept upon the stretch of expectation, now resigned itself to despair. She gently opened the door of her closet, and looked upon the gallery; but all was lonely and silent. It appeared that Robert had refused to be accessary to their scheme; and it was probable that he had betrayed it to the marquis. Overwhelmed with bitter reflections, she threw herself upon the sopha in the first distraction of despair. Suddenly she thought she heard a noise in the gallery; and as she started from her posture to listen to the sound, the door of her closet was gently opened by Ferdinand. 'Come, my love,' said he, 'the keys are ours, and we have not a moment to lose; our delay has been unavoidable; but this is no time for explanation.' Julia, almost fainting, gave her hand to Ferdinand, and Hippolitus, after some short expression of his thankfulness, followed. They passed the door of madame's chamber; and treading the gallery with slow and silent steps, descended to the hall. This they crossed towards a door, after opening which, they were to find their way, through various passages, to a remote part of the castle, where a private door opened upon the walls. Ferdinand carried the several keys. They fastened the hall door after them, and proceeded through a narrow passage terminating in a stair-case.

They descended, and had hardly reached the bottom, when they heard a loud noise at the door above, and presently the voices of several people. Julia scarcely felt the ground she trod on, and Ferdinand flew to unlock a door that obstructed their way. He applied the different keys, and at length found the proper one; but the lock was rusted, and refused to yield. Their distress was not now to be conceived. The noise above increased; and it seemed as if the people were forcing the door. Hippolitus and Ferdinand vainly tried to turn the key. A sudden crash from above convinced them that the door had yielded, when making another desperate effort, the key broke in the lock. Trembling and exhausted, Julia gave herself up for lost. As she hung upon Ferdinand, Hippolitus vainly endeavoured to sooth her—the noise suddenly ceased. They listened, dreading to hear the sounds renewed; but, to their utter astonishment, the silence of the place remained undisturbed. They had now time to breathe, and to consider the possibility of effecting their escape; for from the marquis they had no mercy to hope. Hippolitus, in order to ascertain whether the people had quitted the door above, began to ascend the passage, in which he had not gone many steps when the noise was renewed with increased violence. He instantly retreated; and making a desperate push at the door below, which obstructed their passage, it seemed to yield, and by another effort of Ferdinand, burst open. They had not an instant to lose; for they now heard the steps of persons descending the stairs. The avenue they were in opened into a kind of chamber, whence three passages branched, of which they immediately chose the first. Another door now obstructed their passage; and they were compelled to wait while Ferdinand applied the keys. 'Be quick,' said Julia, 'or we are lost. O! if this lock too is rusted!'—'Hark!' said Ferdinand. They now discovered what apprehension had before prevented them from perceiving, that the sounds of pursuit were ceased, and all again was silent. As this could happen only by the mistake of their pursuers, in taking the wrong route, they resolved to preserve their advantage, by concealing the light, which Ferdinand now covered with his cloak. The door was opened, and they passed on; but they were perplexed in the intricacies of the place, and wandered about in vain endeavour to find their way. Often did they pause to listen, and often did fancy give them sounds of fearful import. At length they entered on the passage which Ferdinand knew led directly to a door that opened on the woods. Rejoiced at this certainty, they soon reached the spot which was to give them liberty.

Ferdinand turned the key; the door unclosed, and, to their infinite joy, discovered to them the grey dawn. 'Now, my love,' said Hippolitus, 'you are safe, and I am happy.'—Immediately a loud voice from without exclaimed, 'Take, villain, the reward of your perfidy!' At the same instant Hippolitus received a sword in his body, and uttering a deep sigh, fell to the ground. Julia shrieked and fainted; Ferdinand drawing his sword, advanced towards the assassin, upon whose countenance the light of his lamp then shone, and discovered to him his father! The sword fell from his grasp, and he started back in an agony of horror. He was instantly surrounded, and seized by the servants of the marquis, while the marquis himself denounced vengeance upon his head, and ordered him to be thrown into the dungeon of the castle. At this instant the servants of the count, who were awaiting his arrival on the seashore, hearing the tumult, hastened to the scene, and there beheld their beloved master lifeless and weltering in his blood. They conveyed the bleeding body, with loud lamentations, on board the vessel which had been prepared for him, and immediately set sail for Italy.

Julia, on recovering her senses, found herself in a small room, of which she had no remembrance, with her maid weeping over her. Recollection, when it returned, brought to her mind an energy of grief, which exceeded even all former conceptions of sufferings. Yet her misery was heightened by the intelligence which she now received. She learned that Hippolitus had been borne away lifeless by his people, that Ferdinand was confined in a dungeon by order of the marquis, and that herself was a prisoner in a remote room, from which, on the day after the morrow, she was to be removed to the chapel of the castle, and there sacrificed to the ambition of her father, and the absurd love of the Duke de Luovo.

This accumulation of evil subdued each power of resistance, and reduced Julia to a state little short of distraction. No person was allowed to approach her but her maid, and the servant who brought her food. Emilia, who, though shocked by Julia's apparent want of confidence, severely sympathized in her distress, solicited to see her; but the pain of denial was so sharply aggravated by rebuke, that she dared not again to urge the request.

In the mean time Ferdinand, involved in the gloom of a dungeon, was resigned to the painful recollection of the past, and a horrid anticipation of the future. From the resentment of the marquis, whose passions were wild and terrible, and whose rank gave him an unlimited power of life and death in his own territories, Ferdinand had much to fear. Yet selfish apprehension soon yielded to a more noble sorrow. He mourned the fate of Hippolitus, and the sufferings of Julia. He could attribute the failure of their scheme only to the treachery of Robert, who had, however, met the wishes of Ferdinand with strong apparent sincerity, and generous interest in the cause of Julia. On the night of the intended elopement, he had consigned the keys to Ferdinand, who, immediately on receiving them, went to the apartment of Hippolitus. There they were detained till after the clock had struck one by a low noise, which returned at intervals, and convinced them that some part of the family was not yet retired to rest. This noise was undoubtedly occasioned by the people whom the marquis had employed to watch, and whose vigilance was too faithful to suffer the fugitives to escape. The very caution of Ferdinand defeated its purpose; for it is probable, that had he attempted to quit the castle by the common entrance, he might have escaped. The keys of the grand door, and those of the courts, remaining in the possession of Robert, the marquis was certain of the intended place of their departure; and was thus enabled to defeat their hopes at the very moment when they exulted in their success.

When the marchioness learned the fate of Hippolitus, the resentment of jealous passion yielded to emotions of pity. Revenge was satisfied, and she could now lament the sufferings of a youth whose personal charms had touched her heart as much as his virtues had disappointed her hopes. Still true to passion, and inaccessible to reason, she poured upon the defenceless Julia her anger for that calamity of which she herself was the unwilling cause. By a dextrous adaptation of her powers, she had worked upon the passions of the marquis so as to render him relentless in the pursuit of ambitious purposes, and insatiable in revenging his disappointment. But the effects of her artifices exceeded her intention in exerting them; and when she meant only to sacrifice a rival to her love, she found she had given up its object to revenge.

CHAPTER IV

The nuptial morn, so justly dreaded by Julia, and so impatiently awaited by the marquis, now arrived. The marriage was to be celebrated with a magnificence which demonstrated the joy it occasioned to the marquis. The castle was fitted up in a style of grandeur superior to any thing that had been before seen in it. The neighbouring nobility were invited to an entertainment which was to conclude with a splendid ball and supper, and the gates were to be thrown open to all who chose to partake of the bounty of the marquis. At an early hour the duke, attended by a numerous retinue, entered the castle. Ferdinand heard from his dungeon, where the rigour and the policy of the marquis still confined him, the loud clattering of hoofs in the courtyard above, the rolling of the carriage wheels, and all the tumultuous bustle which the entrance of the duke occasioned. He too well understood the cause of this uproar, and it awakened in him sensations resembling those which the condemned criminal feels, when his ears are assailed by the dreadful sounds that precede his execution. When he was able to think of himself, he wondered by what means the marquis would reconcile his absence to the guests. He, however, knew too well the dissipated character of the Sicilian nobility, to doubt that whatever story should be invented would be very readily believed by them; who, even if they knew the truth, would not suffer a discovery of their knowledge to interrupt the festivity which was offered them.

The marquis and marchioness received the duke in the outer hall, and conducted him to the saloon, where he partook of the refreshments prepared for him, and from thence retired to the chapel. The marquis now withdrew to lead Julia to the altar, and Emilia was ordered to attend at the door of the chapel, in which the priest and a numerous company were already assembled. The marchioness, a prey to the turbulence of succeeding passions, exulted in the near completion of her favorite scheme. — A disappointment, however, was prepared for her, which would at once crush the triumph of her malice and her pride. The marquis, on entering the prison of Julia, found it empty! His astonishment and indignation upon the discovery almost overpowered his reason. Of the servants of the castle, who were immediately summoned, he enquired concerning her escape, with a mixture of fury and sorrow which left them no opportunity to reply. They had, however, no information to give, but that her woman had not appeared during the whole morning. In the prison were found the bridal habiliments which the marchioness herself had sent on the preceding night, together with a letter addressed to Emilia, which contained the following words:

'Adieu, dear Emilia; never more will you see your wretched sister, who flies from the cruel fate now prepared for her, certain that she can never meet one more dreadful. — In happiness or misery — in hope or despair — whatever may be your situation — still remember me with pity and affection. Dear Emilia, adieu! — You will always be the sister of my heart — may you never be the partner of my misfortunes!'

While the marquis was reading this letter, the marchioness, who supposed the delay occasioned by some opposition from Julia, flew to the apartment. By her orders all the habitable parts of the castle were explored, and she herself assisted in the search. At length the intelligence was communicated to the chapel, and the confusion became universal. The priest quitted the altar, and the company returned to the saloon.

The letter, when it was given to Emilia, excited emotions which she found it impossible to disguise, but which did not, however, protect her from a suspicion that she was concerned in the transaction, her knowledge of which this letter appeared intended to conceal.

The marquis immediately dispatched servants upon the fleetest horses of his stables, with directions to take different routs, and to scour every corner of the island in pursuit of the fugitives. When these exertions had somewhat quieted his mind, he began to consider by what means Julia could have effected her escape. She had been confined in a small room in a remote part of the castle, to which no person had been admitted but her own woman and Robert, the confidential servant of the marquis. Even Lisette had not been suffered to enter, unless accompanied by Robert, in whose room, since the night of the fatal discovery, the keys had been regularly deposited. Without them it was impossible she could have escaped: the windows of the apartment being barred and grated, and opening into an inner court, at a prodigious height from the ground. Besides, who could she depend upon for protection — or whither could she intend to fly for concealment? — The associates of her former elopement were utterly unable to assist her even with advice. Ferdinand himself a prisoner, had been deprived of any means of intercourse with her, and Hippolitus had been carried lifeless on board a vessel, which had immediately sailed for Italy.

Robert, to whom the keys had been entrusted, was severely interrogated by the marquis. He persisted in a simple and uniform declaration of his innocence; but as the marquis believed it impossible that Julia could have escaped without his knowledge, he was ordered into imprisonment till he should confess the fact.

The pride of the duke was severely wounded by this elopement, which proved the excess of Julia's aversion, and compleated the disgraceful circumstances of his rejection. The marquis had carefully concealed from him her prior attempt at elopement, and her consequent confinement; but the truth now burst from disguise, and stood revealed with bitter aggravation. The duke, fired with indignation at the duplicity of the marquis, poured forth his resentment in terms of proud and bitter invective; and the marquis, galled by recent disappointment, was in no mood to restrain the impetuosity of his nature. He retorted with acrimony; and the consequence would have been serious, had not the friends of each party interposed for their preservation. The disputants were at length reconciled; it was agreed to pursue Julia with united, and indefatigable search; and that whenever she should be found, the nuptials should be solemnized without further delay. With the character of the duke, this conduct was consistent. His passions, inflamed by disappointment, and strengthened by repulse, now defied the power of obstacle; and those considerations which would have operated with a more delicate mind to overcome its original inclination, served only to encrease the violence of his.

Madame de Menon, who loved Julia with maternal affection, was an interested observer of all that passed at the castle. The cruel fate to which the marquis destined his daughter she had severely lamented, yet she could hardly rejoice to find that this had been avoided by elopement. She trembled for the future safety of her pupil; and her tranquillity, which was thus first disturbed for the welfare of others, she was not soon suffered to recover.

The marchioness had long nourished a secret dislike to Madame de Menon, whose virtues were a silent reproof to her vices. The contrariety of their disposition created in the marchioness an aversion which would have amounted to contempt, had not that dignity of virtue which strongly characterized the manners of madame, compelled the former to fear what she wished to despise. Her conscience whispered her that the dislike was mutual; and she now rejoiced in the opportunity which seemed to offer itself of lowering the proud integrity of madame's character. Pretending, therefore, to believe that she had encouraged Ferdinand to disobey his father's commands, and had been accessary to the elopement, she accused her of these offences, and stimulated the marquis to reprehend her conduct. But the integrity of Madame de Menon was not to be questioned with impunity. Without deigning to answer the imputation, she desired to resign an office of which she was no longer considered worthy, and to quit the castle immediately. This the policy of the marquis would not suffer; and he was compelled to make such ample concessions to madame, as induced her for the present to continue at the castle.

The news of Julia's elopement at length reached the ears of Ferdinand, whose joy at this event was equalled only by his surprize. He lost, for a moment, the sense of his own situation, and thought only of the escape of Julia. But his sorrow soon returned with accumulated force when he recollected that Julia might then perhaps want that assistance which his confinement alone could prevent his affording her.

The servants, who had been sent in pursuit, returned to the castle without any satisfactory information. Week after week elapsed in fruitless search, yet the duke was strenuous in continuing the pursuit. Emissaries were dispatched to Naples, and to the several estates of the Count Vereza, but they returned without any satisfactory information. The count had not been heard of since he quitted Naples for Sicily.

During these enquiries a new subject of disturbance broke out in the castle of Mazzini. On the night so fatal to the hopes of Hippolitus and Julia, when the tumult was subsided, and all was still, a light was observed by a servant as he passed by the window of the great stair-case in the way to his chamber, to glimmer through the casement before noticed in the southern buildings. While he stood observing it, it vanished, and presently reappeared. The former mysterious circumstances relative to these buildings rushed upon his mind; and fired with wonder, he roused some of his fellow servants to come and behold this phenomenon.

As they gazed in silent terror, the light disappeared, and soon after, they saw a small door belonging to the south tower open, and a figure bearing a light issue forth, which gliding along the castle walls, was quickly lost to their view. Overcome with fear they hurried back to their chambers, and revolved all the late wonderful occurrences. They doubted not, that this was the figure formerly seen by the lady Julia. The sudden change of Madame de Menon's apartments had not passed unobserved by the servants, but they now no longer hesitated to what to attribute the removal. They collected each various and uncommon circumstance attendant on this part of the fabric; and, comparing them with the present, their superstitious fears were confirmed, and their terror heightened to such a degree, that many of them resolved to quit the service of the marquis.

The marquis surprized at this sudden desertion, enquired into its cause, and learned the truth. Shocked by this discovery, he yet resolved to prevent, if possible, the ill effects which might be expected from a circulation of the report. To this end it was necessary to quiet the minds of his people, and to prevent their quitting his service. Having severely reprehended them for the idle apprehension they encouraged, he told them that, to prove the fallacy of their surmises, he would lead them over that part of the castle which was the subject of their fears, and ordered them to attend him at the return of night in the north hall. Emilia and Madame de Menon, surprised at this procedure, awaited the issue in silent expectation.

The servants, in obedience to the commands of the marquis, assembled at night in the north hall. The air of desolation which reigned through the south buildings, and the circumstance of their having been for so many years shut up, would naturally tend to inspire awe; but to these people, who firmly believed them to be the haunt of an unquiet spirit, terror was the predominant sentiment.

The marquis now appeared with the keys of these buildings in his hands, and every heart thrilled with wild expectation. He ordered Robert to precede him with a torch, and the rest of the servants following, he passed on. A pair of iron gates were unlocked, and they proceeded through a court, whose pavement was wildly overgrown with long grass, to the great door of the south fabric. Here they met with some difficulty, for the lock, which had not been turned for many years, was rusted.

During this interval, the silence of expectation sealed the lips of all present. At length the lock yielded. That door which had not been passed for so many years, creaked heavily upon its hinges, and disclosed the hall of black marble which Ferdinand had formerly crossed. 'Now,' cried the marquis, in a tone of irony as he entered, 'expect to encounter the ghosts of which you tell me; but if you fail to conquer them, prepare to quit my service. The people who live with me shall at least have courage and ability sufficient to defend me from these spiritual attacks. All I apprehend is, that the enemy will not appear, and in this case your valour will go untried.'

No one dared to answer, but all followed, in silent fear, the marquis, who ascended the great stair-case, and entered the gallery. 'Unlock that door,' said he, pointing to one on the left, 'and we will soon unhouse these ghosts.' Robert applied the key, but his hand shook so violently that he could not turn it. 'Here is a fellow,' cried the marquis, 'fit to encounter a whole legion of spirits. Do you, Anthony, take the key, and try your valour.'

'Please you, my lord,' replied Anthony, 'I never was a good one at unlocking a door in my life, but here is Gregory will do it.' — 'No, my lord, an' please you,' said Gregory, 'here is Richard.' — 'Stand off,' said the marquis, 'I will shame your cowardice, and do it myself.'

Saying this he turned the key, and was rushing on, but the door refused to yield; it shook under his hands, and seemed as if partially held by some person on the other side. The marquis was surprized, and made several efforts to move it, without effect. He then ordered his servants to burst it open, but, shrinking back with one accord, they cried, 'For God's sake, my lord, go no farther; we are satisfied here are no ghosts, only let us get back.'

'It is now then my turn to be satisfied,' replied the marquis, 'and till I am, not one of you shall stir. Open me that door.' — 'My lord!' — 'Nay,' said the marquis, assuming a look of stern authority — 'dispute not my commands. I am not to be trifled with.'

They now stepped forward, and applied their strength to the door, when a loud and sudden noise burst from within, and resounded through the hollow chambers! The men started back in affright, and were rushing headlong down the stair-case, when the voice of the marquis arrested their flight. They returned, with hearts palpitating with terror. 'Observe what I say,' said the marquis, 'and behave like men. Yonder door,' pointing to one at some distance, 'will lead us through other rooms to this chamber — unlock it therefore, for I will know the cause of these sounds.' Shocked at this determination, the servants again supplicated the marquis to go no farther; and to be obeyed, he was obliged to exert all his authority. The door was opened, and discovered a long narrow passage, into which they descended by a few steps. It led to a gallery that terminated in a back stair-case, where several doors appeared, one of which the marquis unclosed. A spacious chamber appeared beyond, whose walls, decayed and discoloured by the damps, exhibited a melancholy proof of desertion.

They passed on through a long suite of lofty and noble apartments, which were in the same ruinous condition. At length they came to the chamber whence the noise had issued. 'Go first, Robert, with the light,' said the marquis, as they approached the door; 'this is the key.' Robert trembled — but obeyed, and the other servants followed in silence. They stopped a moment at the door to listen, but all was still within. The door was opened, and disclosed a large vaulted chamber, nearly resembling those they had passed, and on looking round, they discovered at once the cause of the alarm. — A part of the decayed roof was fallen in, and the stones and rubbish of the ruin falling against the gallery door, obstructed the passage. It was evident, too, whence the noise which occasioned their terror had arisen; the loose stones which were piled against the door being shook by the effort made to open it, had given way, and rolled to the floor.

After surveying the place, they returned to the back stairs, which they descended, and having pursued the several windings of a long passage, found themselves again in the marble hall. 'Now,' said the marquis, 'what think ye? What evil spirits infest these walls? Henceforth be cautious how ye credit the phantasms of idleness, for ye may not always meet with a master who will condescend to undeceive ye.' — They acknowledged the goodness of the marquis, and professing themselves perfectly conscious of the error of their former suspicions, desired they might search no farther. 'I chuse to leave nothing to your imagination,' replied the marquis, 'lest hereafter it should betray you into a similar error. Follow me, therefore; you shall see the whole of these buildings.' Saying this, he led them to the south tower. They remembered, that from a door of this tower the figure which caused their alarm had issued; and notwithstanding the late assertion of their suspicions being removed, fear still operated powerfully upon their minds, and they would willingly have been excused from farther research. 'Would any of you chuse to explore this tower?' said the marquis, pointing to the broken stair-case; 'for myself, I am mortal, and therefore fear to venture; but you, who hold communion with disembodied spirits, may partake something of their nature; if so, you may pass without apprehension where the ghost has probably passed before.' They shrunk at this reproof, and were silent.

The marquis turning to a door on his right hand, ordered it to be unlocked. It opened upon the country, and the servants knew it to be the same whence the figure had appeared. Having relocked it, 'Lift that trapdoor; we will desend into the vaults,' said the marquis. 'What trapdoor, my Lord?' said Robert, with increased agitation; 'I see none.' The marquis pointed, and Robert, perceived a door, which lay almost concealed beneath the stones that had fallen from the stair-case above. He began to remove them, when the marquis suddenly turning – 'I have already sufficiently indulged your folly,' said he, 'and am weary of this business. If you are capable of receiving conviction from truth, you must now be convinced that these buildings are not the haunt of a supernatural being; and if you are incapable, it would be entirely useless to proceed. You, Robert, may therefore spare yourself the trouble of removing the rubbish; we will quit this part of the fabric.'

The servants joyfully obeyed, and the marquis locking the several doors, returned with the keys to the habitable part of the castle.

Every enquiry after Julia had hitherto proved fruitless; and the imperious nature of the marquis, heightened by the present vexation, became intolerably oppressive to all around him. As the hope of recovering Julia declined, his opinion that Emilia had assisted her to escape strengthened, and he inflicted upon her the severity of his unjust suspicions. She was ordered to confine herself to her apartment till her innocence should be cleared, or her sister discovered. From Madame de Menon she received a faithful sympathy, which was the sole relief of her oppressed heart. Her anxiety concerning Julia daily encreased, and was heightened into the most terrifying apprehensions for her safety. She knew of no person in whom her sister could confide, or of any place where she could find protection; the most deplorable evils were therefore to be expected.

One day, as she was sitting at the window of her apartment, engaged in melancholy reflection, she saw a man riding towards the castle on full speed. Her heart beat with fear and expectation; for his haste made her suspect he brought intelligence of Julia; and she could scarcely refrain from breaking through the command of the marquis, and rushing into the hall to learn something of his errand. She was right in her conjecture; the person she had seen was a spy of the marquis's, and came to inform him that the lady Julia was at that time concealed in a cottage of the forest of Marentino. The marquis, rejoiced at this intelligence, gave the man a liberal reward. He learned also, that she was accompanied by a young cavalier; which circumstance surprized him exceedingly; for he knew of no person except the Count de Vereza with whom she could have entrusted herself, and the count had fallen by his sword! He immediately ordered a party of his people to accompany the messenger to the forest of Marentino, and to suffer neither Julia nor the cavalier to escape them, on pain of death.

When the Duke de Luovo was informed of this discovery, he entreated and obtained permission of the marquis to join in the pursuit. He immediately set out on the expedition, armed, and followed by a number of his servants. He resolved to encounter all hazards, and to practice the most desperate extremes, rather than fail in the object of his enterprize. In a short time he overtook the marquis's people, and they proceeded together with all possible speed. The forest lay several leagues distant from the castle of Mazzini, and the day was closing when they entered upon the borders. The thick foliage of the trees spread a deeper shade around; and they were obliged to proceed with caution. Darkness had long fallen upon the earth when they reached the cottage, to which they were directed by a light that glimmered from afar among the trees. The duke left his people at some distance; and dismounted, and accompanied only by one servant, approached the cottage. When he reached it he stopped, and looking through the window, observed a man and woman in the habit of peasants seated at their supper. They were conversing with earnestness, and the duke, hoping to obtain farther intelligence of Julia, endeavoured to listen to their discourse. They were praising the beauty of a lady, whom the duke did not doubt to be Julia, and the woman spoke much in praise of the cavalier. 'He has a noble heart,' said she; 'and I am sure, by his look, belongs to some great family.'—'Nay,' replied her companion, 'the lady is as good as he. I have been at Palermo, and ought to know what great folks are, and if she is not one of them, never take my word again. Poor thing, how she does take on! It made my heart ache to see her.'

They were some time silent. The duke knocked at the door, and enquired of the man who opened it concerning the lady and cavalier then in his cottage. He was assured there were no other persons in the cottage than those he then saw. The duke persisted in affirming that the persons he enquired for were there concealed; which the man being as resolute in denying, he gave the signal, and his people approached, and surrounded the cottage. The peasants, terrified by this circumstance, confessed that a lady and cavalier, such as the duke described, had been for some time concealed in the cottage; but that they were now departed.

Suspicious of the truth of the latter assertion, the duke ordered his people to search the cottage, and that part of the forest contiguous to it. The search ended in disappointment. The duke, however, resolved to obtain all possible information concerning the fugitives; and assuming, therefore, a stern air, bade the peasant, on pain of instant death, discover all he knew of them.

The man replied, that on a very dark and stormy night, about a week before, two persons had come to the cottage, and desired shelter. That they were unattended; but seemed to be persons of consequence in disguise. That they paid very liberally for what they had; and that they departed from the cottage a few hours before the arrival of the duke.

The duke enquired concerning the course they had taken, and having received information, remounted his horse, and set forward in pursuit. The road lay for several leagues through the forest, and the darkness, and the probability of encountering banditti, made the journey dangerous. About the break of day they quitted the forest, and entered upon a wild and mountainous country, in which they travelled some miles without perceiving a hut, or a human being. No vestige of cultivation appeared, and no sounds reached them but those of their horses feet, and the roaring of the winds through the deep forests that overhung the mountains. The pursuit was uncertain, but the duke resolved to persevere.

They came at length to a cottage, where he repeated his enquiries, and learned to his satisfaction that two persons, such as he described, had stopped there for refreshment about two hours before. He found it now necessary to stop for the same purpose. Bread and milk, the only provisions of the place, were set before him, and his attendants would have been well contented, had there been sufficient of this homely fare to have satisfied their hunger.

Having dispatched an hasty meal, they again set forward in the way pointed out to them as the route of the fugitives. The country assumed a more civilized aspect. Corn, vineyards, olives, and groves of mulberry-trees adorned the hills. The vallies, luxuriant in shade, were frequently embellished by the windings of a lucid stream, and diversified by clusters of half-seen cottages. Here the rising turrets of a monastery appeared above the thick trees with which they were surrounded; and there the savage wilds the travellers had passed, formed a bold and picturesque background to the scene.

To the questions put by the duke to the several persons he met, he received answers that encouraged him to proceed. At noon he halted at a village to refresh himself and his people. He could gain no intelligence of Julia, and was perplexed which way to chuse; but determined at length to pursue the road he was then in, and accordingly again set forward. He travelled several miles without meeting any person who could give the necessary information, and began to despair of success. The lengthened shadows of the mountains, and the fading light gave signals of declining day; when having gained the summit of a high hill, he observed two persons travelling on horseback in the plains below. On one of them he distinguished the habiliments of a woman; and in her air he thought he discovered that of Julia. While he stood attentively surveying them, they looked towards the hill, when, as if urged by a sudden impulse of terror, they set off on full speed over the plains. The duke had no doubt that these were the persons he sought; and he, therefore, ordered some of his people to pursue them, and pushed his horse into a full gallop. Before he reached the plains, the fugitives, winding round an abrupt hill, were lost to his view. The duke continued his course, and his people, who were a considerable way before him, at length reached the hill, behind which the two persons had disappeared. No traces of them were to be seen, and they entered a narrow defile between two ranges of high and savage mountains; on the right of which a rapid stream rolled along, and broke with its deep resounding murmurs the solemn silence of the place. The shades of evening now fell thick, and the scene was soon enveloped in darkness; but to the duke, who was animated by a strong and impetuous passion, these were unimportant circumstances. Although he knew that the wilds of Sicily were frequently infested with banditti, his numbers made him fearless of attack. Not so his attendants, many of whom, as the darkness increased, testified emotions not very honourable to their courage: starting at every bush, and believing it concealed a murderer. They endeavoured to dissuade the duke from proceeding, expressing uncertainty of their being in the right route, and recommending the open plains. But the duke, whose eye had been vigilant to mark the flight of the fugitives, and who was not to be dissuaded from his purpose, quickly repressed their arguments. They continued their course without meeting a single person.

The moon now rose, and afforded them a shadowy imperfect view of the surrounding objects. The prospect was gloomy and vast, and not a human habitation met their eyes. They had now lost every trace of the fugitives, and found themselves bewildered in a wild and savage country. Their only remaining care was to extricate themselves from so forlorn a situation, and they listened at every step with anxious attention for some sound that might discover to them the haunts of men. They listened in vain; the stillness of night was undisturbed but by the wind, which broke at intervals in low and hollow murmurs from among the mountains.

As they proceeded with silent caution, they perceived a light break from among the rocks at some distance. The duke hesitated whether to approach, since it might probably proceed from a party of the banditti with which these mountains were said to be infested. While he hesitated, it disappeared; but he had not advanced many steps when it returned. He now perceived it to issue from the mouth of a cavern, and cast a bright reflection upon the overhanging rocks and shrubs.

He dismounted, and followed by two of his people, leaving the rest at some distance, moved with slow and silent steps towards the cave. As he drew near, he heard the sound of many voices in high carousal. Suddenly the uproar ceased, and the following words were sung by a clear and manly voice:

SONG

Pour the rich libation high;

    The sparkling cup to Bacchus fill;

His joys shall dance in ev'ry eye,

    And chace the forms of future ill!

Quick the magic raptures steal

    O'er the fancy-kindling brain.

Warm the heart with social zeal,

    And song and laughter reign.

Then visions of pleasure shall float on our sight,

    While light bounding our spirits shall flow;

And the god shall impart a fine sense of delight

    Which in vain sober mortals would know.

The last verse was repeated in loud chorus. The duke listened with astonishment! Such social merriment amid a scene of such savage wildness, appeared more like enchantment than reality. He would not have hesitated to pronounce this a party of banditti, had not the delicacy of expression preserved in the song appeared unattainable by men of their class.

He had now a full view of the cave; and the moment which convinced him of his error served only to encrease his surprize. He beheld, by the light of a fire, a party of banditti seated within the deepest recess of the cave round a rude kind of table formed in the rock. The table was spread with provisions, and they were regaling themselves with great eagerness and joy. The countenances of the men exhibited a strange mixture of fierceness and sociality; and the duke could almost have imagined he beheld in these robbers a band of the early Romans before knowledge had civilized, or luxury had softened them. But he had not much time for meditation; a sense of his danger bade him fly while to fly was yet in his power. As he turned to depart, he observed two saddle-horses grazing upon the herbage near the mouth of the cave. It instantly occurred to him that they belonged to Julia and her companion. He hesitated, and at length determined to linger awhile, and listen to the conversation of the robbers, hoping from thence to have his doubts resolved. They talked for some time in a strain of high conviviality, and recounted in exultation many of their exploits. They described also the behaviour of several people whom they had robbed, with highly ludicrous allusions, and with much rude humour, while the cave re-echoed with loud bursts of laughter and applause. They were thus engaged in tumultuous merriment, till one of them cursing the scanty plunder of their late adventure, but praising the beauty of a lady, they all lowered their voices together, and seemed as if debating upon a point uncommonly interesting to them. The passions of the duke were roused, and he became certain that it was Julia of whom they had spoken. In the first impulse of feeling he drew his sword; but recollecting the number of his adversaries, restrained his fury. He was turning from the cave with a design of summoning his people, when the light of the fire glittering upon the bright blade of his weapon, caught the eye of one of the banditti. He started from his seat, and his comrades instantly rising in consternation, discovered the duke. They rushed with loud vociferation towards the mouth of the cave. He endeavoured to escape to his people; but two of the banditti mounting the horses which were grazing near, quickly overtook and seized him. His dress and air proclaimed him to be a person of distinction; and, rejoicing in their prospect of plunder, they forced him towards the cave. Here their comrades awaited them; but what were the emotions of the duke, when he discovered in the person of the principal robber his own son! who, to escape the galling severity of his father, had fled from his castle some years before, and had not been heard of since.

He had placed himself at the head of a party of banditti, and, pleased with the liberty which till then he had never tasted, and with the power which his new situation afforded him, he became so much attached to this wild and lawless mode of life, that he determined never to quit it till death should dissolve those ties which now made his rank only oppressive. This event seemed at so great a distance, that he seldom allowed himself to think of it. Whenever it should happen, he had no doubt that he might either resume his rank without danger of discovery, or might justify his present conduct as a frolic which a few acts of generosity would easily excuse. He knew his power would then place him beyond the reach of censure, in a country where the people are accustomed to implicit subordination, and seldom dare to scrutinize the actions of the nobility.

His sensations, however, on discovering his father, were not very pleasing; but proclaiming the duke, he protected him from farther outrage.

With the duke, whose heart was a stranger to the softer affections, indignation usurped the place of parental feeling. His pride was the only passion affected by the discovery; and he had the rashness to express the indignation, which the conduct of his son had excited, in terms of unrestrained invective. The banditti, inflamed by the opprobium with which he loaded their order, threatened instant punishment to his temerity; and the authority of Riccardo could hardly restrain them within the limits of forbearance.

The menaces, and at length entreaties of the duke, to prevail with his son to abandon his present way of life, were equally ineffectual. Secure in his own power, Riccardo laughed at the first, and was insensible to the latter; and his father was compelled to relinquish the attempt. The duke, however, boldly and passionately accused him of having plundered and secreted a lady and cavalier, his friends, at the same time describing Julia, for whose liberation he offered large rewards. Riccardo denied the fact, which so much exasperated the duke, that he drew his sword with an intention of plunging it in the breast of his son. His arm was arrested by the surrounding banditti, who half unsheathed their swords, and stood suspended in an attitude of menace. The fate of the father now hung upon the voice of the son. Riccardo raised his arm, but instantly dropped it, and turned away. The banditti sheathed their weapons, and stepped back.

Riccardo solemnly swearing that he knew nothing of the persons described, the duke at length became convinced of the truth of the assertion, and departing from the cave, rejoined his people. All the impetuous passions of his nature were roused and inflamed by the discovery of his son in a situation so wretchedly disgraceful. Yet it was his pride rather than his virtue that was hurt; and when he wished him dead, it was rather to save himself from disgrace, than his son from the real indignity of vice. He had no means of reclaiming him; to have attempted it by force, would have been at this time the excess of temerity, for his attendants, though numerous, were undisciplined, and would have fallen certain victims to the power of a savage and dexterous banditti.

With thoughts agitated in fierce and agonizing conflict, he pursued his journey; and having lost all trace of Julia, sought only for an habitation which might shelter him from the night, and afford necessary refreshment for himself and his people. With this, however, there appeared little hope of meeting.

CHAPTER V

The night grew stormy. The hollow winds swept over the mountains, and blew bleak and cold around; the clouds were driven swiftly over the face of the moon, and the duke and his people were frequently involved in total darkness. They had travelled on silently and dejectedly for some hours, and were bewildered in the wilds, when they suddenly heard the bell of a monastery chiming for midnight-prayer. Their hearts revived at the sound, which they endeavoured to follow, but they had not gone far, when the gale wafted it away, and they were abandoned to the uncertain guide of their own conjectures.

They had pursued for some time the way which they judged led to the monastery, when the note of the bell returned upon the wind, and discovered to them that they had mistaken their route. After much wandering and difficulty they arrived, overcome with weariness, at the gates of a large and gloomy fabric. The bell had ceased, and all was still. By the moonlight, which through broken clouds now streamed upon the building, they became convinced it was the monastery they had sought, and the duke himself struck loudly upon the gate.

Several minutes elapsed, no person appeared, and he repeated the stroke. A step was presently heard within, the gate was unbarred, and a thin shivering figure presented itself. The duke solicited admission, but was refused, and reprimanded for disturbing the convent at the hour sacred to prayer. He then made known his rank, and bade the friar inform the Superior that he requested shelter from the night. The friar, suspicious of deceit, and apprehensive of robbers, refused with much firmness, and repeated that the convent was engaged in prayer; he had almost closed the gate, when the duke, whom hunger and fatigue made desperate, rushed by him, and passed into the court. It was his intention to present himself to the Superior, and he had not proceeded far when the sound of laughter, and of many voices in loud and mirthful jollity, attracted his steps. It led him through several passages to a door, through the crevices of which light appeared. He paused a moment, and heard within a wild uproar of merriment and song. He was struck with astonishment, and could scarcely credit his senses!

He unclosed the door, and beheld in a large room, well lighted, a company of friars, dressed in the habit of their order, placed round a table, which was profusely spread with wines and fruits. The Superior, whose habit distinguished him from his associates, appeared at the head of the table. He was lifting a large goblet of wine to his lips, and was roaring out, 'Profusion

513

and confusion,' at the moment when the duke entered. His appearance caused a general alarm; that part of the company who were not too much intoxicated, arose from their seats; and the Superior, dropping the goblet from his hands, endeavoured to assume a look of austerity, which his rosy countenance belied. The duke received a reprimand, delivered in the lisping accents of intoxication, and embellished with frequent interjections of hiccup. He made known his quality, his distress, and solicited a night's lodging for himself and his people. When the Superior understood the distinction of his guest, his features relaxed into a smile of joyous welcome; and taking him by the hand, he placed him by his side.

The table was quickly covered with luxurious provisions, and orders were given that the duke's people should be admitted, and taken care of. He was regaled with a variety of the finest wines, and at length, highly elevated by monastic hospitality, he retired to the apartment allotted him, leaving the Superior in a condition which precluded all ceremony.

He departed in the morning, very well pleased with the accommodating principles of monastic religion. He had been told that the enjoyment of the good things of this life was the surest sign of our gratitude to Heaven; and it appeared, that within the walls of a Sicilian monastery, the precept and the practice were equally enforced.

He was now at a loss what course to chuse, for he had no clue to direct him towards the object of his pursuit; but hope still invigorated, and urged him to perseverance. He was not many leagues from the coast; and it occurred to him that the fugitives might make towards it with a design of escaping into Italy. He therefore determined to travel towards the sea and proceed along the shore.

At the house where he stopped to dine, he learned that two persons, such as he described, had halted there about an hour before his arrival, and had set off again in much seeming haste. They had taken the road towards the coast, whence it was obvious to the duke they designed to embark. He stayed not to finish the repast set before him, but instantly remounted to continue the pursuit.

To the enquiries he made of the persons he chanced to meet, favorable answers were returned for a time, but he was at length bewildered in uncertainty, and travelled for some hours in a direction which chance, rather than judgment, prompted him to take.

The falling evening again confused his prospects, and unsettled his hopes. The shades were deepened by thick and heavy clouds that enveloped the horizon, and the deep sounding air foretold a tempest. The thunder now rolled at a distance, and the accumulated clouds grew darker. The duke and his people were on a wild and dreary heath, round which they looked in vain for shelter, the view being terminated on all sides by the same desolate scene. They rode, however, as hard as their horses would carry them; and at length one of the attendants spied on the skirts of the waste a large mansion, towards which they immediately directed their course.

They were overtaken by the storm, and at the moment when they reached the building, a peal of thunder, which seemed to shake the pile, burst over their heads. They now found themselves in a large and ancient mansion, which seemed totally deserted, and was falling to decay. The edifice was distinguished by an air of magnificence, which ill accorded with the surrounding scenery, and which excited some degree of surprize in the mind of the duke, who, however, fully justified the owner in forsaking a spot which presented to the eye only views of rude and desolated nature.

The storm increased with much violence, and threatened to detain the duke a prisoner in his present habitation for the night. The hall, of which he and his people had taken possession, exhibited in every feature marks of ruin and desolation. The marble pavement was in many places broken, the walls were mouldering in decay, and round the high and shattered windows the long grass waved to the lonely gale. Curiosity led him to explore the recesses of the mansion. He quitted the hall, and entered upon a passage which conducted him to a remote part of the edifice. He wandered through the wild and spacious apartments in gloomy meditation, and often paused in wonder at the remains of magnificence which he beheld.

The mansion was irregular and vast, and he was bewildered in its intricacies. In endeavouring to find his way back, he only perplexed himself more, till at length he arrived at a door, which he believed led into the hall he first quitted. On opening it he discovered, by the faint light of the moon, a large place which he scarcely knew whether to think a cloister, a chapel, or a hall. It retired in long perspective, in arches, and terminated in a large iron gate, through which appeared the open country.

The lighting flashed thick and blue around, which, together with the thunder that seemed to rend the wide arch of heaven, and the melancholy aspect of the place, so awed the duke, that he involuntarily called to his people. His voice was answered only by the deep echoes which ran in murmurs through the place, and died away at a distance; and the moon now sinking behind a cloud, left him in total darkness.

He repeated the call more loudly, and at length heard the approach of footsteps. A few moments relieved him from his anxiety, for his people appeared. The storm was yet loud, and the heavy and sulphureous appearance of the atmosphere promised no speedy abatement of it. The duke endeavoured to reconcile himself to pass the night in his present situation, and ordered a fire to be lighted in the place he was in. This with much difficulty was accomplished. He then threw himself on the pavement before it, and tried to endure the abstinence which he had so ill observed in the monastery on the preceding night. But to his great joy his attendants, more provident than himself, had not scrupled to accept a comfortable quantity of provisions which had been offered them at the monastery; and which they now drew forth from a wallet. They were spread upon the pavement; and the duke, after refreshing himself, delivered up the remains to his people. Having ordered them to watch by turns at the gate, he wrapt his cloak round him, and resigned himself to repose.

The night passed without any disturbance. The morning arose fresh and bright; the Heavens exhibited a clear and unclouded concave; even the wild heath, refreshed by the late rains, smiled around, and sent up with the morning gale a stream of fragrance.

The duke quitted the mansion, re-animated by the cheerfulness of morn, and pursued his journey. He could gain no intelligence of the fugitives. About noon he found himself in a beautiful romantic country; and having reached the summit of some wild cliffs, he rested, to view the picturesque imagery of the scene below. A shadowy sequestered dell appeared buried deep among the rocks, and in the bottom was seen a lake, whose clear bosom reflected the impending cliffs, and the beautiful luxuriance of the overhanging shades.

But his attention was quickly called from the beauties of inanimate nature, to objects more interesting; for he observed two persons, whom he instantly recollected to be the same that he had formerly pursued over the plains. They were seated on the margin of the lake, under the shade of some high trees at the foot of the rocks, and seemed partaking of a repast which was spread upon the grass. Two horses were grazing near. In the lady the duke saw the very air and shape of Julia, and his heart bounded at the sight. They were seated with their backs to the cliffs upon which the duke stood, and he therefore surveyed them unobserved. They were now almost within his power, but the difficulty was how to descend the rocks, whose stupendous heights and craggy steeps seemed to render them impassable. He examined them with a scrutinizing eye, and at length espied, where the rock receded, a narrow winding sort of path. He dismounted, and some of his attendants doing the same, followed their lord down the cliffs, treading lightly, lest their steps should betray them. Immediately upon their reaching the bottom, they were perceived by the lady, who fled among the rocks, and was presently pursued by the duke's people. The cavalier had no time to escape, but drew his sword, and defended himself against the furious assault of the duke.

The combat was sustained with much vigour and dexterity on both sides for some minutes, when the duke received the point of his adversary's sword, and fell. The cavalier, endeavouring to escape, was seized by the duke's people, who now appeared with the fair fugitive; but what was the disappointment—the rage of the duke, when in the person of the lady he discovered a stranger! The astonishment was mutual, but the accompanying feelings were, in the different persons, of a very opposite nature. In the duke, astonishment was heightened by vexation, and embittered by disappointment:—in the lady, it was softened by the joy of unexpected deliverance.

This lady was the younger daughter of a Sicilian nobleman, whose avarice, or necessities, had devoted her to a convent. To avoid the threatened fate, she fled with the lover to whom her affections had long been engaged, and whose only fault, even in the eye of her father, was inferiority of birth. They were now on their way to the coast, whence they designed to pass over to Italy, where the church would confirm the bonds which their hearts had already formed. There the friends of the cavalier resided, and with them they expected to find a secure retreat.

The duke, who was not materially wounded, after the first transport of his rage had subsided, suffered them to depart. Relieved from their fears, they joyfully set forward, leaving their late pursuer to the anguish of defeat, and fruitless endeavour. He was remounted on his horse; and having dispatched two of his people in search of a house where he might obtain some relief, he proceeded slowly on his return to the castle of Mazzini.

It was not long ere he recollected a circumstance which, in the first tumult of his disappointment, had escaped him, but which so essentially affected the whole tenour of his hopes, as to make him again irresolute how to proceed. He considered that, although these were the fugitives he had pursued over the plains, they might not be the same who had been secreted in the cottage, and it was therefore possible that Julia might have been the person whom they had for some time followed from thence. This suggestion awakened his hopes, which were however quickly destroyed; for he remembered that the only persons who could have satisfied his doubts, were now gone beyond the power of recall. To pursue Julia, when no traces of her flight remained, was absurd; and he was, therefore, compelled to return to the marquis, as ignorant and more hopeless than he had left him. With much pain he reached the village which his emissaries had discovered, when fortunately he obtained some medical assistance. Here he was obliged by indisposition to rest. The anguish of his mind equalled that of his body. Those impetuous passions which so strongly marked his nature, were roused and exasperated to a degree that operated powerfully upon his constitution, and threatened him with the most alarming consequences. The effect of his wound was heightened by the agitation of his mind; and a fever, which quickly assumed a very serious aspect, co-operated to endanger his life.

CHAPTER VI

The castle of Mazzini was still the scene of dissension and misery. The impatience and astonishment of the marquis being daily increased by the lengthened absence of the duke, he dispatched servants to the forest of Marentino, to enquire the occasion of this circumstance. They returned with intelligence that neither Julia, the duke, nor any of his people were there. He therefore concluded that his daughter had fled the cottage upon information of the approach of the duke, who, he believed, was still engaged in the pursuit. With respect to Ferdinand, who yet pined in sorrow and anxiety in his dungeon, the rigour of the marquis's conduct was unabated. He apprehended that his son, if liberated, would quickly discover the retreat of Julia, and by his advice and assistance confirm her in disobedience.

Ferdinand, in the stillness and solitude of his dungeon, brooded over the late calamity in gloomy ineffectual lamentation. The idea of Hippolitus — of Hippolitus murdered — arose to his imagination in busy intrusion, and subdued the strongest efforts of his fortitude. Julia too, his beloved sister — unprotected — unfriended — might, even at the moment he lamented her, be sinking under sufferings dreadful to humanity. The airy schemes he once formed of future felicity, resulting from the union of two persons so justly dear to him — with the gay visions of past happiness — floated upon his fancy, and the lustre they reflected served only to heighten, by contrast, the obscurity and gloom of his present views. He had, however, a new subject of astonishment, which often withdrew his thoughts from their accustomed object, and substituted a sensation less painful, though scarcely less powerful. One night as he lay ruminating on the past, in melancholy dejection, the stillness of the place was suddenly interrupted by a low and dismal sound. It returned at intervals in hollow sighings, and seemed to come from some person in deep distress. So much did fear operate upon his mind, that he was uncertain whether it arose from within or from without. He looked around his dungeon, but could distinguish no object through the impenetrable darkness. As he listened in deep amazement, the sound was repeated in moans more hollow. Terror now occupied his mind, and disturbed his reason; he started from his posture, and, determined to be satisfied whether any person beside himself was in the dungeon, groped, with arms extended, along the walls. The place was empty; but coming to a particular spot, the sound suddenly arose more distinctly to his ear. He called aloud, and asked who was there; but received no answer. Soon after all was still; and after listening for some time without hearing the sounds renewed, he laid himself down to sleep. On the following day he mentioned to the man who brought him food what he had heard, and enquired concerning the noise. The servant appeared very much terrified, but could give no information that might in the least account for the circumstance, till he mentioned the vicinity of the dungeon to the southern buildings. The dreadful relation formerly given by the marquis instantly recurred to the mind of Ferdinand, who did not hesitate to believe that the moans he heard came from the restless spirit of the murdered Della Campo. At this conviction, horror thrilled his nerves; but he remembered his oath, and was silent. His courage, however, yielded to the idea of passing another night alone in his prison, where, if the vengeful spirit of the murdered should appear, he might even die of the horror which its appearance would inspire.

The mind of Ferdinand was highly superior to the general influence of superstition; but, in the present instance, such strong correlative circumstances appeared, as compelled even incredulity to yield. He had himself heard strange and awful sounds in the forsaken southern buildings; he received from his father a dreadful secret relative to them — a secret in which his honor, nay even his life, was bound up. His father had also confessed, that he had himself there seen appearances which he could never after remember without horror, and which had occasioned him to quit that part of the castle. All these recollections presented to Ferdinand a chain of evidence too powerful to be resisted; and he could not doubt that the spirit of the dead had for once been permitted to revisit the earth, and to call down vengeance on the descendants of the murderer.

This conviction occasioned him a degree of horror, such as no apprehension of mortal powers could have excited; and he determined, if possible, to prevail on Peter to pass the hours of midnight with him in his dungeon. The strictness of Peter's fidelity yielded to the persuasions of Ferdinand, though no bribe could tempt him to incur the resentment of the marquis, by permitting an escape. Ferdinand passed the day in lingering anxious expectation, and the return of night brought Peter to the dungeon. His kindness exposed him to a danger which he had not foreseen; for when seated in the dungeon alone with his prisoner, how easily might that prisoner have conquered him and left him to pay his life to the fury of the marquis. He was preserved by the humanity of Ferdinand, who instantly perceived his advantage, but disdained to involve an innocent man in destruction, and spurned the suggestion from his mind.

Peter, whose friendship was stronger than his courage, trembled with apprehension as the hour drew nigh in which the groans had been heard on the preceding night. He recounted to Ferdinand a variety of terrific circumstances, which existed only in the heated imaginations of his fellow-servants, but which were still admitted by them as facts. Among the rest, he did not omit to mention the light and the figure which had been seen to issue from the south tower on the night of Julia's intended elopement; a circumstance which he embellished with innumerable aggravations of fear and wonder. He concluded with describing the general consternation it had caused, and the consequent behaviour of the marquis, who laughed at the fears of his people, yet condescended to quiet them by a formal review of the buildings whence their terror had originated. He related the adventure of the door which refused to yield, the sounds which arose from within, and the discovery of the fallen roof; but declared that neither he, nor any of his fellow servants, believed the noise or the obstruction proceeded from that, 'because, my lord,' continued he, 'the door seemed to be held only in one place; and as for the noise—O! Lord! I never shall forget what a noise it was!—it was a thousand times louder than what any stones could make.'

Ferdinand listened to this narrative in silent wonder! wonder not occasioned by the adventure described, but by the hardihood and rashness of the marquis, who had thus exposed to the inspection of his people, that dreadful spot which he knew from experience to be the haunt of an injured spirit; a spot which he had hitherto scrupulously concealed from human eye, and human curiosity; and which, for so many years, he had not dared even himself to enter. Peter went on, but was presently interrupted by a hollow moan, which seemed to come from beneath the ground. 'Blessed virgin!' exclaimed he: Ferdinand listened in awful expectation. A groan longer and more dreadful was repeated, when Peter started from his seat, and snatching up the lamp, rushed out of the dungeon. Ferdinand, who was left in total darkness, followed to the door, which the affrighted Peter had not stopped to fasten, but which had closed, and seemed held by a lock that could be opened only on the outside. The sensations of Ferdinand, thus compelled to remain in the dungeon, are not to be imagined. The horrors of the night, whatever they were to be, he was to endure alone. By degrees, however, he seemed to acquire the valour of despair. The sounds were repeated, at intervals, for near an hour, when silence returned, and remained undisturbed during the rest of the night. Ferdinand was alarmed by no appearance, and at length, overcome with anxiety and watching, he sunk to repose.

On the following morning Peter returned to the dungeon, scarcely knowing what to expect, yet expecting something very strange, perhaps the murder, perhaps the supernatural disappearance of his young lord. Full of these wild apprehensions, he dared not venture thither alone, but persuaded some of the servants, to whom he had communicated his terrors, to accompany him to the door. As they passed along he recollected, that in the terror of the preceding night he had forgot to fasten the door, and he now feared that his prisoner had made his escape without a miracle. He hurried to the door; and his surprize was extreme to find it fastened. It instantly struck him that this was the work of a supernatural power, when on calling aloud, he was answered by a voice from within. His absurd fear did not suffer him to recognize the voice of Ferdinand, neither did he suppose that Ferdinand had failed to escape, he, therefore, attributed the voice to the being he had heard on the preceding night; and starting back from the door, fled with his companions to the great hall. There the uproar occasioned by their entrance called together a number of persons, amongst whom was the marquis, who was soon informed of the cause of alarm, with a long history of the circumstances of the foregoing night. At this information, the marquis assumed a very stern look, and severely reprimanded Peter for his imprudence, at the same time reproaching the other servants with their undutifulness in thus disturbing his peace. He reminded them of the condescension he had practised to dissipate their former terrors, and of the result of their examination. He then assured them, that since indulgence had only encouraged intrusion, he would for the future be severe; and concluded with declaring, that the first man who should disturb him with a repetition of such ridiculous apprehensions, or should attempt to disturb the peace of the castle by circulating these idle notions, should be rigorously punished, and banished his dominions. They shrunk back at his reproof, and were silent. 'Bring a torch,' said the marquis, 'and shew me to the dungeon. I will once more condescend to confute you.'

They obeyed, and descended with the marquis, who, arriving at the dungeon, instantly threw open the door, and discovered to the astonished eyes of his attendants — Ferdinand! — He started with surprize at the entrance of his father thus attended. The marquis darted upon him a severe look, which he perfectly comprehended. — 'Now,' cried he, turning to his people, 'what do you see? My son, whom I myself placed here, and whose voice, which answered to your calls, you have transformed into unknown sounds. Speak, Ferdinand, and confirm what I say.' Ferdinand did so. 'What dreadful spectre appeared to you last night?' resumed the marquis, looking stedfastly upon him: 'gratify these fellows with a description of it, for they cannot exist without something of the marvellous.' 'None, my lord,' replied Ferdinand, who too well understood the manner of the marquis. ''Tis well,' cried the marquis, 'and this is the last time,' turning to his attendants, 'that your folly shall be treated with so much lenity.' He ceased to urge the subject, and forbore to ask Ferdinand even one question before his servants, concerning the nocturnal sounds described by Peter. He quitted the dungeon with eyes steadily bent in anger and suspicion upon Ferdinand. The marquis suspected that the fears of his son had inadvertently betrayed to Peter a part of the secret entrusted to him, and he artfully interrogated Peter with seeming carelessness, concerning the circumstances of the preceding night. From him he drew such answers as honorably acquitted Ferdinand of indiscretion, and relieved himself from tormenting apprehensions.

The following night passed quietly away; neither sound nor appearance disturbed the peace of Ferdinand. The marquis, on the next day, thought proper to soften the severity of his sufferings, and he was removed from his dungeon to a room strongly grated, but exposed to the light of day.

Meanwhile a circumstance occurred which increased the general discord, and threatened Emilia with the loss of her last remaining comfort—the advice and consolation of Madame de Menon. The marchioness, whose passion for the Count de Vereza had at length yielded to absence, and the pressure of present circumstances, now bestowed her smiles upon a young Italian cavalier, a visitor at the castle, who possessed too much of the spirit of gallantry to permit a lady to languish in vain. The marquis, whose mind was occupied with other passions, was insensible to the misconduct of his wife, who at all times had the address to disguise her vices beneath the gloss of virtue and innocent freedom. The intrigue was discovered by madame, who, having one day left a book in the oak parlour, returned thither in search of it. As she opened the door of the apartment, she heard the voice of the cavalier in passionate exclamation; and on entering, discovered him rising in some confusion from the feet of the marchioness, who, darting at madame a look of severity, arose from her seat. Madame, shocked at what she had seen, instantly retired, and buried in her own bosom that secret, the discovery of which would most essentially have poisoned the peace of the marquis. The marchioness, who was a stranger to the generosity of sentiment which actuated Madame de Menon, doubted not that she would seize the moment of retaliation, and expose her conduct where most she dreaded it should be known. The consciousness of guilt tortured her with incessant fear of discovery, and from this period her whole attention was employed to dislodge from the castle the person to whom her character was committed. In this it was not difficult to succeed; for the delicacy of madame's feelings made her quick to perceive, and to withdraw from a treatment unsuitable to the natural dignity of her character. She therefore resolved to depart from the castle; but disdaining to take an advantage even over a successful enemy, she determined to be silent on that subject which would instantly have transferred the triumph from her adversary to herself. When the marquis, on hearing her determination to retire, earnestly enquired for the motive of her conduct, she forbore to acquaint him with the real one, and left him to incertitude and disappointment.

To Emilia this design occasioned a distress which almost subdued the resolution of madame. Her tears and intreaties spoke the artless energy of sorrow. In madame she lost her only friend; and she too well understood the value of that friend, to see her depart without feeling and expressing the deepest distress. From a strong attachment to the memory of the mother, madame had been induced to undertake the education of her daughters, whose engaging dispositions had perpetuated a kind of hereditary affection. Regard for Emilia and Julia had alone for some time detained her at the castle; but this was now succeeded by the influence of considerations too powerful to be resisted. As her income was small, it was her plan to retire to her native place, which was situated in a distant part of the island, and there take up her residence in a convent.

Emilia saw the time of madame's departure approach with increased distress. They left each other with a mutual sorrow, which did honour to their hearts. When her last friend was gone, Emilia wandered through the forsaken apartments, where she had been accustomed to converse with Julia, and to receive consolation and sympathy from her dear instructress, with a kind of anguish known only to those who have experienced a similar situation. Madame pursued her journey with a heavy heart. Separated from the objects of her fondest affections, and from the scenes and occupations for which long habit had formed claims upon her heart, she seemed without interest and without motive for exertion. The world appeared a wide and gloomy desert, where no heart welcomed her with kindness — no countenance brightened into smiles at her approach. It was many years since she quitted Calini — and in the interval, death had swept away the few friends she left there. The future presented a melancholy scene; but she had the retrospect of years spent in honorable endeavour and strict integrity, to cheer her heart and encouraged her hopes.

But her utmost endeavours were unable to express the anxiety with which the uncertain fate of Julia overwhelmed her. Wild and terrific images arose to her imagination. Fancy drew the scene;—she deepened the shades; and the terrific aspect of the objects she presented was heightened by the obscurity which involved them.

[End of Vol. I]

CHAPTER VII

Towards the close of day Madame de Menon arrived at a small village situated among the mountains, where she purposed to pass the night. The evening was remarkably fine, and the romantic beauty of the surrounding scenery invited her to walk. She followed the windings of a stream, which was lost at some distance amongst luxuriant groves of chesnut. The rich colouring of evening glowed through the dark foliage, which spreading a pensive gloom around, offered a scene congenial to the present temper of her mind, and she entered the shades. Her thoughts, affected by the surrounding objects, gradually sunk into a pleasing and complacent melancholy, and she was insensibly led on. She still followed the course of the stream to where the deep shades retired, and the scene again opening to day, yielded to her a view so various and sublime, that she paused in thrilling and delightful wonder. A group of wild and grotesque rocks rose in a semicircular form, and their fantastic shapes exhibited Nature in her most sublime and striking attitudes. Here her vast magnificence elevated the mind of the beholder to enthusiasm. Fancy caught the thrilling sensation, and at her touch the towering steeps became shaded with unreal glooms; the caves more darkly frowned—the projecting cliffs assumed a more terrific aspect, and the wild overhanging shrubs waved to the gale in deeper murmurs. The scene inspired madame with reverential awe, and her thoughts involuntarily rose, 'from Nature up to Nature's God.' The last dying gleams of day tinted the rocks and shone upon the waters, which retired through a rugged channel and were lost afar among the receding cliffs. While she listened to their distant murmur, a voice of liquid and melodious sweetness arose from among the rocks; it sung an air, whose melancholy expression awakened all her attention, and captivated her heart. The tones swelled and died faintly away among the clear, yet languishing echoes which the rocks repeated with an effect like that of enchantment. Madame looked around in search of the sweet warbler, and observed at some distance a peasant girl seated on a small projection of the rock, overshadowed by drooping sycamores. She moved slowly towards the spot, which she had almost reached, when the sound of her steps startled and silenced the syren, who, on perceiving a stranger, arose in an attitude to depart. The voice of madame arrested her, and she approached. Language cannot paint the sensation of madame, when in the disguise of a peasant girl, she distinguished the features of Julia, whose eyes lighted up with sudden recollection, and who sunk into her arms overcome with joy. When their first emotions were subsided, and Julia had received answers to her enquiries concerning Ferdinand and

Emilia, she led madame to the place of her concealment. This was a solitary cottage, in a close valley surrounded by mountains, whose cliffs appeared wholly inaccessible to mortal foot. The deep solitude of the scene dissipated at once madame's wonder that Julia had so long remained undiscovered, and excited surprize how she had been able to explore a spot thus deeply sequestered; but madame observed with extreme concern, that the countenance of Julia no longer wore the smile of health and gaiety. Her fine features had received the impressions not only of melancholy, but of grief. Madame sighed as she gazed, and read too plainly the cause of the change. Julia understood that sigh, and answered it with her tears. She pressed the hand of madame in mournful silence to her lips, and her cheeks were suffused with a crimson glow. At length, recovering herself, 'I have much, my dear madam, to tell,' said she, 'and much to explain, 'ere you will admit me again to that esteem of which I was once so justly proud. I had no resource from misery, but in flight; and of that I could not make you a confidant, without meanly involving you in its disgrace.'—'Say no more, my love, on the subject,' replied madame; 'with respect to myself, I admired your conduct, and felt severely for your situation. Rather let me hear by what means you effected your escape, and what has since be fallen you.'—Julia paused a moment, as if to stifle her rising emotion, and then commenced her narrative.

'You are already acquainted with the secret of that night, so fatal to my peace. I recall the remembrance of it with an anguish which I cannot conceal; and why should I wish its concealment, since I mourn for one, whose noble qualities justified all my admiration, and deserved more than my feeble praise can bestow; the idea of whom will be the last to linger in my mind till death shuts up this painful scene.' Her voice trembled, and she paused. After a few moments she resumed her tale. 'I will spare myself the pain of recurring to scenes with which you are not unacquainted, and proceed to those which more immediately attract your interest. Caterina, my faithful servant, you know, attended me in my confinement; to her kindness I owe my escape. She obtained from her lover, a servant in the castle, that assistance which gave me liberty. One night when Carlo, who had been appointed my guard, was asleep, Nicolo crept into his chamber, and stole from him the keys of my prison. He had previously procured a ladder of ropes. O! I can never forget my emotions, when in the dead hour of that night, which was meant to precede the day of my sacrifice, I heard the door of my prison unlock, and found myself half at liberty! My trembling limbs with difficulty supported me as I followed Caterina to the saloon, the windows of which being low and near to the terrace, suited our purpose. To the terrace we easily got, where Nicolo awaited us with the rope-ladder. He fastened it to the ground; and having climbed to the top of the parapet, quickly slided down on the other side. There he held it, while we ascended and descended; and I soon breathed the air of freedom again. But the apprehension of being retaken was still too powerful to permit a full enjoyment of my escape. It was my plan to proceed to the place of my faithful Caterina's nativity, where she had assured me I might find a safe asylum in the cottage of her parents, from whom, as they had never seen me, I might conceal my birth. This place, she said, was entirely unknown to the marquis, who had hired her at Naples only a few months before, without any enquiries concerning her family. She had informed me that the village was many leagues distant from the castle, but that she was very well acquainted with the road. At the foot of the walls we left Nicolo, who returned to the castle to prevent suspicion, but with an intention to leave it at a less dangerous time, and repair to Farrini to his good Caterina. I parted from him with many thanks, and gave him a small diamond cross, which, for that purpose, I had taken from the jewels sent to me for wedding ornaments.'

CHAPTER VIII

'About a quarter of a league from the walls we stopped, and I assumed the habit in which you now see me. My own dress was fastened to some heavy stones, and Caterina threw it into the stream, near the almond grove, whose murmurings you have so often admired. The fatigue and hardship I endured in this journey, performed almost wholly on foot, at any other time would have overcome me; but my mind was so occupied by the danger I was avoiding that these lesser evils were disregarded. We arrived in safety at the cottage, which stood at a little distance from the village of Ferrini, and were received by Caterina's parents with some surprise and more kindness. I soon perceived it would be useless, and even dangerous, to attempt to preserve the character I personated. In the eyes of Caterina's mother I read a degree of surprise and admiration which declared she believed me to be of superior rank; I, therefore, thought it more prudent to win her fidelity by entrusting her with my secret than, by endeavouring to conceal it, leave it to be discovered by her curiosity or discernment. Accordingly, I made known my quality and my distress, and received strong assurances of assistance and attachment. For further security, I removed to this sequestered spot. The cottage we are now in belongs to a sister of Caterina, upon whose faithfulness I have been hitherto fully justified in relying. But I am not even here secure from apprehension, since for several days past horsemen of a suspicious appearance have been observed near Marcy, which is only half a league from hence.'

Here Julia closed her narration, to which madame had listened with a mixture of surprise and pity, which her eyes sufficiently discovered. The last circumstance of the narrative seriously alarmed her. She acquainted Julia with the pursuit which the duke had undertaken; and she did not hesitate to believe it a party of his people whom Julia had described. Madame, therefore, earnestly advised her to quit her present situation, and to accompany her in disguise to the monastery of St Augustin, where she would find a secure retreat; because, even if her place of refuge should be discovered, the superior authority of the church would protect her. Julia accepted the proposal with much joy. As it was necessary that madame should sleep at the village where she had left her servants and horses, it was agreed that at break of day she should return to the cottage, where Julia would await her. Madame took all affectionate leave of Julia, whose heart, in spite of reason, sunk when she saw her depart, though but for the necessary interval of repose.

At the dawn of day madame arose. Her servants, who were hired for the journey, were strangers to Julia: from them, therefore, she had nothing to apprehend. She reached the cottage before sunrise, having left her people at some little distance. Her heart foreboded evil, when, on knocking at the door, no answer was returned. She knocked again, and still all was silent. Through the casement she could discover no object, amidst the grey obscurity of the dawn. She now opened the door, and, to her inexpressible surprise and distress, found the cottage empty. She proceeded to a small inner room, where lay a part of Julia's apparel. The bed had no appearance of having being slept in, and every moment served to heighten and confirm her apprehensions. While she pursued the search, she suddenly heard the trampling of feet at the cottage door, and presently after some people entered. Her fears for Julia now yielded to those for her own safety, and she was undetermined whether to discover herself, or remain in her present situation, when she was relieved from her irresolution by the appearance of Julia.

On the return of the good woman, who had accompanied madame to the village on the preceding night, Julia went to the cottage at Farrini. Her grateful heart would not suffer her to depart without taking leave of her faithful friends, thanking them for their kindness, and informing them of her future prospects. They had prevailed upon her to spend the few intervening hours at this cot, whence she had just risen to meet madame.

They now hastened to the spot where the horses were stationed, and commenced their journey. For some leagues they travelled in silence and thought, over a wild and picturesque country. The landscape was tinted with rich and variegated hues; and the autumnal lights, which streamed upon the hills, produced a spirited and beautiful effect upon the scenery. All the glories of the vintage rose to their view: the purple grapes flushed through the dark green of the surrounding foliage, and the prospect glowed with luxuriance.

They now descended into a deep valley, which appeared more like a scene of airy enchantment than reality. Along the bottom flowed a clear majestic stream, whose banks were adorned with thick groves of orange and citron trees. Julia surveyed the scene in silent complacency, but her eye quickly caught an object which changed with instantaneous shock the tone of her feelings. She observed a party of horsemen winding down the side of a hill behind her. Their uncommon speed alarmed her, and she pushed her horse into a gallop. On looking back Madame de Menon clearly perceived they were in pursuit. Soon after the men suddenly appeared from behind a dark grove within a small distance of them; and, upon their nearer approach, Julia, overcome with fatigue and fear, sunk breathless from her horse. She was saved from the ground by one of the pursuers, who caught her in his arms. Madame, with the rest of the party, were quickly overtaken; and as soon as Julia revived, they were bound, and reconducted to the hill from whence they had descended. Imagination only can paint the anguish of Julia's mind, when she saw herself thus delivered up to the power of her enemy. Madame, in the surrounding troop, discovered none of the marquis's people, and they were therefore evidently in the hands of the duke. After travelling for some hours, they quitted the main road, and turned into a narrow winding dell, overshadowed by high trees, which almost excluded the light. The gloom of the place inspired terrific images. Julia trembled as she entered; and her emotion was heightened, when she perceived at some distance, through the long perspective of the trees, a large ruinous mansion. The gloom of the surrounding shades partly concealed it from her view; but, as she drew near, each forlorn and decaying feature of the fabric was gradually disclosed, and struck upon her heart a horror such as she had never before experienced. The broken battlements, enwreathed with ivy, proclaimed the fallen grandeur of the place, while the shattered vacant window-frames exhibited its desolation, and the high grass that overgrew the threshold seemed to say how long it was since mortal foot had entered. The place appeared fit only for the purposes of violence and destruction: and the unfortunate captives, when they stopped at its gates, felt the full force of its horrors.

They were taken from their horses, and conveyed to an interior part of the building, which, if it had once been a chamber, no longer deserved the name. Here the guard said they were directed to detain them till the arrival of their lord, who had appointed this the place of rendezvous. He was expected to meet them in a few hours, and these were hours of indescribable torture to Julia and madame. From the furious passions of the duke, exasperated by frequent disappointment, Julia had every evil to apprehend; and the loneliness of the spot he had chosen, enabled him to perpetrate any designs, however violent. For the first time, she repented that she had left her father's house. Madame wept over her, but comfort she had none to give. The day closed—the duke did not appear, and the fate of Julia yet hung in perilous uncertainty. At length, from a window of the apartment she was in, she distinguished a glimmering of torches among the trees, and presently after the clattering of hoofs convinced her the duke was approaching. Her heart sunk at the sound; and throwing her arms round madame's neck, she resigned herself to despair. She was soon roused by some men, who came to announce the arrival of their lord. In a few moments the place, which had lately been so silent, echoed with tumult; and a sudden blaze of light illumining the fabric, served to exhibit more forcibly its striking horrors. Julia ran to the window; and, in a sort of court below, perceived a group of men dismounting from their horses. The torches shed a partial light; and while she anxiously looked round for the person of the duke, the whole party entered the mansion. She listened to a confused uproar of voices, which sounded from the room beneath, and soon after it sunk into a low murmur, as if some matter of importance was in agitation. For some moments she sat in lingering terror, when she heard footsteps advancing towards the chamber, and a sudden gleam of torchlight flashed upon the walls. 'Wretched girl! I have at least secured you!' said a cavalier, who now entered the room. He stopped as he perceived Julia; and turning to the men who stood without, 'Are these,' said he, 'the fugitives you have taken?' — 'Yes, my lord.' — 'Then you have deceived yourselves, and misled me; this is not my daughter.' These words struck the sudden light of truth and joy upon the heart of Julia, whom terror had before rendered almost lifeless; and who had not perceived that the person entering was a stranger. Madame now stepped forward, and an explanation ensued, when it appeared that the stranger was the Marquis Murani, the father of the fair fugitive whom the duke had before mistaken for Julia.

The appearance and the evident flight of Julia had deceived the banditti employed by this nobleman, into a belief that she was the object of their search, and had occasioned her this unnecessary distress. But the joy she now felt, on finding herself thus unexpectedly at liberty, surpassed, if possible, her preceding terrors. The marquis made madame and Julia all the reparation in his power, by offering immediately to reconduct them to the main road, and to guard them to some place of safety for the night. This offer was eagerly and thankfully accepted; and though faint from distress, fatigue, and want of sustenance, they joyfully remounted their horses, and by torchlight quitted the mansion. After some hours travelling they arrived at a small town, where they procured the accommodation so necessary to their support and repose. Here their guides quitted them to continue their search.

They arose with the dawn, and continued their journey, continually terrified with the apprehension of encountering the duke's people. At noon they arrived at Azulia, from whence the monastery, or abbey of St Augustin, was distant only a few miles. Madame wrote to the Padre Abate, to whom she was somewhat related, and soon after received an answer very favourable to her wishes. The same evening they repaired to the abbey; where Julia, once more relieved from the fear of pursuit, offered up a prayer of gratitude to heaven, and endeavoured to calm her sorrows by devotion. She was received by the abbot with a sort of paternal affection, and by the nuns with officious kindness. Comforted by these circumstances, and by the tranquil appearance of every thing around her, she retired to rest, and passed the night in peaceful slumbers.

In her present situation she found much novelty to amuse, and much serious matter to interest her mind. Entendered by distress, she easily yielded to the pensive manners of her companions and to the serene uniformity of a monastic life. She loved to wander through the lonely cloisters, and high-arched aisles, whose long perspectives retired in simple grandeur, diffusing a holy calm around. She found much pleasure in the conversation of the nuns, many of whom were uncommonly amiable, and the dignified sweetness of whose manners formed a charm irresistibly attractive. The soft melancholy impressed upon their countenances, pourtrayed the situation of their minds, and excited in Julia a very interesting mixture of pity and esteem. The affectionate appellation of sister, and all that endearing tenderness which they so well know how to display, and of which they so well understand the effect, they bestowed on Julia, in the hope of winning her to become one of their order.

Soothed by the presence of madame, the assiduity of the nuns, and by the stillness and sanctity of the place, her mind gradually recovered a degree of complacency to which it had long been a stranger. But notwithstanding all her efforts, the idea of Hippolitus would at intervals return upon her memory with a force that at once subdued her fortitude, and sunk her in a temporary despair.

Among the holy sisters, Julia distinguished one, the singular fervor of whose devotion, and the pensive air of whose countenance, softened by the languor of illness, attracted her curiosity, and excited a strong degree of pity. The nun, by a sort of sympathy, seemed particularly inclined towards Julia, which she discovered by innumerable acts of kindness, such as the heart can quickly understand and acknowledge, although description can never reach them. In conversation with her, Julia endeavoured, as far as delicacy would permit, to prompt an explanation of that more than common dejection which shaded those features, where beauty, touched by resignation and sublimed by religion, shone forth with mild and lambent lustre.

The Duke de Luovo, after having been detained for some weeks by the fever which his wounds had produced, and his irritated passions had much prolonged, arrived at the castle of Mazzini.

When the marquis saw him return, and recollected the futility of those exertions, by which he had boastingly promised to recover Julia, the violence of his nature spurned the disguise of art, and burst forth in contemptuous impeachment of the valour and discernment of the duke, who soon retorted with equal fury. The consequence might have been fatal, had not the ambition of the marquis subdued the sudden irritation of his inferior passions, and induced him to soften the severity of his accusations, by subsequent concessions. The duke, whose passion for Julia was heightened by the difficulty which opposed it, admitted such concessions as in other circumstances he would have rejected; and thus each, conquered by the predominant passion of the moment, submitted to be the slave of his adversary.

Emilia was at length released from the confinement she had so unjustly suffered. She had now the use of her old apartments, where, solitary and dejected, her hours moved heavily along, embittered by incessant anxiety for Julia, by regret for the lost society of madame. The marchioness, whose pleasures suffered a temporary suspense during the present confusion at the castle, exercised the ill-humoured caprice, which disappointment and lassitude inspired, upon her remaining subject. Emilia was condemned to suffer, and to endure without the privilege of complaining. In reviewing the events of the last few weeks, she saw those most dear to her banished, or imprisoned by the secret influence of a woman, every feature of whose character was exactly opposite to that of the amiable mother she had been appointed to succeed.

The search after Julia still continued, and was still unsuccessful. The astonishment of the marquis increased with his disappointments; for where could Julia, ignorant of the country, and destitute of friends, have possibly found an asylum? He swore with a terrible oath to revenge on her head, whenever she should be found, the trouble and vexation she now caused him. But he agreed with the duke to relinquish for a while the search; till Julia, gaining confidence from the observation of this circumstance, might gradually suppose herself secure from molestation, and thus be induced to emerge from concealment.

CHAPTER IX

Meanwhile Julia, sheltered in the obscure recesses of St Augustin, endeavoured to attain a degree of that tranquillity which so strikingly characterized the scenes around her. The abbey of St Augustin was a large magnificent mass of Gothic architecture, whose gloomy battlements, and majestic towers arose in proud sublimity from amid the darkness of the surrounding shades. It was founded in the twelfth century, and stood a proud monument of monkish superstition and princely magnificence. In the times when Italy was agitated by internal commotions, and persecuted by foreign invaders, this edifice afforded an asylum to many noble Italian emigrants, who here consecrated the rest of their days to religion. At their death they enriched the monastery with the treasures which it had enabled them to secure.

The view of this building revived in the mind of the beholder the memory of past ages. The manners and characters which distinguished them arose to his fancy, and through the long lapse of years he discriminated those customs and manners which formed so striking a contrast to the modes of his own times. The rude manners, the boisterous passions, the daring ambition, and the gross indulgences which formerly characterized the priest, the nobleman, and the sovereign, had now begun to yield to learning—the charms of refined conversation—political intrigue and private artifices. Thus do the scenes of life vary with the predominant passions of mankind, and with the progress of civilization. The dark clouds of prejudice break away before the sun of science, and gradually dissolving, leave the brightening hemisphere to the influence of his beams. But through the present scene appeared only a few scattered rays, which served to shew more forcibly the vast and heavy masses that concealed the form of truth. Here prejudice, not reason, suspended the influence of the passions; and scholastic learning, mysterious philosophy, and crafty sanctity supplied the place of wisdom, simplicity, and pure devotion.

At the abbey, solitude and stillness conspired with the solemn aspect of the pile to impress the mind with religious awe. The dim glass of the high-arched windows, stained with the colouring of monkish fictions, and shaded by the thick trees that environed the edifice, spread around a sacred gloom, which inspired the beholder with congenial feelings.

As Julia mused through the walks, and surveyed this vast monument of barbarous superstition, it brought to her recollection an ode which she often repeated with melancholy pleasure, as the composition of Hippolitus.

SUPERSTITION

AN ODE

High mid Alverna's awful steeps,
 Eternal shades, and silence dwell.
Save, when the gale resounding sweeps,
 Sad strains are faintly heard to swell:
Enthron'd amid the wild impending rocks,
 Involved in clouds, and brooding future woe,
The demon Superstition Nature shocks,
 And waves her sceptre o'er the world below.
Around her throne, amid the mingling glooms,
 Wild—hideous forms are slowly seen to glide,
She bids them fly to shade earth's brightest blooms,
 And spread the blast of Desolation wide.
See! in the darkened air their fiery course!
 The sweeping ruin settles o'er the land,
Terror leads on their steps with madd'ning force,
 And Death and Vengeance close the ghastly band!
  Mark the purple streams that flow!
  Mark the deep empassioned woe!
  Frantic Fury's dying groan!
  Virtue's sigh, and Sorrow's moan!
Wide—wide the phantoms swell the loaded air
With shrieks of anguish—madness and despair!
Cease your ruin! spectres dire!
 Cease your wild terrific sway!

Turn your steps—and check your ire,

    Yield to peace the mourning day!

She wept to the memory of times past, and there was a romantic sadness in her feelings, luxurious and indefinable. Madame behaved to Julia with the tenderest attention, and endeavoured to withdraw her thoughts from their mournful subject by promoting that taste for literature and music, which was so suitable to the powers of her mind.

But an object seriously interesting now obtained that regard, which those of mere amusement failed to attract. Her favorite nun, for whom her love and esteem daily increased, seemed declining under the pressure of a secret grief. Julia was deeply affected with her situation, and though she was not empowered to administer consolation to her sorrows, she endeavoured to mitigate the sufferings of illness. She nursed her with unremitting care, and seemed to seize with avidity the temporary opportunity of escaping from herself. The nun appeared perfectly reconciled to her fate, and exhibited during her illness so much sweetness, patience, and resignation as affected all around her with pity and love. Her angelic mildness, and steady fortitude characterized the beatification of a saint, rather than the death of a mortal. Julia watched every turn of her disorder with the utmost solicitude, and her care was at length rewarded by the amendment of Cornelia. Her health gradually improved, and she attributed this circumstance to the assiduity and tenderness of her young friend, to whom her heart now expanded in warm and unreserved affection. At length Julia ventured to solicit what she had so long and so earnestly wished for, and Cornelia unfolded the history of her sorrows.

'Of the life which your care has prolonged,' said she, 'it is but just that you should know the events; though those events are neither new, or striking, and possess little power of interesting persons unconnected with them. To me they have, however, been unexpectedly dreadful in effect, and my heart assures me, that to you they will not be indifferent.

'I am the unfortunate descendant of an ancient and illustrious Italian family. In early childhood I was deprived of a mother's care, but the tenderness of my surviving parent made her loss, as to my welfare, almost unfelt. Suffer me here to do justice to the character of my noble father. He united in an eminent degree the mild virtues of social life, with the firm unbending qualities of the noble Romans, his ancestors, from whom he was proud to trace his descent. Their merit, indeed, continually dwelt on his tongue, and their actions he was always endeavouring to imitate, as far as was consistent with the character of his times, and with the limited sphere in which he moved. The recollection of his virtue elevates my mind, and fills my heart with a noble pride, which even the cold walls of a monastery have not been able to subdue.

'My father's fortune was unsuitable to his rank. That his son might hereafter be enabled to support the dignity of his family, it was necessary for me to assume the veil. Alas! that heart was unfit to be offered at an heavenly shrine, which was already devoted to an earthly object. My affections had long been engaged by the younger son of a neighbouring nobleman, whose character and accomplishments attracted my early love, and confirmed my latest esteem. Our families were intimate, and our youthful intercourse occasioned an attachment which strengthened and expanded with our years. He solicited me of my father, but there appeared an insuperable barrier to our union. The family of my lover laboured under a circumstance of similar distress with that of my own — it was noble — but poor! My father, who was ignorant of the strength of my affection, and who considered a marriage formed in poverty as destructive to happiness, prohibited his suit.

'Touched with chagrin and disappointment, he immediately entered into the service of his Neapolitan majesty, and sought in the tumultuous scenes of glory, a refuge from the pangs of disappointed passion.

'To me, whose hours moved in one round of full uniformity — who had no pursuit to interest — no variety to animate my drooping spirits — to me the effort of forgetfulness was ineffectual. The loved idea of Angelo still rose upon my fancy, and its powers of captivation, heightened by absence, and, perhaps even by despair, pursued me with incessant grief. I concealed in silence the anguish that preyed upon my heart, and resigned myself a willing victim to monastic austerity. But I was now threatened with a new evil, terrible and unexpected. I was so unfortunate as to attract the admiration of the Marquis Marinelli, and he applied to my father. He was illustrious at once in birth and fortune, and his visits could only be unwelcome to me. Dreadful was the moment in which my father disclosed to me the proposal. My distress, which I vainly endeavoured to command, discovered the exact situation of my heart, and my father was affected.

'After a long and awful pause, he generously released me from my sufferings by leaving it to my choice to accept the marquis, or to assume the veil. I fell at his feet, overcome by the noble disinterestedness of his conduct, and instantly accepted the latter.

'This affair removed entirely the disguise with which I had hitherto guarded my heart; — my brother — my generous brother! learned the true state of its affections. He saw the grief which prayed upon my health; he observed it to my father, and he nobly — oh how nobly! to restore my happiness, desired to resign a part of the estate which had already descended to him in right of his mother. Alas! Hippolitus,' continued Cornelia, deeply sighing, 'thy virtues deserved a better fate.'

'Hippolitus!' said Julia, in a tremulous accent, 'Hippolitus, Count de Vereza!' — 'The same,' replied the nun, in a tone of surprize. Julia was speechless; tears, however, came to her relief. The astonishment of Cornelia for some moment surpassed expression; at length a gleam of recollection crossed her mind, and she too well understood the scene before her. Julia, after some time revived, when Cornelia tenderly approaching her, 'Do I then embrace my sister!' said she. 'United in sentiment, are we also united in misfortune?' Julia answered with her sighs, and their tears flowed in mournful sympathy together. At length Cornelia resumed her narrative.

'My father, struck with the conduct of Hippolitus, paused upon the offer. The alteration in my health was too obvious to escape his notice; the conflict between pride and parental tenderness, held him for some time in indecision, but the latter finally subdued every opposing feeling, and he yielded his consent to my marriage with Angelo. The sudden transition from grief to joy was almost too much for my feeble frame; judge then what must have been the effect of the dreadful reverse, when the news arrived that Angelo had fallen in a foreign engagement! Let me obliterate, if possible, the impression of sensations so dreadful. The sufferings of my brother, whose generous heart could so finely feel for another's woe, were on this occasion inferior only to my own.

'After the first excess of my grief was subsided, I desired to retire from a world which had tempted me only with illusive visions of happiness, and to remove from those scenes which prompted recollection, and perpetuated my distress. My father applauded my resolution, and I immediately was admitted a noviciate into this monastery, with the Superior of which my father had in his youth been acquainted.

'At the expiration of the year I received the veil. Oh! I well remember with what perfect resignation, with what comfortable complacency I took those vows which bound me to a life of retirement, and religious rest.

'The high importance of the moment, the solemnity of the ceremony, the sacred glooms which surrounded me, and the chilling silence that prevailed when I uttered the irrevocable vow—all conspired to impress my imagination, and to raise my views to heaven. When I knelt at the altar, the sacred flame of pure devotion glowed in my heart, and elevated my soul to sublimity. The world and all its recollections faded from my mind, and left it to the influence of a serene and, holy enthusiasm which no words can describe.

'Soon after my noviciation, I had the misfortune to lose my dear father. In the tranquillity of this monastery, however, in the soothing kindness of my companions, and in devotional exercises, my sorrows found relief, and the sting of grief was blunted. My repose was of short continuance. A circumstance occurred that renewed the misery, which, can now never quit me but in the grave, to which I look with no fearful apprehension, but as a refuge from calamity, trusting that the power who has seen good to afflict me, will pardon the imperfectness of my devotion, and the too frequent wandering of my thoughts to the object once so dear to me.'

As she spoke she raised her eyes, which beamed with truth and meek assurance to heaven; and the fine devotional suffusion of her countenance seemed to characterize the beauty of an inspired saint.

'One day, Oh! never shall I forget it, I went as usual to the confessional to acknowledge my sins. I knelt before the father with eyes bent towards the earth, and in a low voice proceeded to confess. I had but one crime to deplore, and that was the too tender remembrance of him for whom I mourned, and whose idea, impressed upon my heart, made it a blemished offering to God.

'I was interrupted in my confession by a sound of deep sobs, and rising my eyes, Oh God, what were my sensations, when in the features of the holy father I discovered Angelo! His image faded like a vision from my sight, and I sunk at his feet. On recovering I found myself on my matrass, attended by a sister, who I discovered by her conversation had no suspicion of the occasion of my disorder. Indisposition confined me to my bed for several days; when I recovered, I saw Angelo no more, and could almost have doubted my senses, and believed that an illusion had crossed my sight, till one day I found in my cell a written paper. I distinguished at the first glance the handwriting of Angelo, that well-known hand which had so often awakened me to other emotions. I trembled at the sight; my beating heart acknowledged the beloved characters; a cold tremor shook my frame, and half breathless I seized the paper. But recollecting myself, I paused—I hesitated: duty at length yielded to the strong temptation, and I read the lines! Oh! those lines prompted by despair, and bathed in my tears! every word they offered gave a new pang to my heart, and swelled its anguish almost beyond endurance. I learned that Angelo, severely wounded in a foreign engagement, had been left for dead upon the field; that his life was saved by the humanity of a common soldier of the enemy, who perceiving signs of existence, conveyed him to a house. Assistance was soon procured, but his wounds exhibited the most alarming symptoms. During several months he languished between life and death, till at length his youth and constitution surmounted the conflict, and he returned to Naples. Here he saw my brother, whose distress and astonishment at beholding him occasioned a relation of past circumstances, and of the vows I had taken in consequence of the report of his death. It is unnecessary to mention the immediate effect of this narration; the final one exhibited a very singular proof of his attachment and despair;—he devoted himself to a monastic life, and chose this abbey for the place of his residence, because it contained the object most dear to his affections. His letter informed me that he had purposely avoided discovering himself, endeavouring to be contented with the opportunities which occurred of silently observing me, till chance had occasioned the foregoing interview.—But that since its effects had been so mutually painful, he would relieve me from the apprehension of a similar distress, by assuring me, that I should see him no more. He was faithful to his promise; from that day I have never seen him, and am even ignorant whether he yet inhabits this asylum; the efforts of religious fortitude, and the just fear of exciting curiosity, having withheld me from enquiry. But the moment of our last interview has been equally fatal to my peace and to my health, and I trust I shall, ere very long, be released from the agonizing ineffectual struggles occasioned by the consciousness of sacred vows imperfectly performed, and by earthly affections not wholly subdued.'

Cornelia ceased, and Julia, who had listened to the narrative in deep attention, at once admired, loved, and pitied her. As the sister of Hippolitus, her heart expanded towards her, and it was now inviolably attached by the fine ties of sympathetic sorrow.

Similarity of sentiment and suffering united them in the firmest bonds of friendship; and thus, from reciprocation of thought and feeling, flowed a pure and sweet consolation.

Julia loved to indulge in the mournful pleasure of conversing of Hippolitus, and when thus engaged, the hours crept unheeded by. A thousand questions she repeated concerning him, but to those most interesting to her, she received no consolatory answer. Cornelia, who had heard of the fatal transaction at the castle of Mazzini, deplored with her its too certain consequence.

CHAPTER X

Julia accustomed herself to walk in the fine evenings under the shade of the high trees that environed the abbey. The dewy coolness of the air refreshed her. The innumerable roseate tints which the parting sun-beams reflected on the rocks above, and the fine vermil glow diffused over the romantic scene beneath, softly fading from the eye, as the nightshades fell, excited sensations of a sweet and tranquil nature, and soothed her into a temporary forgetfulness of her sorrows.

The deep solitude of the place subdued her apprehension, and one evening she ventured with Madame de Menon to lengthen her walk. They returned to the abbey without having seen a human being, except a friar of the monastery, who had been to a neighbouring town to order provision. On the following evening they repeated their walk; and, engaged in conversation, rambled to a considerable distance from the abbey. The distant bell of the monastery sounding for vespers, reminded them of the hour, and looking round, they perceived the extremity of the wood. They were returning towards the abbey, when struck by the appearance of some majestic columns which were distinguishable between the trees, they paused. Curiosity tempted them to examine to what edifice pillars of such magnificent architecture could belong, in a scene so rude, and they went on.

There appeared on a point of rock impending over the valley the reliques of a palace, whose beauty time had impaired only to heighten its sublimity. An arch of singular magnificence remained almost entire, beyond which appeared wild cliffs retiring in grand perspective. The sun, which was now setting, threw a trembling lustre upon the ruins, and gave a finishing effect to the scene. They gazed in mute wonder upon the view; but the fast fading light, and the dewy chillness of the air, warned them to return. As Julia gave a last look to the scene, she perceived two men leaning upon a part of the ruin at some distance, in earnest conversation. As they spoke, their looks were so attentively bent on her, that she could have no doubt she was the subject of their discourse. Alarmed at this circumstance, madame and Julia immediately retreated towards the abbey. They walked swiftly through the woods, whose shades, deepened by the gloom of evening, prevented their distinguishing whether they were pursued. They were surprized to observe the distance to which they had strayed from the monastery, whose dark towers were now obscurely seen rising among the trees that closed the perspective. They had almost reached the gates, when on looking back, they perceived the same men slowly advancing, without any appearance of pursuit, but clearly as if observing the place of their retreat.

This incident occasioned Julia much alarm. She could not but believe that the men whom she had seen were spies of the marquis; — if so, her asylum was discovered, and she had every thing to apprehend. Madame now judged it necessary to the safety of Julia, that the Abate should be informed of her story, and of the sanctuary she had sought in his monastery, and also that he should be solicited to protect her from parental tyranny. This was a hazardous, but a necessary step, to provide against the certain danger which must ensue, should the marquis, if he demanded his daughter of the Abate, be the first to acquaint him with her story. If she acted otherwise, she feared that the Abate, in whose generosity she had not confided, and whose pity she had not solicited, would, in the pride of his resentment, deliver her up, and thus would she become a certain victim to the Duke de Luovo.

Julia approved of this communication, though she trembled for the event; and requested madame to plead her cause with the Abate. On the following morning, therefore, madame solicited a private audience of the Abate; she obtained permission to see him, and Julia, in trembling anxiety, watched her to the door of his apartment. This conference was long, and every moment seemed an hour to Julia, who, in fearful expectation, awaited with Cornelia the sentence which would decide her destiny. She was now the constant companion of Cornelia, whose declining health interested her pity, and strengthened her attachment.

Meanwhile madame developed to the Abate the distressful story of Julia. She praised her virtues, commended her accomplishments, and deplored her situation. She described the characters of the marquis and the duke, and concluded with pathetically representing, that Julia had sought in this monastery, a last asylum from injustice and misery, and with entreating that the Abate would grant her his pity and protection.

The Abate during this discourse preserved a sullen silence; his eyes were bent to the ground, and his aspect was thoughful and solemn. When madame ceased to speak, a pause of profound silence ensued, and she sat in anxious expectation. She endeavoured to anticipate in his countenance the answer preparing, but she derived no comfort from thence. At length raising his head, and awakening from his deep reverie, he told

545

her that her request required deliberation, and that the protection she solicited for Julia, might involve him in serious consequences, since, from a character so determined as the marquis's, much violence might reasonably be expected. 'Should his daughter be refused him,' concluded the Abate, 'he may even dare to violate the sanctuary.'

Madame, shocked by the stern indifference of this reply, was a moment silent. The Abate went on. 'Whatever I shall determine upon, the young lady has reason to rejoice that she is admitted into this holy house; for I will even now venture to assure her, that if the marquis fails to demand her, she shall be permitted to remain in this sanctuary unmolested. You, Madam, will be sensible of this indulgence, and of the value of the sacrifice I make in granting it; for, in thus concealing a child from her parent, I encourage her in disobedience, and consequently sacrifice my sense of duty, to what may be justly called a weak humanity.'

Madame listened to pompous declamation in silent sorrow and indignation. She made another effort to interest the Abate in favor of Julia, but he preserved his stern inflexibility, and repeating that he would deliberate upon the matter, and acquaint her with the result, he arose with great solemnity, and quitted the room.

She now half repented of the confidence she had reposed in him, and of the pity she had solicited, since he discovered a mind incapable of understanding the first, and a temper inaccessible to the influence of the latter. With an heavy heart she returned to Julia, who read in her countenance, at the moment she entered the room, news of no happy import. When madame related the particulars of the conference, Julia presaged from it only misery, and giving herself up for lost—she burst into tears. She severely deplored the confidence she had been induced to yield; for she now saw herself in the power of a man, stern and unfeeling in his nature: and from whom, if he thought it fit to betray her, she had no means of escaping. But she concealed the anguish of her heart; and to console madame, affected to hope where she could only despair.

Several days elapsed, and no answer was returned from the Abate. Julia too well understood this silence.

One morning Cornelia entering her room with a disturbed and impatient air, informed her that some emissaries from the marquis were then in the monastery, having enquired at the gate for the Abate, with whom, they said, they had business of importance to transact. The Abate had granted them immediate audience, and they were now in close conference.

At this intelligence the spirits of Julia forsook her; she trembled, grew pale, and stood fixed in mute despair. Madame, though scarcely less distressed, retained a presence of mind. She understood too justly the character of the Superior to doubt that he would hesitate in delivering Julia to the hands of the marquis. On this moment, therefore, turned the crisis of her fate!—this moment she might escape—the next she was a prisoner. She therefore advised Julia to seize the instant, and fly from the monastery before the conference was concluded, when the gates would most probably be closed upon her, assuring her, at the same time, she would accompany her in flight.

The generous conduct of madame called tears of gratitude into the eyes of Julia, who now awoke from the state of stupefaction which distress had caused. But before she could thank her faithful friend, a nun entered the room with a summons for madame to attend the Abate immediately. The distress which this message occasioned can not easily be conceived. Madame advised Julia to escape while she detained the Abate in conversation, as it was not probable that he had yet issued orders for her detention. Leaving her to this attempt, with an assurance of following her from the abbey as soon as possible, madame obeyed the summons. The coolness of her fortitude forsook her as she approached the Abate's apartment, and she became less certain as to the occasion of this summons.

The Abate was alone. His countenance was pale with anger, and he was pacing the room with slow but agitated steps. The stern authority of his look startled her. 'Read this letter,' said he, stretching forth his hand which held a letter, 'and tell me what that mortal deserves, who dares insult our holy order, and set our sacred prerogative at defiance.' Madame distinguished the handwriting of the marquis, and the words of the Superior threw her into the utmost astonishment. She took the letter. It was dictated by that spirit of proud vindictive rage, which so strongly marked the character of the marquis. Having discovered the retreat of Julia, and believing the monastery afforded her a willing sanctuary from his pursuit, he accused the Abate of encouraging his child in open rebellion to his will. He loaded him and his sacred order with opprobrium, and threatened, if she was not immediately resigned to the emissaries in waiting, he would in person lead on a force which should compel the church to yield to the superior authority of the father.

The spirit of the Abate was roused by this menace; and Julia obtained from his pride, that protection which neither his principle or his humanity would have granted. 'The man shall tremble,' cried he, 'who dares defy our power, or question our sacred authority. The lady Julia is safe. I will protect her from this proud invader of our rights, and teach him at least to venerate the power he cannot conquer. I have dispatched his emissaries with my answer.'

These words struck sudden joy upon the heart of Madame de Menon, but she instantly recollected, that ere this time Julia had quitted the abbey, and thus the very precaution which was meant to ensure her safety, had probably precipitated her into the hand of her enemy. This thought changed her joy to anguish; and she was hurrying from the apartment in a sort of wild hope, that Julia might not yet be gone, when the stern voice of the Abate arrested her. 'Is it thus,' cried he, 'that you receive the knowledge of our generous resolution to protect your friend? Does such condescending kindness merit no thanks—demand no gratitude?' Madame returned in an agony of fear, lest one moment of delay might prove fatal to Julia, if haply she had not yet quitted the monastery. She was conscious of her deficiency in apparent gratitude, and of the strange appearance of her abrupt departure from the Abate, for which it was impossible to apologize, without betraying the secret, which would kindle all his resentment. Yet some atonement his present anger demanded, and these circumstances caused her a very painful embarrassment. She formed a hasty excuse; and expressing her sense of his goodness, again attempted to retire, when the Abate frowning in deep resentment, his features inflamed with pride, arose from his seat. 'Stay,' said he; 'whence this impatience to fly from the presence of a benefactor?—If my generosity fails to excite gratitude, my resentment shall not fail to inspire awe.—Since the lady Julia is insensible of my condescension, she is unworthy of my protection, and I will resign her to the tyrant who demands her.'

To this speech, in which the offended pride of the Abate overcoming all sense of justice, accused and threatened to punish Julia for the fault of her friend, madame listened in dreadful impatience. Every word that detained her struck torture to her heart, but the concluding sentence occasioned new terror, and she started at its purpose. She fell at the feet of the Abate in an agony of grief. 'Holy father,' said she, 'punish not Julia for the offence which I only have committed; her heart will bless her generous protector, and for myself, suffer me to assure you that I am fully sensible of your goodness.'

'If this is true,' said the Abate, 'arise, and bid the lady Julia attend me.' This command increased the confusion of madame, who had no doubt that her detention had proved fatal to Julia. At length she was suffered to depart, and to her infinite joy found Julia in her own room. Her intention of escaping had yielded, immediately after the departure of madame, to the fear of being discovered by the marquis's people. This fear had been confirmed by the report of Cornelia, who informed her, that at that time several horsemen were waiting at the gates for the return of their companions. This was a dreadful circumstance to Julia, who perceived it was utterly impossible to quit the monastery, without rushing upon certain destruction. She was lamenting her destiny, when madame recited the particulars of the late interview, and delivered the summons of the Abate.

They had now to dread the effect of that tender anxiety, which had excited his resentment; and Julia, suddenly elated to joy by his first determination, was as suddenly sunk to despair by his last. She trembled with apprehension of the coming interview, though each moment of delay which her fear solicited, would, by heightening the resentment of the Abate, only increase the danger she dreaded.

At length, by a strong effort, she reanimated her spirits, and went to the Abate's closet to receive her sentence. He was seated in his chair, and his frowning aspect chilled her heart. 'Daughter,' said he, 'you have been guilty of heinous crimes. You have dared to dispute — nay openly to rebel, against the lawful authority of your father. You have disobeyed the will of him whose prerogative yields only to ours. You have questioned his right upon a point of all others the most decided — the right of a father to dispose of his child in marriage. You have even fled from his protection — and you have dared — insidiously, and meanly have dared, to screen your disobedience beneath this sacred roof. You have prophaned our sanctuary with your crime. You have brought insult upon our sacred order, and have caused bold and impious defiance of our high prerogative. What punishment is adequate to guilt like this?'

The father paused — his eyes sternly fixed on Julia, who, pale and trembling, could scarcely support herself, and who had no power to reply. 'I will be merciful, and not just,' resumed he, — 'I will soften the punishment you deserve, and will only deliver you to your father.' At these dreadful words, Julia bursting into tears, sunk at the feet of the Abate, to whom she raised her eyes in supplicating expression, but was unable to speak. He suffered her to remain in this posture. 'Your duplicity,' he resumed, 'is not the least of your offences. — Had you relied upon our generosity for forgiveness and protection, an indulgence might have been granted; — but under the disguise of virtue you concealed your crimes, and your necessities were hid beneath the mask of devotion.'

These false aspersions roused in Julia the spirit of indignant virtue; she arose from her knees with an air of dignity, that struck even the Abate. 'Holy father,' said she, 'my heart abhors the crime you mention, and disclaims all union with it. Whatever are my offences, from the sin of hypocrisy I am at least free; and you will pardon me if I remind you, that my confidence has already been such, as fully justifies my claim to the protection I solicit. When I sheltered myself within these walls, it was to be presumed that they would protect me from injustice; and with what other term than injustice would you, Sir, distinguish the conduct of the marquis, if the fear of his power did not overcome the dictates of truth?'

The Abate felt the full force of this reproof; but disdaining to appear sensible to it, restrained his resentment. His wounded pride thus exasperated, and all the malignant passions of his nature thus called into action, he was prompted to that cruel surrender which he had never before seriously intended. The offence which Madame de Menon had unintentionally given his haughty spirit urged him to retaliate in punishment. He had, therefore, pleased himself with exciting a terror which he never meant to confirm, and he resolved to be further solicited for that protection which he had already determined to grant. But this reproof of Julia touched him where he was most conscious of defect; and the temporary triumph which he imagined it afforded her, kindled his resentment into flame. He mused in his chair, in a fixed attitude. — She saw in his countenance the deep workings of his mind — she revolved the fate preparing for her, and stood in trembling anxiety to receive her sentence. The Abate considered each aggravating circumstance of the marquis's menace, and each sentence of Julia's speech; and his mind experienced that vice is not only inconsistent with virtue, but with itself — for to gratify his malignity, he now discovered that it would be necessary to sacrifice his pride — since it would be impossible to punish the object of the first without denying himself the gratification of the latter. This reflection suspended his mind in a state of torture, and he sat wrapt in gloomy silence.

The spirit which lately animated Julia had vanished with her words — each moment of silence increased her apprehension; the deep brooding of his thoughts confirmed her in the apprehension of evil, and with all the artless eloquence of sorrow she endeavoured to soften him to pity. He listened to her pleadings in sullen stillness. But each instant now cooled the fervour of his resentment to her, and increased his desire of opposing the marquis. At length the predominant feature of his character resumed its original influence, and overcame the workings of subordinate passion. Proud of his religious authority, he determined never to yield the prerogative of the church to that of the father, and resolved to oppose the violence of the marquis with equal force.

He therefore condescended to relieve Julia from her terrors, by assuring her of his protection; but he did this in a manner so ungracious, as almost to destroy the gratitude which the promise demanded. She hastened with the joyful intelligence to Madame de Menon, who wept over her tears of thankfulness.

CHAPTER XI

Near a fortnight had elapsed without producing any appearance of hostility from the marquis, when one night, long after the hour of repose, Julia was awakened by the bell of the monastery. She knew it was not the hour customary for prayer, and she listened to the sounds, which rolled through the deep silence of the fabric, with strong surprise and terror. Presently she heard the doors of several cells creak on their hinges, and the sound of quick footsteps in the passages — and through the crevices of her door she distinguished passing lights. The whispering noise of steps increased, and every person of the monastery seemed to have awakened. Her terror heightened; it occurred to her that the marquis had surrounded the abbey with his people, in the design of forcing her from her retreat; and she arose in haste, with an intention of going to the chamber of Madame de Menon, when she heard a gentle tap at the door. Her enquiry of who was there, was answered in the voice of madame, and her fears were quickly dissipated, for she learned the bell was a summons to attend a dying nun, who was going to the high altar, there to receive extreme unction.

She quitted the chamber with madame. In her way to the church, the gleam of tapers on the walls, and the glimpse which her eye often caught of the friars in their long black habits, descending silently through the narrow winding passages, with the solemn toll of the bell, conspired to kindle imagination, and to impress her heart with sacred awe. But the church exhibited a scene of solemnity, such as she had never before witnessed. Its gloomy aisles were imperfectly seen by the rays of tapers from the high altar, which shed a solitary gleam over the remote parts of the fabric, and produced large masses of light and shade, striking and sublime in their effect.

While she gazed, she heard a distant chanting rise through the aisles; the sounds swelled in low murmurs on the ear, and drew nearer and nearer, till a sudden blaze of light issued from one of the portals, and the procession entered. The organ instantly sounded a high and solemn peal, and the voices rising altogether swelled the sacred strain. In front appeared the Padre Abate, with slow and measured steps, bearing the holy cross. Immediately followed a litter, on which lay the dying person covered with a white veil, borne along and surrounded by nuns veiled in white, each carrying in her hand a lighted taper. Last came the friars, two and two, cloathed in black, and each bearing a light.

When they reached the high altar, the bier was rested, and in a few moments the anthem ceased. 'The Abate now approached to perform the unction; the veil of the dying nun was lifted — and Julia discovered her beloved Cornelia! Her countenance was already impressed with the image of death, but her eyes brightened with a faint gleam of recollection, when they fixed upon Julia, who felt a cold thrill run through her frame, and leaned for support on madame. Julia now for the first time distinguished the unhappy lover of Cornelia, on whose features was depictured the anguish of his heart, and who hung pale and silent over the bier. The ceremony being finished, the anthem struck up; the bier was lifted, when Cornelia faintly moved her hand, and it was again rested upon the steps of the altar. In a few minutes the music ceased, when lifting her heavy eyes to her lover, with an expression of ineffable tenderness and grief, she attempted to speak, but the sounds died on her closing lips. A faint smile passed over her countenance, and was succeeded by a fine devotional glow; she folded her hands upon her bosom, and with a look of meek resignation, raising towards heaven her eyes, in which now sunk the last sparkles of expiring life — her soul departed in a short deep sigh.

Her lover sinking back, endeavoured to conceal his emotions, but the deep sobs which agitated his breast betrayed his anguish, and the tears of every spectator bedewed the sacred spot where beauty, sense, and innocence expired.

The organ now swelled in mournful harmony; and the voices of the assembly chanted in choral strain, a low and solemn requiem to the spirit of the departed.

Madame hurried Julia, who was almost as lifeless as her departed friend, from the church. A death so sudden heightened the grief which separation would otherwise have occasioned. It was the nature of Cornelia's disorder to wear a changeful but flattering aspect. Though she had long been declining, her decay was so gradual and imperceptible as to lull the apprehensions of her friends into security. It was otherwise with herself; she was conscious of the change, but forbore to afflict them with the knowledge of the truth. The hour of her dissolution was sudden, even to herself; but it was composed, and even happy. In the death of Cornelia, Julia seemed to mourn again that of Hippolitus. Her decease appeared to dissolve the last tie which connected her with his memory.

In one of the friars of the convent, madame was surprised to find the father who had confessed the dying Vincent. His appearance revived the remembrance of the scene she had witnessed at the castle of Mazzini; and the last words of Vincent, combined with the circumstances which had since occurred, renewed all her curiosity and astonishment. But his appearance excited more sensations than those of wonder. She dreaded lest he should be corrupted by the marquis, to whom he was known, and thus be induced to use his interest with the Abate for the restoration of Julia.

From the walls of the monastery, Julia now never ventured to stray. In the gloom of evening she sometimes stole into the cloisters, and often lingered at the grave of Cornelia, where she wept for Hippolitus, as well as for her friend. One evening, during vespers, the bell of the convent was suddenly rang out; the Abate, whose countenance expressed at once astonishment and displeasure, suspended the service, and quitted the altar. The whole congregation repaired to the hall, where they learned that a friar, retiring to the convent, had seen a troop of armed men advancing through the wood; and not doubting they were the people of the marquis, and were approaching with hostile intention, had thought it necessary to give the alarm. The Abate ascended a turret, and thence discovered through the trees a glittering of arms, and in the succeeding moment a band of men issued from a dark part of the wood, into a long avenue which immediately fronted the spot where he stood. The clattering of hoofs was now distinctly heard; and Julia, sinking with terror, distinguished the marquis heading the troops, which, soon after separating in two divisions, surrounded the monastery. The gates were immediately secured; and the Abate, descending from the turret, assembled the friars in the hall, where his voice was soon heard above every other part of the tumult. The terror of Julia made her utterly forgetful of the Padre's promise, and she wished to fly for concealment to the deep caverns belonging to the monastery, which wound under the woods. Madame, whose penetration furnished her with a just knowledge of the Abate's character, founded her security on his pride. She therefore dissuaded Julia from attempting to tamper with the honesty of a servant who had the keys of the vaults, and advised her to rely entirely on the effect of the Abate's resentment towards the marquis. While madame endeavoured to soothe her to composure, a message from the Abate required her immediate attendance. She obeyed, and he bade her follow him to a room which was directly over the gates of the monastery. From thence she saw her father, accompanied by the Duke de Luovo; and as her spirits died away at the sight, the marquis called furiously to the Abate to deliver her instantly into his hands, threatening, if she was detained, to force the gates of the monastery. At this threat the countenance of the Abate grew dark: and leading Julia forcibly to the window, from which she had shrunk back, 'Impious menacer!' said he, 'eternal vengeance be upon thee! From this moment we expel thee from all the rights and communities of our church. Arrogant and daring as you are, your threats I defy — Look here,' said he, pointing to Julia, 'and learn that you are in my power; for if you dare to violate these sacred walls, I will proclaim aloud, in the face of day, a secret which shall make your heart's blood run cold; a secret which involves your honour, nay, your very existence. Now triumph and exult in impious menace!' The marquis started involuntarily at this speech, and his features underwent a sudden change, but he endeavoured to recover himself, and to conceal his confusion. He hesitated for a few moments, uncertain how to act — to desist from violence was to confess himself conscious of the threatened secret; yet he dreaded to inflame the resentment of the Abate, whose menaces his own heart too surely seconded. At length — 'All that you have uttered,' said he, 'I despise as the dastardly subterfuge of monkish cunning. Your new insults add to the desire of recovering my daughter, that of punishing you. I would proceed to instant violence, but that would now be an imperfect revenge. I shall, therefore, withdraw my forces, and appeal to a higher power. Thus shall you be compelled at once to restore my daughter and retract your scandalous impeachment of my honor.' Saying this, the turned his horse from the gates, and his people following him, quickly withdrew, leaving the Abate exulting in conquest, and Julia lost in astonishment and doubtful joy. When she recounted to madame the particulars of the conference, she dwelt with emphasis on the threats of the Abate; but madame, though her amazement was heightened at every word, very well understood how the secret, whatever it was, had been obtained. The confessor of Vincent she had already observed in the monastery, and there was no doubt that he had disclosed whatever could be collected from the dying words of Vincent. She knew, also, that the secret would never be published, unless as a punishment for immediate violence, it being one of the first principles of monastic duty, to observe a religious secrecy upon all matters entrusted to them in confession.

When the first tumult of Julia's emotions subsided, the joy which the sudden departure of the marquis occasioned yielded to apprehension. He had threatened to appeal to a higher power, who would compel the Abate to surrender her. This menace excited a just terror, and there remained no means of avoiding the tyranny of the marquis but by quitting the monastery. She therefore requested an audience of the Abate;

and having represented the danger of her present situation, she intreated his permission to depart in quest of a safer retreat. The Abate, who well knew the marquis was wholly in his power, smiled at the repetition of his menaces, and denied her request, under pretence of his having now become responsible for her to the church. He bade her be comforted, and promised her his protection; but his assurances were given in so distant and haughty a manner, that Julia left him with fears rather increased than subdued. In crossing the hall, she observed a man hastily enter it, from an opposite door. He was not in the habit of the order, but was muffled up in a cloak, and seemed to wish concealment. As she passed he raised his head, and Julia discovered — her father! He darted at her a look of vengeance; but before she had time even to think, as if suddenly recollecting himself, he covered his face, and rushed by her. Her trembling frame could scarcely support her to the apartment of madame, where she sunk speechless upon a chair, and the terror of her look alone spoke the agony of her mind. When she was somewhat recovered, she related what she had seen, and her conversation with the Abate. But madame was lost in equal perplexity with herself, when she attempted to account for the marquis's appearance. Why, after his late daring menace, should he come secretly to visit the Abate, by whose connivance alone he could have gained admission to the monastery? And what could have influenced the Abate to such a conduct? These circumstances, though equally inexplicable, united to confirm a fear of treachery and surrender. To escape from the abbey was now inpracticable, for the gates were constantly guarded; and even was it possible to pass them, certain detection awaited Julia without from the marquis's people, who were stationed in the woods. Thus encompassed with danger, she could only await in the monastery the issue of her destiny.

While she was lamenting with madame her unhappy fate, she was summoned once more to attend the Abate. At this moment her spirits entirely forsook her; the crisis of her fate seemed arrived; for she did not doubt that the Abate intended to surrender her to the marquis, with whom she supposed he had negotiated the terms of accommodation. It was some time before she could recover composure sufficient to obey the summons; and when she did, every step that bore her towards the Abate's room increased her dread. She paused a moment at the door, 'ere she had courage to open it; the idea of her father's immediate resentment arose to her mind, and she was upon the point of retreating to her chamber, when a sudden step within, near the door, destroyed her hesitation, and she entered the closet. The marquis was not there, and her spirits revived. The flush of triumph was diffused over the features of the Abate, though a shade of unappeased resentment yet remained visible. 'Daughter,' said he, 'the intelligence we have to communicate may rejoice you. Your safety now depends solely on yourself. I give your fate into your own hands, and its issue be upon your head.' He paused, and she was suspended in wondering expectation of the coming sentence. 'I here solemnly assure you of my protection, but it is upon one condition only — that you renounce the world, and dedicate your days to God.' Julia listened with a mixture of grief and astonishment. 'Without this concession on your part, I possess not the power, had I even the inclination, to protect you. If you assume the veil, you are safe within the pale of the church from temporal violence. If you neglect or refuse to do this, the marquis may apply to a power from whom I have no appeal, and I shall be compelled at last to resign you.

'But to ensure your safety, should the veil be your choice, we will procure a dispensation from the usual forms of noviciation, and a few days shall confirm your vows.' He ceased to speak; but Julia, agitated with the most cruel distress, knew not what to reply. 'We grant you three days to decide upon this matter,' continued he, 'at the expiration of which, the veil, or the Duke de Luovo, awaits you.' Julia quitted the closet in mute despair, and repaired to madame, who could now scarcely offer her the humble benefit of consolation.

Meanwhile the Abate exulted in successful vengeance, and the marquis smarted beneath the stings of disappointment. The menace of the former was too seriously alarming to suffer the marquis to prosecute violent measures; and he had therefore resolved, by opposing avarice to pride, to soothe the power which he could not subdue. But he was unwilling to entrust the Abate with a proof of his compliance and his fears by offering a bribe in a letter, and preferred the more humiliating, but safer method, of a private interview. His magnificent offers created a temporary hesitation in the mind of the Abate, who, secure of his advantage, shewed at first no disposition to be reconciled, and suffered the marquis to depart in anxious uncertainty. After maturely deliberating upon the proposals, the pride of the Abate surmounted his avarice, and he determined to prevail upon Julia effectually to destroy the hopes of the marquis, by consecrating her life to religion. Julia passed the night and the next day in a state of mental torture exceeding all description. The gates of the monastery beset with guards, and the woods surrounded by the marquis's people, made escape impossible. From a marriage with the duke, whose late conduct had confirmed the odious idea which his character had formerly impressed, her heart recoiled in horror, and to be immured for life within the walls of a convent, was a fate little less dreadful. Yet such was the effect of that sacred love she bore the memory of Hippolitus, and such her aversion to the duke, that she soon resolved to adopt the veil. On the following evening she informed the Abate of her determination. His heart swelled with secret joy; and even the natural severity of his manner relaxed at the intelligence. He assured her of his approbation and protection, with a degree of kindness which he had never before manifested, and told her the ceremony should be performed on the second day from the present. Her emotion scarcely suffered her to hear his last words. Now that her fate was fixed beyond recall, she almost repented of her choice. Her fancy attached to it a horror not its own; and that evil, which, when offered to her decision, she had accepted with little hesitation, she now paused upon in dubious regret; so apt we are to imagine that the calamity most certain, is also the most intolerable!

When the marquis read the answer of the Abate, all the baleful passions of his nature were roused and inflamed to a degree which bordered upon distraction. In the first impulse of his rage, he would have forced the gates of the monastery, and defied the utmost malice of his enemy. But a moment's reflection revived his fear of the threatened secret, and he saw that he was still in the power of the Superior.

The Abate procured the necessary dispensation, and preparations were immediately began for the approaching ceremony. Julia watched the departure of those moments which led to her fate with the calm fortitude of despair. She had no means of escaping from the coming evil, without exposing herself to a worse; she surveyed it therefore with a steady eye, and no longer shrunk from its approach.

On the morning preceding the day of her consecration, she was informed that a stranger enquired for her at the grate. Her mind had been so long accustomed to the vicissitudes of apprehension, that fear was the emotion which now occurred; she suspected, yet scarcely knew why, that the marquis was below, and hesitated whether to descend. A little reflection determined her, and she went to the parlour—where, to her equal joy and surprise, she beheld—Ferdinand!

During the absence of the marquis from his castle, Ferdinand, who had been informed of the discovery of Julia, effected his escape from imprisonment, and had hastened to the monastery in the design of rescuing her. He had passed the woods in disguise, with much difficulty eluding the observation of the marquis's people, who were yet dispersed round the abbey. To the monastery, as he came alone, he had been admitted without difficulty.

When he learned the conditions of the Abate's protection, and that the following day was appointed for the consecration of Julia, he was shocked, and paused in deliberation. A period so short as was this interval, afforded little opportunity for contrivance, and less for hesitation. The night of the present day was the only time that remained for the attempt and execution of a plan of escape, which if it then failed of success, Julia would not only be condemned for life to the walls of a monastery, but would be subjected to whatever punishment the severity of the Abate, exasperated by the detection, should think fit to inflict. The danger was desperate, but the occasion was desperate also.

The nobly disinterested conduct of her brother, struck Julia with gratitude and admiration; but despair of success made her now hesitate whether she should accept his offer. She considered that his generosity would most probably involve him in destruction with herself; and she paused in deep deliberation, when Ferdinand informed her of a circumstance which, till now, he had purposely concealed, and which at once dissolved every doubt and every fear. 'Hippolitus,' said Ferdinand, 'yet lives.'—'Lives!' repeated Julia faintly,—'lives, Oh! tell me where—how.'—Her breath refused to aid her, and she sunk in her chair overcome with the strong and various sensations that pressed upon her heart. Ferdinand, whom the grate withheld from assisting her, observed her situation with extreme distress. When she recovered, he informed her that a servant of Hippolitus, sent no doubt by his lord to enquire concerning Julia, had been lately seen by one of the marquis's people in the neighbourhood of the castle. From him it was known that the Count de Vereza was living, but that his life had been despaired of; and he was still confined, by dangerous wounds, in an obscure town on the coast of Italy. The man had steadily refused to mention the place of his lord's abode. Learning that the marquis was then at the abbey of St Augustin, whither he pursued his daughter, the man disappeared from Mazzini, and had not since been heard of.

It was enough for Julia to know that Hippolitus lived; her fears of detection, and her scruples concerning Ferdinand, instantly vanished; she thought only of escape—and the means which had lately appeared so formidable—so difficult in contrivance, and so dangerous in execution, now seemed easy, certain, and almost accomplished.

They consulted on the plan to be adopted, and agreed, that in attempting to bribe a servant of the monastery to their interest, they should incur a danger too imminent, yet it appeared scarcely practicable to succeed in their scheme without risquing this. After much consideration, they determined to entrust their secret to no person but to madame. Ferdinand was to contrive to conceal himself till the dead of night in the church, between which and the monastery were several doors of communication. When the inhabitants of the abbey were sunk in repose, Julia might without difficulty pass to the church, where Ferdinand awaiting her, they might perhaps escape either through an outer door of the fabric, or through a window, for which latter attempt Ferdinand was to provide ropes.

A couple of horses were to be stationed among the rocks beyond the woods, to convey the fugitives to a sea-port, whence they could easily pass over to Italy. Having arranged this plan, they separated in the anxious hope of meeting on the ensuing night.

Madame warmly sympathized with Julia in her present expectations, and was now somewhat relieved from the pressure of that self-reproach, with which the consideration of having withdrawn her young friend from a secure asylum, had long tormented her. In learning that Hippolitus lived, Julia experienced a sudden renovation of life and spirits. From the languid stupefaction which despair had occasioned she revived as from a dream, and her sensations resembled those of a person suddenly awakened from a frightful vision, whose thoughts are yet obscured in the fear and uncertainty which the passing images have impressed on his fancy. She emerged from despair; joy illumined her countenance; yet she doubted the reality of the scene which now opened to her view. The hours rolled heavily along till the evening, when expectation gave way to fear, for she was once more summoned by the Abate. He sent for her to administer the usual necessary exhortation on the approaching solemnity; and having detained her a considerable time in tedious and severe discourse, dismissed her with a formal benediction.

CHAPTER XII

The evening now sunk in darkness, and the hour was fast approaching which would decide the fate of Julia. Trembling anxiety subdued every other sensation; and as the minutes passed, her fears increased. At length she heard the gates of the monastery fastened for the night; the bell rang the signal for repose; and the passing footsteps of the nuns told her they were hastening to obey it. After some time, all was silent. Julia did not yet dare to venture forth; she employed the present interval in interesting and affectionate conversation with Madame de Menon, to whom, notwithstanding her situation, her heart bade a sorrowful adieu.

The clock struck twelve, when she arose to depart. Having embraced her faithful friend with tears of mingled grief and anxiety, she took a lamp in her hand, and with cautious, fearful steps, descended through the long winding passages to a private door, which opened into the church of the monastery. The church was gloomy and desolate; and the feeble rays of the lamp she bore, gave only light enough to discover its chilling grandeur. As she passed silently along the aisles, she cast a look of anxious examination around—but Ferdinand was no where to be seen. She paused in timid hesitation, fearful to penetrate the gloomy obscurity which lay before her, yet dreading to return.

As she stood examining the place, vainly looking for Ferdinand, yet fearing to call, lest her voice should betray her, a hollow groan arose from apart of the church very near her. It chilled her heart, and she remained fixed to the spot. She turned her eyes a little to the left, and saw light appear through the chinks of a sepulchre at some distance. The groan was repeated—a low murmuring succeeded, and while she yet gazed, an old man issued from the vault with a lighted taper in his hand. Terror now subdued her, and she utterred an involuntary shriek. In the succeeding moment, a noise was heard in a remote part of the fabric; and Ferdinand rushing forth from his concealment, ran to her assistance. The old man, who appeared to be a friar, and who had been doing penance at the monument of a saint, now approached. His countenance expressed a degree of surprise and terror almost equal to that of Julia's, who knew him to be the confessor of Vincent. Ferdinand seized the father; and laying his hand upon his sword, threatened him with death if he did not instantly swear to conceal for ever his knowledge of what he then saw, and also assist them to escape from the abbey.

'Ungracious boy!' replied the father, in a calm voice, 'desist from this language, nor add to the follies of youth the crime of murdering, or terrifying a defenceless old man. Your violence would urge me to become your enemy, did not previous inclination tempt me to be your friend. I pity the distresses of the lady Julia, to whom I am no stranger, and will cheerfully give her all the assistance in my power.'

At these words Julia revived, and Ferdinand, reproved by the generosity of the father, and conscious of his own inferiority, shrunk back. 'I have no words to thank you,' said he, 'or to entreat your pardon for the impetuosity of my conduct; your knowledge of my situation must plead my excuse.'—'It does,' replied the father, 'but we have no time to lose;—follow me.'

They followed him through the church to the cloisters, at the extremity of which was a small door, which the friar unlocked. It opened upon the woods.

'This path,' said he, 'leads thro' an intricate part of the woods, to the rocks that rise on the right of the abbey; in their recesses you may secrete yourselves till you are prepared for a longer journey. But extinguish your light; it may betray you to the marquis's people, who are dispersed about this spot. Farewell! my children, and God's blessing be upon ye.'

Julia's tears declared her gratitude; she had no time for words. They stepped into the path, and the father closed the door. They were now liberated from the monastery, but danger awaited them without, which it required all their caution to avoid. Ferdinand knew the path which the friar had pointed out to be the same that led to the rocks where his horses were stationed, and he pursued it with quick and silent steps. Julia, whose fears conspired with the gloom of night to magnify and transform every object around her, imagined at each step that she took, she perceived the figures of men, and fancied every whisper of the breeze the sound of pursuit.

They proceeded swiftly, till Julia, breathless and exhausted, could go no farther. They had not rested many minutes, when they heard a rustling among the bushes at some distance, and soon after distinguished a low sound of voices. Ferdinand and Julia instantly renewed their flight, and thought they still heard voices advance upon the wind. This thought was soon confirmed, for the sounds now gained fast upon them, and they distinguished words which served only to heighten their apprehensions, when they reached the extremity of the woods.

The moon, which was now up, suddenly emerging from a dark cloud, discovered to them several man in pursuit; and also shewed to the pursuers the course of the fugitives. They endeavoured to gain the rocks where the horses were concealed, and which now appeared in view. These they reached when the pursuers had almost overtaken them—but their horses were gone! Their only remaining chance of escape was to fly into the deep recesses of the rock. They, therefore, entered a winding cave, from whence branched several subterraneous avenues, at the extremity of one of which they stopped. The voices of men now vibrated in tremendous echoes through the various and secret caverns of the place, and the sound of footsteps seemed fast approaching. Julia trembled with terror, and Ferdinand drew his sword, determined to protect her to the last. A confused volley of voices now sounded up that part of the cave were Ferdinand and Julia lay concealed. In a few moments the steps of the pursuers suddenly took a different direction, and the sounds sunk gradually away, and were heard no more. Ferdinand listened attentively for a considerable time, but the stillness of the place remained undisturbed. It was now evident that the men had quitted the rock, and he ventured forth to the mouth of the cave. He surveyed the wilds around, as far as his eye could penetrate, and distinguished no human being; but in the pauses of the wind he still thought he heard a sound of distant voices. As he listened in anxious silence, his eye caught the appearance of a shadow, which moved upon the ground near where he stood. He started back within the cave, but in a few minutes again ventured forth. The shadow remained stationary, but having watched it for some time, Ferdinand saw it glide along till it disappeared behind a point of rock. He had now no doubt that the cave was watched, and that it was one of his late pursuers whose shade he had seen. He returned, therefore, to Julia, and remained near an hour hid in the deepest recess of the rock; when, no sound having interrupted the profound silence of the place, he at length once more ventured to the mouth of the cave. Again he threw a fearful look around, but discerned no human form. The soft moon-beam slept upon the dewy landscape, and the solemn stillness of midnight wrapt the world. Fear heightened to the fugitives the sublimity of the hour. Ferdinand now led Julia forth, and they passed silently along the shelving foot of the rocks.

They continued their way without farther interruption; and among the cliffs, at some distance from the cave, discovered, to their inexpressible joy, their horses, who having broken their fastenings, had strayed thither, and had now laid themselves down to rest. Ferdinand and Julia immediately mounted; and descending to the plains, took the road that led to a small seaport at some leagues distant, whence they could embark for Italy.

They travelled for some hours through gloomy forests of beech and chesnut; and their way was only faintly illuminated by the moon, which shed a trembling lustre through the dark foliage, and which was seen but at intervals, as the passing clouds yielded to the power of her rays. They reached at length the skirts of the forest. The grey dawn now appeared, and the chill morning air bit shrewdly. It was with inexpressible joy that Julia observed the kindling atmosphere; and soon after the rays of the rising sun touching the tops of the mountains, whose sides were yet involved in dark vapours.

Her fears dissipated with the darkness. — The sun now appeared amid clouds of inconceivable splendour; and unveiled a scene which in other circumstances Julia would have contemplated with rapture. From the side of the hill, down which they were winding, a vale appeared, from whence arose wild and lofty mountains, whose steeps were cloathed with hanging woods, except where here and there a precipice projected its bold and rugged front. Here, a few half-withered trees hung from the crevices of the rock, and gave a picturesque wildness to the object; there, clusters of half-seen cottages, rising from among tufted groves, embellished the green margin of a stream which meandered in the bottom, and bore its waves to the blue and distant main.

The freshness of morning breathed over the scene, and vivified each colour of the landscape. The bright dewdrops hung trembling from the branches of the trees, which at intervals overshadowed the road; and the sprightly music of the birds saluted the rising day. Notwithstanding her anxiety the scene diffused a soft complacency over the mind of Julia.

About noon they reached the port, where Ferdinand was fortunate enough to obtain a small vessel; but the wind was unfavourable, and it was past midnight before it was possible for them to embark.

When the dawn appeared, Julia returned to the deck; and viewed with a sigh of unaccountable regret, the receding coast of Sicily. But she observed, with high admiration, the light gradually spreading through the atmosphere, darting a feeble ray over the surface of the waters, which rolled in solemn soundings upon the distant shores. Fiery beams now marked the clouds, and the east glowed with increasing radiance, till the sun rose at once above the waves, and illuminating them with a flood of splendour, diffused gaiety and gladness around. The bold concave of the heavens, uniting with the vast expanse of the ocean, formed, a coup d'oeil, striking and sublime magnificence of the scenery inspired Julia with delight; and her heart dilating with high enthusiasm, she forgot the sorrows which had oppressed her.

The breeze wafted the ship gently along for some hours, when it gradually sunk into a calm. The glassy surface of the waters was not curled by the lightest air, and the vessel floated heavily on the bosom of the deep. Sicily was yet in view, and the present delay agitated Julia with wild apprehension. Towards the close of day a light breeze sprang up, but it blew from Italy, and a train of dark vapours emerged from the verge of the horizon, which gradually accumulating, the heavens became entirely overcast. The evening shut in suddenly; the rising wind, the heavy clouds that loaded the atmosphere, and the thunder which murmured afar off terrified Julia, and threatened a violent storm.

The tempest came on, and the captain vainly sounded for anchorage: it was deep sea, and the vessel drove furiously before the wind. The darkness was interrupted only at intervals, by the broad expanse of vivid lightnings, which quivered upon the waters, and disclosing the horrible gaspings of the waves, served to render the succeeding darkness more awful. The thunder, which burst in tremendous crashes above, the loud roar of the waves below, the noise of the sailors, and the sudden cracks and groanings of the vessel conspired to heighten the tremendous sublimity of the scene.

Far on the rocky shores the surges sound,

The lashing whirlwinds cleave the vast profound;

While high in air, amid the rising storm,

Driving the blast, sits Danger's black'ning form.

Julia lay fainting with terror and sickness in the cabin, and Ferdinand, though almost hopeless himself, was endeavouring to support her, when aloud and dreadful crash was heard from above. It seemed as if the whole vessel had parted. The voices of the sailors now rose together, and all was confusion and uproar. Ferdinand ran up to the deck, and learned that part of the main mast, borne away by the wind, had fallen upon the deck, whence it had rolled overboard.

It was now past midnight, and the storm continued with unabated fury. For four hours the vessel had been driven before the blast; and the captain now declared it was impossible she could weather the tempest much longer, ordered the long boat to be in readiness. His orders were scarcely executed, when the ship bulged upon a reef of rocks, and the impetuous waves rushed into the vessel:—a general groan ensued. Ferdinand flew to save his sister, whom he carried to the boat, which was nearly filled by the captain and most of the crew. The sea ran so high that it appeared impracticable to reach the shore: but the boat had not moved many yards, when the ship went to pieces. The captain now perceived, by the flashes of lightning, a high rocky coast at about the distance of half a mile. The men struggled hard at the oars; but almost as often as they gained the summit of a wave, it dashed them back again, and made their labour of little avail.

After much difficulty and fatigue they reached the coast, where a new danger presented itself. They beheld a wild rocky shore, whose cliffs appeared inaccessible, and which seemed to afford little possibility of landing. A landing, however, was at last affected; and the sailors, after much search, discovered a kind of pathway cut in the rock, which they all ascended in safety.

The dawn now faintly glimmered, and they surveyed the coast, but could discover no human habitation. They imagined they were on the shores of Sicily, but possessed no means of confirming this conjecture. Terror, sickness, and fatigue had subdued the strength and spirits of Julia, and she was obliged to rest upon the rocks.

The storm now suddenly subsided, and the total calm which succeeded to the wild tumult of the winds and waves, produced a striking and sublime effect. The air was hushed in a deathlike stillness, but the waves were yet violently agitated; and by the increasing light, parts of the wreck were seen floating wide upon the face of the deep. Some sailors, who had missed the boat, were also discovered clinging to pieces of the vessel, and making towards the shore. On observing this, their shipmates immediately descended to the boat; and, putting off to sea, rescued them from their perilous situation. When Julia was somewhat reanimated, they proceeded up the country in search of a dwelling.

They had travelled near half a league, when the savage features of the country began to soften, and gradually changed to the picturesque beauty of Sicilian scenery. They now discovered at some distance a villa, seated on a gentle eminence, crowned with woods. It was the first human habitation they had seen since they embarked for Italy; and Julia, who was almost sinking with fatigue, beheld it with delight. The captain and his men hastened towards it to make known their distress, while Ferdinand and Julia slowly followed. They observed the men enter the villa, one of whom quickly returned to acquaint them with the hospitable reception his comrades had received.

Julia with difficulty reached the edifice, at the door of which she was met by a young cavalier, whose pleasing and intelligent countenance immediately interested her in his favor. He welcomed the strangers with a benevolent politeness that dissolved at once every uncomfortable feeling which their situation had excited, and produced an instantaneous easy confidence. Through a light and elegant hall, rising into a dome, supported by pillars of white marble, and adorned with busts, he led them to a magnificent vestibule, which opened upon a lawn. Having seated them at a table spread with refreshments he left them, and they surveyed, with surprise, the beauty of the adjacent scene.

The lawn, which was on each side bounded by hanging woods, descended in gentle declivity to a fine lake, whose smooth surface reflected the surrounding shades. Beyond appeared the distant country, arising on the left into bold romantic mountains, and on the right exhibiting a soft and glowing landscape, whose tranquil beauty formed a striking contrast to the wild sublimity of the opposite craggy heights. The blue and distant ocean terminated the view.

In a short time the cavalier returned, conducting two ladies of a very engaging appearance, whom he presented as his wife and sister. They welcomed Julia with graceful kindness; but fatigue soon obliged her to retire to rest, and a consequent indisposition increased so rapidly, as to render it impracticable for her to quit her present abode on that day. The captain and his men proceeded on their way, leaving Ferdinand and Julia at the villa, where she experienced every kind and tender affection.

The day which was to have devoted Julia to a cloister, was ushered in at the abbey with the usual ceremonies. The church was ornamented, and all the inhabitants of the monastery prepared to attend. The Padre Abate now exulted in the success of his scheme, and anticipated, in imagination, the rage and vexation of the marquis, when he should discover that his daughter was lost to him for ever.

The hour of celebration arrived, and he entered the church with a proud firm step, and with a countenance which depictured his inward triumph; he was proceeding to the high altar, when he was told that Julia was no where to be found. Astonishment for awhile suspended other emotions—he yet believed it impossible that she could have effected an escape, and ordered every part of the abbey to be searched—not forgetting the secret caverns belonging to the monastery, which wound beneath the woods. When the search was over, and he became convinced she was fled, the deep workings of his disappointed passions fermented into rage which exceeded all bounds. He denounced the most terrible judgments upon Julia; and calling for Madame de Menon, charged her with having insulted her holy religion, in being accessary to the flight of Julia. Madame endured these reproaches with calm dignity, and preserved a steady silence, but she secretly determined to leave the monastery, and seek in another the repose which she could never hope to find in this.

The report of Julia's disappearance spread rapidly beyond the walls, and soon reached the ears of the marquis, who rejoiced in the circumstance, believing that she must now inevitably fall into his hands.

After his people, in obedience to his orders, had carefully searched the surrounding woods and rocks, he withdrew them from the abbey; and having dispersed them various ways in search of Julia, he returned to the castle of Mazzini. Here new vexation awaited him, for he now first learned that Ferdinand had escaped from confinement.

The mystery of Julia's flight was now dissolved; for it was evident by whose means she had effected it, and the marquis issued orders to his people to secure Ferdinand wherever he should be found.

CHAPTER XIII

Hippolitus, who had languished under a long and dangerous illness occasioned by his wounds, but heightened and prolonged by the distress of his mind, was detained in a small town in the coast of Calabria, and was yet ignorant of the death of Cornelia. He scarcely doubted that Julia was now devoted to the duke, and this thought was at times poison to his heart. After his arrival in Calabria, immediately on the recovery of his senses, he dispatched a servant back to the castle of Mazzini, to gain secret intelligence of what had passed after his departure. The eagerness with which we endeavour to escape from misery, taught him to encourage a remote and romantic hope that Julia yet lived for him. Yet even this hope at length languished into despair, as the time elapsed which should have brought his servant from Sicily. Days and weeks passed away in the utmost anxiety to Hippolitus, for still his emissary did not appear; and at last, concluding that he had been either seized by robbers, or discovered and detained by the marquis, the Count sent off a second emissary to the castle of Mazzini. By him he learned the news of Julia's flight, and his heart dilated with joy; but it was suddenly checked when he heard the marquis had discovered her retreat in the abbey of St Augustin. The wounds which still detained him in confinement, now became intolerable. Julia might yet be lost to him for ever. But even his present state of fear and uncertainty was bliss compared with the anguish of despair, which his mind had long endured.

As soon as he was sufficiently recovered, he quitted Italy for Sicily, in the design of visiting the monastery of St Augustin, where it was possible Julia might yet remain. That he might pass with the secrecy necessary to his plan, and escape the attacks of the marquis, he left his servants in Calabria, and embarked alone.

It was morning when he landed at a small port of Sicily, and proceeded towards the abbey of St Augustin. As he travelled, his imagination revolved the scenes of his early love, the distress of Julia, and the sufferings of Ferdinand, and his heart melted at the retrospect. He considered the probabilities of Julia having found protection from her father in the pity of the Padre Abate; and even ventured to indulge himself in a flattering, fond anticipation of the moment when Julia should again be restored to his sight.

He arrived at the monastery, and his grief may easily be imagined, when he was informed of the death of his beloved sister, and of the flight of Julia. He quitted St Augustin's immediately, without even knowing that Madame de Menon was there, and set out for a town at some leagues distance, where he designed to pass the night.

Absorbed in the melancholy reflections which the late intelligence excited, he gave the reins to his horse, and journeyed on unmindful of his way. The evening was far advanced when he discovered that he had taken a wrong direction, and that he was bewildered in a wild and solitary scene. He had wandered too far from the road to hope to regain it, and he had beside no recollection of the objects left behind him. A choice of errors, only, lay before him. The view on his right hand exhibited high and savage mountains, covered with heath and black fir; and the wild desolation of their aspect, together with the dangerous appearance of the path that wound up their sides, and which was the only apparent track they afforded, determined Hippolitus not to attempt their ascent. On his left lay a forest, to which the path he was then in led; its appearance was gloomy, but he preferred it to the mountains; and, since he was uncertain of its extent, there was a possibility that he might pass it, and reach a village before the night was set in. At the worst, the forest would afford him a shelter from the winds; and, however he might be bewildered in its labyrinths, he could ascend a tree, and rest in security till the return of light should afford him an opportunity of extricating himself. Among the mountains there was no possibility of meeting with other shelter than what the habitation of man afforded, and such a shelter there was little probability of finding. Innumerable dangers also threatened him here, from which he would be secure on level ground.

Having determined which way to pursue, he pushed his horse into a gallop, and entered the forest as the last rays of the sun trembled on the mountains. The thick foliage of the trees threw a gloom around, which was every moment deepened by the shades of evening. The path was uninterrupted, and the count continued to follow it till all distinction was confounded in the veil of night. Total darkness now made it impossible for him to pursue his way. He dismounted, and fastening his horse to a tree, climbed among the branches, purposing to remain there till morning.

He had not been long in this situation, when a confused sound of voices from a distance roused his attention. The sound returned at intervals for some time, but without seeming to approach. He descended from the tree, that he might the better judge of the direction whence it came; but before he reached the ground, the noise was ceased, and all was profoundly silent. He continued to listen, but the silence remaining undisturbed, he began to think he had been deceived by the singing of the wind among the leaves; and was preparing to reascend, when he perceived a faint light glimmer through the foliage from afar. The sight revived a hope that he was near some place of human habitation; he therefore unfastened his horse, and led him towards the spot whence the ray issued. The moon was now risen, and threw a checkered gleam over his path sufficient to direct him.

Before he had proceeded far the light disappeared. He continued, however, his way as nearly as he could guess, towards the place whence it had issued; and after much toil, found himself in a spot where the trees formed a circle round a kind of rude lawn. The moonlight discovered to him an edifice which appeared to have been formerly a monastery, but which now exhibited a pile of ruins, whose grandeur, heightened by decay, touched the beholder with reverential awe. Hippolitus paused to gaze upon the scene; the sacred stillness of night increased its effect, and a secret dread, he knew not wherefore, stole upon his heart.

The silence and the character of the place made him doubt whether this was the spot he had been seeking; and as he stood hesitating whether to proceed or to return, he observed a figure standing under an arch-way of the ruin; it carried a light in its hand, and passing silently along, disappeared in a remote part of the building. The courage of Hippolitus for a moment deserted him. An invincible curiosity, however, subdued his terror, and he determined to pursue, if possible, the way the figure had taken.

He passed over loose stones through a sort of court till he came to the archway; here he stopped, for fear returned upon him. Resuming his courage, however, he went on, still endeavouring to follow the way the figure had passed, and suddenly found himself in an enclosed part of the ruin, whose appearance was more wild and desolate than any he had yet seen. Seized with unconquerable apprehension, he was retiring, when the low voice of a distressed person struck his ear. His heart sunk at the sound, his limbs trembled, and he was utterly unable to move.

The sound which appeared to be the last groan of a dying person, was repeated. Hippolitus made a strong effort, and sprang forward, when a light burst upon him from a shattered casement of the building, and at the same instant he heard the voices of men!

He advanced softly to the window, and beheld in a small room, which was less decayed than the rest of the edifice, a group of men, who, from the savageness of their looks, and from their dress, appeared to be banditti. They surrounded a man who lay on the ground wounded, and bathed in blood, and who it was very evident had uttered the groans heard by the count.

The obscurity of the place prevented Hippolitus from distinguishing the features of the dying man. From the blood which covered him, and from the surrounding circumstances, he appeared to be murdered; and the count had no doubt that the men he beheld were the murderers. The horror of the scene entirely overcame him; he stood rooted to the spot, and saw the assassins rifle the pockets of the dying person, who, in a voice scarcely articulate, but which despair seemed to aid, supplicated for mercy. The ruffians answered him only with execrations, and continued their plunder. His groans and his sufferings served only to aggravate their cruelty. They were proceeding to take from him a miniature picture, which was fastened round his neck, and had been hitherto concealed in his bosom; when by a sudden effort he half raised himself from the ground, and attempted to save it from their hands. The effort availed him nothing; a blow from one of the villains laid the unfortunate man on the floor without motion. The horrid barbarity of the act seized the mind of Hippolitus so entirely, that, forgetful of his own situation, he groaned aloud, and started with an instantaneous design of avenging the deed. The noise he made alarmed the banditti, who looking whence it came, discovered the count through the casement. They instantly quitted their prize, and rushed towards the door of the room. He was now returned to a sense of his danger, and endeavoured to escape to the exterior part of the ruin; but terror bewildered his senses, and he mistook his way. Instead of regaining the arch-way, he perplexed himself with fruitless wanderings, and at length found himself only more deeply involved in the secret recesses of the pile.

The steps of his pursuers gained fast upon him, and he continued to perplex himself with vain efforts at escape, till at length, quite exhausted, he sunk on the ground, and endeavoured to resign himself to his fate. He listened with a kind of stern despair, and was surprised to find all silent. On looking round, he perceived by a ray of moonlight, which streamed through a part of the ruin from above, that he was in a sort of vault, which, from the small means he had of judging, he thought was extensive.

In this situation he remained for a considerable time, ruminating on the means of escape, yet scarcely believing escape was possible. If he continued in the vault, he might continue there only to be butchered; but by attempting to rescue himself from the place he was now in, he must rush into the hands of the banditti. Judging it, therefore, the safer way of the two to remain where he was, he endeavoured to await his fate with fortitude, when suddenly the loud voices of the murderers burst upon his ear, and he heard steps advancing quickly towards the spot where he lay.

Despair instantly renewed his vigour; he started from the ground, and throwing round him a look of eager desperation, his eye caught the glimpse of a small door, upon which the moon-beam now fell. He made towards it, and passed it just as the light of a torch gleamed upon the walls of the vault.

He groped his way along a winding passage, and at length came to a flight of steps. Notwithstanding the darkness, he reached the bottom in safety.

He now for the first time stopped to listen — the sounds of pursuit were ceased, and all was silent! Continuing to wander on in effectual endeavours to escape, his hands at length touched cold iron, and he quickly perceived it belonged to a door. The door, however, was fastened, and resisted all his efforts to open it. He was giving up the attempt in despair, when a loud scream from within, followed by a dead and heavy noise, roused all his attention. Silence ensued. He listened for a considerable time at the door, his imagination filled with images of horror, and expecting to hear the sound repeated. He then sought for a decayed part of the door, through which he might discover what was beyond; but he could find none; and after waiting some time without hearing any farther noise, he was quitting the spot, when in passing his arm over the door, it struck against something hard. On examination he perceived, to his extreme surprize, that the key was in the lock. For a moment he hesitated what to do; but curiosity overcame other considerations, and with a trembling hand he turned the key. The door opened into a large and desolate apartment, dimly lighted by a lamp that stood on a table, which was almost the only furniture of the place. The Count had advanced several steps before he perceived an object, which fixed all his attention. This was the figure of a young woman lying on the floor apparently dead. Her face was concealed in her robe; and the long auburn tresses which fell in beautiful luxuriance over her bosom, served to veil a part of the glowing beauty which the disorder of her dress would have revealed.

Pity, surprize, and admiration struggled in the breast of Hippolitus; and while he stood surveying the object which excited these different emotions, he heard a step advancing towards the room. He flew to the door by which he had entered, and was fortunate enough to reach it before the entrance of the persons whose steps he heard. Having turned the key, he stopped at the door to listen to their proceedings. He distinguished the voices of two men, and knew them to be those of the assassins. Presently he heard a piercing skriek, and at the same instant the voices of the ruffians grew loud and violent. One of them exclaimed that the lady was dying, and accused the other of having frightened her to death, swearing, with horrid imprecations, that she was his, and he would defend her to the last drop of his blood. The dispute grew higher; and neither of the ruffians would give up his claim to the unfortunate object of their altercation.

The clashing of swords was soon after heard, together with a violent noise. The screams were repeated, and the oaths and execrations of the disputants redoubled. They seemed to move towards the door, behind which Hippolitus was concealed; suddenly the door was shook with great force, a deep groan followed, and was instantly succeeded by a noise like that of a person whose whole weight falls at once to the ground. For a moment all was silent. Hippolitus had no doubt that one of the ruffians had destroyed the other, and was soon confirmed in the belief—for the survivor triumphed with brutal exultation over his fallen antagonist. The ruffian hastily quitted the room, and Hippolitus soon after heard the distant voices of several persons in loud dispute. The sounds seemed to come from a chamber over the place where he stood; he also heard a trampling of feet from above, and could even distinguish, at intervals, the words of the disputants. From these he gathered enough to learn that the affray which had just happened, and the lady who had been the occasion of it, were the subjects of discourse. The voices frequently rose together, and confounded all distinction.

At length the tumult began to subside, and Hippolitus could distinguish what was said. The ruffians agreed to give up the lady in question to him who had fought for her; and leaving him to his prize, they all went out in quest of farther prey. The situation of the unfortunate lady excited a mixture of pity and indignation in Hippolitus, which for some time entirely occupied him; he revolved the means of extricating her from so deplorable a situation, and in these thoughts almost forgot his own danger. He now heard her sighs; and while his heart melted to the sounds, the farther door of the apartment was thrown open, and the wretch to whom she had been allotted, rushed in. Her screams now redoubled, but they were of no avail with the ruffian who had seized her in his arms; when the count, who was unarmed, insensible to every pulse but that of a generous pity, burst into the room, but became fixed like a statue when he beheld his Julia struggling in the grasp of the ruffian. On discovering Hippolitus, she made a sudden spring, and liberated herself; when, running to him, she sunk lifeless in his arms.

Surprise and fury sparkled in the eyes of the ruffian, and he turned with a savage desperation upon the count; who, relinquishing Julia, snatched up the sword of the dead ruffian, which lay upon the floor, and defended himself. The combat was furious, but Hippolitus laid his antagonist senseless at his feet. He flew to Julia, who now revived, but who for some time could speak only by her tears. The transitions of various and rapid sensations, which her heart experienced, and the strangely mingled emotions of joy and terror that agitated Hippolitus, can only be understood by experience. He raised her from the floor, and endeavoured to soothe her to composure, when she called wildly upon Ferdinand. At his name the count started, and he instantly remembered the dying cavalier, whose countenance the glooms had concealed from his view. His heart thrilled with secret agony, yet he resolved to withhold his terrible conjectures from Julia, of whom he learned that Ferdinand, with herself, had been taken by banditti in the way from the villa which had offered them so hospitable a reception after the shipwreck. They were on the road to a port whence they designed again to embark for Italy, when this misfortune overtook them. Julia added, that Ferdinand had been immediately separated from her; and that, for some hours, she had been confined in the apartment where Hippolitus found her.

The Count with difficulty concealed his terrible apprehensions for Ferdinand, and vainly strove to soften Julia's distress. But there was no time to be lost—they had yet to find a way out of the edifice, and before they could accomplish this, the banditti might return. It was also possible that some of the party were left to watch this their abode during the absence of the rest, and this was another circumstance of reasonable alarm.

After some little consideration, Hippolitus judged it most prudent to seek an outlet through the passage by which he entered; he therefore took the lamp, and led Julia to the door. They entered the avenue, and locking the door after them, sought the flight of steps down which the count had before passed; but having pursued the windings of the avenue a considerable time without finding them, he became certain he had mistaken the way. They, however, found another flight, which they descended and entered upon a passage so very narrow and low, as not to admit of a person walking upright. This passage was closed by a door, which on examination was found to be chiefly of iron. Hippolitus was startled at the sight, but on applying his strength found it gradually yield, when the imprisoned air rushed out, and had nearly extinguished the light. They now entered upon a dark abyss; and the door which moved upon a spring, suddenly closed upon them. On looking round they beheld a large vault; and it is not easy to imagine their horror on discovering they were in a receptacle for the murdered bodies of the unfortunate people who had fallen into the hands of the banditti.

The count could scarcely support the fainting spirits of Julia; he ran to the door, which he endeavoured to open, but the lock was so constructed that it could be moved only on the other side, and all his efforts were useless. He was constrained, therefore, to seek for another door, but could find none. Their situation was the most deplorable that can be imagined; for they were now inclosed in a vault strewn with the dead bodies of the murdered, and must there become the victims of famine, or of the sword. The earth was in several places thrown up, and marked the boundaries of new-made graves. The bodies which remained unburied were probably left either from hurry or negligence, and exhibited a spectacle too shocking for humanity. The sufferings of Hippolitus were increased by those of Julia, who was sinking with horror, and who he endeavoured to support to apart of the vault which fell into a recess — where stood a bench.

They had not been long in this situation, when they heard a noise which approached gradually, and which did not appear to come from the avenue they had passed.

The noise increased, and they could distinguish voices. Hippolitus believed the murderers were returned; that they had traced his retreat, and were coming towards the vault by some way unknown to him. He prepared for the worst — and drawing his sword, resolved to defend Julia to the last. Their apprehension, however, was soon dissipated by a trampling of horses, which sound had occasioned his alarm, and which now seemed to come from a courtyard above, extremely near the vault. He distinctly heard the voices of the banditti, together with the moans and supplications of some person, whom it was evident they were about to plunder. The sound appeared so very near, that Hippolitus was both shocked and surprised; and looking round the vault, he perceived a small grated window placed very high in the wall, which he concluded overlooked the place where the robbers were assembled. He recollected that his light might betray him; and horrible as was the alternative, he was compelled to extinguish it. He now attempted to climb to the grate, through which he might obtain a view of what was passing without. This at length he effected, for the ruggedness of the wall afforded him a footing. He beheld in a ruinous court, which was partially illuminated by the glare of torches, a group of banditti surrounding two persons who were bound on horseback, and who were supplicating for mercy.

One of the robbers exclaiming with an oath that this was a golden night, bade his comrades dispatch, adding he would go to find Paulo and the lady.

The effect which the latter part of this sentence had upon the prisoners in the vault, may be more easily imagined than described. They were now in total darkness in this mansion of the murdered, without means of escape, and in momentary expectation of sharing a fate similar to that of the wretched objects around them. Julia, overcome with distress and terror, sunk on the ground; and Hippolitus, descending from the grate, became insensible of his own danger in his apprehension for her.

In a short time all without was confusion and uproar; the ruffian who had left the court returned with the alarm that the lady was fled, and that Paulo was murdered, The robbers quitting their booty to go in search of the fugitive, and to discover the murderer, dreadful vociferations resounded through every recess of the pile.

The tumult had continued a considerable time, which the prisoners had passed in a state of horrible suspence, when they heard the uproar advancing towards the vault, and soon after a number of voices shouted down the avenue. The sound of steps quickened. Hippolitus again drew his sword, and placed himself opposite the entrance, where he had not stood long, when a violent push was made against the door; it flew open, and a party of men rushed into the vault.

Hippolitus kept his position, protesting he would destroy the first who approached. At the sound of his voice they stopped; but presently advancing, commanded him in the king's name to surrender. He now discovered what his agitation had prevented him from observing sooner, that the men before him were not banditti, but the officers of justice. They had received information of this haunt of villainy from the son of a

Sicilian nobleman, who had fallen into the hands of the banditti, and had afterwards escaped from their power.

The officers came attended by a guard, and were every way prepared to prosecute a strenuous search through these horrible recesses.

Hippolitus inquired for Ferdinand, and they all quitted the vault in search of him. In the court, to which they now ascended, the greater part of the banditti were secured by a number of the guard. The count accused the robbers of having secreted his friend, whom he described, and demanded to have liberated.

With one voice they denied the fact, and were resolute in persisting that they knew nothing of the person described. This denial confirmed Hippolitus in his former terrible surmise; that the dying cavalier, whom he had seen, was no other than Ferdinand, and he became furious. He bade the officers prosecute their search, who, leaving a guard over the banditti they had secured, followed him to the room where the late dreadful scene had been acted.

The room was dark and empty; but the traces of blood were visible on the floor; and Julia, though ignorant of the particular apprehension of Hippolitus, almost swooned at the sight. On quitting the room, they wandered for some time among the ruins, without discovering any thing extraordinary, till, in passing under the arch-way by which Hippolitus had first entered the building, their footsteps returned a deep sound, which convinced them that the ground beneath was hollow. On close examination, they perceived by the light of their torch, a trapdoor, which with some difficulty they lifted, and discovered beneath a narrow flight of steps. They all descended into a low winding passage, where they had not been long, when they heard a trampling of horses above, and a loud and sudden uproar.

The officers apprehending that the banditti had overcome the guard, rushed back to the trapdoor, which they had scarcely lifted, when they heard a clashing of swords, and a confusion of unknown voices. Looking onward, they beheld through the arch, in an inner sort of court, a large party of banditti who were just arrived, rescuing their comrades, and contending furiously with the guard.

On observing this, several of the officers sprang forward to the assistance of their friends; and the rest, subdued by cowardice, hurried down the steps, letting the trapdoor fall after them with a thundering noise. They gave notice to Hippolitus of what was passing above, who hurried Julia along the passage in search of some outlet or place of concealment. They could find neither, and had not long pursued the windings of the way, when they heard the trapdoor lifted, and the steps of persons descending. Despair gave strength to Julia, and winged her flight. But they were now stopped by a door which closed the passage, and the sound of distant voices murmured along the walls.

The door was fastened by strong iron bolts, which Hippolitus vainly endeavoured to draw. The voices drew near. After much labour and difficulty the bolts yielded — the door unclosed — and light dawned upon them through the mouth of a cave, into which they now entered. On quitting the cave they found themselves in the forest, and in a short time reached the borders. They now ventured to stop, and looking back perceived no person in pursuit.

CHAPTER XIV

When Julia had rested, they followed the track before them, and in a short time arrived at a village, where they obtained security and refreshment.

But Julia, whose mind was occupied with dreadful anxiety for Ferdinand, became indifferent to all around her. Even the presence of Hippolitus, which but lately would have raised her from misery to joy, failed to soothe her distress. The steady and noble attachment of her brother had sunk deep in her heart, and reflection only aggravated her affliction. Yet the banditti had steadily persisted in affirming that he was not concealed in their recesses; and this circumstance, which threw a deeper shade over the fears of Hippolitus, imparted a glimmering of hope to the mind of Julia.

A more immediate interest at length forced her mind from this sorrowful subject. It was necessary to determine upon some line of conduct, for she was now in an unknown spot, and ignorant of any place of refuge. The count, who trembled at the dangers which environed her, and at the probabilities he saw of her being torn from him for ever, suffered a consideration of them to overcome the dangerous delicacy which at this mournful period required his silence. He entreated her to destroy the possibility of separation, by consenting to become his immediately. He urged that a priest could be easily procured from a neighboring convent, who would confirm the bonds which had so long united their hearts, and who would thus at once arrest the destiny that so long had threatened his hopes.

This proposal, though similar to the one she had before accepted; and though the certain means of rescuing her from the fate she dreaded, she now turned from in sorrow and dejection. She loved Hippolitus with a steady and tender affection, which was still heightened by the gratitude he claimed as her deliverer; but she considered it a prophanation of the memory of that brother who had suffered so much for her sake, to mingle joy with the grief which her uncertainty concerning him occasioned. She softened her refusal with a tender grace, that quickly dissipated the jealous doubt arising in the mind of Hippolitus, and increased his fond admiration of her character.

She desired to retire for a time to some obscure convent, there to await the issue of the event, which at present involved her in perplexity and sorrow.

Hippolitus struggled with his feelings and forbore to press farther the suit on which his happiness, and almost his existence, now depended. He inquired at the village for a neighbouring convent, and was told, that there was none within twelve leagues, but that near the town of Palini, at about that distance, were two. He procured horses; and leaving the officers to return to Palermo for a stronger guard, he, accompanied by Julia, entered on the road to Palini.

Julia was silent and thoughtful; Hippolitus gradually sunk into the same mood, and he often cast a cautious look around as they travelled for some hours along the feet of the mountains. They stopped to dine under the shade of some beach-trees; for, fearful of discovery, Hippolitus had provided against the necessity of entering many inns. Having finished their repast, they pursued their journey; but Hippolitus now began to doubt whether he was in the right direction. Being destitute, however, of the means of certainty upon this point, he followed the road before him, which now wound up the side of a steep hill, whence they descended into a rich valley, where the shepherd's pipe sounded sweetly from afar among the hills. The evening sun shed a mild and mellow lustre over the landscape, and softened each feature with a vermil glow that would have inspired a mind less occupied than Julia's with sensations of congenial tranquillity.

The evening now closed in; and as they were doubtful of the road, and found it would be impossible to reach Palini that night, they took the way to a village, which they perceived at the extremity of the valley.

They had proceeded about half a mile, when they heard a sudden shout of voices echoed from among the hills behind them; and looking back perceived faintly through the dusk a party of men on horseback making towards them. As they drew nearer, the words they spoke were distinguishable, and Julia heard her own name sounded. Shocked at this circumstance, she had now no doubt that she was discovered by a party of her father's people, and she fled with Hippolitus along the valley. The pursuers, however, were almost come up with them, when they reached the mouth of a cavern, into which she ran for concealment. Hippolitus drew his sword; and awaiting his enemies, stood to defend the entrance.

In a few moments Julia heard the clashing of swords. Her heart trembled for Hippolitus; and she was upon the point of returning to resign herself at once to the power of her enemies, and thus avert the danger that threatened him, when she distinguished the loud voice of the duke.

She shrunk involuntarily at the sound, and pursuing the windings of the cavern, fled into its inmost recesses. Here she had not been long when the voices sounded through the cave, and drew near. It was now evident that Hippolitus was conquered, and that her enemies were in search of her. She threw round a look of unutterable anguish, and perceived very near, by a sudden gleam of torchlight, a low and deep recess in the rock. The light which belonged to her pursuers, grew stronger; and she entered the rock on her knees, for the overhanging craggs would not suffer her to pass otherwise; and having gone a few yards, perceived that it was terminated by a door. The door yielded to her touch, and she suddenly found herself in a highly vaulted cavern, which received a feeble light from the moon-beams that streamed through an opening in the rock above.

She closed the door, and paused to listen. The voices grew louder, and more distinct, and at last approached so near, that she distinguished what was said. Above the rest she heard the voice of the duke. 'It is impossible she can have quitted the cavern,' said he, 'and I will not leave it till I have found her. Seek to the left of that rock, while I examine beyond this point.'

These words were sufficient for Julia; she fled from the door across the cavern before her, and having ran a considerable way, without coming to a termination, stopped to breathe. All was now still, and as she looked around, the gloomy obscurity of the place struck upon her fancy all its horrors. She imperfectly surveyed the vastness of the cavern in wild amazement, and feared that she had precipitated herself again into the power of banditti, for whom along this place appeared a fit receptacle. Having listened a long time without hearing a return of voices, she thought to find the door by which she had entered, but the gloom, and vast extent of the cavern, made the endeavour hopeless, and the attempt unsuccessful. Having wandered a considerable time through the void, she gave up the effort, endeavoured to resign herself to her fate, and to compose her distracted thoughts. The remembrance of her former wonderful escape inspired her with confidence in the mercy of God. But Hippolitus and Ferdinand were now both lost to her — lost, perhaps, for ever — and the uncertainty of their fate gave force to fancy, and poignancy to sorrow.

Towards morning grief yielded to nature, and Julia sunk to repose. She was awakened by the sun, whose rays darting obliquely through the opening in the rock, threw a partial light across the cavern. Her senses were yet bewildered by sleep, and she started in affright on beholding her situation; as recollection gradually stole upon her mind, her sorrows returned, and she sickened at the fatal retrospect.

She arose, and renewed her search for an outlet. The light, imperfect as it was, now assisted her, and she found a door, which she perceived was not the one by which she had entered. It was firmly fastened; she discovered, however, the bolts and the lock that held it, and at length unclosed the door. It opened upon a dark passage, which she entered.

She groped along the winding walls for some time, when she perceived the way was obstructed. She now discovered that another door interrupted her progress, and sought for the bolts which might fasten it. These she found; and strengthened by desparation forced them back. The door opened, and she beheld in a small room, which received its feeble light from a window above, the pale and emaciated figure of a woman, seated, with half-closed eyes, in a kind of elbow-chair. On perceiving Julia, she started from her seat, and her countenance expressed a wild surprise. Her features, which were worn by sorrow, still retained the traces of beauty, and in her air was a mild dignity that excited in Julia an involuntary veneration.

She seemed as if about to speak, when fixing her eyes earnestly and steadily upon Julia, she stood for a moment in eager gaze, and suddenly exclaiming, 'My daughter!' fainted away.

The astonishment of Julia would scarcely suffer her to assist the lady who lay senseless on the floor. A multitude of strange imperfect ideas rushed upon her mind, and she was lost in perplexity; but as she examined the features of the stranger; which were now rekindling into life, she thought she discovered the resemblance of Emilia!

The lady breathing a deep sigh, unclosed her eyes; she raised them to Julia, who hung over her in speechless astonishment, and fixing them upon her with a tender earnest expression—they filled with tears. She pressed Julia to her heart, and a few moments of exquisite, unutterable emotion followed. When the lady became more composed, 'Thank heaven!' said she, 'my prayer is granted. I am permitted to embrace one of my children before I die. Tell me what brought you hither. Has the marquis at last relented, and allowed me once more to behold you, or has his death dissolved my wretched bondage?'

583

Truth now glimmered upon the mind of Julia, but so faintly, that instead of enlightening, it served only to increase her perplexity.

'Is the marquis Mazzini living?' continued the lady. These words were not to be doubted; Julia threw herself at the feet of her mother, and embracing her knees in an energy of joy, answered only in sobs.

The marchioness eagerly inquired after her children, 'Emilia is living,' answered Julia, 'but my dear brother —' 'Tell me,' cried the marchioness, with quickness. An explanation ensued; When she was informed concerning Ferdinand, she sighed deeply, and raising her eyes to heaven, endeavoured to assume a look of pious resignation; but the struggle of maternal feelings was visible in her countenance, and almost overcame her powers of resistance.

Julia gave a short account of the preceding adventures, and of her entrance into the cavern; and found, to her inexpressible surprize, that she was now in a subterranean abode belonging to the southern buildings of the castle of Mazzini! The marchioness was beginning her narrative, when a door was heard to unlock above, and the sound of a footstep followed.

'Fly!' cried the marchioness, 'secret yourself, if possible, for the marquis is coming.' Julia's heart sunk at these words; she paused not a moment, but retired through the door by which she had entered. This she had scarcely done, when another door of the cell was unlocked, and she heard the voice of her father. Its sounds thrilled her with a universal tremour; the dread of discovery so strongly operated upon her mind, that she stood in momentary expectation of seeing the door of the passage unclosed by the marquis; and she was deprived of all power of seeking refuge in the cavern.

At length the marquis, who came with food, quitted the cell, and relocked the door, when Julia stole forth from her hiding-place. The marchioness again embraced, and wept over her daughter. The narrative of her sufferings, upon which she now entered, entirely dissipated the mystery which had so long enveloped the southern buildings of the castle.

'Oh! why,' said the marchioness, 'is it my task to discover to my daughter the vices of her father? In relating my sufferings, I reveal his crimes! It is now about fifteen years, as near as I can guess from the small means I have of judging, since I entered this horrible abode. My sorrows, alas! began not here; they commenced at an earlier period. But it is sufficient to observe, that the passion whence originated all my misfortunes, was discovered by me long before I experienced its most baleful effects.

'Seven years had elapsed since my marriage, when the charms of Maria de Vellorno, a young lady singularly beautiful, inspired the marquis with a passion as violent as it was irregular. I observed, with deep and silent anguish, the cruel indifference of my lord towards me, and the rapid progress of his passion for another. I severely examined my past conduct, which I am thankful to say presented a retrospect of only blameless actions; and I endeavoured, by meek submission, and tender assiduities, to recall that affection which was, alas! gone for ever. My meek submission was considered as a mark of a servile and insensible mind; and my tender assiduities, to which his heart no longer responded, created only disgust, and exalted the proud spirit it was meant to conciliate.

'The secret grief which this change occasioned, consumed my spirits, and preyed upon my constitution, till at length a severe illness threatened my life. I beheld the approach of death with a steady eye, and even welcomed it as the passport to tranquillity; but it was destined that I should linger through new scenes of misery.

'One day, which it appears was the paroxysm of my disorder, I sunk in to a state of total torpidity, in which I lay for several hours. It is impossible to describe my feelings, when, on recovering, I found myself in this hideous abode. For some time I doubted my senses, and afterwards believed that I had quitted this world for another; but I was not long suffered to continue in my error, the appearance of the marquis bringing me to a perfect sense of my situation.

'I now understood that I had been conveyed by his direction to this recess of horror, where it was his will I should remain. My prayers, my supplications, were ineffectual; the hardness of his heart repelled my sorrows back upon myself; and as no entreaties could prevail upon him to inform me where I was, or of his reason for placing me here, I remained for many years ignorant of my vicinity to the castle, and of the motive of my confinement.

'From that fatal day, until very lately, I saw the marquis no more — but was attended by a person who had been for some years dependant upon his bounty, and whom necessity, united to an insensible heart, had doubtless induced to accept this office. He generally brought me a week's provision, at stated intervals, and I remarked that his visits were always in the night.

'Contrary to my expectation, or my wish, nature did that for me which medicine had refused, and I recovered as if to punish with disappointment and anxiety my cruel tyrant. I afterwards learned, that in obedience to the marquis's order, I had been carried to this spot by Vincent during the night, and that I had been buried in effigy at a neighbouring church, with all the pomp of funeral honor due to my rank.'

At the name of Vincent Julia started; the doubtful words he had uttered on his deathbed were now explained — the cloud of mystery which had so long involved the southern buildings broke at once away: and each particular circumstance that had excited her former terror, arose to her view entirely unveiled by the words of the marchioness. — The long and total desertion of this part of the fabric — the light that had appeared through the casement — the figure she had seen issue from the tower — the midnight noises she had heard — were circumstances evidently dependant on the imprisonment of the marchioness; the latter of which incidents were produced either by Vincent, or the marquis, in their attendance upon her.

When she considered the long and dreadful sufferings of her mother, and that she had for many years lived so near her, ignorant of her misery, and even of her existence — she was lost in astonishment and pity.

'My days,' continued the marchioness, 'passed in a dead uniformity, more dreadful than the most acute vicissitudes of misfortune, and which would certainly have subdued my reason, had not those firm principles of religious faith, which I imbibed in early youth, enabled me to withstand the still, but forceful pressure of my calamity.

'The insensible heart of Vincent at length began to soften to my misfortunes. He brought me several articles of comfort, of which I had hitherto been destitute, and answered some questions I put to him concerning my family. To release me from my present situation, however his inclination might befriend me, was not to be expected, since his life would have paid the forfeiture of what would be termed his duty.

'I now first discovered my vicinity to the castle. I learned also, that the marquis had married Maria de Vellorno, with whom he had resided at Naples, but that my daughters were left at Mazzini. This last intelligence awakened in my heart the throbs of warm maternal tenderness, and on my knees I supplicated to see them. So earnestly I entreated, and so solemnly I promised to return quietly to my prison, that, at length, prudence yielded to pity, and Vincent consented to my request.

'On the following day he came to the cell, and informed me my children were going into the woods, and that I might see them from a window near which they would pass. My nerves thrilled at these words, and I could scarcely support myself to the spot I so eagerly sought. He led me through long and intricate passages, as I guessed by the frequent turnings, for my eyes were bound, till I reached a hall of the south buildings. I followed to a room above, where the full light of day once more burst upon my sight, and almost overpowered me. Vincent placed me by a window, which looked towards the woods. Oh! what moments of painful impatience were those in which I awaited your arrival!

'At length you appeared. I saw you — I saw my children — and was neither permitted to clasp them to my heart, or to speak to them! You was leaning on the arm of your sister, and your countenances spoke the sprightly happy innocence of youth. — Alas! you knew not the wretched fate of your mother, who then gazed upon you! Although you were at too great a distance for my weak voice to reach you, with the utmost difficulty I avoided throwing open the window, and endeavouring to discover myself. The remembrance of my solemn promise, and that the life of Vincent would be sacrificed by the act, alone restrained me. I struggled for some time with emotions too powerful for my nature, and fainted away.

'On recovering I called wildly for my children, and went to the window — but you were gone! Not all the entreaties of Vincent could for some time remove me from this station, where I waited in the fond expectation of seeing you again — but you appeared no more! At last I returned to my cell in an ecstasy of grief which I tremble even to remember.

'This interview, so eagerly sought, and so reluctantly granted, proved a source of new misery — instead of calming, it agitated my mind with a restless, wild despair, which bore away my strongest powers of resistance. I raved incessantly of my children, and incessantly solicited to see them again — Vincent, however, had found but too much cause to repent of his first indulgence, to grant me a second.

'About this time a circumstance occurred which promised me a speedy release from calamity. About a week elapsed, and Vincent did not appear. My little stock of provision was exhausted, and I had been two days without food, when I again heard the doors that led to my prison creek on their hinges. An unknown step approached, and in a few minutes the marquis entered my cell! My blood was chilled at the sight, and I closed my eyes as I hoped for the last time. The sound of his voice recalled me. His countenance was dark and sullen, and I perceived that he trembled. He informed me that Vincent was no more, and that henceforward his office he should take upon himself. I forbore to reproach — where reproach would only have produced new sufferings, and withheld supplication where it would have exasperated conscience and inflamed revenge. My knowledge of the marquis's second marriage I concealed.

'He usually attended me when night might best conceal his visits; though these were irregular in their return. Lately, from what motive I cannot guess, he has ceased his nocturnal visits, and comes only in the day.

'Once when midnight increased the darkness of my prison, and seemed to render silence even more awful, touched by the sacred horrors of the hour, I poured forth my distress in loud lamentation. Oh! never can I forget what I felt, when I heard a distant voice answered to my moan! A wild surprize, which was strangely mingled with hope, seized me, and in my first emotion I should have answered the call, had not a recollection crossed me, which destroyed at once every half-raised sensation of joy. I remembered the dreadful vengeance which the marquis had sworn to execute upon me, if I ever, by any means, endeavoured to make known the place of my concealment; and though life had long been a burden to me, I dared not to incur the certainty of being murdered. I also well knew that no person who might discover my situation could effect my enlargement, for I had no relations to deliver me by force; and the marquis, you know, has not only power to imprison, but also the right of life and death in his own domains; I, therefore, forbore to answer the call, though I could not entirely repress my lamentation. I long perplexed myself with endeavouring to account for this strange circumstance, and am to this moment ignorant of its cause.'

Julia remembering that Ferdinand had been confined in a dungeon of the castle, it instantly occurred to her that his prison, and that of the marchioness, were not far distant; and she scrupled not to believe that it was his voice which her mother had heard. She was right in this belief, and it was indeed the marchioness whose groans had formerly caused Ferdinand so much alarm, both in the marble hall of the south buildings, and in his dungeon.

When Julia communicated her opinion, and the marchioness believed that she had heard the voice of her son — her emotion was extreme, and it was some time before she could resume her narration.

'A short time since,' continued the marchioness, 'the marquis brought me a fortnight's provision, and told me that I should probably see him no more till the expiration of that term. His absence at this period you have explained in your account of the transactions at the abbey of St Augustin. How can I ever sufficiently acknowledge the obligations I owe to my dear and invaluable friend Madame de Menon! Oh! that it might be permitted me to testify my gratitude.'

Julia attended to the narrative of her mother in silent astonishment, and gave all the sympathy which sorrow could demand. 'Surely,' cried she, 'the providence on whom you have so firmly relied, and whose inflictions you have supported with a fortitude so noble, has conducted me through a labyrinth of misfortunes to this spot, for the purpose of delivering you! Oh! let us hasten to fly this horrid abode — let us seek to escape through the cavern by which I entered.'

She paused in earnest expectation awaiting a reply. 'Whither can I fly?' said the marchioness, deeply sighing. This question, spoken with the emphasis of despair, affected Julia to tears, and she was for a while silent.

'The marquis,' resumed Julia, 'would not know where to seek you, or if he found you beyond his own domains, would fear to claim you. A convent may afford for the present a safe asylum; and whatever shall happen, surely no fate you may hereafter encounter can be more dreadful than the one you now experience.'

The marchioness assented to the truth of this, yet her broken spirits, the effect of long sorrow and confinement, made her hesitate how to act; and there was a kind of placid despair in her look, which too faithfully depicted her feelings. It was obvious to Julia that the cavern she had passed wound beneath the range of mountains on whose opposite side stood the castle of Mazzini. The hills thus rising formed a screen which must entirely conceal their emergence from the mouth of the cave, and their flight, from those in the castle. She represented these circumstances to her mother, and urged them so forcibly that the lethargy of despair yielded to hope, and the marchioness committed herself to the conduct of her daughter.

'Oh! let me lead you to light and life!' cried Julia with warm enthusiasm. 'Surely heaven can bless me with no greater good than by making me the deliverer of my mother.' They both knelt down; and the marchioness, with that affecting eloquence which true piety inspires, and with that confidence which had supported her through so many miseries, committed herself to the protection of God, and implored his favor on their attempt.

They arose, but as they conversed farther on their plan, Julia recollected that she was destitute of money — the banditti having robbed her of all! The sudden shock produced by this remembrance almost subdued her spirits; never till this moment had she understood the value of money. But she commanded her feelings, and resolved to conceal this circumstance from the marchioness, preferring the chance of any evil they might encounter from without, to the certain misery of this terrible imprisonment.

Having taken what provision the marquis had brought, they quitted the cell, and entered upon the dark passage, along which they passed with cautious steps. Julia came first to the door of the cavern, but who can paint her distress when she found it was fastened! All her efforts to open it were ineffectual. — The door which had closed after her, was held by a spring lock, and could be opened on this side only with a key. When she understood this circumstance, the marchioness, with a placid resignation which seemed to exalt her above humanity, addressed herself again to heaven, and turned back to her cell. Here Julia indulged without reserve, and without scruple, the excess of her grief. The marchioness wept over her. 'Not for myself,' said she, 'do I grieve. I have too long been inured to misfortune to sink under its pressure. This disappointment is intrinsically, perhaps, little — for I had no certain refuge from calamity — and had it even been otherwise, a few years only of suffering would have been spared me. It is for you, Julia, who so much lament my fate; and who in being thus delivered to the power of your father, are sacrificed to the Duke de Luovo — that my heart swells.'

Julia could make no reply, but by pressing to her lips the hand which was held forth to her, she saw all the wretchedness of her situation; and her fearful uncertainty concerning Hippolitus and Ferdinand, formed no inferior part of her affliction.

'If,' resumed the marchioness, 'you prefer imprisonment with your mother, to a marriage with the duke, you may still secret yourself in the passage we have just quitted, and partake of the provision which is brought me.'

'O! talk not, madam, of a marriage with the duke,' said Julia; 'surely any fate is preferable to that. But when I consider that in remaining here, I am condemned only to the sufferings which my mother has so long endured, and that this confinement will enable me to soften, by tender sympathy, the asperity of her misfortunes, I ought to submit to my present situation with complacency, even did a marriage with the duke appear less hateful to me.'

'Excellent girl!' exclaimed the marchioness, clasping Julia to her bosom; 'the sufferings you lament are almost repaid by this proof of your goodness and affection! Alas! that I should have been so long deprived of such a daughter!'

Julia now endeavoured to imitate the fortitude of her mother, and tenderly concealed her anxiety for Ferdinand and Hippolitus, the idea of whom incessantly haunted her imagination. When the marquis brought food to the cell, she retired to the avenue leading to the cavern, and escaped discovery.

CHAPTER XV

The marquis, meanwhile, whose indefatigable search after Julia failed of success, was successively the slave of alternate passions, and he poured forth the spleen of disappointment on his unhappy domestics.

The marchioness, who may now more properly be called Maria de Vellorno, inflamed, by artful insinuations, the passions already irritated, and heightened with cruel triumph his resentment towards Julia and Madame de Menon. She represented, what his feelings too acutely acknowledged, — that by the obstinate disobedience of the first, and the machinations of the last, a priest had been enabled to arrest his authority as a father — to insult the sacred honor of his nobility — and to overturn at once his proudest schemes of power and ambition. She declared it her opinion, that the Abate was acquainted with the place of Julia's present retreat, and upbraided the marquis with want of spirit in thus submitting to be outwitted by a priest, and forbearing an appeal to the pope, whose authority would compel the Abate to restore Julia.

This reproach stung the very soul of the marquis; he felt all its force, and was at the same time conscious of his inability to obviate it. The effect of his crimes now fell in severe punishment upon his own head. The threatened secret, which was no other than the imprisonment of the marchioness, arrested his arm of vengeance, and compelled him to submit to insult and disappointment. But the reproach of Maria sunk deep in his mind; it fomented his pride into redoubled fury, and he now repelled with disdain the idea of submission.

He revolved the means which might effect his purpose — he saw but one — this was the death of the marchioness.

The commission of one crime often requires the perpetration of another. When once we enter on the ladyrinth of vice, we can seldom return, but are led on, through correspondent mazes, to destruction. To obviate the effect of his first crime, it was now necessary the marquis should commit a second, and conceal the imprisonment of the marchioness by her murder. Himself the only living witness of her existence, when she was removed, the allegations of the Padre Abate would by this means be unsupported by any proof, and he might then boldly appeal to the pope for the restoration of his child.

He mused upon this scheme, and the more he accustomed his mind to contemplate it, the less scrupulous he became. The crime from which he would formerly have shrunk, he now surveyed with a steady eye. The fury of his passions, unaccustomed to resistance, uniting with the force of what ambition termed necessity—urged him to the deed, and he determined upon the murder of his wife. The means of effecting his purpose were easy and various; but as he was not yet so entirely hardened as to be able to view her dying pangs, and embrue his own hands in her blood, he chose to dispatch her by means of poison, which he resolved to mingle in her food.

But a new affliction was preparing for the marquis, which attacked him where he was most vulnerable; and the veil, which had so long overshadowed his reason, was now to be removed. He was informed by Baptista of the infidelity of Maria de Vellorno. In the first emotion of passion, he spurned the informer from his presence, and disdained to believe the circumstance. A little reflection changed the object of his resentment; he recalled the servant, whose faithfulness he had no reason to distrust, and condescended to interrogate him on the subject of his misfortune.

He learned that an intimacy had for some time subsisted between Maria and the Cavalier de Vincini; and that the assignation was usually held at the pavilion on the sea-shore, in an evening. Baptista farther declared, that if the marquis desired a confirmation of his words, he might obtain it by visiting this spot at the hour mentioned.

This information lighted up the wildest passions of his nature; his former sufferings faded away before the stronger influence of the present misfortune, and it seemed as if he had never tasted misery till now. To suspect the wife upon whom he doated with romantic fondness, on whom he had centered all his firmest hopes of happiness, and for whose sake he had committed the crime which embittered even his present moment, and which would involve him in still deeper guilt—to find her ungrateful to his love, and a traitoress to his honor—produced a misery more poignant than any his imagination had conceived. He was torn by contending passions, and opposite resolutions:—now he resolved to expiate her guilt with her blood—and now he melted in all the softness of love. Vengeance and honor bade him strike to the heart which had betrayed him, and urged him instantly to the deed—when the idea of her beauty—her winning smiles—her fond endearments stole upon his fancy, and subdued his heart; he almost wept to the idea of injuring her, and in spight of appearances,

pronounced her faithful. The succeeding moment plunged him
again into uncertainty; his tortures acquired new vigour from
cessation, and again he experienced all the phrenzy of despair.
He was now resolved to end his doubts by repairing to the
pavilion; but again his heart wavered in irresolution how to
proceed should his fears be confirmed. In the mean time he
determined to watch the behaviour of Maria with severe
vigilance.

They met at dinner, and he observed her closely, but
discovered not the smallest impropriety in her conduct. Her
smiles and her beauty again wound their fascinations round his
heart, and in the excess of their influence he was almost
tempted to repair the injury which his late suspicions had done
her, by confessing them at her feet. The appearance of the
Cavalier de Vincini, however, renewed his suspicions; his heart
throbbed wildly, and with restless impatience he watched the
return of evening, which would remove his suspence.

Night at length came. He repaired to the pavilion, and
secreted himself among the trees that embowered it. Many
minutes had not passed, when he heard a sound of low
whispering voices steal from among the trees, and footsteps
approaching down the alley. He stood almost petrified with
terrible sensations, and presently heard some persons enter the
pavilion. The marquis now emerged from his hiding-place; a
faint light issued from the building. He stole to the window,
and beheld within, Maria and the Cavalier de Vincini. Fired at
the sight, he drew his sword, and sprang forward. The sound of
his step alarmed the cavalier, who, on perceiving the marquis,
rushed by him from the pavilion, and disappeared among the
woods. The marquis pursued, but could not overtake him; and
he returned to the pavilion with an intention of plunging his
sword in the heart of Maria, when he discovered her senseless
on the ground. Pity now suspended his vengeance; he paused in
agonizing gaze upon her, and returned his sword into the
scabbard.

She revived, but on observing the marquis, screamed and
relapsed. He hastened to the castle for assistance, inventing, to
conceal his disgrace, some pretence for her sudden illness, and
she was conveyed to her chamber.

The marquis was now not suffered to doubt her infidelity,
but the passion which her conduct abused, her faithlessness
could not subdue; he still doated with absurd fondness, and
even regretted that uncertainty could no longer flatter him with
hope. It seemed as if his desire of her affection increased with

his knowledge of the loss of it; and the very circumstance which should have roused his aversion, by a strange perversity of disposition, appeared to heighten his passion, and to make him think it impossible he could exist without her.

When the first energy of his indignation was subsided, he determined, therefore, to reprove and to punish, but hereafter to restore her to favor.

In this resolution he went to her apartment, and reprehended her falsehood in terms of just indignation.

Maria de Vellorno, in whom the late discovery had roused resentment, instead of awakening penitence; and exasperated pride without exciting shame—heard the upbraidings of the marquis with impatience, and replied to them with acrimonious violence.

She boldly asserted her innocence, and instantly invented a story, the plausibility of which might have deceived a man who had evidence less certain than his senses to contradict it. She behaved with a haughtiness the most insolent; and when she perceived that the marquis was no longer to be misled, and that her violence failed to accomplish its purpose, she had recourse to tears and supplications. But the artifice was too glaring to succeed; and the marquis quitted her apartment in an agony of resentment.

His former fascinations, however, quickly returned, and again held him in suspension between love and vengeance. That the vehemence of his passion, however, might not want an object, he ordered Baptista to discover the retreat of the Cavalier de Vincini on whom he meant to revenge his lost honor. Shame forbade him to employ others in the search.

This discovery suspended for a while the operations of the fatal scheme, which had before employed the thoughts of the marquis; but it had only suspended—not destroyed them. The late occurrence had annihilated his domestic happiness; but his pride now rose to rescue him from despair, and he centered all his future hopes upon ambition. In a moment of cool reflection, he considered that he had derived neither happiness or content from the pursuit of dissipated pleasures, to which he had hitherto sacrificed every opposing consideration. He resolved, therefore, to abandon the gay schemes of dissipation which had formerly allured him, and dedicate himself entirely to ambition, in the pursuits and delights of which he hoped to bury all his cares. He therefore became more earnest than ever for the marriage of Julia with the Duke de Luovo, through whose means he designed to involve himself in the interests of the state, and determined to recover her at whatever consequence. He resolved, without further delay, to appeal to the pope; but to do this with safety it was necessary that the marchioness should die; and he returned therefore to the consideration and execution of his diabolical purpose.

He mingled a poisonous drug with the food he designed for her; and when night arrived, carried it to the cell. As he unlocked the door, his hand trembled; and when he presented the food, and looked consciously for the last time upon the marchioness, who received it with humble thankfulness, his heart almost relented. His countenance, over which was diffused the paleness of death, expressed the secret movements of his soul, and he gazed upon her with eyes of stiffened horror. Alarmed by his looks, she fell upon her knees to supplicate his pity.

Her attitude recalled his bewildered senses; and endeavouring to assume a tranquil aspect, he bade her rise, and instantly quitted the cell, fearful of the instability of his purpose. His mind was not yet sufficiently hardened by guilt to repel the arrows of conscience, and his imagination responded to her power. As he passed through the long dreary passages from the prison, solemn and mysterious sounds seemed to speak in every murmur of the blast which crept along their windings, and he often started and looked back.

He reached his chamber, and having shut the door, surveyed the room in fearful examination. Ideal forms flitted before his fancy, and for the first time in his life he feared to be alone. Shame only withheld him from calling Baptista. The gloom of the hour, and the death-like silence that prevailed, assisted the horrors of his imagination. He half repented of the deed, yet deemed it now too late to obviate it; and he threw himself on his bed in terrible emotion. His head grew dizzy, and a sudden faintness overcame him; he hesitated, and at length arose to ring for assistance, but found himself unable to stand.

In a few moments he was somewhat revived, and rang his bell; but before any person appeared, he was seized with terrible pains, and staggering to his bed, sunk senseless upon it. Here Baptista, who was the first person that entered his room, found him struggling seemingly in the agonies of death. The whole castle was immediately roused, and the confusion may be more easily imagined than described. Emilia, amid the general alarm, came to her father's room, but the sight of him overcame her, and she was carried from his presence. By the help of proper applications the marquis recovered his senses and his pains had a short cessation.

'I am dying,' said he, in a faultering accent; 'send instantly for the marchioness and my son.'

Ferdinand, in escaping from the hands of the banditti, it was now seen, had fallen into the power of his father. He had been since confined in an apartment of the castle, and was now liberated to obey the summons. The countenance of the marquis exhibited a ghastly image; Ferdinand, when he drew near the bed, suddenly shrunk back, overcome with horror. The marquis now beckoned his attendants to quit the room, and they were preparing to obey, when a violent noise was heard from without; almost in the same instant the door of the apartment was thrown open, and the servant, who had been sent for the marchioness, rushed in. His look alone declared the horror of his mind, for words he had none to utter. He stared wildly, and pointed to the gallery he had quitted. Ferdinand, seized with new terror, rushed the way he pointed to the apartment of the marchioness. A spectacle of horror presented itself. Maria lay on a couch lifeless, and bathed in blood. A poignard, the instrument of her destruction, was on the floor; and it appeared from a letter which was found on the couch beside her, that she had died by her own hand. The paper contained these words:

TO THE MARQUIS DE MAZZINI

Your words have stabbed my heart. No power on earth could restore the peace you have destroyed. I will escape from my torture. When you read this, I shall be no more. But the triumph shall no longer be yours—the draught you have drank was given by the hand of the injured

MARIA DE MAZZINI.

It now appeared that the marquis was poisoned by the vengeance of the woman to whom he had resigned his conscience. The consternation and distress of Ferdinand cannot easily be conceived: he hastened back to his father's chamber, but determined to conceal the dreadful catastrophe of Maria de Vellorno. This precaution, however, was useless; for the servants, in the consternation of terror, had revealed it, and the marquis had fainted.

Returning pains recalled his senses, and the agonies he suffered were too shocking for the beholders. Medical endeavours were applied, but the poison was too powerful for antidote. The marquis's pains at length subsided; the poison had exhausted most of its rage, and he became tolerably easy. He waved his hand for the attendants to leave the room; and beckoning to Ferdinand, whose senses were almost stunned by this accumulation of horror, bade him sit down beside him. 'The hand of death is now upon me,' said he; 'I would employ these last moments in revealing a deed, which is more dreadful to me than all the bodily agonies I suffer. It will be some relief to me to discover it.' Ferdinand grasped the hand of the marquis in speechless terror. 'The retribution of heaven is upon me,' resumed the marquis. 'My punishment is the immediate consequence of my guilt. Heaven has made that woman the instrument of its justice, whom I made the instrument of my crimes; — — that woman, for whose sake I forgot conscience, and braved vice — for whom I imprisoned an innocent wife, and afterwards murdered her.'

At these words every nerve of Ferdinand thrilled; he let go the marquis's hand and started back. 'Look not so fiercely on me,' said the marquis, in a hollow voice; 'your eyes strike death to my soul; my conscience needs not this additional pang.' — 'My mother!' exclaimed Ferdinand — 'my mother! Speak, tell me.' — 'I have no breath,' said the marquis. 'Oh! — Take these keys — the south tower — the trapdoor. — 'Tis possible — Oh! — '

The marquis made a sudden spring upwards, and fell lifeless on the bed; the attendants were called in, but he was gone for ever. His last words struck with the force of lightning upon the mind of Ferdinand; they seemed to say that his mother might yet exist. He took the keys, and ordering some of the servants to follow, hastened to the southern building; he proceeded to the tower, and the trapdoor beneath the stair-case was lifted. They all descended into a dark passage, which conducted them through several intricacies to the door of the cell. Ferdinand, in trembling horrible expectation, applied the key; the door opened, and he entered; but what was his surprize when he found no person in the cell! He concluded that he had mistaken the place, and quitted it for further search; but having followed the windings of the passage, by which he entered, without discovering any other door, he returned to a more exact examination of the cell. He now observed the door, which led to the cavern, and he entered upon the avenue, but no person was found there and no voice answered to his call. Having reached the door of the cavern, which was fastened, he returned lost in grief, and meditating upon the last words of the marquis. He now thought that he had mistaken their import, and that the words "'tis possible,' were not meant to apply to the life of the marchioness, he concluded, that the murder had been committed at a distant period; and he resolved, therefore, to have the ground of the cell dug up, and the remains of his mother sought for.

When the first violence of the emotions excited by the late scenes was subsided, he enquired concerning Maria de Vellorno.

It appeared that on the day preceding this horrid transaction, the marquis had passed some hours in her apartment; that they were heard in loud dispute;—that the passion of the marquis grew high;—that he upbraided her with her past conduct, and threatened her with a formal separation. When the marquis quitted her, she was heard walking quick through the room, in a passion of tears; she often suddenly stopped in vehement but incoherent exclamation; and at last threw herself on the floor, and was for some time entirely still. Here her woman found her, upon whose entrance she arose hastily, and reproved her for appearing uncalled. After this she remained silent and sullen.

She descended to supper, where the marquis met her alone at table. Little was said during the repast, at the conclusion of which the servants were dismissed; and it was believed that during the interval between supper, and the hour of repose, Maria de Vellorno contrived to mingle poison with the wine of the marquis. How she had procured this poison was never discovered.

She retired early to her chamber; and her woman observing that she appeared much agitated, inquired if she was ill? To this she returned a short answer in the negative, and her woman was soon afterwards dismissed. But she had hardly shut the door of the room when she heard her lady's voice recalling her. She returned, and received some trifling order, and observed that Maria looked uncommonly pale; there was besides a wildness in her eyes which frightened her, but she did not dare to ask any questions. She again quitted the room, and had only reached the extremity of the gallery when her mistress's bell rang. She hastened back, Maria enquired if the marquis was gone to bed, and if all was quiet? Being answered in the affirmative, she replied, 'This is a still hour and a dark one!—Good night!'

Her woman having once more left the room, stopped at the door to listen, but all within remaining silent, she retired to rest.

It is probable that Maria perpetrated the fatal act soon after the dismission of her woman; for when she was found, two hours afterwards, she appeared to have been dead for some time. On examination a wound was discovered on her left side, which had doubtless penetrated to the heart, from the suddenness of her death, and from the effusion of blood which had followed.

These terrible events so deeply affected Emilia that she was confined to her bed by a dangerous illness. Ferdinand struggled against the shock with manly fortitude. But amid all the tumult of the present scenes, his uncertainty concerning Julia, whom he had left in the hands of banditti, and whom he had been withheld from seeking or rescuing, formed, perhaps, the most affecting part of his distress.

The late Marquis de Mazzini, and Maria de Vellorno, were interred with the honor due to their rank in the church of the convent of St Nicolo. Their lives exhibited a boundless indulgence of violent and luxurious passions, and their deaths marked the consequences of such indulgence, and held forth to mankind a singular instance of divine vengeance.

CHAPTER XVI

In turning up the ground of the cell, it was discovered that it communicated with the dungeon in which Ferdinand had been confined, and where he had heard those groans which had occasioned him so much terror.

The story which the marquis formerly related to his son, concerning the southern buildings, it was now evident was fabricated for the purpose of concealing the imprisonment of the marchioness. In the choice of his subject, he certainly discovered some art; for the circumstance related was calculated, by impressing terror, to prevent farther enquiry into the recesses of these buildings. It served, also, to explain, by supernatural evidence, the cause of those sounds, and of that appearance which had been there observed, but which were, in reality, occasioned only by the marquis.

The event of the examination in the cell threw Ferdinand into new perplexity. The marquis had confessed that he poisoned his wife—yet her remains were not to be found; and the place which he signified to be that of her confinement, bore no vestige of her having been there. There appeared no way by which she could have escaped from her prison; for both the door which opened upon the cell, and that which terminated the avenue beyond, were fastened when tried by Ferdinand.

But the young marquis had no time for useless speculation—serious duties called upon him. He believed that Julia was still in the power of banditti; and, on the conclusion of his father's funeral, he set forward himself to Palermo, to give information of the abode of the robbers, and to repair with the officers of justice, accompanied by a party of his own people, to the rescue of his sister. On his arrival at Palermo he was informed, that a banditti, whose retreat had been among the ruins of a monastery, situated in the forest of Marentino, was already discovered; that their abode had been searched, and themselves secured for examples of public justice—but that no captive lady had been found amongst them. This latter intelligence excited in Ferdinand a very serious distress, and he was wholly unable to conjecture her fate. He obtained leave, however, to interrogate those of the robbers, who were imprisoned at Palermo, but could draw from them no satisfactory or certain information.

At length he quitted Palermo for the forest of Marentino, thinking it possible that Julia might be heard of in its neighbourhood. He travelled on in melancholy and dejection, and evening overtook him long before he reached the place of his destination. The night came on heavily in clouds, and a violent storm of wind and rain arose. The road lay through a wild and rocky country, and Ferdinand could obtain no shelter. His attendants offered him their cloaks, but he refused to expose a servant to the hardship he would not himself endure. He travelled for some miles in a heavy rain; and the wind, which howled mournfully among the rocks, and whose solemn pauses were filled by the distant roarings of the sea, heightened the desolation of the scene. At length he discerned, amid the darkness from afar, a red light waving in the wind: it varied with the blast, but never totally disappeared. He pushed his horse into a gallop, and made towards it.

The flame continued to direct his course; and on a nearer approach, he perceived, by the red reflection of its fires, streaming a long radiance upon the waters beneath—a lighthouse situated upon a point of rock which overhung the sea. He knocked for admittance, and the door was opened by an old man, who bade him welcome.

Within appeared a cheerful blazing fire, round which were seated several persons, who seemed like himself to have sought shelter from the tempest of the night. The sight of the fire cheered him, and he advanced towards it, when a sudden scream seized his attention; the company rose up in confusion, and in the same instant he discovered Julia and Hippolitus. The joy of that moment is not to be described, but his attention was quickly called off from his own situation to that of a lady, who during the general transport had fainted. His sensations on learning she was his mother cannot be described.

She revived. 'My son!' said she, in a languid voice, as she pressed him to her heart. 'Great God, I am recompensed! Surely this moment may repay a life of misery!' He could only receive her caresses in silence; but the sudden tears which started in his eyes spoke a language too expressive to be misunderstood.

When the first emotion of the scene was passed, Julia enquired by what means Ferdinand had come to this spot. He answered her generally, and avoided for the present entering upon the affecting subject of the late events at the castle of Mazzini. Julia related the history of her adventures since she parted with her brother. In her narration, it appeared that Hippolitus, who was taken by the Duke de Luovo at the mouth of the cave, had afterwards escaped, and returned to the cavern in search of Julia. The low recess in the rock, through which Julia had passed, he perceived by the light of his flambeau. He penetrated to the cavern beyond, and from thence to the prison of the marchioness. No colour of language can paint the scene which followed; it is sufficient to say that the whole party agreed to quit the cell at the return of night. But this being a night on which it was known the marquis would visit the prison, they agreed to defer their departure till after his appearance, and thus elude the danger to be expected from an early discovery of the escape of the marchioness.

At the sound of footsteps above, Hippolitus and Julia had secreted themselves in the avenue; and immediately on the marquis's departure they all repaired to the cavern, leaving, in the hurry of their flight, untouched the poisonous food he had brought. Having escaped from thence they proceeded to a neighbouring village, where horses were procured to carry them towards Palermo. Here, after a tedious journey, they arrived, in the design of embarking for Italy. Contrary winds had detained them till the day on which Ferdinand left that city, when, apprehensive and weary of delay, they hired a small vessel, and determined to brave the winds. They had soon reason to repent their temerity; for the vessel had not been long at sea when the storm arose, which threw them back upon the shores of Sicily, and brought them to the lighthouse, where they were discovered by Ferdinand.

On the following morning Ferdinand returned with his friends to Palermo, where he first disclosed the late fatal events of the castle. They now settled their future plans; and Ferdinand hastened to the castle of Mazzini to fetch Emilia, and to give orders for the removal of his household to his palace at Naples, where he designed to fix his future residence. The distress of Emilia, whom he found recovered from her indisposition, yielded to joy and wonder, when she heard of the existence of her mother, and the safety of her sister. She departed with Ferdinand for Palermo, where her friends awaited her, and where the joy of the meeting was considerably heightened by the appearance of Madame de Menon, for whom the marchioness had dispatched a messenger to St Augustin's. Madame had quitted the abbey for another convent, to which, however, the messenger was directed. This happy party now embarked for Naples.

From this period the castle of Mazzini, which had been the theatre of a dreadful catastrophe; and whose scenes would have revived in the minds of the chief personages connected with it, painful and shocking reflections — was abandoned.

On their arrival at Naples, Ferdinand presented to the king a clear and satisfactory account of the late events at the castle, in consequence of which the marchioness was confirmed in her rank, and Ferdinand was received as the sixth Marquis de Mazzini.

The marchioness, thus restored to the world, and to happiness, resided with her children in the palace at Naples, where, after time had somewhat mellowed the remembrance of the late calamity, the nuptials of Hippolitus and Julia were celebrated. The recollection of the difficulties they had encountered, and of the distress they had endured for each other, now served only to heighten by contrast the happiness of the present period.

Ferdinand soon after accepted a command in the Neapolitan army; and amidst the many heroes of that warlike and turbulent age, distinguished himself for his valour and ability. The occupations of war engaged his mind, while his heart was solicitous in promoting the happiness of his family.

Madame de Menon, whose generous attachment to the marchioness had been fully proved, found in the restoration of her friend a living witness of her marriage, and thus recovered those estates which had been unjustly withheld from her. But the marchioness and her family, grateful to her friendship, and attached to her virtues, prevailed upon her to spend the remainder of her life at the palace of Mazzini.

Emilia, wholly attached to her family, continued to reside with the marchioness, who saw her race renewed in the children of Hippolitus and Julia. Thus surrounded by her children and friends, and engaged in forming the minds of the infant generation, she seemed to forget that she had ever been otherwise than happy.

* * * * *

Here the manuscript annals conclude. In reviewing this story, we perceive a singular and striking instance of moral retribution. We learn, also, that those who do only THAT WHICH IS RIGHT, endure nothing in misfortune but a trial of their virtue, and from trials well endured derive the surest claim to the protection of heaven.

FINIS

Milton Keynes UK
Ingram Content Group UK Ltd.
UKHW021938081024
449407UK00008B/152